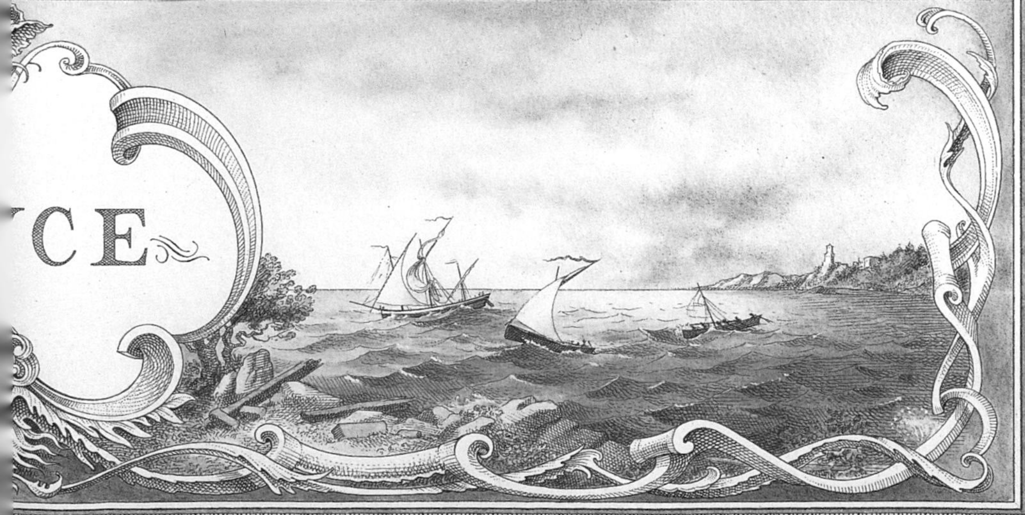

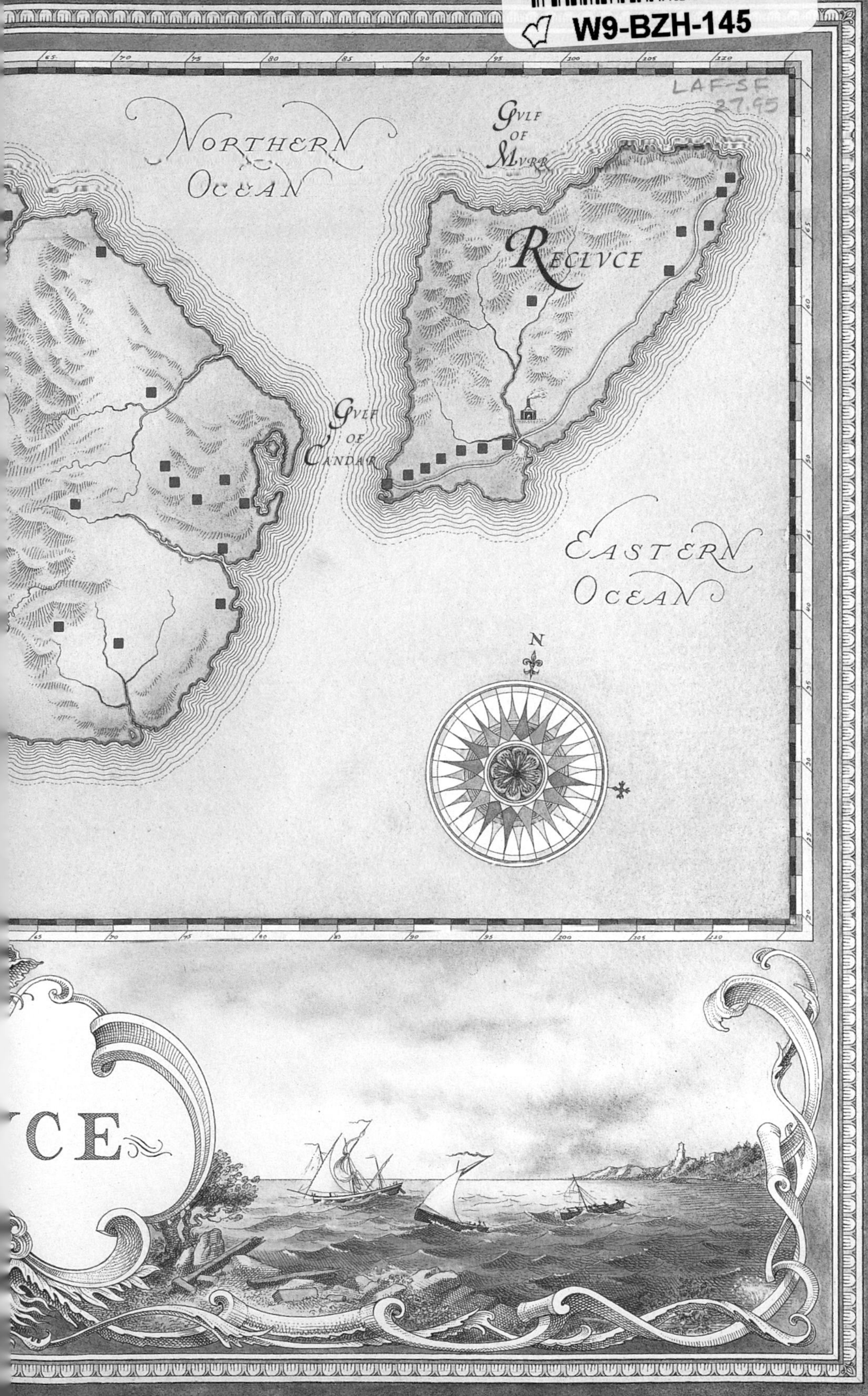
Northern Ocean
Gvlf of Mvrr
Recluce
Gvlf of Candar
Eastern Ocean
N
CE

ORDERMASTER

Tor Books by L. E. Modesitt, Jr.

The Saga of Recluce

The Magic of Recluce
The Towers of the Sunset
The Magic Engineer
The Order War
The Death of Chaos
Fall of Angels
The Chaos Balance
The White Order
Colors of Chaos
Magi'i of Cyador
Scion of Cyador
Wellspring of Chaos
Ordermaster

The Corean Chronicles

Legacies
Darknesses
Scepters
*Alector's Choice**

The Spellsong Cycle

The Soprano Sorceress
The Spellsong War
Darksong Rising
The Shadow Sorceress
Shadowsinger

The Ecolitan Matter

The Ecologic Envoy
The Ecolitan Operation
The Ecologic Secession
The Ecolitan Enigma

The Forever Hero

Dawn for a Distant Earth
The Silent Warrior
In Endless Twilight

GHOSTS OF COLUMBIA

Of Tangible Ghosts

The Ghost of the Revelator

Ghost of the White Nights

TIMEGODS' WORLD

The Timegod

Timediver's Dawn

The Green Progression

(with Bruce Scott Levinson)

The Parafaith War

The Hammer of Darkness

Adiamante

Gravity Dreams

The Octagonal Raven

Archform: Beauty

The Ethos Effect

Flash

*Forthcoming

L. E. Modesitt, Jr.

ORDERMASTER

A Tom Doherty Associates Book / New York

ORDERMASTER

This book is printed on acid-free paper.

Edited by David G. Hartwell

Maps by Ellisa Mitchell

A Tor Book
Published by Tom Doherty Associates, LLC
175 Fifth Avenue
New York, NY 10010

www.tor.com

Tor® is a registered trademark of Tom Doherty Associates, LLC.

ISBN 0-765-31213-1
EAN 978-0765-31213-6

First Edition: January 2005

Printed in the United States of America

0 9 8 7 6 5 4 3 2 1

For Nancy and Kennet,
in the trinity of time

Northern
Candar
Gulf of Murr
Gulf of Candar
Recluce
Eastern Ocean
The WORLD
EMitchell 1995

Ocean

Gulf of Austra

Austra

Brysta

Valmurl

Nordla

Western Ocean

Swartheld

Luba

Cigoerne

Afrit

Atla

Swarth River

Merowey

Hamor

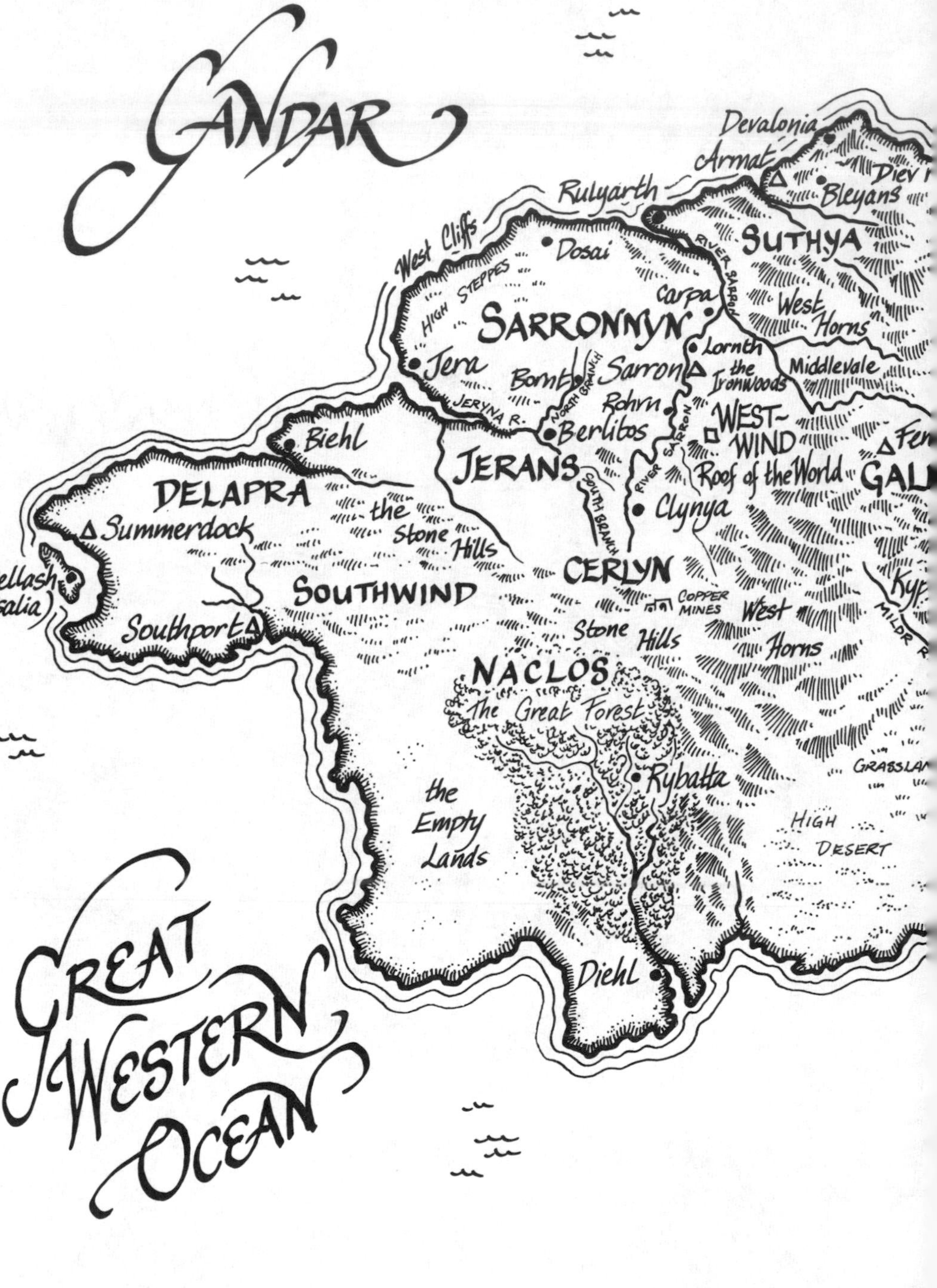

Gandar
Devalonia
Armat
Diev
Bleyans
Rulyarth
West Cliffs
Dosai
SUTHYA
River Sarron
High Steppes
Carpa
West Horns
SARRONNYN
Lornth
Jera
Bornt
North Branch
Sarron
the Ironwoods
Middlevale
Jeryna R.
Rohrn
Berlitos
WEST-WIND
Biehl
JERANS
River Sarron
Roof of the World
South Branch
DELAPRA
the Stone Hills
Clynya
Summerdock
CERLYN
Dellash (Esalia)
SOUTHWIND
Copper Mines
West Horns
Southport
Stone Hills
NACLOS
The Great Forest
Rybatta
Grasslan
the Empty Lands
High Desert
Diehl
Great Western Ocean

Northern Ocean
Gulf of Murr
Land's End
Black Holding
Extina
Alberth
Reflin
Lydkler
Alaren
Feyn R.
Iron Works
Mattra
Feyn
Wandernaught
Clarion
Enstronn
Sigil
Nylan
Southpoint
Recluce
Spidlaria
Quend
East Horns
Tyrhavven
Gulf of Candar
Sligo
Rytel
Certis
Lavah
Great North Bay
Montgren
Vergren
Jellico
Weevett
Fiven
Freetown
Hydolar
Tellura
Freetown (Lydiar)
Meltosia
Ohyde River
Renklaar
Hydlen
Dasir
Telsen
Arastia
Asula
Pyrdya
Sunta
Fakhlaar
Fakla River
High Desert
Worrak
Eastern Ocean
EMitchell 1995

Lord Ghrant's Mage

I

"You sure you'd not be wanting more, ser?" The ample Adelya stood in the archway from the kitchen to the breakfast room.

Kharl smiled as he eased back the straight-backed oak chair and stood. He glanced down at the green-trimmed white plate—it was the plain china—on which remained a half slice of egg toast. "More, Adelya? I couldn't finish everything you cooked. It's been a long time since I've eaten so well." That wasn't quite true. He'd eaten that well as Lord Ghrant's guest in Dykaru, but, he reflected, he'd never eaten under his own roof as he had for the last two eightdays.

He still had trouble believing that he was lord of Cantyl. He'd studied the figures laid out in the ledger by Speltar, the estate steward, and seen and counted the golds in the strong room below. He was wealthy, if modestly so by the standards of lords, and that was something he'd never expected, never dreamed. Not for a man who had been a cooper in Brysta most of his life, and a carpenter's assistant on the *Seastag* after he'd been forced into exile by Lord West's son Egen.

From that exile had come all the events—and the magely talents—that had led him to become lord and master of Cantyl and its lands. Cantyl was a modest estate, as estates went, roughly some ten kays by five, with timberlands and vineyards, enough fertile ground to provision the lands, and more than a few rugged and rocky hills. There were a handful of fruit trees on the slope south of the main house, but they were barely an orchard.

The only things missing were his sons, but he had no way to reach Arthal, and he'd sent a message on Hagen's *Seastag*, the next ship of the lord-chancellor's merchant fleet scheduled to port in Brysta. It was chancy as to whether his letter would actually reach Merayni in Peachill, where Warrl stayed with his aunt, but Kharl had to try.

"You be sure you've had enough, ser?" asked Adelya. "The way you've been working, more like a field hand than a lord . . ."

"Hard work makes me feel better," Kharl replied.

"You could have someone—"

"I'm a better cooper and carpenter than anyone I could pay." Kharl grinned. "And I'm more trustworthy, too."

Adelya tried not to smile, and failed.

"Besides, how can I learn about Cantyl if I don't work it?"

"You sound like Lord Koroh. He was Lord Julon's father."

Hagen had mentioned in passing that Julon had held the estate before Lord Ghrant, but had not mentioned any details.

"Good lord, Koroh was." Adelya straightened. "You sure you don't need any more?"

"I'm most certain." With a smile, Kharl turned and walked from the breakfast room down the rear hall to the south doorway. It was really a service entrance, but it was closest to the small barn that he was converting into his private cooperage. He enjoyed working with wood, and once he received the oak he had ordered, he could begin to make barrels for the vineyard. That would save Glyan, the head vintner, more than a few golds over the course of the year, and it would give Kharl the sense that he was adding to the worth of Cantyl.

Once outside in the chill sunlight, he walked briskly down the gravel path toward the small barn. Although the first days of spring had been cool for Austra, the heavy sandstone walls of the house had kept it pleasant during the past eightdays as Kharl had worked to learn about his holding, studying the accounts, walking the lands, and building his cooperage.

Without hesitation, Kharl slid back the barn door and stepped into what had once been a secondary stable. At some point, he'd need to put in a better set of doors, but his first task was to finish removing the remaining stalls.

For a good two glasses, Kharl worked in the small barn, carefully loosening and breaking down the last of the stall walls, taking out pegs and the occasional nail, so that the planks and cut timbers could be reused. He had three piles in the center of the dirt floor.

After finishing with the eighth stall, he straightened. Despite the coolness of the day, sweat beaded on his forehead, and he blotted it away with the sleeve of the heavy gray shirt he'd worn as the carpenter's assistant on the *Seastag*.

"Ah . . . ser?"

Kharl turned to see Speltar, the estate steward, standing in the open doorway. "Good morning, Speltar."

"That it is, ser. You've been working hard."

"I can't build a cooperage here until I've got the space ready."

The steward nodded. "I should have the listing ready this afternoon." He paused. "For the equipment we talked about yesterday."

"What did we forget?" Kharl grinned. "Or I forgot?"

"We'd talked about varnish or shellac for the flooring here. . . ."

Kharl looked at the dirt floor inside the east end of the barn, a space where there had been ten stalls, then glanced to Speltar. "I can't believe there were so many stalls. There were ten here, and there are twenty in the main barn."

"Lord Julon had four teams," replied the short and slim steward, nervously pushing back his wispy reddish brown hair, not that there was enough to cover his balding pate. "He had four horses to a team, and they weren't used for work around the lands. So we needed stalls for the shire horses, mostly in winter, and stalls for the fancy teams."

"Where did he drive them?"

"Oh, he took two teams to Valmurl. One team pulled the carriage most of the way, and then he made his entrance with the other." Speltar cleared his throat. "About the varnish?"

"What about it?"

"I was talking to Dorwan about it. He had a suggestion."

Kharl nodded. He'd already learned that Dorwan never volunteered anything directly to him, but always suggested things to Speltar. The forester, for all his size and bulk, was almost painfully shy, and it would take a while before he was at ease with Kharl—or anyone new to the estate. "It was probably a good one."

"Yes, ser. You know the flagstone walk in front? Well . . . years back, Lord Julon had flagstone squares cut, big thick squares, and he was going to have them polished for a summer porch. Ah . . . the porch never got built. Dorwan says that the flags, more than enough to floor your cooperage anyway, are still there, in the back of the storage shed above the vineyard building. They were smoothed, but never polished."

Kharl laughed. "Those would be better than a timber floor, especially around the forge." He paused. "I know how to lay a plank floor. I can't say I know how to lay a stone floor that well."

"Dorwan says his boy Bannat and he can do it. Take less than an eightday. Need some lime for the mortar, but that's a sight cheaper than varnish."

"Does he have the time, without neglecting what he does in the woodlands?"

"Still early for poachers, and word's out that Lord Kharl's a mage." Speltar grinned shyly. "Dorwan says that he and Bannat can start leveling and packing the clay underneath tomorrow."

"What do you think?"

"Stone'll last longer than wood, ser. We already have the flags. If we have to cut the timbers . . . all we have is softwood."

"What you're trying to tell me is that a softwood floor won't last, and that we could sell the good spruce timbers to the carpenters and shipyards in Valmurl for good coins, and besides that, you can get some use out of the flagstones stored in the shed, and free up some storage space."

"There is that, ser."

Kharl shook his head. "It's a good idea. We should do it. If I don't see Dorwan today, and you do, tell him that I appreciate his thoughtfulness. I'll tell him, but . . ."

"Yes, ser. He's a mite . . . reserved."

"Begging your pardon, ser . . ." came a young voice from behind Kharl. "There's a vessel under steam headed for the pier. Da said you'd want to know, ser."

Kharl turned to see a dark-haired girl of ten or so—Glyan's daughter Rona. She was the unofficial messenger around Cantyl. "Thank you."

"Yes, ser." Rona smiled. "Do you want me to tell Da anything?"

"Not yet. Why don't you come down to the pier with us? That way, if I need you to take a message . . ."

"Yes, ser!"

Kharl and Speltar walked up the rise from the small barn to the main house, then took the graveled lane that led down to the east and to the pier. Rona followed several paces behind. The lane split a large sloping meadow into two sections of roughly equal size—although the grass was still winter brown, with just the barest hints of green showing beneath the dead thatch. The meadows were bordered by stone walls, beyond which, on the south-facing slopes, were the vineyards that produced much of the income from the estate, mainly from the sale of the pale amber Rhynn, considered a desirable wine with poultry and fish by those well-off in Valmurl and Bruel. In the brief time he'd been at Cantyl, Kharl had discovered that he actually liked good wine, and he suspected that his past dislike of wine had not been a distaste for wine but a repugnance for bad wine—and that had been all that he'd ever tasted. Still, a good lager was his favorite.

The incoming vessel was already well past the harbor mouth and steaming toward the pier, a thin trail of smoke dispersing into the blue-green sky.

"You weren't expecting a ship?" asked Kharl.

"No, ser."

Kharl tried to make out the vessel. It wasn't the *Seastag*, but with the twin masts, and the midships paddle wheels, it could have been her twin. "Looks like one of Lord Hagen's vessels."

"Aye," offered Speltar. "Looks much like the *Seacat*. Captain Druen stops here now and again for timbers, and for the wine."

Kharl and Speltar reached the pier before the ship, but not before Dorwan and his assistant, the wiry Norgal.

"You'll be handling the lines?" Kharl asked.

"Yes, ser," replied Dorwan.

"Good." Kharl paused. "Dorwan . . . Speltar told me about your idea for the cooperage floor. Using the old flagstones, that's much better than using softwood. Thank you."

Dorwan nodded. "My duty, ser."

"That may be, but I appreciate how well you do it."

"Thank you, ser." Dorwan turned toward the end of the pier, watching as the vessel approached with bare steerageway.

When the ship drew within ten rods or so of the pier, Kharl made out the name under the bowsprit—*Seafox*. Within moments after making out the name, Kharl recognized Hagen, standing just aft of the bow, wearing the same dark gray jacket he'd often worn as master of the *Seastag*, rather than the finery of the lord-chancellor of Austra. Why was he coming to Cantyl? Or was he stopping on his way to Valmurl?

That was unlikely, Kharl thought, because Hagen had been obliged to ride northward from Dykaru with Lord Ghrant in almost a processional return to Valmurl.

The master of the *Seafox* backed down the paddle wheels expertly, and the vessel came to rest less than three cubits from the pier. Dorwan and Norgal caught the lines and made them fast to the bollards.

"Walk her in! Lively now!" came the commands from the deck.

When the gangway was down, Hagen was the first one onto the water-whitened timbers of the pier.

Kharl stepped forward, inclining his head to Hagen, out of respect for both the man and the office. "Lord-chancellor."

"Ser Kharl and mage." Hagen smiled broadly. "No sooner than you're out of sight, and you're back in working grays." He shook his head in mock-despair.

"I don't see any lord-chancellor's finery on you, ser," Kharl replied.

"Not in traveling," Hagen said with a laugh. "What's your excuse, ser Kharl?"

"I was working on turning part of a barn into a cooperage. If we make our own barrels, we can bring in more coins from the wine. We can also save on storage barrels. . . ."

Hagen shook his head. "Lord Ghrant will be disappointed to hear that his mage has returned to coopering."

"I can't be a mage all the time, not when matters here are peaceful." Kharl gestured toward the *Seafox*. "I'm not sure that we have any cargo for your ship." He turned toward the steward. "Speltar? Do we have cargo that should go?"

"Not right now, ser."

"That makes us even," replied Hagen. "We don't have anything to offload, either. Or so I'm told."

Kharl gestured toward the house. "Would you like to see the house? You haven't seen it before, have you?"

"No. I wasn't exactly favored by either Lord Julon or Lord Estloch." Hagen's voice was dry. "I'd like to see it. I do need a few words with you, as well. That's why I'm here, but we can talk while you give me a private tour."

Kharl caught the slight emphasis on *private*. Of course, Hagen had a reason for stopping in Cantyl. He turned to Speltar. "Speltar, if you and Rona would let Adelya know that the lord-chancellor will be having the midday meal with me. We'll eat in the breakfast room, just the two of us."

"Yes, ser."

As Rona and Speltar hurried ahead of them, Kharl and Hagen started up the lane toward the house at a more measured pace.

After several moments, Kharl glanced at Hagen. "You can stay for a midday meal, at least, can't you? I didn't ask you . . . I just thought . . ." His eyes flicked back, but Dorwan and Norgal had remained on the pier.

"That would be about all," replied Hagen, with a laugh. "Lord Ghrant expects me for tomorrow afternoon's audience." Hagen paused. "He expects you as well."

"Me?"

Lord Ghrant had told Kharl his services might be required, but within two eightdays of coming to Cantyl?

"He has a problem," Hagen said. "The problem is Guillam."

"The head of the factors' council?" As Kharl recalled, perhaps according to Lyras, the black mage who had claimed he was but a minor mage, if that, Guillam had been quietly backing Ilteron and had slipped out of Valmurl during the revolt.

"Guillam claims that he is a most faithful subject. For obvious reasons, Lord Ghrant has his doubts. You are known to be a mage, and Lord Ghrant wishes you present when he receives Guillam."

"He expects I will know if Guillam lies, then?"

"Will you not? You knew when Asolf was lying about stealing Reisl's coins."

Again, Kharl was reminded of how thorough Hagen was, and how he had known everything aboard the *Seastag*. Doubtless, that attention to detail was what had made him the owner of ten ships and lord-chancellor. "I usually can tell."

"That could be a problem," mused Hagen.

"That I might not be able to tell?"

"No. That you could. Let us say that Guillam did support Ilteron. What else can Lord Ghrant do but execute or exile him?" Hagen cocked his head, waiting for an answer from Kharl.

"If he does either, then, that will upset the other factors."

"All regarded Ghrant as weak."

"He still is," suggested Kharl. "He has a strong lord-chancellor."

"And a black mage," added Hagen.

"So . . . you are suggesting that my presence is more important than my judgment?"

"Your presence is most important."

Kharl realized that. It had to be, with Hagen diverting one of his ships to get Kharl. "Does it matter so much what Guillam has done as what he will do? Does his past matter as much as his loyalty?"

Hagen fingered his chin, smiling broadly. "So you would have him questioned about both his past and his loyalty?"

"If he lies about his past, but honestly believes that he is loyal," Kharl said slowly, "Lord Ghrant might overlook his lies."

"That is possible, but what if Guillam lies about his loyalty?"

"Then Ghrant is better off if he is dead or exiled, I would judge," Kharl replied carefully.

"Dead. Traitorous exiles can return."

Kharl wasn't so sure that he liked having Guillam's life put in his hands.

"You see, Kharl," Hagen went on, "there is a price to wealth and position. There is always a price. Those who do not attain either seldom see that price, and at times, the price is deferred, often for generations, but when it is deferred the cost falls upon the descendants manyfold."

Kharl couldn't help but wonder if Lord West of Nordla and his sons had ever paid such a price, or if it had been deferred in the manner Hagen suggested.

Adelya hurried up as Kharl and Hagen stepped onto the front porch. "Ser Kharl . . . ser Kharl . . ." Abruptly, she stopped and bowed. "Lord-chancellor . . . I'd not be meaning . . ."

"Whatever we have will be fine," Kharl said to Adelya. "I didn't know that Lord Hagen was coming, and he didn't know before yesterday. That didn't give him time to send a messenger."

"Whatever you cook will be far better than we ate on board ship."

Adelya did not look mollified, not completely.

"I'll come back—with notice—for one of your finest meals," Hagen offered with a smile. "Then you will have time to offer your best."

Adelya bowed again. "Your lordship is most kind."

"Please don't blame Lord Kharl. He did not know I was coming."

Kharl could hear the words under her breath as Adelya backed away, "But he's a mage. . . ." He resisted replying.

Hagen laughed softly. "You see. There is a price for being a mage, too. People come to expect the impossible."

"She isn't happy that I like working with my hands."

"People aren't ever happy when you don't meet their expectations." Hagen's voice was matter-of-fact, almost dismissive. "How do you find Cantyl?"

Kharl gestured toward the bay. "It's more than I ever expected. I'm still learning about the lands, and I haven't been through all the timberlands and the southern hills yet."

"If you do, you'll have seen more of them than any of the lords who've held Cantyl in generations," Hagen said dryly.

"How can a man not know his lands?" asked Kharl.

"That's a good question. It's also why at least some of them didn't keep them."

"Let me show you the house and the nearer outbuildings," offered Kharl.

"If you would . . ."

Kharl began the informal tour by showing Hagen the first-floor study with the wide window overlooking the bay, directly below the master suite, which had an even grander view, and took him through the entire two-story stone structure. By the time they had walked through the house, toured the barns, viewed the vineyards, and returned to the house, the midday meal was waiting.

Adelya hovered in the archway as the two seated themselves.

"This looks to be a feast, not a midday meal!" Hagen exclaimed, taking in the platters that Adelya set between them, with cutlets, fowl breasts, cheese lace potatoes, honeyed pearapples, and rye and dark bread with the honey-butter that was Adelya's pride. There were two goblets, with a pitcher of Cantyl's full red wine set on one side of the table.

"It's little enough, ser."

"It's a great deal, Adelya," Kharl said firmly, "and we both appreciate it. Thank you."

"I am hungry," Hagen admitted as he began to serve himself, "and we won't have anything near this good on the return voyage to Valmurl."

"How long will that take?"

"We'll be using both the engines and sails. If the winds hold, we might reach the harbor by midnight."

Kharl filled both goblets, then lifted one. "To you, for all of this . . ."

Hagen flushed as he lifted his goblet. "To you, ser Kharl . . . for saving Austra."

"And to friendship . . ."

Hagen nodded, then took a sip of the wine. "It's a good solid wine."

"I like it. Glyan says that the Rhynn is better, but to me, they're both good." Kharl broke off a chunk of the dark bread and passed the basket to the other. "Do you know how Tarkyn, Furwyl, and Rhylla are doing?"

"The *Seastag* is on its way to Land's End on Recluce. Only want to port there in spring and summer. I heard that there was some black wool to be had there. Doesn't come on the market often. A good weaver can make cloth for a lord from it."

At the reference to weavers, Kharl couldn't help thinking about Jeka, wondering how she was doing with Gharan—hoping that she had been able to stay with his former neighbor. He just wished he'd been able to do more for Jeka. She'd certainly saved his life and befriended him at a time when no one else would lift a hand. Beneath the hard surface . . .

"Kharl?"

"I'm sorry. I was . . . thinking. Was everyone all right when they cast off from Valmurl?"

"Furwyl left a report for me, and everything was fine. He did say that he needed to look for another carpenter. Tarkyn was complaining that there was too much work for any one carpenter." Hagen shook his head. "No one will ever be as good a ship's carpenter as you were, not for Tarkyn."

"Nothing is ever as good as it was," Kharl said dryly. "Even when it wasn't that good."

"You are almost as cynical as I am, ser mage." Hagen took another sip of wine. "That's saying a great deal."

Kharl feared he would need that cynicism when he reached Valmurl.

II

Thrap!

"Ser Kharl? Ser Kharl?"

Kharl struggled out of sleep. Where was he? How early was it?

"Ser Kharl?" The feminine voice was unfamiliar.

He squinted in the light pouring into the unfamiliar bedchamber, before everything came back. He was in the north wing of Lord Ghrant's Great House. For just himself, he had not only a large bedchamber, but a sitting room with a desk, as well as a lavishly equipped bath chamber.

"Ser?"

"Coming . . ." Kharl pulled himself out of the triple-width bed and yanked on his traveling trousers, shambling through the sitting room to the door, aware of the old but thick carpet beneath his bare feet.

"Your breakfast, sir."

Kharl concentrated, hard as it was, with his order-senses, but so far as he could tell, the young woman stood alone outside his door. He eased the lock plate back. A dark-haired young woman, barely out of girlhood, stood there holding an enormous tray.

"If you'd let me bring it in, ser. If you would, ser."

Kharl watched as she eased through the doorway and set the tray on the table desk. "Thank you."

"My pleasure, ser." The girl bowed and slipped away.

After locking the door again, Kharl crossed the sitting room. He looked at the tray, taking in the slices of ham, the egg toast, fillets of some sort of fish, a basket of black bread, a pot of jam, and the twin pitchers, one of pale ale, and the other of cider, with an empty beaker. He hadn't expected a breakfast to be delivered, but he couldn't say he was displeased, not as late as he had arrived in Valmurl the night before.

The winds had not been as favorable as Hagen had hoped, and the *Seafox* had not reached Valmurl until a good two glasses past midnight, even pushing the engines. A coach had been waiting, though, to take them to the Great House. For all that, or because of it, he had not slept that well, fretting as he had about the upcoming audience. Then, just when he had drifted off, or so it had seemed, the young woman had knocked on his door, carrying a tray with his breakfast.

A faint smile crossed his lips. A former cooper, being served by the servants of the Lord of Austra—that was something that Charee would never have believed. The pain he felt when he thought of his dead consort was not so much grief as a deep sadness over something that had never been quite right for years—and for the fact that she had been killed because Egen had wanted to punish Kharl. Her death had led to his losing both boys. Charee's sister Merayni had claimed the younger Warrl just before Kharl had been forced into hiding. Arthal, bitter at his mother's death, had signed on to the *Fleuryl* as a carpenter's apprentice without even telling Kharl until the morning he had left.

Kharl could only hope that Warrl was doing well as a grower's boy at Peachill. Once the rebel lords were subdued—if they were—then he could look into sending for Warrl. Going back to Brysta in person to get Warrl wasn't a good idea, but if all else failed, he'd try that as well. As for Arthal . . . he didn't even know where his older son was—or that Arthal would even talk to him if he could find the boy—except Arthal was a young man, an angry young man. Then, Arthal had always been angry, and Kharl had never understood why.

He shook his head and looked down at the breakfast tray. After a moment, he frowned.

There was something about the tray.

He studied it, both with his eyes and his order-senses. His eyes and nose insisted that everything was as it should be. His order-senses told him that there were pockets of reddish white spread through most of the food.

He left the tray on the table and went into the bath chamber.

In less than half a glass he was washed up and dressed. The tray and food remained untouched on the desk, and Kharl used the big brass key to lock the door behind him. He doubted that would stop whoever had poisoned the food.

He found the staircase down to the main level without any difficulty and made his way southward, toward what he thought was the center of the Great House. He stopped in a large hexagonal hallway, off which branched four corridors.

"Ser mage?" asked the guard in the yellow and black of Ghrant's personal guard.

"I'm looking for the lord-chancellor. Lord-chancellor Hagen."

The guard looked at Kharl's face, then at his black garments—those of a mage—once more. "Ah . . . yes, ser. His chamber is this way. I'd best take you."

Kharl studied the man with his order-senses, but the fellow seemed honest.

The guard turned down a narrower corridor that stretched a good fifty cubits, but he stopped after thirty at an unmarked ironbound door.

"The mage Kharl to see you, ser."

"Have him come in."

"Ser." The guard nodded and stepped back.

Kharl found himself inside a small chamber, no more than ten cubits square, without even a window. There was a second door, also of golden oak, at the rear of the room. Wearing a black velvet jacket trimmed in gold, with a heavy gold chain with a gold medallion at the end around his neck, Hagen stood beside the small table desk.

"You look upset, Kharl. What is it?"

"I had a breakfast tray delivered. I'm fairly sure it's poisoned. I just left it in the sitting room."

Hagen walked to the wall and yanked on the yellow-and-black bellpull. "I'll send Charsal up with you. He'll bring back the tray, and we'll feed it to the rats."

"The rats?"

"Lord Estloch keeps them for just such purposes. Anything that kills a rat will certainly kill a person."

Kharl hadn't thought about the possibility of an organized system for dealing with poison, but the moment that Hagen had mentioned it, he realized that he should have.

Hagen fingered his chin. "I wouldn't put it past Guillam. I can't think of anyone else who would know—or want to—that you were coming—or what that might mean. But that doesn't mean it was he."

"There's something he doesn't want discovered," Kharl suggested. "Why else . . . ?"

Hagen laughed. "Were it only that simple. A mage reduces everyone's influence with Lord Ghrant. Many will feel themselves threatened." The lord-chancellor moved back toward the desk. "How did you sleep?"

"I must have slept. I don't recall anything."

"Good. It's likely to be a long day. Lord Ghrant has confirmed that he expects Guillam at the second glass past noon."

"Early afternoon," Kharl mused. "Does Guillam have a dwelling near here in Valmurl?"

"Not that close. He has a country house fifteen kays west of Valmurl, and a small mansion off the Factors' Square. That's three kays from here—" Hagen broke off at the knock on the chamber door. "Yes?"

"Charsal, ser."

"Come in."

The door opened, and a trim young man, half a head shorter than Kharl, entered. He wore the yellow and black of the Ghrant's personal guard.

"Undercaptain . . . this is ser Kharl of Cantyl, the mage. He believes that a breakfast tray that was delivered to his quarters may be poisoned. If you would take one of your serjeants . . ."

"The rats, ser?"

"Exactly, and have him watch them closely."

"Ah . . . after that . . . where can I get breakfast?" Kharl asked sheepishly.

"Charsal will take you to the kitchen. It's probably best if the cooks fix something for you while you're there. I'll send a messenger to find you before the audience. If you'd just stay somewhere in the Great House." Hagen nodded to Charsal. "Undercaptain."

"Yes, ser."

Because Hagen was clearly preoccupied, Kharl inclined his head. "Until later, ser."

Hagen offered a wry smile in return.

Charsal stepped back and opened the door, holding it for Kharl. Outside, an older armsman, with a short but grizzled beard, stood. Without a word, the serjeant followed the undercaptain and Kharl.

Kharl led the way back up the stairs. Outside the chamber, Kharl took out the heavy brass key and unlocked the door. His order-senses confirmed that the room was empty. The tray remained where he had left it and did not look as though it had been touched.

"Is this it, ser?" asked Charsal, gesturing toward the tray.

"That's it."

Charsal nodded to the serjeant. "Everything gets fed to the rats. You're to watch them and report to me."

"Yes, ser." The serjeant lifted the tray and carried it out.

"Now for the kitchen." Charsal smiled.

"I hope this isn't too much of a problem."

"No, ser. We can't have people being poisoned here in the Great House."

"I'm not sure it is poisoned, but there's something not right about it."

"When a mage says something's not right, best to listen." Charsal smiled. "You were asking about breakfast, I believe."

"I had thought about it," Kharl replied with a grin.

"This way, ser."

The kitchen was on the lower level of the north side of the Great House, a large stone-walled room already uncomfortably warm even before midmorning.

"The mage here needs some breakfast," Charsal announced. "Prepared now."

A round-faced woman looked up, then nodded. "Be right on it. We could have prepared a tray if we'd 'a known."

Kharl kept his frown to himself, but noted the slightest nod from Charsal.

"Anything you'd be liking, ser?" asked the cook.

"Whatever you do best, except I'd rather not have any fish."

"We can do that. Egg toast, good ham, fresh bread, and cool cider? Jam, too."

"That would be fine," Kharl replied.

Both Charsal and Kharl stood against the stone wall and watched as the cooks bustled around the huge cast-iron stove.

Seemingly in moments, the cook had two heaping platters, pitcher and goblet, a basket of the black bread, and a pot of jam all set on a tray. She looked around, as if for a serving maid.

"I can take it," Kharl said.

"But . . . ser . . ."

"I'm escorting the mage." Charsal stepped forward and took the tray, then turned and led the way to the northwest corner of the kitchen, through an archway, and up a circular set of stone steps into an airy room with wide windows overlooking a stone terrace. "This is one of the dining rooms, ser. For those guests and staff here who are not being fed at various functions."

Two younger men were seated at a circular table in one corner, clearly finished with eating, but talking in low and intense voices. Besides Kharl and the undercaptain, they were the only ones in the room.

Charsal set the tray on a table before the windows. "Is this all right, ser?"

"That's fine. Thank you, undercaptain. I can find my way back to my chambers, and there's no need to keep you from your other duties." Kharl paused. "You have eaten, haven't you? There's more than enough—"

"I ate just a little while ago, ser, but I appreciate your kindness." Charsal bowed. "If you would not mind . . ."

Kharl smiled. "Go."

After Charsal turned, Kharl settled into the breakfast. While he had thought the portions large, he was surprised to find that he left little enough, except for half a loaf of bread. The black bread was heavy and sweetish, some of the best he recalled having, and he'd appreciated it. He still recalled all too well the days of hiding between the renderer's walls in Brysta, when he and Jeka had gone days with little sustenance.

With his hunger satisfied, using his order-senses, he tried to pick up the conversation of the two men in the corner, both wearing dark green tunics and trousers, the same color as the green of the Austran armsmen and lancers.

". . . taking a chance to stay here . . . Lord Ghrant . . . be vindictive . . ."

". . . not that bad . . . worse to worry about Fostak . . ."

". . . say Guillam has audience with Ghrant . . . what if . . ."

Kharl strained, but could not make out the words for the next several moments. He refilled his goblet with cider.

". . . wouldn't know a mage . . . saw one . . . not here in Austra . . ."

". . . wear black or white sometimes . . . Lyras does . . . black . . . not much of a mage . . ."

". . . say the new one killed Ilteron with a thunderbolt . . ."

Kharl wanted to snort. He couldn't create a spark, let alone a lightning bolt. He'd just surrounded Ilteron and his wizard with an impermeable barrier of solid air and let them suffocate. It had been the only thing he'd known how to do.

". . . fellow who's over there wearing black . . ."

There was a strangled gulp. Kharl did not look up as the two young men hurried out of the breakfast room.

A wry smile crossed his face. From the fragments of the conversation he'd overheard, he doubted that either man had been the one who had tried to poison him. On the other hand, the younger man had glanced back worriedly, and his hand had been held close to the hilt of the sabre at his side.

Kharl got up slowly, glancing around. As he did, a serving girl, not even so old as his younger boy Warrl, dashed out from the archway at the top of the steps from the kitchen.

Kharl held out a hand.

"Ser?"

"Those two men who were seated in the corner. Do you know who they are?"

"Ser?"

"Do you know who they are?"

The girl looked down, then up. She did not meet Kharl's eyes. "The taller one, ser, that was ser Zerlin. He's the youngest son of Lord Woren. The other man . . . I have seen him, but I don't know his name."

Kharl sensed the truth. "Thank you." Unfortunately, he could have used the name she didn't know. He stepped back and let the scullery girl collect his tray and the dishes on the table the two men had vacated.

He'd been in the Great House less than half a day, and he was beginning to see why Hagen had never wanted to serve as lord-chancellor. He thought about attempting to use his order-abilities to shield himself from view; but that was hard work, and he'd have to move slowly. For what? Because he was worried?

Still . . . he needed to be watchful.

He passed two guards in yellow and black on the main level as he made his way toward the staircase up to his chamber. Both nodded politely, and he returned the nods.

For the residence of the Lord of Austra, the Great House was surprisingly stark and simple. The walls on the main level were of simple polished stone, as were the floors. There were occasional niches, set shoulder high, in which there were busts of figures Kharl did not recognize. The ceilings were of a white plaster, and unadorned. All the doors were of ancient golden oak, and the fixtures upon them were brass, tarnished in many cases.

Kharl was halfway up the closed circular staircase when he thought he heard something below. He stopped and looked back over his shoulder. He couldn't see the bottom of the staircase because of the curvature and the walls, but there was no one on the steps as far down as he could see.

He turned and continued up the stairs, stopping at the top landing, and listening. Then he extended his order-senses. Two figures were frozen around the curve of the stairs, as if waiting for him to go on. Kharl considered. Now what? He wasn't carrying any weapons, not that he was any good with anything except a staff or a cudgel, and even if he had been, he couldn't very well attack someone for merely following him.

He smiled, then turned and walked quickly through the archway at the end of the landing, turning left and heading toward the north wing.

He swallowed. Ahead of him was a figure in the shadows of the space where the corridor ended, intersecting the narrower hallway that served the north wing. The figure was lifting something. Behind him, he could hear boots racing up the staircase.

Kharl concentrated, first hardening the very air on each side of him into a barrier, but with a good three cubits between each barrier, then wrapping himself in darkness—and invisibility. He also flattened himself against the wall, as an added, if unnecessary, precaution.

Clank! Something had struck the barrier. *Clank! Clank!*

"Frig!" The single word was half-whispered, half-hissed, and came from the hallway, probably at the top of the staircase, but Kharl could not see, not wrapped in the darkness of invisibility, and he was having enough trouble managing the barrier and invisibility, without trying to extend his order-senses forty or sixty cubits.

". . . gone . . ."

". . . friggin' mage . . . get out of here . . ."

At the sound of boots on stone, Kharl dropped the invisibility, but, even so, could only catch the vaguest glimpse of two figures in dark green or gray as they darted from the hallway down the staircase. He turned back toward the north wing, but that figure had vanished as well. He could not see or sense anyone else nearby.

With more than a little trepidation, he released the barriers, quickly. He was breathing as hard as if he had run half a kay, but that was to be expected. Using order-magery the way he had took strength and endurance.

Kharl collected the three bent crossbow quarrels, then, with his order-senses extended, made his way to the end of the central corridor and down the narrower hallway back to his own chamber. His order-senses told him that it was empty. He unlocked it and stepped inside, sliding the lock plate into place.

He sat down in a straight-backed chair to catch his breath and collect his thoughts.

Should he tell Hagen?

He decided against immediately telling the lord-chancellor. What good would that do? Hagen already knew that someone didn't want Kharl at the Great House. Kharl didn't want to run down to Hagen and once more convey news about which Hagen could do little. Doubtless crossbows and men in green were all too common in Valmurl and probably in the Great House. Also, he wouldn't be surprised if someone had planned for him to do exactly that.

Besides, Kharl needed to prepare for the audience with Guillam. He needed to think about what he might say, and, if given a chance, what questions he might need to ask.

Also, he didn't want to create more consternation in the Great House. That would not help him, Hagen, or Lord Ghrant. No . . . it might better be handled quietly. That was also something else he had learned from experience. Bitterly.

III

Kharl studied his image in the mirror of the bedchamber. His dark brown hair was cut tastefully short, his beard neatly trimmed. The silvery gray shirt and black waistcoat, and even the black trousers—bestowed by Lord Ghrant in Dykaru—were far finer than any raiment he had ever worn.

Was Guillam so worried about Kharl that he had attempted two assassination attempts in one morning? Or was Kharl so much of a threat that more than one person wanted him dead? Was truth—or disclosure—that deadly?

He laughed. Egen had certainly not wished certain things to become known and had killed Charee and Tyrbel to quell that information, as well as hounded Kharl out of Brysta. The Lord Justicer Reynol had seen what Egen wanted and had made sure that Charee could not reveal anything before she had been hanged.

Why would people be any different in Austra and Valmurl?

He took a deep breath, thinking once more about the past. He shook his head. At the moment, he could do nothing about it. He never could do anything for Charee, but he had hopes for Warrl, and Jeka . . . if he could ever get back to Brysta. As for Arthal . . . what would be would be.

As he waited, Kharl leafed through *The Basis of Order*, seeking a passage that might shed some light on the issues of truth and justice, even as he doubted that Lord Ghrant truly wanted justice or truth from Guillam.

> . . . there is order, and there is chaos, and those who follow each will declare that either order is truth or chaos is truth. A truth that holds for all does not exist, not in the world, nor in the stars, nor on the surface of the land, nor beneath the waves of the ocean. That which is exists, but those who search for truth that applies to all seek what never was and never will be. That is because truth is an image of what is, and that image is painted in the colors of the seeker's beliefs. Each seeks a different truth, and each claims that his is the only truth. In that the seeker is surely correct . . .

No such thing as truth?

Kharl frowned, then nodded slowly.

As midday came and passed, Kharl read, and thought, and considered. He spent close to a glass just thinking about how to word questions for the chief factor. He'd been a cooper, not a justicer or a minstrel.

Thrap!

"Lord Kharl?" The voice was that of Charsal. "I'm to take you to see the lord-chancellor, ser."

Kharl used his order-senses to make sure the undercaptain was alone. Then he picked up the three bent quarrels and unlocked the door to his chamber, stepping out into the stone-walled corridor and relocking the door.

Charsal glanced at the bent metal quarrels.

"I thought the lord-chancellor should see these."

"Those are standard quarrels, ser. Why—"

"That is why he should see them. We should go."

"Yes, ser." Charsal's voice expressed puzzlement.

The two walked silently to the central staircase, then down to the main level. There were more bodies—and more guards—in the large hall at the base of the staircase.

When Kharl entered Hagen's modest space, the lord-chancellor was seated behind the small table desk. He looked up from the papers before him, but did not rise, gesturing to the chairs across the table desk from him.

Kharl set the three quarrels on the desk. "Three men tried to kill me after breakfast this morning. They missed, but I thought you'd like to see these."

"Why didn't you tell me earlier?"

"What good would it have done? They were too far away and in too much shadow for me to recognize anyone. It would have distracted you. We already know that people want me dead." Kharl shrugged.

"We might have—" Hagen broke off the words. "You're right. They just shot at you and ran?"

"Something like that."

"I knew things were bad here, but . . ." Hagen shook his head. "You were right about the food. There was enough vicin in your meal to kill an entire company. I'm not surprised that you are regarded as an enemy, but I was surprised that Guillam knew you were here and moved so quickly."

"You didn't tell anyone when you left to fetch me?"

"No one. I did say that I was going out on the *Seafox* to test the new condensers."

"Did you talk to the girl who brought the tray?"

"I couldn't." Hagen's face clouded. "The guards found her body in the outer garden. She was garrotted. The cooks thought the tray was for the armsmaster of the Great House, but he spent the night outside Valmurl, with his brother. They swear that no one had touched it when they gave it to her to deliver."

A dead serving girl and two attempts on his life—scarcely a promising beginning to his first day in Lord Ghrant's Great House. "Does the name Fostak mean anything to you?"

"Where did you hear that?" Hagen's eyebrows furrowed.

"I overheard it in a conversation, from a young man named Zerlin. I had the feeling I wasn't supposed to hear it."

"Fostak is the private secretary of Lord Joharak. Joharak is the Hamorian envoy to Austra. There have been rumors that Fostak is a duelist, as well as the one who funneled golds to Ilteron to encourage him to take up arms against Ghrant."

"He is still in Valmurl?"

"Of course. Would you wish to upset the Emperor of Hamor, with all his iron-hulled warships? Without a shred of proof?" Hagen's tone was gently ironic.

There hadn't been any real proof against Kharl when he'd been unjustly accused of murdering Jenevra, but that hadn't stopped Egen and Lord West. But then, Kharl reminded himself, there were different standards when rulers and power were involved.

"The other reason I wanted to talk to you was to brief you on what will happen shortly. As we discussed earlier, Lord Ghrant will be seeing Chief Factor Guillam in a formal audience. That means that no one else can speak unless addressed first by Lord Ghrant. Even if he looks at you, that does not give you permission to speak. He may ask you if you have any questions for Guillam. That means that he expects you to have a question or two, three at the most. When you speak to Guillam, or offer more than a word or two, you step forward slightly. If Lord Ghrant wishes you to continue with questions, he will let you know by saying something like, 'Please continue, ser Kharl.' You should ask several more questions, then look at Lord Ghrant and either suggest that you have a few more questions or say that you have nothing further to ask the chief factor. Oh, and during an audience, Lord Ghrant is addressed as 'your lordship.' "

Kharl nodded. "Do you know what Lord Ghrant wants to know?"

Hagen laughed. "He wants proof that Guillam was a traitor and will be loyal."

"And if he will not be loyal?"

"Some way to show Guillam's treachery to all present."

"He does not wish much."

"Rulers never do. Neither do lords-chancellor." Hagen stood and straightened the gold-trimmed, black velvet jacket. "We should go. Lord Ghrant expects us to be in the audience chamber a quarter glass before he appears."

Rather than take the front door, Hagen stepped to the rear door, opening it. Kharl followed the lord-chancellor down the narrow, oak-paneled corridor.

"This is a private entrance to the audience chamber. When we reach the dais, you stand to my left and about a half pace back, if you would."

"I can do that."

At the end of the short passageway was an armsman, wearing the yellow and black of Ghrant's personal guard.

"Lord-chancellor . . . how should I announce . . . ?"

"The lord-chancellor and ser Kharl of Cantyl."

"Ser mage." The guard inclined his head, then turned and opened the door, stepping into the audience hall. His voice boomed out. "The lord-chancellor, Lord Hagen, and ser Kharl of Cantyl."

As directed, Kharl followed Hagen out into the audience hall, a high-ceilinged chamber close to sixty cubits in length and half that in width. The ceiling rose to an arched height of perhaps thirty cubits. The archway through which he and Hagen had entered opened directly onto a dais that was ten cubits deep and stretched the width of the chamber, two cubits above the main floor. In the center was a simple high-backed carved chair. It was empty.

The area below the dais contained close to a hundred men, and no more than a handful of women. All stood facing the dais, but most continued to talk to each other in low voices. Only a handful even looked in Kharl or Hagen's direction as the two walked into the hall. At first glance, Kharl recognized no one, but then, after a moment, he did see Commander Vatoran near the rear of the group on the right side.

When Hagen stopped, Kharl halted as well, positioning himself as directed.

"In a moment," Hagen said quietly, "some of them will recognize who you are, and they will begin to study you. There was a reason I did not have you announced as a mage."

"I only recognize Commander Vatoran."

"They do not know your face, but some know your name, and that will spread through them. Trust me. Watch."

Kharl watched. As Hagen predicted, more and more sets of eyes focused on him, but in passing, as if no one wanted to be caught looking at Kharl for long. The effect was mildly unsettling, especially as Kharl could hear fragments of murmured conversations.

"... big man for a mage ..."

"... said he was a cooper and a marine ... lord-chancellor's ships ..."

"... Hagen's more than Ghrant's ... you ask me ..."

"... not all bad that way ..."

In a sense that was right, because without Hagen's support and kindness, Kharl would either have been starving in the back alleys of Brysta or dead.

"His Lordship, Ghrant of Dykaru, Lord of Austra and Scion of the North."

The murmurs died away as Ghrant entered the hall from the other rear door—opposite the one through which Kharl and Hagen had entered. The Lord of Austra was attired in dark green, trimmed in black, and the green was the same shade as worn by the two men whose conversation Kharl had overheard, although the cloth itself looked to be of the finest velvet.

Without a word, Ghrant seated himself in the ancient high-backed chair. He nodded to the chamberlain, who had followed him and stood to the right of the chair, roughly the same distance from Ghrant as were Hagen and Kharl.

"Summon Guillam of Desfor."

The hall remained silent for a time, without even the lowest of murmurs.

"Guillam of Desfor, chief factor of Austra," announced one of the guards in yellow and black stationed just inside the double doors.

"Have him enter."

Guillam stepped through the doors, which closed behind him, and into the audience chamber. He was an angular figure, with thinning gray hair and deep-set eyes. Over his trousers and jacket, he wore a sleeveless open robe of purple. Since no one else in the audience hall wore anything like it, Kharl assumed the robe was a symbol of his position as chief factor.

From the moment the chief factor stepped into the hall, Kharl could sense the whiteness of chaos that drifted around him. That whiteness felt wrong to Kharl, almost like an itching that he could not scratch.

Guillam glanced toward the mage, then away. As he headed toward the high-backed chair, and Lord Ghrant, his eyes flickered toward Kharl several times Even so, the chief factor walked deliberately, without a hint of haste, to the foot of the six wide and carpeted steps that rose from the floor to the dais. There he halted.

"You had requested my presence, your lordship?" Guillam's voice was a smooth yet resonant baritone. He bowed slightly after speaking.

"We did, chief factor." Ghrant's voice was thin by comparison to those of Guillam, the guard, and the chamberlain.

"At your request I am here." Guillam emphasized the word *request* ever so slightly.

"I always attempt to be courteous, wherever possible," Ghrant replied smoothly. "During the recent uprising, your early absence from Valmurl was noted. I had hoped that you might enlighten us as to the reasons for your departure . . . and, of course, your destination."

"I had received word that my eldest son was most ill. It was feared that he might not live, and I repaired to my country house."

Guillam was but six cubits from Kharl, and the falsity of his reply shivered through the mage.

"How is your son? I assume that he recovered, since we have not heard otherwise."

"He is on the path to recovery, your lordship."

"And you remained at your country house during the entire period of unpleasantness?"

"Of course, your lordship."

That also was false, strongly so.

"Some have questioned your loyalty and stated that you had favored the would-be usurper. I would not wish to make a judgment on such without hearing from you."

"Your lordship, I favored and supported your father. You are his rightful heir, and I have likewise supported you. I will continue to support you, as I have from the beginning." Guillam bowed again.

Kharl managed to keep his face absolutely immobile in the face of the chaos and falsity that filled and lay beneath Guillam's words, words so smoothly delivered.

"I am most pleased to hear that, chief factor." Ghrant turned slightly in the chair. "Do you have any questions you might wish to ask the chief factor, ser Kharl?"

"Yes, your lordship." Kharl was very glad that he had thought over carefully what Guillam might say.

Ghrant nodded at Kharl.

Kharl stepped forward a pace. "Chief factor, you are a man who knows a great deal and a great number of people in Austra. Because you do know so many, you might be most helpful. This morning, there was a poisoned tray offered to a guest at the Great House. Before she could be questioned, the server who offered it was found strangled. Did you have any knowledge of this?"

"No, ser mage. Why would I have any knowledge of something that sordid?" Contempt oozed from Guillam, along with a sense of chaos, not the chaos of magic, but the sort of chaos that Kharl was coming to associate with evil. While Guillam seemed to be looking at Kharl, his eyes avoided those of the mage. He was also lying.

"What is your relationship with a man named Fostak?" After a slight pause, Kharl added, "Or what was it?"

For the slightest moment, Guillam did not move, a moment almost imperceptible. "I have no relationship with anyone called Fostak. I never have."

Another lie. Kharl was beginning to feel that he was making the chief factor uncomfortable, but that might have been because of the questions.

"This morning, three crossbowmen fired quarrels within the Great House. While no one was hurt, this sort of matter could be considered to reflect poorly upon Lord Ghrant, and your knowledge could be most helpful in resolving this. Have you any knowledge of this?"

"Crossbowmen in the Great House? Hardly."

That was also a lie, if not so pronounced as the other two. Kharl could see that there was no way to get Guillam to admit his guilt, and if he could not, Lord Ghrant would not be terribly pleased with Kharl. That didn't bother Kharl so much as the fact that Guillam was not only a liar, but someone who had ordered two murders and was and would be a traitor.

"Ser mage?" asked Ghrant, a slight hint of irritation in his voice.

"One more question, if you please, your lordship."

"Go ahead."

Kharl forced a hard smile. "Chief Factor, why have you lied in answering every question you have been asked? Have your misdeeds been so great that honest answers would have condemned you to execution for treason and treachery?"

Kharl could hear the indrawn breaths from some standing below the dais.

"I have answered most truthfully, ser mage. Surely, you of all people must know that."

"I know that you will choke on your treachery, your lies, and that your smooth tongue will not save you from the poison within you. Speak the truth or be suffocated by it." With his last words, Kharl turned the air around Guillam solid, so solid that the factor stood immobile, unmoving.

Silence filled the chamber. Kharl could feel Guillam struggling, unmoving as he was. The chief factor's face slowly turned red, then redder, then blue. Only when Kharl could feel the emptiness of death did he dissolve the barriers.

Guillam toppled forward, hitting the floor with a sickening dull thud. He did not move. Kharl knew he never would.

The stillness in the chamber stretched out.

"What . . . what did you do, ser mage?" Ghrant's voice was thin.

"I did nothing out of the ordinary," Kharl said. "I merely commanded him to speak the truth or to choke on his untruths. He could not bear to speak the truth. He died, rather than speak the truth." Kharl had to struggle to keep his voice steady. His entire body seemed ready to shake, and his knees felt watery. He'd forgotten how much effort magery of that sort took, and he'd done almost none since the battle at Dykaru—four eightdays earlier.

Ghrant turned slightly, his eyes fixing on a darker-skinned individual in crimson-and-gold silks, standing in the group of envoys on the south side of the audience. "Lord Joharak . . . apparently, there are times when the truth must out—if one is to live."

"So it might seem, your lordship. Yet one man's truth is another's traitor. All rulers who have succeeded have come to understand that."

"That is most true, Lord Joharak, and the truth that must be in Austra is that which serves Austra." Ghrant stood. "Chamberlain . . ." He gave the slightest nod to the body sprawled at the foot of the steps from the dais. "The audience is over." Ghrant turned and departed.

The moment Ghrant vanished into the one archway, Hagen turned. "This way," he murmured.

Kharl followed.

Hagen said nothing until the two were alone in the lord-chancellor's chamber. "Do I wish to know what you did to Guillam?"

"Every word he spoke was a lie," Kharl replied. "He had no intention of being loyal. He knew Fostak and knew him well. He had also ordered my death and the serving girl's."

"You realize that you have now become a danger to most of the lords and merchants?" asked Hagen dryly. "They have all lied to Lord Ghrant, in more ways than one. I imagine that many of them will have urgent reasons to leave Valmurl before tomorrow."

"I'm sure Lyras could do what I did."

"He probably could tell who was lying, but he couldn't do what you did about it, and he has no magery capable of protecting himself. You will have to be most careful in the days ahead."

"It might be best if I returned to Cantyl, at least for a time," Kharl suggested.

"Not quite yet. We will have to act quickly."

Kharl raised his eyebrows.

"There will be more than one attempt to kill Ghrant within days, if not sooner, or a revolt in his personal guard, or one by the regular guard. Perhaps all three." Hagen shook his head.

"Because I can tell if someone is lying?"

Hagen nodded slowly.

Kharl had thought he was resolving Ghrant's problem with Guillam, as well as getting rid of a man who had tried to kill him twice—and now Hagen was telling him that he'd made the situation worse. "I'm sorry. I'd thought—"

Hagen raised his hand. "Don't worry about it. There would have been problems either way. If Guillam had walked out of the audience hall, everyone would be claiming that Ghrant was afraid to act. If Ghrant had ordered his execution, without any proof, then there might well have been something else."

"You make it sound like ruling fairly is impossible."

"It is. Everyone has a different idea of what fairness is." Hagen walked to the bellpull and gave it three measured tugs. "We'll start with Vatoran, Casolan, and Norgen. You know Vatoran. Casolan is the commander of the western district, and Norgen commands Ghrant's personal guards." Hagen looked mildly at Kharl. "This time, just let me know if someone is lying."

"While they're here, or after they leave?"

"While they're here. We don't have time for indirection. I take it that you can immobilize or kill one of them if he turns violent?"

"I can, but if you want me to do much, I'll need to eat something. Bread or cheese, but something."

"I'll have some brought. Then we'll see how much treachery we can sniff out."

Kharl managed not to shake his head. He just swallowed. He'd never even considered that the truth would have such far-reaching and dangerous consequences—or so quickly.

IV

Almost half a glass had passed before the three commanders stood in Hagen's small chamber. Kharl had choked down some bread and cheese, and a mug of ale, enough food that he was no longer feeling weakened.

Vatoran stood in the middle, a gray-haired officer with a broad forehead, pointed chin, and perfect mustache. Casolan, to Vatoran's right, was short and blocky, square-faced. Both Vatoran and Casolan wore the green-and-black uniforms, while on the left stood Norgen, a slender man in black and yellow, whose once-red hair had faded to strawberry and whose freckles had faded into pale splotches on a face that had seen too much sun.

While Hagen stood behind the desk, Kharl was to the side, his back to the north wall.

"Commander Vatoran," Hagen began, "you were at the audience earlier this afternoon. What did you think of the chief factor's attitude toward Lord Ghrant?"

Vatoran squinted slightly. Clearly, the question puzzled the officer, Kharl felt.

After a moment, Vatoran replied. "His words were polite. They were not truthful, but they have never been. He was never that truthful to Lord Estloch." The commander coughed, several times, then stepped back, trying to clear his throat. When he finally straightened up, he was to the left of Norgen.

Kharl could sense the falsity of the cough, but why had Vatoran moved to one side? There was a hint of chaos around the commander, but Kharl had found that many people occasionally showed such hints. While he did not know why, he had surmised that occurred because they had been near a source of chaos.

"What was your impression of the chief factor, Commander Norgen?"

"Guillam was always well-spoken, ser. He chose his words with care. His own interests were always more important to him than the interests of Austra, but I have found that to be true of most factors and merchants."

"Were you surprised to find that he was plotting against Lord Ghrant and ser Kharl?"

"No, ser. He is the sort that believes he is superior to others. He believes that, even if they know he opposes them, they will not dare to act against him."

"You are charged with the safety of Lord Ghrant, Commander Norgen. One of your more trusted armsmen was suborned and tried to murder his consort and heirs. The performance of a number of your companies and their officers has left something to be desired. Under these conditions, I have to ask two questions. First, are you willing to do what is necessary to improve the personal guard? Second, are you personally completely loyal to Lord Ghrant?"

Norgen smiled ironically. "If I were not loyal to the Lord of Austra, I would not be in this room. It is clear that ser Kharl can tell falsehoods more quickly than they can be uttered. Because I understand this, I will tell the truth as I see it. I am loyal to the Lord of Austra, and I will do all that I can to improve the personal guard. I am greatly concerned that Lord Ghrant is not the leader that his sire was, but I always felt that Ilteron would have plunged Austra into chaos and that we would have ended as either a Hamorian pawn or part of their empire. Any other leader would not have the support of all those necessary to rule effectively. Lord Ghrant, unless he is most careful, and unless he heeds your advice, may still have great difficulty."

Kharl could sense the truth of Norgen's words, even to the fact that Norgen did not particularly care for Ghrant, but would be loyal.

Norgen looked to Kharl, not to Hagen. Then Hagen nodded at Kharl.

"Commander Norgen is bound by his duty, and will be loyal, even though he does not have the deepest of affection for Lord Ghrant."

Vatoran shifted his weight from one boot to the other, and his lips tightened.

Hagen turned to Casolan. "The Western Division armsmen and lancers had the best performance in dealing with Ilteron's forces, but they were not as good as they should have been."

"No, ser. I have already removed three captains, and one overcaptain, and we have stepped up training for all companies."

"I know," Hagen said dryly. "The Lords Fergyn, Kenslan, and Sterolan have already complained that there was no reason to dismiss their sons. I've suggested, politely, that there was reason, and that the lords and their sons might well not wish those reasons to become public. They agreed, reluctantly." The lord-chancellor paused, then asked, "How do you see your duty to Lord Ghrant, commander?"

"Guess I'm like Norgen. Lord Ghrant's got a lot to learn, and he didn't want to learn it until circumstances forced him. Ilteron was the worst of a bad lot, and I can't thank the mage enough for putting an end to that problem. I'm loyal to the Lord of Austra. I just hope he's worth that loyalty."

Along with truthfulness, Casolan conveyed a rock-hard solidity. On the far side of the other two commanders, Vatoran shifted his weight once more, almost imperceptibly, his eyes avoiding Kharl.

"Ser mage?" asked Hagen.

"Commander Casolan has stated his feelings most truthfully, ser."

"I would expect no less from a distinguished officer." Hagen smiled. "Ser Kharl . . . do you have any questions for Commander Vatoran?"

Kharl thought he understood what was coming. "Commander Vatoran, the last time we met, I had told you about the officers who were eating a lavish meal in Dykaru when a battle was about to begin. I also told you about the officer who had given poor direction to the driver of a wagon carrying wounded. Could you tell me what you did about those incidents?"

Vatoran looked at Kharl, coldly, then at Hagen. "You are allowing this . . . mage . . . to question my command?"

"Can you suggest anyone more honest, and more interested in the truth, commander?" replied Hagen.

Kharl could sense the faintest hint of ironic amusement from Casolan, but he kept his eyes and senses upon Vatoran.

"Truth means nothing without understanding," Vatoran replied.

"That is very true," Kharl said. "That is why I asked what you did. You could certainly explain matters to me so that I could understand. What did you do?"

Vatoran stiffened. "My officers insist that you were mistaken, mage. Honestly mistaken, but mistaken."

Vatoran was lying, but Kharl could not understand why, not under the circumstances. "I am confused, commander." Kharl paused. "The uniforms of Austran officers are very distinctive. I did see those uniforms. Does that mean that someone else was wearing them?"

"You had to be mistaken."

"Did you actually inquire?"

"Of course."

That was a blatant lie. "I see. Would you say that your loyalty is more to your officers, or more to the Lord of Austra?"

"I must be loyal to both. If my officers do not trust me, then I can do nothing for my lord."

Kharl had to think. Vatoran was right about that. "How do you enforce discipline, then, when they have done wrong?"

"Done wrong? You were mistaken, mage." Vatoran's voice was tight.

Kharl half turned to Hagen, not totally taking his eyes and senses off Vatoran. "I may have been mistaken. I do not think so, not when there were others in Dykaru who also saw those officers and spoke of it. Whether I was mistaken or not, Commander Vatoran is not telling the truth, and he knows that he is not."

Vatoran turned to Casolan. "Will you let them do this? Listen to a cooper who has never commanded a single armsman?"

Casolan smiled sadly. "The mage has been in more battles than you have, Vatoran. He doesn't lie, either."

Vatoran looked to Norgen.

Norgen shook his head.

Kharl cleared his throat. "I have one last question. Have you been involved in any of the plots against Lord Ghrant?"

Vatoran looked from Kharl to Hagen. "I do not have to answer such an insulting question."

"Yes, you do," Hagen said. "If you do not answer, you are admitting guilt."

"Ghrant is a weakling. Who would not oppose him?" Vatoran shrugged. "You can imprison me, but you will not hold me."

"My guards will," said Norgen.

Vatoran looked stunned. "You don't even like Ghrant."

"That has nothing to do with loyalty and duty," replied Norgen.

Casolan nodded.

Hagen moved to the bellpull and tugged it once.

Vatoran looked at Kharl, except that his eyes darted away from meeting Kharl's directly. "You will destroy Austra, mage, you and your truth-telling."

Kharl said nothing. He well might destroy the Austra that Vatoran represented, but could he do less, after what he had experienced?

"If that is the Austra you represent, Vatoran, it might as well be destroyed," Hagen said, "because it will fall to the first gale of winter."

At the knock on the door, Hagen ordered, "Enter."

Undercaptain Charsal opened the door. Behind him were four guards, two in green and black and two in yellow and black.

"Commander Vatoran is to be held," Hagen stated. "In the deep cell for now."

"Yes, ser."

Vatoran looked around the small chamber. "None of you will survive this. Not even you, mage. There are always greater mages." He turned to the undercaptain. "I am in your care, undercaptain. For now."

No one in the room spoke until the door closed.

"He never did like real armsmen," Casolan said.

"That may be," replied Hagen. "But some of his companies may attempt to attack the Great House. He has three nearby. Can you two get companies you trust in place here immediately?"

"I have one company standing by, ser," offered Norgen. "I can get another in place within two glasses."

"I only have one near here. Most of mine are nearer to Bruel," said Casolan dryly.

"You'd best go and form up what you can." Hagen nodded. "The mage and I need to see what else we can do."

"Best start with Lord Kenslan," suggested Norgen.

The two bowed and departed.

Hagen tilted his head, and began speaking, almost to himself. "Both Hedron and Kenslan left the Great House right after the audience. Majer Fuelt is Kenslan's middle son. He's a majer in command of three companies under Vatoran."

Kharl frowned. "Fuelt? Wasn't he in that meeting in Dykaru? Was he the one who was contemptuous—"

"That would be Fuelt. His father is worse."

Kharl looked to Hagen. "I'm sorry. It seems as if—"

"Don't be sorry. It would have happened sooner or later. Better now than later. If . . . if we can weather this storm, it may be for the best."

Kharl wasn't so certain. He recalled what Lyras and Taleas had said to him, how setting forth the truth was a good way to get killed, and to upset everyone. Well, he'd exposed too many truths in the past day. That was clear.

"You look doubtful, Kharl."

"I was thinking about the dangers of truth."

"It's a little late for that. I need to brief Lord Ghrant. He won't be happy, but I think I can convince him that it's better to face this head-on than to get a knife or a crossbow quarrel in the back in a season or two. You need to get more to eat. We'll need all the strength you have in the glasses ahead. Go on down to the kitchen. Then come back here. If I'm not here, wait for me."

"Yes, ser."

"Don't fret so much. We might as well face this storm as run from it."

As if we have much choice, thought Kharl.

V

Kharl made his way to the kitchen, where he ate heartily, if guiltily, then hurried back to his chamber—carefully—to recover *The Basis of Order* before returning to Hagen's small chamber. The pair of guards in yellow and black who had been posted there since his departure a half glass before opened the door for him.

"The lord-chancellor said it might be longer than he thought, ser mage."

"Thank you."

Kharl didn't mind the quiet of the chamber. He needed to think. If armsmen did attack or storm the Great House, what could he do? His skill of hardening air—or anything—was of limited use, except against a very few individuals, and it tired him quickly. He was good with a staff, but that would only be useful in defending himself while he did something else.

The one thing that would be useful would also be the most dangerous—and it would work only if there were but one or two leaders of the attackers. He could use his ability to move unseen and attack the leaders.

That worked only if the attackers did not have a mage who could detect him—and if someone didn't detect him by other means and fill the air with arrows. His ability to order-harden air and other things was useful only for defense or against one or two people from a very close distance.

What else could he do? The ability to know and tell the truth had only created more problems—or perhaps it had simply made obvious problems that were already there. But sometimes, it was clear, revealing the truth directly was not the best course. Very few people liked hearing the truth.

His thoughts skittered back to the passage in *The Basis of Order* that he had read earlier in the day. What if there were no such thing as truth? He shook his head. That was not what the words had meant, because the book had said that what was, indeed was. Did that mean that there was something wrong with the idea of truth? That it was something beyond what was?

He nodded. When people talked about truth, there was a righteousness in their words, a belief that the truth was absolutely the way they saw it. That was what the book had meant, and *that* was why revealing what in fact had happened or what someone believed could be so dangerous. It was not because of the rightness of what was revealed, but because revealing that kind of truth showed people's weaknesses. So often what one person saw as truth was another person's failing.

Kharl smiled wryly. That was an interesting insight, and one he should have understood years earlier, but that was the sort of thinking that wasn't usually required of coopers. Interesting or not, it didn't offer a way to solve the immediate problem of what he could do to help defend the Great House.

He opened *The Basis of Order* and began to leaf through the pages, hoping that something, on some page, might spur an idea. After several pages, his eyes caught on several lines.

> . . . when chaos that is bound to nothing strikes an object, it loosens the bonds that hold the object together. Order holds all together. Without order, stone would be as sand, water as mist or rain. Thus, order can strengthen what is beyond its natural strength, while chaos weakens it . . .

That didn't help, except to confirm what he already knew. That additional order was what made the staff of a beginning mage as strong as iron, if far lighter. He might be able to strengthen a weapon or two, but that was all, and someone still had to wield those weapons, and it wouldn't be him, unless it was a staff. He certainly wasn't that good with weapons like sabres.

Kharl skimmed through nearly thirty pages before he found something else.

> Light from the sun is thought by the learned to be chaos, but it is not that. Rather it is not precisely that. Light is composed of tiny particles of order that can be thought to flow like water in a millrace from the sun—or from a lamp. The flow is chaotic, but the light itself is not. Could the light be ordered, in a fashion similar to what a burning glass will do, except within itself, its power would be almost without limit . . .

Kharl pursed his lips. He wasn't sure exactly what the words meant, but they did mean that sun and light itself were somehow linked to order. How that might benefit him . . . or how he could use it . . . that was another question. The words suggested that there was a way to make the light from the sun terribly powerful, but the book did not say how. Or did it?

He read on, but there was nothing in *The Basis of Order* that suggested *how* sunlight might be ordered to create such power. Had anyone ever done so? Kharl smiled faintly. With all the secrets Recluce kept, how would he or anyone else ever know?

The mage who knew that he knew too little kept reading, searching, but, as he had suspected, order was far better suited to protection of an individual than to attacks against an army. Or . . . whoever had written it had hidden the aspects of order suited to attack so that each had to be ferreted out in the way that Kharl had figured out how to use the hardening of air as a weapon as well as a defense.

Kharl straightened in the chair, then rose, as the door opened, and Hagen entered.

"I apologize for being so long, Kharl."

"I'm the one who should be sorry. If I hadn't—"

Hagen waved off Kharl's protest. "You may have staved off a worse disaster. Some of my scouts report that a number of the midlands lords have been riding west to meet with Lord Malcor."

"Wasn't he the lord who killed Lord Estloch?"

"It was suspected, but there was no way to prove it. Once word got out about your ability to discern the truth, several of the more dissatisfied lords scurried off to tell Malcor. Since he's avoided Lord Ghrant, I think we can take it that he did murder Lord Estloch."

"They wouldn't be plotting another revolt if it weren't for me, because they could just cover up what happened."

"There's some truth in that," Hagen admitted, "and Ghrant could have used some time to deal with it quietly. But he hates conflict and scheming, and there's a good chance he would have done nothing."

Kharl could tell that Hagen believed his own words, and that was both disturbing and a relief of sorts for the mage.

"I've talked it over with Ghrant. We've sent Casolan west to gather his forces. Casolan's confident that most of the western lords will either back Lord Ghrant or remain out of the conflict." Hagen laughed. "Strange, isn't it? The lords who backed Ilteron are likely to support Ghrant against Malcor and his allies. They don't want years of squabbling. Most of them backed Ilteron because they felt he was stronger. The way he fought Ghrant weakened their support. Casolan thinks the way that you and Ghrant handled Guillam will add to their backing of Ghrant. They've been worried about the power that the factors have been gaining, anyway."

"But . . . trade . . . doesn't it help all Austra?"

"It does, but it helps the east more than the west."

As Hagen talked, Kharl felt as though he stood in the middle of a storm at sea, with lightning likely to come from anywhere and waves and treacherous currents all about him.

"They also back you," Kharl suggested.

"That doesn't hurt, but it's not enough."

"What do you think will happen next?" asked Kharl.

"We won't see an attack today. Perhaps not even tomorrow. We will see one," Hagen said tiredly. "Vatoran threatened the guards who imprisoned him. He had already ordered the eastern companies to obey Lord Kenslan if anything happened to him."

"He wasn't threatening them. He was bargaining for his own safety."

"Kenslan, unfortunately, is a better arms-commander than Vatoran, and his son is one of the subcommanders."

"What if something happens to Kenslan?"

Hagen shook his head. "If it happens in battle, everyone will accept it.

If you kill him with magery, without even an audience, that will just stir things up more."

"He can start a revolt, take over some of Lord Ghrant's armsmen, but if I use magery . . . ?"

"Exactly." Hagen snorted. "I know. It makes no sense, but that's the way people are. Everyone knows Malcor killed Lord Estloch; but there was no proof, and without it, no one wanted to act."

"So we wait?"

"We gather forces, strengthen our position, and see where they plan to attack. There is little doubt that they will attack."

Kharl could tell he would not be headed back to Cantyl anytime soon.

VI

Threeday passed, and so did fourday. Kharl found nothing else of use in *The Basis of Order.* On fiveday, right after breakfast, in the chill of the spring morning, under a gray sky with high clouds, Kharl stood in the front courtyard of the Great House, studying the walls, only about five cubits high and but a double course of stone in width—designed to keep out casual intruders, but certainly not an attacking force. But then, Hagen had already pointed out that it would be foolish—both politically and practically—for the rebels to begin with an open attack within the general confines of Valmurl.

"Good day, ser Kharl."

The mage turned. Undercaptain Charsal stood ten cubits away.

"Good day, undercaptain. What news do you have?"

"No more than you, probably. No one's moving armsmen toward Valmurl yet. Lord Malcor leveled Lord Vertyn's country place because Vertyn voiced support for Lord Ghrant. Folk are worried about fighting. Most in Valmurl support Lord Ghrant." Charsal shrugged. "Then, they might well be telling me that because they know I do."

"What about the factors?"

"My cousin works for Gessryn. He's a small wool factor. He says that all the factors are upset about what happened to Guillam. Half are mad at Guillam, dead as he may be, because he thought only of himself. The other half are mad because they think Lord Ghrant and the other lords want to tariff them more heavily . . . and keep all the power to themselves."

"No one thinks about the people or Austra?"

Charsal laughed. "Have they ever, ser mage?" He nodded. "Need to be reporting to Commander Norgen."

Kharl returned the nod and watched as the young undercaptain hurried toward the main entrance to the Great House. The mage took a last look at the low walls and turned, making his way through the side service entrance and along the back corridors he was beginning to learn until he reached Hagen's chamber.

The two men in yellow and black were new to Kharl, but the shorter inclined his head. "Ser mage, would you be wanting to see Lord Hagen?"

"If he's not with someone."

The guard turned, knocked once, and said, "The mage to see you, lord-chancellor."

"Have him come in."

The guard opened the door, and Kharl entered. The guard closed the door behind Kharl.

Hagen sat behind the table desk, a map spread before him. "Sit down, Kharl. Please." He returned his attention to the map, then dipped the metal pen into the inkpot and wrote something on the long paper set to one side of the map. He continued to make notes for a quarter glass or so. Finally, he looked up.

"Undercaptain Charsal told me that Malcor had destroyed Lord Vertyn's estate," Kharl said.

"He did," Hagen replied. "He also killed Vertyn and his eldest son. The middle son is a junior captain under Norgen."

"Charsal said no one was moving toward Valmurl. What is Malcor doing?" asked Kharl.

"Word is that he and Lord Kenslan look to be marching northward toward Lord Lahoryn's lands."

"If they attack Lord Lahoryn, is that a battle?" asked Kharl. "Will Lord Ghrant see it so?"

Hagen looked sharply at Kharl. "You have something in mind?"

"I do. I don't like it, but what is . . . is."

"Go ahead, ser mage."

"It's simple, honored lord-chancellor. As a mage, that is, with what I know now, I can do very little against companies and armies. I can sometimes do a great deal against individuals. In most battles, lots and lots of armsmen get killed and wounded. Most of the time the commanders and lords don't, not from the little I've seen and what the armsmen say."

"That's true, but once you leave the Great House, you're going to be the target of every crossbow that Malcor and his allies can find."

"That's if they know I'm leaving."

Hagen looked at Kharl. "That could still be very dangerous. Why are you volunteering for something like this?"

Kharl laughed, a sound holding amusement and irony. "If Lord Ghrant is overthrown, after all that I've already done, how long before I'm dead or skulking down alleys looking over my shoulder—or back at sea on a vessel far worse than the *Seastag*?"

"Not long, I'd judge." Hagen's smile was sympathetic. "So you want to increase the stakes for Lord Malcor and the discontents? Is that it?"

"They're the ones causing the troubles, aren't they?"

"Depends on who's talking."

"From what I've seen, Lord Ghrant's biggest problem is that he doesn't look or talk like a leader. He's not out making free with every girl, and he's not lining his pockets with everyone else's coins. Or have I missed something?"

"No. Ghrant doesn't want to hurt anyone. He just wants his comfortable life to go on, and he doesn't want to be betrayed or removed."

"That's more reasonable than most lords," Kharl said dryly.

"You have a high opinion of rulers," Hagen replied dryly. "So high that I'm surprised that you suggested this . . . expedition."

"Will things get better for what I need to do if I wait?"

"No." Hagen took a deep breath.

"Do you know if they have any wizards or mages?"

"No one has said anything about wizardry. If Malcor was supporting Ilteron, there might be another white wizard from Hamor around. Supposedly, there were two left, but there's been no sign of either yet."

Kharl had hoped there weren't any, but he'd have to deal with whatever was, wizards or not. He still didn't like the thought of running up against a powerful white wizard. There was so much he still didn't know.

"Charsal knows the area. What about sending you with him and a squad on what look to be road patrols? You'd have to wear Ghrant's personal livery, the yellow and black."

Kharl fingered his beard. He'd considered going alone, dressed as a carpenter, but carpenters couldn't afford mounts, and it took a long time to walk anywhere. "That might be best."

"You don't have to do this, you know?"

"I know. But what I might have to do later, if I don't, could be worse."

"I'll see if Charsal is willing, and then the three of us can talk about where you should go and which roads and lanes to take."

Kharl nodded. He didn't like the idea much. He just liked far less what he feared would happen if he didn't act soon.

VII

Sixday morning found Kharl wearing the yellow-and-black uniform of Ghrant's personal guard as he rode northwest beside Charsal along a rutted clay road barely wider than a lane. Kharl was doing his best not to bounce in the saddle, but his riding experience had been most limited. Instead of a sabre, there was a cudgel in the lance holder, since Kharl had never learned either lances or blades. Behind him rode ten other lancers, a half squad.

A fine cold spring mist drifted down from low-lying clouds, leaving a thin sheen of water on the lower and more level sections of the road. The flat light gave the water-covered parts of the road a silver cast. The air was still cold and damp enough that at times the breath of the horses steamed.

What was he doing riding out again to do something that could easily get himself killed if anything at all went wrong? Kharl wondered. He'd had to risk his life just to stay alive when he had been running from Egen. Then he'd risked his life in saving Lord Ghrant to repay Hagen. Now he was risking his life, in a sense, to keep what he'd earned so that he didn't end up back in poverty and on the run. Was life just a continuing series of situations where he had to wager himself for higher and higher stakes—just to avoid losing what he had? Was that why rulers in difficulties ended up making bad decisions?

After a time, Kharl began to notice an acrid odor in the air. Something was burning, and it didn't smell like a hearth fire or a forge. He turned to Charsal. "How much farther do we need to ride along this road?"

"A good two kays more, maybe three. Then we'll be taking a lane to the back side of the orchards. The scouts reported that Malcor and Kenslan have got their forces north of there. The trees have started to leaf out, but they're mostly still winter-gray."

"That will provide some cover?"

"Enough so they won't see us from afar, anyway. They don't have pickets out more than half a kay. Leastwise, they didn't yesterday. Wouldn't count on that, though. Kenslan'll begin whipping 'em into better discipline."

"Vatoran didn't do that?"

"Vatoran came up through the ranks. Learned that you got further if you didn't piss off the officers who came from lordly families and if you always said yes to lords. Gets you promoted. Doesn't make for good discipline." Charsal laughed. "That's what Commander Norgen says, anyway. But . . . back then, who was worrying about discipline? Hadn't been anyone to fight in years."

"It's late to instill discipline after the fighting starts," Kharl said dryly.

"Yes, ser. Commander Norgen said that Lord Estloch should have kept Lord Hagen as arms-commander, but too many of the younger sons of lords complained that he was too strict."

So Hagen had once been arms-commander of Austra? Hagen had alluded to his past, but that was something he hadn't mentioned.

"That's when he went to sea, they say." Charsal frowned, then held up a hand. "Halt."

Kharl managed to rein up his mount, far less smoothly than did the riders behind him. He glanced northward. The narrow road sloped upward to a crest a good ten rods ahead. He thought he could make out the beginning of a hedgerow beyond on the left side of the road.

In the silence, the undercaptain listened for several moments before speaking. "Riders . . . headed this way."

Kharl could not only hear the drumbeat of hoofs, but also, for the first time, could clearly sense something like a faint white fog—a white wizard.

Had they been detected by sorcery? How many wizards were there supporting the rebel lords? He could hope that there was only one remaining.

"They're still almost a kay away, from the sound. We'll head up just short of where the road crests, so we can look over and see how many and how far away they are."

Kharl had hoped they would have been able to get closer to the rebel forces. From what Charsal said, he was almost three kays away. Still, he'd walked three kays many a time, and more than once just to save a few coppers.

When they reined up short of the road crest, Kharl tried to make out the riders who headed down the long and gentle incline that was opposite the low hillcrest from where he watched. Against the low clouds, he found it hard to take an accurate count, but there were clearly far more armsmen headed toward them than in the small force behind him.

He looked ahead to his left, where the hedgerow began, bordering the road on the west. Behind the hedgerow was a meadow, one not terribly tidy, with winter-browned grass. Farther to the west, at the end of the meadow, was a grove of trees—or an ill-tended orchard whose leaves had yet to turn from winter-gray to green. Apples, he thought. Beyond the trees were several buildings, barely visible. Kharl looked more to the north. After a moment, he realized that what he'd first thought had been fog was smoke from the buildings that had already been burned.

"They've burned that place."

"Lord Lahoryn's country house," said Charsal. "We've got other problems. Two whole squads riding toward us, and they look to be fresh."

Kharl asked quickly, "What would happen if they rode into a wall that they couldn't see?"

"They'd still outnumber us."

"But that would stop them for a bit, get them confused, even if the wall vanished, wouldn't it?"

Charsal nodded.

"Then, let's try this. I'll get off by that hedgerow there. You take my mount and ride just a little farther, then turn around and ride back. Not too fast at first, as if your horses are more tired than they are."

"What if they see you, ser?"

"They won't." Kharl paused, trying to work out his strategy. "If they turn back, you can come and get me. If they don't . . . just head back toward the Great House. You remember that corner where the meeting house of the one-god believers is?"

"You want us to meet you there?"

"Not until close to sundown, anyway, and it might be later. That's if they try to follow you."

"You don't need to do the wall-like thing, ser. We can just ride."

"It's better if I do. It should make them cautious in following you. That will be easier on your mounts. Also, I'm hoping that I can create the impression that I'm still with you, and that they'll not think I'm where I am."

"If you say so, ser." Charsal turned in his saddle. "We're riding forward about twenty rods. Then we'll turn and head back . . . slow trot. The mage is going to work a diversion. Forward!"

Not a word or a murmur came from the lancers.

Kharl half turned in the saddle, almost falling off as he struggled to extract some of the cheese, biscuits, and dried apples from the saddlebag. Then he thrust those and the water bottle inside the yellow-trimmed black riding jacket. He had to steady himself by grabbing the gray's mane. A rider he was not.

When Kharl and Charsal had almost reached the hedgerow, the mage eased his mount toward the undercaptain. "Slow down for a moment."

"Ah . . . yes, sir."

Kharl leaned right in the saddle and handed the gray's reins to Charsal. "Don't be surprised." With that, he slipped the sight shield around himself, and, once more, was in the dark and sightless, relying on his order-senses to get him off his mount, off the road, and behind the hedgerow.

". . . gone . . ."

". . . course . . . he's a mage . . . do our part . . ."

Once he was in place behind the hedgerow, mostly hidden, Kharl released the sight shield. If he couldn't see the road, whoever was on the road was unlikely to see him, and it was unlikely the holders or tenants in the buildings beyond the trees would see him against the back of the hedgerow.

Kharl knelt behind the twisted mass of branches and vines that had barely begun to show green, using his order-senses to watch what happened on the road. Within moments, Charsal and his squad trotted back southward past the spot where Kharl waited behind the hedgerow. From the north came the growing sound of hoofs, and a stronger sense of the chaos whiteness.

As he stood next to the foliage that separated him from the road, Kharl concentrated on creating not so much an image, but a projection of order, set close to the now-riderless mount that Charsal led, hoping that the white wizard who rode with the rebels would focus on that order.

The pursuing lancers did not slow as they neared Kharl's hiding place—a good sign. He waited until the lancers were within five rods of him before he struggled to create a solid barrier of air, based on linking the air together with twists of order. The barrier ran from the road surface to more than head height of a mounted man.

"We're gaining . . ."

A series of dull *thuds,* followed by screaming from downed horses and yells as riders tried to rein up and avoid becoming entangled in the mass of fallen mounts and unhorsed men. At least two of the rebel armsmen were dead. Kharl had felt the emptiness, the wash of red-tinged death. Several others were injured, perhaps severely.

Kharl was trembling when he released the barrier. He took a deep breath and began to move northward at a quick walk. He did not let go of the order projection moving with Charsal until he was a good thirty rods north of the milling confusion. As he moved away from the pileup of men and mounts, he kept checking with both eyes and senses to see if anyone had chanced to look behind the hedgerow, but no one did.

"After them . . . !"

The riders who had not suffered—or perhaps the second squad—resumed the pursuit of Charsal.

Kharl kept walking, hurriedly, through the damp grass of the meadow. Already, the lower parts of his trousers were wet. The ill-tended meadow extended down a slight slope for almost a kay, until it reached a small stream, so small that it was a mere rivulet running across a muddy depression. Just short of the stream, which Kharl could sense, but not see, the hedgerow stopped, or rather turned westward at a right angle. So thick was the vegetation that the mage had to walk almost ten rods westward before he came to a gate in the hedgerow.

The iron latch was broken, and the gate had been secured with a length of twine. Kharl used his belt knife to cut it, but quickly retied the twine once he was through.

His legs were wobbly.

He glanced around, then leaned against the stone pillar that held the gate hinges and took the water bottle out from inside his jacket. After a long swallow, he munched on some dried apple slices and took a bite of the hard yellow cheese. He finished with a biscuit that was mostly fragments and crumbs, and another swallow of water.

Ahead, near the hilltop almost a kay away, he could make out a large orchard with trees set precisely in rows—the orchard on the southern border of Lord Lahoryn's lands, he thought. If so, the rebel forces were less than a kay north from where he stood.

Before setting out northward, Kharl scanned the area nearby once more, taking in the path that led through the muddy depression holding the tiny stream, the stone-walled meadow on the far side, one wall of which bordered the road—without a hedgerow. The hedgerow through which he had just passed continued westward, then turned north once more on the far side of the meadow. In order not stand out to any observer, Kharl would have to walk westward, then follow the hedgerow uphill and north toward the orchard—and the rebel forces beyond. He took another swallow of water, corked the water bottle, and slipped it back inside the riding jacket. He turned westward, following the hedgerow.

When he reached the spot where the hedgerow started northward once more, he crossed the middle strip that held the stream. He had only covered ten or fifteen rods, walking beside the twisted and intertwined branches and through the damp grass, before his trousers below the knee were thoroughly soaked, and water oozed down into his boots. He was also sweating under the riding jacket from his exertions and the damp spring air.

He kept close to the hedgerow as he moved uphill. He was still a quarter of a kay from the stone wall between the meadow and the orchard when he began to sense that there were sentries set at intervals along the wall. Once more he drew upon his skills and let the light flow around him so that the sentries could not see him. He had to move more slowly because he was relying on his order-senses, rather than his sight.

Kharl moved even more carefully when he neared the wall. While the sentry a hundred cubits to the east could not see him, the man could certainly hear if the mage knocked off a stone or made any other significant noise. Kharl still felt strange climbing over the low stone wall so close to a sentry.

Once over the wall he made his way from tree to tree, always headed northward. Outside of the sentries, no other armsmen were in the orchard. At the north end of the orchard, on the west end, there was a small section of a hedgerow. There, Kharl found a spot that was sheltered from casual view and released the sight shield. While he did not feel as weak as he had after the encounter with the rebel lancers and the white wizard, he could sense that he needed to rest. He drank some more from the water bottle and finished the cheese and dried apples—and another biscuit that was also mostly pieces and crumbs.

After he had refreshed himself, he peered northward through the screen of branches and winter-gray leaves. A handful of tents rose from the highest point in the meadow to the northwest of the hedgerow, and around them were mounts on tie-lines and armsmen in groups, seemingly waiting. Beyond the meadow were the smoldering ruins of what had been Lord Lahoryn's large country house.

Kharl had to wonder why they had burned it, rather than just taking it. Or was the rebels' plan to make an example of Lord Ghrant's supporters? It didn't make much sense to him.

Beyond the hedgerow was more of the damp meadow grass, and he would have to cross a good half kay of open ground. He just hoped there were no dogs around because they would sniff him out, even if they couldn't see him.

He took a long and deep breath, then drew the sight shield around himself and stepped away from the hedgerow.

Step by step, he made his slow way toward the tents. After less than ten rods he had to circle more to the east to avoid a line of mounts and the lancers tending them. He listened as well as he could as he slipped past.

". . . not that hard . . ."

". . . just an old man and his people . . ."

". . . would have liked to have gotten that girl before . . ."

". . . she's spoils for the lords . . ."

By the time Kharl had circled around more lancers and mounts, reoriented himself, and headed back toward the low crest in the middle of the meadow, he felt soaked inside and out, from the high damp grass, from the damp mist that was becoming more like a fine rain, and from his own sweat. With each step, his feet sank into the soft ground, and he could feel the chill dampness inside his boots.

From what his order-senses told him, there were but five tents, the two in the center being the largest. He eased between two of the smaller tents, both empty, and toward the nearer of the larger pair. There, he paused near the rear canvas wall. There was no need for him to enter the tents, but the first larger tent was vacant as well.

At the sound and sense of someone coming, Kharl edged closer to the canvas, standing beside a guy rope. An armsman strode past. The man paused, looked around, shook his head, then continued toward the next large tent.

Kharl waited, then followed. While the armsman circled to the front of the tent and the two guards stationed there, Kharl made his way close to the rear canvas, where he listened.

"Lord Kenslan, Undercaptain Giron, ser."

"Yes, undercaptain?" The voice was simultaneously surprisingly high and yet hard.

"You had asked for a report. Lord Ghrant's black mage came up the orchard road. He set some sort of trap that killed a handful of our lancers. The mage Alborak and the lancers chased him back south. We don't have a report on what happened yet."

"Thank you, undercaptain. Let us know what occurred as soon as you hear."

"Yes, ser."

There was silence within the tent until the undercaptain was well away.

"Where is Yarak? Alborak is barely a wizard. That mage of Ghrant's could be more than he can handle."

"Yarak had another task. He went to make sure that our plans are not revealed. What Ghrant's mage can do is limited. He is black, not white." There was a laugh. "Kenslan, you worry too much."

"Malcor, you worry too little. I have good reports on what that mage did. That's why I suggested to Fostak that a stronger wizard would be necessary if we were to be successful. And you sent him off on this . . . fool's errand."

"Vatoran was the fool."

Kharl nodded. There were only two men in the tent, and they were Malcor and Kenslan. He took a slow deep breath and concentrated, forming an impermeable barrier of hard air around each lord.

All sound from within the tent stopped.

Kharl felt light-headed, but continued to hold the hardened air barrier around the two lords.

At last came one red-tinged void of death, then another.

Kharl immediately released the barrier. From inside the tent came two dull *thuds*, followed by a muffled crash.

The mage found himself trembling once more. The effort to remove the two rebel leaders, combined with the requirement to keep himself shielded, had once more left his legs feeling like jelly. That wouldn't do, not when he had a good five kays to walk back to the crossroads—avoiding armsmen the entire way and going much of the distance without being able to see and having to rely on his order-senses to navigate.

Besides, it would only be moments before the guards raised an alarm.

Kharl forced himself to move quickly back the way he had come, but he had covered less than a handful of rods before he heard the yelling, although he could not make out the words.

He kept walking, as fast as he could, knowing that he could not cover as much ground as he needed at any faster pace. He'd known that using magery would take strength, but what choice had he had? He'd have to practice more in the future. He couldn't afford to be tired so quickly, not when he had to deal with Lord Ghrant's enemies one at a time.

By the time he reached the southeast edge of the meadow and the hedgerow where he'd stopped before, he was staggering, and he was so light-headed he wasn't certain how much longer he could even hold his sight shield.

Like it or not, he had to rest, even on the matted wet grass and dirt in the small niche in the hedgerow. He released the sight shield and sank onto the damp soil behind the twisted branches and winter foliage, which offered but minimal cover.

His fingers trembled as he fumbled out the water bottle. The water helped some. He only had one biscuit left, and half of a dried apple slice. He ate both, then just sat there, breathing hard.

The rain was coming down more heavily, and water drizzled off the branches overhead and down the back of his neck. He could hear and sense more yells, orders being barked. Before long, if someone hadn't started looking already, they would be looking for traces, and they well might find his boot prints. Or someone might think about a tracking dog. The rain and the imprints of other boots might confuse them, but Kharl couldn't count on that.

He wasn't quite so light-headed.

He glanced around, looking to the orchard and toward the sentries and the stone wall. The rain made it harder to see clearly, and no one was nearby, not that he could see. He decided against raising the sight shield. It was tiring, and he might need it more later.

He stepped around the end of the hedgerow and began to walk quickly toward the stone wall, as if he were headed on an errand or carrying a message. That was safer than skulking from tree to tree and looking guilty. Besides, with the mist and rain, at a distance his riding jacket was not that different from those of the rebels, and the black trousers were the same. The sentries most likely wouldn't look behind themselves too much, and in the rain, they might even concentrate more on the meadow to the south.

Kharl kept walking through the muddy grass and dirt of the orchard, through a rain that slowly continued to grow in intensity. He tried to ignore the hubbub behind him, a snarling confusion that followed him, growing neither louder nor quieter. Before long, he could see the nearest pair of sentries, one less than a hundred cubits ahead, and slightly to his right, the other barely visible twice that distance away and well to the left.

He watched the nearer sentry closely as he neared the rebel. He was less than thirty cubits away when the man started to turn. Kharl pulled the sight shield around himself and angled his steps more to the right so that he would pass behind the man and reach the wall on the south border of the orchard close to the hedgerow bounding the west end of the meadow.

He was almost abreast of the sentry when he heard the mud-muffled hoofs of a horse behind him.

"Sentries! Eyes sharp! Eyes sharp! Got a scout, maybe a spy. Might be coming this way. See him . . . raise the alarm."

Kharl kept moving.

"You, at the point, see anyone?"

"No, ser! Just rain."

The rider moved eastward away from Kharl. He found himself almost stumbling and forced himself to concentrate on maintaining the sight shield as he eased over the low stone wall and began to make his way down the west side of the meadow. The going was slower, because the winter-dead grass had gotten slicker with the rain, and the dirt in the bare patches had turned to slippery mud.

Still, he made it down the side of the meadow and back through the gate, which he forced himself to secure once more. Once he was out of any possible sight of the sentries to the north, he released the sight shield. He followed the hedgerow eastward, then south.

He made it halfway up the slope, within a few hundred cubits of where he had set the ambush, when he heard hoofs and riders on the road. He sensed a squad of riders. They reined up almost on the other side of the hedgerow from him.

"There's no one on the road. Not any tracks in the mud."

"What about the fields, behind the hedgerow there? Someone could walk or ride there and not be seen."

Kharl looked around. He certainly couldn't move fast enough to outrun a horse, especially the rain, and he had real doubts about how long he could hold a sight shield.

"Senstyn! Take your four and check out the fields to the west. Derk, you check the east fields there."

The hedgerow closest to where Kharl was offered no real concealment. He looked back north. That was too open. To the south, perhaps a hundred cubits ahead, the hedgerow widened, just slightly, and it looked like there was an opening of some sort. Maybe.

He picked up his steps and hurried toward what he hoped would provide cover.

On the road, the riders also began to move.

Kharl began to run, if slowly, trying to pick his way over and through the muddy grass and uneven ground toward what looked to be his only chance of hiding without using the magery that he knew he could not hold for long.

He was within cubits of the slight overhang in the hedgerow and a depression that looked to be hidden from view, especially from the south, and he looked toward the end of the hedgerow, hoping that the riders had not started to turn past the hedgerow.

At that moment, with his eyes off the ground, Kharl's boot caught on something, and he found himself flying forward, helplessly. The ground came up and hit him—hard.

A flash of pain—and then blackness—washed over him.

When he woke, for a moment, he wasn't certain where he was. But the patter of rain on the hedgerow told him that he was partly under cover. His clothes and jacket were soaked, and he was shivering. Each shudder sent dull spasms through his chest.

He was sprawled in a muddy depression overhung by the hedgerow, and he could taste the mud in his mouth and on his lips.

He started to move, to wipe it away, and dull reddish fire surged over the left side of his chest, all the way into his shoulder and down almost to his waist. His eyes blurred. Then, slowly, very slowly, he rolled to his right side and gathered his knees under him.

It took him some time to get to his feet.

He glanced around. Up the short slope was a root, thick as a heavy rope, and below it was the heavy gray rock he'd come down on. From what he could tell, someone had tried to dig out the rock, and failed, leaving a hole between the rock and the hedgerow. Over time the hole had softened into a depression and the grass had mostly overgrown the buried boulder—except for the part where he had hit, then slid down out of sight.

He studied the area around him quietly, but he didn't see or hear or sense anyone nearby, or on the road to the east of the twisted foliage. The cloudy gray afternoon was slightly lighter, and the rain had let up. He guessed it might be midafternoon, but it was hard to tell without seeing the sun.

Slowly, he eased himself out of the depression and back onto the grass beside the hedgerow and south of where he had fallen. He took a step, then a breath. Step and breath . . . step and breath.

He had covered almost two kays, slowly, when the sky began to darken, not from another storm, but from the sun dropping behind the hills to the west. He'd had to hide, several times, but most of the riders had been solitary, and for the one rebel patrol, he'd managed to hold the sight shield until they had ridden well past to the north. He'd had to sit behind the stone wall for a time after that, regaining his strength.

Now he was almost to the crossroads. Once there, he would have to find somewhere to wait, either until the lancers returned, or to rest. He hoped they would. He couldn't count on walking all the way back to the Great House, not with his ribs the way they were.

Kharl settled behind the hedge around the meeting house, in a corner invisible from any of the windows, although no one was inside the place. He was soaked, muddy, shivering, and flushed.

Just as full twilight had descended over the crossroads area, and Kharl was gathering himself together to begin walking again, he heard mounts. Cautiously, he peered out. It took him a while to determine that eight riders in yellow and black approached the crossroads, one leading a riderless mount. Charsal was not among the riders.

Kharl rose from behind the low hedge. "Over here."

"Ser mage?"

"It's me." Kharl tried not to wince or limp as he made his way toward the riders.

"Weren't sure you'd be here." The speaker was an older guard, one Kharl recognized by his face, but not by his name.

"I managed. Undercaptain Charsal . . . ?"

"Wizard got him and Zolen with a firebolt . . . Tiersyn got burned, sent him back to Commander Norgen with message."

Kharl swallowed silently.

"You get done . . . what you needed, ser mage?" The lancer rode led the mount for Kharl closer.

"It's done." Kharl had to lever himself into the saddle with his right arm and hand. Even so, his vision was blurring, and his head was light once more as he tried to steady himself on his mount. He had to grasp twice for the reins extended by the other.

"You wounded, ser mage?"

"Injured," Kharl replied. "Had some of the rebels chasing me. Stupid. Fell and smashed my side. Ribs."

"We'd better get moving." The squad leader shook his head. "That's war. Gets you in ways you'd never think."

Kharl had to admit that the squad leader was right. He held on to the reins and tried not to lurch in the saddle. He *would* ride back, even if every sway of the mount sent another wave of pain through his chest.

VIII

Kharl sat on a stool in his sitting room at the Great House, stripped to the waist, while a healer finished binding his chest. On the table was a small tray which had held the good dark bread and cheese, and a cold fowl breast. There was also an empty pitcher of ale and an empty beaker. He had eaten while he had waited for the healer. The food and ale had helped.

"How bad . . . ?"

"You're a mage. Can't you tell?" asked the gray-haired Istya. "I'm a poor healer at best, and I can even feel some of it."

"I'm a very ill-educated mage. Healing's something I don't know too much about."

"You keep getting banged up like this, and you'd better learn, ser mage."

The heavy cloth did seem to help, and Kharl thought that he could probably speed the healing some by infusing some order into the injured ribs.

"From the bruising, and chaos there, I'd say you cracked two ribs. They're not out of place, but you get hit there again, and they could splinter, maybe go right into your lungs. Mages aren't supposed to be fighting like lancers."

"I was doing the best I could. I didn't do it as well as I should." Kharl had refrained from explaining what had happened in detail. He'd said that he'd been trying to get back to Great House, and he'd been chased by lancers and fallen and hit a boulder. Tripping over a root and his own boots was hardly noble—or smart—especially when lancers were getting slain by sabre, crossbow, and firebolts.

"Better not do it again, ser mage." Istya straightened. "That should do it. Don't be getting the binding wet."

"Yes, healer."

After Istya left, stepping out past the pair of guards now stationed outside his door, Kharl eased himself back into the chair, most carefully. Despite the long day and the darkness outside, he wasn't ready for sleep, and he hadn't yet talked to Hagen.

Charsal's death bothered him. Kharl hadn't thought that the white wizard could have gotten that close or that he'd been strong enough to throw a firebolt from a distance. Had he exposed Charsal unnecessarily by suggesting that the lancer ride slowly at first? Were firebolts that easy for chaos-wizards? Even Kenslan had said that the white wizard chasing Charsal and his half squad hadn't been that strong.

Kharl knew life was not fair, but he wondered about how a weak white wizard could create so much damage. It seemed to be such an imbalance, but was it? So long as his strength held out, he could block anything the wizards he'd encountered could throw, and against any single white wizard he was probably stronger than one of comparable power in a one-on-

one situation, but the chaos-wizard could spray destruction against scores, and Kharl could not. That was balance . . . of a sort.

At the sound of voices, Kharl's head turned toward the door.

Thrap. "The lord-chancellor, ser."

"He's more than welcome," Kharl called back.

The door opened, and Hagen stepped into the sitting room, closing the door behind him.

"Kharl."

"You'll excuse me if I don't rise."

"Don't fret about it. I'm sorry I was late getting up to see you, but Lord Ghrant had some concerns." Hagen looked at Kharl, propped up carefully in the armchair. "You have this habit of creating havoc, then getting injured."

"I didn't plan it that way." Kharl started to shake his head, then stopped at the warning twinges. "I tripped over a root and fell on a half-buried boulder because I was trying to make sure I didn't get seen by lancers who were chasing me."

"Might I ask why they were chasing you?"

"Malcor and Kenslan are dead."

"I thought—I hoped—it might be something like that. Lord Ghrant will be happy to learn of the deaths, especially of Malcor's. That will help . . . some."

"Some?" Kharl could sense more trouble.

"While you were gone, Vatoran escaped. Three of the guards were killed—one by a firebolt."

Kharl wanted to sigh, but he was afraid it would hurt his bruised ribs too much. "So . . . while I was after the lords, their wizard came in here?"

"From what we can tell, he had a squad dressed in the uniforms of the personal guard, and they killed the guards who challenged them."

That didn't speak very highly of the defenses of the Great House, but Kharl let that pass. "I overheard a few words between Malcor and Kenslan. They had sent a newly arrived wizard out. Kenslan called it a fool's errand. Malcor said that it was necessary to make sure that their plans were not revealed. Oh . . . and they both had been talking to Fostak. He was the one who made sure they got another wizard. You can't do anything about him, can you?"

"If we did, the emperor would have our envoy in Cigoerne killed or imprisoned."

Kharl did sigh. What was he supposed to do? What was anyone supposed to do?

"You can't be everywhere, Kharl," Hagen added. "They have more mages than we do."

"We're different kinds of mages. That's the problem. They can spray chaos at a number of people. Mostly, what I can do is defend."

"You defended Malcor and Kenslan to death?" Hagen raised his eyebrows.

"What I did is really a perverted way of using order. It works, but only against one or two people at a time, and I can't do much else."

"Something like what happened to Guillam?"

"In a way," Kharl said tiredly. "So far as I know, not that I know much about it, it's not something that very many mages have figured out." He paused. "Is there any good news?"

"Norgen managed to ambush Vatoran's third and fifth companies with his two companies. Between that and your disorganization of the rebels' leadership, we may have enough time for the nearer companies under Casolan to reach Valmurl before there's an attack on Valmurl or the Great House." Hagen looked to Kharl, then stood. "You need some rest. This revolt is going to last longer than anyone thought, and we'll need your skills."

"Even with Malcor and Kenslan dead?"

"Vatoran is free, and there are lords like Fergyn and Hensolas who were looking for an excuse to overthrow Ghrant. Casolan cannot possibly reach Valmurl with all his forces until late spring, at the earliest."

"I thought—"

"He has three companies that will be here in another two eightdays, perhaps less, but they will only allow us to defend Valmurl."

"How did it come to this? I thought that once Ilteron was dead . . ."

"Fostak, Lord Joharak . . . they've been spreading rumors and golds, I'd wager, even promises to support a new ruler."

"How could anyone believe them?"

"The ambitious believe anything that fuels their dreams, and the Hamorians will take full advantage of that." Hagen stepped toward the door. "You need your rest. I'll talk to you tomorrow."

After Hagen departed, Kharl sat for a time in the chair, thinking. Why was it that everything he did seemed to create as many problems as it resolved—if not more?

IX

On sevenday morning, Kharl woke in the grayness before dawn. His entire chest was one dull aching mass, but that was not what had wakened him. He could sense chaos . . . somewhere beyond the Great House . . . and it seemed to be getting nearer.

Much as he tried to hurry, dressing was a chore. Bending enough to get on his boots was near agony, and getting on his tunic was almost as bad. He didn't bother with much in the way of washing up, not when he knew time was short, and not after what had happened to Charsal and the armsmen guarding Vatoran.

As Kharl made his way stiffly to the outer door of his quarters, he could have used the black staff he'd destroyed in fighting Ilteron and one of the Hamorian white wizards—but just for support. He felt old and tired—and all because of one moment of carelessness.

"Ser?" The guards stiffened as Kharl stepped out.

"I'm headed up to the north tower. Could one of you find the lord-chancellor and tell him that there's a white wizard headed this way?"

"Ah . . ."

The two exchanged glances. Then the taller and dark-haired sentry nodded. "Will you be wanting to meet with him?"

"Just tell him that there's a white wizard and that I'll be in the north tower. On top."

"Yes, ser."

Kharl turned and headed toward the stone stairs that would take him to the third level. Then he'd have to take another passageway to reach the circular steps that led to the top of the tower. Behind him, he could hear the low murmurs, words he could not have made without his order-senses.

". . . mages . . . strange . . ."

". . . leastwise, ours goes out and fights . . ."

Kharl wasn't so sure that what he'd done merited being called fighting, but he was glad they thought of him as one of theirs. He moved deliberately, but it took him twice as long, if not longer, to climb to the top of the tower as it would have normally, and he had to stop twice. Breathing was harder with his chest bound and sore.

His breath steamed as he stepped through the narrow doorway and walked to the eastern side of the tower. From there, standing behind battlements that were more decorative than functional, on the open top of the north tower, Kharl had a sweeping view of both the grounds of the Great House and of Valmurl. Walls a third of a kay on a side surrounded the Great House, with the main eastern gates in the front on the avenue. There was also a delivery gate on the avenue, but near the south end of the wall, and a small bailey gate in the middle of the north wall. Lawns and gardens extended immediately behind the main structure, with outbuildings farther to the rear against the north and south walls.

The Great House stood on a rise more than a kay west of the center of Valmurl, and nearly two kays from the harbor. From his viewpoint, Kharl could just barely make out the dry docks to the north of the harbor where the *Seastag* had been repaired and refitted more than a season earlier. He could also discern Traders' Square and the Guard Barracks to the south, barracks now empty because Kenslan had earlier marched the armsmen west, then north.

The eastern horizon lightened as Kharl made his survey. Then the top edge of the white disc that was the sun flared above the dark waters of the harbor and the western ocean beyond. Overhead, the sky was mostly clear, with only a hint of hazy clouds over the hills to the west of Valmurl, hills still dotted with snow near their crests.

Kharl walked around the parapets, slowly, letting his order-senses extend beyond the low gray stone walls around the Great House. To the north, beyond where the avenue that passed in front of the Great House turned into the winding road that eventually led to the Nierran Hills, Kharl could sense a concentration of chaos. He could see nothing.

He frowned. That was not quite right. His eyes seemed to dart away, to avoid one spot on the road. So the white wizard had something like a sight shield as well? Kharl had thought that had to be the case. Otherwise, how else had they managed to get close enough to kill the armsmen guarding Vatoran?

He tried to judge the distance, but he wasn't that familiar with Valmurl. The white wizard was more than a kay away, closer to two. As Kharl watched and sensed, occasionally, he thought he saw a puff of dust, but that could have been his imagination.

At the sound of boots on the stones of the tower, he turned.

"A white wizard headed this way?" Hagen, wearing a black jacket trimmed in green, walked toward Kharl.

The mage waited until Hagen was almost beside him. "There . . . out on the north road, I'd say half a kay beyond where the avenue ends."

Hagen leaned forward. "I don't see anything."

"He has a sight shield. Your eyes feel like they're moving away from the road."

Hagen blinked several times. "Hmmm . . . I feel something, but I still don't see anything. How big a force does he have with him?"

"It's hard to tell. It's less than a company, I think. This wizard feels stronger than the one that attacked Charsal. He might be the one that Kenslan mentioned."

"Or another one from Hamor."

Kharl didn't like that possibility at all.

"What can you do about him?" asked Hagen.

"To do much of anything, I'd have to get close to him."

"It would be better if you didn't," Hagen said. "They have two mages. They may have more." The lord-chancellor frowned. "Will you be able to see exactly where this white wizard is when he gets closer to the Great House?"

"Not exactly see," Kharl admitted. "I'll know where he is."

"Can you describe it? Well enough so that crossbowmen can aim a quarrel?"

"I could. What about rifles— No. I suppose he could set off the powder."

"That's why no one uses rifles against white wizards, and why cannon are used sparingly and set apart. Except on iron-hulled warships." Hagen's voice turned dry. "It's also why there are never very many experienced artillerymen. Even without mages around, it's still possible for free chaos to set off the powder."

Kharl used his order-senses to study the approaching wizard. "I'd say two squads are with him. That's a guess, though."

"We could put a half score of crossbowmen in the gate towers with you, and we could have others wind and cock."

"We can try. If he heads for the main gates. If he doesn't . . . then I can always try something else," Kharl admitted.

"We'd better get moving," Hagen said.

"I'll meet you there."

"You're still sore, aren't you?"

"Yes." Kharl was more than sore, but what was the point of admitting it? It had been his own carelessness, and he still had to do something about the white wizards, whether he was hurt or not. "I'll be there."

Hagen nodded, hurried across the top of the tower, and vanished through the door in the archway. He left the door ajar in his haste.

Kharl followed, not quite so swiftly, descending the steep steps with care, since there were no railings, and the centers of the stone treads had been hollowed out by years of usage.

The corridors of the Great House seemed empty, even emptier than he might have expected nearing end-day. Was that because people were slipping away, afraid that the rebel lords would overthrow Lord Ghrant?

Kharl made his way down to the main level, then out across the front courtyard. As he crossed the stone-paved expanse, a half squad of armsmen in yellow and black bearing crossbows hurried past him. By the time Kharl reached the gate tower, its lower entrance was guarded by two armsmen in yellow and back.

"The lord-chancellor is waiting topside for you, ser mage."

"You a former sailor?"

"Yes, ser."

"I know I'll be in good hands, then." Kharl smiled and stepped through the narrow doorway. The stone steps up the gate tower were even narrower and steeper than the north tower, although the gate tower itself only rose some thirty cubits above the courtyard and the avenue it overlooked.

The small room at the top of the stairs held four armsmen serving as loaders. Kharl saw that they had more than ten crossbows set out, ready to wind and cock. He nodded as he eased past them in the crowded space and out onto the semicircular battlement overlooking the avenue.

Standing behind the center merlon, Kharl began to search for the rebel wizard, with both order-senses and eyes.

Directly across the avenue from the gate towers was the Lord's Park—almost a garden with topiary and grass and stone paths. Around the park were the town dwellings of various lords and wealthy merchants and factors, none over two stories, by decree. Kharl studied the avenue to the north. While someone might have expected so little traffic just after dawn on eightday—that there were so few out on sevenday, usually a market day, was disturbing. He could see a servant hanging out wash in the side court of a modest dwelling across the avenue and perhaps thirty rods to the northeast, and a doorman standing on the porch of a dwelling even farther north, but no riders or carriages were visible on the avenue—not to the eye. After a moment, Kharl could sense the wizard and the riders who accompanied him, now on the avenue itself, and less than a kay away.

"They're about three quarters of a kay to the north," he said, before Hagen could ask him. "They're moving at a quick walk."

"A quarter glass before they're in range," Hagen announced. "I've had all the other guards stationed behind stone and out of sight."

Kharl should have thought of that. Stone was about the only thing, besides thick and heavy iron or an order shield, that could stop a large firebolt.

Silently, Kharl and Hagen watched the avenue.

Kharl concentrated for a moment, just briefly, on throwing up a weaker shield, one that partly hardened the air but was coated with a thin layer of order to deflect something like a firebolt. He dropped it instantly, but he had wanted to make sure that he was ready.

"I don't see any signs of them, not even any dust off the stones," Hagen said, after a time. "Shouldn't they be fairly close by now?"

"No sound, either . . ." murmured an armsman behind them.

Kharl frowned. "They've split. The riders are headed down a lane to the east."

"There they are! On the lane north of the Lord's Park," called one of the armsmen.

"They're headed toward Lord Lahoryn's dwelling," murmured Hagen. "Right in the open." He turned. "Theragon! Get a squad over to Lord Lahoryn's dwelling! Now!"

"Yes, ser!" came back a call from lower in the tower.

"Close the main gates behind our squad!" Hagen glanced at Kharl. "The rebels will ride off, but it will stop the destruction."

Even as he spoke, the riders fired several times. After a moment, one of the riders dismounted and opened the iron gates to the courtyard in front of the mansion.

Why were they attacking a supporter of Lord Ghrant, and so close to the Great House? With the others, Kharl watched. Then he shook his head. Where was the white wizard? Outside of a vague feeling that the wizard was somewhere north of the Great House, he could not pin down where the other was.

"Kharl?" asked Hagen.

"The white wizard . . . he's disappeared."

"Disappeared? Where?"

"I can't tell."

"A diversion! Do you have any idea where he was?" demanded Hagen.

"To the north . . . somewhere."

"The bailey gate—that has to be it. We need to get there before he does." The lord-chancellor whirled and headed for the stairs. After a moment, Kharl followed, trying to ignore his various aches.

"Send a squad right behind us!" Hagen snapped at the senior squad leader at the top of the tower stairs. "We're headed for the north bailey gate."

"Third squad! After the lord-chancellor! Loaders, too!"

Kharl felt as though he were more staggering than anything else as he followed Hagen down the gate-tower steps, back across the courtyard, then around the north side of the Great House. By the time they neared the bailey gate, Kharl was breathing hard, and every breath was agony against his bruised ribs.

Even from a good fifty cubits away, he could see that there was no one at the bailey gate, a gate far too small for mounted entry, and that the gate was ajar.

Then the solid oak gate flew open, and rebel armsmen in the green-and-black uniforms of Austra rushed through.

Kharl could feel chaos building. A shadowy figure appeared behind the armsmen, and a firebolt flew toward Hagen, Kharl, and the armsmen flanking the lord-chancellor.

"Fire!" snapped Hagen.

Four armsmen with crossbows halted and fired. Quarrels flew past Kharl. Most of them missed, and Kharl could see several skitter off the paving stones short of the bailey gate. One bounced away from the indistinct figure of the white wizard, who had created a shield.

At the same time, Kharl did the same.

Chaos flared outward from the bailey gate and nearly simultaneously, two quarrels struck the back side of the shield and rebounded toward Kharl and Hagen, one dropping but a few cubits from Kharl's boots.

"Have them stop firing!" Kharl said, still holding the shield as another firebolt flared across the north courtyard.

"Reload and hold!"

Yet another blast of chaos flared against Kharl's shields, but it was weaker than the earlier chaos-fire.

Kharl tried to reach out to see if he could harden the air around the white wizard, but the distance was either just a trace too far—or perhaps it was because the white wizard had his own shields.

A third blast of chaos flared against Kharl's shields, still weaker than the first two.

As Kharl sensed that the white wizard was trying to recover, he dropped his own shields. "Have them fire now!"

"Resume fire!"

This time, the quarrels began to strike the handful of rebel lancers.

Another firebolt arced over the rebels toward Kharl, and he deflected it back toward the white wizard.

Chaos flared around the wizard, and one of the rebel armsmen flared into flame, screaming, if only for a moment, before pitching onto the stones.

"Back! Now!" ordered someone, and within moments, the area inside the bailey gate held only those loyal to Lord Ghrant.

"Secure the gate!" ordered Hagen. "Two of you hold it!"

The sound of hoofs on stone echoed through the still-open gate, but faded quickly as the gate closed and the riders departed northward along the back lane.

Four rebels lay on the stones of the courtyard, just inside the gate.

". . . won't try that again . . ." murmured one of the crossbowmen to Kharl's left.

Kharl had his doubts about that. The rebels might well try another sneak attack. They knew that Ghrant only had one mage. He looked at Hagen.

The older man offered a crooked smile. "Best we take what we can," he said in a low voice.

Kharl realized that sweat was streaming down his forehead and that his ribs were aching more than they had—but not too much more. Carefully raising his right arm, he blotted the sweat away with his sleeve. He extended his order-senses, just to make sure that the attackers were continuing northward. While he could not tell if all the riders continued away from the Great House, the white wizard certainly had.

"They're still riding north?" asked Hagen.

"The wizard is."

"Stand by here. Don't open that gate for anyone until either the captain or I tell you to," Hagen ordered. "The mage and I need to check on some matters." He nodded to Kharl. "You go first. I'll be right behind you." His voice lowered to barely more than a murmur. "You need to eat. You're as pale as those dressings on your chest."

Belatedly, Kharl realized that he did feel slightly light-headed. "I didn't have time to eat."

"Neither did I. Would you join me?"

"I'd be happy to."

Before long the two were in a small dining room less than thirty cubits from Hagen's receiving chamber. There were but two circular tables, and no one else was there—except for a serving girl.

"Two full breakfasts, with hot spiced cider," Hagen said, even before he seated himself.

Kharl sank gratefully into the chair across the table from the lord-chancellor.

"This morning's skirmish will hearten the personal guard," Hagen noted. "They'll all be saying how you were stronger than the rebel mage."

"Order is better at defending, I think."

"It also may buy us some time." Hagen paused. "Why couldn't you sense him for a time there?"

"He knew I was looking. He stopped using chaos at all. That was how I found him to begin with. He needed it to get the armsmen close to the Great House, but then he dropped all his shields and stopped using chaos. He and the smaller force slipped behind the bigger dwellings to the north, where we couldn't see them, and circled around to come down the lane behind the houses toward the bailey gate."

"That's probably how they got in to take Vatoran. They had to bribe someone. I'd wager that the armsman who left the gate open is long gone." Hagen shook his head. "None of this helps. It was very clever. Even if the attempt to get into the Great House failed, they attacked one of Lord Ghrant's supporters right here in Valmurl, and they got inside the Great House—twice, if anyone tells about how Vatoran escaped. Word will get around that Lord Ghrant can't even protect those close to him."

All of it had started with Kharl showing that the chief factor had lied, and matters just kept getting worse . . . "What did you want to talk about?"

Hagen smiled. "Nothing. I just wanted to get you fed. I also didn't want anyone to notice how much that cost you."

"I'll be better in a few days. I should have kept up practicing using magery."

"You'll get plenty of practice in the next few eightdays."

Kharl had no doubts about that.

"Here comes the hot cider."

Kharl let Hagen fill both mugs, then drank slowly. He *was* hungry.

X

Eightday dawned far more quietly than had sevenday, for which Kharl was most grateful, since his chest and ribs did not seem much improved. There was less sharp pain and more of a dull aching. Since Hagen had told him to eat in the smaller dining room, he had enjoyed a hot breakfast there.

As Kharl had finished eating, Hagen had peered in, a somber look on his face. "I thought I might find you here."

"You look worried."

Hagen nodded as he slid into the chair across from Kharl. "Vatoran is dead. I just got a messenger from Norgen."

"I thought Vatoran had escaped."

"He did. He didn't live very long after he escaped. He was garrotted."

"Like the serving girl," Kharl said.

"It might have been the same person, someone whom they both trusted. Or they were with someone they trusted, and off guard." Hagen frowned. "I don't see why they'd help Vatoran escape, then kill him. If they were worried about what he'd told us, they'd have found out—" Hagen looked at Kharl. "Chaos-wizards have a hard time telling if someone is telling the truth, don't they?"

Kharl considered, then recalled what he had seen in Hamor, where a wizard had destroyed an innocent man who had been telling the truth. At the time, he'd just thought it cruel, but what if Hagen happened to be right? "Some of them probably do. Maybe a lot. I don't know for sure."

"So they couldn't be sure that he hadn't betrayed them. That would explain it. Once you'd talked to him, they couldn't trust him."

The rebels had killed Vatoran because Kharl had talked to him? "But he never told anyone anything."

"They don't know that. Lords like Malcor and Kenslan don't trust anyone. Neither do Fergyn and Hensolas, and I'd wager that they've taken over leadership of the rebels."

"There were that many lords who opposed Ghrant?"

"These things take on a life of their own. Hensolas in particular is too calculating ever to start a revolt, but he might encourage others and let them take the lead. That was why Estloch had sent him off as envoy to Brysta. Once he came back, he'd stayed in the background, but he had to have worried about Malcor's treachery and Kenslan's brutality. With both of them dead, and with the quiet support of Hamor—and seeing what you've done to Malcor, Kenslan, and Guillam, he and Fergyn wouldn't trust Lord Ghrant. They'd feel that they had no choice. They don't." Hagen's words were level.

"You're telling me that I caused this revolt? Because I caught Guillam lying in his teeth?" Kharl set down the mug of warm cider without taking a swallow.

"Lords fear the truth at times more than death or their ruler." Hagen offered a faint smile. "You didn't cause the revolt. It would have happened before long."

Kharl understood all too well that Hagen and Lord Ghrant would have liked more time before the rebel lords had acted. He just shook his head. "I was afraid that if Guillam walked out of the audience hall, there would have been a revolt within eightdays. I didn't realize that I'd cause it to occur immediately."

"Lord Ghrant is aware of that." Hagen fingered his chin. "As I told you earlier, if we can get through this, matters may turn out for the best." He laughed softly. "The next few eightdays will be the test."

"What else has happened?"

"Norgen's scouts have reported several Hamorian vessels off the coast just north of here. They landed a small party, then departed."

"Golds . . . and more white wizards," Kharl suggested.

"The golds I can see. They're cheaper than soldiers and less costly."

"So are white wizards. The one wizard with Malcor wasn't that strong. Neither was the one with Ilteron. The one who attacked yesterday wasn't as strong as the one with Ilteron in Dykaru." Kharl felt that any white wizard he'd bested couldn't be that powerful. After all, he'd been working with order for less than a year.

"You think so?"

"The emperor keeps his wizards under tight rein. I saw that in Hamor. What better way to suggest that they stay in line than by sending those who are not as . . . obedient as he might like to Austra?"

"And if they refuse to follow orders once they're here," Hagen added, "it just creates more chaos here in Austra, and anything that does that weakens Austra."

Kharl nodded.

"Always Hamor . . ." Hagen shook his head. "They want to hold the entire world."

"What about Recluce?"

"Hamor will try to take over everyone else first. It may take generations, but the emperors have all been patient, and they have wizards and iron-hulled warships and golds." Hagen rose. "How are your ribs?"

"Still sore."

"You'll have a few days, I'd judge. I'd like more, but I'm not counting on it."

Neither was Kharl.

XI

As Hagen had predicted, there were no more attacks on the Great House—or nearby—on oneday, or on the days following. Fortunately, the damage at Lord Lahoryn's city house had been minimal, and not even his guards had been wounded.

Kharl spent the time practicing his order-skills, particularly his shields, and in studying *The Basis of Order* in the manner in which he had found most effective—by questioning. Sometimes he read in his quarters, but when he could, he preferred the sheltered area on the top of the north tower.

On fiveday, after midday dinner, he was in the bright and cool sunlight of the tower, his back against sun-warmed stone, perusing a particularly obvious section, wondering why the writer had felt it necessary to emphasize the point so thoroughly.

Every strength is a weakness, every weakness a strength, for under the Balance there cannot be more order than chaos. Thus, if order is concentrated in one place, there must be another place where there is less and where it will take less effort for chaos to prevail. Likewise, the same is true of chaos . . .

That had certainly been the case in his own experience. If he concentrated order into a shield, for him to resist the firebolts of the white wizards, that order had to be restricted to a very small area. On the other hand, he asked himself, was there a time or place where the use of additional order spread over a large area, almost like seasoning over a large piece of meat, would prove useful? Kharl considered it, but could not think of a situation where it might be useful. Perhaps he might in time.

He continued reading, until he came to a passage which seemed both direct and obscure, simultaneously.

Because chaos reflects the absence of order, it can manifest itself in two fashions, or both at once. The first is as what appears as white fire, and that is chaos free of all order and all constraints, but chaos drawn from elsewhere by one who is able to do so and imposed upon what order may exist in a given place. The second is that chaos caused by the withdrawal of order from the place itself. Both methods produce that force known as chaos, and the unrestrained chaos created by either means cannot be differentiated, one from the other. The first method is the easiest, and the one most widely practiced, but the amount of chaos that can be mustered is limited by the strength of the wizard, because by nature such free chaos is widely dispersed. The second method does not require strength alone, but great mastery of both order and chaos, and has seldom been employed because failure to attain mastery is almost inevitably fatal.

Kharl understood the concepts well enough, but there was no explanation of *why* attempting the second method was so dangerous. He read on, but nowhere could he find any explanation of the dangers—or even of the reasons behind the caution.

He frowned. The book seemed to suggest that technique was the key to the second method. As a cooper, he certainly understood that the key to any craft was skill and not brute force, but exactly what sort of skill was required to remove order from an area or an object? What would happen if he did?

He marked his place in the book and closed it slowly, thinking.

What sort of danger was involved? Why hadn't the book explained? Or was it like so much else—something that the writer had not wanted to spell out? Or could not?

"Ahhh . . ."

Kharl turned his head, then rose from where he had been seated.

Hagen was walking across the stones of the tower.

"You look worried—again," offered Kharl.

Hagen nodded. "These days . . . I'm worried all the time. The rebel lords look to be trying something else. Hensolas has gathered his forces, and they include half of the regular Austran lancers from the eastern district, the ones who were under Vatoran. Norgen's scouts are reporting that the rebels are moving around Valmurl to the southeast."

Kharl didn't know enough about the local geography to understand what that meant. "Where are they heading?"

"I'd judge that they're planning to use the southern high road into the harbor. If they take the harbor, they can claim they hold Valmurl. It also makes it much easier for the Hamorians to send them supplies."

"What about Lord Fergyn?"

"No one seems to know. I'd wager that he's moving through the area just south of the Nierran Hills toward the north road. That's closer than we'd like"

"It's closer to the dockyards."

"And most of the factors' warehouses."

"Are they short of supplies?"

"I'd imagine so, and their armsmen haven't been paid in several eightdays."

"Have you heard from Commander Casolan?"

"We're still looking at almost an eightday before his forces arrive." Hagen offered a laugh, a sound somewhere between sardonic and humorous. "I was wondering if you have any other magely stratagems that might work against an attack on the road into the harbor."

"Are there any places where the road is narrow? Any bridges that they have to cross?"

"Only the causeway, and that's not really that narrow. It was built by Lord Estloch's great-grandfather through the marshes. For ten years he just had anyone convicted of crimes sent there to cart rocks. It's two kays long, and between three and five rods wide. If we blocked it, though, they could just ride through the city. In any case, the causeway is so open that they could see anyone waiting there for them. You couldn't hide us, could you?"

"I could hide you from sight, but it would be hard on the armsmen, because they wouldn't be able to see, and any wizard could still tell that I was doing it."

"I had hoped . . ."

"Let me think about it. How long do I have?"

"Norgen thinks they'll begin before dawn tomorrow."

Kharl nodded.

"If you need supplies of any sort, let me know."

After Hagen left, the mage and former cooper tucked *The Basis of Order* inside his tunic and walked to the eastern side of the tower. The sun warmed his back as he studied Valmurl and the harbor. In the distance, he could barely make out the causeway, just a darker line through the dark waters of the harbor.

What could he do? How?

He glanced at the stones of the parapets, catching sight of a fragment of dried leaf that had been blown into a corner in the stone, doubtless by a winter storm. He'd had luck in working with leaves before. Could he try removing the order from a fragment of a leaf, leaving only chaos? Would it be like hardening the leaf, then infusing the order elsewhere?

With his order-senses, Kharl reached out for the piece of dried leaf, no larger than perhaps a quarter of his palm. Carefully, he tried to sense the order links within the bleached and ragged tan fragment. The dark links felt faded, but so did the whitish points of chaos.

Rather than strengthening the links between the minute segments of order, as he did when creating shields, Kharl concentrated on the ties between two points. He tried to break the linkage, but all that happened was that he felt warmer, as if he had been walking uphill. He paused. Mere force wasn't the answer.

Technique—that was what worked. But what kind of technique? He considered for a moment. When he strengthened air into a barrier, he reinforced the hooks and links. Was there a way to unlink one small segment from another? He tried visualizing two segments of darkness as linked by interlocking open hooks, then concentrating on turning them so that they separated.

Once more, he could feel himself getting hotter, but nothing happened with the leaf.

Were the ordered sections of the leaf, faded as they were, tied together more like a hook and eye? He tried that, but the results were the same. Nothing happened, except he was sweating more than before.

What about some sort of latch structure? He realized that he was trying to visualize the unknown, but order had to have some pattern or structure. Didn't it? The latch idea didn't work either.

For a time, he just leaned on the stones of the parapet, letting himself cool back down, thinking about how many ways order could be structured. When he felt somewhat refreshed, he tried not forcing his concepts of linkage on the leaf, but instead concentrated on trying to receive, to sense, the order-structure of the leaf. For a time, he could sense nothing except the darkness of order and the reddish white of chaos. Instead of turning away, he took a deep breath and let himself and his senses drift toward the leaf.

In time, he began to get an impression of linkages, of hundreds of rows of tiny twisted hooks. Instead of immediately trying to use that image, he willed himself to gather in an even more detailed understanding of the order linkages of the leaf, trying to gather an image of just how the links twisted and how much each needed to be turned to be unlinked from the next. The leaf seemed to have frayed barbs on the tips of the hooks. That was the way Kharl perceived them, at least.

Ever so gently, he began to press, then push and twist. One of the minute linkages released, and then another. The third and fourth were easier, and, almost immediately, Kharl could feel heat rising from the leaf. Despite the cool breeze coming from the ocean and across Valmurl, he had begun to sweat even more heavily.

The heat was far greater than if the leaf had caught fire and burned on the spot. Involuntarily, Kharl stepped back.

He could feel a surge of chaos—stronger than even that thrown by the chaos-wizard who had tried to attack the Great House—and he threw himself to the side. A jolt of pain flashed through his ribs at the sudden movement, and he staggered farther to his right.

A vortex of white chaos flared upward from where the leaf fragment had been, and the force of the chaos-explosion flung Kharl onto the stones that paved the top of the tower. He lay there for a moment, letting the pain subside. The explosive force had not been that powerful, and he might not even have sprawled on the stones had he not already been off-balance.

From what he could tell, his ribs had not suffered any worse damage, thanks to the heavy binding around them.

He lifted his head, then slowly and carefully rose. He could sense no more free chaos—or none that was concentrated, for there was a white miasma of scattered chaos slowly drifting westward above the tower.

After a short time, the mage and cooper eased back toward the lower part of the embrasure in the parapet where the leaf fragment had been. There was no trace of the leaf. Five black lines, each a fingernail's width in depth, had been scored in the granite above where the leaf had been, radiating out from a small pit in the stone, also blackened.

Kharl shook his head slowly. All that chaos from such a small fragment of a leaf? No wonder so few mages survived trying to release chaos from objects. What if he had been experimenting with wood—or metal?

Kharl's legs were trembling, and his vision was blurring. Slowly, he sat down and rested his back against the parapet. He could also feel that his face was reddened, as if he had spent the day under a hot summer sun.

Was what he had done possible to replicate from a greater distance?

His lips curled into a wry smile. What he had done wasn't something he wanted to try if he couldn't do it from a distance—and from behind a stone wall or the like.

All that chaos, he marveled, just from a winter-dried fragment of a leaf.

Had the mage from Recluce who had destroyed Fairven released chaos in such a fashion? Or had he used something even more terrible?

After a time, Kharl rose, moving slowly toward the stairs down to the kitchen. He needed to practice what he had tried, but not without some more to eat—and certainly not without even greater care—and more distance between him and what he was working on.

XII

By the time the sun hung over the hills to the west of Valmurl, Kharl was exhausted. He had trouble focusing his eyes. He'd spent most of the afternoon on the tower, working on how to release chaos from various substances through the manipulation of the order bonds that held all objects together. It hadn't taken him long to discover that the amount of chaos within a substance was almost directly proportional to its size and density. The difficulty of releasing the order bonds was more than proportionally harder with denser materials, like metals, and even harder with mixed materials, like rocks or alloys like bronze.

He'd enlisted the armorer to cut him minute scraps of copper, iron, bronze, and tin, and he'd also taken his own wood samples from the workroom of the Great House's carpenter. No one had asked him what he wanted the materials for, almost as if no one even wanted to hazard a guess as to what a mage had in mind.

Kharl smiled wryly. He was definitely learning, and he'd discovered things that weren't in *The Basis of Order* . . . or rather, tricks that were barely hinted at in the order manual. Although the book's lack of clear directions for technique had bothered him in the beginning, he was beginning to understand why whoever had written it had avoided describing techniques except for a few relatively basic points.

Wood was easier to work with, but the chaos-energy released wasn't that much greater for most pieces of wood than for a leaf the same size, except for a tiny fragment of lorken, and that had almost been as hard to handle as iron, although the "feel" had been different. On the other hand, the chaos released from a small fragment of an iron nail had blown off a quarter of one of the granite parapet stones and cracked the remainder of the stone. Kharl was just glad that he had had the presence of mind to use very small bits of metal and crouch behind one of the granite parapet braces several cubits away. Even so, he'd suffered several small cuts from flying stone fragments.

Even with all the work and experimentation he had done, Kharl had been unable to release the order bonds from much farther than a rod away for the heavier substances, such as metals, and perhaps twice that for woods. Exactly how what he had discovered would help Hagen, he was unsure, but perhaps the lord-chancellor might have an idea or two.

Kharl found himself shivering as the wind picked up. The spring day had started out cold, but the morning breeze had died away, and the cloudless sky and sun had joined to turn the afternoon almost as hot as early summer. Nearing sunset, the wind had risen and shifted, blowing out of the north and cooling the top of the tower.

"Will it work?" came a voice from the west side of the north tower.

The other's figure was blurred to Kharl's sight, but he recognized Hagen's voice. "Will what work?"

"Whatever you've been doing up here all day that has everyone in the Great House afraid to get near the tower, or even beneath it." Hagen laughed. "I told them that the only time to worry would be if you fled the tower."

As Hagen moved nearer, and Kharl's vision cleared, the mage could make out the dark circles under the lord-chancellor's eyes. "You're tired. And worried."

"Wouldn't you be? Hensolas has moved his forces to Kiford. That's less than five kays from the southern end of the harbor causeway."

"Why was it built? Does it go anywhere?"

"It's a direct road south. They say that Lord Esthaven built it so that he could move armsmen from the southern barracks directly to the harbor." Hagen laughed. "The barracks were never used after Esthaven, and Lord Estloch tore them down and reused the stones for rebuilding the barracks in the city. They were wood before."

"How soon will Hensolas attack?"

"Tomorrow, I'd wager."

"You didn't tell me until now?" said Kharl.

"Why? You're doing the best you can, and I just would have wasted your time and mine. You understand what's happening."

"I may have wasted it anyway. I've been trying to work out how to release chaos from objects."

Hagen frowned. "Is that something black mages can do?"

Kharl understood the question Hagen hadn't asked, the one he hadn't wished to ask, and replied, "There is one way that is acceptable for a black mage. That is not to handle the chaos directly, but to remove the order bonds from an object and leave the chaos." Kharl offered a crooked smile. "It's not recommended. According to the . . . to what I've heard and learned, trying to do that could kill a mage."

"You've been doing it."

"I couldn't think of anything else that might be helpful," Kharl admitted. "I don't know how useful it will be."

"You blew pieces of granite off the tower. Stone shards were falling in the courtyard."

Kharl nodded. "I have to be close, somewhere within twenty or thirty cubits."

Hagen fingered his clean-shaven chin, tilting his head to one side. "We still might be able to figure out something. Let's go get something to eat, and we'll see what we can work out."

"I am hungry," Kharl admitted. He was ready to listen. Besides, he was too tired to try anything else.

"Good. You look like you could use a good meal." Hagen turned.

Kharl followed the lord-chancellor down the stone steps from the tower.

XIII

In the darkness before dawn, Kharl used his order-senses check the causeway to the east of the flat-bottomed boat. Using them was necessary, because the boat had been covered with reeds and grass, from which jutted straggly cattails that remained from the fall before. In the mist that covered the marshes bordering the causeway, the concealed boat looked like another marshy hump, one of a number, if the only one in the immediate area. Under the canvas covered with grass and clumps of plants, the fetid mixed odors of marsh and harbor backwaters were almost unbearable.

Kharl swallowed.

"How much longer, ser mage?" asked Dorfal, the young armsman and former crabber, his voice low.

"They're still a good kay or more south of us," Kharl whispered back. As he waited with the clammy fog all around him, Kharl wondered, once more, how he'd managed to get himself where he was—sitting in a flat-bottomed boat less than thirty cubits off the causeway, essentially alone. There was a squad of armsmen waiting well to the west of the marsh, but they were out of sight, and too far away to be of much immediate assistance. They were there to protect Kharl once he returned—and to escort him back to the Great House.

How had he gotten into this mess? By the way he had dealt with Guillam, everything else had followed. While it might not have been his fault, not totally, it was certainly his responsibility. More important, if he didn't support Ghrant, he'd have nothing, and he didn't want to go back to that.

Hiding, not having enough to eat, watching every corner, listening to every sound—no, he'd had enough of that, even if it had only been for a season.

He could only hope the plan he and Hagen had developed would work out.

The plan itself was simple. Kharl and Dorfal waited in the concealed boat, a craft built like a scow, but far smaller, with two hastily mounted winches fore and aft. Cables were attached to the winches. One was anchored—underwater—to a massive boulder at the edge of the causeway. The other, more than ten rods to the west and also underwater, was tied to a huge and ancient stump that barely protruded from the water. Beyond the stump was a low hillock, behind which the armsmen waited. Between the small scow and the trunk was one of the few stretches where the murky swamp water was a good three or four rods in depth. Kharl would make sure that no order or chaos could be sensed by the Hamorian white wizard—or wizards. He and Dorfal would wait until the bulk of the rebel forces passed. Then Dorfal would winch the craft to the causeway, and Kharl would begin to release order from the nails and other small scraps of metal in the pouch at his belt—after he'd thrown or otherwise placed them in the right spots among and behind the rebels. With the winch and cables, the scow would stay where it was supposed to, and could be moved more quietly.

The idea was to push the rebels forward, toward the harbor front, which appeared largely undefended. It was, in fact, scarcely defended at all—except for the dozen or so old cannon that Hagen had taken from the armories. But those cannon were set to rake the end of the causeway with grapeshot. Hagen had also managed to dig out cold-iron powder canisters, the kind that could be closed after each load was measured and set. While there were still risks involved, from what Kharl and seen and sensed, the Hamorian mages weren't likely to be able to set much of the powder off at any one time. But he'd told Hagen that it was most likely that some of the powder would still be fired by chaos.

"We're still risking less this way," the lord-chancellor had replied.

Kharl had wondered, but with the first companies of Casolan's main force still at least four days away—and that was if dry weather held—Hagen had few enough choices. He didn't have forces adequate to defend both the Great House and the harbor, and Fergyn's forces in the north were uncomfortably close to the Great House. Yet, if Hensolas and the rebel lords took and held Valmurl harbor, before all that long the Hamorians would be pouring arms and aid to the rebels—as well as slipping in the Hamorian forces that would soon make Austra part of Hamor.

Kharl's "diversion" had two possible favorable outcomes. It either pushed the rebels into the cannon or forced them to stop and regroup. In the second instance, Kharl would need to get back to the concealed boat in some haste and beat a quiet retreat. That was if matters went their way, and Kharl wasn't all that confident about that, but he didn't wish to think about what might happen if they didn't.

Dorfal said nothing, just shifted his weight uneasily, and the scow tilted slightly.

"Someone's coming . . . riders . . ." Kharl murmured. "Two squads . . . could be more."

"How far?"

"Half a kay, maybe a little less."

The two waited and listened, and Kharl let his order-senses receive, but he offered no probes, nothing active, as the lancers neared. There was no sense in alerting a white wizard if one accompanied the oncoming forces. Before long he could sense the armsmen marching behind them, several companies, at least. "Quiet now," he murmured.

Dorfal nodded.

Kharl wasn't certain how much of the gesture he caught with night vision that had improved dramatically since he had begun to work with order and how much had come directly from his order-senses.

The sound of hoofs on the flat stones of the road in the center of the causeway rose from the faintest hint to semiregular dull clicks. Kharl could only sense a company of lancers, followed by perhaps three companies of armsmen on foot. That was half of what Hagen had expected.

The mage frowned, because he could not sense any other lancers or armsmen—and there was no sign of a white wizard. That would make his task easier, but it also disturbed him. Where were the white wizards? Were the armsmen coming up the causeway from the south some sort of feint? How would Kharl know? How could he? All he could do was wait until the force passed, then decide whether he could carry out his mission.

More than half a glass passed before the last of the foot neared the concealed scow.

"Winch us in, Dorfal, slowly," Kharl finally whispered.

"Yes, ser."

So far as Kharl could sense, no one had even looked in their direction across the ten rods that separated the road from the edge of the causeway. In the misty grayness just before dawn, Kharl slipped from under the canvas flap covered with tannish marsh grass. His boots splashed slightly as he stumbled in the span-deep water at the edge of the causeway. He was wearing the heavy winter grays that he had once used as a ship's carpenter, because the gray would blend with the morning fog and mist and help in concealing him.

After scrabbling up the yard or so of rip-rap at the edge of the causeway, Kharl studied the area around him. The misty fog was still thick enough that the armsmen to the north and east of Kharl were but indistinct forms. He checked the leather pouch at his belt and began to move toward the rear of the column of armsmen. With no wizards around, he could throw up a sight shield once he got closer—or if the fog began to thin.

He had decided to begin by releasing the order linkages in the nails he carried in the pouch. Metal was easier to handle than were small stones, at least with his level of ability. He'd thought about releasing the order in the nails, then using a sling to throw them; but the moment he finished unlinking the order within anything, the chaos flared out instantaneously, and he couldn't unlock order from any great distance.

As he eased along the causeway, angling toward the road, Kharl took care that his boots did not skid on the uneven surface that was mossy rock and slime, with occasional patches of honest soil. He couldn't see or sense anyone to the south, not nearby, although he thought there might be others another two kays or so to the south.

After a tenth of a glass, Kharl was within perhaps fifteen cubits of the stragglers in the rear guard, five or six back, and less than ten to one side. With the sun yet to rise and with mist all around, the carpenter's grays had so far provided all the concealment Kharl needed.

The voices of the foot carried in the mist and stillness.

". . . don't have any armsmen at the harbor . . . what Vuran said . . ."

". . . got that mage . . ."

". . . phaw . . . order-mage . . . not like a chaos type . . ."

". . . hope you're right . . ."

Kharl's lips tightened. He still wasn't close enough. With a muted deep breath, he drew the sight shield around himself and, in the darkness, made his way onto the road, turning northward and closing the gap between him and the stragglers. As he neared the last rank, he decided that such a position was unwise, that he needed to move so that he was more toward the middle of the column.

"You in the rear!"

For a moment, Kharl thought that the mounted officer had seen him, but the man was calling to the stragglers in front of Kharl.

"Close it up! Don't make me keep coming back here, or you'll not be lying on your backs for a season or so."

". . . frigging undercaptain . . ."

". . . just move . . . don't want a floggin' . . ."

"Keep it close!" ordered the officer, even as his turned his mount back northward.

Kharl eased back to the west side of the road and began to hurry along the shoulder, trying not to breathe hard as he moved past one rank, then another. By the time the mage had caught up to the middle of the second company, the captain or undercaptain had ridden even farther toward the front of the column.

Kharl kept walking, but pulled the first nail from his pouch, letting his order-senses range over it. The linkages in the iron nails were more like clips than hooks, but he had discovered how to unlink whole segments. The nails were small enough, and he was quick enough, that he could handle a nail all at once. He couldn't have done that with a much larger piece of metal, and that didn't take into account the fact that his shields wouldn't have been able to protect him from that much chaos.

Kharl took the nail and threw it. None of the armsmen seemed to hear the faint *clink* as it landed two ranks ahead of where he stood.

With a deftness he would not have believed possible an eightday earlier, he used his "unclipping" technique to release the order bonds in the first nail. Immediately, intense heat radiated from the nail, but none of the armsmen seemed to notice.

As the last of the order unlinked, Kharl raised his own order shield.

Crumpt! Soil and chaos flared from the nail as it fragmented into an explosive white miasma. Dirt and rock fragments pattered against Kharl's order shield.

One of the armsmen dropped, and those near him scattered.

Kharl threw another nail, and then unclipped the order bonds.

At the second explosion, the confusion and yells began to mount.

"Cannon! They're shelling us!"

"How?"

"Magery!"

"... don't have any white wizards ..."

"... cannon ... somewhere in the marshes!"

Kharl threw another nail, and removed the order.

Crumpt!

He winced as he felt the red-white chaos-void of death sweep over him, but he followed with another nail, and yet another.

Invisible to those around him, Kharl continued to rain forth random destruction for a time yet. When he stopped, he could feel that he was close to his own limits, and the rebel force had split—or he had split it. All the rebel armsmen were moving quickly, but the lancers and the leading foot continued toward the harbor. The latter half or so of the column had turned back southward, heading away from Kharl and past the disguised boat, seemingly not even looking at it.

Kharl had only covered more than twenty rods of the distance back to Dorfal and the boat before it had become a chore just to lift one leg, then the other. He had long since released the order shield, but holding the sight shield had become a major effort. Keeping himself erect and not falling was also becoming harder and harder.

The toe of one boot caught on something, and he sprawled forward. He managed to break his fall, somewhat, with his hands, but he had the feeling he'd slashed one palm on a sharp rock, and his left knee throbbed as he scrambled erect, shambling toward the straggly cattails protruding from marsh-grass-covered canvas. He knew he wasn't *that* clumsy, but tiredness and uneven ground could make the strongest man awkward.

His legs were shaking, and his eyes blurring as he clumsily struggled under the canvas flap, and released the sight shield.

Dorfal had to help him into the scow.

"Winch ... us ... back ..."

"All the way?"

"If ... you do it slow-like ... still might see us ... some close ..." Each word was an effort.

As Dorfal began to crank the return winch, Kharl could feel the boat moving away from the causeway.

Nothing had gone the way it had been planned. Half the rebels had gone one way, and half the other. As a mixture of whiteness and darkness swirled around him, Kharl thought he heard cannon. Had Hagen been more successful?

He tried to concentrate, to use his senses to find out, but then, a deeper blackness pulled him under, as though he had sunk silently into the marshes through which Dorfal winched the concealed scow.

XIV

Kharl's head was splitting when he woke. He opened his eyes, but the room remained black. He turned his head, but that didn't help. He tried to reach out with his order-senses, but a line of fire slammed through his skull, and his head dropped back onto the pillow. Another wave of darkness swallowed him.

When he drifted back awake later, he still could not see, but the headache was only a dull throbbing. He did not try to use his order-senses.

"Ser?"

The voice was female, slightly throaty—and unfamiliar.

"Yes?" His voice was croaking and hoarse.

"I have some ale . . . Istya said you should drink as much as you can."

"You'll have to put the mug in my hands. I can't see right now."

There was a momentary silence, followed by a *clink* and a scraping sound.

"Ah . . . ser."

"Oh . . ." Kharl raised both hands.

The unseen woman guided the mug to his right hand.

Kharl grasped the heavy mug with both hands before slowly moving it to his lips, tilting it slowly until he could feel the ale. He took a small swallow at first, then a larger one.

"What time is it? What day?"

"Midafternoon, ser. On eightday."

Eightday. He'd been sleeping or unconscious for two days. "What's happened? The rebels . . . ?"

"The lord-chancellor . . . he said to tell you not to worry. He's been stopping by."

Kharl belatedly remembered his manners. "I'm sorry. I can't see you. Could you tell me who you are?"

"Yes, ser. I'm Renella. I'm an apprentice to Istya. A new apprentice, ser."

"You've been most kind, Renella." Kharl took another swallow of ale. Outside of the headache, which had begun to fade with the ale, and his lack of vision, he didn't feel that poorly, although his left hand was also sore. But what had he done that had left him unable to see? Had it come from being surrounded by all the chaos he had released? Or was there a problem for an order-mage to handle chaos—even indirectly?

"I haven't done much, ser. I've just been watching you."

"Thank you." A scuffing followed, with a slight breeze wafting over Kharl. "Lord-chancellor . . . he's awake, ser." After the briefest of pauses, she added, "If you need anything, ser Kharl, I'll be back shortly."

Kharl heard Hagen's boots on the polished stone of the floor and the shoes of the departing apprentice.

"You look all right," offered Hagen.

"I can't see," Kharl said. "Other than that . . ."

"Did you get hit in the head?"

"It has to do with magery, I think. I couldn't see for a day or two after the battle in Dykaru, either."

"Are you sure you didn't hit your head?"

"I'm sure." Kharl tried to keep the irritation out of his voice. "Too much chaos is what causes the problem."

"You're an order-mage."

"What I did, remember . . . it released chaos."

"You had said . . ." ventured Hagen.

"I said I could do it. I hadn't realized what would happen. Most of this is still new to me."

Hagen said nothing, and Kharl wished that he could see the lord-chancellor's face. "What happened at the harbor?" he finally asked.

"We got off two complete volleys from all the cannon," Hagen said dryly. "They stopped and marched back down the causeway. They lost around a hundred armsmen."

"You don't sound that happy."

"I'm not. It was a feint. Hensolas had sent half his armsmen north to join the troops Fergyn already had. That was so that Fergyn could leave enough in place to threaten the Great House and still take the dockyards and warehouses."

"But not the harbor?"

"They got the supplies from the warehouses, and they have enough armsmen that they can take the harbor anytime." Hagen laughed, bitterly. "They've put you out of action for at least a while. It only cost them a hundred men, and those armsmen really were Lord Ghrant's armsmen."

"You think they're waiting for help from Hamor?"

"I'd not be surprised."

"What else?"

"They want us to attack them and be the ones that destroy the warehouses and dockworks?"

"So Lord Ghrant is the one who is hurting people?"

There was silence, although Kharl had the feeling that Hagen had nodded.

This time, Kharl waited, taking a sip of the ale from the mug that he still held.

"Casolan's been delayed. Forces under Lord Azeolis have been harassing him, and that has slowed his progress toward Valmurl."

"Azeolis?" Kharl had never heard the name.

"He's a distant cousin of Malcor. His holdings are in the high hills to the south of the mountains that border Vizyn."

"That's a long way north. How did he get far enough south to attack Casolan unless . . ."

"Unless he'd been ordered to do so from the beginning? He couldn't have."

The more Kharl heard, the less he liked what was happening, and the bad news seemed unending.

"So there are more lords involved than you thought, and they've planned this out in more detail?"

"It would seem so." Hagen's voice was flat.

Kharl took another long swallow of ale, almost finishing the mug. "What do you think they'll do next?"

"If they've planned this carefully . . . then they must have something worked out to wipe out Casolan's forces."

"Can you change his marching route?"

"I'd thought of that. They'll think that he'll take the shortest route. If he takes another way, that will at least give them pause." Hagen's sigh was soft, but audible. "All I can do is give them pause."

Kharl took a last swallow and finished the ale.

"How soon . . . ?"

"I don't know," the mage admitted. "It could be tomorrow; it could be an eightday." He had to think out what he was doing with his order-skills far better than he had before—and that was if he got his sight back—before the rebellion took over all of Austra.

"I'll talk to you later," offered Hagen. "I hope you're up and can see before long."

So did Kharl. He also hoped that he could offer Hagen and Ghrant much more aid than he had so far—and that he could find a way to remedy the damage he had inadvertently caused.

He sat in the bed, in his darkness, fretting over the rebellion he had sparked and pondering what lay ahead.

XV

Oneday came and went, and twoday dawned warmer and clearer. While Kharl was up and out of bed, he still could not see, but he could employ his order-senses—sparingly—to get around. The need for deliberation in movement made him think about Jeka, although he could not have said why, and about Warrl. He did understand why he had thought about his younger son. His own lack of deliberation and understanding had been one of the reasons that had forced the boy into seeking shelter with Merayni. He couldn't have explained why he'd thought about Jeka, but he did.

At the moment, there was little Kharl could do about either Jeka or Warrl, and if he didn't find a way to be more effective in helping Lord Ghrant, he might never be in a position to help either of them. Yet, without seeing, he could not read *The Basis of Order*, and his reflections on what he had recalled seemed to spin him in circles.

Finally, when he had not heard from Hagen by late morning on twoday, he decided to make his way down to the lord-chancellor's study. He had to wait outside for close to half a glass before the lord-chancellor was free, and, using just his order-senses, he did not recognize either of the lords who left, although he caught the names—Shachar and Harunis.

"I'm glad you're up and around." Those were the first words from

Hagen, even before Kharl eased into the chair across the table desk from the lord-chancellor.

"I still can't see, but the headaches are gone. What are the rebels doing?"

"Having their own problems, thankfully. According to the scouts and various rumors, Lord Hedron doesn't trust Hensolas, and threatened to withhold supplies and support if Fergyn wasn't given the right of summary refusal on any of Hensolas's plans. That might gain us another few days."

"How long before the first companies of Casolan's forces near Valmurl?"

"I don't know. I sent word to him. I ordered him to take a different route. I left it up to him as to what route it should be since I cannot be certain that any choice I made might not be passed to Hensolas or Fergyn." Hagen cleared his throat. "I also got a messenger from him, and the report that he crushed a company of rebels under Azeolis. He's very cautious, though. He didn't pursue, because he had reports that Azeolis had five more companies."

"That would make sense to me," Kharl replied. "Lord Ghrant needs those forces here more than he needs to defeat five companies away from Valmurl." After a moment of silence, he asked, "Is that not so . . . or is there something I don't know?" He almost had said "don't see."

"No. With the disunity among the rebels, Casolan's companies may be enough to stop their attacks." Hagen laughed ironically. "Now . . . if only you could find a way to remove them from the dockworks and warehouse areas."

"Order doesn't seem to work that way." Kharl paused before adding, "Not for most mages, anyway, and the ones who can do more with it haven't shared how they did."

"I've heard that," replied Hagen. "One of the traders out of Recluce said that just two mages destroyed Fairven, and only one returned, and he never spoke a word about it." Hagen shook his head. "I was younger then, and I asked why the rulers of Recluce, their council or whatever it is, hadn't forced him to tell them. The trader gave me this funny look, and then he asked me exactly how I would propose to force that from a mage who had destroyed an empire." Hagen's chuckle was anything but humorous. "Take you, Kharl. Someone might be able to take you off guard and kill you, but could anyone force you to tell them how you do what you do?"

"No." Kharl didn't explain that was because so much of what he did was through order-senses, and that the directions would have been meaningless to anyone without that ability.

"That's the problem with wizards and mages. They can only be controlled by other mages or wizards—or by their own beliefs. That bothers lords. They don't like to deal with powers they can't control."

"That's why Lord Ghrant prefers to have you deal with me?"

"Of course." Hagen laughed, once, brusquely. "That way, if anything goes wrong, it was my fault."

Kharl waited to see if Hagen would say more.

"Ghrant's basically honest," the lord-chancellor went on. "Weak about some things, but honest. Your presence doesn't bother him, except that he'd rather have me give orders. Vatoran and Guillam, though, you made them uncomfortable just by being around. Do you feel that way around the white wizards?"

Kharl frowned. "I can feel them. Don't know as they make me uncomfortable." He paused and reconsidered his words. "I don't know as I'd be comfortable around chaos all the time."

"That makes sense. I'd wager they'd not be comfortable around you, either." Hagen stood. "I need to go and see Norgen."

After a moment, Kharl stood, belatedly realizing that the lord-chancellor had many demands upon him, and Kharl was in no position to help with those demands—not at the moment, not until he recovered. "I'll try to see if I can discover some other way to help." He stepped around the chair, deliberately.

"That would be useful."

Kharl appreciated the understatement. Hagen and Lord Ghrant needed something that was more than merely useful.

After leaving the lord-chancellor, Kharl walked slowly back up the steps to the upper level, past his own quarters, and toward the north tower. He took the stone steps carefully, one at a time. Once he was out in the late-morning air, he crossed the tower to the east side.

There, he leaned forward, his forearms on the parapet stones, with the spring sun warming him and the breeze in his face. For a time, he faced eastward, in the direction of the city and the harbor he could not see, thinking.

What could he do? Unbinding order to release chaos was definitely a bad idea—except as the sort of last resort when he might be killed if he didn't. A chaos-wizard could spray free chaos everywhere, and it could wound or kill. Doing the same with order would only strengthen things. It might help people who were ill. As Hagen had pointed out, order did seem to make people who were chaos-driven uncomfortable, but Kharl didn't see that as terribly useful in a battle. From what he'd been able to do so far, his only effective use of order seemed to be to use it to kill Ghrant's enemies through confinement, and he could only do that to one or two people at a time. Still . . . if he removed enough of the rebel lords . . .

He shrugged. He couldn't do anything until he recovered more.

XVI

By threeday, Kharl could see—intermittently. His vision came and went unpredictably. At least, he could not discern the reasons for its presence or absence, although he had no doubt that his ability to see was affected by some deeper interrelation between order and chaos. In time, he suspected, he would understand, and wonder why he had not seen sooner. That seemed to be his lot in life, to understand, imperfectly and late.

As he made his way toward the small dining room for a midday meal, in one of his moments of clear vision, he noticed Commander Norgen leaving Hagen's study.

"Commander?"

"Ser mage." Norgen bowed.

"Have you a moment to join me in eating?" asked Kharl.

"Ah . . ." Norgen paused. "I cannot take long."

"You have not eaten, have you?"

"No. Sometimes, I end up missing meals here and there."

"That can't be good. I won't take much of your time, and it won't hurt for you to eat something."

"I suppose not." The slender commander's laugh was good-natured.

Once they entered the larger of the small dining rooms, Norgen led the way to a corner table. Only one other table was occupied, and that by two men in dark blue, one with white hair, and the other much younger, perhaps Kharl's age. The mage recognized neither.

". . . does not understand that law favors precedent and example . . ."

". . . consistency over the wishes of a ruler . . ."

Kharl kept his frown to himself, but even as he did, his sight vanished, and he had to rely on his order-senses to seat himself.

"Advocates, magistrates, justicers," said Norgen, "always talking about law. They think it's the same as justice."

Kharl's laugh was short and bitter.

"Your laugh says more than my words," added Norgen.

"Why are they here?" asked Kharl, not wishing to discuss his past experiences with justicers, or rather, Lord Justicer Reynol of Nordla.

"They come to brief Lord Ghrant on the cases they have already decided. Always in open audiences."

"He's not in the Hall of Justice?"

"No. Everyone knows that's not good. They might decide the cases on what Lord Ghrant wants, or what they think he wants."

Norgen's reply confused Kharl. "But . . . if they tell him . . . ?"

"Oh . . . there's a procedure for that. Lord Ghrant sits behind a screen and never speaks. If he has a question, he whispers to the lord-chancellor or whoever's attending him, and they ask it. His questions are always about the facts or the law."

That seemed better than what happened in Nordla, but Kharl still suspected that in some cases, Lord Ghrant might well be able to get his views across.

"Sers?"

Kharl turned toward the server's voice.

"We just have a boar stew today," announced the serving girl.

"I'll have that with ale," said Norgen.

"The same," added Kharl. "The pale ale." He liked the lager better most times, but occasionally had ale.

After she had left, Norgen cleared his throat.

"I'm sorry," Kharl said. "At times, I'm still having trouble seeing. It comes and goes."

"Did you hit your head? That sometimes . . ."

"No. What I did on the causeway released too much chaos. I'm pretty much an order-mage. Handling too much chaos affects how I see for a while."

"I wondered why we hadn't seen much of you lately."

"Sers . . ." The server set the two ales on the table. "I'll be back with the stew."

"Thank you," Kharl said. He had to use his order-senses to locate the mug. He took a swallow, enjoying the coolness.

"You had something in mind, ser mage?" asked Norgen gently.

"I did. I don't know how to be subtle. How do the armsmen and lancers feel about this rebellion?"

As Kharl took another swallow of the ale, enjoying it, he could see once more. He blinked.

"You know, ser mage, that is a dangerous question?" Norgen lifted his eyebrows, white and bushy, in contrast to his thin and faded—and wispy—strawberry blond hair.

"Dangerous? I'm just a cooper and a beginning mage. Why would wanting to know how troops feel be dangerous?"

Norgen smiled. "My father always told me to watch the man who began with words like that. Just a beginning mage? Just a cooper? Hagen said you were one of the best, and Lyras says you're far more than a beginning mage."

Kharl laughed. "He also told you to avoid telling people what they don't want to hear."

"Sometimes." Norgen took a sip of his ale, then tilted his head slightly. "You would understand. The lord-chancellor might. Lord Ghrant would not." He offered a faint smile and took another sip of ale.

Kharl thought he understood. "The armsmen don't see why all this is necessary. In the end, whoever rules, their situation will be the same. They might stand a better chance of getting paid by Lord Ghrant, but they also might think they stand a greater chance of getting killed. Is that it?"

"Close enough. Most armsmen serve because they've little choice in life. True of many of the officers, too. Lands go to the eldest, and that leaves being a guard officer or going into trade. Sons of lords have this worry about trade. It's . . . unbecoming. Me . . . never saw how honestly making or selling something of use to others was unbecoming. But I'm better with a mount and blade than with figures or crafting." Norgen broke off as the serving girl, painfully thin, returned with two large bowls and a basket heaped with dark bread still warm from the ovens.

As Kharl watched her approach, he saw that the two justicers, or magistrates or whatever they had been, had left the small dining room.

"Here you are, sers. Would you like more ale?"

Kharl realized his mug was almost empty. He hadn't been aware of drinking so much, good as the ale had tasted. "Yes, please."

"I've enough, thank you," added Norgen.

Once she departed, Kharl cleared his throat. "You were saying about officers . . ."

"I was." Norgen waited again.

"All but the most senior feel like their armsmen? That rebellion is meaningless to them, and they'd prefer to survive it with the fewest casualties?"

"Many feel that way, or so it's said. Why are you so interested in that, ser mage?"

"I'm trying to think of a way to end the rebellion that won't blind me for life and won't kill thousands of armsmen and their officers."

"You do that, and you'd have many happy troops. Happier officers." Norgen snorted. "That'd be true magery." He took a mouthful of stew. After eating for a time, he added, "Not bad. Glad you dragged me in here."

Kharl was, too. The stew, if slightly too peppery, was hot and filling, and he could use the nourishment. He also had a feeling, or part of one . . . about what he could do . . . if he could just figure out how to present it to Hagen. "It seemed the thing to do. I don't know much about armsmen and lancers. I know more about trade and barrels, and even sailing."

"At times, I wish I did."

"You didn't want to be a lancer?"

"It was the best choice open to me. My father was a cabinetmaker. After I'd ruined too many pieces, he suggested that I might be better as a renderer's apprentice, because no one cared what anything looked like once it got to the renderer. If I didn't like that, he said, then being an armsman or lancer would be a good second choice." Norgen took another mouthful of stew.

"He must have had quite a tongue."

"He did. He was always too quick for me. So was my brother. Figured it was better for me to listen to orders and have a blade do the talking."

"Are you from Valmurl?"

"No. I grew up in Nasloch. About a hundred kays south of Bruel, along the west coast. My brother's still there, still making cabinets."

"Do you ever go back?"

"No. My consort's from Valmurl. Her family thinks what I do is honorable. Mine doesn't."

Kharl nodded.

"That nod says more than words." Norgen stood. "I need to be getting back." A faint smile appeared on his narrow face. "Anything you can do will be better than what's going to happen otherwise. Good day, ser mage."

Kharl sat for a time at the circular table, sipping the last of his ale.

XVII

Early on fourday, after his breakfast, Kharl walked to the study Hagen used and waited outside in the corridor for the lord-chancellor, who was expected soon.

A quarter glass passed without Hagen's appearance, but Kharl continued to wait.

After a time, one of the guards—an older man—spoke. "They say the rebels have some wizards."

"They do. From what I know, they still have two left."

"Ah . . . are they pretty good, ser?"

Kharl caught the unspoken question behind the one asked. "They're white wizards. Black and white are different. White is better for attacking. Black is usually better at defending."

"You think that's why they haven't attacked the Great House? Except that one time?"

"It might be. I wouldn't wish to guess," Kharl said with a laugh. "That's something the lord-chancellor and Commander Norgen would know better than I would."

The guard closed his mouth as Hagen turned the corner at the end of the corridor.

Kharl waited until the lord-chancellor was within a few cubits. "Good morning, ser."

"Good morning, ser mage. I take it that you're better?"

"So it would seem. I would like a few moments if you can spare them."

"For you, I can always spare a few moments. This morning, those moments may have to be fewer, unfortunately." Hagen opened the study door, leaving it open for Kharl.

The mage closed it after he followed Hagen into the chamber.

"I am glad to see that you are recovered." Hagen settled into chair behind the table desk.

"So am I."

"What did you have in mind? You're not one for idle talk," Hagen observed.

"Who are the best leaders left among the rebel lords?"

"Hensolas is probably better at tactics and strategy, but Fergyn is better at inspiring officers and troops."

"Do you have pictures or likenesses of them?"

"Ser Kharl . . ." Hagen's voice was even, almost flat.

"I've thought about this, lord-chancellor. I've thought about it a great deal. I am not that great a help against large forces." Kharl offered a wry chuckle. "In fact, I've proved to be as great a danger to myself as to them. But there is another way . . . If the wizards and the rebel leaders cannot survive, neither can the revolt."

"What you're suggesting is a great risk for Lord Ghrant, and a greater risk for you."

Kharl snorted. "Anything else is a greater risk. I know what I can do, and I know what I cannot. When Ilteron was threatening Lord Ghrant, you told me that if he did not win quickly, then he would lose support throughout Austra. Is not that the situation Lord Ghrant now faces?"

"It's possible," Hagen conceded.

"If this revolt is put down without the lives of many more armsmen being taken, whom will that benefit?"

"You are sounding more like an advocate than a mage," replied Hagen, his voice containing a testy edge. "Yet you are suggesting government by murder."

Kharl forced a laugh. "You murdered a hundred armsmen with cannon on the causeway. I have murdered a score or more through order-magery. What is the difference between one death and another?"

"Lords . . . are not treated that way."

"Oh? Then it is good—or acceptable—to kill mere armsmen, who have no choice and who never had much of a say in matters, but it is wrong to kill the leaders who created the problem and have already sent hundreds to their deaths?"

Hagen did not answer.

"Will the armsmen serving the rebels be more likely to be supportive of a ruler who butchers them and their mates or one who removes their leaders and demands their allegiance?" Kharl snorted. "More to the point . . . how long will it take to subdue this rebellion by force of arms? Can it be done?"

"Can what you propose be done?" countered Hagen.

"Who knows? But I cannot do more to slaughter large numbers of armsmen. So what do you and Lord Ghrant have to lose by letting me try?"

"We could lose you."

"I would personally dislike that a great deal, but if I cannot be useful to you and Lord Ghrant, I do not see a great loss for either of you."

"Just . . . for the purpose of discussion . . . how would you propose this . . . effort?"

Kharl laughed. "In the reverse of what is normally done, from what I have seen."

Hagen's brow furrowed.

"Most times, it seems to me, a mage or a wizard is used to position the enemy's forces in such a fashion that it allows action by regular lancers and armsmen. On the causeway, I created chaos with the purpose of moving the armsmen into range of your cannon. I propose that you use your forces to decoy Hensolas or Fergyn or their wizards into positions where they are easier for me to reach."

"And . . . if you fail?"

"You withdraw. Is that not done? You tell no one why the companies are where they are, not even Norgen or Casolan, when he arrives."

"You are suggesting a novel approach, ser Kharl."

"I'm suggesting the only approach I can think of that might work."

"You're suggesting assassinating lords."

"And mages. Why not?"

"What if they return the favor?"

"I'll have to go for the wizards first, won't I? That would be better, anyway."

"Perhaps we could discuss the matter of lords after your success with the wizards."

Kharl leaned back in the chair and looked at Hagen. "You weren't this concerned in Dykaru. What don't I see?"

"Every action creates the need for another action," Hagen said dryly. "If you are successful, then assassination will return as an accepted tool for gaining power. In case you have not noticed, Lord Ghrant is not terribly prepossessing. He's barely adequate as a swordsman and less than that using his hands. He's an easy target for the poorest assassin. Then there's the problem of the example that you'd create. Or create once more. For the first five generations after Austra was unified, not a single ruler died in his bed or peacefully. I'm not terribly interested in returning to that kind of . . . chaos."

Kharl waited.

"I don't have a problem with your taking on the white wizards. First, they're nothing more than Hamorian spies and tools. Second, any conflicts between them and you will be regarded as battles between equals. Not even Ghrant's worst detractors will gainsay your acts against the wizards, but against lords . . ." Hagen shook his head. "Austra will end up in fragments again."

Kharl had his doubts—strong doubts—but then, Hagen did know Austra and power better than Kharl—and Kharl had been the one to touch off the rebellion by his unwise use of power.

"I'll see what I can do about the white wizards."

Hagen nodded. "Before you do more than that . . . we should consider what might happen." He stood. "Come back right after midday, and I'll give you the best information we have on where the troops and wizards are."

The lord-chancellor wasn't quite saying no, and he could well be right, Kharl reflected, as he stood. "I'll be here."

XVIII

Barely after dawn on sixday, Kharl rode yet another borrowed mount through the damp air of the late-spring morning. This time, the mage wore the green and black of the regular Austran lancers. Given the cloudless day and the stillness of the air, the coolness would doubtless turn into a warm and slightly uncomfortable noon, and a sticky and sultry afternoon. For the moment, Kharl appreciated the cool stillness as he rode beside Undercaptain Demyst. The soreness in his ribs had subsided enough that he was reminded of their tenderness only when he moved suddenly—or lurched in the saddle.

The afternoon before, Kharl and three companies under the command of Majer Ghenal had moved to the northeast of the Great House, settling into the estate of one Buvert, a sympathizer of the late Lord Malcor. Buvert's consort had fled, along with the staff and children. Once there, the three companies had begun visible preparations for an attack upon the dockyards, still held by forces commanded by Lord Fergyn. Hagen had told Majer Ghenal that the majer was not to attack under any circumstances, that the maneuver was designed to make sure that Fergyn and Hensolas did not unite their forces—not until Casolan arrived with reinforcements, at least.

Kharl and Undercaptain Demyst's two squads were riding due east, conducting a reconnaissance in force. Those were the orders that Hagen had given the undercaptain, along with the observation that, as necessary, Kharl might undertake his own reconnaissance efforts independently at any time.

The hoofs of the two squads created a muted thunderlike sound as they struck the heavy planks set in clay that formed the hard surface of the Cross-Stream Pike.

"Are there many roads like this?" asked Kharl. He'd heard of timbered pikes, but never run across one.

"This used to be a true pike, maybe a hundred years back, and the only way to get to the part of Valmurl north of the dockworks in times of rain." Demyst laughed. "Story is that the shamblers burned Lord Lysaran's stables one night, and the barns an eightday later in protest of the fees. Lord Esthaven stripped Lysaran of his lands and gave him an eightday to leave Austra. Said that anyone who couldn't control rabble didn't deserve lands."

"A hard lord, it sounds like. Wasn't Esthaven the one who built the harbor causeway?"

"He was hard, but he did much for Austra. He united east and west . . ."

"I thought that was Isthel—"

Demyst shook his head. "Isthel was his grandsire. Isthel conquered the west, but Esthaven was the one who united Austra. He gave the new western lords the same privileges as those in the east and abolished the special tariffs laid on the west. He even set up schools in Bruel and along the west coast."

Kharl wondered if he'd ever understand Austra. But then, he hadn't really understood Nordla, and he'd been born and raised in Brysta.

"There! One of their scouts."

Kharl glanced ahead, toward the southeast, following the undercaptain's gesture. A rider in green and black, wearing the blue sash of the rebel forces, galloped southward along a narrow lane that ran between two ragged hedgerows for half a kay, before the ancient hedgerows ended at a welter of ramshackle wooden structures. A handful of people in the middle of the lane scattered just before the lancer bore down on them.

"That's Tinkertown," offered the undercaptain. "All the peddlers and tinkers, and the men who offer their backs for a day's work at the dockyards—most of 'em come from there."

"And the land used to belong to Lord Lysaran?" Kharl's tone was dry.

"So they say." After a moment, Demyst added, "Scout's riding hard. He'll be turning at the crossroads there, come back onto the pike, and make for the northern corner of the dockworks."

Reportedly, Lord Fergyn had made one of the old factor's warehouses, one with living quarters above and behind it, into his temporary headquarters.

"You think they'll move against us today?" asked Kharl.

"I don't see how. That's the only scout we've seen. They weren't expecting us to move before Commander Casolan reached Valmurl."

"We might as well keep riding and see how close we can get."

"Not too close to their wizards, if you please, ser Kharl."

That was exactly what Kharl wanted—or at least to discover where they were—but he couldn't admit that. So he nodded, and said, "We don't want to lose any men to wizardry."

"No, ser."

At the moment, Kharl was using no active order-magery at all. From what he had observed so far, the white mages had trouble pinpointing order-users unless the black mages were actively engaged in some sort of magery. Certainly, it was far harder for Kharl to determine the exact location of a white wizard if the wizard wasn't using chaos. Given the distances involved, Kharl had decided that he would continue on horseback toward the dockworks. He had a bright blue sash tucked inside his tunic. Once he separated from Demyst and the two squads, he hoped that the uniform and the sash would suffice as a disguise until he got close enough to need to use his sight shield. He'd tried the shield with the mount before leaving Buvert's estate. The gelding hadn't bucked or tried to throw Kharl, but he had come to a stop, and Kharl had only been able to coax him along at a slow walk. Kharl thought that, if necessary, he could dismount and lead the gelding. He'd seen horses blindfolded and led, but he didn't want to have to walk too far. Not after his last use of magery in rebel-held territory.

As he rode, Kharl took in the land around him, looking for lanes leading off the pike to the south that might curve eastward or intersect other smaller roads or lanes. He didn't recall taking the pike when he had sought out Lyras, and that meant that there were other ways to the dockworks than the route they were taking.

He was also trying to sense where the white wizards were. He'd felt nothing immediately after leaving Buvert's estate, but as they left Tinkertown behind and neared the outskirts of Valmurl, he could sense two separate areas of chaos—presumably the two white wizards. One was less than two kays from where he rode, closer to the dockworks. The other—and stronger—influence was somewhere to the south of Valmurl. To Kharl, that meant that the stronger white wizard was with Lord Hensolas, and the weaker with Fergyn's forces.

Ahead of them, the pike began to descend slightly into a lower meadow area between two stone walls. The grass showed the lighter green of spring. At the crest of a gentle rise some sixty rods farther along the pike to the southeast, scarcely more than half a kay away, a low wall of greenery lay across the road.

"They've blocked the pike," said Demyst. "Felled firs or something and dragged them into place."

Kharl studied the makeshift barrier, catching sight of men behind the ragged green barrier. "They've got armsmen there."

"We need to pull up. If they have cannon and rifles, we'll be too exposed on the downslope ahead." Demyst turned in the saddle, raising his right arm. "Squads halt! To the rear, ride!"

As they turned back the way they had come, Kharl studied the area to the south of the pike even more closely. Ahead, he saw a narrow way, wider than a path, but barely a lane, that bordered an ill-tended pearapple orchard.

"It's time for me to head off," Kharl said. "I need to look into this more closely. Can you have a squad stand by for me, starting in two glasses?"

"Ah . . . ser . . . where did you have in mind?"

"Nowhere close to the rebel forces. What about where the lane from Tinkertown leaves the pike?"

Demyst nodded. "That'd not be a problem, not unless they attack, and I don't see that happening."

"If they do, I'm on my own."

"You say two glasses, ser?"

"Probably be closer to three," Kharl admitted.

"We'll be there, ser."

With a nod to Demyst, Kharl turned his mount off the pike and onto the lane that led past the pearapple orchard. He did not hear a word from the lancers, even using his order-senses. Once he was well away from the lancers, he extracted the blue sash from his tunic and smoothed it in place across his chest. As he neared the southern end of the orchard, he saw a cot and a small barn to his right. A woman with a babe in her arms turned, then rushed back to the cot.

The door closed with a muffled *thud*.

Beyond the orchard were fields, recently tilled. Kharl could not see anything sprouting yet, and he had no idea what crops the smallholders might grow. The sun continued to beat down, and the black-and-green-wool uniform was far warmer than Kharl had expected. He blotted the dampness from his forehead and kept riding.

He rode south almost a kay, watching as holders and their consorts and children either fled or watched him pass stolidly. With each rod he rode, the huts and cots were closer and closer together, until they stood almost as close together as in Valmurl itself, with barely space for small gardens between each dwelling. At the first wider way, one rutted with the tracks of carts and wagons, he turned eastward. Ahead, he could see the taller warehouses and the cranes of the dock area. Only a few people were out and about, and they stayed well clear of the road.

Another rider, also in uniform and with a blue sash, rode toward Kharl. As he neared the mage, the younger lancer called out to Kharl, "Careful when you get to the square. Old ironbritches 'bout to bust a gut."

"Thanks. Need to watch out to the north. There's a road patrol farther out on the pike."

"Thanks to you."

With a nod, Kharl passed the lancer, letting his order-senses track the man until they were several rods apart, but the man never looked back.

The nearer Kharl rode to the docking area, the quieter and emptier the streets became. A good three blocks short of the square to the north of the dockworks proper, Kharl turned his mount southward along a side street, one lined with modest dwellings. Most were shuttered and locked. A prudent precaution, the mage reflected.

As he rode he used his order-senses to gather in impressions of chaos. A well of whiteness was centered almost due east of where he rode, and at the next corner, he turned his mount back eastward, toward the square and the northern end of the harbor—the part holding the shipworks and dry docks and the majority of the factors' warehouses. That was where he and the crew of the *Seastag* had refitted the ship some two seasons before. Had it only been two seasons?

He could see lancers in green and black, with the blue sashes, riding back and forth, as if on a post set across the southern side of the square. Glancing ahead, Kharl looked for a place to tie his mount. He settled on a hitching rail outside a felter's shop because the shop was shuttered and seemed empty. There he dismounted and began to walk toward the square.

He was now somewhat west and south of the center of the whitish fount of chaos, which he felt was less than a block to the north of where he was. At the corner of the square, where one of the other lancers glanced in his direction, Kharl turned and nodded northward, half-shrugging.

A wry expression crossed the sentry's face. "Good luck."

"Need it," Kharl replied, and kept walking, past a row of three shops, a wool factor's, a leather factor's, and a small brassworks.

Ahead of him to his left was a three-story building—its bricks painted a faded light green. The sign hung over the large double doors read OSSAFAL AND SONS, FACTORS, and the letters were a faded dark green. Two armsmen stood before the doors.

Kharl did not wish to use any active order-skills until he was far closer to the white wizard. Before reaching the southern end of the building, as he passed the brassworks, Kharl turned left and down the narrow lane between the brassworks and larger factor's structure. The loading dock to the brassworks was closed, and there was no doorway on the south side of the green-brick building—the structure within which was one of the white wizards.

At the end of the side lane on the north side was an enclosed yard, with a gate. The lock on the gate had already been broken. Kharl paused, letting his order-senses receive a feeling for the rear yard. It was empty, except for three mounts tethered to a beam protruding from a sagging dock that had not been used in years. The former loading dock door had been boarded shut, leaving just a smaller door to one side.

The steps up to the smaller door creaked as Kharl took them. He did not sense anyone just inside the building. Still, he opened the door and paused before stepping inside. Beyond the door was an oblong room half-filled with pallets on which bales had been roped, amphorae, crates, and a number of boxes clearly wrenched open. Scuff marks in the dust on the scarred wooded floors showed where pallets had been recently moved.

An armsman straightened up from where he'd been rummaging through one of the boxes. He frowned.

"Message for the wizard," Kharl offered, ready to clamp shields around the other at the slightest sign of alarm.

"His mightiness the white wizard, the almighty Alborak?"

"Guess he's the one."

"Take the stairs in front." There was a pause. "Why'd you come in back?"

"They said I could tie my mount out back," Kharl explained, hoping the other did not check immediately.

"Figures."

Kharl walked toward the only door he saw, still holding himself ready to use the shields if he needed to. Nothing happened, and he stepped into another corridor, even more dimly lit. The staircase was to his left.

While there were no guards on the lower level, a single armsman stood at the top of the steps. He had not seen Kharl, or not looked in the mage's direction.

Kharl formed a sight shield, hoping that Alborak would not notice, and began to climb the steps, quietly, slowly, one at a time. As he climbed, he could hear voices from above him. He tried to listen as he moved.

". . . you didn't even know he was there?"

"He was only a cooper," said a second voice, hard and conveying arrogance. "How can he possibly know that much about order, let alone chaos?"

"I'm but an undercaptain, ser wizard," came the reply, "but Captain

Fegaro said that there was chaos-fire everywhere on that causeway, and he's seen most everything in his years."

Kharl moved up several more steps. He had the feeling that he would be able to get close enough to the white wizard without going all the way to the top of the ancient stairs.

"It had to be cannon fire, like in the harbor. Order-mages cannot handle chaos."

"He said it was chaos."

Kharl took two more steps.

"He's not a wizard or a mage. How would he know?"

"Ser . . . you'd have to ask him."

"There's something strange—"

Kharl hardened the air around the young wizard before he could say more.

Hssst! White fire appeared from nowhere, as if it had formed in the air less than three cubits from Kharl, and flashed downward toward him.

His shields barely deflected the chaos-bolt, and he took a hard step sideways on the staircase.

"Chaos-fire!" called the guard.

"There's a mage somewhere! Look for him!" called the undercaptain.

Another blast of chaos flared toward Kharl, if slightly weaker than the first.

Kharl struggled to maintain his barrier around the white wizard and to maintain the sight shield. He could sense the sentry moving to the top of the stairs, less than two cubits from where Kharl stood, and looking down.

"There's no one here, ser! Just chaos-fire everywhere!"

"There's a mage somewhere! There has to be!"

"I don't see no one, ser!"

A third blast of chaos-fire rocked Kharl, one hurled with a desperation that Kharl could feel, but his defenses held.

"Has to be somewhere!"

Leaning in darkness against the side of the staircase, Kharl kept his shields in place. He could smell something burning farther down the staircase.

"The stairs are catching fire, ser!" called the guard.

More chaos, this time more diffuse and less focused, splashed around Kharl. He could also feel heat from the wall behind him, and he edged forward. He knew he couldn't retreat yet. He was close to the limit at which he could hold the hardened air barrier around Alborak, and if he loosened that barrier, the white wizard would escape. That would make any later efforts much, much harder, if not impossible.

"Find the wizard!"

"But . . . ser . . . there's no one here!"

A grim smile crossed Kharl's lips, one erased by the effort of holding his shields as another desperate blast of chaos flared around him.

Two more weaker blasts followed.

The sound of crackling flames began to rise, and Kharl struggled not to cough as smoke filled the staircase.

"Ser . . . we got to get out of here!" called the armsman at the top of the staircase.

Abruptly, the reddish white void of death washed over Kharl. He almost sagged as he released the hardened air barrier that had killed Alborak. Flames licked at him and the old and dry wood as he staggered down to the bottom of the steps and toward the front double doors.

He scrambled forward and let his sight shield drop just as he pushed open the right-hand door. "Fire! Fire! Stairs are on fire!"

The two guards standing beyond the archway just looked at him.

"Can't you smell it? See the flames? Get a bucket brigade . . . or something . . . whole place'll burn." A well of heat rushed out from behind Kharl.

The guard who had been at the top of the stairs charged out, beating out small patches of flame on his uniform. "Call the fire brigade!"

"We . . . we're . . ." stammered one of the guards.

"I'll do it." Kharl dashed past them, heading south. "Fire in headquarters! Fire in the building!"

Others took up the cry.

Once he was past the woolen factor's, Kharl raised his sight shield for a short time, just long enough to get around the corner and closer to his mount. The gelding had remained where he tied it, doubtless only because he had only been gone for a short time and possibly because the locals feared that it had belonged to the rebels and that taking it would have led to great reprisals.

Kharl dropped the sight shield, mounted, and rode away at a fast trot, a pace he judged likely enough for a messenger or a scout. He tried not to bounce in the saddle.

As he made his way north and west, watching for rebel lancers, and for pursuit, he couldn't help thinking about the young white wizard he'd killed. The young man hadn't had a chance, not really. He hadn't known what had struck him, not until it was effectively too late.

Yet what else could Kharl do? He didn't know any method to capture a white wizard, or to hold one once captured, and he couldn't just let the man continue to use chaos to kill Lord Ghrant's and Hagen's lancers and armsmen. And Kharl didn't have any other weapons that would be effective. A staff was useless in close quarters, and, besides, neither a staff nor a cudgel could stand up against chaos-fire.

He glanced over his shoulder. A column of thick gray smoke rose from the dockworks area. Kharl could only hope that the fire did not spread beyond the one building, but how could he have predicted that Alborak's chaos-bolts would turn the old factoring building into an inferno?

Kharl shook his head. Chaos-fire was hotter than fire in a hearth or a stove, perhaps as hot as a forge. With that much of it being flung around an old building, fire was highly likely—but that was a chance he'd had to take.

He kept riding, and looking back over his shoulder. The column of smoke had gotten larger, but not markedly so. He could only hope the damage was limited, but he kept glancing back.

In time, he returned to the Cross-Stream Pike, where he removed the blue sash and tucked it back into his tunic.

Undercaptain Demyst was waiting—with both squads—at the rendezvous point.

Kharl reined up. "Thank you."

"Our pleasure, ser mage." Demyst frowned slightly. "Your face is a shade red, ser Kharl." He glanced eastward toward the column of grayish smoke that still rose over the north harbor area.

"Matters were somewhat hotter where I was," Kharl replied, slowly easing his mount beside that of the undercaptain. "Did you see any rebel forces?"

"Not except for the ones at that barrier. We saw one messenger. He saw us and turned due south."

"I think I saw him, too," Kharl said. "We can head back to Buvert's estate."

The undercaptain nodded, then gestured. The two squads fell in behind the mage and the undercaptain.

Kharl forced himself not to look back toward the fire. He regretted so much destruction, but what else could he have done?

XIX

After he had returned to Buvert's estate and taken care of the mount, Kharl made his way to the kitchen in the main house. His legs were shaky. His eyes blurred, and his ribs had begun to ache again. All were signs that he needed to eat. A servingwoman from the Great House, wearing Ghrant's livery, suggested that he seat himself at the dining table to be served.

Kharl walked into the dining room, where the only other person was the lord-chancellor.

"Good afternoon, Kharl."

"The same to you, lord-chancellor." Kharl sank into the chair across the dining room table from Hagen. Absently, Kharl noted that the polished surface of the dark wooden table was covered with a thin golden haze of oak pollen.

"You look tired," Hagen observed.

"You don't," Kharl replied.

"It is helpful to leave the Great House occasionally. How did your reconnaissance go?"

"It was successful. Fergyn no longer has a white mage at the dockyards. I killed him. That leaves the stronger one in the south with Hensolas." Kharl's voice was flat. "In the fight, the mage—Alborak was his name—his chaos-fire turned the factor's place into flames. I hope they were able to limit the fire to that one building, but there was a lot of smoke."

The door behind Kharl opened, and the servingwoman appeared with two crystal beakers of dark ale that she set quickly before the men, then departed.

"I had reports of fire," Hagen said. "I've already had my people start spreading word that it was caused by chaos-fire and that sort of thing happens when white wizards are around. With a few coppers to the street boys, they'll pass it on to anyone who will listen."

"Do you think that will help?" Kharl did not ask whether Lord Ghrant had decided to be easier on the street children than his sire had been. He took a long swallow of the ale.

"It will help, perhaps more than winning another skirmish with the rebels."

"You don't think they'll attack?"

"No. They want us to attack."

"Then I'd better head south and find the other white wizard. I heard his name once, but I can't remember it."

"You don't sound so confident as you did when you proposed this. Do you wish to continue?" Hagen raised his eyebrows.

"I'm confident enough." Kharl's throat was dry, and he took another swallow of the ale before continuing. "It almost seems . . . I don't know. I was going to say that it was pointless, but it's not. If I do what I do carefully and well . . . I'll probably be successful, and fewer people will die. I don't like doing it, but I still don't see any other way of dealing with the rebels. Or the white wizards. Or Hamor." Kharl took a deep breath. "Do you?"

"That is often the way of ruling. What is carefully planned and distasteful is often the most effective strategy. It is effective because it is distasteful, and because it is distasteful others do not consider the possibility."

"It doesn't make sense." Kharl held the beaker, but let it rest on the wide wooden coaster. "Everyone seems to think that battles are glorious—"

"No. A handful of popinjays think so. The wise commanders see them as necessary, and the experienced troops accept them, but as a last resort. Only the minstrels and poets who have not seen the blood and the broken bodies glorify battle. There is little glorious about battle." Hagen snorted. "The only virtue a battle has is when it puts an end to more battles that otherwise might have to be fought."

"After all this . . . if they lose their wizards and their leadership, you think the rebel lords will just surrender . . . or flee?"

"They're unlikely to surrender. They might flee."

"Have you told Lord Ghrant? About our plans?"

"There's no need to do so, not until the wizards are no longer a problem."

"You're still worried about my using magery on Hensolas and Fergyn?"

"I can hope that they will see the writing in the flames they have created."

"If they don't?"

"We'll face that problem when the time comes."

Kharl could sense that Hagen was disturbed, but that he was not deceiving Kharl. The lord-chancellor was worried. Gravely worried, but it did not seem as though he were worried about what Kharl had done. "You don't care for the white wizards, do you?"

"The ones used by Hamor? No. The fewer of them, the better for the rest of the world."

Although the Hagen's voice was level, Kharl could sense the anger—or cold hatred—behind the words.

"But you worry that Fergyn and Hensolas won't flee? That they'll keep fighting?"

"After what happened with Guillam and Malcor and Kenslan . . . wouldn't you be worried?" countered Hagen.

"I would." Kharl had to admit that he could see Hagen's concerns. But if removing the white wizards and the two lords leading the rebels did not suffice to break the revolt, what would it take? Turning half of Austra into ashes and graves?

"When one deals with passion, ser mage," Hagen said heavily, "reason is blinded. Care, thoughtfulness, and compassion are forgotten, and the sole thirst is that for blood."

Kharl looked down at the half-empty crystal beaker.

"I would not see reason blinded by anger," Hagen went on, "or compassion inundated under a flood of hatred. Yet I fear that already the finer traits have been swept away, and that what you propose may well be necessary—and only the first step. But . . . first deal with the other white wizard, and then we will see."

"Then we will see . . ." Those words echoed in Kharl's ears long after he had eaten and left the dining room to walk alone through the gardens at the rear of the estate. To the east, the smoke from the dockyards area had subsided, but a haze lay over Valmurl, and the sun shone with a tinge of red in its rays.

XX

On sevenday, wearing the blacks of an order-mage, Kharl had ridden back to the Great House, accompanying the lancers who had been used as the cover for his attack on Alborak. Hagen had left earlier, late on sixday, without telling Kharl.

Kharl had worried about Hagen's silent departure during his own ride, and even after he'd eaten his midday meal—alone at the Great House—and had returned to his quarters there. Although Hagen had always been his superior, in one way or another, Kharl felt that a distance had grown between them. Was that because Hagen was lord-chancellor? Because as lord-chancellor he had to balance so much? Or because Kharl had changed, because he had become less accommodating and more willing to speak out?

When he had been just a cooper, perhaps the best in Brysta, but only a cooper, people had talked to him. They had been his superiors or his equals or his inferiors, but no one had hesitated to say what they had thought. Even his sons and Charee had spoken. Now . . .

For a time, the mage who had been a cooper had paced back and forth in his quarters. Then, he opened *The Basis of Order* and paged through the volume, not exactly certain what he might be looking for, but letting his eyes flow over the words. Before long, a passage stopped him, and he reread it deliberately and slowly.

> Magery is no different from any other craft. Each action must be constructed with care, and all the components must be finely finished before being assembled into the final form . . .

"Magery is no different," murmured Kharl.

Was that another of his problems? That he had not approached magery as a craft, as he did coopering, where the staves had to be shaped and fitted perfectly, the chimes trimmed exactly, the hoops fitted precisely? No . . . that was not it exactly. He had tried to do anything involving order and chaos as precisely and as perfectly as he knew how, but he had not seen the pieces, the separate acts, as a part of a whole. Just as a stave was but one part of the barrel, so was one use of magery just a part of the whole framework of order. And he had seen sight shields as separate from hardening air. While the acts were separate, each affected the other.

More important, each act of magery affected the world around him, in ways that he still had great trouble foreseeing. He had had no idea that his public revelation of Guillam's falseness would immediately set off a revolution. While Kharl had occasionally stretched the truth, or embroidered it, he'd steered away from out-and-out falsehoods his entire life. That had not been because he was that good a person, he felt, but because lying about his craft and what his barrels could and could not do would create more harm than being truthful, even if his honesty and accuracy had occasionally cost him a sale.

Now, he was dealing with rulers and politics, where deception seemed to be accepted, and where so often truth was to be avoided at all costs. Why was that?

Kharl had shied away from that question before, not even wanting to think about it, but his most recent experiences made it clear that it was not a question he could avoid facing. Not any longer. There had to be a reason why truth was avoided.

He paused. Maybe the word itself was the problem, as the one passage in *The Basis of Order* had suggested.

He shook his head. That might be part of the problem, because what people saw as "truth" varied from individual to individual, but that self-righteousness associated with the word *truth* also did not explain why lords and rulers said things that were not factually so. Did those who had power come to believe that what they wished to be was already so? Or did they tell lies because they could?

Or was it simply the fact that even a powerful ruler could not make everything work out as everyone wanted, and lies were easier for people to accept than words that were accurate and painful?

Did that mean that, in effect, telling the "truth" created chaos?

Kharl closed the book slowly, turning and looking out the window, out at the darkening clouds rolling in from the west toward Valmurl.

What did "truth" have to do with order? Or power? Or magery?

Kharl already knew that lying made him uncomfortable and probably reduced his power as a mage. Yet those in power, either in Nordla or Austra, used lies to bolster their power. Those in Recluce did not seem to use lies, but all of Hamor was based on chaos and deception, from what he had seen in Swartheld, at least. Were lies a manifestation of chaos? A form of disorder?

That would grant liars and their lies a measure of power.

What of honesty and truth? Or perhaps accuracy and lack of falsehood were better terms. In what aspect of order did their power lie?

Abruptly, Kharl smiled broadly. In its own way, order created chaos. His acts with Guillam had proved that. Order could disrupt chaos. He just had not recognized what had happened.

His smile faded. That belated realization did not solve his problems in dealing with the white wizards—and the rebel lords.

His eyes went to the windows and the oncoming storm. Storms, really, for there would be many.

XXI

On eightday, Kharl was in his quarters, seated in the more comfortable armchair, his back to the window, once more studying *The Basis of Order*, and thinking about possible strategies for dealing with the remaining—and stronger—chaos-mage with the rebel forces. He would have preferred to spend the time up on the north tower, but the previous day's clouds had brought a cold and steady spring rain that settled in and showed no sign of soon clearing.

From what he could tell through his order-senses, the remaining white mage was still somewhere to the south of Valmurl, but not too far from the city. Kharl had noticed that the sense of chaos was less when it rained, and he had paged through the pages of *The Basis of Order*, seeking an explanation. The first section dealing with rain was not what he recalled:

> Water is chaos bound in two levels of order. Thus, an ocean or a lake conveys order, as does rain, and will provide a barrier against lesser chaos, but not against greater . . .

Like everything in the book, or so it seemed, the words twisted back upon themselves. Several pages farther along, he found the words he half remembered.

> Chaos fares best upon the dry land, and least in a steady rain or snowfall . . . Even a fog will affect a chaos-wielder, but only those who are of the weaker sort. A steady rain is a patterned fall of ordered chaos. A raindrop is ordered, and the fall of each is unpatterned, chaotic, yet all raindrops falling together results in a pattern ordered by chaos, and that order can weaken or destroy many of the links of power created by those who wield chaos . . .

He couldn't exactly call up rain, or expect the white wizards to attack during a storm.

There was a tentative rap on the door. "Ser Kharl?"

"Yes?" Kharl extended his order-senses, as much for practice as anything, but also to assure himself that the figure beyond the door was not another would-be assassin. While Kharl had a sturdy oak bar on the inside of his door, added after the earlier trouble, he no longer had guards stationed outside—at his own request.

The figure on the far side of the door was alone—and young—and replied quickly, "The lord-chancellor would like to see you, ser."

Kharl rose. "Now?"

"At your soonest convenience, ser."

"I'll be right with you." Kharl laid aside the book, still as frustrating as enlightening, and straightened his jacket before going to the door and opening it.

The young armsman in yellow and black was scarcely older than the boys used as messengers in the Great House and a good head shorter than Kharl. He stepped back, involuntarily, as Kharl left the quarters. "Ser . . ."

"Lead the way," Kharl said, with a cheeriness he did not quite feel.

"Yes, ser." The young man turned and headed down the corridor toward the staircase.

Kharl followed, absently noting the damp chill that permeated the hallway and wondering what else had gone wrong for Hagen to summon him in such a peremptory fashion. Was Hagen growing wary of Kharl? Or was the lord-chancellor just pressed with all he had to handle?

Even before Kharl reached the door to the lord-chancellor's study, one of the two guards stationed there stepped forward and opened the door.

After glancing at Hagen, alone in the chamber and seated behind the table desk, Kharl entered and closed the door behind him.

"Please be seated, Kharl." Hagen's voice was gentle.

"You look worried, ser."

"I am." Hagen took a sip from the goblet on the table desk. "This rain . . . my throat is raw. The healer says this should help."

"What is it?"

"Honeyed brandy with chaos knows what else in it."

Kharl let his senses range over both the lord-chancellor and the potion, but he could feel only the faintest hint of whiteness in the older man's throat. The liquid in the goblet held no chaos at all. "It may be irritating, ser, but it is only a small rawness. The potion should help."

"You sound like Istya." Hagen took another sip. "I was about to tell you. The rain has slowed Casolan, but his first companies will be here on threeday. The bulk of his forces should arrive by the end of this eightday."

"That's good, isn't it?"

"Hensolas is already moving his forces west to intercept Casolan. In this rain, there are only two safe ways for Casolan to reach Valmurl. I worry about the white wizard. If he stays near Valmurl, either you or some of Norgen's forces need to remain here, but if you do, and the white wizard accompanies Hensolas . . ."

"Then should I not go south so that I can move to shadow the wizard, whatever he does?"

"If only there were two of you . . ." murmured the lord-chancellor.

"Did something else happen?"

"I just got word. One of Norgen's squads, one he uses for scouting, disappeared. This happened while you were dealing with the one wizard. That squad was checking the dam on the Southwest Branch and the Lord's Millrace. We'd heard that Hensolas had sent sappers to start undermining the dam. If it went, all the mills would be without power."

Kharl nodded, not really understanding.

"Kharl . . . a quarter of what golds flow into Valmurl from trade come from the cloth woven in those mills. The mills are powered by the waterwheels on the Lord's Millrace." Hagen's voice was even, but Kharl recognized the strain behind the forced patience.

This time, Kharl's nod conveyed comprehension. "It was a diversion?"

"Exactly. That chaos-spawned wizard flamed down almost the entire squad." A grim smile preceded Hagen's next words. "Lord Ghrant has suggested that anything you can do to remove the white wizards would be appreciated."

Kharl felt vaguely uncomfortable at first, then angry. Less than half an eightday before, he had practically had to force Hagen to accept his ideas about dealing with the wizards. Now, he felt as though he were being blamed indirectly for not having done enough soon enough. He almost spoke, then swallowed, forcing himself to take a slow deep breath. After a moment, he spoke quietly. "I would be happy to do what I can, ser, as I suggested earlier."

"You did." Hagen paused and took another sip from the goblet. "I did not mention your suggestion for dealing with Hensolas and Fergyn. I did tell Lord Ghrant of your willingness to take on the white wizards. He supports that. He did ask me to suggest to you that it might be unwise to extend your talents to either lord, except in the heat of battle."

"Does he fear that the lords who now support him might think I would be turned against them in time?"

"He did not say, and it was not a question that was prudent to ask. He was not in the best of humors. I would judge that he has fears along those lines." Hagen took a deep breath.

Kharl said nothing for a moment, understanding belatedly that, in his own way, Hagen was trying to balance what needed to be done against the temperament of a ruler who feared to act most of the time, then rushed into unwise action—as Ghrant had in Dykaru. Kharl also understood the message within the words. If Kharl could dispose of either Fergyn or Hensolas in a way associated with battle, he was not only free to do so, but such a course of action was highly desirable.

Was that the way all successful ruling was handled? By hint and indirection, so that a ruler could deny ordering what he had wished? Or so that he had the choice of taking credit or denying responsibility?

"Do you think we should leave immediately?"

"I would judge that dawn tomorrow would be adequate. The rain may have abated by then."

"Dawn tomorrow," Kharl affirmed.

"Will one squad be enough to accompany you?" asked Hagen. "I propose assigning Undercaptain Demyst once more. He seems suited to such duty."

Kharl thought he understood that message as well. The undercaptain wasn't that good in combat and needed direction. Or he had some other fault. "One squad and Undercaptain Demyst. We will deal with the wizard and keep him and Lord Hensolas from interfering with Commander Casolan's forces." He just hoped he wasn't promising more than he could accomplish.

"I can count on you, Kharl. I wish there were more about whom I could say that." Hagen offered a wan smile. He coughed several times. "Chaos-fired throat."

"You'll be better."

"I'm sure I will be, especially once this rain ends." Hagen stood. "I need to get ready to discuss some matters with Commander Norgen."

Kharl rose. "I'll need to prepare a few things myself."

Once he was outside Hagen's study, Kharl walked deliberately toward the staircase to the upper levels and his own quarters. He was being given leave—quietly—to carry out what he had proposed. Could he do it?

XXII

The clouds that had brought eightday's rain had lifted, but not vanished, by dawn on oneday, and the air was warm and damp, enough so that even without direct sunlight Kharl was sweating in the green-and-black uniform by the time he had ridden less than a glass southward. The white wizard had left the spot where he had been, nearly due south of Valmurl, and appeared to be moving westward, generally toward the Southwest Branch, the stream that fed the Lord's Millrace before joining the River Val.

From the maps Kharl had studied and from what Hagen had said, the wizard could be accompanying rebel troops heading to join battle against Casolan's forces or riding westward to destroy the millrace and dam. Kharl doubted that a Hamorian wizard would want to destroy something that produced golds—especially not as a first resort—but he had been wrong before in his judgments, often enough that he wasn't about to discard either possibility.

"Warm, it is, for such a cloudy day," offered Undercaptain Demyst. The stocky and square-faced man had been blotting his forehead even more often than Kharl.

"It's likely to get even warmer once the clouds clear." Kharl paused. "How much longer before we reach the River Val?" To reach the Southwest Branch and the Lord's Millrace, Kharl and the lancers accompanying him had to cross the River Val first. Then they would turn east if they wished to reach the Southwest Branch, or westward on the south river road if it appeared that the wizard's forces were heading out to intercept Casolan's advance force.

"Less than a glass, ser. Less than a glass. The scouts say that the way is clear. No rebel lancers, leastwise. Not this side of the river."

Kharl nodded and concentrated on riding, and in taking in the countryside west of Valmurl. For at least a score of kays to the west of where they rode, the land stretched out in a nearly flat valley that extended a good eighty kays to the south of the River Val and slightly less than forty to the north. In places, there were low hills, but none rose more than a few rods above the road. Fields, recently tilled, and meadows were everywhere, with cots set at almost regular intervals. While he could see both men and women working in more distant fields, the peasants or smallholders of those lands closest to the road were wisely remaining out of sight.

To the northwest, when he looked back over his shoulder, Kharl could make out the distant hills, and a few snowcapped peaks behind them. He could see nothing but fields and meadows ahead of them—and a line of trees several kays to the south. The trees, he suspected, marked the River Val. While there were some woodlots on the holdings, and a few orchards, most of the land was marked out in squarish fields set aside for crops, and there were almost no hedgerows at all. Those appeared to have been created only in the north and west of Valmurl.

"Why aren't there any hedgerows here?" he asked the undercaptain.

"Lord Esthaven forbid them here in the valley proper. Said that they gave holders airs. Had to kill a few before they got the idea."

The more Kharl heard about Esthaven, the less he liked what he heard. "What do they grow here?"

"Maize and oats, mostly, besides gardens. Everyone has a garden. There's wheat corn south of the river. Doesn't do as well here on the north side. No one knows why. Around the river, where it's wet, there's sorghum. Best molasses in the world here, and that's why there's none better than Austran black bread."

Kharl had enjoyed the dark bread, but hadn't connected it to the quality of molasses in Austra—although that made sense. With a faint smile at the thought, and the realization that there was much he had never questioned, he shifted his weight in the saddle. He still wasn't that used to riding, and the saddle got hard after a while. Awkwardly, he stood in the stirrups, trying to stretch his legs and give his backside a respite. He glanced ahead, hoping that the river wasn't that far ahead.

"Really won't be that far, ser," offered Demyst.

"I'm not a lancer," Kharl said dryly. "Riding is harder on me than coopering all day."

"You'll get used to it, ser."

Kharl wasn't certain he wanted to get that used to riding. As he struggled to make himself comfortable in the saddle, he sensed something. Except that wasn't it. He tilted his head, trying to focus on what he'd felt. Then he realized that for the past quarter glass or so, as he had ridden southward toward the river, he had lost the distant sense of the white wizard—just as if the wizard had vanished.

"Chaos . . ." he muttered under his breath. He'd been so preoccupied with his own discomfort that he hadn't even realized when he'd lost the sense of the other wizard. He tried to gather in a sense of that chaos, but he could feel absolutely nothing.

Had the wizard gone into a cave or something? Or behind a waterfall? That might provide a shield of some sort. Or had he created his own shield?

"Ser? Something wrong?"

"Not yet," Kharl replied. Now he'd have to be more alert than ever, and especially after they crossed the River Val.

Almost half a glass passed before they neared the river. During that time, they had seen no one nearby on the road, although one cart and another wagon had turned down side lanes to avoid the lancers. While Kharl had gotten a quick impression of faint traces of chaos several times, the traces had vanished so quickly that he only knew that the wizard was somewhere to the south. Were the rebels moving farther south and trying to circle behind Casolan's forces? Or were they already west of the bridge and heading out to attack Casolan? Kharl couldn't be certain, and that worried him.

It was most likely that the wizard had some sort of shield and did not want Kharl to track him easily. But why now? Had he just discovered that Kharl was near?

Kharl blotted his forehead. The clouds had thinned, and at times, faint hazy sunlight had oozed over the riders. The day had continued to warm, and the heavy armsman's uniform had gotten less and less comfortable.

Kharl took in the raised earthen causeway that led to the bridge itself, then the river that stretched away from the bridge. The River Val wound in wide, sweeping arcs, its course meandering through the river plain, its banks clearly marked by earthen levees and trees planted behind the levees. The bridge itself was an old and heavy timber structure that was supported by three stone piers evenly spaced across the riverbed. The roadway was broad enough for a large wagon or three horses abreast, and the side rails were weathered heavy timbers. The watercourse itself was perhaps ten rods wide under the bridge. The plank roadbed was worn, and in places, as he crossed, Kharl could see the swirling gray of the water below through gaps in the planking. While the bridge creaked slightly as the squad rode across the spans, he could feel no swaying or give, but he was glad to reach the causeway on the south side.

Kharl caught the faintest sense of whiteness to the south and west, but when he tried to focus on it, the feeling was gone.

"You be wanting us to head back toward Valmurl, ser, or out west."

"West," Kharl said with a certainty he did not feel. "They're past here and headed west." He glanced back toward Valmurl, but the river road was empty.

"No tracks on the road, ser. Doesn't look as though they came this way."

"Not by the road," Kharl admitted. He somehow *knew* that the rebel forces had not returned to Valmurl, but where could they be? The fields immediately to the south of the river road were flat and open, and the smell of turned bottomland occasionally came to Kharl on the intermittent light breeze from the west.

Another kay or so to the west, he could see a stand of trees. As they rode closer, he realized that the trees extended nearly a kay to the south, and certainly that far west, if not even farther.

"What are those trees?"

"Red pears, ser. Don't grow many places."

Kharl had heard of red pears, but never seen one. The orchard was old, and the trees seemed close together, so much so that he could not see more than a few trees into the mass of foliage, despite the thinner early-spring leaves.

As the squad passed the eastern edge of the orchard and continued westward on the river road, the clouds thinned more, and Kharl could feel the spring sun on his back. He had to blot his forehead more frequently, and he had lost all track of the white wizard, except for traces of white that felt almost due south, and closer. What had happened? Where was the wizard?

Demyst coughed, then swallowed. "Back there, to the east, ser . . ." Demyst's voice was almost apologetic as he pointed.

Pouring out of the orchard less than a half kay behind them was a column of lancers—men in black and green, with the blue sashes and behind a blue banner bearing a device Kharl did not recognize, not that he was familiar with heraldry, especially Austran heraldry.

"That'd be Lord Hensolas. That's his banner, ser. Looks to be three companies." Demyst swallowed. "And there's another company to the west, maybe two. They're riding toward us."

Somewhere among the eastern group was the faintest trace of chaos. Then, a blaze of white appeared among the larger force.

Kharl wanted to hit his forehead with his palm. He'd known that the white wizard had hidden his chaos behind some sort of shield, but he'd thought that the wizard had done that to conceal his approach to Casolan's force or to keep Kharl from tracking him. Instead . . . the wizard was after him—with five companies. And Kharl and his squad were trapped, with a thick orchard that was close to impossible to ride through to the south, at least at any speed, and with the river to the north.

"How deep is the river?" Kharl snapped.

"Two to three rods, five in places. Current's real strong here, ser. We'd be sitting ducks for crossbows. They got crossbows, ser."

Kharl understood the unspoken. Most of the lancers couldn't swim. Even Kharl wasn't that good a swimmer, although he might have been able to manage the river. But . . . he'd been the one to get them into the trap.

He looked toward the orchard, and the ancient and crooked split rail fence between the trees and the road. His order-senses did not find any other chaos, except that of the single wizard, but . . . he frowned. There was the thinnest mist of blackness all across the orchard. Order. From the orchard itself? From the spring growth? Behind that order was something else, not quite chaos, or a different kind of chaos, or order. He wasn't certain, and he didn't have time to puzzle it out.

"Form up right between the fence and the trees. Make it tight!"

"Ser . . ."

"We'll try magery. If it doesn't work, the men will at least have a chance of escaping through the trees. The rebels can't ride through them, not at any speed."

"Ah . . . yes, ser. You pick the spot, and we'll form around you."

"Just behind me." Kharl turned the gelding toward a gap in the fence, not exactly a gate, but an opening wide enough for a wagon. He glanced to the east, but the rebel lancers were not galloping or even trotting, but closing in inexorably at a fast walk. He looked to the west, but that force was also closing in on them.

Kharl decided against staying at all in the open, even just in front of the trees. He rode right up to one of the gnarled and ancient pear trees. There, he dismounted and walked the gelding back toward the second row of trees. The trees had been pruned just enough to allow him to walk between them, but riding at more than a walk would have been dangerous, as he had guessed. He tied the gelding and hurried back to the front row.

"Ser?" Demyst looked puzzled. "We can't get that close to you, not with all the trees."

"Get into the trees—in back of the first row." Kharl studied the oncoming riders.

The white wizard was hanging back, with a full company of lancers between him and Kharl and the lancer squad. Kharl could also see a score of crossbowmen dismounting less than twenty rods away. That didn't surprise him. The white wizard clearly knew about Kharl's shields and wanted to exhaust the black mage before using chaos-fire. Or perhaps he would just watch for an opportunity.

Could Kharl tap the order of the orchard? He reached out, nodding as he gathered in some of the orchard's order, then waited. Both forces drew closer, then reined up, waiting, except for the crossbowmen, who continued to set up.

Finally, the crossbowmen lifted their weapons. Kharl smiled grimly. Just before the quarrels sleeted toward them, Kharl raised a shield of hardened air, only long enough to halt the quarrels. Bent quarrels and iron shafts rained down short of the trees. He hoped that the attackers would continue to fire in volleys, but he watched closely as the crossbowmen rewound their weapons.

The white wizard had done nothing—except remain well back from the center of the orchard, as if he knew that Kharl's ability to strike was limited in distance.

"Oh . . ." murmured one of the lancers.

Kharl continued to consider what he could do. Before long, either armsmen or lancers would charge in force, and he could not hold shields for that long, not around even a small group. His last efforts with releasing chaos had not been totally successful, but perhaps . . . maybe . . . using the order of the orchard . . . and his own shields . . .

His lips tightened. He would have to see.

Three more volleys flew toward Kharl and the lancers. Between the thick foliage and Kharl's quickly raised and lowered shields, none reached the defenders.

Then a horn sounded, and a full company of rebel lancers dressed their lines, then unsheathed blades.

"Don't leave the trees until I tell you!" Kharl hissed to Demyst.

"You heard the mage," the undercaptain ordered. "Stay under cover till you get the word."

"Sitting ducks . . ." murmured someone.

"Not yet," replied a deeper voice.

There came two blasts on the horn—off-key—and lancers trotted toward the orchard, blades at the ready.

Kharl disliked what he was seeing, because Hensolas and the white wizard were sacrificing troops—essentially Ghrant's troops—to wear down Kharl. Yet, Kharl reminded himself, the same thing would have happened, and might anyway, in a pitched battle between Casolan's forces and those of the rebels.

Kharl concentrated on a single section of the split rail fence, waiting until the lancers were almost upon it, when he unlinked the order in a section a third of a yard long, erecting a curved hardened air shield behind that fence section.

Whhhsssttt! . . . Crumptt!

The glare was so bright that, for a moment, Kharl could not see, and even behind the shield, he could barely stand.

Belatedly, he dropped the shield, and almost collapsed as the wave of death swept over him.

A blackened quarter circle radiated from the section of the fence a rod in front of Kharl. Nothing remained except blackened heaps and fine ash for a good five rods. For another ten rods beyond that, everything was blackened, as if a fire had swept across everything.

The air was filled with screams of mounts and groans of men—not from the attackers, for none of them remained, but from the second company of lancers, those almost twenty rods back.

Point stars of brilliant light flashed before Kharl, and he had to squint to try to focus on the remainder of the attackers' forces. He could feel a wave of fatigue somewhere, but he called on more of the order from the orchard and walled off that tiredness.

Hssttt! A firebolt flared toward the orchard—aimed directly at Kharl.

The mage flung up an order shield, and fire sheeted to both sides.

The branches and leaves that protruded forward of Kharl flared into flame and ashes, and Kharl found himself standing in the open, if half-concealed by fine gray ash floating everywhere. He took a step backward, under a heavy branch. He was breathing deeply, trying to catch a solid gulp of air as ashes finer than dust swirled around him.

Hssst! Another firebolt slashed through the ash-filled air.

Kharl staggered. He couldn't keep up the defenses much longer, and no one was moving close enough for him to use the order-release of chaos effectively. What else could he do? He was limited in how he could create chaos, and he couldn't fling it the way the white mage was.

He swallowed, coughing, blocking yet another chaos-bolt.

There was one other possibility . . .

He waited for the next bolt, and as it flashed toward him, he formed a curving tube, almost like an invisible curved cannon that was aimed back toward the banner that showed—he hoped—where Hensolas was. As the firebolt slid through the tube, Kharl released a touch of order from the very air behind the firebolt, adding speed and force to it, then juggled the tube, trying to focus it on the banner.

But . . . Kharl had overdone it, and the firebolt flared behind the banner.

He went to his knees, under the storm of death and anguish that slammed into him, a wave almost as great as the effect of his one order-released chaos blast—and far more deadly, landing as it had in the midst of two companies of waiting lancers.

The banner had fallen, and mounts and men scattered.

Kharl could sense the white wizard, could feel that the other's shields had weakened.

Almost without thinking, Kharl began to move, walking swiftly through the gray ash and dust that was everywhere, straight toward the white wizard. He was just trying to get close enough to clamp hardened air around the other.

Another firebolt flared toward Kharl, and he redirected it, this time, toward the two other remaining intact companies of lancers, those on the west side of the road.

Drawing even more strength from the orchard, the last of that black mist of order, Kharl staggered when a deep groan, an anguished wail, emanated from the very earth itself, or so it seemed. Even with that anguish shivering through him, he managed to remain upright and cover another ten rods before the next firebolt came, a slightly weaker blast that he directed toward a group of officers who had clustered around a single figure—Hensolas, Kharl thought.

White chaos-fire splashed directly into the center of the officers, and more death washed over Kharl. The remaining lancers and armsmen, those still alive, were scattering away from the wizardly battle.

Kharl could feel, solidly now, the shredding shields of the white wizard, and he clamped the air hard around the other, throwing back one chaos-bolt then another, then, later, a third, one that guttered out even as it splashed around the dead form of the white mage, a form that vanished in white ash as Kharl released the hardened air around the wizard.

Kharl coughed, trying to clear his throat and lungs.

Ash was everywhere, ash and the odor of death and burned flesh. Ash and blackened forms that had been men and mounts.

Kharl couldn't help retching as he turned and stumbled back toward the orchard—except it was no longer there. Where the orchard had been was also an ashen wasteland. All that was left were two ash-covered oblong shapes that might have been barns.

Twenty-one riders waited, covered in gray, still mounted, as Kharl stumbled back toward them. Brilliant point stars flashed before his eyes, flaring, and each flaring star sent a dagger through his eyes and deep into his skull. Every muscle, and every part of his body, even down to his toenails, ached.

"Ser . . . that you?"

"It's me." Who else would it be, he wanted to scream. Who else?

Demyst guided the gelding toward Kharl. The mage had to clamp his jaws together to climb into the gelding's saddle, and his legs almost gave way before he got his boots in the stirrups.

The undercaptain turned from side to side, his mouth open, staring at the wasteland of ashes and blackened stumps and fallen figures, and at the lines of blackness seared through the very earth to the southeast of the river road. "Never seen . . . never . . ." His voice faded away.

"Chaos-fire . . . what the white wizards use." Kharl realized his words were dull, stating the obvious, but his throat and jaws throbbed when he spoke, and he didn't feel like explaining more. He doubted he could, or would ever want to.

"Now . . . what do we do, ser mage?" asked Demyst.

"We head back to the Great House." Kharl turned his mount eastward. In the few moments when he could see, in between the lightstars and pain daggers that blinded him, causing involuntary tears that carved lines in the ash covering his face, he thought he made out a handful of riders moving eastward, back toward Valmurl.

Kharl felt as though he should be elated, or at least satisfied. Hensolas and the white wizard were dead, and so were most of the rebel armsmen and lancers. But most of those troops had not been rebels. They had served the rebels, and Kharl doubted that they had been given much choice.

His mouth tasted like ashes, and each breath he drew in, raggedly, reeked of ashes and death. When he could see, he saw lancers gray-coated in ashes, and when he could not, he could remember all too vividly the pain of all the deaths, and the last groaning from within the earth as he had gutted, unknowing, the vast orchard for the force necessary to prevail.

He tried to wash the taste of ashes out of his mouth with a long swallow from his water bottle, but the water tasted like ash and death going down his throat.

XXIII

Somewhere, along the road back to the bridge over the River Val, Kharl passed out. Or fell asleep. Or dropped out of the saddle.

He knew that because he found himself lying on something hard and cold—the ground. Someone was washing and blotting his face with cool water. But the water tasted and smelled like ashes.

"Ser Kharl . . . ser."

Kharl managed to turn his head to the side and cough out some of the water that had been choking him. Despite the hazy sunlight, there were large irregular patches of darkness drifting across his eyes. The lightstars and the daggers that they jabbed into his skull seemed to have subsided a little. Rather than being agonizing, they had become more like the lashes of a tiny whip.

"Sorry . . ." he mumbled.

"Are you all right, ser?"

Of course he wasn't all right. No one who fell out of a saddle was all right. He could tell that his left leg was sore and bruised, and that there was a large lump on his forehead above his right eye. ". . . getting there . . ."

"One moment, you were riding," Demyst said, "and the next you weren't."

"Happens sometimes after magery," Kharl said slowly, coughing some more.

After a time, he struggled into a sitting position. He'd thought that he wouldn't collapse anymore after doing magery. He'd been wrong. Again. "There's some bread and cheese in my saddlebags . . . might help."

"Sileen . . . get the provisions from the mage's saddlebags."

"Yes, ser."

Kharl just sat on the ground on the shoulder of the road, looking blankly eastward. The River Val bridge was less than ten rods away. He supposed he'd been lucky. He could have fallen off on the bridge, hit his head on the railing, and gone into the water and drowned. At least, that way, he wouldn't have to explain how he'd been trapped by Hensolas. He hoped Hagen and Norgen didn't ask too many questions . . . but Hagen didn't miss much.

"Ser . . ." As the undercaptain extended the provisions bag, and a water bottle, his voice was both solicitous and respectful.

Kharl wondered why. He'd led the squad into a trap, almost gotten them burned to ashes, and then he'd collapsed and fallen right out of the saddle. That sort of behavior shouldn't have created respect. "Thank you."

He forced down the bread, which tasted of ashes, like the water had, and chewed off several morsels of the hard yellow cheese. The black patches that drifted across his field of vision shrank, but did not disappear entirely. Much to his surprise, he did finish everything in the bag, as well as empty the water bottle.

After eating, he took a damp rag and wiped the blood from the gash over his forehead and the ashes from his face.

"We could wait here a while," suggested Demyst.

"No. I should have eaten right after the . . . fight. Magery takes food." Except that he doubted he could have kept anything down then.

"You're in charge, ser."

"In a moment, we'll start back."

Demyst nodded.

Kharl's legs were still a bit weak when he finally stood and walked toward the gelding, but he remounted, if carefully. He patted the horse's shoulder. "Be trying not to fall out of the saddle again," he said to the gelding. "Makes us both look bad."

XXIV

Kharl and his small force reached the Great House less than a glass before sunset. They'd had to stop several times for Kharl to rest. His left leg was sore and getting stiffer, and the lump on his forehead was tender, occasionally throbbing, as he made his way into the Great House from the stables.

He decided to report to Hagen on the expedition, first, but when he made his way to Hagen's first-floor study, there were no guards there, and the heavy oak door was locked. That meant the lord-chancellor was off somewhere and unlikely to return soon. With a shrug, Kharl went off to get some supper. He'd have to talk to Hagen in the morning—or whenever the lord-chancellor returned.

After eating in the small dining room, alone, Kharl checked to see if Hagen had returned, but the lord-chancellor was nowhere to be found. So Kharl retired to his quarters, took a lukewarm bath, trying to clean out his scrapes and bruises, and finally climbed into bed. His sleep was fitful, but undisturbed by outside influences.

When he woke the next morning, his left leg was almost as sore as it had been the night before, and far stiffer. The black holes in his vision had diminished to large spots, but his mouth still tasted like ashes.

There were guards stationed back outside Hagen's study, but Kharl decided to eat before reporting to Hagen. Then, he stood outside, silently, for almost half a glass before a lord he did not know departed. The man shot Kharl a quick glare, then strode off without a word.

"You can go in, ser. The lord-chancellor . . . he's waiting," offered one of the guards.

Hagen didn't say a word until Kharl had seated himself. "I understand that you had a pitched battle with Hensolas and his forces and the white wizard. You've got more bruises and scrapes, I see."

"We did. They were tracking us while we were tracking them . . ." Kharl described, as briefly as he could what had happened—but not how. ". . . there were but a few armsmen left on their side after it was all over. Most everything around us got burned to ashes." He decided against explaining how he had been injured.

Hagen laughed, harshly. "So I just heard. Lord Sheram is less than perfectly pleased."

Kharl had no idea even who the lord was—unless he was the man who had left just before Kharl had entered. "Why?"

"Your battle with Hensolas and the white wizard destroyed his red pear orchard. That orchard is one of the few that survived the red blight of twenty years ago, and the yearly crop of those pears provided Lord Sheram with several hundred golds a year." Hagen's voice was level, with little sign of either wry humor or anger.

"I certainly didn't intend to destroy the orchard. Hensolas and the white wizard attacked us."

"That may be, but Lord Ghrant does not like to create more unhappy lords."

Kharl suppressed his reaction to snap back. Hagen was only stating facts. After a moment, he said, "Hensolas was the one responsible. He rebelled. He attacked. Why not allow this Lord . . ." Kharl hadn't caught the lord's name, or perhaps he hadn't wanted to.

"Sheram," Hagen supplied.

". . . this Lord Sheram to pick a property of comparable value from Hensolas's lands and estates?"

"That might be acceptable to Sheram. Lord Ghrant will doubtless find it so, because it will further weaken Hensolas's son's ability to raise arms in the future."

"If they had all stood behind Ghrant, none of this would have happened," Kharl declared.

"That is true," Hagen agreed, "but that is not the way they will see matters. They will claim that Ghrant's weakness led to the revolt."

"They were revolting and following Ilteron before Ghrant even had a chance to show strength or weakness," Kharl pointed out.

"They do not see it that way. They never will. They perceived Ghrant as weak, and they hold him responsible for their perceptions."

Kharl could see no point in arguing against that. "And now they're angry because I show that he has strength?"

Hagen laughed. "That makes them twice as angry, because they have found they were wrong, and your actions have shown them to have been mistaken for all of Austra to see."

Kharl took a long and deep breath.

"Do you see why I would rather be back on the bridge of the *Seastag*?" asked Hagen.

The mage nodded. "Nothing pleases any of them, and yet they are largely responsible for what has happened."

"As I said, that may be true, but they do not see it that way."

"Do they ever?" Kharl was convinced that most lords were that way. Certainly, Lord West and his son Egen had been. It had all been Kharl's fault that Egen had been humiliated, when Egen had been in fact assaulting and raping young women at will. But Kharl had been the one flogged, and his consort executed for a murder that had been committed by an assassin hired by Egen—not that Kharl would ever be able to prove such.

"No," admitted Hagen.

"Does Lord Ghrant know about Hensolas?"

"The circumstances of Hensolas's death were acceptable to Lord Ghrant."

"Acceptable?"

"That was the word he used," replied the lord-chancellor, not disguising the sardonic tone of his words. "Acceptable," Hagen glanced at the goblet on the table desk.

"How is your throat?"

"Better. So long as I don't have to talk too much placating lords who wish everything and risk nothing. None of them would last a season as traders." The lord-chancellor took a sip from the goblet. "Lord Ghrant wishes to know how long before you can arrange an equally suitable incident for Fergyn."

"I'll need a few days to rest. I sometimes still can't see straight."

"It's a good thing you were a cooper, ser mage. Any mage less strong than you wouldn't have survived what you've created."

"Sometimes, I almost haven't," Kharl admitted.

Hagen laughed. "Get some rest and some more food. We'll talk tomorrow. That is, unless something else happens before then." He stood.

Kharl smiled. He wished Hagen hadn't added the last sentence, although he couldn't imagine what else could happen that had not already. More of the same, perhaps, and that would be bad enough.

XXV

On threeday, Kharl decided against trying to see Hagen immediately after breakfast, and instead returned to his quarters to study—and to think. While the problem of the white mages was solved, for the moment, Fergyn remained in revolt and was avoiding any semblance of battle. At the same time, Kharl realized how fortunate he had been in his encounters, though he had not thought so at the time. He also understood that he could not continue to draw the order out of living things, even trees and crops, not for long and remain welcome in Austra. He needed to find a better technique for dealing with chaos-fire and white mages. Whatever technique that might require was not described in *The Basis of Order*. But then, very few techniques were.

Kharl settled into the most comfortable chair in his sitting room and, once more, began to leaf through the black book that was far more worn than he would ever have believed possible when it had fallen into his hands less than a year before. He turned page after page. The light coming through the window behind him strengthened as the morning sun burned away the mists. He paused at the paragraph near the bottom of one page.

> One might also say it yet another way. Chaos is power without form, and order is the form that enables chaos to inspire the spirit

of life, to allow the crafting of tools and of all manner of devices that improve the way of life of man and woman . . .

That was true enough, Kharl reflected, but not exactly helpful. He kept reading. Some twenty pages later, he came across another few words. He had seen them before, but there was something about them that had nagged him before . . . and still did.

One danger of order-magery or chaos-magery is that the mage who handles either in mighty efforts may become what he attempts to control. For a part of that mage must accompany the order or chaos that he infuses or creates. An order-mage may become so fixated upon order that he can do nothing without a structure so rigid that he accomplishes nothing of value . . .

Kharl skipped farther down the page.

. . . more unnoticed is the danger that order or chaos may rebound upon him who casts it forth, for there is a tie between what is cast forth and the one who casts it . . .

The mage frowned. If there were such ties . . . could he use order to strengthen them? Ties had to have a basis in order. That *might* be far easier than creating hardened air tubes.

He laughed silently. Once he developed such a technique, it *might* be easier, but could he do so? How? What would happen if he did?

Thrap.

"Ser Kharl? Are you there?"

Kharl looked up in irritation. "Yes?" He cast forth his order-senses without rising from the chair. A man, an armsman, stood outside his door.

"The lord-chancellor'd be seeing you right quick."

"I'll be with you in a moment." Kharl closed *The Basis of Order,* set it on the side table, and slowly rose from the chair. The stiffness was worse when he hadn't moved for a time. He made his way to the door and out into the corridor.

As he closed the door behind him, the armsman, another he had not seen before, turned without speaking. Kharl followed him down to Hagen's study.

There, one of the guards spoke. "The lord-chancellor said for you to go right in, ser Kharl. The other mage is already there."

"Thank you."

The other mage? Lyras? Could there be any other in Austra? What was he doing in the Great House? From Lyras's own words, he avoided the Great House and the Lords of Austra in any way possible. As Kharl stepped into Hagen's study, even before he closed the door behind himself, his eyes took in Lyras first. The older mage looked even more gray than Kharl recalled.

Lyras rose from the chair on one side of the table desk and bowed. "Ser Kharl."

"Lyras. I had not expected to find you here." Kharl inclined his head out of respect.

"I had not expected to be here."

"We have news that is less than good." Hagen gestured to the other empty chair.

Kharl settled into it, gingerly, and, without a word, waited for Hagen to explain.

"While you and Undercaptain Demyst were dealing with Hensolas," Hagen said, his eyes on Kharl, "the Hamorians landed a force at Northbay. That's fifteen kays to the northeast of Valmurl, just east of the Nierran Hills. The harbor there is small, with just one pier, mostly for fishing craft. They've taken over the town for now, but they'll likely start their march on Valmurl tomorrow or the next day. Lyras was telling me that there are two more white wizards with them."

Two more? How many did Hamor have that the emperor could keep sending them? Kharl glanced at Lyras.

"One doesn't seem that powerful. The other one—I've never sensed a white wizard that strong." Lyras turned to Kharl apologetically. "Begging your pardon, ser Kharl."

"They also brought another company of lancers, doubtless to serve as his personal guard. I'd wager that Fergyn and his forces will move north and that they'll join the Hamorians at Ghalmat. That's a town about eight kays up the Fahsa River from the harbor at Valmurl. Ghalmat's where the northeast road from Valmurl ends. The river road from there to Northbay isn't much better than a cart path."

Kharl didn't pretend to understand totally the geography, but it was clear enough that the Hamorians had picked the small harbor because it would not be easy for Ghrant to send forces there, even if he had known about the landing.

Hagen added, "Fostak and Lord Joharak departed from Valmurl last night on a Nordlan trader."

"That's . . ." Kharl wasn't sure what it was, except a sign of trouble.

"As close to war as Hamor will go," Hagen replied. "It's also a sign that Lord Joharak realized that his position here was about to become untenable. He didn't wait for a Hamorian ship."

"The emperor would just have left him here if he hadn't left on his own?"

"There are privileges associated with being an envoy, but there are also risks." Hagen's smile was brief and cold.

"The Hamorians intend to make Fergyn their puppet, you think?" asked Kharl.

"Oh . . . the emperor might even let him have some real power, so long as he serves Hamor," replied Hagen. "Or . . . he might just be trying to foment so much internal warfare and bloodshed that everyone would welcome the stability that Hamor would bring."

"The lords would not like that," Lyras pointed out.

"There won't be any of them left," Hagen said. "They'll either die in the fighting or flee before Hamor takes total control of Austra."

Kharl said nothing. It seemed as though, with each success he had, matters just got worse.

"What do you suggest, ser mage?" Hagen looked at Kharl.

"That we attack," Kharl said tiredly. "There's little to be gained by waiting."

"Attack? Just like that?" An ironic tone colored Hagen's words.

"Attack," Kharl repeated. "Most of the rebel armsmen and lancers were with Hensolas, you said. Fergyn doesn't have that many left."

"We may not, either, not after attacking."

"Do you think these white wizards—especially the powerful one—will let me just ride up to wherever they are and attack them?"

"Why will they meet us?"

"Because Lyras is going to be with the attacking force," Kharl said.

Lyras paled. His swallow was audible in the stillness of the chamber.

"These two wizards have never sensed me, not up close, and most whites don't seem to be that good at locating blacks. Lyras will show some order-magery, and I'll do what I need to do while they're concentrating on our force."

"That could be dangerous," Hagen said. "They could wipe out our entire force."

"If I can't do what I need to do, you can order a retreat. Or Casolan or Norgen can."

"It's best, I think, if I'm there." Another grim smile crossed the lord-chancellor's lips. "One way or another."

Kharl understood.

Hagen rose. "We may not need to ride out until fiveday, but you should be ready tomorrow, mages." His eyes went to Lyras.

"Yes, lord-chancellor." Lyras's voice carried resignation. He looked to Kharl. "Ser Kharl."

"I will see you both in the morning," Hagen added, in dismissal.

Kharl inclined his head, then turned and left the study. Lyras followed.

Outside, in the corridor, the older mage turned to Kharl. After a moment, he said, "You have learned much, ser Kharl, but do you think you can face one of the most powerful mages from Hamor?"

"I can certainly face him," Kharl said, with a laugh. "Whether I can prevail . . . that is another question. If I can, it is best to end this now. If I cannot, then it is also for the best."

"For the best?"

"We could retreat, and harass, and attack, and in a year all of Austra would be in flames, and most would be starving." Kharl did not add that there was already too much blood on his hands, and too many deaths weighing upon him. At times, his mouth, his food, everything still tasted of ashes.

"You are saying . . ."

"I am saying that there are worse things than being conquered. I would rather not live under the emperor. I will do my best so that does not happen. What we do does not affect us alone. Already, Lord Ghrant has lost more than half his lancers and armsmen, one way or another. Hundreds of women are already widows, and thousands of children are orphans. How many will there be in a season, in a year? What sort of land will Lord Ghrant have then, if he has any at all?"

Lyras looked away.

XXVI

For all of his words to Lyras, Kharl was worried. Just how would he be able to stand up to a mighty white wizard? He was wagering on his ability to make something out of a few words in *The Basis of Order* and out of the few abilities he had perfected.

Unlike most black mages, he had learned little about healing, no matter how he had tried, and he could barely sense what the weather might do, let alone change it or influence it. He had no idea how to help things grow, the way Lyras and the druids did. He could not feel what was deep beneath the earth, nor in the water. All he had learned was how to sense order and chaos, to harden substances, especially air, to create shields against chaos, and to release chaos by unbinding order.

After he and Lyras parted outside of Hagen's chamber, Kharl had gone to the top of the north tower, but he had been unable to discover a way to put into action the words in *The Basis of Order*.

Still thinking about Hagen's revelations and his own too-proud words to Lyras, Kharl had left the tower and walked slowly through the corridors of the Great House. He crossed the rear courtyard and made his way out to the smithy, an armorer's smithy, although the forge was shared at times by the estate smith and the farrier. If the forge happened to be hot, perhaps studying the chaos within the coals might give him some hints. Besides, he had spent enough time in his quarters, and sitting down for any length of time would just leave his leg stiff again.

The armorer was not using the forge, but the farrier was, shaping a horseshoe. The horse to be reshod was a dun mare, one that Kharl thought might be the mount that Lady Hyrietta often rode. Since he had returned to Valmurl, he had seldom seen the dark-haired lady with the heart-shaped face, or Lord Ghrant's two sons, even at a distance.

The farrier glanced at Kharl, nodded, and went about his business, thrusting the tongs holding the shoe into the forge.

Kharl stood in the doorway to the smithy, letting his senses range over the forge fire. The energy of the forge was what he would have called honest chaos, without the reddish overshades of the chaos-fire spewed forth by the white wizards. Or by what he had done in unbinding order to release chaos.

The farrier's hammer struck the horseshoe on the forge, and Kharl sensed the change in both order and chaos within the iron. There was a flow, an ordering, in the metal . . . but why? Kharl continued to follow the farrier's actions for a time. He could sense the slight ordering in the shoes, and he could tell that the mount's feet would be protected by more than the shoe, if only slightly. But why?

He frowned and let his senses take in the farrier himself. There was the faintest sense of blackness about the man. In a way, Kharl decided, the farrier had a touch of the order-mage within him. Only the slightest touch, but a little. Did all the best crafters have a trace of order-talent? Kharl wouldn't have been surprised at that, but that observation and its application would have to wait.

As he took in the smithy, and especially what was happening with the horseshoes, he began to pick up the pattern, a faint pattern, but it was there. There were ties between the farrier and the horseshoe, and even though the farrier had added but the slightest trace of order from himself to the shoe, there was a link. Kharl tried to follow that link, but it was so delicate that even reaching out to touch it shattered the connection, and it was so faint that the farrier didn't even seem to feel it.

After a while longer, Kharl nodded and stepped back, thinking as he began to walk back through the warm noon sunlight toward the small dining room. *The Basis of Order* had been right. There was a connection or a tie. That suggested that the linkage might be used. Could it be a way back through the white wizard's shields? How could he find out?

He laughed, briefly. There wasn't any way to find out, not short of trying, and failure could be costly, and probably deadly.

He turned toward the small dining room. Whatever might happen, he needed to eat, and he needed to make sure he had plenty of provisions on the ride—or campaign—against the rebels and the Hamorians.

XXVII

Fourday found Kharl back in the saddle before dawn, in the green-and-black uniform of an Austran armsman, riding with Undercaptain Demyst and his squad on a side road at the south edge of the Nierran Hills, not all that far from Lyras's cottage. Kharl smiled briefly as he recalled the meeting with the older mage in the small cottage of red sandstone, with its glass windows and green-painted shutters and front door. Lyras had offered refreshments, hospitality, and almost no advice, except how to determine where Kharl's skills might lie. While he had always suspected the reason for that, Kharl was truly beginning to understand why. Handling of order—or of chaos—had to come from understanding, and that could never be taught, only experienced.

There was barely enough space for two mounts abreast on the clay track that wound under the sandstone cliffs on the north side of the fast-moving and swirling dark waters of the rod-wide stream. The road was no more than two cubits above the spring runoff. Immediately to the south of the stream were low meadows, some of which were still partly underwater, and beyond them a long sloping expanse of firs along the north side of a narrow ridge. South beyond the ridge, Kharl knew, were the open hills that rolled down toward the northeastern part of Valmurl. Those hills held kay upon kay of orchards and berry patches.

Once again, Demyst rode alongside Kharl. The square-faced captain looked morosely ahead, into the lighter gray sky to the east. "This circles north of the main road, comes out where the stream joins the Fahsa. That's a bit west of Ghalmat. Should be there well before the rebels." Demyst paused. "Should be. No telling until then, though."

"The Hamorians are still somewhere to the east of Ghalmat," noted Kharl. "They're not moving that fast." He could sense the two focal points of chaos, even though they were several kays to the south and east. Both were far stronger than the white wizards he had faced before, although the lesser chaos-focus was not that much stronger than the last white wizard.

But that was the lesser of the two, and he had no idea if the two might even be hiding part of their power, the way the last white wizard had, and as Kharl was attempting.

Kharl could also sense Lyras and the comparatively faint but solid black order around the older mage. Lyras was stronger than he claimed, Kharl was convinced, but still nowhere near as powerful as he needed to be—not if the older mage had to hold off the oncoming white wizards if Kharl failed. Then, Kharl himself wasn't exactly a youth, either, he reflected.

"What about Lord Fergyn?" asked Demyst.

"I can't tell. He doesn't have a white wizard with him."

"You think this'll be as bad as the last time, ser?" asked the undercaptain.

"No," Kharl replied. "If we're fortunate, it will only be about twice as bad." As soon as he'd spoken, even before the undercaptain shook his head, Kharl wished he'd been less truthful and more tactful. But why did people ask such stupid questions, then get upset when they got a truthful reply?

Truth, again. Always seemingly what people claimed they wanted, but only when it confirmed what they wished to believe. "It might not be that bad," Kharl said quickly, "but they do have two powerful white wizards and a company of heavy Hamorian horse." Demyst already knew that, but it wouldn't hurt to repeat it.

"What did Lord Ghrant do to Hamor, that they'd send such against us?"

"He did nothing. Hamor wants to rule the world. The emperor thinks that, if he can unseat Lord Ghrant, he can rule through Lord Fergyn. Even if we win, it will take years to rebuild Austra, and Lord Ghrant will be in no position to move against Hamor in trade or other matters."

"Some folks, they never seem to have enough."

"Usually, they're already the ones who have more than most," Kharl replied, thinking of Egen and Lord West.

"Saw that growing up. Biggest orchards belonged to old Khosen, but he was always trying something to get more."

"It's like that." Kharl nodded, trying still to gather in a sense of the white wizards without actively using or creating excess order.

The road began to angle more to the southeast, and the steep cliffs on the north, to Kharl's left, gave way first to hillsides of red sand, scrub, and fir, then to lower hills covered by an older forest, mostly of evergreens.

They covered another kay or so before the edge of the sun, tinged white-orange by the mists hanging over both valleys and hills, rose over the old forest to the east of the narrow road. Ahead of them the narrow way curved even more southward, following the stream as it angled southeast toward a low gap between the hills to the north and east and the ridgeline to the south. Beyond the gap, according to the maps, was where the stream met the River Fahsa, roughly half a kay west of Ghalmat. Hagen had called Ghalmat a hamlet of but a few hundred people that basically served as a center for the berry patches and the orchards that covered the surrounding hills and ridges.

As they neared the gap between the ridge and hills, a lancer rode toward them, then slowed as he approached. Kharl recognized the scout by face, but not by name.

"Undercaptain . . . ser . . . there's no one in the town. Not more 'n a few, anyway. The rest were clearing out when I got there. They must have heard about the Hamorians."

Or Hagen's force. Or the white wizards, Kharl thought.

"Did you see any other lancers?"

"No, ser. There's dust on the road to the east, mayhap a kay east of the town. I didn't see any to the west or south. Wagon tracks in the roads, carts, but not more than a few mounts."

The undercaptain looked to Kharl. "We'll be getting there a little before the Hamorians."

"If we do, we'll let them pass, and we'll do what we need to once they've headed toward the lord-chancellor."

Demyst nodded, then looked at the scout. "Fall in." He'd turned in the saddle. "Herles!"

"Yes, ser?" answered the left-hand rider of the pair of lancers riding immediately behind Kharl and the undercaptain.

"Ride forward and watch the gap ahead. Make sure that no one heads toward us. If they don't, just wait for us."

"Yes, ser." Herles pulled out and past Kharl and Demyst, then eased his mount into a faster pace.

Almost another half glass went by before Kharl reined up just beyond the gap between the ridge to the west and the low hills to the east. Looking south, he studied the gentle slope running down to the river and the narrow cart bridge that arched over the Fahsa. On the far side was the crossroad that linked the north road and the northeast road out of Valmurl. The woodlots and orchards stretching to the south seemed to extend to the horizon, yet they were less than five kays north of the dockworks area of the harbor.

Just south of the river, and to the east, he could make out the outlines of the houses and buildings of Ghalmat—and the dust rising on the east side of the hamlet. The dust seemed to match what his order-senses told him about where the white wizards were. "They're coming into the east side of the town."

"Yes, ser. Lot of dust, ser."

After several moments, Kharl pointed to a thicker patch of evergreens on a knoll to the west of the road, no more than twenty rods north of the bridge. "We'll take cover there, and wait."

"Take a while to cross the bridge, ser."

"It'll take longer for the Hamorians."

"Ser?"

"If they discover us and come after us, they'll have trouble getting to us quickly, and it won't take that long for us to cross going south."

"Yes, ser."

Kharl urged the gelding forward, toward the heavily wooded knoll. Again, they would wait; but waiting, Kharl was learning, was often better than rushing into disaster.

A quarter glass went by, then another quarter glass, and the surge of white chaos drew nearer and nearer. At the same time, from gathering in impressions of Lyras, Kharl could sense that Hagen had stopped almost a glass earlier. He hoped that meant that Casolan's first companies and those remaining forces of Norgen—all under Hagen's command—had reached the hill to the west of where the northeast road and the river road intersected. There was a low outcropping of sandstone there on the east side of the hillcrest, which might give cover from chaos-fire, and the flanks and front of the hill were steep enough, and so covered by thornberries, that an easy and swift charge was not possible.

As Kharl reflected on those precautions, hoping they were sufficient, the Hamorian outriders appeared. Two posted themselves at the narrow bridge, but made no attempt to cross. The other six rode westward on the Fahsa River road. Before long, the column of lancers appeared.

From what Kharl could tell, the Hamorians had close to two companies of their lancers. Unlike the armsmen of either Austra or Nordla, whose uniforms were shaded more dramatic colors, such as green and black and blue, the Hamorians wore pale tan, with black belts and boots. Their tan caps had black visors as well. They bore sabres and long belt knives, as well as black lances in their stirrup holders.

"The squad leaders and officers have rifles," murmured Demyst.

"Not the lancers?"

"Don't see any."

Kharl knew that few armies used firearms, either the kind fired by cammabark or by powder, because a chaos-mage could trigger any powder not contained within iron—and sometimes even propellant that *was* so contained. Yet the Hamorian officers and squad leaders had rifles. Because they were so confident that their own mages would prevail? Or for special situations?

Kharl suspected the latter. He might find out in time, and probably when he least wanted to do so. Without extending any order-energy beyond himself, he concentrated on trying to get a better impression of the two white wizards, both of whom rode roughly in the middle of the Hamorian lancers. What he could only have described as lines of unseen white flashed from the two, but those energies were directed more to the west.

"How long are we waiting?" asked the undercaptain.

"Until they're far enough away that we can attack the bridge guards and get across before the main body could turn and get back to us." In some ways, Kharl would have preferred to have been on the south side of the river; but there was no cover there, not nearby, and nowhere to go if they had been discovered and immediately attacked. There was no other bridge across the Fahsa, not within kays, not except the north road bridge to the west, and the river was also more than three rods wide, and the spring runoff was violent and deep—close to two rods deep in midstream.

Kharl watched.

The main body of Hamorian column, riding three abreast on the wider river road, was more than a half a kay in length. With the outriders, and the squad or so of the trailing rearguard, the Hamorians took up nearly a kay of road.

Almost a third of a glass passed before the rear guard passed the bridge. When the last of the rear guards were about fifty rods west of the bridge, the bridge guards turned their mounts and began to trot westward to rejoin the main body.

"Now?"

"Not quite yet," Kharl said. "We'll wait until they're another half kay west. They'll still be short of the lord-chancellor." Not that short of Hagen's forces, he reflected, but he didn't want to call attention to himself or the squad until he had to.

Kharl used his order-senses once more, but there were no signs of other Hamorians—or of Lord Fergyn's lancers. Finally, once the distance between the Hamorian rear guard and bridge reached more than half a kay, Kharl turned to Demyst. "Now."

"Forward! To the bridge."

The Hamorians did not look back, not so far as Kharl could determine, and none of the column was detached to fight a rearguard action against the squad, even though someone must have seen them. Were the Hamorians that oblivious to Kharl? Or that confident, or did they know that Kharl—or anyone—would have to come to them? The latter, probably, Kharl surmised.

Once across the narrow bridge, a span that did in fact creak and sway with each passing rider, the squad re-formed in double files and headed after the Hamorians, who maintained a quick walk westward.

"Don't seem to care about us, do they?" ventured the undercaptain.

"Not for now," Kharl replied, his concentration on the column ahead and the unseen chaos-probes that flashed from the two white mages.

Another half glass passed as Kharl's small force slowly closed the gap. Kharl could sense the growing closeness of Lyras and, presumably, Hagen's forces. The morning sun was beating out of a clear sky, bringing a summerlike heat to the road, and sweat plastered the armsman's tunic against his back.

"They've halted."

Kharl could see that. The Hamorians waited on a flat of the road. Beyond was the intersection with the northeast road out of Valmurl, and farther to the west was the hillside on which Hagen and Lyras and their forces had taken a position. A quick glance showed riders in black and green—with blue sashes—withdrawing downhill. Kharl had to wonder how many attacks Fergyn's forces had already made—or if they had just begun, then withdrawn at the approach of the Hamorians.

Kharl wrenched himself away from futile speculations because he could also see that the rear ranks of the Hamorians had turned, and several squads faced eastward—toward Kharl. Immediately behind them was a smaller group, which included one of the white mages.

"Ser?"

"Keep riding. We need to get closer." Kharl could smell, seemingly for the first time, the road dust, the odor of fresh horse droppings, and the faintly acrid odor of chaos. Or was that odor only in his thoughts?

Ahead, the Hamorian lancers facing him lifted their lances but remained in place.

A bolt of chaos-fire flashed from the white wizard. Kharl waited, and at the last moment, lifted an order shield, letting the chaos splash away. The impact was enough to drive him back in the saddle. He leaned forward, trying to concentrate on finding the chaos tie that led back to the white wizard.

"Ser . . . ?"

"Keep riding," Kharl snapped. "Unless you want to be ashes."

"Yes, ser." Demyst raised his voice, "Follow ser Kharl. Keep riding!"

Hssst! Another chaos-bolt, every bit as powerful as the first, slammed against Kharl's shields. His readiness kept him in the saddle, but even as he sensed what he was looking for, he had to wonder how many more firebolts he could deflect—and he was only facing the lesser wizard.

A trumpet sounded, somewhere, and the Hamorian rear guard charged.

"Keep riding! Same pace!" Kharl ordered. The closer to the wizards, the better, because, while they could incinerate at any distance, or at least at a far greater distance than could he, what he could do had to be done at close range.

"Keep riding! Same pace!" echoed Demyst. "Blades at the ready! At the ready!"

Kharl waited, knowing what was about to happen.

The Hamorians thundered toward the Austran squad, still moving forward at a fast walk. Then, when the lancers in tan were but fifty cubits from Kharl—or less—an enormous firebolt arced in over them.

Kharl smiled grimly, and hardened the air before him, into the slippery tube shape that turned and focused the chaos back on the charging Hamorians.

Whhhssst!

The chaos-fire flared across the close-packed Hamorians, so quickly that there were not even screams as men and mounts turned to burned meat and charcoal, then ashes and blackened forms. The reddish white emptiness of a score or more of deaths shivered through Kharl, and he swallowed, trying to regain his concentration.

". . . demon-spawn!"

"Friggin' sowshit!"

"Quiet! Keep riding!" snapped Demyst.

Within moments, the squad was through and past the ashes and blackened remnants of the fallen Hamorians.

For all his success so far, Kharl knew his strengths and resources were limited.

Another trumpet sounded, and Kharl glanced beyond the Hamorian forces at the hill where Hagen and Lyras held out—so far. He could sense an enormous gathering of power—of mighty raw chaos. Then, a firebolt, more like wave of fire, washed over the front of the hillside. When the fire subsided, the hillside was black and gray—bare except for a few tree trunks at each side. The thornberry patches that would have slowed lancers had vanished into powdery ash.

Kharl found himself momentarily awed at the power and the amount of chaos released, far more than he had seen from other white wizards.

But the remaining Hamorian lancers did not charge. They remained on the flat to the east of the slope, their lines dressed.

Fergyn's lancers rode northward, and re-formed.

Kharl could see all too well what was about to happen. Both Austran forces would fight—and tear each other down—until either Fergyn was repulsed and defeated or until the lord-chancellor was. Either way, the Hamorian casualties would be far less.

What could Kharl do?

Hssst!

Kharl barely managed to get just an order shield up. Stupid! He needed to concentrate on one wizard at a time. He and his squad were less than thirty rods from the lesser wizard and his personal guard. He forced his eyes and his senses on the nearer wizard, trying to find the line of chaos that had to be there.

Hssst!

This time, Kharl managed to deflect the chaos-bolt back toward the white wizard, forcing the white to use his shields against his own chaos-fire. Two Hamorian lancers and their mounts, out to the side of the white wizard, went down in flames. One of the mounts screamed—an agonizing cry that went on and on.

Kharl ignored it, concentrating on the wizard, feeling, using all his order-senses, as the other drew upon chaos, seemingly from deep within the earth, formed it, and hurled it toward Kharl, now less than ten rods from the white wizard.

Kharl caught the chaos-tie between that ball of chaos and the wizard who had cast it, but lost the tie before he could fully sense it, when he had to throw up another order shield. If only he had a moment more, but the closer he got the less time he had, and yet, from a distance, he could do nothing.

Ahead, he could sense another huge wave of chaos bursting across the hillside—and this time, the redness of Austran deaths flashed across him. He could also sense more Hamorian lancers turning, raising lances, but Kharl forced his concentration back to the nearer wizard, watching the man in white. As Kharl rode ever nearer, this time, he caught the tie and link, but, again, he was too slow, and had to release that link—barely in time—to throw up another order shield. He was drenched in sweat and breathing heavily, and he had not even lifted a cudgel or a staff—or anything.

He forged his attention into a narrow line, ignoring the oncoming Hamorian lancers, waiting. As the white wizard drew upon the chaos of the earth deep beneath, Kharl seized the linkage and created an order shield within the channel, throwing the chaos back upon the white wizard, within the wizard's own shields.

Whhhsst!

Kharl flung up his own shields, around him and the squad, as an expanding blast of chaos radiating from where the lesser white wizard had stood.

The impact of that force against his shields jerked him back in the saddle, braced as he was. The reddish white voids of scores of deaths washed across Kharl, and tears streamed down his face from the pain and the brightness of that explosion.

Kharl shook his head, blotted the dampness from his eyes with the rough fabric of his uniformed sleeve. Everything around him was faint, washed out, but he immediately began to look for the other white wizard, both with eyes and order-senses. The lancers who had been charging Kharl were gone, seared into ashes or less, and perhaps half the Hamorian forces had already died. That didn't matter, not so long as a single white wizard remained.

Kharl could feel another massive wave of chaos rising, and it was not directed at the hillside, where Hagen and his forces held out, crouched and hiding behind the sandstone ridge—those that had survived thus far. It was directed toward Kharl and no other.

Find the link . . . don't think of shields . . . Find the link, Kharl kept telling himself. *Let the chaos flow back along that link . . . and return to me. Let it flow.* He kept concentrating on the wizard facing him.

For a long moment, he could see—as if they were less than a rod apart—the smooth-skinned wizard with the angular face, and the deep black eyes that had seen more than Kharl ever wanted to see.

Then . . . that vision was gone, and reddish-tinged white chaos fountained from beneath the ground, rising skyward in a plume, unseen except by the two mages and the white wizard. The earth trembled, then rocked beneath the gelding's hoofs. Somewhere, another mount screamed.

Kharl kept concentrating, reaching for the link between wizard and chaos, between power and the depths from which it came beneath the earth. He had eyes and senses only for that link, even as he rode forward, ever closer to the figure that glowed eerily in more chaos than Kharl could ever have imagined, could ever have wanted to imagine.

Time seemed frozen, with chaos towering over him, ready to fall and crush him.

Kharl struck, twisting through that undefended back linkage, opening it and letting all the chaos that had been gathered from the depths rush to and through the white wizard.

As the whiteness of that chaos burned more brightly than the sun for that instant, Kharl threw up an order shield, one that held all the strength and will that remained in him, one to block out the fires that seemed hotter than any forge, any boiler, any sun.

NO!!!!

Kharl shuddered under the assault of will and chaos, under a wave of heat that stopped somewhere short of him, but still burned. The very earth groaned, twisted, and heaved. Sheets of flame flared skyward from the ground.

As fire flared everywhere, as Kharl could feel himself toppling in the saddle, and someone grabbing for him, he also realized something else. The greater white wizard had been a woman. How he knew that . . . he did not know, but the thought flashed through his mind, just before the blackness slammed across him.

Somewhere in that hot blackness, ashes and death sifted down across him, and distant voices he could not make out called out in languages he could not understand. Then, there was a silence, and he could feel that he was on his back.

"Eyes moving . . ."

The first thing Kharl felt was water, warmish water, across his forehead and face, as he lay on his back on a hard surface—the road, he thought.

"Ser Kharl?"

He opened his eyes, but the light seared them, and he closed them immediately. He tried to speak, but all that came out was a growl, followed by a paroxysm of coughing. After a moment, he coughed out matter, perhaps fine ashes. Then, as the coughing subsided, he managed to sit up, assisted by someone he could not see.

Slowly, he tried to open his eyes again, slitting them and squinting against the light. The all-too-familiar daggers stabbed into his skull.

"Ser . . . best you drink some water."

Kharl didn't argue, either about the water or about eating the bread and cheese that a lancer handed him in small morsels. Everything tasted like ashes—again—but he put the food in his mouth and chewed, methodically. He swallowed the water in between mouthfuls. Finally, he slowly rose to his feet on legs that felt as weak as water.

"You think you should be standing, ser?" asked Undercaptain Demyst from his mount.

"No. I probably ought to get mounted and let the horse do the standing."

A lancer laughed, quietly, but the laugh died away as Demyst turned his head and glared to his right.

Kharl closed his eyes for a moment. That helped relieve the pain and the glare, although he knew that the sun wasn't that bright.

"Just a moment, ser," said another voice. "Janos is bringing your mount."

"Thank you."

Kharl stood there, waiting, his eyes still closed, with the odors of ashes and death swirling around him. There was no sense of chaos. He still could not quite take in what had happened, or the stillness around him.

"The lord-chancellor's on his way down, ser. Had to go around the back side of the hill, a long way. That's what Stevras said. Sent him as a messenger."

"I'd better get mounted." Kharl slit his eyes again. The pain daggers were still there, but he tried not to wince as he turned and took two steps toward the gelding. Mounting was easier than seeing what he was doing.

Once in the saddle, he had to cough again, and, for a moment, he thought he might not be able to hold down what he had eaten, but he closed his eyes, and the coughing subsided. As he sat in the saddle, waiting for Hagen, he realized that he could sense no chaos. None. That was good, he supposed.

After a time, he slit his eyes again to look around him, first uphill to the southwest, then along the road to the south. Everywhere he saw gray—ashes, smoke and ashes, and with the faint breeze came even more strongly the stench of burned flesh, both of men and mounts. The entire front of the hill beyond the northeast road and the flat below were smoldering charnel heaps, and the gray of ashes as fine as dust had settled over everything.

Farther west, the top of the hill shimmered in the afternoon sunlight, shimmered like a mirror, a glassy surface of red and black, a surface created by the chaos blasts of the dead white wizard—or should she have been termed a sorceress?

Kharl had heard of the Legend, and the tales of Megaera, but . . . those had always just been stories. Who could have believed that such a mighty sorceress had existed in his own time? Or that she had been sent to Austra?

Slowly, he eased the mount along the road toward the ragged column coming from the west along the river road.

When he caught sight of Kharl, the lord-chancellor motioned for the other lancers to halt, then rode alone toward Kharl.

"I'll meet the lord-chancellor alone," Kharl said to Demyst.

"Lancers halt! The mage and the lord-chancellor will meet alone."

Kharl forced himself to take another swallow from the water bottle. The water still tasted like liquid ashes, but he swallowed with a gulp, then put it back in the looped holder above his knee.

Hagen reined up, letting Kharl come the last few rods to him. The mage eased the gelding to a halt a rod or so from the lord-chancellor.

"Ser Kharl . . . What . . . what did . . . ?" Hagen could not finish the question.

"What was necessary." Kharl's voice was flat. "Both the white wizards are dead. From their own chaos." He closed his eyes. Talking intensified the sight-daggers jabbing into his skull.

"That last . . . it seared everything below the hillcrest—except your squad. We lost a third of ours then. It's all glass—a hillside of glass."

"And ashes." Kharl paused. "We lost more than that. We lost all of the lancers in Lord Fergyn's forces."

"I see . . . why few would wish a war with either Hamor or Recluse."

Kharl offered a weary smile, except the expression was more grimace than smile. "No. That is clear. I am certainly not as great a mage as those of Recluce, and the white wizard could not have been the greatest in Hamor."

"No. The emperor would not send his greatest," Hagen agreed.

"Will this end the rebellion?" asked Kharl.

"I would judge so." Hagen glanced to his right, out across the grayness and devastation. "One can never tell, but all those who led it or were in the councils of the rebels are dead. The lancers and armsmen who followed them are dead."

Kharl just nodded. Then, a wave of weakness and dizziness swept over him, and he lowered his head until his forehead was almost resting against the gelding's mane.

"Kharl . . . are you all right?"

"Be . . . a while . . . before . . . I get my strength . . . back." Even those few words seemed to exhaust him, and he sat in the saddle, his eyes closed, trying just to hang on. After several moments, the worst of the dizziness passed, and he gradually straightened.

"Are you sure?" asked Hagen.

"I'll . . . be riding . . . slowly." Kharl managed a faint smile.

XXVIII

There is a Balance, too, among those who can master order or chaos. There are few who have the talent and the discipline to claim even minor skills in handling such forces. There are even fewer who can boast of some limited degree of mastery, and fewer still who attain great mastery, especially of order, for mastery of chaos is far easier than the same level of mastery of order . . .

The balance is this: A mage may have a wide range of skills, but his breadth of skills will limit great skill in one area of mastery. Conversely, a mage may have great mastery in one area, but most limited abilities in others, where lesser mages may in fact show greater skill.

This Balance of mastery, then, must be considered in all things. A great weather mage may not be able to spur the slightest growth in plants nor heal the simplest cut. A mighty metal mage may not be capable of even sensing when the weather will change.

Yet a possessor of minor order abilities may be able to heal a cut, strengthen the wool of sheep, find the bad pearapples from among the good without touching a one, and always know when the weather will change. But he can do no great mageries, though he can accomplish some magery in all areas where order may be fruitfully used.

That often is the weakness of those of great single magely skills, that they fail to understand that they cannot be great in all areas, and that they may make great errors if they fail to recognize that the Balance applies to them as well as to the relation between order and chaos.

As in all matters of order, chaos, and the affairs of men and women, there is a Balance, and a price to be paid for greatness and great accomplishments.

—*The Basis of Order*

XXIX

Kharl slept poorly on fourday night, even though they had not reached the Great House until after sunset, what with the clouds and the downpour that had swept in, seemingly from nowhere, turning the roads into muddy quagmires and extending a journey of perhaps two glasses into one three times that long. By the time he reached his quarters, he was soaked and shivering. Even before the fire in his small hearth, a good glass had passed before he had been warm enough to climb into bed.

Then, after he had dropped off, uneasily, the image of the white sorceress appeared before him, time after time, then vanished in a swirl of chaos and ashes. Twice he woke, drenched in sweat, with every muscle in his body aching. Even in the darkness of his quarters, when he opened his eyes, the sight-daggers jabbed into his skull. In fact, in the darkness it was worse, because each dagger exploded in a flash of light.

Morning was not much better, although a visit to the bath chamber and breakfast improved his being somewhat. The egg toast only tasted lightly of ashes. The pale ale might have helped as well. Then he went back to his quarters, to rest. Outside the windows of his quarters, the rain continued to fall, almost in sheets at times.

Rest eluded him. Too many thoughts swirled through his skull. Why had the Emperor of Hamor sent a white sorceress? She had been far more powerful than any of the white wizards, and the emperor had risked her on a revolt in Austra? Did Hamor have that many whites so powerful? Or had she been a danger to the emperor? Every time Kharl thought he had learned something, he found that there was so much more he did not know.

So far as Kharl knew, how he had applied order had seemed straightforward. He'd read from *The Basis of Order*, then tried to work things out. Some things hadn't worked. Some had, but had almost prostrated him, or worse, and one or two others had worked well. In most magely things, Kharl had just been middling, and only good in a few. That was life. The same had been true when he'd just been a simple cooper.

"Ser Kharl?"

Even without much effort, Kharl could sense the blackness of Lyras beyond the door. His order-senses were sharper than ever, but that sharpness was so clear that it was almost painful. He did not want to think about what it might feel like to deal with another white wizard.

"Come in, Lyras. It's unbolted. Unbarred, too."

Lyras, in the browns he always wore, opened the door and stepped inside.

Kharl motioned to the other chair and watched as Lyras seated himself.

"You're feeling better?" asked Lyras.

"Not sure I could have felt worse . . ." Kharl closed his eyes as the sight-daggers jabbed into his skull even more sharply. "I feel better."

Lyras laughed. "The more powerful a black mage is, the harder it is to say something that is not accurate. You have become very powerful, ser Kharl, and in a shorter time than perhaps any mage since the great Creslin."

Kharl wanted to deny the other's words, but . . . was there any truth in them? He finally spoke. "I would not know. I do know that it is uncomfortable not to tell . . . what is accurate." He was having a hard time with the word *truth* and wanted to avoid using it, at least aloud.

Lyras smiled. "You have not had the time to become accustomed to the results of power."

"That is so. Unfortunately." While Kharl still wasn't certain how much real power he had, there was no doubt that he had not had time to become accustomed to dealing personally and directly with those of power. He closed his eyes for a moment.

"Too much use of power, especially in dealing with chaos, often affects a mage's sight. Creslin lost his, on and off, for much of his later life."

"When I look at anything, there are daggers stabbing in through my eyes," Kharl admitted.

"Hmmm . . . that's one I never heard of. Then, everything about you is . . . a little different."

"I wouldn't know."

"No . . . you wouldn't," Lyras agreed cheerfully. "That's why I'm here."

"Oh?"

"Lord Hagen, he said . . ."

Kharl waited.

"You said that you were far from the great mages of Recluce."

"I did. I've been a mage something like a year, Lyras. I can do a few things passably, and one or two fairly well. The great mages of Recluce certainly can do more than that." Kharl felt confident about that statement, and his eyes certainly didn't pain him any more than they had.

"I hesitate to tell you this, ser Kharl, but what I have to say . . . there is no one else who has seen what I have and knows what it portends."

Kharl didn't like the words, or the caution behind them. "What are you going to tell me?"

"You are the greatest mage—or the most powerful in what you do—in two generations, and possibly among the handful of truly great order-mages."

"Me?"

"Not since Fairven fell has a black mage faced the kind of chaos that I felt yesterday."

Had it been only yesterday? Just yesterday? Kharl shrugged, helplessly. "I wouldn't know. I find that hard to believe."

"A stretch of hillside almost a kay square was fused into glass. More than six companies of lancers and two white wizards were burned to ashes. People will ride by there for generations to come and marvel. Not many mages can handle that kind of power." Lyras gestured to the rain outside. "Out of a clear sky this torrent swept in. That happens when mighty order and mighty chaos meet. Crops all across eastern Austra will be washed out if it continues."

"But . . . I didn't create it. The white wizards did. All I did was turn it against them."

"All?" Lyras's laugh was warm, rather than hard, and somehow sad. "Those were great white wizards. The greater one was, I think, perhaps even a chaos-focus. He was probably sent here to keep him out of Hamor. No ruler likes that kind of power too close."

"I had thought about that." Although Kharl could understand that, he wondered if he was the only one who had realized that the greater wizard had actually been a sorceress, and if he should correct Lyras. He decided against saying anything. What difference would it make whether the white had been man or woman? Power was power. The more important point was the one about rulers distrusting great wizardry too near to them. "I had hoped to return to Cantyl as soon as I can."

"That is a good thought." Lyras smiled again. "You need time to rest, and to consider what you have learned and how it has changed you and how it will continue to change you." He stood. "Until later."

"You're going home."

"Lord Ghrant does not need me. Nor does the lord-chancellor. They have you. I would rather spend my efforts on my berry bushes."

"Give my best to your consort," Kharl offered.

"Oh, I will, and we'll send you some of the best preserves in the fall. It's the least we can do." With those words, and another smile, the black mage was gone.

Kharl closed his eyes and leaned back in the chair.

Thrap!

He jerked awake at the rap on the door. He'd dozed off, but from the light coming through the window, it couldn't have been for long.

"Ser Kharl?"

"Yes?" The word came out as a croak. Kharl cleared his throat and tried again. "Yes?"

"The lord-chancellor wanted to know if you would join him for a private midday meal in his study."

"Now?"

"He had thought so."

"I'll be right there." Kharl eased himself out of the chair and to his feet. He walked slowly to the door, and the armsman who stood outside waiting.

Neither spoke on the way along the corridor and down the stone steps, although Kharl could sense the young man's gaze falling upon him more than once.

The two guards outside the lord-chancellor's study stiffened as Kharl approached.

"He's expecting you, ser Kharl," said the older one, half-opening the door.

"Thank you." Kharl managed a smile he hoped was warm and friendly.

As Kharl stepped inside Hagen's study, the lord-chancellor stood. "Kharl. Please join me."

Set on each side of the table desk was a platter, and a beaker of lager by each. As Hagen seated himself, so did Kharl.

"How are you feeling?" asked Hagen.

"Passable," Kharl admitted. "A bit tired, too. How about you? How are things going here? With Lord Ghrant?"

Hagen laughed, sardonically. "All the leading rebel lords are dead. The others have all sent messengers and messages, pledging their allegiance and claiming that they had no choice, because, like Lord Vertyn and Lord Lahoryn, they would have lost everything had they not reluctantly agreed to support the rebellion."

"For some it was probably true." Kharl took a swallow of the lager, enjoying it mainly just because it did not taste like ashes. "But what about lords like Azeolis?"

"He was one of the first to pledge allegiance and to offer reparations."

"And Lord Ghrant will accept both, I take it."

"For now, blaming the dead makes for a convenient apology and explanation."

Kharl understood. Ghrant couldn't afford to lay low all the dissatisfied lords in Austra, and they certainly didn't want to end up like Fergyn or Hensolas. Kharl took a bite of the lamb cutlet in a white cheese sauce. He had to admit that the food was welcome. He also ate several of the fried lace potatoes, dipping them in the sauce as well.

Hagen ate several mouthfuls before he spoke. "What do you plan to do next?"

Kharl sipped some of the ale before replying. "I'd thought it might be best for me to return to Cantyl. Quietly. Seems to me that I've done enough for now."

"That might be for the best." A faint smile quirked the lips of the lord-chancellor. "After Lord Ghrant's audiences with Lord Deroh and a few of the lords who tacitly supported Kenslan, Malcor, Hensolas, and Fergyn."

"After the last audience . . . you want me there? Lord Ghrant does?" Kharl found that hard to believe.

"Want?" Hagen laughed. "I doubt Lord Grant *wants* you there, but he needs you there. He needs all of Austra to see that you stand behind him, and that you are indeed a presence. Then he will doubtless grant you some other boon and suggest that you rest and enjoy your lands."

Kharl wasn't looking forward to another audience, but he could see the reasons for Hagen's request—or command. "When will these audiences be?"

"An eightday or so from now. It will take Lord Azeolis some time to reach Valmurl, and somewhat longer for my scouts to report. In the meantime, enjoy your food." Hagen smiled.

Kharl returned the smile. He could use the time to recover more fully—and the lamb was excellent.

XXX

On sixday and sevenday, Kharl did little but rest, eat, sleep—and reflect. Trying to read hurt his eyes too much. After two days, the torrential rain had subsided into gray mist and fog that matched Kharl's melancholy. He told himself that he shouldn't feel that way. He'd helped put down a rebellion that would have left Austra in far worse shape. He'd stopped—for the time, anyway—the Emperor of Hamor from taking the first steps to subdue Austra, and he'd preserved his own lands and future, lands he would never have dreamed of having a year before. He'd bested some of the most powerful white wizards seen outside of Hamor in years. Weren't those worthy accomplishments?

Yet, with each accomplishment, he felt more distant from those around him. The guards stepped back and stiffened. Some people who once smiled bowed thoughtfully. Others stepped into side corridors, as if they had errands elsewhere.

He eased himself out of the chair in his sitting room and turned to face the window, looking out into the gray afternoon. He could still see the face of the white sorceress, and hear her single word of protest, as if what he had done was not supposed to have happened.

Was Lyras right? Certainly, the older mage had believed he was telling the truth. That Kharl had sensed. But . . . how could that be? How could a former cooper, who had not even studied magery, have gained that much power?

Kharl laughed softly. He had not gained that much power. He had mastered one or two abilities well enough to turn chaos-power against its users. At the risk of blinding himself, he could release some chaos by loosening order bonds, and he could shield himself and a small group. That was power, but it was limited power.

Lyras disliked using power. According to legend, the mage who had brought down Fairven had survived and vanished. Creslin had seldom used his powers in later years. Kharl himself worried about what might happen if he faced more white wizards. At some point, did a black mage become strong enough that the greatest bar to his use of power was his understanding of what that power could do?

At the same time, Kharl had seen enough to know that most people respected only power. Was that why power so easily came to be abused, reflected the mage, and why the great mages of the past had vanished, or become recluses? He paused. Did the very name of *Recluce* signify something like that? Was that why it had a council, rather than a ruler, because it had been created by Creslin, supposedly the greatest air mage of all time? Because shared power was less easily abused?

Kharl turned away from the window, closing his eyes to relieve them, his thoughts still swirling within his skull.

XXXI

Not until eightday did the weather clear fully, and by then Kharl was able to see more distinctly, and the frequency of the sight-daggers knifing into his skull had diminished, although each jab felt as painful as any of those he had endured earlier. He had not seen Hagen, and he knew few within the Great House, and those he did not know were both polite, friendly—and distant. That was to be expected, he had come to understand.

Late on eightday afternoon, Kharl strolled through the formal gardens on the south side of the main building, gardens enclosed by a four-cubit-high redstone wall. Despite the wall, the winds and rains had taken their toll on the flowers and the more delicate shrubs. Stems and leaves littered the white gravel pathway. Not a single one of the maroon bellflower stems remained erect, all flattened before the buds had opened.

He stopped before a bed of early pink roses. Beneath the plants was a carpet of petals, still damp from the rain. A single bloom remained largely intact, if with a disheveled appearance, and it drooped on a lower branch, slightly sheltered. Kharl could smell but the faintest scent.

He studied the bedraggled pink rose, still waterlogged. It might have opened into a perfect blossom, once, but the wind and rain of the previous days had put a stop to that. Even so, the rosebushes held the faintest of black auras, the same order that had infused the red pear orchard. He stood on the path, sensing that particular rosebush. He shifted his weight, and the white gravel under his boots crunched.

He had been able to sense the order and chaos within people for some time, an ability that had begun almost the moment he had taken Jenevra's black staff and fled from Egen's Watch. The feeling for other aspects of living order—he had become aware of that only recently, and most dramatically, when he had drained the pear orchard of its life order to stop the white wizard supporting Hensolas.

At a cough coming from his left, Kharl straightened and turned.

Hagen stood there.

"Lord-chancellor."

"Ser mage." Hagen inclined his head, somberly. "How do you feel?"

"Better, each day."

"That's good. Lord Ghrant has set the first audience for fiveday. For Lord Deroh."

Kharl remembered Hagen mentioning Deroh, but he didn't recall anything about the lord.

"His estates are midway between Dykaru and Valmurl. He didn't raise men or arms for the rebels, but he did send golds to Hensolas. He has pleaded that he had to do that in order to keep from having his lands ravaged."

"It sounds like his lands were in no immediate danger," Kharl observed.

"I doubt they were. I'd wager a few of the audiences will be like that. You will be there, of course."

"This time, I'll whisper what I think to you."

A sardonic grin crossed Hagen's face. "I had already suggested that to Lord Ghrant. He agreed most readily."

"Is there anything else I should know?"

"No. It's probably better if you don't know about the backgrounds of any of the lords who will be appearing."

"You don't sound like their backgrounds speak well for them."

"For them, perhaps, but not for their support of Lord Ghrant." Hagen shook his head. "I should not even have said that. The less said the better." After a moment, he looked to the battered roses and the single remaining bloom. "The gardens will be spectacular later in the year after so much early rain."

"If there isn't too much more rain," Kharl replied cautiously. With all the flattened plants and stems he had seen, he had his doubts even if the summer days to come were temperate.

"Lyras said that there wouldn't be. Not unless you have to deal with more white wizards. That appears unlikely." Hagen laughed sardonically, a trace more bitterness in the sound than usual, even recently.

"Why do you say that?"

"Lord Ghrant received a message from a Lord Fynarak."

From the sound of the name, Kharl suspected that the lord was Hamorian. "What did it say?"

"It was vaguely worded, something to the effect that he was conveying the solicitude of the emperor about the internal difficulties that Lord Ghrant had recently faced, but congratulating him on his fortitude and resourcefulness in dealing with the rebel lords. This Lord Fynarak went on to say that the emperor was committed to measures that would ensure peace between Austra and Hamor."

Kharl smiled, somewhat faintly.

Hagen continued. "The message also conveyed the news that the ship taken by Lord Joharak and his assistant Fostak had apparently been lost at sea with all aboard perishing, and that, shortly, the emperor would name a new envoy to Austra, one who would be committed to ensuring warm and cordial relations."

"So they sank a Nordlan ship to bury any evidence of Hamor's treachery?"

"Not exactly. Too much of the world already knows what the emperor attempted. The sinking was another message of sorts. The first was to his own people. He won't tolerate failure, and trying to escape to other lands is futile. The second was to the rest of the world, suggesting that interfering in Hamor's affairs can bear a heavy price."

Kharl understood Hagen's words, but he had his doubts. "That seems . . . strange. Dishonest, rather. They interfered in Austra, and we stopped them."

"And we paid a heavy price, did we not?"

"But a Nordlan ship?"

"Oh . . . the *Fleuryl* has been a thumb-thorn for Hamor before, and more than once. Her master barely escaped from Swartheld several years back, something about dreampowder—"

The *Fleuryl*? Kharl could feel his entire body chill. The *Fleuryl*?

Hagen fell silent for a moment, before asking, "What's the matter, Kharl?"

The *Fleuryl*? Why the *Fleuryl*? Kharl swallowed.

Hagen waited.

"There . . . weren't any survivors?"

"No. The missive made that most clear." Once more, Hagen waited.

Finally, Kharl spoke, slowly. "My eldest, Arthal. He was a carpenter's assistant. On the *Fleuryl*."

This time, Hagen was silent for some time before speaking. When he did, his words were deliberate, but soft. "I am sorry, Kharl. I had no idea. Rhylla told me your boy had left to go to sea, but not the ship. I didn't know."

"You couldn't. I didn't tell her. He wasn't happy with me. Not after everything that happened."

"I lost one of my boys. Not something like this, though." Hagen reached out and touched Kharl's shoulder, gently.

The mage could feel the older man's concern. It helped—some. "I . . . I always worried about him . . . going off because he was angry. Leaving . . . like that. Not going to something, but from something."

Hagen nodded. "It doesn't matter how it happens, or why. It hurts. It always will. It just hurts less often after a while." The lord-chancellor stood quietly, not offering, not pushing, but not leaving.

Kharl could feel a numbness inside. He didn't want to think about it, and yet he couldn't not. After a time, he looked up at Hagen.

"I'm sorry," the lord-chancellor said again.

"I know. I know." Kharl swallowed. "I think I'd just like to be alone . . . for a bit."

"You'll have supper with me," Hagen said firmly. "At the first glass of evening."

"Thank you."

The lord-chancellor nodded, then stepped back.

Kharl listened as Hagen's boots crunched through the damp white gravel, the sound getting fainter until it was gone, and the garden was still once more.

He wondered if he could have accepted Arthal's death more easily if Arthal had died in a storm or even a brawl. But to be killed . . . as a result of what Kharl himself had done? Even indirectly?

And the *Fleuryl*? It had been in the harbor at Valmurl not days before. Arthal had been there, and Kharl had not even known, not even suspected, so preoccupied had he been in dealing with white wizards and rebel lords. So close . . .

The mage looked back at the single rose, drooping, above the carpet of fallen petals. A single survivor, of sorts, of the storm that Kharl had created. Would that Arthal had been so fortunate.

Arthal . . . dead. Because of Kharl. Because of a petulant emperor.

Dead . . .

Slowly, Kharl walked back up to his chambers.

He took his time washing up and preparing for dinner, not that Hagen would care, but because it was easier than doing nothing and thinking about Arthal. He wanted to be alone, and yet he didn't.

He still thought about his son, even as he later walked down to meet Hagen in the smaller dining room. Why the *Fleuryl*? Why Arthal?

The lord-chancellor was waiting.

Hagen gestured toward the table, on which there were two goblets of red wine, then seated himself. "It's hard, when something like this happens."

Kharl nodded, slipping into the chair opposite the lord-chancellor. "I hadn't thought . . ."

"We never do." Hagen went on. "People say that you need to be alone. It could be that I'm mistaken, but there's more than enough time to be alone. The nights can be long." He lifted a goblet. "It's a sad time, but to better times . . . and friendship."

Kharl lifted his own goblet. "To better times and friendship." He was glad for Hagen's friendship, and for the way in which the lord-chancellor had immediately responded.

Even from the first small swallow, the wine was warming. "This is good."

"I hope so." Hagen smiled.

For a long moment, there was silence.

"You lost a son," Kharl said, wanting to talk about Arthal, and yet, not wanting to.

"With some boys, Kharl," Hagen said slowly, "it seems like a man can do nothing right. If you're strict, then you don't understand what they feel. If you're not strict, they'll go out and do foolish things. Not that we all didn't as young fellows. We were more fortunate."

Had Kharl been too strict? "I didn't think that I was all that strict with Arthal. I wanted him to understand that he had to do what was expected. People don't pay unless you do the job and do it well." Kharl shook his head. "Charee was always saying that he was just a boy, even when he'd reached his double-eight."

"To them, they're always boys." Hagen took the smallest sip of his wine. "It was my second son. Narlan. Tall and strapping. He had a smile that would melt any girl's heart—her mother's, too. He worked hard, and he learned quickly." The lord-chancellor's voice softened. "He listened to everyone but me."

"I don't know who Arthal listened to," Kharl said, after a moment. "He didn't listen to me."

Hagen nodded for Kharl to go on.

"Everything happened so fast," Kharl mused. "One night, I heard singing and loud voices in the alley behind the cooperage, just as I was getting ready to go up for supper. I went out. Two bravos were making free with my neighbor's daughter, had her blouse half–ripped off. I stopped them and got her home. I didn't think much about it, didn't even tell Charee or the boys. A few days later, I heard moaning in another alley, found another girl. She was a blackstaffer, and she'd been taken by force, beaten badly, and left to die. I brought her back to the cooperage. Charee didn't want me to. She said it would cause trouble. She was right, but how could I let the girl die?" Kharl stopped and looked down at the wine goblet.

"What happened then?" Hagen's voice was gentle.

"It turned out that it was the same bravo, lord's second son. He hired an assassin. They set a fire in my neighbor's shop. I went to help. The assassin killed the girl with one of my shop knives. The Watch hauled me off, and put me up for murder. There were witnesses, though. They came to the Hall of Justice and said I couldn't have done it. One was well known to Lord West." Kharl shrugged helplessly. "They found blood on Charee's blouse, said she'd done it. Hanged her and flogged me. Arthal took it hard. He blamed me. He said that it was all my fault, that I should have listened to his mother. Wasn't that long before he walked out and shipped on the *Fleuryl* as a carpenter's boy. Lord West raised my tariffs so high I would have lost the cooperage. Except I killed the assassin. I didn't even know it was him until later. He'd murdered my neighbor for speaking up for me at the Hall of Justice. I caught him coming out of the scriptorium. Had to run then, and hid till you and the *Seastag* ported in Brysta. You know the rest."

"You did the honorable thing," Hagen pointed out. "More than once."

"No one else thought so. Not Charee, not Warrl, not Arthal." Kharl sipped the wine. "Especially not Arthal. He said I never listened and that nothing could be worse than staying with me. I should have stopped him."

"For how long?" asked Hagen. "He would have left when you were not around." His laugh was sad and rueful. "That was what Narlan did. He left a note. He wrote that since I could talk him out of anything, he couldn't say good-bye except in writing."

"You said . . . you lost him . . ." offered Kharl.

"He sailed with a Delapran merchanter—except it wasn't a merchanter. She was a sometime pirate, and one of the black ships of Recluce sank her in less than a season after he left."

"I'm sorry." What else could Kharl say?

"It was a good ten years ago. You don't ever get over it. It always hurts. It just doesn't hurt as often." Hagen offered a faint smile. "You have to remember, Kharl, hard as it is, hard as it will be, that young men make their own choices. We did, and they will. When you've done your best—and you're a man who always tries to do what's right—in the end, they have to choose for themselves. The hard thing is when they don't choose well, and there's nothing you can do about it."

What could Kharl have done differently? He still couldn't see ignoring Sanyle or Jenevra. Nor could he have not tried to help fight the fire that had threatened Tyrbel's scriptorium. After that . . . nothing would have changed, and Arthal would never have understood, no matter what Kharl had said.

Yet . . .

He looked at the wine. That was no answer, either. He was just glad that Hagen was there.

XXXII

Each day brought Kharl greater recovery, and by threeday, he was only occasionally finding holes in his vision, and the sight-daggers had become infrequent, and more like momentary wasp stings. He still brooded about Arthal, wondering if there had been anything he could have done that would have persuaded his son against leaving the cooperage. Even if Arthal had waited . . . for a later ship . . . anything . . . Every time he recalled their parting, he came to the same conclusion that Hagen had voiced. Arthal had been so angry that nothing short of chaining the youth would have stopped him from taking the billet on the *Fleuryl*.

And then, to find after his death, that his son had been within a handful of kays, and Kharl had not even known it.

Slightly after midday, Kharl was sitting alone in the small dining room, sipping light ale from a beaker and waiting for his meal when Norgen entered and walked over to his table.

"Might I join you, ser Kharl?"

"Please do." Kharl gestured to the seat across the table from him. He was more than glad to see the commander of Ghrant's personal guard. Everyone else, except Hagen, had been most polite, most courteous, and most distant.

"Thank you." As Norgen seated himself, he absently brushed back the thin and fine hair that had once been far redder. He gestured to the serving girl. "An ale, here, when you have a moment."

"Yes, ser."

Norgen smiled at Kharl. "You're looking better. Your face was blistered all over after the battle."

"An eightday's worth of rest helps. Or almost an eightday."

"That can be a long time. I imagine it's been rather quiet for you." Norgen paused as the server set a beaker of ale before him. "Thank you," he said to her.

The server inclined her head and slipped away.

"Not many people wish to talk to you, I'd think, and those few that do aren't the ones you'd wish to exchange words with."

Kharl raised his eyebrows. "Those words come from experience."

Norgen laughed, a harsh sound, for all that the laugh was not that loud. "Commander . . . surely you could have prevailed without losing so many lancers? Commander, if you had been more effective, Lord Ghrant might not have had to rely so heavily on the mage . . ."

"That's not the lord-chancellor," Kharl said.

"No. It's lords like Vhint and Ferosyl. They had to supply lancers and armsmen to replace casualties in the personal guard. Like all armsmen in a battle, some didn't survive, and now the lords are complaining—as if casualties in battle were a great surprise."

"I did the best I could," Kharl said.

"Ser Kharl . . . you'll get no complaint from me. If you hadn't prevailed, all of our forces would be ashes, and I'm not sure that the ones with Hensolas and Fergyn wouldn't still have been as well."

Both men looked up as the server returned and set platters before each, and a basket of bread between them. Dark bread, and freshly baked, Kharl noted with satisfaction. On each platter were three cutlets in brown gravy, cheese mashed potatoes, and soggy-looking beans.

"Thank you," Kharl said to the server, offering a smile.

"Yes, ser." The young woman's eyes avoided Kharl's, even as she half bowed and backed away.

"The terrible mage," murmured Kharl.

"It's the same folk who want you—or me—to use whatever force is necessary so that their lives can go on, undisturbed," said Norgen cheerfully. He broke off a section of the dark bread and handed the basket to Kharl. "I've been in service long enough to see how fickle folk are. When there's peace, they see no use for lancers—or mages. When there's war, they'll promise you anything and look the other way if what you do is too bloody for their sensibilities. But if you suggest that a campaign will be too bloody, you're accused of cowardice or sympathizing with the enemy. Afterwards, they all say that you didn't have to be so brutal . . . or something like that."

After taking a chunk of bread, Kharl set it on the edge of his platter. "Gratitude doesn't last long."

"If you get it at all," replied Norgen. "Most people are like small children. They want things their way, and they don't like to be reminded of their duties, or that they should be grateful to those who have protected them. Children don't ever appreciate their parents, not until they have children of their own. The problem with ruling—or fighting for a ruler—is that most people never get that kind of responsibility. So they never understand the choices and the costs." He took a sip of the ale before continuing. "There are folktales that go back as long as people have told them. In them, most rulers are evil and greedy. Ever hear one that talks about evil and greedy subjects?" He laughed.

"You don't think much of people, then?" asked Kharl.

Norgen smiled, sadly. "I'm one of them. I get as greedy and as upset as the next person when things don't go my way. You remind yourself of that, and don't expect people to do more at their best than you at your worst, and you'll be pleasantly surprised in life. People are people. Those who expect goodness from everyone all the time—they're the ones who die bitter and unhappy."

"Do most commanders think the way you do?"

"The good ones do—like Casolan—not that I'm as good as he is."

"You both believe in doing the best you can," observed Kharl.

"So do you, ser mage. I've seen that." After a pause, the lean commander added, "What else is there in life, other than doing your best? Youth doesn't last. Neither does good fare or ale. Gratitude certainly doesn't. Fame doesn't. About all that does is the satisfaction of knowing you did your best."

"You should have been a scholar," Kharl suggested.

Norgen grinned sheepishly. "I was for a time. Don't tell people. Upset my folks something awful. Couldn't stand all the older scholars arguing about things they'd never known and couldn't prove. Far as I know, you only get one life. Decided I'd rather live mine than study and write about the lives and acts of dead men and women. Or about the way languages or laws have changed. Or . . ." The commander shrugged.

"You have any children?"

"Two daughters, one son. He's a scholar. Thinks his father's crazy, but he's scared to say so. My daughters, they just shake their heads when they think I'm not looking. Kasrina understands, and that's enough."

"If she understands, you're a fortunate man," Kharl said, after finishing a mouthful of a too-chewy cutlet. "None of mine did . . . or have, not so far, anyway."

"I know that, too." Norgen took another sip from the beaker. "You had to leave your family behind?" The word were not quite a question.

"My consort died, and my eldest son . . . he left. He blamed me." Kharl swallowed. He'd wanted just to mention Arthal and let it go. He shook his head. "The Nordlan merchanter, the one that had the Hamorian envoy on it. The Hamorians . . . they sank it. He was a carpenter's apprentice."

Norgen nodded slowly and gravely. "I'm sorry. I had wondered. You have been quiet and withdrawn, even for a mage with much to think about."

"I wouldn't have thought they would destroy an entire ship, just to punish a failed envoy."

"They are without compassion. I am sorry." Norgen lifted his beaker.

Kharl couldn't help noticing that the commander, for all the number of times he had sipped the ale, had drunk less than half. He swallowed and pushed away the thoughts of Arthal, for the moment, at least. "Do you think there will be any more rebellion?"

"There's no one left to rebel—not with enough golds and armsmen to stand against even what's left of Lord Ghrant's personal guard. No . . . things will be quiet here for a while, maybe a long while. Hamor will go make trouble somewhere else, Nordla or Candar, most likely. The lord-chancellor will keep Lord Ghrant from being too vindictive and from tariffing too much. Lord Ghrant will try to forget that you're around, except to summon you to the Great House now and again, just to remind the lords of your power, and on those days, we'll get our blades and harnesses polished and parade, and the young lancers will think that they're getting paid for doing little—and when the next trouble comes, the ones who learned the least will die, and we'll start all over again. But, by that time, I hope, I'll be stipended or even long gone."

Kharl found Norgen's cheerful cynicism refreshing—and depressing. Perhaps what made his words even more depressing was the honesty behind them. The commander saw life as it was, not as he wished it to be—and he didn't seem to hate those who were cruel and stupid.

What was it that the druid had said? Not to act out of anger and hatred? Kharl wished he had listened to the druids more carefully. He half nodded, more to himself than to Norgen. "I hope you're right."

"Oh . . . things will go that way. Lord Ghrant's not the brightest who ever ruled, but he's far from the dimmest, and he's come to understand that he'd do far worse with anyone else as lord-chancellor."

Was Norgen being too charitable to Lord Ghrant? Kharl couldn't say. So he took another mouthful of the potatoes. Time would tell.

XXXIII

On fiveday afternoon, Kharl stood to the right of Hagen in the audience hall, a half pace back, watching as Lord Deroh walked toward Lord Ghrant, who remained seated in the high-backed chair. Unlike the last time, Ghrant was attired almost entirely in black, with but just enough green trim that he would not be mistaken for a mage.

The angular and dark-bearded Deroh stopped several paces short of the dais and turned his head. He stared directly at Kharl, and his face seemed to narrow. After a long moment, he spoke, in a hard and deep bass voice, "Are you going to strike me dead, mage? The way you did Guillam."

The sardonic words seemed to fill the chamber.

Kharl looked steadily back at Deroh. He felt no guilt about what happened to the corrupt chief factor, and his eyes did not answer.

"Lord Deroh," said Ghrant, his voice thin by comparison, "you answer to me, not to my mages."

"Of course, your lordship." Deroh turned and bowed deeply, then took two more steps and bowed again.

Kharl understood exactly what Deroh had done. In a way, he had to respect the lord for making that statement, and in another way, it irritated Kharl, because it implied that Kharl was just a tool of execution. The mage repressed an ironic smile as he realized that irritation had also been planted by Deroh's question. Once more, Kharl had gotten a lesson in the halls of power.

"I am here at your request, your lordship." Deroh inclined his head after his words.

"Your presence was commanded because of your apparent support for the late and rebellious lords. Rather than begin with questions, I give you leave to explain, as I am most certain you will, Lord Deroh."

"My support, as you termed it, my lordship, was more apparent than real. I did not provide armsmen or lancers. Nor did I encourage any other lord to become disrespectful of your lordship or rebellious."

Kharl watched and listened. Only the last words bore a hint of untruth, but those preceding them had felt accurate to Kharl.

Hagen glanced sideways at Kharl.

The mage leaned forward and murmured, "He tells the truth. So far."

In turn, Hagen nodded ever so slightly to Lord Ghrant.

"Why did you grant such *apparent* support, Lord Deroh?"

"What choice did I have, your lordship? Malcor and Hensolas had armies at my door. Your forces were far removed from my lands. I dared not profess open loyalty, not after I saw what happened to Vertyn and Lahoryn."

"Would you have provided such apparent support if you had not been so coerced?"

"Why would any sensible lord do otherwise?" A touch of sardonicism edged the dark and lean lord's words.

"I do not believe you answered my question, Lord Deroh."

"No. Matters as they had been were much to be preferred over what those rebelling promised."

Again, Kharl could sense some equivocation, and he definitely had the impression that while Deroh probably had to have been coerced, it had not taken much pressure. Still . . . the lord was being fairly accurate as to how he had acted and felt.

"That is less than a ringing declaration of support for your lord." Ghrant's voice dripped acid.

"It is support, your lordship. I had great fondness for your sire, but I had not had the chance to come to know you."

"I did not notice you hurrying to Valmurl to pay your respects, Lord Deroh."

"No, your lordship. Before I could, I found Lord Malcor and Lord Hensolas on my doorstep."

That statement rang as true as anything Deroh had said, if not more so, and Kharl whispered that to Hagen.

"Yet you did not warn me?"

"Had I risked sending a message such as that, your lordship, I risked everything. They had four white wizards, and none knew then of the power of Lord Kharl."

"That is true. None did. A sad thing it is when the lords of a land must weigh power over duty. We shall make sure that none of you ever face that choice again."

Deroh paled slightly at Ghrant's words, but did not reply.

"We will consider your statements, Lord Deroh, and reflect upon them overnight. You will remain here as our guest until I offer my judgment in the morning."

Deroh bowed. "I await your judgment, your lordship."

"You may retire."

After Deroh had left the chamber, Lord Ghrant rose, without another word, and departed as well.

Kharl followed Hagen back to the lord-chancellor's study. Neither man spoke until after Kharl had closed the door, and they were seated across the table desk from each other.

"What is your feeling about the most honorable Lord Deroh?" Hagen's voice was dry.

"He cares little for Lord Ghrant, but he cared far less for Malcor and Hensolas. He was loyal, I would judge, only so long as it suited him."

"That could be said of many lords over the history of Austra, indeed, of any land." Hagen leaned back in his chair, just slightly, but his eyes never left Kharl. "What would you do?"

Kharl didn't want to answer directly. "All of those who joined the revolt are guilty to some degree. That includes those like Deroh who provided golds. He's less guilty, by far. I'm not a justicer or a ruler, but if you punish them all, what reason is there for anyone to support Lord Ghrant? Yet, if he ignores their guilt, he might appear either weak or stupid. Also, if he pardons them, some might say that shows weakness."

"After what you did to the white wizards and the four lords who spearheaded the revolt, some form of mercy might not be considered as weak as it might otherwise."

"Then he should pardon them, but require some golds to repay him for all the costs of the rebellion." Kharl offered a crooked smile. "After all, if they were willing to part with golds to those they did not support willingly, they should certainly be willing to help rebuild Austra and support the rightful ruler."

Hagen laughed. "For a former cooper, ser Kharl . . ."

"How *will* Lord Ghrant deal with Deroh, do you think?" Kharl paused. "Or should I ask what you will suggest as punishment?"

Hagen shrugged. "As you have said, most of them are guilty. I would suggest that Lord Ghrant find him guilty, technically, but pardon his actions because of the necessity facing him."

"What of the others he will see?"

"Much the same. I would hope that he finds them all guilty, then pardons all of them, save Azeolis."

"What of Azeolis? The last I heard, he was harassing Casolan."

"Casolan, once he heard of your victory, turned and crushed Azeolis's forces. He captured Azeolis and brought him to the Great House, trussed like a fowl."

"I thought Azeolis had pledged to Lord Ghrant?"

"He did so in haste as Casolan was bearing down upon him." Hagen laughed. "It is easy to do so when you fear worse."

"Does he have heirs?"

"He has two sons living, and a daughter. His consort died three years ago. I imagine Lord Ghrant will be merciful and allow them exile. The lands . . . Lord Ghrant will grant as he sees fit."

"Perhaps to Norgen or Casolan? Or split them between the two?"

"That might be too generous. The lands are extensive." Hagen frowned. "He should keep some for a time. His coffers are near empty. Perhaps an eighth part each to his faithful commanders."

"What if he suggested that he was holding that part only for a time? Perhaps appoint an honest custodian, but one not beholden to him. He could still take the golds until he bestowed the lands, and by giving some to Casolan and Norgen . . . ?"

"That might be best." Hagen nodded. "Lord Ghrant will reward you, as well."

"I have enough land, with Cantyl," Kharl replied.

"The forest to the south of Cantyl is now Lord Ghrant's. It was Ilteron's, and so seldom mentioned that I was not even aware that it had come to Lord Ghrant, and"—Hagen grinned momentarily—"I understand that there are a few squares where there are white oaks. Not enough for commercial timbering, but enough for a cooper. There is also a cherry orchard, which has been neglected."

"I leave that in your hands, ser. I have been well rewarded."

"A modest additional reward, and the gratitude of Lord Ghrant. That is not too much for the mage who saved a land for its ruler." Hagen's tone was firm. "A ruler must always be seen to be fair." He rose. "I am to meet Lord Ghrant. We will talk later."

After leaving Hagen, Kharl walked slowly toward the steps to the north tower. He needed time to think, in a place where he didn't feel walls all around him.

His steps were slow as he climbed to the top of the tower, then crossed to the eastern side, from where he could see all of Valmurl.

He had very mixed feelings about greater rewards. By the standards of what he had done, what Hagen had proposed was fair. Yet Kharl couldn't help feeling uneasy about it. He'd received what amounted to a fortune, albeit smaller than that of a greatholder, for destroying Ghrant's enemies. He'd accomplished that through the twisted application of order, uses which he doubted that true order-mages would have approved. When he had been a cooper, providing honest crafting for folk like himself, he'd needed to worry over every copper. If he had not had to worry so much, then perhaps Arthal . . .

He shook his head. More coppers would not have changed what had happened or what Arthal felt.

Now he needed to worry about coins little, provided he was even halfway careful, although he had done little constructive, and great destruction. He paused in thought. Yet . . . was not preserving a land from rebellion and chaos constructive?

He shook his head. It had been the lesser of two evils, and he disliked having been put in that position. But was that what having power meant? In a way, he envied Lyras, with his berry bushes. Yet . . . the white wizards would have killed Lyras had Kharl not come to Austra and done as he did.

Kharl looked out over Valmurl, the afternoon sun on his back.

XXXIV

The next two days were filled with audiences. Standing beside Hagen, Kharl watched, and occasionally made quiet observations to the lord-chancellor as Lord Ghrant heard the pleas of those lords who had not been so loyal as they might have been. The one guilty lord who did not appear before Lord Ghrant—and Kharl and Hagen—was Azeolis.

Several glasses after the last audience on sevenday, Kharl and Hagen were sharing a small evening meal in the lord-chancellor's study. Kharl's thoughts went back to the last audience, the one for a Lord Benin, a round-faced man who had seemed more ineffectual than lordly to Kharl. As he had with the others, Ghrant had found Benin guilty of not fully supporting his Lord, had pardoned Benin, and like the others, required a slightly higher annual tariff from the lord for the next five years.

"How much longer will he hold audiences?" Kharl asked, after taking a sip of the lager he preferred over wine—at least the wine he had tasted at the Great House. "There can't be many lords left, guilty ones who are still alive, anyway."

"There's only Azeolis," Hagen said. "His audience will be the very last. For the first days on the coming eightday, Ghrant will be seeing the loyal lords—and the regents for those who were killed by the rebels for being loyal. He will praise them and honor them." Hagen's voice turned sardonic. "He will try not to have to honor them excessively, or with more golds or lands than he plans to take from the estates of the rebel lords."

"Am I to be there?"

Hagen laughed. "How could you not be there? The most powerful mage in the history of Austra? That is part of the performance. You will not have to say anything, unless you discover something that is highly untoward, but part of the reason for the audiences is to remind each lord of what happened to the rebels."

Kharl could see the need for that—unfortunately. "What about Azeolis?" He had an idea, but he was still learning about the politics of governing, and he felt more comfortable having Hagen explain than trying to guess.

"There will be one long audience to deal with the dead rebel lords, and their heirs—and with Azeolis. Lord Ghrant wants the most unpleasant aspects handled at one time."

"Will he take all their lands?"

Hagen paused to take a mouthful of the duck confit before replying. "He has already let that be known, if quietly."

"So that the heirs will leave Austra? Isn't he afraid that they'll plunder their estates to raise golds?"

"There are guards at all the rebel estates. If the heirs slip away . . . so long as the estates remain intact . . ." Hagen shrugged. "Most of the value is in the lands and the livestock and equipment."

"He'd prefer that they leave, rather than being exiled?"

"They will be exiled, and if they try to remain, they face a lifetime in gaol."

Kharl found that he had little sympathy for the rebel lords, or for their heirs. They had all held great wealth and lands, and the heirs had enjoyed that wealth as well. Lord Ghrant, while not the most prepossessing of men, had certainly not acted cruelly or wantonly, not from what anyone had said. Nor had Kharl found chaos or evil within the young ruler. He did worry that Ghrant was not so strong as a ruler should be; but after having suffered under the cruel strength of Lord West and his son Egen in Brysta, Kharl was willing to deal with a ruler who did not rely solely on the iron fist or the whip.

At that thought, his lips curled slightly. He had provided that sort of force, if only against the rebels and the Hamorians. Force had its necessary place, but it was a question of balance. He almost laughed. For a man who had never thought about balance, he had come to consider its place in everything in recent eightdays.

"You find the exile amusing?" asked Hagen.

"No, ser. I was thinking about force, and how it must be balanced. I was also wondering why men with so much wealth and such great lands would revolt against a ruler who had done nothing to them."

"He seemed to show weakness. Weakness—or the appearance of weakness—is an invitation to some. That is why Azeolis's audience will be the last."

Kharl sensed the darkness behind Hagen's words. "He'll be made an example, then."

"Yes. It will be ugly—and unhappily necessary." After a pause, the lord-chancellor asked, "How do you like the duck?"

"Very much. I've never had it before, not like this."

"I persuaded the cooks to try an old family recipe."

"It's good." The mage could tell that Hagen was not pleased with the idea of making Azeolis into an example, and yet that the lord-chancellor was convinced that it was necessary. Or was it that Hagen was disturbed that such an example was required?

He hesitated to ask the next question, knowing the answer already. Still . . . "You haven't any word from the *Seastag*?"

"No. We won't unless they port in Lydiar at the same time as the *Seasprite*. You worry about the boy, I know, but . . ."

Kharl nodded. Warrl should be safe with his aunt and uncle, but Kharl would have felt much better to have his son at Cantyl. Yet there was no way he could travel to Nordla, not at the moment.

He glanced down at the remaining portion of the duck on the green-bordered white bone china. Finally, he took another sip of the lager, then slowly cut a thin slice of the duck.

XXXV

On sixday, Kharl stood in the audience hall beside Hagen, half a pace back, as he looked out at the group gathered together on the right side of the audience hall. Stationed around them were a squad of armsmen in the yellow and black of the personal guard. Roughly half of those standing in custody were women of all ages; the remainder were children. They were the heirs, consorts, and offspring of the rebel lords, standing and waiting for the judgments to come. Less than a half score were men, and they were all young, not much older than Arthal would have been. At the thought of Arthal, a wave of sadness swept across Kharl.

"His Lordship, Ghrant of Dykaru, Lord of Austra and Scion of the North."

In silence, Ghrant entered the hall from the rear door across from the one through which Kharl had followed Hagen. Once more, the Lord of Austra was attired in black, trimmed in dark green. He took his seat in the ancient high-backed chair on the dais without a word, then nodded to the chamberlain, who stood to his right.

"Summon the traitor Azeolis," announced the chamberlain.

The hall remained hushed, even after the doors opened, and two burly armsmen in the yellow and black of Ghrant's personal guard marched in a stocky figure dressed in nearly shapeless gray trousers and undertunic. Azeolis's hands were manacled behind him. A wide and thick band of cloth was tied across his lower face, effectively gagging him.

Before the doors closed, Kharl caught a glimpse of a full squad of the personal guard stationed outside the audience hall.

"Azeolis, former lord and traitor," announced the chamberlain once the captive had reached a spot a cubit or so short of the foot of the dais.

Azeolis looked directly at Ghrant.

The young ruler stood and began to speak, his own eyes fixed, not on Azeolis, but on the group to the right and behind Azeolis. "Azeolis—you who were once a lord, privileged and exalted above others—you were not satisfied with wealth and power. You lacked the courage to be loyal and the wisdom to ignore the vain promises of others. Have you anything to say for yourself?"

Kharl noted that Hagen nodded, as if to himself.

Ghrant motioned to the armsmen.

The taller deftly unknotted the heavy gag.

Azeolis cleared his throat, but did not speak.

In turn, Ghrant waited.

Silence weighed upon the entire chamber before Azeolis finally spoke. "I was loyal—once. Before a weakling became Lord of Austra." The still-stocky man did not bother to disguise the contempt in his voice. "Even now, you do not rule. Your power lies in the judgment of a merchant with a title and a mage from another land."

"That may well be," Ghrant replied. "It shows that I have better judgment about who serves me well than you did. I have chosen loyalty and talent over privilege and position."

Kharl caught several looks of surprise on the faces of those in the audience hall.

For a moment, even Azeolis was silent. That did not last. "You admit you have debased your heritage—"

"Silence him." Ghrant's voice was not hard, but almost tired, the voice of a man who recognized that Azeolis would not hear what was said.

"Yes . . . silence me." Azeolis got no further before one of warders wrapped a heavy gag across his mouth and lower face.

"I silence you because you have already spoken," Ghrant went on calmly. "You spoke when you joined a revolt that began with the despicable murder of my sire. You spoke when you supported the pretender who wanted to usurp this seat so that he could rule with fire and fear. You spoke when you joined with those who murdered loyal lords and their families. You spoke when you tried to ambush loyal lancers. It is said that actions speak louder than words. Your actions have indeed spoken for you. And for those actions you will pay. You cannot live long enough to suffer as did all those for whom you caused suffering, but you will suffer. You will be flogged like the common criminal you have become. Then you will have all the limbs in your body broken, and then you will be beheaded. Even that is too merciful for someone who has betrayed his heritage and his family. Your estates will be divided. Half will return to the Great House, and half will be broken into holdings. Many of those lands will be distributed to those who worked them, for they should not suffer for your treachery. All the heirs of your body and all those consorted to them and all issue are hereby banned from Austra. Their lives or their freedom, or both, are forfeit should they be found within Austra at the end of the next eightday." Ghrant gestured. "Take him away. Let his sentence begin within the glass, and let it be carried out before sunset."

Once more, Hagen nodded.

Raw hatred blazed from the gagged former lord—hatred so intense that to Kharl it resembled chaos. Was hatred the chaos of thought—corrosive and destructive, yet with a power to move men to great deeds of devastation? If so, what was the order of thought? Anticipation and thoughtful planning? Or merely good judgment? Kharl wasn't certain that he knew.

Ghrant did not seat himself, but waited until Azeolis had been marched out and the doors closed behind the last of the rebel lords. Then he surveyed those remaining, his eyes seeming to move from one face to another, letting the silence drag out.

In time, he spoke once more, slowly, carefully, with pauses at the end of each sentence. "Your consorts and sires were disloyal. They were disloyal not because I had inflicted harm upon them. Not because I had imposed excessive tariffs. Not because I had abused my position and seized daughters for my pleasure. Not for any reason except that I was considered young and because they sought greater wealth and power. For that, they have paid. For that, all of you will also pay. A mad boar begets other madness, both in the sows and the boars that come from him. Such madness is not acceptable in Austra."

Again, the young lord let silence fill the chamber before he continued, repeating his last words before going on. "Such madness is not acceptable in Austra. It will never be acceptable. All of you, save those from the household of the traitor Azeolis, have two eightdays from oneday to leave Austra. You may take with you only what you can carry in one bag. You may not sell lands or equipment, nor may you take more than a hundred golds with you. All the lands that your consorts and lords held have reverted to the Great House." Ghrant stopped and surveyed the group once again.

No one cried. Several swallowed. The children glanced from their parents to Ghrant and back again.

"That is all. You may go and prepare for your exile." Ghrant nodded to the armsmen, then turned his back on the group, as if in another form of dismissal, and walked from the dais.

Slowly, silently, the group shuffled out of the audience hall.

Kharl had to admit to himself that he had been impressed by the young Lord Ghrant, and by the clarity with which he had expressed himself; but it was also clear that those words had not been crafted by Lord Ghrant, or not just by the young ruler. Hagen's nods had indicated that the audience had been as planned as a minstrel's song—or even a cooper's barrel.

But, Kharl reflected, that was not necessarily bad. When words affected people, should they not also be considered and crafted?

"Kharl?" murmured Hagen.

The mage started, then turned, realizing that he had to precede the lord-chancellor from the audience chamber.

XXXVI

After the last audience, Kharl retired to his quarters in the Great House. There he wrestled with all that had happened in the eightdays since he had come to Austra, with all that he had done. Just before sunset, the bell tolled to mark Azeolis's death.

Kharl left his sitting room, quietly, and made his way to the top of the north tower. First, he watched the sunset, a sunset without brilliantly lit clouds. For a time, he looked to the hills to the north and west. Then he crossed the tower and studied Valmurl, with the evening breeze at his back, as the city darkened and the first lamps were lit. He had skipped the evening meal, neither feeling hungry nor wanting to talk to anyone.

The rebellion was over, the rebellion that his thoughtless words had sparked. The clenching of his stomach and the uneasiness of his thoughts forced him to correct his thoughts—the rebellion that his thoughtless words had helped spark far earlier than might otherwise have occurred.

There had been so many dead. So many. Nearly half of Ghrant's regular Austran lancers and armsmen had perished, one way or another. A third of the personal guard had been killed or wounded, many disabled for life. Kharl had long since lost count of the lords and their heirs who had been killed by one side or the other—and all too many had died from his own efforts. Ilteron, Malcor, Kenslan, Fergyn, Hensolas—and that didn't count the loyal lords such as Lahoryn and Vertyn and their sons and daughters, killed by the rebels.

And all of it sparked over truth? Because Kharl had revealed that he could tell when they lied? Did those in power fear so greatly their deceptions being made known? Did being a lord or ruling require that much deception? Was justice a charade?

He laughed softly, bitterly. It certainly had been in Brysta. But did it have to be? Could justice not be administered, if not impartially, at least with greater understanding and fairness?

His eyes surveyed Valmurl once more. Did it seem strangely quiet, or was he just imagining what he felt it should be?

So many questions . . . so few answers.

He turned as he sensed someone else stepping out onto the open tower top—Hagen.

"I thought I might find you here," offered the lord-chancellor. "The servers said that you had not eaten, but no one had seen you leave the Great House, not that they would, were you minded to leave without being seen."

"I've been thinking."

"That can be very dangerous." Hagen's words were without a trace of humor, sarcasm, or mockery.

"I had not realized how dangerous truth can be."

"Ah, yes. We all tell our children to tell the truth, even as we conceal it ourselves. Yet none can bear to admit that too much truth is as dangerous as too little."

Kharl frowned.

"Does it do well to tell your consort that she is tired-looking or aging? Does truth serve there, my friend? Do you tell a child that his first effort at . . . whatever it may be . . . is totally without merit? Does it serve to tell a people that many of them are self-centered and lazy? Yet, at times, such is indeed the truth."

Even truth was subject to the Balance, it seemed, Kharl reflected. He took a slow breath before speaking again. "You told Ghrant what words to say at the audience, didn't you?"

"Yes. What he said was important. He's not experienced enough to know what to say, but he is bright enough to understand that he needed the right words. We worked on them together." Hagen paused. "You don't seem surprised."

"Should I be?"

"No. You would have been surprised a year ago, but you are not the same man today as you were then." The lord-chancellor laughed, softly. "Neither am I."

"I was thinking that I should return to Cantyl before long."

"You should, but not until Lord Ghrant summons you. That is likely to be tomorrow, but at the moment, I cannot press him."

"Did today . . . ?"

"Like all young men of privilege, he is of two minds. Part of him is still furious at the effrontery of the rebels, and part of him is grateful to have survived and retained his hold on Austra. I am hoping that he will be the wiser for what he has been through."

Kharl could sense Hagen's doubts and concerns. "If he is not?"

"Nothing will happen for years, possibly not until after his death."

"Or yours," Kharl suggested.

"That is possible," Hagen admitted blandly, if honestly. "Unless I can find and train a successor. That will be difficult."

"I can see that. Most would only see the power, and not the duty."

"There are some who understand the duty, but they have not the power to rein in a lord, and most who have some power either would not take my position, or they would abuse it, as you have said." Hagen smiled. "But . . . there will be time to talk of such for years to come. I had hoped you would join me for a late supper, and if you are not hungry, at least to keep me company."

Kharl smiled in return. "I might have some supper, at that."

XXXVII

Lord Ghrant did not summon Kharl until twoday afternoon.

In the meantime, Kharl had taken the time to work out an arrangement with Hagen that, the next time one of Hagen's ships ported in Brysta, he would pay for someone to travel to Merayni's and Dowsyl's with a message for Warrl—and passage to Valmurl, or if possible, to Cantyl itself. He still had no word on whether his earlier message had reached Peachill.

"You realize that my man can't force the boy?" Hagen said.

"I know, but if his aunt knows I have lands here . . ."

"They may not agree."

Kharl had taken a deep breath. "I know, but I have to try."

"We'll do what we can," Hagen had replied.

Kharl could only hope that it would suffice.

After taking care of that detail, all he could do was study *The Basis of Order* and wait for the meeting with Lord Ghrant. When he was summoned, he was surprised to find that their meeting was not in the audience hall, but in Ghrant's private study, a room that was far larger than the sitting rooms of some mansions, Kharl realized as he glanced around a chamber measuring a good thirty cubits in length and twenty in width. Dark wood paneling covered the walls, except for the ceiling-to-floor bookshelves on the long inside wall, shelves of the same dark wood as the paneling. The outside long wall was mainly of windows, separated by stretches of bookshelves, also floor to ceiling.

Ghrant was seated at an ornate desk of black oak and lorken. The pedestal legs were ornately carved with figures that Kharl did not recognize. Kharl sat in a wooden armchair upholstered in dark green, directly across the desk from Ghrant. None of the lamps in the study had been lit, despite the heavy gray clouds and the sullen drizzling rain that had fallen most of the day. Ghrant's face was in shadow as he looked at Kharl, although the mage could see the lord clearly enough.

"Ser Kharl . . . all of Austra should be most grateful to you. Most will not be, but I am a grateful ruler." A faint smile crossed the younger man's face.

"I did what I thought was best, ser."

"That is to your credit, and to our benefit." The slender lord coughed once, then cleared his throat. "The lord-chancellor has conveyed your concerns. Those concerns also speak well of you. Still . . . I must honor you, if only for my own sake, foremost as an upper lord, and with tangible reward as well." Ghrant forced a laugh. "I cannot allow it to be said that I was a lord who did not reward the mage who saved his land."

Kharl nodded, knowing from whom those words had come.

"Your actions in defense of Austra were greater magery than has been seen in generations, and even I know that such magery risked your life—and more. Your skill and courage kept Austra from falling under the mailed fist of Hamor. While I respect your modesty and prudence, I must reward you. You have expressed fondness for forests. I inherited a great woods from my late brother. I have had little time to treat it as it should have been. In fact, until recently, I was not even aware that it had come to me. Since it adjoins Cantyl, and I have no other holdings nearby, it would seem to be a perfect match for me to transfer that woodland to you."

"Your lordship is most generous. Most generous."

"I'm not generous at all, Lord Kharl. But these are hard times for Austra, as you have recognized, and I am happy to be able to reward you in a manner that is good for us both. Your modesty and forbearance are also received with great gratitude. For those, not only will you receive my thanks, but also a purse of five hundred golds to help you and your retainers in taking over and managing the forest. Lord Hagen will provide that to you." Ghrant smiled. "And I will listen most favorably to any reasonable request you put forth, either now or in the future."

"Thank you, your lordship." Kharl inclined his head.

"What had you thought to do, now?"

"I had thought to return to Cantyl, your lordship. I had scarcely time to learn of the lands, before . . . this."

Ghrant laughed, more warmly than before. "That is true. You have been so great a help that it is hard to remember that you are not from Austra. But your loyalty is far greater than that of many whose families have lived and prospered here for many generations."

"I have seen justice abused, your lordship. I saw wrongs committed because a lord had greater power than others. I could do nothing about it in Nordla. I would not see that happen here in Austra. You should have the right to rule justly."

Ghrant smiled—faintly, once more. "Between you and my lord-chancellor, I doubt that I will have much choice but to rule justly. I am fortunate that your support has allowed me that ability."

Kharl realized that Ghrant had read more into Kharl's words than the mage had meant. "I fear you misunderstood, your lordship. I had only meant to say that your heart told you to rule justly, but that others would have preferred an unjust rule so that they could gain from it."

Ghrant's smile widened slightly. "You speak as you believe, ser Kharl, and that is rare indeed in dealing with rulers."

"That is also dangerous, ser, and as I have learned, not always to your benefit."

"You have learned, and that is more than most in these days." Ghrant nodded and rose.

Kharl quickly stood, bowing slightly.

"I wish you well on your return to Cantyl. I trust that will enjoy your lands without interruption and hope that I will not soon need to call upon your talents."

"Begging your pardon, ser, I hope the same. I wish you and your family a warm spring and a pleasant summer, and I thank you for all that you have provided for me."

Kharl could feel the lord's eyes on his back as he left the study, but he did not sense either anger or chaos.

Scholar of Justice

XXXVIII

Summer had finally come, and even right after an early breakfast, the day was warm as Kharl stood just inside the east end of the cooperage. For a time, he surveyed the work benches, the fire pots, and the tool racks. After more than an eightday's worth of hard work on the interior, everything—including the white and red oak he had ordered a season earlier—was finally ready for him to work on his barrels. He'd even replaced the doors. At least the heavy flagstone flooring had been laid and waiting for him when he had returned from Valmurl. Dorwan and Bannat had done a good workmanlike job, and Kharl had paid them a handsome bonus immediately after his return to Cantyl.

"Ser . . . we were just doing . . ." Dorwan had protested.

"You did it well, and I appreciate good work. I especially appreciate it when I'm not here."

"Be thanking you, ser. Kariana will be most pleased. She's been thinking about a chest and a bed for Bannat. He'll be consorted to Fiana come fall."

"Fiana? I don't recall . . ." Kharl was well aware that he knew less than he should about his tenants and retainers. Then, he hadn't exactly been at Cantyl that much.

"Ah . . . you wouldn't, ser. She's Chyhat's daughter."

"The forester on the new forest?" asked Kharl. Those were the words Dorwan had taken to using when referring to the forestland that Kharl had received from Lord Ghrant. Kharl had only met with Chyhat twice, an older man, slim and wiry, unlike the burly Dorwan, who stood even a span taller than Kharl, and few men reached the mage's height and breadth.

"Yes, ser."

"How are you two getting on?" Kharl had insisted that each forester retain control over the forests that they had always supervised, but that they meet and work out how much timber should be harvested as a total each year.

"Same as we always did." Dorwan laughed. "We think the same about which trees should be cut, and where lands ought to be thinned, and we don't talk about much else except our bairns. Better that way."

Kharl smiled at the recollection of Dorwan's words. He'd been fortunate. Speltar was a good steward, and he'd kept the good people. Probably the wisest thing Lord Estloch had done had been to leave Cantyl alone under Speltar's care.

The last of the basic tools Kharl had ordered from Valmurl had arrived at Cantyl long before he had been able to return to there. While the forge was adequate, he'd need to do more over the next season or so. Still, he'd been able to forge some of his cooper's tools, and he had two adzes, a chiv, three hollowing knives, and his planer. The shaver had been the hardest because of the thinness required, and he would have to forge his own hoops from scratch, rather than just trimming and riveting the iron strips he'd bought at his cooperage in Brysta. Still, he'd made three red oak barrels for slack uses, as much to renew his skills as for use at Cantyl. But he hadn't wanted to start with tight cooperage, not given the time since he had last worked on barrels.

Given what it had cost to equip his new cooperage, he doubted that it would pay for itself for several years, but he had wanted to do something productive and not just live off the fruits of the land. According to Chyhat, there was indeed a small stand of white oak on the western edge of the new forest, with enough trees to supply billets for cooperage and cabinetry, but not enough for consistent timber sales. That was fine with Kharl.

"Ser?" Speltar stood at the door to the cooperage.

"Yes, Speltar?"

"I should have the figures for the improvements this afternoon, ser."

"Improving the sawmill here, and adding the cots? And the roads? Chyhat agreed with you and Dorwan?"

"Yes, ser. He'd asked Lord Ilteron for golds to improve the old mill there for years. Said it was too dangerous."

"What about closing it?"

"He said that was fine, just so the millmen kept their places." Speltar grinned. "When I told him about the new cots, he asked if we'd consider tossing in a few golds so he could add a room and fix his roof. I said I would ask you."

"He seems honest. I'd think so, unless you have a reason not to grant his request."

"I'd grant his request, ser, and add a gold for furnishings."

"Then do so." Kharl paused. "What about you? Have you ever received a bonus for all your work?"

"I have the house, ser, and it's far grander than what most stewards ever see."

"That may be, but when I compare what the new forest shows and what Cantyl shows . . ."

"I have been fortunate, ser."

Kharl snorted. "Do you find a ten-gold bonus fair?"

Speltar swallowed, his Adam's apple bobbing in his thin throat.

"Let's make it fifteen."

Speltar bowed. "Thank you. I have never . . . you are most generous."

Kharl could sense the truth of his words. "I cannot be so generous with all, but as part of your duties, I would request that you recommend a small bonus for those on the lands who deserve it. We would pay it after harvest."

"Lord Koroh did so, but that was before my time."

"Do you think it is a bad idea?"

"No, ser. The lands were most productive under Lord Koroh."

"Or his steward," Kharl suggested dryly. "Was the steward from your family?"

"No, ser. Lord Estloch brought me here fifteen years ago. I was the assistant to the steward at Dykaru."

"How did Lord Estloch end up with the lands? I'd heard that Lord Julon . . ." Kharl left the sentence unfinished.

"Lord Julon spent far too many golds on his horses, and upon pleasures in Valmurl. He owed over a thousand golds, it was said, and none of the lenders in Valmurl would advance him more golds. Then, when he was murdered, his lands reverted to Lord Estloch because his consort and heirs could not pay off the debts. Lord Estloch settled the debts and set me here." Speltar shrugged, as if his words explained everything.

"What happened to his consort?"

"She was most beautiful, and she became the second consort of Lord Malcor." Speltar smiled sadly. "She died ten years later, of a mysterious illness, and he consorted a third time. She had but two daughters by Lord Julon, and no children by Lord Malcor."

Was everyone in Austra tied to everything, or was that just the way of the noble families everywhere? Kharl suspected the latter.

Speltar cleared his throat. "If you don't need anything else, ser . . ."

"Go do what you need to, Speltar." Kharl grinned. "You know where to find me."

The steward bowed slightly. "Yes, ser."

After Speltar had left, Kharl went to the racks on the left at the rear of his new cooperage, somewhat smaller than the space he had had in Brysta but more than adequate for his present needs.

After several moments, he pulled down enough white oak billets for several standard barrels. He'd try tight cooperage, this time. He was smiling as he set the billets on the bench next to the planer.

XXXIX

Kharl had just finished trimming the chime on a white oak barrel and was blotting his forehead when he noticed Speltar standing in the doorway to the cooperage, nervously shifting his weight from one foot to the other.

"Lord Kharl?"

"Come in, Speltar. It's a cooperage, not a bedchamber or a study. When I'm working here, just come inside. I may have to finish something, but there's no reason for you to stand outside."

As he stepped into the cooperage, Speltar lifted a square of heavy paper with a florid purple wax seal on one edge. "I have a missive from ser Arynal. His man is waiting for a response."

A response? "What do you know of Arynal?" Kharl had run across the name, but he didn't know where. He was fairly sure that Arynal had not been among the collaborators with the rebels, but he couldn't recall why he would have known a lord's name.

"He holds the lands to the north and west of yours, ser . . ."

That was where Kharl had seen the name, on the maps that Speltar had gone over with him almost a season earlier.

". . . He is a minor lord, most properly."

"Like me?"

"Ah . . . ser. If I read the proclamation correctly, you are a lord of the upper level."

"Proclamation?" Kharl hadn't even realized that there was such.

"Oh, yes, ser. I thought you knew. A lord or a grant must be proclaimed. I thought you had sent the proclamations to me. I have both the proclamation of your title as a lower lord—that was when you received Cantyl—and the one at the end of spring when you were elevated to an upper lord and received the new forest."

"Hmmm . . ." Kharl recalled Lord Ghrant saying something about an upper lord, but he had paid more attention to the grant of the lands. Then, abruptly, he recalled Ghrant and several others addressing him as Lord Kharl. He'd passed that off as a compliment, but he should have known that Ghrant would not have addressed him as such through courtesy. Again . . . it showed what he didn't know and the subtleties of lordship. The deliberate use of the term *lord* by Lord Ghrant would have been so obvious to any lord, lower or upper, and Kharl hadn't even noticed what it had meant. "What's the advantage of being an upper lord? Is there one?"

"Well . . . ser . . . if you do something wrong, like murder, they have to behead you, rather than hang you." A faint smile crossed the steward's face.

Kharl laughed. "Is that all?"

"You have the right to administer low justice on your lands."

"For minor things, like theft?"

"If the theft is less than ten golds."

That wasn't such a small amount, Kharl reflected.

"And you have to supply services or armsmen to the Lord of Austra." Speltar's smile turned wry. "At times, in the past, the Lord of Austra has elevated lords to the upper level only to require armsmen that the lord could not support."

Kharl could see someone like Lord West doing that.

"In your case, that would not be a problem, I would judge," Speltar added.

"Not any more of a problem than it already is." Kharl gestured toward the missive. "I suppose I should read the letter."

The steward extended it.

Kharl took it and broke the seal, carefully. He didn't want purple wax on his new flag floor. The note within was short, if written in an elegant hand that was not Arynal's, since the signature differed from the text.

> Lord Kharl,
> With the deepest respect, and begging your indulgence, I would like to call upon you late this afternoon to pay my respects to you.

> I have not wished to impose upon you, but as your nearest neighbor thought that I should present myself and offer what information you might find useful.

Kharl looked up. "Does he expect supper?"

"That, or afternoon refreshments, would be in order."

"Am I expected to invite his family?"

"His consort would be acceptable." Speltar smiled.

"What you are telling me is that I should invite everyone. How many?"

"He has two consortable daughters, and a son who has already been consorted."

Kharl took a deep breath. "Can Adelya handle that?"

"She would be upset, ser, if you thought otherwise."

"Would you write a response that says that I would be happy to have them all for supper this evening? And tell Adelya to prepare as she sees fit." Kharl shook his head. He could sense Speltar's concealed laughter at the resignation in Kharl's voice.

"She will be pleased that you've chosen to entertain, ser."

"And you?"

"It is always beneficial to be on good terms with neighbors."

Speltar's words, once more, were dry.

"Are you telling me that Lord Julon was not always on the best of terms?"

"I would not know, not for certain, ser. There are stories, but one never can tell how true they might be, and I would not be the one to pass them on."

Kharl laughed. "I have my answer. You are most astute, and most tactful, Speltar."

Speltar did grin, if but for the briefest of moments. "And you, Lord Kharl, see more than most lords."

To Kharl that was a frightening thought, because Speltar meant it. Kharl knew how much he missed. He'd even missed his own elevation. Part of that was because of his unfamiliarity with Austra, and part was because he hadn't paid enough attention. "I fear for them, then." He glanced around the cooperage, then toward the open doorway where the midmorning sun cast an oblong of light across the stone floor. "If you would write what is necessary and bring me a pen? Your writing will be far better than mine."

"I can do that." Speltar nodded slightly, then stepped away.

Kharl wanted to shake his head. He supposed he was fortunate to have few neighbors, or his lack of understanding of both lordly and Austran customs would have become much more apparent far earlier. He glanced around the cooperage. He could still get in most of a day's work before bathing and changing into his magely finery, although he doubted it was as fine as whatever ser Arynal and his family might be wearing.

Then, he cautioned himself, Arynal and his consort might well be people he'd like. Certainly, Kharl had liked Hagen from the beginning. He'd just have to see about Arynal.

XL

Two glasses before sunset, roughly, and barely after Kharl had bathed and finished dressing, young Bannat had run up to the main house to announce that ser Arynal's coach was less than a kay away.

Kharl hurried from his study back to the kitchen. "They're about a kay away, Adelya."

"I know, Lord Kharl. Bannat told Heldya. You just greet your guests, and we will have everything in readiness, ser."

Kharl couldn't help but grin. "That's all you've left for me to do."

"That is as it should be."

In the corner, Heldya, barely eleven and dressed in gray trousers and tunic, nodded solemnly, not looking up from the crystal wine goblets she was polishing a last time.

Kharl shook his head, ruefully, then left the kitchen and walked through the sitting room and past the serving table laid out with refreshments for the time before supper. From there he made his way out through the foyer and onto the wide porch, from where he could look at both the harbor and the narrow road that wound to the south of the barns before turning westward and past the mill, then crossing the stream and eventually joining the inner coast road to Valmurl.

The dust of the coach was visible before the four-horse team itself appeared coming down the gentle slope to the millrace bridge. As the coach neared the main house, Kharl walked out the flagstone walk from the front porch, then waited as the driver pulled up where the walk ended at the lane. The coach was older, painted in light and dark gray, bearing more than a few scrapes and worn places on the bodywork. The grizzled coachman wore a faded burgundy jacket and brown trousers. His boots were scuffed.

An older man, with black hair greased back from the temples of his thin face, opened the coach door and stepped out, pulling the mounting stool from its bracket and setting it beneath the door. Then he straightened, smoothed his burgundy velvet jacket, and looked at Kharl. "You must be Lord Kharl, from all that black. I'm Arynal."

"I'm Kharl. Welcome to Cantyl."

"I'd forgotten how long the drive was. Two solid glasses." Arynal turned and extended a hand to a long-faced but stout woman with striking gray-and-black hair. "My consort, Jacelyna. This is Lord Kharl, my dear."

"You met us, yourself, Lord Kharl," replied Jacelyna, in a thin and high voice. "How charming."

"Who else would meet guests?"

"A doorman or a retainer," suggested Jacelyna.

"I have very few retainers, Lady," replied Kharl.

"Lord Kharl has had these lands for but half a year, dear," interjected Arynal, "and he has spent most of that time serving with Lord Ghrant." The thin-faced lord turned to the younger women who had left the coach. "My daughters Norelle and Meyena. Norelle is the elder, but only by two years."

Slightly stocky, buxom, with shoulder-length jet-black hair, strong features, and a long face, Norelle clearly took after her mother. Meyena was slighter in build, with long brown hair set in ringlets. All three women wore ankle-length dresses in various shades of green, a color that suited Meyena, but not her sister or her mother.

Both sisters inclined their heads to Kharl, almost together.

Bannat reappeared. "I'll be taking care of the coach and driver, ser. Adelya will have some fare for him, and we've grain in the guest barn."

"Thank you." Kharl hadn't even thought about that, another aspect of being a lord with which he had little familiarity. He nodded to Bannat and turned to Arynal. "There are refreshments in the sitting room . . . before dinner." He motioned to the three women. "Up the walk and across the porch."

". . . always called it a portico," murmured Norelle.

Kharl ignored the comment and turned back to Arynal, letting the women walk in front of them.

"I always thought mages were little fellows," offered Arynal, his eyes measuring Kharl.

"Some are, and some aren't. That's like lords. Some are large, and some aren't," replied Kharl.

Lady Jacelyna giggled, a high-pitched sound that grated on Kharl's ears. She turned her head, and said, "He has you on that, dearest."

The higher heels of the ladies' boots clicked on the stone tile of the porch. Only the youngest, Meyena, turned before entering the house. She stepped aside and looked out across the harbor. "The view is quite lovely, Lord Kharl."

The late-afternoon sun had turned the harbor water, smooth because there was no wind, into a silvered expanse that seemed to meld into the trees on the north shore.

"It is, and there are times when I have stood here and watched for almost a glass." Kharl offered a polite smile, waiting for her to enter the foyer that opened onto the sitting room to the right. On the left was the study, where, out of prudence, he'd tucked the ledgers into the larger drawer on the right side of the desk.

Adelya's daughter Heldya was standing behind the serving table in the sitting room as the five entered. She did not speak.

"This is most elegant, if spare," remarked Jacelyna. "It reflects a man's taste."

More than anything, Kharl reflected, the house showed the absence of anyone living in it for any length of time, but he merely nodded.

After Heldya handed a delicate goblet filled with the amber Rhynn wine from the estate to Jacelyna, the lady took a sip, then said, "This is quite good."

"Thank you. Glyan is an outstanding vintner, and I'm fortunate in that. He claims that the Rhynn is as good as that anywhere." Kharl stood back as Heldya offered goblets to Arynal and his daughters as well.

"Arynal had said that you have been serving Lord Ghrant most of the time since you gained Cantyl," Jacelyna continued.

Kharl noted that the lady had only made a statement, but decided to answer the question that had not been asked. "I did what was necessary."

"Emelor—he's Lord Vertyn's son," Arynal said, "and I guess that makes him lord now, or will once Lord Ghrant proclaims it—he was saying that you took on something like five white wizards."

Kharl thought for a moment, then nodded. "I was fortunate."

Arynal laughed, and his wine almost slopped out of the crystal goblet. "Most times, white wizards turn black mages into charcoal. Been years since a black took on so many whites and won. Leastwise, that's what Emelor said. Is that so, Lord Kharl?"

"That's something I wouldn't know. There haven't been many fights between wizards and mages in the last few years. I don't know of any."

"Hmmm . . ." mused the older lord. "Might be true at that. Not since the fall of Fairven, anyway." He laughed again. "Still . . . it's good to know that our Lord of Austra has a mage of power. It can't hurt to have you here, either, not that we've seen brigands in more than a score of years."

"You came from Nordla, did you not?" asked Jacelyna, before her consort could say more.

"Brysta," Kharl replied. "It's very different. Lord West is not the fairest of lords. Lord Ghrant, for all his youth, seems to me to be a far better ruler." He really didn't want to discuss his past, not with people he'd never met.

"Is it true," asked Norelle, "that you were once in . . . trade?"

Kharl offered a laugh. "That's fair to say. I once had a cooperage in Brysta. It was the best in the city—until I rescued a young woman who'd been attacked by Lord West's son." He shrugged. "I had to leave Brysta, then." Actually, he'd rescued three young women, if one counted Jeka as well as Sanyle and Jenevra. He couldn't forget Jeka, or her fierce green eyes.

Meyena's eyes widened. Norelle appeared unbelieving, and while Kharl was not attracted to either young woman, he was rapidly developing a dislike for Norelle, little as she had said.

"You were exiled?"

"No. I might as well have been. My consort died, and Lord West took my cooperage. My eldest went to sea, and my younger boy went to live with his aunt. It was time for me to leave."

"You were an officer on one of the lord-chancellor's ships, I understand," Arynal said smoothly, after a sharp look at Norelle.

"I was. After I joined the *Seastag*, I began to learn about being a mage."

"You didn't know before?" Meyena's voice was gentle, and not critical.

Kharl offered her a smile. "No. I was later told by other mages that I had always had the talent, but I had not known I had it." After a pause, he looked to Arynal. "I must confess that I know little about your lands. Could you tell me a bit?"

Arynal finished a sip of the wine. "Good stuff." He moistened his lips. "Well . . . you've got mostly hills and timberlands here, except for the valley and the vineyards. We're west of your hills, and it's mostly rolling meadows. Sheep, that's what fits our lands best. Some cattle as well."

"And the peach orchards," added Jacelyna.

"Best peaches this side of Bruel, they say, except they only grow well on the south side of the ridge in the red soil there." The older lord took another sip of the amber wine. "Meadows run about eight kays north–south, and ten east–west. Not really, but that's close enough . . ."

Kharl listened, asking a question or two, for almost half a glass, until Adelya slipped into place in the archway from the sitting room to the dining room. When Arynal paused, she looked to Kharl. "Lord . . . at your pleasure, ser."

"Thank you." Kharl inclined his head to his guests, gesturing toward the long cherry table that dominated the dining room. The ancient bronze oil lamps in the wall sconces had already been lit and supplied a golden glow to the chamber.

Kharl took his seat at the head of the table, with Arynal to his left and Jacelyna to his right. Meyena was beside her father. Both Heldya and Adelya served. There were two main dishes. One was the honeyed and cheese-stuffed fowl breasts, and the other was flaankar—thin tubes of rarish beef filled with soft white cheese and parsley and covered with a white butter sauce. Then came the cheese lace potatoes, and the pickled beans—since it was too early in the year for any fresh vegetables.

Adelya set two pitchers of wine on the table, and looked at Kharl as she did.

"You can choose between the white and the red wine," he said. "I like the red, myself, but many prefer the white, especially with fowl. It's the same Rhynn as you had earlier." He wouldn't have known that, but for Adelya's words to him earlier in the afternoon.

"White is always better with fowl," observed Norelle. "For those with delicate palates."

"It is a matter of taste, dear child," replied Arynal, emphasizing the word *child* ever so slightly. "Tastes do differ."

"That is what makes the world an interesting place," added Jacelyna.

"I think I would prefer the red," said Meyena.

Kharl managed to keep a straight face as he handed the pitcher with the red in it to Arynal. "Lord Hagen is also quite fond of the red."

"The lord chancellor is known to be a man of good taste." Arynal half filled Meyena's goblet.

When all the goblets had been filled, Kharl lifted his glass. "It may not be exactly proper, but I'd like to drink to you all, the first of my neighbors to have shared a meal with me."

"Excellent idea!" Arynal lifted his goblet as well.

For a time, conversation lagged as Kharl had several bites of both fowl and flaankar, as well as a chunk of the sweet dark bread that held juicy raisins.

"I've not had flaankar this tasty in years," Arynal said, after several mouthfuls.

"I'm most fortunate in having Adelya."

"A good cook is a gem. That's always been true."

"Pardon me, Lord Kharl, but I've not seen anyone else here, and there is the rumor . . ." ventured Jacelyna.

"I am a widower, that's true." Kharl did not elaborate, especially since he had indicated that earlier. Had Jacelyna missed that, or was she making sure that he was single?

"Be a shame if you had no sons to hold the lands," murmured Arynal.

"It would be, but I'm hoping my . . . younger son will be joining me before the end of the year."

"Oh . . . where is he?"

Once more, Kharl ignored the fact that he'd already mentioned that fact. "He's in Nordla, with his aunt and uncle. They have an orchard, mostly peaches, but some pearapples."

"You don't have that much in the way of fruit here, do you?"

"Besides the berry patches, there's a small cherry orchard in the western lands, and a handful of fruit trees on the south slopes here—apple, pearapple, and a quince. Maybe two quinces," he added.

"Quinces make good jelly," offered Meyena.

Kharl laughed gently. "From what I've tasted, Adelya can make anything taste good."

"What are your plans for the summer, Lord Kharl?" asked Arynal.

"We'll be improving the sawmill here, and making some other

changes. I'll be seeing if the white oaks on the new lands are suitable for barrels for the vineyard, and we may need some better roads in places."

"You don't plan to return to Valmurl . . . Lord Ghrant?"

"If Lord Ghrant needs me, I will certainly attend him, but he and the lord-chancellor have seasons' worth of work before them, I think, in repairing the damage caused by the rebellion. For now, it is better that I remain here at Cantyl. I have done what was necessary. For now, at least."

"Some had thought, after the defeat of the Hamorian wizards . . ."

Kharl laughed. "Hamor sent five wizards. The emperor has scores, and hundreds of iron-hulled warships with mighty guns. Austra can defend itself." He hoped it could. "But waging war elsewhere would be foolhardy."

The older lord nodded. "So you plan to be here for a time."

"I do. There's much to do here."

"There always is. The sheep . . . you know that we have the best white wool in the east. Some say that it is as good a white as Recluce produces black . . ."

From that point on, the conversation turned to the lands, the weather, how Lord Julon had wasted his inheritance on horses and women.

Kharl managed to smile his way through the rest of dinner, and the sweets afterward, then see his guests to their coach.

Once the coach's side-lamps vanished from sight, Kharl walked back up to the porch. He looked at the pin-lights that were the stars, then at the darkness of the harbor. Arynal's motives—or those of his consort—were clear enough. Kharl was a lord and a widower. They had two consortable daughters.

He shook his head. Norelle was the better-looking, and he doubted if he could have stayed in the same room alone with her for a glass without wanting to strangle her. The younger one was sweeter, but he knew he would feel nothing for her . . . except perhaps pity.

If he had to consort, he would have taken Sanyle or Jeka—young as they were—over either of Arynal's daughters, but that wasn't the question. He just hoped that Hagen's men could get a message to Warrl.

After a time, he walked back into the house, sliding the door bolt into place behind him. It was quiet, and all the lamps had been wicked out, except a carry-lamp in the study. He lifted it and headed for the stairs up to his chambers.

XLI

By the end of another two eightdays, Kharl had the cooperage working the way he wanted, in most fashions, although he needed a better hollowing knife, and he was short on charcoal for the toasting and the forge. He'd ordered coal, because he didn't want to turn his few hardwood trees into charcoal, but coal came by ship from Colton, a good hundred kays north of Valmurl, and he had no idea when it might arrive.

He had already turned out a score of white oak barrels, as well as several of red oak and spruce. The red oak and spruce were for slack cooperage around Cantyl.

Glyan, the estate vintner, was looking over the white oak barrels, turning them so that the morning light from the open door illuminated the insides of the staves. "Good barrel, ser. I'd not be saying that because you made it, either."

Kharl could tell that Glyan mean it. The barrels were good, not his very best, but that would come, once he got back into better form.

The gray-bearded Glyan looked up from the barrel he had been examining, his deep brown eyes fixing on Kharl. "Ser . . . we'd make more golds by selling your barrels and buying from Dezant, even counting the shipping costs."

Kharl shook his head. "We wouldn't. People won't pay for the best barrels. They say they will, but they don't. They buy barrels that are just good enough."

"I forget. You've been the cooper." Glyan scratched his head. "I've been thinking, ser. I'd like to try a few barrels that are toasted different-like, a touch darker for the Rhynn, and lighter for the red."

"You think it will make a difference?"

The vintner nodded. "Don't know as what the difference will be. Know that the vintners in the Cetarn Hills like their barrels that way. Might not work here. Grapes, soil, sun, they're all different, even on different sides of the same hill. That's why I want to see."

"We can do that. I can toast some scrap oak first, and you can tell me what darkness you want." Kharl paused. "Maybe I should make them half barrels or kegs, if you're going to try something new."

Glyan furrowed his brow. "Half barrels'd be better. Keg might be too small."

Kharl could see that. "How many?"

"Just four, I think." Glyan offered a slow smile. "Doesn't beat all. Finally get a real say on the barrels, and that's cause the lord's making 'em." He laughed.

So did Kharl.

Once Glyan had left, humming under his breath, Kharl began laying out the billets for some smaller kegs. He'd planned to do one for Speltar anyway, who asked if it were possible because his consort had a weak arm and had trouble with a full-sized flour barrel. Then Dorwan had mentioned that three of the smaller kegs would be useful. That was as close as the forester would ever come to asking. So Kharl would be making kegs for the next day or so, not that he minded.

He'd already discovered that he couldn't spend all his time in the cooperage—not if he wanted to learn about Cantyl. He'd spent two full days walking the southern boundaries of the estate with Dorwan and half a day for an eightday trailing Glyan, watching and listening as the vintner explained everything from the stone troughs that fed just the right amount of water to the grapes in times of no rainfall to the need for Rona to inspect the leaves of every plant and use a fine brush to sweep away the webs of the brown spider—just the brown spider.

Kharl doubted that he would ever learn all that was necessary, but the more he learned the better.

After checking the oak billets, both with his eyes and order-senses, he moved to the planer and began to rough shape the staves.

XLII

Almost another eightday had passed, and, in addition to his travels around his lands with Glyan, Dorwan, and Chyhat, Kharl had finished another score of various types of barrels, as well as the six half barrels for the vintner, two each with different amounts of toasting. Of course, the mage and cooper reflected, it would be more than a year before Glyan would have any idea as to whether the toasting mattered, and how much. Then, too, because the grapes changed some every year, depending on the weather, it might well be years before they really knew. He was just beginning to understand why Glyan was so cautious.

Kharl had blotted his forehead with the sleeve of his working gray shirt and turned to reach for another stave when he noticed that Heldya stood just inside the doorway of the cooperage, her figure outlined by the late-morning sunlight.

He stopped and stepped away from the bench. "Yes, Heldya? What is it? Does your mother need something?"

"No, Lord Kharl. Ser Arynal's daughter is here. She's waiting for you up at the main house."

"Which daughter? Did she say?"

"Mother said it was the younger one, the nicer one."

Meyena? Kharl took a deep breath. At least it wasn't Norelle. "If you would run back and tell her that I'll be there shortly."

"Yes, ser." Heldya scurried off.

Kharl glanced at the staves for the unfinished hogshead, then shook his head. He reracked his tools and left the cooperage, making his way up the last part of the hill to the main house, where he entered through the rear service door.

"She is in the sitting room," Adelya said quietly from the kitchen. "I will have a midday meal for you and your company."

"Thank you. I didn't expect her," replied Kharl.

"You are a widower, Lord Kharl," Adelya pointed out. "You are also thought to be a powerful man, and you're handsome."

Handsome? Kharl certainly didn't consider himself good-looking. He wasn't ugly, but handsome?

"I'll tell them you'll be with them shortly."

"Thank you," he said again, before turning to take the rear stairs to the upper level.

Kharl undressed and washed quickly, using the basin and pitcher Adelya or Heldya had set out for him—he didn't have time for a real bath. Then he dried and donned a clean set of blacks, before heading down the front staircase.

Meyena was still waiting on the love seat in the sitting room. Beside her was an older woman who looked like Lady Jacelyna, but with a more pinched face, and totally white hair. Both women rose the moment they saw Kharl. The older woman wore a long gray traveling dress with a muted purple jacket.

Ser Arynal's younger daughter wore flowing black trousers, a cream shirt, and a dark maroon vest. "Lord Kharl."

"Lady Meyena."

"You're kind. I'm not the heiress. Only Mama is properly a lady." Her smile was tentative. "This is my aunt Aylena."

Kharl inclined his head to the older woman. "I'm pleased to meet you."

"And I you, Lord Kharl. One seldom encounters a mage who is also a lord."

Kharl wasn't quite sure what to say to that, but after a moment that felt all too long and awkward, he managed to reply. "That was Lord Ghrant's choice, and who am I to second-guess his decisions?" After another silence, he added, "I must apologize. I didn't expect company, and I've been working in the cooperage."

"It was quite rude of us to come unannounced," the young woman replied. "I know, but I brought you three bushels of redberries. We had so many of them, and I just thought it would be a shame if you didn't have some. You can make juice if you can't eat them all, and it will keep in a cellar for eightdays." Meyena offered another tentative smile.

"Redberries—that was very thoughtful of you, and to come all that way."

"No one was using the coach, and Aunt Aylena was kind enough to accompany me. Besides, it is a lovely day, and there are so few neighbors who are close."

What she meant, Kharl realized, was that there were few neighbors who were well-off or lords. "There are few close to Cantyl, and not many, I would wager, close to your father's lands."

"Yes, Feldingdon is most isolated, especially in the winter. That is why I like to visit when we can."

"I can imagine." Kharl turned to the older woman, who was probably closer to his age than was Meyena. "Do you live at Feldingdon, or are you visiting?"

"Me? Ser Arynal was kind enough to let me have a cottage there after Durulat passed on. It is different. We had lived in Valmurl ever since we were consorted—in Hilldale, you understand."

Kharl assumed that Hilldale was one of the better areas. "I would judge that Feldingdon is very different."

"That it is, but Arynal has been most kind, as have the girls." Aylena smiled at Meyena. "I was delighted to accompany her here. You know that it's been years since a lord was in residence here?"

"So I have been told. Would you like a short tour of the grounds near the house?" Kharl smiled politely.

"That would be—" Aylena turned to her niece. "This was your idea, dear, and I should not be deciding for you."

"Oh, no," protested the younger woman, "I would very much like to see what you have done here, Lord Kharl."

"I've only done a few things, but I'd be happy to show you around; then perhaps you two would join me for a midday dinner."

"You're most gracious, Lord Kharl," offered Meyena.

Kharl could sense that the young woman meant what she said, and that she was a sweet and sincere young lady. The only problem was that he did not have the faintest interest in her, and that would make it hard on her, since her parents were clearly hoping that he would. He smiled. "Then we should start by walking down to the pier. You get a better view of the harbor from there . . ."

Without a doubt, Kharl reflected, as he opened the door to the front porch—or portico, as Norelle had called it—the day would be moderately pleasant . . . and very long.

XLIII

A single bronze lamp illuminated the study, spilling amber-gold light over the ledger in front of Kharl. In the quiet of the night, his fingers brushed his short and square-cut brown beard as he perused the entries and figures set out in black ink on the pages before him. Speltar's figures went back more than a decade. They were neat, and the entries clear—just another of the steward's many virtues.

When his eyes reached the bottom of the last column, he nodded and closed the ledger. For a time, he sat behind the antique desk. Then he stood and took a last look at the closed account book he had been studying for the last glass.

By any rendering he could imagine, he was well-off. Not wealthy, for the coins necessary to operate Cantyl were not insignificant, but over the past ten years, the lands, the vineyard, and the sawmill had produced an annual income above expenses of almost two hundred golds. He didn't have many of those golds. They'd gone to Lord Estloch, but the strongbox in the cellar counting room now held almost seven hundred golds—one hundred remaining from the previous wine sales and the timber loaded on the *Seastag* from the time when Kharl had first come to Cantyl, the hundred remaining from the hundred and fifty Kharl had received initially from Lord Ghrant, and the most recent five hundred.

Even with the year's timbering and planting costs ahead, and the wages for the retainers and the sawmill, there would have been some golds remaining out of the original hundred, and that was without sales of the aged red wine scheduled for the fall, and the payment for the timber consignment being readied for midsummer.

The new forest produced far less in golds, showing a profit of twenty to thirty golds a year after costs. That suggested another reason why Ghrant had been happy to settle the forestlands on Kharl. Chyhat, while a good forester, had not been the best of stewards and had been happy to relinquish those duties to Speltar, especially after Kharl had explained that his stipend would not be reduced. Speltar had recommended building several roads, closing the ancient sawmill in the new forest, improving the Cantyl sawmill, and adding another drying barn. Those changes were likely to run close to a hundred golds, including the costs of building several cots for the sawmill workers to be moved from the old sawmill to the one at Cantyl. Despite Glyan's fears, they would actually save some golds through Kharl's barrels. Kharl also hoped that, with the better barrels and changes in the toasting, Glyan could improve the red wine enough that they could get a better price in Valmurl, one equal to what the Rhynn received already.

He moved around the desk and stood at the window, looking out into the darkness, out at the hillside leading down to the thin black line that was the narrow pier where, little more than a season before, he had stepped off the *Seastag* to become ser Kharl. His eyes, with a night sight sharpened by order-magery, took in the small, nearly enclosed bay, its entrance less than a kay in width. The water was black and calm on the early-summer night, with a silverlike sheen he suspected only he—or another mage—could have seen.

For reasons he could not fully explain, Meyena's visit had nagged at him. Yet she and her aunt had been pleasant, certainly not pushy, and the amount of redberry that they had brought had been closer to five bushels. With that, Adelya had been pleased.

"You should eat some in the morning. Plenty for juice, too. It keeps off the summer fevers," she had told him more than once.

He had tried the juice, but it was almost too sweet for him. The apple-and-redberry pie had been more to his liking.

Meyena was less than ten years older than Arthal, he had discovered.

His lips tightened. How could he ever have foreseen that his actions in saving Lord Ghrant would have led to Arthal's death? Was that the cruelty of the Balance—or just his own terrible misfortune? If Arthal had stuck with Kharl, it wouldn't have happened. Jeka would have said that. Kharl knew that from the way Jeka had talked about her own mother. He'd seen the love, the pain, and the devotion in that gamine face. Yet Jeka was also practical—and honest—even after the years on the streets of Brysta.

Had his efforts to place her as a weaver with Gharan worked out? That had been the best he had been able to manage, and he wished he could have done more. Without her guidance, when he'd had to flee from Egen, he doubted that he would have survived long enough to have caught the *Seastag*. In a way, he owed everything he had to three people—Jenevra, the dead blackstaffer, Jeka, and Hagen.

He'd done his best to repay Hagen, although he doubted he had done near enough, but there would never be a way to repay Jenevra, and he doubted that he would be headed back to Brysta anytime soon. Not with Lord Ghrant needing him, and not with Lord West and Egen still in power in Brysta.

So why did Kharl feel so restless? Because he'd righted wrongs—or tried to—for everyone but himself and those he had loved? But how much had he loved them? Or was it as the druids of Naclos had told him—that he could not decide his future without facing his past and the land where it had occurred?

He turned back to the desk, gently blowing out the lamp, before walking up to his bedchamber in the dark.

Tomorrow, he would begin work on a simple chest for young Heldya. Adelya had hinted that every young woman needed a dower chest, and while it would be more than several years before the young woman was consorted, it was something he could do.

In the dimness of the staircase, he laughed. That was a problem he could address.

XLIV

Kharl stood on the narrow harbor pier in the midday sun, watching as a vessel he had not seen before—the *Seahound*—eased to the pier at Cantyl. With that name, and the side paddle wheels, even if he had not seen Hagen near the bow, he could have guessed that the ship belonged to the lord-chancellor's merchant fleet. His stomach tightened as he wondered what problems Hagen's presence signified because the lord-chancellor would not have left Valmurl for anything insignificant.

"We were expecting the *Seafox* and not for another eightday." Standing at Kharl's shoulder, Speltar brushed back his wispy reddish hair, although it did little to cover his bald pate. "The lord-chancellor's there. I'd wager that they didn't come for the timber." The steward paused. "You think they'll take the timber, and that they'll stay long enough for us to get the timbers from the mill? The timber is ready to load."

"All we can do is ask," said Kharl. "How long will it take to get the timber up here?"

"Less than a glass, and a glass to load."

The two watched as Bannat caught the first line and snugged it to the inshore bollard, then ran out to the end of the pier, where he caught the second. Before long, the fenders were in place against the hull, and the *Seahound* was tight to the pier. Hagen was the first down the gangway.

Kharl stepped forward. "Welcome to Cantyl."

"Thank you."

"What brings you here again?" asked Kharl, smiling.

"You, of course," returned Hagen. "It was a short trip, but thirsty."

"You'd like some of my red wine? Is that it?"

"I'd not turn it down."

"Before you tell me why you're here?"

"Kharl . . ." Hagen counterfeited mock surprise. "Do you think so uncharitably of me?"

"As a friend, as a captain, and as a factor . . . no. As lord-chancellor, I have some doubts."

The lord-chancellor laughed. "You understand the difference too well, lord mage."

Kharl gestured to Speltar. "We have some timbers. They were supposed to go on the *Seafox* on her next pass."

Hagen tilted his head. "Let's see. That'd be outbound from Valmurl." He nodded. "We can take them. The *Fox* would port in Valmurl first anyway. We'll save Nysat a port call. Tell Captain Haroun that I said you could load them."

Kharl looked at Speltar. "There's your answer."

"Thank you, ser." Speltar inclined his head to the lord-chancellor. "If you lords will excuse me . . ."

"Go." Kharl and Hagen spoke almost simultaneously.

"We might as well walk back to the house and get that wine," Kharl suggested. "So you can soothe your throat before you tell me what I don't want to hear."

Hagen grinned. "It's the best wine anywhere I port."

"I am glad that you think so."

"How are you liking Cantyl?" asked Hagen, as they turned up the lane from the pier to the house.

"I'm finding a lot to do. I've got the cooperage working, and I've made some different barrels for Glyan. He wants to see if the amount of toasting changes the wine."

"Don't change what's already good," warned Hagen.

"Oh . . . he's only going to try it on a few half barrels."

"Doesn't work, and you can turn it to vinegar, I suppose. Be a waste of what could have been good wine."

"If he doesn't try, how will we know if it could be better? And if it doesn't work, then we'll know what not to try. And . . ." Kharl drew out the word, "if it's better, we can raise the price."

Hagen chuckled. "You learned something besides ship's carpentry on the *Seastag*."

"Some," Kharl admitted.

After the two men reached Kharl's study, and Adelya had brought up a pitcher of the red wine, drawn from the barrel in the cellar, Kharl closed the study door. He half filled two goblets and let Hagen take his choice.

The lord-chancellor took a sip, then a healthy swallow. "Almost worth the trip for the wine."

"Almost? Has someone else revolted? Or misled Lord Ghrant?" Kharl looked directly at Hagen. "You wouldn't have come here if it weren't a matter of import."

"Nothing like that," Hagen protested. "Not exactly, anyway." He held up a missive. The seal had already been broken. "I received this yesterday. From Furwyl through Jeksum—he's the master of the *Seasprite*. It's about your boy."

Kharl could feel every muscle in his body tighten.

Hagen shook his head. "No. It's not bad news."

"Then . . . what?"

"It's no news. Furwyl apologized for not trying to send a messenger or one of his crew to Peachill, but he felt it would have been most unwise. There has been brigandage and murder of travelers on the roads outside Brysta, especially to the south, and the harbor inspectors suggested that the crew remain close to the harbor. They were most insistent, particularly about the south roads. Furwyl also noted several large Hamorian trading vessels in the harbor."

"They trade everywhere you do, don't they? Or did Furwyl think that they were there for other purposes? That they might be connected to the unsafe roads?"

"He did not say, other than that the Hamorians had ported two eight-days before the *Seastag* and had not yet made preparations to set to sea when he was about to cast off."

"Do you think that the emperor has turned his eyes on Nordla? So soon?"

Hagen shrugged. "I do not know. Not for certain. From your experiences in Brysta, I would wager that those who would support Lord West—or his sons—might be fewer than the lord imagines. Or perhaps the son you ran afoul of is plotting something. Or Lord West is trying to enlist Hamorian support for some venture or another." He took another sip of the red wine. "Most prefer the Rhynn, but for me, the red is far better."

On that, Kharl had to agree with Hagen.

"You're worried about your boy, aren't you?" asked the lord-chancellor.

"Wouldn't you be? He's all I have. I've already lost Arthal."

"You must have mulled over going back to Brysta," suggested Hagen.

"I've given it some thought," replied Kharl warily, not certain he liked the direction the conversation was turning. "Lord West would not like to see me back."

"Lord West—or his younger son?"

Kharl smiled, faintly. "Egen, most likely. Lord West has probably forgotten that there was a cooper named Kharl who ever lived in Brysta."

"If you could go back . . . what would you do there?"

"I still have the feeling that things ought to be set right." Kharl shook his head. "Before I . . . became a mage, I'd thought about taking the Justicer's Challenge."

Hagen laughed. "You wouldn't have to now."

"I think I would. Still. Or do something about justice. Unless you are a ruler, people don't much care for others using force or magery to get their way. Besides, unless you replace the justicers, how do you get better justice?"

Hagen cocked his head.

"You're thinking about something, honored lord-chancellor."

"I am. Would you consider being Lord Ghrant's envoy in Brysta?"

"Me? Why me? What could I do? I've barely been a lord for half a year, if that. What if Lord West found out who I am?"

"There are good answers to your questions," Hagen replied calmly, then paused and took another swallow from the goblet.

Kharl refilled it. As he did, he realized that he'd never seen Hagen drink so much so quickly. In the past, the lord-chancellor had barely drunk a full goblet.

"First," Hagen went on, "you know more about Brysta than anyone else Lord Ghrant or I can trust. Second, Lord Ghrant has received some disturbing reports from Brysta, about Hamorian mercenaries being added to Lord West's regular lancers, or something like that—and that they are being paid with Hamorian golds. Third, envoys traditionally cannot be held accountable for actions taken in the past. Fourth, there are reports of Brystan troops being moved southward."

"Toward Lord South's lands?"

"We do not know, and that's part of the problem. There's much we do not know."

"Lord South is old . . . and he has no sons . . ." ventured Kharl. "Lord West and Egen are ambitious."

"Lord South rejected an offer to consort his youngest daughter to one of Lord West's sons, the one you encountered."

"Lord West was offended?"

"We do not know, but what we have heard from other merchanters and factors suggest that the mercenaries began arriving after that."

"Why does this concern Lord Ghrant?" Kharl asked, although he had a good idea.

"Lord South has never been a strong ruler, and the south is the weakest of the four lands of the Quadrant. All too easily, between the west and the south, half of Nordla could fall to Hamor. Once Hamor held half of Nordla, the rest would soon follow. Nordla's ports are far closer to Bruel and Valmurl than Swartheld is." Hagen took another swallow of his wine. "As envoy, you could find out more than others. Also, Kharl is not an uncommon name, and it is most unlikely that Lord West or his sons will connect an Austran lord from a small estate with a former cooper. If you shaved your beard, I doubt anyone would recognize you, save perhaps your son or a close friend."

"This will take some thinking," Kharl stopped. "Who was the envoy?

What happened to him?" He recalled Hagen telling him once, but he didn't remember who it had been.

"Lord Estloch had recalled Lord Hensolas," Hagen said slowly. "He never told Ghrant why. He'd summoned Ghrant to talk over matters, but he was killed before they met."

"Do you think that Ilteron was planning to topple his sire? That Hensolas was part of the plot?"

"That well might have been. Ilteron certainly resented Ghrant being named as heir, and many lords were not that happy under Lord Estloch."

"You were not pleased with the way he ruled," Kharl pointed out.

"No, I was not. I advised him against many things he did. He told me I did not understand what ruling was." Hagen laughed, bitterness in the sound.

Kharl had another thought. "I have a few golds laid by, but you had told me that being an envoy was costly."

"Lord Ghrant will send you with a purse, and with a draw on the Factors' Exchange in Brysta."

Kharl looked at Hagen blankly.

"On your signature, you can draw up to a thousand golds over each year, but never more than a hundred an eightday. Only for matters befitting an envoy, of course."

Draw or take a hundred golds an eightday?

"Now . . . if you wish to consider this, you would need some education, and some protection."

"Education? I'll need much of that."

"You know more than enough about most things. But, in addition to being Lord Ghrant's envoy, it would be good for you to be a scholar of the law. That way, you can present yourself as a scholar as well as an envoy . . ."

"Since I know little about either," Kharl pointed out, "it will seem as if Lord Ghrant appointed me to repay a debt."

"That perception will be to your advantage," Hagen said. "Also, if you do choose to undertake the Justicer's Challenge, you will be prepared. If not, you will still be able to quote from the law as an envoy, and that is useful. Also, as a scholar, you can frequent the Hall of Justice in Brysta. Often more can be discovered there than in bedrooms or salons."

"I still don't see why Lord Ghrant . . ." Kharl shook his head.

"After all that has happened here, he feels that he needs to know what is happening in Brysta. He cannot send an envoy who might join forces with Lord West, or even Lord South, and he needs someone who can protect himself. You will, of course, have a secretary with you, and several lancers. I understand that Undercaptain Demyst is an excellent blade."

"He is not bright enough to be a captain?"

Hagen shook his head. "He is more than bright enough. He will be devoted to you, and he is as honest as it is possible for an officer to be."

"I have not said that I wanted to be an envoy," Kharl pointed out.

"I have proposed to Lord Ghrant that you spend the next season studying with one of the justicer's clerks in Valmurl."

"But . . ." Kharl couldn't help but protest.

"Lord Ghrant owes you everything. He didn't pay you nearly what he owes, especially after the way you settled the rebel lords, and he would like to settle you with more. He could do that, if you acquitted yourself well as an envoy. He also needs you, because . . ." Hagen paused. "There is no one else he can trust."

"No one?"

"You sat through the audiences. Did you see a single man you would trust in Brysta? One who is even a lesser lord? Or a factor?"

Kharl didn't even have to think to answer that. "No. The good ones were probably the ones Malcor and Kenslan killed at the beginning."

"Vertyn would have made a good envoy, I think, and so would have Lord Lahoryn's eldest son." Hagen looked bleakly at Kharl. "Do you think I like asking this of you?"

Kharl sat there for a moment, realizing why Hagen had drunk so much wine and why the lord-chancellor had come himself.

"I do worry about you," Hagen said. "I would not wish you to return to Brysta without being fully prepared. Law is not the same as magery. You would not leave immediately. You would be in Valmurl for a good season, and you would have quarters in the Great House."

Kharl understood. He was perceived as one reason behind Ghrant's success. If he departed Valmurl too soon, there was the possibility of more unrest. Later, some might be relieved to see him go. What the lord-chancellor said made sense, and both Hagen's concern and his desperation were real.

"Also," Hagen added, "you should tell no one that you are a mage. Word and rumor will filter to Brysta, but the longer it takes, the better for you. And . . . a power never mentioned is far more fearsome than one discussed openly."

Kharl was not certain about that, but Hagen had far more experience in dealing with lords and rulers and their retainers. "How long is one an envoy?"

"Usually it is for two years."

"Two years?" asked Kharl involuntarily. Two years away from Cantyl? Then he found himself smiling involuntarily. Already, he was thinking of it as home. What did that tell him?

"I doubt you will need to be there that long. Not nearly that long."

That meant, Kharl thought, that one way or another, he was expected to solve the problems at hand sooner than in two years. Still . . . that would give him time to find Warrl . . . and to help Jeka . . . if he could. Kharl had worried about his younger boy, but with his own guards and abilities, he could certainly travel to Peachill directly, although it might be wise to wait an eightday or longer after his arrival before undertaking such a journey. As in the case with battles against the rebel lords, the guards would provide a certain cover for his use of his magely talents, if he even needed them.

Then . . . outside of the need to recover Warrl, did he really want to return to Brysta and Nordla?

Another thought crossed his mind, words he had not considered for a time.

"You haven't said much, Kharl," Hagen said.

"I was thinking. Do you remember the druids in Diehl?"

Hagen's brow wrinkled in puzzlement. "The ones who healed you? Yes."

"They told me that I could never really leave Brysta behind, not until I returned. So . . . that is perhaps another reason I should become an envoy. If that is what Lord Ghrant wishes."

"I do not know that it is what he would wish in his heart, were there other choices," Hagen said evenly, "but there are none." He offered a faint smile as he fingered his chin. "I also don't think I'd argue against a druid."

"Two druids," Kharl said dryly.

"That's even worse." Hagen took another sip of the wine before speaking. "Does that mean that you will accept Lord Ghrant's offer?"

Kharl nodded slowly. "It's as much for Warrl as for Lord Ghrant."

"I would not have thought otherwise."

Kharl glanced out through the window toward the harbor and the *Seahound*. The wagon with timber had not yet reached the pier. "Do I return with you?"

"You can."

"I might as well. I've little enough to pack, and Speltar and Dorwan will need time to load the timber."

"You'll have much more. You'll have to have a full wardrobe as an envoy."

Kharl hadn't even thought of that, and he wondered how many other matters he hadn't even considered. But . . . with what had happened to Warrl already, did Kharl have that much choice? And did he dare to continue to disregard the advice of the druids?

XLV

Threeday morning was cloudy, and a fine warm drizzle drifted from the low gray clouds that hung over Valmurl. Kharl glanced around his new quarters in the Great House, larger than the ones he had used before, still on the second level, but on the north wing, not far from the staircase to the tower. The sitting room was set in the northwest corner of the building and had windows on both sides. The evening before, Kharl had seen how that arrangement had provided a cooling breeze for both the sitting room and bedchamber.

He had not seen Lord Ghrant, but on the short voyage back from Cantyl to Valmurl, Hagen had warned Kharl that such meetings would be infrequent.

"He's heard all the old stories about how his great-grandsire fell under the spell of a mage," Hagen had said. "He's more afraid of others believing that of him than of it actually happening. Much of the rebellion was stirred up by tales of his weakness and indecisiveness. He doesn't want to feed such stories."

Kharl could understand the young ruler's concerns, but he also worried that Ghrant might worry too much about what his people thought and not enough about what needed to be done. Still, Kharl reflected, the rebellion had proved that a ruler could not ignore what people thought.

The mage and lord stepped up to the tall mirror in its stand beside the single chest in the bedchamber. He took in his own reflection—broad shoulders, squarish chin, dark hair thinning in front, dark green eyes . . .

He paused. Had his eyes always been that dark? He didn't think so, but he hadn't really looked at himself in the mirror that much.

After several moments, he turned from the mirror, with its faded gilt frame, and walked into the sitting room. There, he looked out through the window, down at the lawns and fountains. With the misty drizzle falling he could not see westward much beyond the stables and barracks, and the long sloping lawn that extended from the terraces.

Well beyond the fine warm rain, across the breadth of the land, and across the Gulf of Austra, lay Nordla—and Brysta. In some ways, his life in Brysta felt as though it had happened to someone else—and long ago. Until he thought about Arthal . . . and Warrl . . . and even Jeka. Yet, even if he'd had no sons, he needed to go back, if only to see the city once more. Would it look different after all he had been through?

Why did he now feel so impelled to return to Brysta? Had Charee still lived, she would have settled into Cantyl, and she would have called him a fool for ever going close to Lord West again. Maybe he was a fool to agree to be an envoy. But there was Hagen . . . who would far rather have been upon the *Seastag*, than standing behind Ghrant, advising and maneuvering, and risking displeasure day after day. And the image of Tyrbel remained in Kharl's mind. The scrivener had in effect given his life for Kharl when no one would have been the wiser if he had not. Kharl would not even have blamed the scrivener had the older man not chosen to speak up. But Tyrbel had, and he had been murdered by Egen's assassin. It didn't matter that Kharl had killed the assassin. Tyrbel was dead.

He half turned from the window, his eyes falling to *The Basis of Order*. There wasn't anything in the book about envoys, nor about serving a ruler, not directly, anyway.

On fourday, he was to present himself to the lord justicer's chief clerk in Valmurl to begin his hurried study of law. He had to wonder whether it would be of that much use. But then, Hagen felt so, and the lord-chancellor had seen far more of the world—and those who controlled it—than had Kharl.

Kharl looked back out through the window. The rain was beginning to fall more heavily.

XLVI

Kharl rode down Casters Way, a street whose shops offered no reason for the name. Riding beside him was Dorfal, again assigned to accompany Kharl.

"Quiet this morning, ser. Always is this time of day."

"Most are at work or doing chores, I'd imagine." Kharl could sense more than a few eyes on him, although they had to have been trained on him from behind window hangings or shutters, for he saw no one actually looking at him. He did not sense any large amounts of chaos, but Valmurl, like any city, was filled with small pockets of chaos—and order.

He did catch, through his order-sense boosted hearing, a few words and phrases here and there.

". . . that's him . . . all in black . . ."

". . . mages everywhere wear the black . . ."

". . . big fellow . . . more like an armsman . . ."

". . . good at that, too . . . some say . . ."

". . . Lord Ghrant . . . fortunate . . ."

". . . we're the lucky ones . . . lords still be fighting . . ."

Kharl couldn't keep a faint smile from his lips. Whoever the speaker had been, he had been right. Through luck, some limited skill, and arrogance—both his and that of the white mages—he'd stopped the white wizards. If he had not, he had few doubts that the fighting would still be continuing, if only because that would have best suited Hamor.

"The square's just ahead, ser, past the silversmith's on the left."

Kharl nodded. He hadn't wanted an escort, but Norgen and Hagen had insisted. The Hall of Justice was too far from the Great House to walk, and there were no stables nearby. So Dorfal was escorting Kharl.

As the two turned at the silversmith's, the morning sunlight glinted off the puddles remaining in the lower sections of the stone-paved square that fronted the hall of Justice. The gray stone structure was longer and narrower than the Hall in Brysta. Its double doors were of dark oak rather than light, and there were no guards posted either outside or immediately inside.

Kharl reined up outside the doors and dismounted. From the gelding's saddlebags, he took out a small leather case, which contained only blank paper and a markstick.

"I'll be back at noon, ser."

"Thank you." Kharl smiled at the young lancer, then turned and headed for the doors, conscious of Dorfal's eyes on his back.

Inside the doors, a series of polished brass lamps set in wall sconces illuminated the hall-like foyer, and the white plaster walls had been recently painted. There were no decorations.

Kharl glanced around. The foyer was empty.

A thin white-haired man in a green jacket appeared from a narrow archway to the left. "Ser? Might I help you?"

"I'm looking for Jusof, the clerk for—"

"You must be Lord Kharl, I'd imagine." The man bowed. "Most pleased to meet you, ser. Jusof is expecting you, ser. If you would take the narrow stairs to the left over there, the library and his study are just at the top."

"Thank you." Kharl bowed his head.

"Oh, no, ser. Thank you."

Kharl followed the directions and took the stairs, so narrow that his shoulders almost brushed both walls at once. At the top was another foyer, with three archways set in an arc. The archway in the center had a single door, open into a small chamber. Kharl could see someone seated at a table desk on which were stacked piles of books and papers and that half filled the chamber. The ancient oak door set in the archway to the right was closed. The leftmost archway had no door and opened into a long chamber that seemed to run the rest of the distance to the back of the structure. It was filled with shelves, and on those shelves were rows and rows of leather bound volumes, and all the volumes seemed to be the same size—at least from what Kharl could see.

Kharl strode forward toward the occupied chamber. By the time he stood at the doorway, the occupant was standing.

"Lord Kharl, I presume?"

"Yes. You're Jusof."

"None other." Jusof was even thinner, if but slightly younger, than the man who had offered directions. His eyes were gray, large, and luminous, and his hands were enormous, with such long fingers that each hand resembled a spider.

"I had no doubt you were Lord Kharl, the mage." The warmth of the clerk's smile erased immediately the severity of his appearance.

Kharl laughed slightly. "Everyone seems to know who I am, and yet I've not met any of you. It's very strange."

"That will pass, I am most certain, but you not only are attired as befits a mage, but you carry yourself as such. There is a power there . . . one who looks cannot mistake it." The elderly clerk smiled at Kharl. "You look like a mage, not like a cooper, or a carpenter, but I've been assured that you've been successful at all three occupations. I've also been assured that you can read and write with proficiency. Is that accurate?"

"Yes." Kharl wasn't so sure about his proficiency in writing, at least compared to the justicers and advocates who frequented the Hall of Justice.

"The lord-chancellor has stated that he wishes me to guide you in learning as much about justice and its procedures as possible in the season ahead. Lord Justicer Priost has no objections, so long as you do not disrupt the proceedings of any case, and I am willing to do that, if you are willing to apply yourself. It will mean working as hard as at anything you have done, for wrestling with the many-headed beast that is law is more tiring than most would imagine."

A faint smile crossed Kharl's lips as he listened.

"First, I will offer a precept, and an observation. The precept is: Never mistake law for justice. Justice is an ideal, and law is a tool. Absolute justice would be as unjust as applied injustice. Now . . . the observation is that justice is the wellspring of chaos. That is because those who are guilty will do anything to avoid justice, as will most of those who are innocent." The clerk's tone turned even more dry. "The innocent fear justice because of what they might do, or because of what might be done to those they love. The only ones who pursue justice with great vigor are those who would use the law as a weapon, and they are to be more feared than either the innocent or the guilty."

Kharl only had to think about the clerk's words for a moment.

Jusof cleared his throat and asked, "Does that surprise you?"

"No. I can't say that it does," Kharl replied reflectively. "I could not have said it as clearly as you did, but I have wondered about the very ideas you expressed."

"You speak well for a former craftsman. Have you read widely?"

"I have read. Not so widely as I should, I fear."

"That is true of all of us." The clerk coughed. "I will summarize in practical terms what I just told you. Law is a necessary evil. With it, matters are never what they should be. Without it, they are inevitably worse."

Kharl had to wonder, if the clerk of the head justicer in Austra happened to be so cynical, how fairly the judgments of his justicer were arrived at.

"The law is something that is always changing, but its roots date to antiquity. Hamor has an actual code of laws, set forth in great detail by the third emperor. These are periodically updated and recodified. We do not do this in Nordla. The laws of both Austra and Nordla derive originally from the Code of Cyad, such of it as remained, and largely from the ensuing case histories, by precedent, and as amended by any proclamations of the lord, provided that the lord justicer does not issue an opinion suggesting the legal invalidity of such a proclamation . . ."

What was a case history? What did Jusof mean by precedent? And how could a lord justicer invalidate a lord's decree? Kharl feared that what was in *The Basis of Order* was simple in comparison to the arcaneness of law.

"We will need to get you settled. The lord justicer suggested that you spend some time studying the simplified procedures first, then the most important precedents. After that, as there is time, you can look into other cases and observe some of the cases that come before the lord justicer." Jusof smiled. "There is a large table in the northwest corner of the library, right under one of the clerestories, so that on most days you won't need a lamp . . ."

The chief clerk slipped around the table desk, the sleeve of his short jacket brushing a pile of books, which teetered but did not fall.

Kharl took his case in hand and followed the justicer's clerk.

XLVII

Jusof stood beside his table desk, overflowing with the piles of papers and volumes that seemed to have grown even in the two days since Kharl had first seen them. "Now that you have read through the basic clerks' guide, and the summary of important laws, I thought you should learn to use the library while you are studying some of the cases."

Kharl nodded. His head was already spinning after two long days of reading through documents that made *The Basis of Order* seem simple indeed.

"I have listed here some representative cases of each of the major classifications of law." Jusof extended three sheets of paper filled with his precise and small script. "The criminal sections are simple enough. There are crimes against persons, either common or noble; crimes affecting property; and crimes against the Lord—those are effectively crimes against Austra itself, since its lord represents the land. Crimes against the Lord fall into three categories. The first category comprises minorities, such as public drunkenness, vagrancy, disturbing the peace. The second comprises majorities. These are greater offenses, such as destroying public property, begging or soliciting on the streets without a permit from the Lord—"

"I did not know that one could get a permit for begging," Kharl said, recalling the time when he had seen one of the Watch patrollers take away a child for begging.

"There is a precedent for the Lord to grant such, but no lord has granted any since before the time of Lord Esthaven. Generally, they are not given. Begging and street soliciting, if not forbidden, lead to greater offenses."

"What kinds of soliciting are allowed under the law?"

"There is little restriction on soliciting from one's own property or property rented when the owner has consented in writing to the purposes to which the property is put."

"Hmmmm . . ." Kharl could see a few problems there.

Jusof laughed. "Most young advocate scholars don't see that. There is a recommended consent form laid out in the *Salaharat* case. That is a very famous decision by the lord justicer under Lord Isthel."

"I'm supposed to find these cases . . . and read through them?"

"Exactly."

"Ah . . . the library is large."

"Oh . . . I must not have explained. One takes so much for granted. The cases are laid out by section here in the library. Each set of shelves is labeled on the east end. The cases in each set of shelves are arranged alphabetically by the name of the defendant, and the sections correspond generally to the classifications."

"What if a case has more than one classification?"

"Good question. The case will be filed under what we thought was the major issue at law, but a sheet will be filed in the other sections telling where the actual decision and abbreviated proceedings are filed." The clerk pointed to the sheet. "If you search out each of these cases, then read through them, you should gain a very basic understanding of how the law is applied and decided. Please remember that in many instances the situation does not fit the law as it stands, and the lord justicer must decide what aspects of the law and various precedents apply. If you have questions, write them down, in reference to the case, and we will discuss them each afternoon before you leave. I would judge that it will take you close to an eightday to study all those on the list, even if you read quickly."

An eightday more of reading? Most of the daylight hours? "I see that I will be very busy."

"You will, indeed. I only wish that more lords would spend some time trying to understand the law. If they did, there would be fewer cases before the lord justicer."

"People are people," Kharl replied. "They only accept the knowledge that suits them." He'd seen that often enough as a cooper. No one wanted to understand the advantage of a tight red or white oak barrel when they were after cheap cooperage, even when the slightly more costly oak barrel would save them twice the difference over in a few years.

"You are most probably right," Jusof said with a sigh, "but one hopes."

"I had best begin," Kharl said.

Jusof stood watching, a faint and sad smile on his thin face, as Kharl turned away.

Jusof and the clerks were well organized, Kharl thought as he headed for the corner table in the library that had become his immediately two days earlier. Several of the advocate students still looked up from the smaller wall tables when he passed, but fewer did so each day.

Kharl set his case on the table. He wondered if the detail pursued by Jusof and the clerks was that necessary. Then he shook his head. That detail was necessary for a good set of laws, just as the same kind of attention to detail made crafting better barrels possible, and greater magery successful. Did Nordla have a similar system? Jusof had indicated that the legal systems had come from the same general background, but, if they did, how could Lord Justicer Reynol of Brysta have accepted the abuses of Egen and Lord West?

Kharl smiled. Anyone could twist anything. That was something he would have to watch in himself. Perhaps studying the law would help. He just hoped it did not make him too much more cynical about people.

XLVIII

After the first eightday in the Hall of Justice, spent entirely in the library reading, Kharl wasn't sure that he understood any more than when he had first walked inside. He knew more, but the knowledge had not yet deepened his understanding. At least, he didn't think so. His routine was simple. He spent the morning there, rode back to the Great House for a midday meal, then returned and studied some more until close to sunset. The last half glass or so was spent with Jusof.

On fiveday evening he walked slowly into the dining chamber in the Great House. For a moment, he did not recognize anyone. Then he saw Norgen and Casolan seated at the larger table. They had ales before them, but no platters.

Casolan gestured. "If you would join us, Lord Kharl . . ."

"I would not intrude."

"You'd not be intruding," said the square-faced Casolan. "In fact, we insist."

Norgen nodded agreement.

Kharl sat down, gratefully. He hadn't been looking forward to eating alone. He'd been doing that too often, of late.

"An ale"—Norgen glanced from the serving girl to Kharl—"it is an ale, isn't it?"

"Pale ale, please."

"A pale ale for Lord Kharl."

"Yes, sers."

"You don't get to choose tonight," Casolan said. "It's stew. Only stew. They had problems in the kitchen."

"That's fine." Kharl looked at the two commanders. Both had circles under their eyes and appeared thinner than when he had left Valmurl. "How are matters with you both?"

The two officers exchanged glances. Then Casolan burst into a laugh, and Norgen shook his head, his lips twisted into a wry expression.

"We've had to recruit more armsmen and lancers, and retrain most of those who remained," Casolan finally said. "Half the new lancers think horses are wasted on anything but plowing. Half the junior officers have had full stables and have no idea about the need to pace a mount."

"Not half," suggested Norgen. "Just too many."

"The ones who know blades fancy themselves duelists, and those who don't treat a sabre like an ax." Casolan took a swallow of his ale, almost finishing the beaker.

"None of them think that they really need training, because wars don't happen often, and we've just finished one," Norgen added. "They don't see that training and discipline are necessary for more than just fighting. Some of them don't even see the need for training to fight. They just think that you charge with your mount and swing wildly at anything in sight."

The three paused as the server returned with another round of ales, and with three bowls of the stew—and two baskets of bread, only rye.

"No dark bread," observed Casolan. "What's stew without it?"

"I'm so sorry, ser," offered the serving girl, "but the molasses ran out . . ."

"It's not your fault," Casolan said politely. "It's probably not even the cook's fault."

"No, ser. It's not. Thank you." Before anyone could say anything else, she bowed and hurried off.

"What's the problem?" asked Kharl.

"The lord-chancellor discovered that the provisions steward for the Great House was, shall we say, taking a small portion of the accounts for his own uses. Some of the holders had not been paid in eightdays for supplies delivered here. Everything below the stairs is being looked at, and not everything has been ordered as it should have been because the steward kept it all to himself."

"So that no one would know what he was doing?" suggested Kharl.

Norgen nodded. "When someone wants to do everything by himself, it's a good wager that he either doesn't trust those working for him or that he's up to no good. Neither is a good sign."

Kharl understood that. Even as a cooper, if he couldn't train his sons or apprentices to be trusted, he wouldn't have been much of a crafter. "So the Great House has a new provisions steward, and he's having trouble finding everything?"

"So I hear. It doesn't help that some of the holders were favored with a few extra coins, and not because their provender was of better quality."

"It's going to take a while before the lord-chancellor can work things out," interjected Casolan.

Kharl did not envy Hagen.

"Where have you been?" asked Norgen.

Kharl debated momentarily about what he should say, then replied. "I've been studying law at the Hall of Justice."

"Law?" Casolan frowned.

"The lord-chancellor thought it might be helpful. I'm not sure yet, but I think I've learned a bit more about how Austra really works."

"I can see how that might be helpful for a mage," observed Norgen. "Whatever you do may affect someone."

"Glad it's not me," said Casolan, after a mouthful of stew. "Just as soon stay away from the Hall of Justice. You have to settle things there, and it's already more trouble than anyone should want."

"What have you learned?" asked Norgen.

"Mostly, that clerks and advocates and justicers write down everything, and that their writing is very small."

Both commanders laughed.

XLIX

Late on fourday afternoon, Kharl stepped out of the Hall of Justice and looked across the square toward the tavern. After almost another eightday in the library, Kharl's eyes and brain were weary. His initial impression had not changed that much. The law was a tool, as Jusof had stated; but it was a tool that, while varying between the bluntness of a cudgel and the focused deadliness of a stiletto, generally served the interests of those with property and wealth, especially the Lord of Austra. Still, like all tools, it depended on who was using it for what. That had also become clear from his readings.

He had decided that he needed a break from the fare at the Great House and arranged for Dorfal to meet him much later than usual in the square, after having asked Jusof about places to eat nearby.

"A tavern that would be appropriate for a lord? There are few of those." Jusof had paused, mulling over the thought. "The Silver Horse is said to be the best. It is just across the square. I suppose one would not find much trouble with an establishment but a few doors from the Watch Patrollers' headquarters."

Kharl had repressed a laugh at that. His experiences with the Watch in Brysta had left something to be desired.

Dorfal had not been exactly pleased when Kharl had told the young armsman that he would be eating at the tavern and to meet him later, but Kharl had insisted quietly. "I don't know enough about Valmurl, and where people eat tells something. Besides, I need to get out of the Great House more, and not only to the Hall of Justice."

At the recollection of Dorfal's glum agreement, Kharl smiled momentarily. Then he lengthened his stride and crossed the square. The Silver Horse stood out from the brick-fronted buildings on either side, neither of which bore signs identifying them, because its front was of dark timbers framing white plaster. The door was of time-blackened oak. Kharl opened it and stepped inside, closing it behind him.

A muscular woman in nondescript blue, with a gray apron, hurried up to Kharl, then slowed as she took in the black jacket, trousers, and tunic. "Ah . . . ser . . ."

"I'm looking for a meal and a good lager," Kharl offered cheerfully. "I'm told you have both."

The woman smiled. "Yes, ser. Plain fare, but good. No ale any better." She looked over her shoulder. "Early enough we got a corner table." She turned.

Kharl followed her, then sat in the corner chair against the wall, the one from which he could see most of the crowd. "A lager or a light ale, if you have it. What do you suggest for fare?"

"Light ale's better, ser. Tonight, ser, the burhka's pretty good. Hot but not too hot."

Kharl hadn't had burhka in seasons. "That sounds fine. Dark bread?"

"Yes, ser. Five for the fare and bread. Three for the ale. When you please, ser." She hurried off.

She hadn't gotten more than a few cubits away, when another serving-woman, gray-haired, stopped her. "Who's that? Some advocate . . . ?"

". . . think it might be Lord Ghrant's mage . . . you want to ask him?"

". . . think not . . . don't question mages. You keep serving him."

Within moments, the first server returned with Kharl's ale.

"Thank you."

"Yes, ser." She nodded and slipped away, glancing toward the other corner of the tavern.

Kharl's eyes followed hers. Opposite him was a small group of men, young but fairly well dressed. After a moment, he smiled. No wonder Jusof knew about the Silver Horse. Kharl could recognize the faces of several of the student advocates, not that he knew any of their names.

One of the advocates-to-be lifted a guitar and began to strum and sing. After a moment, the others joined in.

Kharl concentrated on the words.

"Our brave Lord Ghrant, he ran away,
came back to fight another day.
His found mage fought wizards and even more,
whupped 'em all in the age's shortest war.

"Our brave Lord Ghrant, he loved his land,
ran and showed it but his left hand.

His brother lost his mages and his head,
and Lord Ghrant came back from the almost dead.

"Our brave Lord Ghrant, he knows so well
when to fight and when to run and tell.
But better a lord who knows where to flee
than his brother who'd slaughter you and me!"

Several of those at the tables in the tavern laughed, heartily, but Kharl could only shake his head. Humorous as the song was, the point applied to him, and, like Lord Ghrant, it was more than clear that his running days were done, and that he needed to return to Brysta before Egen became yet another Ilteron—and before something happened to Warrl.

He paused, thinking. Just how likely was it that such a song could have been sung in Brysta about either Egen or Lord West? He doubted that the singers, wellborn students or not, could have sung such words about the ruler of the West Quadrant of Nordla—not without ending up either in gaol or suffering some other form of Egen's displeasure. In that sense, Austra was much to be preferred to Nordla.

Yet . . . even without his debts to Ghrant and Hagen, Kharl knew he would have had to return to Nordla. Was it just because of Warrl? Or because he needed to see Brysta with fresh eyes? Or because he worried that he had not done enough for Sanyle and Jeka—especially Jeka?

"Your burhka, ser." With the burhka came a small loaf of dark bread in a basket, still warm.

"Oh . . . thank you." Kharl slipped the server a silver and a copper.

"Thank *you*, ser." With a pleased smile, she gave the slightest of bows before leaving Kharl to his evening meal.

Across the tavern, the students were singing another song.

"Oh, clerks and justicers, justicers and clerks,
all that they love are their cases and their perks . . .
With their ink-stained noses as black as a rook's,
their only pleasures lie in their files and their books . . ."

Kharl smiled again and began to enjoy the ale and the burhka.

L

Kharl made his way through the double doors of the Hall of Justice. He hoped to spend some time reading through the next-to-last section of *Austran Justicer Cases*, suggested strongly by Jusof because Jusof had wanted him to finish those cases before they observed the day's proceedings in the Hall of Justice.

The mage used his sight shield to slip by the open chamber door of the lord justicer's chief clerk because he really didn't feel like another long lecture by Jusof on the law as a tool. Kharl had understood that the first time, and he doubted that he could keep from showing some impatience. Kharl knew Jusof was trying to help him, but sometimes what Jusof said lasted a full glass. Kharl suspected that was because Jusof was lonely, and because the older man knew that Kharl was honestly trying to understand the law for itself and not as a way to wealth or fame or both.

He released the sight shield as he neared the corner table, hoping that none of the student advocates happened to be looking his way.

". . . see that?" whispered one of the young men.

"See what?"

"That's him . . . the mage . . . just appeared out of nowhere . . ."

"How'd you know? You were dreaming about Juhlya. Besides, if he's a mage, what does it matter? They do things like that."

". . . say he's studying the law with Jusof . . ."

"A mage . . . studying law?"

"Maybe he figures he needs to, now that he's a lord . . ."

". . . don't know that a mage needs the law . . ."

". . . big fellow, for all the fine clothes . . ."

". . . carried Lord Ghrant three kays on his shoulders . . . killed two wizards and that scum Ilteron . . . gave him a small estate . . . then turned a whole mountain into glass . . ."

Kharl winced at the exaggerations. In the fight in Dykaru, which had brought him Cantyl, he'd been fortunate rather than skillful, and glad enough to have survived. As for the so-called glass mountain, the powers of the two white wizards had been the reason why part of one small hill was glassy. He pushed aside the whispered words, settled himself at the table, and opened volume nine of *Austran Justicer Cases*.

He'd actually read through two of the cases before he sensed Jusof walking into the library and heading toward him.

He closed the volume and rose, then walked past the young advocates toward Jusof.

"You must have been here early, Lord Kharl. I didn't see you come in." Jusof carried a large case under his left arm.

"Not that early. You looked rather intent when I passed."

Jusof sighed. "That must have been when I was copying out Lord Justicer Priost's decision on the rendering case . . . rather involuted, if impeccable logic." The clerk turned toward the narrow staircase leading down to the main floor. "Are you ready to observe?"

"I am." Kharl followed the clerk. "Do you agree with most of the lord justicer's decisions?"

"It is not a clerk's place to agree or not to agree. I would say that I would rather serve under Lord Justicer Priost than any others in recent years."

"Austra doesn't have that many justicers—just one here and one in Bruel. There are that many just in Brysta."

"There are town magistrates and two subjusticers as well, in Vizyn and Dykaru. The decisions of the subjusticers have the same standing as those of the lord justicers, except that their decisions, in cases involving death, must be reviewed by Lord Justicer Priost. Some excellent decisions have been set forth by Subjusticer Dhorast. Those are in the library as well. As you well know, the powers of lords and magistrates are limited to low justice."

At the base of the steps, Jusof turned and crossed the lower foyer toward the double doors.

The bailiff opened the left-hand door to the hall as the two men approached. "Good morning, ser Jusof, Lord Kharl."

"Good morning, Henolt," said Jusof.

"Good morning," added Kharl.

Beyond the double doors was a long and narrow chamber, far more stark than the corresponding hall in Brysta—and smaller. The width was about twenty cubits, the length no more than forty, and the ceiling height but seven or eight. At the south end of the chamber was a single dais, raised but half a cubit. On it rose a podium desk of dark wood, possibly walnut, thought Kharl. The desk was empty. There was no podium for the lord, as there was in Nordla.

A center aisle split eight rows of low-backed wooden benches, and there was a space of about two cubits between the stone walls and the end of the benches. Between the first row of benches and the dais was a space of perhaps a rod, but in that space on each side, set out from the walls about four cubits, were two thin narrow black tables, behind which were straight-backed chairs. The two tables and chairs were parallel to the sidewalls, so that those who sat at the tables would face each other, and not either the lord justicer at the podium desk or the audience in the benches.

Both side tables were empty, and Jusof walked to the narrow black table on the right side, where he seated himself in the chair closest to the dais. Kharl slipped into the wooden straight-backed chair beside Jusof, his eyes running across the narrow hall. No more than half a score of people sat in the benches, and none in the first two rows.

From his case, Jusof took out a portable inkpot, two pens, and several sheets of paper, laying them out before him. "The case at hand this morning concerns Tellark, a tanner accused of murdering a tariff farmer."

Even as the bells from the tower above began to strike the glass, the rear door opened, and the bailiff stepped into the hall. At the south end of the chamber, a small side door opened, and the lord justicer stepped out onto the dais.

"All rise!" intoned the bailiff.

Kharl rose with Jusof, his eyes on the lord justicer.

Priost wore a robe over his own garb, and the robe was almost shapeless black, trimmed in green. From what Kharl could tell, the lord justicer was neither lean and angular, nor large and corpulent, but a man of moderate height with black hair tinged with gray. He walked briskly, but not hurriedly, to the podium desk, where he seated himself.

"You may be seated."

After a moment of silence, Priost cleared his throat. "Before we begin, is there one who would take the Justicer's Challenge?" He looked around, waited, then went on, "There being none, bailiff, bring forth the defendant."

The rear door opened once more, and two armsmen in green and black escorted a thin, wiry man with lank red hair into the chamber.

"Tellark, the tanner, step forward!" called out the bailiff.

Kharl noted that the tanner wore a clean gray undertunic and trousers, boots, and that his hands were not tied or chained. He did not look to be bruised. Kharl could not sense any hints of chaos about the man, and there was no feel of injury. The mage waited as the tanner approached the dais, then halted several cubits short of the lord justicer.

"You are Tellark, the tanner, and your home and business are located at the intersection of Renderers Way and the Southwest Lane?" The justicer's dry voice barely reached Kharl, although the mage was less than a rod from Priost.

"Yes, Lord Justicer." The tanner's response was hardly audible.

"You are charged with the murder of Yeson, the tariff farmer for the southwest quarter of Valmurl." Priost waited several moments. "Did you kill Yeson?"

The wiry tanner looked down at the polished gray granite of the floor, then straight at Priost, but did not reply.

"The accused being mute, and without an advocate, the justicing enters a statement of denial."

Kharl nodded to himself. He approved of the Austran practice of assuming a person charged was innocent until the evidence was provided. According to Jusof, that was supposed to be the code for both Austra and Nordla, but Kharl certainly hadn't seen it in his own case. Nor had Charee.

He glanced to his right, where Jusof was writing quickly, but in a clear, if small, script.

Without a word, the armsmen escorted Tellark to the table opposite the one where Jusof and Kharl were seated and had the tanner sit in the middle chair. Both armsmen remained standing, their backs to the wall, a cubit from Tellark.

"The first witness," ordered Priost.

The hall doors opened, and a large figure of a man, seemingly overflowing his maroon tunic, slouched inside.

"Bebarak, step forward!" commanded the bailiff.

The big man lumbered forward, and Kharl noted that the scabbard at his right side was empty, as was the knife sheath at his left. Bebarak halted short of the dais.

"You are Bebarak, chief guard to the tariff farmer Yeson?"

"Ah . . . yes, your honorship. Well . . . I was."

"Ser or lord justicer will suffice."

Bebarak looked dumbly at Priost.

"Just call me ser."

"Yes, ser."

After several more questions establishing who Bebarak was and that he had seen the incident, Priost asked, "After you entered the tannery, what happened?"

"Well, ser . . . Master Yeson, he walked up to him—the tanner over there—and he told him that his time was up. He said he'd best come up with the ten golds, or it'd be hard on him—"

"Did he say 'ten golds'?"

"Yes, ser. He'd been saying that we needed the ten golds earlier-like, too. Anyway, Master Yeson told him his time was up, and the fellow said no he wouldn't because Yeson was overcharging, and it wasn't right, and that he'd been taking too much for years."

"Then what happened?"

"Well, ser . . . Master Yeson, he laughed. He told the tanner to stop complaining, that everyone paid the tariff farmer. He said he'd be paying like he did every year, and he told him to stop whining, and just like that the tanner bent down; then he straightened up, and he had this hammer. He hit Master Yeson upside his head, and Master Yeson fell over. He weren't breathing, either, pretty soon."

"What did the tanner do?"

"He just stood there."

Priost asked a number of other questions, but the guard's story remained essentially the same—and truthful, Kharl noted. When the guard was finished, he was escorted from the hall. All through the process, Jusof kept writing.

The next witness was Keromont, Lord Ghrant's tariff steward. Even as he stopped before the dais, his eyes darted from the lord justicer to Kharl and back to the lord justicer.

"Steward," Priost said firmly, "so long as you tell what is so, I doubt you have much to fear from Lord Kharl. He is hear to learn how justice is done."

"Yes, ser."

"Now . . . according to your records, what was the tariff assessed on Tellark the tanner?"

"Five golds, Lord Justicer."

"Five." Priost nodded. "Were you aware that Yeson was insisting on ten from Tellark?"

"Ah . . . sir. Not . . . precisely. Might I explain, ser?"

"Go ahead."

"Tariff farmers collect tariffs for the Lord of Austra. They have been allowed to require somewhat more than the assessed tariff in order to cover their expenses. If a tariff farmer has to make many visits to someone, or cover the tariffs due themselves until they can collect, that excess can be larger. I did not know how much more than five golds that Yeson was charging, but it is always more."

"How much more?"

"Usually . . . and this is only what is considered customary, Lord Justicer, the excess is roughly one gold for every ten of tariff. That is, if large sums are not past due."

"So you would not consider it unusual for Yeson to have charged Tellark, say five and a half golds, even six?"

"No, ser."

"Did you know if Tellark happened to be habitually late in paying his tariffs?"

"From what Yeson told me, it would have been unlikely. If what he said was true. He had said that he was fortunate in having no great delinquencies."

"To your knowledge, had Yeson misled you in the past on this fact?"

"No, ser."

Once more the questions went on, but Kharl didn't see that they added that much.

After Keromont came a series of witnesses, including the tanner's wife. She claimed she had not seen the murder, that her consort was a good man, that he would not have murdered any good person, and, in response to Priost's questioning, that her consort had been aware that Yeson was overtariffing, but had not known what to do about it. Then came the other two guards of the tariff farmer and a neighbor who had summoned the Watch patrollers.

Jusof kept writing, scarcely looking up from the growing sheaf of paper that he had created.

Finally, some time near midday, the lord justicer called no more witnesses and instead looked to his right. "Tellark, rise and come forward."

The tanner did not speak as the armsmen escorted him to a position in front of the dais.

"You have heard the evidence against you. Do you have anything to say that justicing should know? Have any of the witnesses said anything that is not true?"

Tellark remained silent.

"Master tanner, this is your last chance to say anything in your own defense."

Kharl could sense Priost's frustration. At least, he thought the thin miasma of order-bounded chaos around the lord justicer was frustration.

"Won't change nothing, ser."

"Let me be the judge of that. You stand accused of murder. All of the witnesses save your consort have testified that you committed this murder. If you have anything to say in defense of yourself, you should speak now."

Tellark shuddered, but did not speak.

Priost waited, far longer than Kharl would have.

Then, finally, the tanner spoke. "He was cheating everyone, ser. Taking golds in the name of the Lord, but keeping 'em. Everyone knew it. Even the steward knew it. No one did nothing. Some years, I could pay it, hard as it was. I couldn't this year. Emela, she lost the baby and couldn't help none, and I had to hire Balsat's boy. I told Yeson that, and all he said was that everyone had a story, and iffin I knew what was good for me, I'd be paying. I knows what he was saying. His guards, they burned down that cooper's place. Kundark couldn't pay, neither. No one did nothing then, neither. Everyone said it was an accident. Wasn't no accident." Tellark closed his mouth sharply, as if he had said too much.

Kharl could sense that the tanner was telling the absolute truth, and he would have wagered that Priost knew it as well.

"Did you come to the Great House and tell anyone this? Did you come here?"

"Wouldn't done no good."

"Did you try?"

Tellark did not look at the justicer. "Got nothing else to say."

"You may be seated."

The guards escorted Tellark back to the other table.

When Jusof had stopped writing, seemingly for the first time since the trial had begun, Kharl cleared his throat, gently.

"Yes, Lord Kharl?"

"What happens next?" Kharl kept his voice low.

"He will decide. There is nothing more to be heard."

"Now?"

"Shortly."

Lord Justicer Priost never left his podium desk, but neither did he look up. Upon occasion he wrote something down, but he did not appear to have written that much. After less than a quarter glass he looked up.

"Master Tellark, come forward."

The guards flanked Tellark when he stopped before the dais, and this time, they were far closer, and far more alert.

"Call forth Steward Keromont."

Kharl wondered about that, but said nothing as the tariff steward returned to the hall and stood beside Tellark. Keromont kept glancing at Kharl.

"Master Tellark and Steward Keromont, here is what the justicing has found. First, the tariff farmer Yeson had made a practice of excessive tariffing. He had used his guards to intimidate those tariffed so that they would not protest. The tariff steward was not aware of the degree of such abuses. Such a practice is not conducive to an orderly collection of tariffs, nor is it to the benefit of Austra." Priost looked hard at Keromont.

The steward swallowed, but did not speak.

"Second," the lord justicer continued, "the tanner Tellark did in fact murder the tariff farmer Yeson with a hammer, and the tanner did so in a manner that showed that he knew what he was doing." He paused and looked at the tanner.

Tellark did not look directly at the justicer.

"Therefore, with regard to the questions of the tariff, this justicing sets forth the following. First, the tariff steward will review the rolls and records of all tariff farmers on a regular basis and, where necessary, require a tariff farmer to explain any tariff that the steward judges as excessive. Second, those rolls will henceforth show both the Lord's tariff and the amount collected. Failure of a tariff farmer to keep accurate records will be deemed a crime against the Lord. Third, the tariff for this year for the tanner Tellark will be deemed paid on the rolls of Yeson's successor and upon the accounts of the Lord of Austra." Priost looked at the tariff steward. "Is that clear, Steward Keromont?"

"Yes, Lord Justicer."

Kharl almost opened his mouth in astonishment that the lord justicer could impose requirements on the Lord of Austra—and expect compliance.

Priost turned his eyes back on Tellark. "Master Tellark, with regard to the murder of the tariff farmer Yeson, you are found guilty of that murder, and hereby sentenced to be hanged at sunset tonight."

Tellark did not move as the two armsmen each took hold of him.

"Let justice be done," Priost stated, rising.

"All rise!" ordered the bailiff.

Priost did not turn and leave the dais until both Keromont and Tellark had been escorted from the hall. Then, without a word, the lord justicer turned and walked to the small doorway from the dais. The few spectators in the hall began to file out in silence.

After several moments, Kharl turned to Jusof.

"You are most agitated, Lord Kharl," suggested Jusof, in the silence of the nearly empty chamber as the clerk straightened his papers and closed the portable inkpot.

"He killed the tariff farmer, but the tariff farmer was charging him far more than he owed. For that he'll be hanged? Not put in gaol or flogged, but hanged?"

"It is true that Yeson was not known to be the most scrupulous of tariff farmers. He had been overtariffing the tanner well beyond his costs and pocketing the difference. There were reports that he had done the same with others." Jusof paused. "In none of those cases did anyone come forward or complain."

"They were afraid," suggested Kharl.

"Doubtless they were, but the law cannot reward fear. It cannot guess what people may think or feel or need. If no one speaks, the law cannot act. Tellark could have come to the Hall of Justice and protested. He could have gone to Lord Ghrant's tariff steward."

"But . . . how would he know that?" Kharl certainly hadn't known that such possibilities existed. Then, in Brysta, he doubted that protesting would have changed anything, because Egen had ordered Fyngel to increase the tariffs on the cooperage so that Kharl could not pay. Kharl had to admit that Tellark had not faced quite as great an injustice—but it was still injustice.

"Did he ever ask? There is no evidence that he did. Rather than try for a better solution, he killed a man. The tariff farmer was not a good man. We know that, but the law must frown on people deciding on their own whose life to take and whose to spare."

"But hanging?"

"What would you have the lord justicer do? Tellark did kill Yeson. Regardless of the reason for the killing, except in self-defense, or in defense of family, a justicer cannot excuse a killing. In a brawl or an accident, the death penalty is not required, but Tellark knew full well what he was doing. The law cannot excuse willful and knowing murder. If the lord justicer allows attacks on tariff farmers, who are not the most beloved of men, that weakens Lord Ghrant and all of Austra. Who would then pay their tariffs? Justicer Priost did what he could under the law. He insisted on an accounting of all the tariff farmers' rolls. He mandated a change in accounting, with penalties, and he dismissed the tanner's tariff for this year, presumably on the grounds that the tariff farmer exceeded the authority granted by Lord Ghrant and that the tariff steward did not exercise adequate supervision. That will ensure that the widow will retain the tannery. The other tariff farmers will receive the message that excessive zeal is not acceptable."

"That does not seem totally fair."

Jusof smiled sadly. "Totally fair or just it is not. You might recall, Lord Kharl, what I said about the law when you came to the Hall of Justice. Law is a tool. It is not justice. Sometimes it can be close to it. At other times, while the law is the best we have, it cannot be just, not without destroying Austra itself." The clerk slipped the papers and inkpot into his case, then withdrew a single sheet, which he extended to Kharl.

Kharl took it.

"The lord justicer has suggested that you write an advocate's brief. You've read enough of them—on a forthcoming case. I have the file in my chamber. Your brief will remain, of course, private to me and the lord justicer."

Kharl looked at Jusof. Write a brief? He'd never written much of anything, except a few letters, one or two short statements when he bid on barrels for the harbor fort at Brysta, and his statement of candidacy to become a master cooper.

"Just use the same format as all the others," Jusof offered. "It's a simple enough pattern. Make it short. Most are too long." The clerk smiled briefly, then stepped away from the table.

As he followed Jusof, Kharl was silent. Write a brief? Why? He wouldn't ever be an advocate. Could he even write three sentences that made sense?

Even as he pondered the lord justicer's request, Kharl was still wondering about Jusof's words about Tellark's fate. The law could not be just without destroying the land? He'd thought he had understood what Jusof had said on the first day, but Priost's death sentence for Tellark cast that understanding in a different light. Was it fair to require people to act when they might suffer? That was what Priost's decision had said, in effect. But Kharl could see what Jusof had meant as well. For years, the tanner had done nothing. Then . . . he had murdered the tariff farmer. Priost had crafted a sentence to reduce the abuse, but did not excuse the murder.

Kharl took a deep breath. Without even the struggle that trying to write a brief would entail, he had more to think about, because what he had seen went far beyond the Hall of Justice.

LI

As Kharl stepped into the lord-chancellor's chamber, he saw standing beside Hagen a young man, one who looked like he'd scarcely reached his first score, for all that his shoulders were broad, and he was less than half a head shorter than Kharl. His hair was a rusty red, and his face was lightly freckled. He was clad in gray trousers and a dark green tunic that brought out the paleness of his skin.

Upon seeing Kharl, even before the door had closed behind the mage, the young man bowed. "Lord Kharl."

"Lord Kharl, this is Erdyl," Hagen said, with a smile. "He will be your secretary, more properly the secretary to the Austran Envoy to the Western Quadrant of Nordla. He also has been told that he is to say nothing of this until it is proclaimed."

Kharl had recalled something about a secretary, but seeing the young man brought home the point that he would scarcely be traveling alone, not when he would be accompanied by Undercaptain Demyst, Erdyl, and guards. He also understood that Hagen had told Erdyl about Kharl's future duties as a form of test. If Erdyl said a word, Kharl suspected he would have a new secretary.

"Lord Hagen had told me I would have a secretary"—Kharl offered a smile—"but little more."

Erdyl stood respectfully, waiting. His eyes appraised Kharl, but the mage could sense no chaos.

"Erdyl is the youngest son of Lord Askyl of Norbruel," Hagen went on. "He has five older brothers, and his father had suggested that he might be most suitable."

Kharl could detect neither untruthfulness nor sarcasm in the older man's words. "Erdyl, with the lord-chancellor's word, I am most certain you'll do well."

"I would hope to do my best and to support you in all that you require."

"Except magery," Hagen added dryly. "And that is something you are to mention not at all. To no one."

"Oh, yes, ser. I did not mean such," Erdyl said quickly.

Hagen gestured to the chair before his table desk, then seated himself. Erdyl waited until Kharl was seated before sitting. The lord-chancellor turned back to the young man. "Erdyl, Lord Kharl's strengths are magery, an understanding of men that few possess, and great strength of will. He is less conversant with the intricacies of etiquette. Your tasks are to write what is needful in a manner that captures what Lord Kharl requires and to provide any insights that will prove useful. You are to obey Lord Kharl in all matters, however. I say this not just as a polite phrase, but as a matter of your survival. There are very few, if any, left alive, who have failed to heed Lord Kharl's warnings, while most of those who have followed his direction are hale and hearty."

Erdyl nodded solemnly.

While Kharl could sense the young man's acquiescence, he also had the feeling that Hagen had already made the same points in private with Erdyl.

"In addition to his duties as envoy, Lord Kharl will also be studying the laws of Nordla while he is in Brysta, as he has been doing with those who serve the lord justicer here."

That, Kharl sensed, was a definite surprise to the young man.

"The way the laws are administered can tell much to an envoy," Hagen went on, "and such investigations are far less dangerous, and less costly, than attempting to play at the game of spying. You will, of course, say nothing of what Lord Kharl does beyond the general observation that he is an envoy—unless he orders you to do so."

"Yes, ser."

"When we are alone, you may ask why I do something," Kharl added, thinking that was something he should have handled better with Arthal.

"But only when you are truly alone," Hagen added. "You will also be tasked with writing the final draft of Lord Kharl's reports in fair hand, and some of them might be quite long."

"Yes, ser."

"You will also be tasked with organizing anything that Lord Kharl wishes done. While he is finishing his work at the Hall of Justice, you will be learning a few matters here at the Great House, from me, and from the commanders, and from the stewards . . ."

Almost a glass passed before Hagen stood. "I have a few words for Lord Kharl, before you two have a quick midday meal. It will be brief, because Lord Kharl is expected back at the Hall of Justice."

Kharl repressed a smile. Hagen was stretching the truth there a little.

Once Erdyl had left them, the lord-chancellor turned to Kharl. "Erdyl writes well, and quickly. Despite his age, he sees much, and his mind is also quick."

"He has enough older brothers that he has no chances of seeing any coins from the family lands," suggested Kharl.

"His father has been loyal to both Lord Estloch and to Lord Ghrant," Hagen added.

Kharl smiled. He understood that Hagen wanted someone who could help Kharl, but whom he could also reward, and someone who would be regarded as very traditional by doubting lords. It made great sense. "Is there anything I need to worry about with him?"

"Don't disappoint him. If you plan to do something to upset his high opinion of you, explain why."

Kharl also understood that. "I'll try."

"Go have your meal with him." Hagen gestured toward the door.

"Yes, most honored lord-chancellor." Kharl grinned.

"Out, troublesome lord mage." Hagen followed his words with a rueful smile.

Kharl laughed and made his way out of the lord-chancellor's chamber.

Erdyl was standing outside in the corridor. "Ser?"

"We'll just go to the smaller dining hall," Kharl said, turning down the corridor. "I only have a glass or so before I need to get back to the Hall of Justice."

Erdyl looked quizzically at Kharl. "Ser . . . might I ask . . . ?"

"I'm trying to learn how to write an advocate's brief." Kharl stopped at the archway into the dining chamber, then saw that the smaller table was empty and headed toward it.

Erdyl followed, but did not speak until they were seated. "Is that part of being a mage, ser?"

"In a fashion, I guess." Kharl motioned to one of the servers.

"A lager, Lord Kharl?"

"Yes, please, and whatever you think is best for the meal." Kharl looked to Erdyl.

"Ah . . . red wine, please, and whatever Lord Kharl is having."

"I'll have your lager and wine in a moment, sers." The woman smiled pleasantly and headed for the back staircase down to the kitchen.

"You're from somewhere near Bruel?" asked Kharl.

Erdyl smiled, seeming almost embarrassed. "It's not so close that I'd call it near. Father's lands lie nearly a hundred and fifty kays north of Bruel along the coast. It takes an eightday by the roads to get to Bruel. That's in good weather in the summertime."

Kharl laughed at his own misunderstanding. "And in the winter?"

"You can't use the roads. The Sudpass is snowed in within a few days after harvest is over, an eightday or two at most. There's a fair harbor in the town. That's Norbruel. The holding house is on the hill to the north of town. We can see the harbor and Seal Island from the terrace."

"Did you want to come to Valmurl? Or was it your father's idea?"

"I asked, ser. He had no objections." Erdyl's voice was even, almost flat.

"He really didn't think it was a good idea," suggested Kharl.

Erdyl looked at Kharl, then shrugged, smiling sheepishly. "No, ser. He said that, if I wanted to make my way among strangers, I might as well try. He sent a letter to Lord Hagen, even before he became lord-chancellor, asking if Lord Hagen might find me a position."

Kharl nodded. "How long have you been in Valmurl?"

"Just three eightdays, ser. Once Commander Casolan sent word that it was safe, Father put me on the *Seafox*. He's known Lord Hagen since they were young, and the lord-chancellor had sent back a letter asking Father if I'd be willing to serve Lord Ghrant."

"I'm scarcely Lord Ghrant," Kharl pointed out.

"You are one of the most loyal lords serving him, it is said."

Kharl still found it jarring to be called a lord, and he wasn't quite certain what to say to Erdyl's statement. He pondered for a moment before answering. "I came to serve Lord Ghrant because Ha— Lord Hagen served him, and Lord Hagen is the most worthy man I have met." He stopped as the server set a pale lager before him and a goblet before Erdyl.

"Did you really turn a mountain into glass?" Erdyl asked.

"Not exactly," Kharl replied. "Order doesn't work like that. A white wizard tried to use chaos to burn up all our forces, and I turned the chaos back on the wizard. Part of a hill behind the wizards turned into glass."

The young man nodded slowly. "I didn't see how a black mage would do that, but everyone kept saying that you had."

Kharl took a sip of his ale before saying more. "I've been told that I'm not exactly like other order-mages. I seem to be a little better with shields, but I don't seem to have much talent for healing or things like that." He felt that he was being truthful in what he said.

"Shields? Like an old-style lancer?"

"No. A way of stopping chaos-fire and, sometimes, things like cross-bow bolts. That's if I know they're coming." Kharl took another sip of lager. "Have you ever been in Nordla, or anyplace else besides Norbruel or Bruel or Valmurl?"

"I went to Vizyn once with Clandal." Erdyl shrugged. "It was even colder than Norbruel, and that was in the summer."

"Nordla can be a dangerous place," Kharl said. "Lord West and his sons have killed many who made the mistake of talking about them in public. The less we speak about ourselves and about them, the better."

"The lord-chancellor said that I was only to say that you were the lord of Cantyl and that you had once been a merchant officer."

"That's right." Kharl nodded. "You should say only that your sire is the lord of Norbruel." He could sense a quiet solidness about the young man, and he had the feeling that Hagen had picked well. "We should let others talk."

Erdyl laughed. "Father is always saying that. He said you couldn't hook the smallest gilly in the brook if it kept its mouth shut."

Kharl found that he was enjoying talking to young Erdyl, and regretted that, after he ate, he would have to go back to the Hall of Justice to work on the brief suggested by Jusof. He supposed he would learn from that, but he was not looking forward to that learning. Writing anything was a chore, and a laborious one at that.

LII

Kharl walked down the main floor corridor of the Great House toward the lord-chancellor's chamber, for the private midday meal to which he had been invited by a messenger. Had his brief for Jusof and the lord-justicer been so bad that Hagen had reconsidered sending him to Brysta as an envoy? Kharl frowned. He knew what he had written had been simple, but all he could write about the law and the case was simple.

As he neared the chamber, the guard on the left opened the door. "He's expecting you, Lord Kharl."

Hagen rose from behind the table desk as Kharl entered the chamber. The mage turned to close the door, but the armsman had already shut it.

"Greetings, Kharl." Hagen smiled. "I'm glad you could join me." He gestured to the place set across from him. Only a goblet and a beaker were on the polished wood surface, and Hagen's goblet held red wine, the beaker for Kharl a lager.

"I appreciate it. Not too many wish to eat with me, except for Casolan and Norgen."

"That's not surprising," Hagen replied, seating himself once more. "You have the power to punish, but not reward. People generally risk the chance of hearing bad news from me because they feel I can also reward them—or provide information or some sort of advantage."

Kharl settled into the chair, studying Hagen.

The lord-chancellor looked tired, with blackish circles under his eyes. His face was thinner, and one eye twitched. "You've met several times with Erdyl now."

"We've talked over meals," Kharl replied. "I've told him what to expect in Brysta, a little about how it's laid out . . . that sort of thing."

"Good." Hagen paused. "You've now been studying under Jusof for almost four eightdays. How have you found it?"

Kharl's lips twisted into a wry smile. "I have found that I write poorly. The more I learn about the law, the less I like it. Yet the less I like it, the more I understand how necessary it is for a land."

"You already understand more than some advocates." Hagen paused to take a sip from his goblet.

Kharl doubted that, but did not say so.

"Be that as it may, I've talked with Lord Justicer Priost and with Jusof. Jusof feels that within the next eightday, it is likely that you will have learned as much as is necessary for an envoy to know. He and the lord justicer are also willing to provide you with a letter of introduction to the lord justicers of Brysta. It will state that you have been a most diligent scholar of the law in Valmurl, and that they hope that their peers in Nordla will extend you every courtesy in allowing you to pursue your studies there, as your other duties permit."

Kharl took a sip of the lager. "You need me to go to Brysta soon, I take it. Are things bad there?"

"Not yet, but they will be, I fear. We had received word that Lord West had fallen ill. That happens. Then we later heard indirectly from a Sarronnese trader that Lord West was poisoned, but will recover." Hagen paused. "When there is an attempt such as this, there is most likely to be another one. From what you have said, I would wager that young Egen has enlisted some Hamorian assistance in the matter of his sire's illness. We do not know this, but as you have seen here, there is a certain pattern to the way the emperor and his minions work. As you can, we need you to discover what is really happening and how deeply Hamor is involved."

"You said you had spies . . ." ventured Kharl.

"We did. That is another reason for concern. Two are dead, and one has vanished. That is why we must rely on indirect reports. That also concerns Lord Ghrant."

"The Hamorians seem to be moving quickly after their defeat here."

"The emperor does not admit defeats. He suffers but temporary setbacks. That is what his late envoy Joharak once told me. I would also imagine that they would like to make such an effort before Lord Ghrant can rebuild Austra."

"Lord Ghrant has no designs on Nordla, does he?"

"Of course not." Hagen snorted. "Because the Hamorians have such designs, though, they imagine everyone else has the same motivations." He paused at the knock on the door.

"Your dinner, sers," came the voice of one of the guards.

"Come on in."

One of the serving girls from the kitchen stepped into the chamber carrying a tray. She inclined her head. "Lord-chancellor, Lord Kharl."

The platters both contained ascalyn—veal thinly sliced, marinated in a mint sauce, braised quickly, and served with a browned butter sauce and fried pearapples. A large basket of bread came with the meal. Kharl had only tasted ascalyn once, and that had been at the consort feast of Charee's cousin Vertya.

Once the server had left, Hagen raised his goblet. "To better days."

"To better days."

They both ate silently for a time. Kharl found the veal far better than he had remembered it, but he suspected that his memory had been accurate, and that the preparation at the Great House was far better.

Hagen broke off a chunk of the brown bread. "You'll have to leave within a few days, as soon as the *Seastag* is loaded. She ported yesterday. She was on a short-leg voyage to Nylan, Lydiar, Renklaar, and Worrak."

"How else do you think I should prepare? Is there anything else I should know? Can I tell Erdyl?"

"You can tell young Erdyl. He has said nothing to anyone, except that he is learning what he can at the Great House. There is little else that we can provide, except that Lord Ghrant will have to proclaim you as an envoy. That will be as late as possible, the day before you depart on the *Seastag*. But you cannot be recognized as an envoy without the audience and proclamation. It will be a short ceremony." Hagen added, "There is one other thing. I shouldn't have to tell you, but we all overlook things. The Hamorians will not wish you in Brysta. I would not put it past them to attempt some action against you."

"How would they find out if the ceremony is just before I leave?"

"We have spies in Swartheld, and they have spies here. Most spies know that it is difficult to kill a mage who is forewarned or alert. I would doubt that you will have much difficulty in such a fashion, but . . . many spies are good at indirection. I know you can detect poison . . . but that ability does little good if you do not realize that even food prepared by close friends can be poisoned without their knowing it. Crossbow bolts kill if you do not see them coming. Even cliffs have been toppled on mages, I've been told." Hagen shook his head.

"Are you trying to tell me not to go to Brysta?"

"No. I want you to come back . . . And one last thing, Kharl. About that beard . . ."

"I know. It would be foolish to go to Brysta looking the way I once did."

"You might also want people here to see what you look like without it, before the audience."

"Do you want me to shave it off tonight?" Kharl asked. "Would that be soon enough?"

"No," parried the lord-chancellor, "tomorrow morning would be most suitable."

They both burst into laughter.

LIII

So hot was the midsummer morning, even before the second glass after dawn, that Kharl was blotting his forehead even before he dismounted outside the Hall of Justice and handed the gelding's reins to Dorfal. He had to admit that on days so warm, he didn't miss having a beard. Winter might be another story.

"I'll just be waiting, ser," offered the young lancer.

"Thank you." The day was to be his last with Jusof, and it would be short, since Kharl's audience with Lord Ghrant was set for the glass before noon.

Kharl walked through the double doors into the cooler main foyer and headed up the narrow stairs to the upper level.

Jusof rose as Kharl entered. "Good morning, Lord Kharl."

"Good morning," returned the mage. "It's hot out."

"It will be warm in here as well by afternoon." Jusof nodded. "Congratulations on your appointment to Brysta as the envoy. We received the proclamation for posting just half a glass ago, not that we had not heard in secrecy several days ago." The clerk smiled. "The lord-chancellor's motives in having you study law are most clear."

"I think I know just enough to be wary of any laws and those who administer them," Kharl replied. "Especially when they are not of such honesty as Lord Justicer Priost."

"That is wise, even for advocates," said Jusof. "Still, you know more than you allow yourself credit for. You seem to have mastered the basics of jurisprudence, the very basics, but many who call themselves advocates often know less."

After almost four eightdays, Kharl hoped he had learned something, but doubted that he had learned much more than to apply what he had already known to the law.

"There is little point in your studying more unless you plan to become an advocate." Jusof smiled. "You must indulge me if I point out that such seems most unlikely. You have a talent for the law, but I cannot see Lord Ghrant—or your own talents—restricting you to the Hall of Justice."

The mage nodded.

Jusof handed Kharl two elaborately sealed letters. "The lord-chancellor had requested that the lord justicer and I both draft and sign these letters commending you as a scholar of the legal system to whatever clerks and justicers you may need to approach in Nordla or elsewhere. Lord Justicer Priost was most impressed with your brief on the Lendyl case. It might have used some more polish, but the logic and the precedents were sound. He did say that you might well be wasted as a mage." Jusof laughed softly.

"But . . . I've never met the lord justicer," Kharl observed, slipping the letters into a jacket pocket.

"That is true, and that is as it should be. Were the Lord's mage ever to have met with the lord justicer, many would think that Lord Ghrant might be pressing for something in the Hall of Justice. Lord Justicer Priost has not met with Lord Ghrant, except at very public dinners at the Great House, or at his blind briefings of Lord Ghrant, since he became lord justicer." Jusof cleared his throat. "That does not mean, in regard to you, Lord Kharl, that he has not been apprised of all you have done, and he was most impressed with your diligence, as well as your understanding."

"I'll accept the diligence," Kharl replied. "I hope the understanding will come."

"As I am most certain you know," Jusof said with a dryness just short of the pedantic, "understanding is the virtue most often claimed and least often exhibited. Since you have already shown it elsewhere, I have no doubts it will surface in the law as well." He smiled once more. "I will not keep you, Lord Kharl, but it has truly been a pleasure to work with you."

"Thank you." Kharl inclined his head. "You have been most understanding."

After taking his leave of the chief clerk and heading back down to the main level, Kharl was still mulling over his surprise that Jusof had been pleased to work with him.

Even after such a short time, the square was even hotter than when he had entered the Hall of Justice, and he was once more blotting his forehead as he and Dorfal rode back toward the Great House.

"You'll not be coming here any longer, ser?" asked the lancer.

"No. Today was the last day."

"Will you be heading back to your lands, then, ser?"

"That is up to the lord-chancellor and Lord Ghrant." Kharl felt uncomfortable with the answer, true as it was, because it was misleading, but he also did not wish to announce what he would be doing on the open streets of Valmurl.

"Yes, ser."

"Are you going to stay a lancer?" Kharl asked.

"I don't know, ser. I've another two years. Then, I have to decide whether to go for five or leave." Dorfal laughed. "Undercaptain Demyst was saying that I ought to stay on. Told me that fighting like we been through only comes every double handful of years, and that I ought to take the easy years that follow."

"Do you want to go back to crabbing?"

"Not really, ser. Don't know as I see myself as a lancer for years either, though."

Kharl smiled faintly. He'd never thought about it at Dorfal's age. He'd just assumed he would be a cooper. Then, that might have been because he'd liked being a cooper, liked the smell and feel of the wood, and the sense of having done something right when a barrel or keg or hogshead had been finished. He didn't presume to offer Dorfal advice. "I'm sure that when the time comes you'll do fine."

Dorfal smiled uneasily.

When they reached the Great House, Kharl dismounted in the front entry and let the young lancer take the mounts. He made his way to his quarters, where he washed up again and changed into his newest magely finery, garb that had been paid for by Lord Ghrant, along with five other sets of clothing deemed suitable for an envoy.

Then he made his way down to the hallway outside the main audience hall, where Hagen found him.

"You look most impressive, Lord Kharl," offered the lord-chancellor.

Kharl felt more like a traitor bird dressed in the plumage of a raven. "I'm not certain I'll ever get used to wearing end-day finery all the time."

"It looks good on you." Hagen's smile dropped away. "The ceremony will be very short. Afterward, there will be a midday dinner with Lord Ghrant, Lady Hyrietta, and a few others."

"You didn't mention that."

An impish smile crossed Hagen's face. "I didn't? It must have slipped my mind."

Kharl shook his head. "If Glyan's experiments with the new wine barrels *don't* work, I'll send a half barrel to you."

Hagen laughed softly. "I need to go so that I can be on the dais before Ghrant enters." With a nod, he slipped away.

Kharl stood in the side hallway, away from the audience hall doors, where he could not see who entered the hall nor be seen by them, for another quarter glass.

"Lord Kharl, ser . . . you've been summoned," called one of the armsmen in the yellow and black of the personal guard.

Kharl walked around the corner and toward the doors. When he was in place, one of the armsmen opened the door, and Kharl stepped through it. The hall had but perhaps a score of people in it, and slightly less than half of those Kharl knew. He had half expected to see Norgen and Casolan, and he did, but he had not expected to see Lady Hyrietta standing behind Lord Ghrant's shoulder as her consort waited for Kharl to reach the dais. Nor had he expected to see Lyras standing beside Casolan, nor Jusof and Lord Justicer Priost.

He squared his shoulders and walked deliberately forward, halting several cubits short of the dais, as he had seen all the others do at various audiences. There he bowed slightly, and waited.

Lord Ghrant smiled, and Kharl could sense that it was a friendly smile, albeit one with a hint of nervousness behind it. "Lord Kharl of Cantyl, are you a true and faithful subject of Austra?"

"I am, your lordship."

"Are you willing to serve, to the fullest and best of your abilities, as an envoy of Austra?"

"I am, your lordship."

"Then, Lord Kharl of Cantyl, you are hereby appointed as the envoy of the Lord of Austra to the West Quadrant of Nordla, governed by Lord

West, with all powers and privileges accorded such envoys, and with the responsibilities required by such powers."

"Thank you, your lordship."

"Thank you, Lord Kharl, for taking on those responsibilities and duties. We wish you well." Ghrant nodded.

Kharl bowed twice, then turned and walked from the audience chamber.

Outside, a messenger was waiting. "Lord Kharl, ser, if you would follow me?"

They had traveled but twenty cubits when Hagen appeared.

"I'll escort him from here," the lord-chancellor suggested.

"Ah . . . yes, ser."

Hagen smiled, and the messenger scurried away.

"How do you feel as an envoy?" asked Hagen.

"Not that different," Kharl admitted. "A little more worried. What about this dinner?"

"Oh, it will be very social. Just don't talk about Brysta or magery unless you're asked. Otherwise, you can talk about anything."

Kharl resolved to listen more than talk.

After the private dinner, which was completely social and without a word of either Brysta or what Kharl would be doing as envoy, Kharl accompanied Hagen back to the lord-chancellor's chamber. He was thinking about being an envoy, and all that it might entail.

Two years in Brysta? It could be much less, Hagen had said. However long it might be, Kharl supposed that it wouldn't be all that bad, certainly not so bad as living between the walls of a renderer's vats and a tannery as he had before escaping Brysta. He did have to find Warrl and make arrangements to get him to Cantyl. He could see what else he might be able to do for Sanyle and Jeka. He hoped that Gharan had been able to keep Jeka on as a weaver.

Once the door to the lord-chancellor's chamber closed, Hagen began immediately by handing Kharl a flat leather case, ornately tooled at the edges and trimmed in gilt. "These are your credentials for presentation to Lord West. No matter what some functionary tries to tell you, insist on a formal presentation. Tell them it can be brief, even but a few moments, but it must be public and formal. If they demur, then suggest that you will be making arrangements to return to Valmurl. If they don't back down, make the arrangements to take passage on the first of my vessels to port there again and learn what you can while you wait." A wry smile crossed the lord-chancellor's lips. "It might come to that, but the moment they learn you intend to leave, you'll get an audience." He paused. "Now . . . there are a few more things we should go over. First, as we have discussed, in my dispatches to the residence steward in Brysta, I have not mentioned you are a mage. I would try to keep that from being widely known for as long as possible. Second, you already understand that you should not trust any other envoys, especially the Hamorian. Also, consider that all Hamorian merchants are effectively spies of the emperor, whether they support him or not."

Kharl frowned momentarily, then nodded. A good mage or wizard could doubtless discover the truth, as could Kharl.

"You are to send back dispatches, but only upon my vessels and only if you or Erdyl hand them personally to the captains. If you feel that a particular captain has been suborned, let me know by a message through another captain. All dispatches are to be sent to me, and you should never mention Lord Ghrant either directly or by reference. Lord Ghrant will read every one, but if they are intercepted, a message addressed to me is less damaging than one directly to Lord Ghrant. He can always claim that he knows nothing . . ."

Kharl could also understand that, little as he liked the idea.

". . . we have already discussed the token gift you will present to Lord West and your purse and your draw upon the Factors' Exchange for the expenses of the envoy's residence and staff. Do not be extravagant, but also do not be foolishly frugal . . ."

As Hagen went on, Kharl forced himself to concentrate not only on the words, most of which he had already heard in one form or another, but also on the reasons behind what the lord-chancellor said.

Envoy

LIV

Kharl had never thought he would be leading an entourage, but as he walked down the pier in the hazy early-morning sunlight of fiveday toward the *Seastag,* Undercaptain Demyst walked before him, Erdyl beside him, and two armsmen from Ghrant's personal guard followed. Cevor and Alynar wore plain gray, rather than yellow and black, while Demyst wore a gray tunic and a darker gray jacket. Erdyl wore his usual dark green and gray.

Behind them came horse drawing a cart filled with baggage. Much as Kharl had tried to limit what he had brought, he still had three bags. He'd never owned so many garments in his life. His fingers strayed to his bare chin. He still wasn't used to not having a beard.

"Hadn't thought I'd ever be leaving Austra, ser," Demyst said, glancing back at Kharl for a moment. "You think we'll be in Brysta long?"

"Envoys are sent for two years, I was told, unless they get in trouble."

"Guess we'll be in Brysta for two years, then. Master Erdyl and I'll have to keep you out of trouble."

Erdyl suppressed a smile.

Kharl doubted that two years would pass, or pass uneventfully, not the way his life had been lately, but it could be a year or more. As he neared the gangway to the *Seastag,* Kharl glanced back over his shoulder. A heavy wagon had turned onto the pier. He frowned. There was something about the wagon . . .

"Lord Kharl!" boomed a voice.

Kharl turned to see Furwyl, who had been the first mate when Hagen had captained the ship, standing at the top of the gangway in the master's jacket. "Furwyl."

"Bring your crew on board."

Even before Kharl had reached the gangway, three crew members were on the pier, beginning to unload the baggage cart. Kharl was first up the gangway, followed by his young secretary and Undercaptain Demyst.

"Every time I see you, you've come up in the world. Gives a man hope," declared the captain.

"You've come up as well. You're master of a fine ship." Kharl turned.

"This is my secretary, Erdyl, and Undercaptain Demyst, and Cevor and Alynar."

"Pleased to meet you all. Crew's already getting your baggage on board," Furwyl said. "Lord Kharl, you'll be in the master's cabin, and the undercaptain and your secretary will share the bunks in the first passenger cabin. Your guards'll have to share the small passenger cabin, but that's better than the fo'c'sle."

"I couldn't take your cabin."

"You don't have a choice. That's what the lord-chancellor ordered, and he owns the ship." Furwyl grinned.

"I still feel strange about taking the master's cabin," Kharl said.

"Strange or not, that's the way it is. Besides, I wouldn't feel right having the Lord's envoy to Brysta in that small cubby for passengers. You can do me a favor someday." Furwyl was grinning broadly.

"You'll have to come to Cantyl for that," Kharl said.

"I'll hold you to that, Lord Kharl. Best get yourself settled into your spaces. We'll be off once we finish loading this last set of pallets. They just arrived. Last-moment cargo." Furwyl gestured toward the winch and hoist gang, then toward the pier, where the heavy wagon that Kharl had noted earlier had halted.

The first pallet swung up off the heavy wagon and over the railing.

"Easy there!" called Bemyr, still the bosun. "Forward more."

Kharl's eyes and senses focused on the single long crate in the hoist sling—and sensed chaos—tightly bound within iron. "There's something wrong with that crate in the sling."

"Lord Kharl?" asked Furwyl.

"Don't let Bemyr load that crate," Kharl said tightly. "Swing it back onto the pier. There's something dangerous in it."

"Bosun! Swing that back to the pier! On the double!"

"Bring her around! Back to the pier. Don't ask questions!" Bemyr hurried down the gangway toward the pier. "Where's that teamster?"

"Stay here!" Kharl ordered Erdyl, before rushing back down the gangway after the bosun, but Demyst immediately turned and followed Kharl. The undercaptain had his blade out at the foot of the gangway.

As he neared the crate, Kharl could sense the chaos within it, massive but restrained. He'd never felt anything quite like it. He turned to the wagon before him, whose driver had vanished, but none of the other crates seemed to contain anything like the first one.

Bemyr approached the crate where it sat on the pier. He turned to Kharl, who had stopped halfway back along the side of the wagon. "This one, right?"

"That's the one. Don't touch—"

Bemyr kicked it with his heavy boot. Nothing happened. "Looks all right."

"It's not. There's something in it."

"It's just this crate, right?" asked the bosun. "Just dump it in the water. That'll take care of it."

"No! Leave it—"

Before Kharl could say anything more, Bemyr had hoisted the heavy crate, grunting as he did, and pitched it off the pier. So heavy was the crate that it splashed into the water just beside the pier, sinking so that the top edge was only a handspan above the water within moments. Bemyr stepped forward, looking down at the water, three cubits or so from the top of the pier.

Kharl could sense chaos building within the crate and threw up a shield, but Bemyr was too far from the mage—too far if Kharl had to cover Demyst and himself.

Chaos flared up from the top of the crate.

"Back!" yelled Kharl, too late, as a wave of destruction and flame roared over the bosun.

Pieces of iron slammed into the sides of the pier. The two horses screamed—if but for an instant—as flames seared them.

Bemyr's charred figure toppled onto the edge of the pier, then dropped into the water. The horses reared, trying to escape both the pain and the wagon traces. Kharl's senses swept over the animals, and his stomach twisted. With so much chaos . . . there was no way to save them.

For a moment, he just stood there. What . . . what could he do?

The wagon lurched as the dying horses tried to escape.

Kharl moved forward along the side of the wagon, then reached out with his order-senses. After a moment, he hardened the area under the nearer horse's chest, around where he felt the heart was. The gelding dropped in the traces. Sweat began to stream down Kharl's forehead as he did the same for the second horse.

Slowly, he looked up, blotting his forehead with the back of his hand.

No one seemed to have moved. Demyst stood to his right, blade in hand. Everyone on the deck of the *Seastag* moved so slowly, as if their feet were anchored in near-solid molasses. The front half of the wagon smoldered, wisps of gray smoke rising from the seared wood and paint. Foglike steam rose from the puddles of water on the pier in front of the wagon.

Kharl swallowed, then turned to look back along the pier. He could not sense any chaos.

"Rhylla! Ghart!" ordered Furwyl. "Get a net. Do what you can for Bemyr."

"He's dead," Kharl said, loudly enough for his voice to carry. He turned slowly back toward the ship.

Erdyl's eyes were wide, fixed on Kharl as he walked up the gangway. So were those of Cevor and Alynar.

Kharl stopped short of Furwyl and looked at the captain. "I'm sorry. I had no idea something like this . . ."

"Wasn't your fault, Lord Kharl." Furwyl moistened his lips. "You told him to lay off. Heard you." The captain looked at the carnage on the pier, then turned to a mate Kharl did not know. "Hysen . . . soon as they get Bemyr in canvas, we'll be casting off. Quick-like. Single up and make ready."

"Yes, ser."

Furwyl looked back to Kharl. "Safest place for a ship in times like these is at sea."

"How long before we cast off?" asked Kharl.

"Less'n quarter glass, if we cast off at all."

Kharl understood that.

Undercaptain Demyst stood at the top of the gangway, his blade out. He jerked his head for the two guards to join him.

Furwyl studied Kharl. "Don't think someone wants you going to Nordla, Lord Kharl. Best we get you there before they try something else. The lord-chancellor warned me."

"Is there anyone who could take a message to him?"

"Cargo-master for all his ships hasn't left with the manifest yet."

"Good." Kharl turned to Erdyl. "Get ready to take down what I say. We've only a few moments." He could already hear the heavy steam engine beginning to turn over, and the smoke from the stacks had begun to thicken.

Without speaking, Erdyl had opened his case and taken out a portable inkpot.

"Best in the cabin," suggested Furwyl.

"Thank you." Kharl glanced to Erdyl. "This has to be quick so that we can give it to the cargomaster within a few moments.

"Yes, ser."

Kharl hurried into the passageway leading to the master's cabin, Erdyl following.

Once his secretary was seated at the narrow desk along the inner bulkhead, Kharl began to speak, trying to organize his thoughts.

> "Honored Lord-chancellor,
> A crate exploded in chaos at the pier when Bemyr threw it into the water. I had felt chaos in the crate as it was being loaded. I told him not to, but my warning was perhaps too late, and he was killed by the chaos. It was the kind of chaos that comes from white wizards. It was set off by water when the bosun threw it into the harbor. I would judge that it was built to do the same thing when bilgewater or seawater seeped into the crate when we were at sea. . . .

As he talked, Kharl could not help but wonder why someone did not want him to arrive in Brysta—and how they had been able to act so quickly—and without a white wizard seemingly nearby. What sort of device had they used, that stored chaos in such a fashion?

Hagen had been right, again.

LV

By midday, the *Seastag* was well away from Valmurl and had long since passed the low headlands marking Cantyl. Bemyr's burial at sea had been swift and quiet, and already Reisl, whom Kharl had known when he had been ship's carpenter under Tarkyn, had taken over as bosun.

"He'll do a good job," predicted Furwyl.

Kharl thought so as well, but he worried that he hadn't been quick enough to warn Bemyr. Still, he'd never seen or sensed anything like the chaos in the crate, and there was little he could do now.

"Hagen ordered you to get me to Nordla, no matter what, didn't he?" Kharl said quietly. He could see Erdyl stiffen with interest, although the secretary was at the starboard poop railing, several cubits away.

"That he did, Lord Kharl. Told me not to let anything stop us." Furwyl scanned the horizon to the south before continuing. "He looks tired-like. Older, too."

"He has to worry about all of Austra," Kharl replied.

"Thought that was what Lord Ghrant was supposed to do." Furwyl shook his head. "He's too young to understand everything that can go wrong. Same thing happens when a ship's master is too young. That's why he needs Lord Hagen. Needs you, too."

"He needs Hagen more," Kharl said.

"Hope we don't see any Hamorian warships this crossing. You think they're the bastards got Bemyr?"

"I don't know, but if I had to wager, that'd be where my coins went."

"Mine, too."

After a time, Kharl eased away, to the railing beside Erdyl. "I'm going below for a bit."

"Do you need me, ser?"

Kharl glanced at the young man, sensing his discomfort. "No. Just stay up here in the fresh air. It helps."

"Did you . . . ?" Erdyl swallowed.

"It takes a while to get used to, especially when we're running with the wind in the long swells."

Kharl did not go to the master's cabin, his temporary quarters, but took the ladder down to the main deck, then headed forward and down the inside ladder to the carpenter's shop. He peered through the open hatch. Tarkyn was working on a carving, his relaxation when the carpentry tasks were light.

"Tarkyn?"

"Lords don't belong in the carpenter's shop." The older man's voice was gruff. "Ser."

Kharl could sense that, despite his tone, Tarkyn was pleased. "They do if they were once carpenters."

"Knew you should have been a mate, at least." Tarkyn laid aside the carving. "Told you that. I didn't think I'd see you as a lord and an envoy."

"I didn't, either," Kharl admitted. "I didn't ask for it."

"Might be why you got it." Tarkyn shook his head. "Terrible thing with Bemyr."

"I tried to protect him, to warn him. I wasn't fast enough."

"Good man," Tarkyn said. "He always did want to do things his way, though. One time, made me replace a capstan bar with spruce. Told him it wouldn't work. It didn't. Broke the first time they used it. Captain Hagen reamed him good."

"How are you doing?"

"I'm getting up there. Told Furwyl to start looking for another carpenter. You hadn't gone and saved Lord Ghrant, and it'd be you." Tarkyn looked up at Kharl. "Best second I ever had."

"I liked working here," Kharl said. "I never thought it would turn out this way."

"Better for you that it did."

Kharl nodded thoughtfully. It might have been better for him, but it hadn't always been better for those around him. Not at all. Charee and Arthal were dead. Warrl had lost his mother and the birthright of the cooperage that had been in the family for generations. Kharl had had to leave Sanyle and Jeka, and he could only hope that they were all right. The young undercaptain who'd been with him on the first attack against the rebels was dead, and so were half of the lancers who'd supported Lord Ghrant.

When he left the carpenter shop, Kharl made his way back up to the main deck, then into the master's cabin. There he sank into the chair beside the built-in desk.

He needed to sort out what he'd been told and what he knew.

Lord Ghrant was worried about what was happening in Nordla. He had few people he could trust to find that out, and none who were experienced as envoys. Hensolas had been the previous envoy, and immediately after he had returned, even before Estloch could talk to Ghrant, Estloch had been murdered, and Hensolas had ended up as one of the lords rebelling against Ghrant, but only after Ilteron's death. Had he been involved with Ilteron from the beginning? What was going on in Nordla that would cause an attack against Kharl? Or did the attack have anything to do with Nordla? Could it have been a scheme merely to kill Kharl in a way in which he could not use his abilities?

If the crate had merely exploded in the hold once the *Seastag* was well at sea, the explosion would not have hurt Kharl, but it would have blown out a chunk of the hull, and set the ship afire. Once the *Seastag* was sunk—or aflame—Kharl's magery could not have done much against the ocean, not for long.

The mage and envoy shook his head. In some ways, the reasons did not matter. It was clear that someone, most probably the Hamorians, wanted him dead. But it would help to know for what reason.

It might, Kharl corrected his thought.

LVI

The rest of the crossing, on a route south of the Gulf of Austra, then up the west coast of Nordla, was uneventful for the entire passage—more than two eightdays.

At various times, he'd talked with both Ghart, the first mate, and Rhylla, the second, as well as Furwyl. While all three were friendly, and clearly happy for Kharl, there was a definite reserve, an understanding that while they had once been shipmates those times were past. That reserve saddened Kharl, because the officers of the *Seastag* had been welcoming and helpful when he'd had nowhere to go.

Kharl also had kept thinking about the chaos explosion in the harbor at Valmurl. While he could imagine a number of reasons for the attack on the *Seastag*, he just didn't know enough to be sure what was behind it. He'd have to assume that no one was to be trusted until he found out differently. That was definitely the safest attitude for an envoy anywhere, but not one that Kharl liked.

In midafternoon on fourday, Kharl and Erdyl stood at the port railing on the poop deck, watching as Furwyl brought the *Seastag* toward the breakwaters that marked the entrance to the harbor at Brysta.

Even with the light breeze off the water, the day was clear and hot—but damp. Clearly, the easterlies were remaining strong over the west of Nordla, and the patches of brown on the hills suggested that there had been little rain in recent eightdays. Kharl glanced at the fair weather banner on the pole on the northern outer breakwater—a green oval against a white background, almost limp. The pole itself rose from the tower on the southeastern corner of the north harbor fort. Something about the fort nagged at him. It took him a moment to realize that there was a concentration of chaos there, somewhere behind the walls. It wasn't the kind that meant a white wizard was present, but more like one had been there. One of Lord West's mages? He shrugged. Lord West had both types, and he'd certainly learn soon enough. He hoped he would.

"Those are both forts, aren't they?" asked Erdyl, glancing from one side of the *Seastag* to the other, his eyes taking in the two structures that faced each other at the mouth of the harbor—the south fort at the end of one breakwater, and the north fort at the end of the other.

"Those are the harbor defenses. There are two chains that lie on a stone channel under the water. Each chain is attached to a capstan in each fort. When the capstan is turned, it raises the chain, and the chains block the harbor. They used to raise the chains once every four eightdays and inspect them." Kharl knew that from the year he had served as an assistant to the cooper at the south fort and had been pressed into the work gang that turned the capstan. "I have some doubts that the chains would work that well against the iron-hulled ships of Hamor or Recluce . . . but those are the harbor defenses." Kharl could see several figures on the battlement in uniforms he did not recognize—maroon and blue, rather than the blue and burgundy of Lord West's armsmen. Or had the uniforms been changed since he had left Brysta?

"Would you say that Brysta is somewhat backward?" asked Erdyl.

"Not in most things," Kharl replied. "Ships and guns and iron cost golds. I don't think that Lord West wishes to spend them."

"That's true," mused Erdyl. "Golds spent on a ship cannot be spent on food or goods or other things."

As the *Seastag* steamed slowly into the harbor proper, Kharl studied the piers, then the city beyond, slowly and carefully. From what he could tell, as the *Seastag* eased toward the three deepwater piers, only four vessels were tied up. A single schooner was at the outermost of the two coastal wharves. Once fall arrived, almost every berth would be taken.

He looked at the two vessels at the innermost deepwater pier. Both looked to be Hamorian merchanters, although he could only see the ensign on one. He'd have wagered that they were the same pair that Hagen had mentioned.

After several moments, Kharl pointed once more. "You can see that all the piers are north of the River Westlich, except for the ferry pier over there. That's for folk who want to cross to the southwest road. Costs a copper each way. North of the piers, over there, where all the ragged tents are, that's the lower market, mostly for poorer folk." He paused for a moment, thinking of the times that he and Jeka had used his few coppers to buy food there, and the first time when he'd saved her from the white wizard.

"Ser?"

"Oh . . . just thinking. Over there is the slateyard." He paused. A new structure had been constructed where the slateyard had been. It looked like some sort of barracks. "It used to be the slateyard. I don't know what that building is." After a moment, he went on. "The main road to the harbor is Cargo Road. Most of the low hill to the west here, that's for crafters and shopkeepers. The grander places are on the east side, overlooking the river and the back bay."

Furwyl eased the *Seastag* toward the first ocean pier, empty on the inshore side. "Back her down! Engines full stop! Lines out!"

"Lines out!" echoed Reisl.

The *Seastag* barely touched the fenders between pier and ship before she was fast to the bollards, the lines doubled up.

Kharl looked at the pier, then toward Cargo Road. Supposedly, the steward at the envoy's residence was to send the carriage and a baggage wagon to the *Seastag*. He suspected that they would have to wait for a time. While he knew about where the residence was, he had seldom been in that part of Brysta and did not recall the area, except that it was an older part of the city with large dwellings—not all that far from where he had confronted the first of the white wizards.

Rhylla scrambled up the ladder to the poop deck, said something to Furwyl, who replied and nodded toward Kharl. The second hurried toward the mage. "Lord Kharl . . . there's some harbor inspectors headed down the pier. They usually don't hit so soon."

"Thank you." Kharl grinned. "Erdyl and I will stay here, discussing the harbor and the weather."

"It's hot and likely to stay so, Lord Kharl. If you would excuse me . . ."

"Go be friendly to the harbor inspectors," Kharl suggested, knowing that no ship's officer cared much for the tariff collectors.

Once Rhylla had headed down to the main deck, ahead of Furwyl, Kharl looked at his secretary. "I don't think an envoy should worry about inspectors, do you?" He blotted his forehead. Now that the *Seastag* was tied to the pier, the faint breeze he had felt earlier had vanished.

Erdyl barely managed to keep a smile from breaking out. "Ah . . . no, ser."

"How many ships are at the deepwater piers?"

"Four, ser."

"How many could the piers hold?"

"That would be hard for me to say, ser, but I'd guess three, four times that many, could be more."

"What do you think about the two closest to shore?"

"They look almost deserted, ser. Are they Hamorian?"

"I'd judge so."

"Are you thinking. . . ." Erdyl glanced in the direction of the quarterdeck, where two men in dark blue tunics stood in the hot afternoon sun, talking to Furwyl. Rhylla stood back slightly from the three men.

"We'll have to see," Kharl said.

After perhaps a quarter glass of talking, then going over manifest lists, seemingly line by line, the two harbor inspectors left the *Seastag,* but one remained on the pier, watching the ship. Shortly after that, a covered carriage painted in green and black and drawn by two grays rolled up the pier. Behind it was an open teamster's wagon.

"Our carriage has arrived," Kharl said.

"Let me check, ser."

Kharl nodded, and Erdyl hurried down the ladder. He was met on the main deck by Undercaptain Demyst. The two made their way down the gangway.

Furwyl made his way up the ladder and joined Kharl. "A carriage yet."

Kharl almost laughed. There had been a time, not all that long ago, when he'd walked from the piers to his cooperage to save two coppers. "It's not mine. It belongs to the envoy's residence, or so they tell me."

"From cooper to carpenter to mage to lord. All in less than two years."

"It seems longer." Kharl didn't mention the flogging or the time in gaol or the season in hiding. "Thank you." He paused. "What did the inspectors want? Why's the one waiting?"

"They insist on watching the cargo being off-loaded," replied the captain. "They didn't say what they were looking for. Just said that we wouldn't have any trouble if the manifest was right."

"Crossbow quarrels and blades, you think? Lances? Rifles?"

"Something like that, I'd guess," replied Furwyl. "Or maybe iron pigs."

Kharl nodded. "Could be. There's no iron in the West Quadrant. Smythal had to buy his rough stock from one of the factors. Came from Recluce or Lydiar, I think." He also wondered if someone had been told that the ship would not arrive—and worried about how it had. Still, it seemed unlikely that the Hamorians would confide in Brystan customs inspectors.

"Don't envy you, Lord Kharl. You can have the carriage and finery and all that."

"That's because you love the sea."

"Could be. Treacherous as she can be, she's not half so treacherous as most lords and rulers, excepting you and Lord Hagen. But you two aren't like most lords."

"You're kind." Kharl wondered if that happened to be because Hagen had been a captain and factor more than a lord, and because Kharl himself had not had a chance to learn treachery.

"I see what I see."

Kharl laughed. "I'd best be getting my gear. I see young Erdyl heading this way. Thank you again for surrendering your cabin."

"For you, I'd do that anytime." Furwyl glanced toward the main deck, where Reisl was directing the deck crew on opening the main hatch and setting up to unload. "Best watch the new bosun."

Kharl thought Reisl would do well, but he just nodded, and let Furwyl head down the ladder. He followed, but went to the master's cabin.

Cevor was waiting in the passage. "Thought we'd be taking your bags, ser."

"They're ready."

Kharl let the guards lead the way off the *Seastag*. He followed, carrying only the large leather case that held documents, letters, and his credentials. Around his waist, inside his tunic and jacket, was a shimmersilk bodybelt that held golds, over five hundred. He felt as though he wore lead. That much gold was heavy.

Furwyl turned from where he watched the deck crew. "You take care, Lord Kharl."

"You, too." Kharl turned and headed down the gangway to the waiting carriage, a carriage that the driver had turned, carefully, on the wide pier, so that it was headed off the pier and toward the city.

Undercaptain Demyst was waiting at the foot of the gangway. "Cevor and Alynar will go with the baggage cart. Don't want your things disappearing."

"Thank you." Kharl looked up at the driver, a small man neither young nor old, with a weathered face, who wore a coachman's jacket of green trimmed in black.

"Ser?"

"I'm Lord Kharl. You're the driver?"

"Yes, your lordship. I'm Mantar. Been with Fundal for near-on half a score."

"You've seen a few envoys come and go, then."

"Yes, ser."

Kharl smiled. "Well . . . I'm pleased to meet you."

"Yes, ser. Thank you, ser."

Kharl stepped into the coach, where he was joined shortly by Erdyl and Demyst. In but a few moments they were under way.

"Brysta looks bigger than Valmurl," Erdyl said.

"Valmurl is more spread out," Kharl suggested. "There are more towns nearby. Not everyone lives in the city, like in Brysta."

"Brysta looks older," added the undercaptain.

"I think many of the buildings and dwellings are."

Kharl cleared his throat.

"Ser?" asked Demyst.

"I'd like to remind you both not to mention . . . my talents with order. Not to the steward or the retainers at the residence. Not to anyone."

"Yes, ser."

Kharl turned to Demyst. "You will remind Cevor and Alynar, as well."

"I have told them both that they will answer to me, to you, and to Lord Hagen if they so much as hint."

"Good. Thank you." It might not help, but Hagen had made the suggestion, and usually what the lord-chancellor suggested was wise.

The carriage rumbled up Cargo Lane until it reached Eighth Cross. There the driver turned westward. Eighth Cross sloped upward for another half kay before descending. After the crest, they traveled two long blocks before the carriage slowed, then turned in through a wide brick gate, before coming to a halt in a brick-paved courtyard on the left side of the dwelling.

From the carriage, Kharl took in the residence, a structure a good three times the size of the main house at Cantyl. The walls were of a rough brownstone, with wide mullioned windows, trimmed in dark green. The pitched roofs were of dark slate, and the front wall was of dark red brick, with two gates, the carriage gate, and a smaller gate with a brick archway above it.

A gray-haired man, wearing a black-trimmed green tunic, hurried down the brick walk. He stumbled on a protruding brick, but caught himself.

Erdyl opened the carriage door and stepped out, holding the door for Kharl. The mage and envoy eased through the narrow door and stepped onto the ancient brick pavement.

"Lord Kharl?" The man took in Kharl slowly.

"I am Lord Kharl." Kharl hated to announce himself as a lord.

"Yes, Lord Kharl. I'm sorry I did not recognize you, but no likeness was sent. I am Fundal, the residence steward."

"I understand. This is Erdyl, my secretary, and this is Undercaptain Demyst. The two guards I brought are with the baggage wagon. It was following us."

"Ah . . . two guards?"

"I thought guards were customary."

"Yes, ser. Lord Hensolas brought half a squad, added more later, and two secretaries, and his . . . cousin . . . Genya, of course."

Kharl smiled. "Then we should have plenty of room."

"More than enough, ser. More than enough." Fundal bowed. "Let me show you the residence."

Undercaptain Demyst smiled politely. "I'll be going first, if you will, steward." He stepped toward the side steps leading up to the covered porch that wrapped around the front of the dwelling.

"Of course, undercaptain, of course."

His case under his arm, Kharl followed the steward.

"This is the front porch. Lovely in the morning. Lord Isel always took breakfast here. The rear porch, of course, is more private. It has seen many summer functions . . ."

Kharl said little as Fundal took Kharl through the main sitting room, the front salon, the library, which also served as the envoy's study, the long dining room, the adjoining breakfast room, the rear salon, which opened onto the covered rear porch, which, in turn, overlooked the small formal garden, the kitchen, and the various pantries. Then Fundal led them to the basement, which held various cellars, as well as a strong room. They returned to the main foyer and climbed the wide grand staircase to the second level, which held five large bedchambers, and two bath chambers, one of which was attached to the envoy's bedchamber and sitting room. The third level held six smaller chambers, including those for Erdyl and the undercaptain.

"Your guards . . . now there's a barracks quarters over the stable . . . and that adjoins the other staff quarters," ventured Fundal.

"With only two, it would be better to have them on the third level," Kharl suggested. "They'd be closer."

"Yes, ser," interjected Demyst.

"Third level, it is," affirmed the steward.

"Do we have mounts for riding?" asked Kharl.

"Why, yes, ser . . . but for your guards and your secretary. That is, when you need the carriage. The past envoys . . . they have not ridden in Brysta."

"I imagine not." Kharl nodded, but was glad to know that the mounts were available.

While the bags were being carried to the various quarters, and before he did more, Kharl drew Fundal aside into the library.

"Yes, ser?"

"I was led to believe, Fundal, that you were concerned that the residence accounts were short of coins?"

"Yes, ser. I can show you the ledgers. We have less than twenty golds on account at the Factors' Exchange. Prices . . . well, for everything . . . they've been higher this year. Almost no produce coming from the south, they say. The brigands . . . or something. You hadn't come in the next few eightdays . . . I can't say that I could see how we'd have lasted."

"Leave the ledgers out on the desk here. I'll look them over after we get settled, and we'll take care of the accounts first thing in the morning."

"Yes, ser." The steward smiled tentatively.

Kharl was glad that he could solve one problem. He had the feeling that, while he didn't know what others he faced, not in detail, setting Fundal's mind at ease would be one of the easier tasks before him.

LVII

Kharl should have been tired, he supposed, after the long trip to Brysta, but he hadn't been. So after unpacking and hanging out his clothes in the capacious wardrobe in his chambers, he had made his way down to the study and gone through the ledgers, line by line. From what he could tell,

Fundal was honest, relatively frugal, and probably without imagination or more than modest initiative. Several of the suppliers of provender and other goods for the residence were not sellers Kharl would have chosen, even with unlimited golds, and over time those would need to be changed.

Nowhere in the residence library were there any records of what previous envoys might have done as envoys, nor was there a history of recent events in Brysta. Even the leather-bound volumes on the dark oak shelves were old and stiff enough that Kharl doubted most had ever been read, even when new.

He, Erdyl, and Demyst had taken an early supper, and Kharl had gone back to the library afterward. There, he had drawn up a listing of what he thought needed to be done, based on what he recalled of the verbal instructions Hagen had given him. Doubtless he would miss things. He'd not been raised as a lord.

Then, for a time, he had just sat in the darkness and thought, wondering about Warrl, Jeka, and Sanyle . . . and, always, there was the sadness about Arthal.

His first inclination was to deal with Warrl and the young women as soon as possible, preferably on the morrow, but, as Taleas the scrivener had pointed out, acting before thinking had been his undoing more than once. Painful as it was, he would do better to proceed carefully. If Warrl remained safe with Merayni and Dowsyl, then rushing in would do no good. If something had happened because of the so-called brigands, whatever Kharl might do was already too late. That thought nagged at him, and he had to force it away.

The same held for Jeka. If she was still working for Gharan as a weaver, then she was safe. If not, he could scour the city for her—or even all of the West Quadrant—and never find her. As for Sanyle, he hadn't even known where she had gone before he'd left Brysta.

Could he employ Erdyl to look around?

Kharl shook his head. The secretary was likely to be watched in some ways even more closely than Kharl himself, and if Kharl gave any premature indication of interest in his son or the young women, Egen or Lord West would not be above using them against Kharl and Austra, even if they had no idea what the linkage was. Nor would the Hamorians. After Kharl had sent Erdyl on various errands, he might be able to work things in, but not first off. That also meant that, when Kharl acted, he would have to act decisively and quickly.

He did not sleep well. He woke early, washed, dressed, and ate, then went to his study-library.

Erdyl was still yawning when Kharl summoned him into the library.

"Have you eaten yet this morning?"

"Yes, ser. I just finished. What would you like of me?"

"You get to scour the hoops," Kharl said. "The dirty work. Write out a fancy letter to Lord West saying that I've just arrived from Valmurl as Lord Ghrant's appointed envoy to the West Quadrant of Nordla and would like to pay my respects to Lord West and present my credentials to him in person, as is usual and customary."

"Ah . . . you shouldn't say it's usual and customary."

"But I can say that I wish to present myself and the credentials in person?"

"Yes, ser."

"Then . . . you write it as you think best, and I'll sign it, and then you get to deliver it. When you do, be charming, but most insistent that Lord West see it. Listen for names. While you're writing that, I'll be at the Factors' Exchange, first, arranging for the transfer of golds to the residence account. After that, we'll come back. I'll sign the letter. Then I'll have the driver take me to the Hall of Justice. I'll introduce myself as a visiting scholar. The driver can take you to deliver the message, and then come back and find me."

"You're not going alone, ser?"

"No. I'll take Undercaptain Demyst. You take either Cevor or Alynar with you."

Erdyl nodded. "Yes, ser."

"You can use the library here to write out that letter." Kharl picked up the leather case that held his credentials and the authorizations to draw on the account at the Factors' Exchange, then walked out into the main foyer, catching sight of himself in one of the full-length mirrors set into the wall. Without the beard, his hair cut short, and wearing the dark gray tunic trimmed in Austran green, and the black jacket, he looked like a different man. Then, in many ways, he was.

"Fundal!"

Even before Kharl's call finished echoing through the main foyer, the steward appeared.

"Ser?"

"We're heading to the Factors' Exchange. They should be open on five-day."

"Yes, ser. They close on sevenday afternoon and on eightday. You want me to accompany you?"

"They know you. They don't know me."

"But everyone has heard that a new envoy has arrived from Valmurl."

"What else have they heard?"

"Just that you are a strong supporter of Lord Ghrant and that you were effective in the battles that ended the rebellion."

Kharl looked hard at Fundal. "How would they know that?"

"Ser . . . you are the envoy. Lord Ghrant is the ruler. Anyone he sent would have to be a supporter who had been effective."

Kharl could detect no sense of deceit or chaos . . . or even something withheld. Still . . . for some reason, Fundal's statement bothered him. Was it because everyone who dealt with power would draw similar conclusions? Or that Kharl would have to accept such sharpness, even in secretaries and stewards—and even greater perception among those whom those underlings served? Those thoughts were disturbing enough, and once Lord West and the other envoys heard from their spies in Austra, more would be known about Kharl than he would have preferred.

"Ser?"

"Let's go. The sooner we get this done, the sooner you have the golds to resupply the residence and pay the retainers, and the sooner I can get on to what I need to do."

"Ser?"

"I'm also a scholar of justice. You *can* tell people that."

Fundal's brow crinkled, but the steward did not say more.

The trip to the Factors' Exchange was short, less than a kay downhill and south to an old structure above the now-unused and marshy waters that had once been the back bay. Not all that far from the White Pony, Kharl reflected although it was farther to the east.

When they alighted from the carriage, Kharl was vaguely surprised to see a pair of Watch patrollers on the opposite corner, wearing maroon-and-blue uniforms of a type he had not seen when he had left Brysta. Yet neither appeared to be watching the Factors' Exchange.

At the Exchange, Fundal introduced him to the bursar and head clerk. Kharl produced his credentials and authentications, then transferred one hundred golds from the drawing account into the residence account. At that, Fundal looked noticeably relieved. Kharl hoped the relief was from normal worry, but he resolved to watch the accounts closely.

By the time they returned to the residence, Erdyl had finished a draft letter, but it took almost a glass before Kharl and Erdyl were both satisfied, and Kharl signed the missive, somewhat more flowery than he would have preferred, but the minimum necessary according to Erdyl.

Then Kharl and Erdyl set off in the residence carriage, accompanied by Undercaptain Demyst and Cevor.

Mantar drove at a measured pace. Demyst kept looking out the carriage window.

Occasionally, Kharl nodded. Mostly, he frowned, especially when he saw the burned-out ruins of what he recalled had been a large factor's warehouse. He couldn't remember the factor's name, because he'd never dealt with the man, but the faint sense of chaos lingering within the burned-out structure bothered him.

Somehow, the Hall of Justice appeared less imposing than Kharl had remembered it, although it was larger than the Hall in Valmurl. After he stepped out of the carriage, his eyes went to the walled courtyard to his left. Behind those walls, Charee had been hanged, and he had been flogged. The leather case under his arm almost forgotten, Kharl studied the walls for a time.

"Ser? Lord Kharl?"

At the sound of the driver's voice, Kharl started, then turned. "I'm sorry. Go ahead and attend to Erdyl's business. We'll be here for a time, at least several glasses."

"How will I know when to come for you?"

"The second glass past noon, unless Erdyl needs me sooner." That was a guess, but as good as any. If he had troubles in getting access to the library, he and Demyst could always walk back to the residence. It wasn't that far, and Kharl had certainly walked far greater distances without even giving it a thought.

"Second glass past noon. Yes, ser."

As the carriage pulled away, Kharl started for the open double doors. Demyst kept pace with him. Once inside the doors, Kharl paused in the foyer, a good thirty cubits long and half that in width. At the end of the foyer was a single set of double doors, guarded by two patrollers, also in the newer maroon uniforms. Before, when he had been at the Hall, where he had been tried by Reynol, the guards had been armsmen.

Kharl decided that viewing the justicers inside the Hall of Justice could wait. He needed to get his introductions and begin his studies in the library.

He had his own plans for Lord Justicer Reynol . . . and for Egen.

One of the patroller guards hurried across the foyer.

Kharl turned and fixed the man, a good head shorter than he was, with his eyes.

The guard stopped. "Blades, weapons are not allowed in the Hall, ser . . . ?"

"This is Lord Kharl, the Austran envoy to Brysta," Demyst announced, his hand on the hilt of his sabre.

Before the guard could protest, Kharl cleared his throat. "We're not going into the Hall itself. I'm here to see the lord justicers' chief clerk."

"Fasyn is the overclerk, ser. His chamber is on the upper level, off the front stairs. I suppose the blade would be all right there . . . but not in the Hall itself."

"Thank you," Kharl said politely. He turned toward the narrow staircase to the left, a stairwell he had not even noticed when he had been in the Hall before.

"No blades . . ." murmured the other guard to the one who had stopped Kharl.

"Austran lord . . . says . . . envoy to Lord West . . . you want to tell him?"

"So long as he doesn't bring it into the Hall . . ."

". . . what I say . . ."

At the top of the staircase was a long and narrow foyer. The first chamber held a table desk piled with papers and volumes, but no one was within. Kharl moved to the doorway of the second.

An older man with sunken cheeks and jowls looked up from the narrow table set against the right sidewall. "Yes?"

"You're Chief Clerk Fasyn?"

"None other, ser."

"I'm Lord Kharl. I'm here from Austra to study the records. Lord Hagen felt that such a measure would be useful."

"Lord Hagen?"

"He's Lord Ghrant's new lord-chancellor."

Undercaptain Demyst cleared his throat. "Lord Kharl tends to be too modest. He is also the Austran envoy to the West Quadrant."

The elderly man rose, almost laboriously. "An envoy and a lord from Austra, up here?"

"I am also a scholar of the law, in a fashion," Kharl said. "I have letters from the Lord Justicer of Austra." He opened the leather case and extracted the heavy envelope.

"Most properly, that should go to one of lord justicers . . . ser."

"I'm sure that your hands are most trustworthy." Kharl smiled.

Fasyn opened the envelope and began to read. Then he looked up. "Most unusual . . . only seen one other of these, and that was years back, some young captain from Certis. He only stayed an eightday or so."

"I'm likely to be here far longer than that."

The elderly man studied Kharl. "What exactly are you looking for, ser?"

"The divergence in case law over the past three centuries, particularly in how it defines the role of the lord justicers." Kharl was very glad for the study with Jusof. He hadn't even known of legal divergence.

"So . . . this Lord Hagen wants greater control over his justicers." Fasyn laughed, with almost a cackling sound.

Kharl smiled politely. "I would not be so bold as to make such a guess."

"I'm sure you wouldn't." After a moment, the clerk added, "Lord or not, ser, you'll need to sign the scholars' register." He took a bound volume from the shelf beside him, opened it, and extended it, nodding toward the inkpot and pen on the forward part of the desk.

Kharl wrote "Kharl of Cantyl, Austra."

The clerk took the book back and read. "Are those lands yours, or is that where you're from?"

"They're mine."

"Well . . . Lord Kharl, we'll do what we can to help you."

"You must be kept busy, Fasyn."

"At times . . . at times. What volumes . . . or cases . . . do you wish first?"

"Is there an interpretive guide that outlines current procedures? I would like to review that, if it exists. That way, I will not be led into false assumptions."

"There aren't that many differences . . . Both Austran and Nordlan justicer codes derive from the Code of Cyad . . . the same as Lydiar and Delapra. They're so close that sometimes merchanters, in civil cases, tariff adjustments and claims, you understand, they bring in their own advocates."

"Could they do so in criminal cases?"

"There's no bar to that." Fasyn tilted his head. "I don't know that it's been done in years. You have someone . . . ?"

"No. I just thought that, as an envoy, it might be useful, if the matter ever came up." Kharl smiled politely. "About the guide?"

"Oh . . . yes, there is a guide of sorts. It's incomplete. My predecessor did not finish it . . . but there are a number of precedents, established since . . . still . . ."

Kharl waited.

"I cannot imagine that there are significant differences, though . . ."

Kharl smiled apologetically. "Small differences in past years can lead . . ."

"You advocates . . ." The clerk shook his head. "We'll go into the library. There's a table in the middle of the back wall. It's handy to most of what would be of the greatest interest to you."

Kharl followed Fasyn, as did Demyst, his hand still on the hilt of his sabre, his eyes checking every shadow in the ancient and musty library.

Unlike the library in the Hall of Justice in Valmurl, there was not a single advocate or student in the library.

"If you would wait a moment . . ." Fasyn walked slowly around one of the freestanding shelves and toward a locked cabinet. From the ring on his belt he took a small key and unlocked the cabinet, extracting a folder and a thick volume bound in faded green leather. After relocking the cabinet, he carried both back, setting them on the table.

He looked to Kharl. "The folder here holds Ghasad's guide. It is not complete, as I said . . . and here is the Code of Cyad. It's not original, course, but it is the first—the only—version, and it's a copy. The original, well, it would be more than a thousand years old, more like seventeen hundred, really, but every new chief clerk has it copied, and I am most certain it is accurate. The first part has the original Cyadoran text. Most of you don't know that, but the translation is in part two, and it's an honest transcription. Honest, but awkward." Fasyn smiled.

"You must be one of the few that know Cyadoran," Kharl said.

"There are not many, and fewer every year."

Kharl looked at the folder, then at the ancient volume. Would they help in his plans, or would they be little more than a cover? He could only read them and see.

LVIII

Again, Kharl, Demyst, and Erdyl ate the evening meal together, using but one end of the long table in the formal dining chamber. Supper was a stew, although Khelaya, the cook, had called it ratouyl. To Kharl, it was a stew, and not bad, but not so good as what Adelya had prepared. Khelaya's brown bread was good, and that helped.

"Tell me again how you were received." Kharl took a swallow of his ale, then a last bite of the bread.

"I presented myself and was shown to Mihalen, Lord West's secretary." Erdyl broke off a chunk of bread, then passed the silver bread tray to Demyst. "He was pleasant, but not warm. He left me in his chamber for several moments while he went into the adjoining study to talk with someone else. The door was ajar when he walked in, and I caught the name . . . I thought he said Lord Osten."

"It might have been," Kharl said. "Osten is Lord West's older son. The youngest is Egen. There's another one, I think, an overcaptain, but no one talks much about him. Does something with the tariff farmers, or he did several years ago." Kharl couldn't help frowning. Was Osten making decisions for Lord West? What was Egen doing? He pushed those thoughts away. He needed to know more. "What did they say?"

"I couldn't hear any more because they closed the door, and I didn't want to get up and try to listen through the door itself. Mihalen came back and said that he expected that Lord West would receive you formally within the eightday, but that it had been noted that you were the representative and envoy for Lord Ghrant. He asked me to convey Lord West's greetings and welcome." Erdyl shrugged. "That was all that happened." Abruptly, he looked down.

"What is it?"

"I am most sorry, Lord Kharl. I had forgotten. There is a missive. I left it on your desk in the library. I was told that it contained an invitation for you to have refreshments with the Sarronnese envoy on threeday afternoon.

I'm most sorry, ser. I meant to tell you as soon as you returned this afternoon."

"That's all right." Kharl smiled. "A few glasses' delay won't matter." Sarronnyn? That was one of the northwestern lands in Candar. Kharl thought it was one of the places that still followed the Legend. The ruler was called the Tyrant, or something like that. But why would he get such an invitation so quickly?

"If it is an invitation," Erdyl said, "you will need to send an acceptance."

"First thing in the morning, then."

"Yes, ser."

"What do you think of Brysta?" Kharl looked to his secretary, then to the undercaptain.

"Sort of . . . old . . . run-down," offered Demyst. "Didn't see many ships in the harbor. Not when we ported. Looked at the docks from the hillside yesterday, and there weren't any more, either. Valmurl's smaller, and there are more ships in the harbor, all the time."

Kharl had noticed the same, but he just nodded. "What struck you, Erdyl?"

The young secretary swallowed, then blushed, but did not speak.

"Erdyl?"

"Well . . . ser." He swallowed again. "I didn't see any girls out. Not any young women. Most places I've been, at least in Austra, you see a few."

Kharl frowned. Now that Erdyl had mentioned that, he couldn't recall seeing any younger women, either.

"I say something wrong, ser?"

"Oh, no. I think you're right. I just hadn't thought that way." Was he getting old before his time, not noticing comely young women? Did dealing with order do that?

"More than a few Watch patrollers out, too," added Demyst. "In pairs, mostly."

More patrollers and no young women, Kharl reflected. That suggested that matters were not well, but, again, in what fashion he could not say. "Anything else that either of you saw or thought about?"

"People don't wear bright colors," offered Erdyl. "Everyone was in gray or brown or maroon." He looked down. "Perhaps that is the custom here. I haven't seen much of the world."

Kharl tried to recall what it had been like when he'd been younger.

He'd had a crimson jacket once, and Charee had often worn a brilliant purple shawl. "We'll have to look more, but . . . folks used to wear brighter colors."

"Could be because of the season?" Demyst asked, then shook his head. "Can't be. Bright garb is for spring and summer."

"What will you be having us do tomorrow?" blurted Erdyl. "Besides the reply to the Sarronnese envoy, I mean."

Kharl smiled, sheepishly. "I'll have to think about that this evening. We've really only a half day tomorrow. Sevenday afternoon is part of the end-day. Many of the shops close in the afternoon, and the Hall of Justice is closed on both sevenday and eightday."

"That's not so different from Austra," ventured Erdyl.

"Some things aren't," Kharl admitted. But some things were very different, and he had the feeling that those differences had gotten worse. He needed to remind himself to be careful, and to think out what he did. He definitely did not wish to repeat his mistakes—not in Brysta.

LIX

Sevenday morning was quiet, and after writing a reply to Luryessa, the Sarronnese envoy, Kharl dispatched Erdyl with the missive. The fact that the envoy was a woman confirmed in Kharl's mind that Sarronnyn, along with Southwind, was a land that still followed the Legend of ancient and vanished Westwind. The invitation, merely for afternoon refreshments, also raised the question of what the envoy wanted. Did she wish merely to learn more about Kharl and what was happening in Austra? Somehow, Kharl doubted that. The invitation had been too immediate.

Once Erdyl had left to tender the acceptance, Kharl went looking for Undercaptain Demyst and found him inspecting the unused barracks section of the space over the stables.

"What do you think?" Kharl asked.

Demyst turned, slowly. "They kept the place clean. Not much wear. Even has an armory off the back hall."

"Ah . . . ser . . ."

Both Kharl and Demyst turned. Fundal stood at the end of the hallway.

"Yes, Fundal?" said Kharl.

"I couldn't help but overhear what the undercaptain said, Lord Kharl. I'm gratified that he finds the barracks space here clean."

Kharl repressed a smile. "It wasn't clean when Lord Hensolas left?"

"No, ser. It was more like a hog pen." The steward shook his head. "Too many armsmen."

At Fundal's expression, Kharl had another thought. "Did you do the cleaning up and the painting by yourself?"

"Mostly, ser. After they all left, things were quiet. Thought it was best to put matters to right. No sense in having someone else do it. Besides, I was worried about the coins."

"You did a good job. We couldn't even tell there were so many here."

"Far too many," Fundal replied. "At the end, there were almost threescore armsmen packed in here. Some of them couldn't even speak properly. Mercenaries. I suggested to Lord Hensolas that it might be wiser to quarter some of them elsewhere, but he just put me off. 'We'll talk of that later, Fundal.' Then, one twoday, they all left, and Lord Hensolas with them. He didn't even leave any extra golds in the residence account. Drew out all the golds he could. The armsmen left some blades and a half score of rifles in a crate that they hadn't even opened. I sold all that and put the golds in the account. Even with that being so, it barely lasted till you got here."

Kharl could sense that the steward was telling the truth—and that he felt strongly about the situation. "Did they leave anything else? Other weapons? Tools?"

"Just an unopened keg of cammabark." Fundal shook his head. "Cammabark, in a place where folk live. Didn't get a bad price for it, though, but half of that went to Guarlt because I had to go through the Armorers' Guild."

Cammabark? A keg of it? In quarters over a stable where it could explode and burn down both the stable and the envoy's residence? That bothered Kharl, not because it confirmed Hensolas's treachery, but because it was so at odds with everything he had heard about the lord's caution. "I'm glad you took care of all that."

"That's what a steward's for, ser." Fundal smiled, if faintly.

"Did you ever find out where all the mercenary guards came from?"

"Seemed like they came from everywhere. I heard one say he was from

Jellico, and another was talking about being glad to leave Analeria. The others . . . they could have come from anywhere."

"Thank you."

"If you'll not be needing me . . ."

"I'll let you know if there's anything," Kharl promised.

He moved on toward the back hall. As Fundal had said, the armory had been repainted recently, and there was but the faintest sense of chaos in the space. In less than half a glass, Kharl finished going through the barracks and retainer quarters, and he and the undercaptain made their way back to the library in the main residence.

Kharl closed the door before speaking. "What do you think about what Fundal said?"

"He was telling the truth, wasn't he?"

"Yes."

"Cammabark? Be an idiot to keep that except in an underground and stone-walled armory, even with what it's worth."

"He didn't take it with him," Kharl mused. "I'd wager he didn't buy it, either."

"Why didn't he sell it, then, the way Fundal did? Why did he leave the rifles?"

Those were good questions, especially since Hensolas had taken out all the golds he could. Kharl could only shrug.

He walked to the study window, the one nearest the rear of the dwelling, and looked out at the corner of the formal gardens. The white roses were in bloom, as were the lilies. One of the gardener's boys was following his father, picking up the clippings that fell from the shears as the older man trimmed the boxwood hedge.

Beyond the garden and the grounds, through the trees, Kharl could just make out a far larger dwelling. For all that he had lived in Brysta most of his life, this was a section of the city about which he knew little.

"Ser?" asked the undercaptain.

"We need to take a ride," Kharl said. "A carriage ride through and around Brysta. Mantar can tell us everything he knows. We need to learn more about Brysta." Especially the parts that Kharl had never frequented.

"I suppose so, ser."

"We might not have time, later."

Demyst nodded.

"If you would tell Mantar to ready the carriage, then find Erdyl."

"Yes, ser." Demyst bowed, then turned.

Kharl had his reasons for the ride. First, he did want Demyst and Erdyl to see more of the city. Second, he wanted to see what had changed. Third, he wanted to see if he could sense any more concentration of chaos. And finally, he wanted to see where the other envoys were, as well as where the lord justicers and others of power and wealth lived. As he'd realized, looking beyond the residence gardens, those were parts of Brysta he'd never known, because the wealthy buyers of his barrels had always sent their retainers to pick up the cooperage—and what cooper ever had time to walk around the city?

LX

The ride on sevenday had proved useful not only to Demyst and Erdyl, but, as Kharl had hoped, to himself as well. Mantar had been happy to show off his knowledge of Brysta, and to point out everything from the Quadrancy Keep—the walled hilltop keep of Lord West and his family and retainers—to the various enclaves below it on the hill, the largest of which was the Hamorian. It had also been recently enlarged. At least, several of the outbuildings and walls looked new, and felt that way to Kharl. He had not sensed a chaos-wizard there, and that had worried him, in some ways, more than if he had, although he could not have said why.

Also, in addition to the new barracks building in the old slateyard, there was another set of barracks and stables on the south side of Brysta, beside the road south to Surien, the same road Kharl had walked to Peachill. Patrollers guarded both.

Kharl had the feeling that they had been followed, but not by wizardry or wizards, and supposed that was to be expected. Only a single additional merchant ship, from Suthya, had ported in the harbor, and the coastal schooner had departed. One of Lord West's two gunships had also ported, looking old, small, and insignificant compared to the Hamorian warships Kharl had seen on the high seas and in port at Swartheld.

Kharl had requested that Mantar take them down Crafters' Lane, but while his old cooperage now bore the name of Mallamet, he had not seen the cooper, nor had he been able to make out the inscription on the adjoining building that had once been Tyrbel's scriptorium. Gharan's shutters had been closed—not at all unusual for a crafter on sevenday afternoon—so that Kharl could not tell whether Jeka still worked for the weaver. The drive itself was all he thought prudent for the present, until he had a better idea of how matters stood—but he wished he had been able to see and sense more.

After returning, Kharl had sampled the leather-bound books in the library, going through and opening them, reading sections at random. Several were merely compilations of folktales. One was called *History of the Ancients,* and Kharl read several pages. One paragraph caught his attention.

> All across Candar, there are people, usually women, who talk about the "Legend." Yet there is no evidence to support this Legend, save for the ruins of Westwind itself, and the ruin of a black tower and a walled keep on the Roof of the World tells nothing of its inhabitants or how they lived . . . They are no written histories dating from that time, except those reputed to be in the archives in Nylan, and no one not of Recluce has ever been granted access to those, if they even exist . . .

So far as Kharl could tell, most of the pages before and after that paragraph were written in the same vein—claiming that years of tales passed down meant nothing. They had to mean something. They just couldn't be dismissed, although what they meant Kharl wasn't certain.

The other volumes were even drier. One was a manual on tanning, and another dealt with rendering. At that, Kharl recalled Werwal, the renderer, who had been one of the few crafters in Brysta who had not turned against Kharl. Another was a thin volume that offered a guide to bookkeeping. There were several hundred volumes on the shelves, and Kharl did not see a one that he found interesting, or likely to be of immediate use, except perhaps the one that dealt with accounts. But he did not wish to spend more time looking through all of them, one at a time, some were so old he could not even make out the titles on their fronts or their spines.

After his brief perusal of the volumes on the shelves, most of which were stuck to the wood on which they rested, Kharl had begun to study the residence ledgers and accounts in greater detail—much greater detail. He continued that effort on eightday. By late afternoon, he was convinced that Fundal was relatively honest. He also felt that the steward was a timid man at heart, and one fearful of changing providers or asking firmly for a better price.

So he sent Erdyl to bring the steward to the library.

Fundal entered, his eyes downcast.

Young as he was, Erdyl clearly understood, because he slipped away, closing the door behind him.

"Ser? Is there something wrong?"

"You haven't done anything wrong," Kharl replied. "I have been studying the accounts."

"Yes, ser." Concern and puzzlement warred on Fundal's face.

"There are some things that trouble me . . ."

"Ser?"

"You've been buying linens from Soret, I see."

"Yes, Lord Kharl. We've always purchased from him."

"Do we need any more?"

"Not soon."

Kharl nodded. "The weaver Gharan does better work, I've heard. Ask him for a price and get a sample of his work before you see Soret."

"But . . . ser . . . we've always . . ."

"Fundal. I've some experience in trade. I'm sure you have heard that. If Gharan does better work or does the same work at less cost, our golds go farther."

Fundal swallowed.

"Now . . . about the flour. I'd like you to consider Wassyt, the miller to the north . . ." Kharl did not explain in detail, either about Wassyt or the other crafters whose names he mentioned in turn, but every name he mentioned was a good and honest provider, the best that Kharl had known. He didn't actually tell Fundal to change providers, but he did suggest very strongly that the steward learn about each man before purchasing more from the current provider. ". . . we're charged with spending Lord Ghrant's golds wisely, and I intend that we should. Is that clear?"

"Yes, ser."

"If you have any ideas that would help, I'd like to hear them."

"I'd have to think about that, ser."

Fundal was almost trembling when he left the study.

Kharl followed, using his sight shield, and listened, with his order-boosted senses, as Fundal talked to Khelaya.

". . . practically told me who to buy provender and the like from . . ."

"That doesn't sound like any lord I've known, but he's a new lord. Maybe he came from trade."

"He might have, but how could he know all those names?"

"You said he was an officer on one of Lord Hagen's ships. They meet everyone. Been on one long enough, he'd know who was good, I'd wager. 'Sides, I told you myself that Soret was cheating you. Told you to go to Chyrent, too."

Kharl smiled at the cook's tone.

". . . weren't for the golds, almost wish we didn't have an envoy." Fundal's voice carried resignation.

"Like him a lot better than Hensolas. Mean-assed bastard. Barely got Sysena off to her aunt's before he ruined her, and him havin' that woman, too. Called her his cousin." The cook snorted, then laughed.

"I don't know as I like him. Seems honest, but he looks right through you, like as he could see your heart."

"Can't take blooms and fruit from the same tree, Fundal. You didn't like Hensolas 'cause he paid no attention and treated you like dust under his boots. You don't like this one because he watches you and wants you to do better."

"Go fix supper." The rear door to the kitchen closed firmly as the steward left.

Kharl frowned as he eased back to the study. Fundal wasn't stealing from the residence, but he certainly didn't want Kharl watching him too closely.

In the kitchen, Khelaya hummed happily as she chopped nuts.

LXI

Kharl glanced around the library that was his to use while he was envoy, then blotted his forehead. Although it was well before midmorning on oneday and the walls of the residence were thick, the rooms were already warm, and the day promised to be more than unpleasantly hot. Too hot to visit the harbor and the Hall of Justice? Kharl shook his head. He needed a better feel for what was happening, and he didn't want to talk to anyone who might recognize him, certainly not just after he had arrived in Brysta. No one he knew closely was likely to be in either place.

"Ser?" Erdyl appeared at the half-open library door. "You have another message, another invitation of some sort, I would judge."

"Do you know who it's from?"

"The messenger who rode up with it wore the black and crimson of Hamor," Erdyl said, extending the envelope that was sealed with black-and-crimson wax.

Hamor? Kharl didn't want to deal with the Hamorians, but he supposed that, so long as he met with their envoy in a relatively public place and kept his guard up, it was as safe as anything else he had been doing—not at all safe, but unavoidable. He broke the seal and extracted the short missive written on a heavy cream-colored paper, a paper more like parchment, but paper nonetheless.

He read the words slowly.

> Most esteemed Lord Kharl,
> On behalf of His Mightiness Sestar, Emperor of Hamor, and Regent of the South, I bid you welcome to Brysta and to the community of envoys gathered here to serve their rulers.
>
> The heat and damp of summer are scarce the best time to arrive in Nordla, and for that reason, we would like to tender an invitation for refreshments on sixday afternoon, the fourth glass past noon, here at the residence. With so many of those of interest and power in Brysta gone until the weather returns to a more temperate state, the afternoon will offer time to become acquainted . . .
>
> As the envoy of Lord Ghrant, you represent a young ruler who has proved that he has resources and wisdom beyond his years, and I look forward greatly to meeting with you.

The letter bore the signature of Whetorak, Lord Councilor. Kharl handed the invitation back to Erdyl. "What do you think?"

After reading it, the secretary looked up. "Ser?"

"He doesn't expect me to say no," Kharl said dryly.

"For a social occasion, ser, it might not be—"

"Oh, I know. Telling him I don't want to see him isn't wise. I learn nothing, and I just make him mad."

"And curious," suggested Erdyl.

There was another aspect to the letter. Whetorak had apologized for there being few others, if any, that he could invite. He was also suggesting that Kharl was unfortunate or unwise for arriving when he had, because so few remained in Brysta during the summer. That was something Kharl never thought about when he had been a cooper. Coopers didn't retreat to the hills or to anywhere else during the heat of summer. They just kept working.

"I suppose you should write a response to Lord Whetorak," Kharl said. "Something like the last one, not too flowery."

"Right now, ser?"

"Please. Use the desk."

While Erdyl began to write, Kharl made another attempt at perusing the books on the library shelves. The third book was entitled *On Philosophy*. He read the first page three times before setting the book back on the shelf. It made *The Basis of Order* seem simple and practical.

Kharl walked to the window and looked out for a time. The green-blue sky was cloudless, but already showing heat haze, and there was not even a hint of a breeze.

"Ser . . . if you would read this?"

Kharl walked to the desk and took the short reply from Erdyl. He read it carefully before speaking. "That's fine. I'll sign it, and you can seal it."

"Yes, ser."

After signing the reply and watching Erdyl apply the envoy's seal, Kharl cleared his throat.

"Erdyl . . . if you would have Mantar ready the carriage."

"Yes, ser. Where are we going?"

Kharl grinned. "The undercaptain and I are going to swing by the harbor to check the ships, then go to the Hall of Justice. You are going to come in the carriage so that Mantar can take you to deliver my reply. After that, you'll locate the residences of the other envoys and make a short call on each, introducing yourself to their secretaries, or whoever acts as such, and finding out what you can. Then you'll come back here and make some notes on what you find out. After that, if you have time, go through the books in the library and make a *short* list of any worth my reading. You can also see if there is anything inside any of them that I should know about."

"Yes, ser." The young secretary looked glumly at the shelves.

"You have more learning than I do," Kharl said. "You can do that far faster."

Erdyl only looked slightly cheered by his envoy's words.

"The carriage . . ." Kharl prompted.

"Oh . . . yes, ser." The redhead turned and was gone.

Kharl went back to the window, taking in the formal gardens in the bright light outside. At times, where he was and what he was doing seemed almost unreal, as if he were in a dream. Coopers didn't become mages and envoys, not in the world in which he had grown up. Except that he had, and the world in which he was living was even more dangerous than that of a cooper had been, perhaps because he'd been raised to be a cooper, not a mage or an envoy.

After a quarter glass or so, Kharl gathered the case he was using for notes, the one that held a portable inkpot, paper, and pens, then left the library.

"Lord Kharl?" Fundal stood in the corridor. "Will you be here for the midday meal?"

"A late midday meal, I'd judge." Kharl had already decided not to spend the entire day at the Hall of Justice, not as hot as it was looking to be.

"Thank you, ser. I'll tell Khelaya."

"Thank you, Fundal."

The carriage was waiting. So were Mantar, Erdyl, and Undercaptain Demyst. Cevor sat outside in the seat beside the driver.

"Mantar," Kharl said with a smile, "we'll start with the harbor, just for a quick look, then to the Hall of Justice. After that, you can take Erdyl to the Hamorian envoy's residence."

"The harbor, Lord Kharl, then the Hall of Justice, that it is."

Kharl settled into the carriage, which, spotless as it seemed, bore a faint odor of mold and age. He rubbed his nose, which had begun to itch, then slid open the side window. Perhaps the movement of the carriage would provide some faint semblance of a breeze, despite the heavy still air.

"You think we'll see more ships in the harbor?" asked Erdyl.

"This isn't the time of year for heavy trading," replied Kharl. "Still, I'd have expected a few more vessels."

Kharl recalled what Erdyl had said about younger women, and he studied the streets and walks, but he saw none. Then, it was fairly early on oneday, and Kharl didn't recall ever seeing that many young women out, particularly alone. Had they always had to fear Egen and others? Had Kharl just not noticed that? He didn't have an answer for that question, and no real way to find out. Not now.

As Mantar turned the carriage onto Cargo Road, Kharl began to study the harbor as he could. By the time they were on the flat south of the lower market, Kharl could see a large merchanter easing into a berth on the other side of the same deepwater pier where Hagen's ship had been tied up.

Kharl studied the ship, then nodded. "It's another Hamorian."

"They've got four in the harbor now," observed Erdyl.

"No ships from any other lands here," added Demyst.

Kharl had noted that the Suthyan vessel had not stayed long, either. He liked what he saw not at all.

Mantar slowed the carriage and turned in the small square short of the piers, to the south of the new patroller barracks, before heading back up Cargo Road. As Kharl looked back, the lower market seemed smaller, but that might have been because Kharl had changed, and not the marketplace itself.

Before long, the carriage slowed outside the Hall of Justice. Demyst opened the door and stepped out, glancing around, his hand on the hilt of his sabre. Kharl followed.

"When should I return, ser?" asked Mantar.

"A glass past noon."

"A glass past noon," repeated the driver. "Very good, ser."

As the carriage pulled away with Erdyl looking glumly from the open window, Kharl turned toward the main doors of the hall. Undercaptain Demyst hurried forward and opened the left one. Inside was cooler than outside under the hot morning sun, but not all that much so, despite the dimness of the main foyer.

One of the two patroller guards in maroon and blue stationed outside the double doors of the inner hall stepped forward, then stopped, as if he recognized Kharl.

"Lord Kharl is going up to the library," Demyst announced.

The guard watched, but said nothing as Kharl and the undercaptain turned and made their way up the narrow staircase.

Neither Fasyn nor the other clerk happened to be in his chambers, although one chamber had a wall lamp lit. They might have been in the Hall of Justice or conferring with the lord justicers.

Just before the library archway, Kharl stopped, recalling the rifles in the residence barracks and Hagen's warnings. He turned to the undercaptain. "I think it might be better if you watched the hallway here, and the top of the stairs. That way, someone can't get too close without being seen."

"Ser . . . ?"

"If you're out here, you can see if anyone is headed my way. You can check the library first, if that will make you feel better."

Demyst frowned, then nodded. "Put that way, it does make sense, ser." He paused. "There aren't any other entrances, are there?"

"No. There used to be a back entrance, but it was walled up years ago, it looks like."

Once inside the library, Kharl began to look through the shelves. Very quickly, he noticed that there were no volumes of cases that appeared to have been bound recently. He searched until he found one that seemed to be the most recent and checked it. There were two dates, a Cyadoran date of 1898 A.F. and a second date. The second date was stated as the 27th year of Ostcrag, Lord West. For a moment, Kharl frowned, then nodded. Every ruler of the West Quadrant was Lord West. Ostcrag was Lord West's personal name, as Osten was that of his eldest son. From what Kharl recalled, Lord West—or Ostcrag—had celebrated his thirtieth year as Lord West only a year before Kharl had left Brysta. That meant that the newest volume was almost four years old.

After almost half a glass of perusing volumes, Kharl could find no newer compilation of cases. By comparison, he was fairly certain that the newest case volumes in Hall of Justice in Valmurl were little more than a year old, if that.

He turned as he sensed Fasyn heading toward him.

"How are you finding things?" asked the chief clerk.

"I think it will take a little while before I know where everything is," Kharl admitted. "I couldn't find any recent cases."

Fasyn did not quite meet Kharl's gaze. "We're somewhat behind in compiling those. There are only the two of us."

"It takes a great deal of work," suggested Kharl, "and a good hand."

"I've heard that the role of the bailiff is different in Austra," suggested Fasyn quickly.

"I haven't seen a case tried here," Kharl replied. "So I couldn't say. There's no difference in the guide you provided and in how it's done in Valmurl. There's generally only one guard at the outer doors, though. Also, the Lord of Austra does not preside in any cases."

"What about the dating?"

Fasyn was clearly going to avoid commenting on Lord West's role in justicing, Kharl reflected.

"From the cases I've read here . . . I've only read a few," Kharl replied. "You're using two dates. All the dating in Austra is from the founding of Valmurl, and that was some sixteen hundred years ago. Only the old cases have Cyadoran dates."

"Hmmm . . . I didn't know that."

Kharl managed to conceal his surprise, because Fasyn was lying. "I'm sure I'll find other differences, especially after I see how the lord justicers handle matters."

"You plan on observing?"

"How else will I see the differences?"

"There is that," murmured the overclerk.

Kharl could tell that Fasyn was not pleased with that thought.

"Do you still follow the Justicer's Challenge?" asked Fasyn.

"The offer is made, but I don't know of a time that it's been taken. What about here?"

"Some would-be advocate who wanted to be lord justicer tried it, I'd say fifteen years back." Fasyn paused. "No. Sixteen, because one of the cases was the Asolin case. He came close, won four out of five. That was right after Lord Justicer Reynol took the dais."

"What was the case he lost? The challenger, I mean, if you recall."

"Oh . . . that was an assault on a tariff farmer." Fasyn laughed. "The challenger claimed that, when a tariff farmer exceeded the authority delegated by the Lord of the Quadrant, he could not act under the mantle of the Lord, and therefore an assault was not a crime against the Lord, but against a person, and therefore, merited but a flogging, since no weapons were used. The precedents state clearly that tariffing is a sole privilege of the Lord, and that when delegated, anything that interferes with that privilege constitutes a crime against the Lord." Fasyn shrugged. "He ended up getting eighty lashes. It took him three days to die."

"He followed the Code of Cyad, and not the more recent precedents?" asked Kharl.

Fasyn frowned.

Kharl decided to explain. It was one of the few cases where he did know something because he'd seen and followed a tariff farmer's case in Austra, and because he'd researched some to find out what would happen if he'd done something to Fyngel, the tariff farmer who had cost him his cooperage. "The Code of Cyad made that an absolute law, but that was when the tariffs were collected directly by officials appointed by the Emperor of Cyador. The Lords of both Nordla and Austra have asserted that precedent, but I never did find a proclamation or a case that actually confirmed that authority." He laughed softly. "Not that I'd challenge a Lord on that point."

"You're a wise advocate in that, Lord Kharl."

Kharl did not correct the clerk's assumption that he was an advocate.

"I can see that you're busy." Fasyn nodded and turned.

As Kharl followed the overclerk with his eyes, he noticed the robed figure of a lord justicer in the hallway outside. Kharl walked around and behind the shelf, out of sight of the two Nordlans and Demyst. There he raised his sight shield and turned back to follow the overclerk.

Both men walked to Fasyn's chamber. Kharl had to hurry to slip inside before Reynol gestured for the overclerk to close the door. The mage had to flatten himself against the wall between two bookcases.

"What more did you find out about this envoy?" Reynol cleared his throat. "He is an envoy. I checked with Overcaptain Osten."

"He knows his way around the cases. He has a recommendation from the lord justicer of Austra. The way it is written, it would be hard to forge. From all that, and the way he speaks, I'd say he's an advocate, or close enough that it makes little difference. He's not lord-born, but not low crafter. He's not practiced much. It could be that he was trained, then was granted lands by Lord Ghrant."

"Payback for supporting Ghrant in the revolt, no doubt." Reynol's words were sneering.

"Why would Ghrant send an advocate and call him a scholar of the law?" mused Fasyn. "Do you think he really might be?"

"I don't know, but Captain Egen says that Lord West will want to know," replied Reynol. "We don't wish to displease Captain Egen."

"No, ser."

"Watch him closely. Find out anything more that you can."

"Yes, your lordship."

"Let us get back to the Hall. We need to dispose of that cabinetmaker." Reynol turned.

Kharl did not move until the two had left. Leaving his sight shield up, he moved back to the library and out of eyeshot from Demyst before releasing it. He doubted he would find much more of immediate interest to him in the library, but he needed to make sure of that.

LXII

Kharl finally returned to the residence sometime closer to two glasses past noon. Before finding Erdyl, he washed up, then came back down the front staircase.

Erdyl was seated at the desk in the library with a stack of books beside him, jotting down notes. He stood quickly. "Ser?"

"You can tell me what you found out while we eat," Kharl said.

"There's not much, ser. No one seems to be in Brysta." Erdyl looked directly at Kharl.

That was a lord's reply, Kharl reflected, meaning no one felt to be of power and real import, for the city still held crafters, servers, tanners, scriveners, and even justicers. Kharl decided against calling that to Erdyl's attention, not at the moment, at least. "Let's go eat, and we can talk at the table."

Kharl was hungry, and a little frustrated. As he'd suspected, the case files in the library not only were old, but there were missing volumes and files in every section. While some of those might well have been stacked on the desks of Fasyn and the other clerk, that still would not have accounted for all the missing documents and volumes.

As Kharl headed for the dining room, both Demyst and Erdyl followed.

Khelaya stood at the door from the service pantry to the dining area. "The bread is not so warm as it should be, ser," she began. "A glass past noon, that was what I was told."

"The bread is not your fault," Kharl said as he seated himself at the end of the dining room table. "I spent more time than I'd planned. I'm sure everything will be fine."

"And the fowl—"

"I was late," Kharl said, taking one of the sauce-covered slices, then adding lace potatoes from the casserole dish. "That wasn't your fault."

Khelaya's knowing glance confirmed that.

Kharl filled his beaker with lager, taking a long swallow, before turning to Erdyl. "Tell me about each one—in the order you visited them."

"First, I went to the Lydian residence. The secretary was there. That was Lyelt. The envoy is Kyanelt, but he returned to Lydiar to meet with the duke, and he isn't expected back for at least three or four eightdays."

"What did you find out from him?"

"He told me that I shouldn't fail to make sure you and I went pheasant hunting in the uplands after harvest, and to take in the ice festival at Kofal at the turn of the year."

"What did he say about Lord West and the Hamorians?"

"Lord West is most charming. The Hamorian envoy never says anything, and what he does say tells you nothing. Lyelt knows that the Hamorian merchanters are selling goods. At least, they're unloading them, but he doesn't know who's buying them. There are usually Lydian iron factors selling iron pigs here, but he hasn't seen any of their vessels all summer . . ."

Kharl nodded. In time, he asked, "Who else did you see?"

"There isn't a secretary at the Sarronnese residence, but the envoy has an assistant. Her name is Jemelya, but she just welcomed me, and said that she'd be most happy to meet with me after you met with Envoy Luryessa." Erdyl took a sip of his white wine, then a mouthful of bread.

"Did she say anything at all beyond pleasantries?"

"She said I would have an interesting year. I didn't like the way she smiled when she said it."

Kharl laughed.

"The residence of the envoy from Hydlen was closed. Not even a steward, just a caretaker. The same was true for Spidlar and Certis."

"Did you meet any others from Candar?"

"The Gallosian secretary was curt. Dour fellow. His name was Ustark. Told me that nothing ever happened here, that the functions all combined second-rate food with third-rate conversation. Not like being an envoy in

Cigoerne, where the entertainment and food were outstanding. He also suggested that, outside of his envoy and the Hamorian envoy, none of the envoys were of particular import or ability. I just listened. That part was hard, but I just listened."

"Good." Kharl waited.

"The Delapran secretary, that was . . ." Erdyl frowned. ". . . Gosperk. All he did was go on and on about how hot and damp Brysta was in the summer, and how cold and inhospitable Lord West and his sons were."

"Did he say why?"

"His envoy had inquired about a Delapran vessel that had been sighted south of Brysta but had never ported. Osten met with this Gosperk and told him that, after all of the problems with Delapran pirates, the Delapran envoy certainly could understand that sometimes ships just didn't make port. Gosperk said that Osten was practically smirking. He didn't have much else to say . . ."

Kharl glanced to the undercaptain, who had remained silent.

"I wouldn't know, ser," said Demyst.

Kharl looked back to his secretary. "What about the Hamorians?"

"I was refused entrance. Both the secretary and the envoy were out. They were conducting business in the south."

"They said that they were in the south?"

Erdyl nodded, then paused. "No . . . it wasn't quite like that. The lancer who met me said that they were in the south, and I made some comment about envoys having to travel, but that it was likely to be hotter in the south. He said that they weren't in the south, that he didn't know exactly where they were, but that they wouldn't be back for several days."

"He wasn't supposed to let anyone know they were in the south." Kharl fingered his bare chin. He was still unused to not having a beard. "Lord South, problems with brigands to the south, piracy or missing vessels, Hamorians in the south . . . hmmm . . ." He took another swallow of the lager. "Anyone else?"

"Far as I could tell, there's no envoy here from Montgren or Southwind, and the Suthyan residence is closed until the first day of fall."

"What about Recluce?"

"They don't have envoys, ser. Not anywhere. They never have had."

"Oh." Kharl hadn't known that, not that it surprised him. Recluce did things its own way, and didn't seem to care what anyone else thought.

After a moment, and another bite of the lace potatoes, which were cold, and that was definitely his fault, he looked to the undercaptain. "You've been listening. What do you think?"

"Doesn't sound like most envoys and their folks want to stay in Brysta in the summer. Also sounds like the white worms from Hamor are up to something—in the south."

"I don't think it's just the Hamorians," mused Kharl. "We'll have to listen and watch closely." He glanced at Erdyl. "Did you look through any of the books in the library?"

"Twoscore or so, ser." The secretary grimaced. "Most of them are pretty bad."

"I'd thought so. The good ones probably disappeared over the years."

"There are two or three decent histories . . ."

Kharl nodded and helped himself to more of the fowl. He needed to find out more about what was happening in the West Quadrant, but he wasn't sure just how else to go about it.

LXIII

Twoday proved very quiet, and even hotter than oneday. Kharl spent only the morning at the Hall of Justice. Already, he was discovering the apparent truth of what both Jusof and Fasyn had said. In terms of the law itself, the proclamations, and the precedents, there was not that much difference between Austra and Nordla. Not to his partly trained eye, anyway, and that told him that the difference lay in its administration, something he'd already half concluded even before returning to Brysta.

After several glasses poring through cases and records, he had Mantar take him and Undercaptain Demyst on another brief tour of the harbor, which still held only the four Hamorian ships. By the time he returned to the residence exactly a glass after noon, to Khelaya's satisfaction, he was soaked in sweat. After eating and taking a cool bath, he studied a history of Brysta that Erdyl had found. The words were less straightforward than many law briefs, and Kharl had to struggle, but he found much of what was in the history fascinating.

Although he had grown up in Brysta, he'd never heard or read about what had happened much before the time of his father. Then, he supposed, that was true of most crafters. He'd been among the few who could actually read and write, only because his sire had insisted—and that because he wanted Kharl to become a mastercrafter. That had not happened, because Kharl had never managed to save enough golds, but the reading ability had made all the difference, if not in the way his father could ever have imagined.

He'd worked in the harbor forts, but he'd never realized that they had been built after the burning of Brysta in the time of Elzart, the fourth Lord West, by a punitive expedition from Sarronnyn, because a Sarronnese trading ship had been sunk at the pier and the crew abused by Elzart and his men.

"Ser?" Erdyl stood in the library door.

"Yes?"

"You have a message from Lord West, ser." Erdyl raised the envelope.

Even from halfway across the library, Kharl could see the blue ribbons and gold wax of the seal. "Let's see when I meet with him—or if he's putting me off."

"I would judge that he will meet with you. It costs him nothing." Erdyl crossed the library and tendered the missive.

Kharl took it. He wasn't that inclined to be charitable to Lord West—or his sons—but Erdyl was probably right about that. The name on the outside was impressive: Lord Kharl of Cantyl, Envoy of Lord Ghrant, Ruler and Potentate of Nordla.

Kharl slit the envelope with his belt knife. Before opening the envelope, he paused, looking down at the knife. It felt strange, as though it were pushing away from his fingers. He looked at the blade with his order-senses. It was ordered enough, and yet . . . there was a sense of something, not quite like chaos. He sheathed the knife before extracting the short but heavy parchment, also sealed at the bottom.

> Lord Kharl of Cantyl,
> His mightiness, Ostcrag, Lord of the Western Quadrant, will receive you and your credentials at the third glass of the morning on twoday, an eightday from today, in the small receiving room of the Quadrant Keep.

Except for the signature and seal, that was all. Kharl studied the signature—Osten, for his sire, Lord Ostcrag. Kharl nodded. After Erdyl's visit to the Quadrant Keep, he wasn't surprised, and he wouldn't be at all surprised if Osten were there. He'd have to consider what to do if Lord West—or, more properly, he guessed, Ostcrag, Lord West—were not there. He handed the missive back to Erdyl.

Erdyl swallowed. "The brevity, that's almost a snub . . . an insult. So is the early-morning time, and the signature."

"I'm not insulted. So long as I present my credentials to Ostcrag, it doesn't matter to me."

"I suppose not," replied the secretary. "It's not as though they'd tell anyone. It would make them look small. But they're counting on your not saying anything."

"Of course." Kharl laughed. "If I say anything, then I'm the one who looks small."

"That is true."

"Make sure that the silver box is polished just before I leave on the morning of the audience. We should not forget the token of Lord Ghrant's esteem." Not when so much thought and care had gone into it.

"Yes, ser. It will be ready."

Kharl set Lord West's reply aside. "Do you know how close to today this history goes?"

"It was written close to thirty years ago, ser."

"Too bad there isn't a more current history, but I suppose writing about any ruler is dangerous while the ruler is still alive. At least one that is accurate." Kharl's lips twisted into a crooked smile.

"Any history written about the near past would have to curry favor."

"Why else would it be written?" asked Kharl.

"You are a most cynical envoy, Lord Kharl."

"Most realistic, young Erdyl. I've seen men considered most honorable murder innocents when they were stopped from having their way with unwilling women, and I've seen so-called equally honorable men look the other way."

"That's something I wouldn't know, ser."

"Have you looked that closely?" Kharl fixed his eyes on his secretary.

Erdyl looked away.

Kharl half regretted pressing the young man, but for all his upbringing it was clear that there was much he had not seen, or had chosen not to see.

Then, that was true of all young men. It had been true of Arthal, and Kharl had not been so understanding as he might have been. He moistened his lips, and paused. "There are matters we would all choose not to see," he added more gently, after a moment, "but the cost of doing so here is far too high. Then, it's high anywhere."

Erdyl nodded, if hesitantly.

"Tell me about the other history, the one on Hamor," Kharl said cheerfully.

LXIV

On threeday, which dawned cloudy, and slightly cooler, Kharl did not attempt to visit the Hall of Justice, but took a longer and slower carriage tour of Brysta, one that lasted until almost noon. The streets and lanes were not empty, but neither were they bustling, and there were few young women about, and none without escorts of some sort.

Had the word about Egen's proclivities come to circulate through the city, or had enough people observed the actions of Lord West's youngest that it was unspoken and common knowledge? Kharl suspected the latter.

Likewise, he saw no beggars, and no one idling on the streets or visible in the alleys and serviceways. While there had always been few, there had been some. For a time, Kharl had been one of them. Now there were none . . . or they were most well hidden.

After returning to the residence, Kharl summoned Erdyl.

The secretary hurried into the study. "Ser?"

"I have another errand for you. I'd like you to stop by several of the cloth factors and weavers. There are two on Crafters' Lane around Fifth Cross. Those are Derdan and Gharan. Then there's Soret. Fundal can give you directions for him."

"Yes, ser." Erdyl paused. "Am I to order something?"

"No. You're to ask about cloth, about the special maroon color used in the patrollers' uniforms, and anything you can find out about who wove it or where it came from."

"Ser?"

"Those uniforms are new in the last year, and there are a lot more patrollers than there used to be. If we start asking about that . . ."

"Yes, ser. But if I ask about the cloth and color . . . and ask who could supply so much . . . that sort of thing."

"That's right. Look and see if any of them have added weavers or let them go. If the cloth came from Hamor, then it might have an effect."

"Yes, ser. You want me to start this afternoon?"

Kharl nodded. "After we eat. You'll have to ride. Try to notice as much as you can."

"Yes, ser."

"Let's go eat."

After eating a light midday meal, Kharl checked the ledgers once more, then read sections of the *History of Hamor*, a thick book that began with the legends of the founders who fled the demons of Candar in search of a better life.

"Why is everyone who opposes a people a demon?" mumbled Kharl to himself. "Or is it just whoever opposes the people of the writer?"

From what he had read so far, the founders of Hamor had fled the ancient chaos-wizards of Cyador, then promptly created a land modeled on Cyador, while denying it all the while—and that was if the writers of the history happened to be accurate. Kharl had his doubts, long before he laid aside the history to get ready for his foray into refreshments with the Sarronnese envoy.

At slightly before the fourth glass of the afternoon, Mantar halted the carriage under the portico of the Sarronnese envoy's residence as the four bells from the back bay tower finished echoing across the upper hillside.

Demyst held the carriage door as Kharl stepped out.

"We'll be waiting with the carriage, Lord Kharl," Demyst announced.

"Thank you." Kharl walked toward the wide white marble steps, where a footman or some sort of attendant in a blue-and-cream uniform waited.

As he neared, he saw that the attendant was a muscular woman, not a man, wearing the twin shortswords of Southwind—or of Westwind, if one believed the Legend. She opened the door, and announced, "Lord Kharl of Cantyl, honored Envoy of Lord Ghrant of Austra."

Kharl stepped inside the high-ceilinged and marble-walled foyer, decidedly cooler than the afternoon outside, to find a silver-haired woman awaiting him.

But a half a head shorter than Kharl, she wore long, flowing trousers of green shimmersilk, a tunic of the same fabric, and a short jacket of a darker green, also of shimmersilk. Despite the silver hair, he doubted that she was much older than he was.

"Envoy Luryessa?" Kharl bowed. He could sense chaos all around the woman, but chaos under tight control—chaos that might be called even orderly. He tried not to show any surprise at learning that the Sarronnese envoy was both a woman and a chaos-wizard or sorceress.

"Lord Kharl, I am most pleased to see you and welcome you to the residence." Luryessa smiled. "Refreshments will be ready shortly. Before that, I would like to show you the public rooms of the residence if you would not mind."

Kharl smiled politely. "I would appreciate that." Even the rooms might tell him something.

She turned through the archway on the far right, walking a good thirty cubits to open double doors set under a square arch, stopping there. The chamber was an oblong a good forty cubits by twenty. The ceiling was ten cubits high, and both walls and ceiling were a creamy off-white, plain plaster finish. The only ornamentation on either walls or ceiling were the crown moldings and a wide but plain chair railing, both painted Sarronnese blue, a brighter color than the dark navy blue of Brysta. The floor was of white marble tiles, but most was covered by thick carpets with designs tending toward green. The chairs and settees were upholstered in dark green, and the wood of the tables and furnishings was all a light cherry. The mirrors—flanked by lamps in wall sconces—were framed in cherry as well. There were no paintings hung on the walls, but ornate green tapestries were suspended from the crown moldings. The hangings did not show scenes, but curved and patterned designs in green and gold.

"This is the formal drawing room, for use in the evenings before large dinners."

Kharl nodded, since he'd never seen a chamber that seemed so cold and formal.

Luryessa continued down the corridor, also marble-tiled, with thin brass strips between the tiles, to the next set of open double doors, where she stopped, without speaking. The dining chamber was larger than the formal drawing room, with a single long table, also of cherry, and flanked with straight-backed wooden chairs, their seats upholstered in dark green. A quick count suggested to Kharl that the table could seat at least fifty people.

Luryessa smiled and continued to the cross corridor, where she turned right, coming to a stop at another open door. "This is the personal dining chamber, and it's used most often."

The smaller chamber held a table that seated close to twenty, but the western-facing windows, the hearth on the south wall, as well as the mauve-and-blue hangings and the cherry-paneled walls, gave it a warmer feeling.

Next came the library, which was almost the size of the main floor of Kharl's house at Cantyl, with oak shelves covering most of the walls. Here, Luryessa stepped inside.

"Some of these volumes date back several centuries."

"So do some in our residence," Kharl said. "I doubt anyone has read most of them in all that time."

The Sarronnese laughed. "There are several thousand here. I've read perhaps two or three hundred, mostly the histories, and some of the essays. Jemelya has read another hundred or so."

Kharl recalled the assistant's name, but did not comment.

Luryessa gestured toward a door set in the middle of the south wall, between the wall cases. "Would you like to see my private study, Lord Kharl?"

Kharl understood. The message was not an invitation to dalliance. "I would be honored, Envoy Luryessa."

After they entered, Luryessa closed the heavy door behind her and turned. "Lord Kharl . . . or should I call you mage?"

"Envoy Luryessa . . . one could also call you sorceress."

The muscular silver-haired woman nodded. "One could. It would not be accurate in many fashions. Shall we fence, or be direct? We are private here, and all of my retainers in the residence at the moment are trustworthy."

Kharl shrugged helplessly. "I cannot fence. My weapons are staff and cudgel, and both are most direct."

"Are you at liberty to tell me why Lord Ghrant sent a powerful mage as his envoy? Has he so many that he can spare one of your strength more than a thousand kays from Valmurl?"

"I cannot look into Lord Ghrant's mind, Envoy Luryessa—"

"Just Luryessa in private, please."

"I know that he is greatly concerned about the intentions of the Emperor of Hamor. All I have seen in the harbor are Hamorian vessels, and there are no other merchanters. That concerns me."

"It would concern all with any intelligence. Your secretary was most polite with Jemelya, but you would not have sent him so soon after your arrival had you not been concerned about matters here in Brysta."

"You are most observant."

She smiled. "Has Lord Ghrant so many mages?"

Kharl smiled, politely. "Does the Tyrant?"

"No. Sorcery and magery are frowned upon in Sarron. I am seldom welcomed home, but find myself honored in my positions as envoy to other lands . . . so long as I do not return home too often or for too long."

Kharl could sense the absolute truth of Luryessa's words . . . and the hidden sadness behind them.

"And what of you?" she asked.

He paused, then said carefully, "Lord Ghrant is wary of mages, but one other of longer service to the Lords of Austra remains in Valmurl." That was certainly true.

"You are most cautious, yet truthful in what you have said." A smile containing a hint of impishness, incongruous in the stately envoy, crossed her lips. "You have not said much, though."

"I have never been an envoy before. I must feel my way with care. Great care."

"Envoys must always be careful. They send us where there are neither fleets nor lancers to support us."

"And some lands have few of either."

Luryessa nodded, then said, "Magery is an acceptable substitute. Great magery was used to defeat the Hamorians in Austra, although Lord Whetorak has claimed that there were no Hamorians in Austra, except for a handful of mercenaries."

"That may be, but those mercenaries wore Hamorian uniforms," Kharl said.

"Did the emperor also send chaos-wizards?"

"I cannot say who sent all of them. Not for certain. Some did arrive on Hamorian ships, and they were chaos-wizards who supported the rebel lords."

"Our envoy reported that Lord Ghrant had a powerful order-master.

No one knows much about what he did or how, except that there are claims that he turned a mountain into solid glass, and when all was over, there were no rebels left living, and no chaos-wizards."

Kharl shrugged. "I can say that he did not turn a mountain into glass."

"I thought not. That is something of chaos. Still . . . a powerful order-master might be able to deflect such forces, and that deflection might turn part of a mountain into glass."

"I suppose that could happen," Kharl admitted. While he suspected that Luryessa was probably more trustworthy than either the Hamorians or Lord West and his retainers, he was uncomfortable dealing with such an astute woman. "I think it is best that I not speak of how Lord Ghrant was able to overcome the rebels and the Hamorians."

"Then we will not. I would not wish to place you in an uncomfortable position." Another smile appeared. "Overcaptain Osten and the Hamorians may wish that. Sarronnyn does not."

"My secretary met with a secretary for Lord West, and he gained the impression that young Osten is greatly involved in governing the West Quadrant."

"In practice, Overcaptain Osten, who is the eldest of Ostcrag's sons, rules Brysta. The youngest, Captain Egen, rules the southern lands of the West Quadrant. Vielam rules the others outside of the south and Brysta, but he defers to his brothers."

"I thought that Egen was the youngest."

"He is, but Vielam defers to him, nonetheless. That has become more true and more frequent since Klarsat departed."

The name meant nothing to Kharl. "Was he a councilor or advisor to Vielam?"

"Of sorts. He was an order-mage. Of moderate abilities. He departed in the spring, on a merchanter from Recluce."

"He supported Vielam, then."

"Let us surmise that he disliked Vielam less than his brothers. He left after the first of the Hamorian white wizards arrived."

The more Kharl heard, the less he liked what he felt was happening in Brysta. "I have heard reports of brigandage. One of our merchanters told the lord-chancellor that his men were prevented from traveling south for goods for that reason."

Luryessa laughed. "All the would-be brigands are working in the quarries that Egen has reopened. Do not have any of your retainers walk the streets alone, particularly at night."

"Every man not a lord and not likely to be missed is a brigand?"

"Or a beggar or a thief."

Kharl could easily believe that of Egen. "Why does he need that many?"

"They're building a road to the south, following the old road to Surien."

"For trade?"

"That is the claim, but work on the road did not begin until Lord South refused to consort his daughter Estelya to young Egen."

"And the Hamorians?"

"They are providing tools and knowledge. So they say."

Kharl snorted.

"You doubt the honorable intentions of Hamor?"

"From what I have seen, Hamor has no intentions that are honorable. Although I have been told that the Emperors of Hamor are patient, I have doubts about this emperor."

"His mightiness Sestar reached his majority less than two years ago. He is little older than your Lord Ghrant. As you surmise, he is not considered patient." The Sarronnese laughed, sardonically, yet good-naturedly. "You have been to Cigoerne, then?"

"Only to Swartheld. Have you seen Cigoerne?"

"I have. It is most beautiful, most cultured, and terrifying in what it represents."

"Oh?" Kharl did not know exactly how to respond to that statement.

"The city is pleasant and beautiful, as is all around it. But, two hundred kays to the north is Luba, where the sky is black with soot and dust and ashes, and where thousands of furnaces and steam engines roar day and night. To the west stretches the Great Highway, a white stone road that will reach all across Hamor to Atla in the east. It, too, is proud and beautiful, and few see the quarries where thousands labor endlessly." Luryessa gave the smallest of shrugs.

"Beauty built on misery and slavery?"

"The Hamorian philosopher Aurelat wrote that most men live lives of misery, and that is indeed the human condition. Since misery has always existed, continues to exist, and always will, he posited that a ruler's task was to harness that misery in the most productive of ways, creating structures of beauty and providing adequate food and lodging for all so that their misery could be most effectively used to improve the land and the world."

"That serves the lords and the emperor most effectively."

"Aurelat has been a favorite of the emperors, especially after he drowned in his bath a hundred years ago."

"I see."

"Do Lord West or his sons know that you are an order-master?"

"I am to present my credentials on twoday. I have not said anything about my small abilities."

"Most wise. Still, it will not be that long before it is rumored that you are a mage. Lord West retains a chaos-wizard, and anything known in that keep does not remain there. Once that becomes known, those who favor greater alliance with Hamor will claim that your presence signifies an alliance between Nordla and Recluce."

"Recluce has never allied with anyone. It is not likely to do so now," Kharl pointed out.

"What is in fact has never changed the minds of those who wish to believe otherwise."

Kharl could not argue that. "Is it known that you are a sorceress?"

"No, but all women envoys of the Legend-following lands are considered sorceresses. So we never affirm or deny it. What good would it do?" Luryessa's lips quirked. "It is said that you have been studying the laws of Nordla. I would not have thought that of much use, since the lord justicers neither know them nor follow them."

"I had heard such," Kharl admitted. "I am hopeful that the way in which they do not follow them might prove helpful in understanding Brysta."

"You have greater hopes than do I." Abruptly, she turned, her hand on the lever of the closed study door. "Come, let us have some refreshments, and I will tell you what I know of Brysta and Ostcrag, Lord West."

"And about Sarronnyn. I know little of Sarronnyn," Kharl confessed.

"We can help with that." Luryessa opened the door to the private study, then led him through the main library and farther down the corridor to a smaller parlorlike room. The chamber held a circular table of black lorken, inlaid with a floral border of white oak. Five chairs were set around the circular table. The only other furnishings were chest tables set against the inside walls. Wide glass windows stretched the length of the outside wall, overlooking a garden, except the garden was almost entirely of stones arranged in a pattern that Kharl thought he should recognize, but didn't.

Luryessa gestured toward the windows and the garden beyond. "The stone garden is a copy of one I once saw in Viela. I tried to have it laid out from my memory, but you never know. The druids are good with sand and stone, for all that they prefer the forest." After the briefest of pauses, she added, "Please sit down. Ziela will be bringing the refreshments. I've taken the liberty of offering you Shyrlan. It's a light white wine, very refreshing on hot sultry days like these. If you don't like it, we can offer other vintages, or pale ale or lager, as well."

"You know more of it than I do." Kharl smiled.

A slender girl, wearing a blue shirt and matching blue trousers, appeared with a tray. Deftly, she set a fluted crystal goblet before Kharl and another before Luryessa, followed by a small blue porcelain plate. Then came three platters, each with different kinds of pastries, which she placed equidistant from the two envoys.

"Thank you, Ziela," said Luryessa.

"Thank you," echoed Kharl.

They received a slight bow, and then Ziela was gone. As the serving girl slipped away, Kharl realized that he had not seen a single boy or man since he had entered the Sarronnese residence.

Luryessa lifted her goblet. "To your success as an envoy, Lord Kharl."

"And to your continued success." Kharl could detect no hint of chaos or anything untoward in the nearly clear wine, nor in the miniature cakes and pastries on the oval platters of blue-tinted porcelain. He took a small sip. While he was no expert on wines, the Shyrlan was light and cool, as Luryessa had promised, with a slight sweetness and a hint of a fragrance that was fruitlike, but not like any fruit he had ever tasted. "This is good."

"You doubted me?" Her voice was light.

"I did not doubt you, but I am no expert on wines."

"You have great knowledge in other matters, I am most certain, else you would not be here."

"I've never heard of a name like Luryessa," Kharl said, not wishing to discuss his expertise or lack of such and hoping that comments about her name were harmless enough.

"You may never hear of it again. It's an old name, and in the tongue of the Legend, it means 'of Ryessa,' or of the lineage of Ryessa."

Having no idea who Ryessa might be, Kharl just nodded and took a sip of the white wine.

"Ryessa was the Tyrant of Sarronnyn and the older sister of Megaera. Megaera was a powerful white sorceress in the days of Westwind. I don't know if you're familiar with the founding of Recluce, but she . . ."

"*That* Megaera? You're related to her?"

"More to her older sister, according to family stories, but that was hundreds and hundreds of years back." Luryessa grinned. "Seven hundred and eight, actually."

Kharl took another sip of the wine, then followed Luryessa's example and lifted one of the white-glazed pastries onto his small plate.

"Sarronnyn went into a period of great decline after Megaera's departure," Luryessa went on. "It was gradual, so gradual that few noticed until just before the great cataclysm. Then the Iron Guard of Fairven and the white wizards began to build the last of their great highways. That was the one through the Westhorns so that they could bring Sarronnyn and all the west of Candar under their rule."

"But that didn't last long," Kharl pointed out, recalling what Tarkyn had once told him. "Only for a few years."

"Less than that, actually, but that was only because Fairven and most of the wizards were destroyed, not because of any strength of Sarronnyn."

"No one knows who did that, do they?"

The faintest smile crossed Luryessa's lips. "It is a fair guess that a renegade black wizard and engineer from Recluce did so. There were . . . artifacts . . . left, and they were of black iron. There were also bodies, but to this day, no one knows more than that."

"I'm sorry. I was asking about your name."

"The name of the Tyrant who let Sarron fall was expunged, never to be used again, according to her heir. So was the name Ryessa."

"Why Ryessa? She didn't have anything to do with the fall of Sarronnyn. She was long dead."

"The thought was that her handling of Megaera created Recluce and made the rise of Fairven possible. My grandmother disagreed. I was named for Ryessa as a protest. Now . . . names that suggest that lineage are frowned upon."

"Just frowned upon?"

"In Sarronnyn, that is as good as an outright prohibition."

That said much to Kharl. "So you still have a Tyrant?"

"Absolutely. And we still follow the Legend."

"How long have you been the envoy here?"

"Six years."

"Isn't that long for an envoy?"

"It is, but . . . everyone feels more comfortable with me being here. That includes me."

"What can you tell me about Brysta that you think I should know?" Kharl took a bite from the pastry. The inside held a pearapple-almond filling. He managed not to lick his lips.

"It seems clear enough that the Hamorians are behind the road-building and the new patroller barracks. They seem to meet mostly with Captain Egen . . ."

That made great sense to Kharl, knowing what he did of Egen.

"They've also been overcharging for the goods they bring to Brysta, and refusing to buy Brystan wares unless they can get them at prices that beggar the sellers."

"But . . . people won't buy then, and they won't sell."

"Oh . . . where will the smiths and factors get iron stock? Or copper? Why do you think Egen has his men patrolling the roads to the south, and why there are some white wizards with his forces? Or why Vielam's road patrols to the north and east are levying road tariffs on all merchant traffic?"

"It's that bad?"

"No. It's worse. More than a half score merchanters have vanished in the past two seasons, all of them nearing or bound for Brysta or Sagana. They were all from smaller lands, places like Suthya and Spidlar."

"I've heard little of that, and neither has the lord-chancellor."

"He and Lord Ghrant doubtless suspect something. Otherwise, why would you be here?" Luryessa smiled once more, knowingly.

Kharl could not argue with either the logic or the smile, and he had no doubts that everything she had told him was true. He could only worry about what she had not said—or did not know.

"While there are details I may have glossed over, Lord Kharl, that is what we face here in Brysta."

There were more than a few details missing, but they wouldn't change the overall view, Kharl suspected as he took another sip of wine. "Could you tell me about the other envoys?"

"I could, but I'd rather not share that information until after you have met them. Then, you can invite me for refreshments, and we can compare what we have seen."

Once more, Kharl could detect no evasions, and none of the chaos that generally signified lying or dishonesty. That was more disturbing than a lie would have been. "Then, if you will not share that information with me now, perhaps you could tell me about Sarronnyn, and about how people conduct their lives under the Legend . . . and how you came to be an envoy."

"You do not ask for much. Histories have been written about Sarronnyn."

"But I have not read them." Kharl smiled. "I have not seen any in Austra, either."

"That is less than surprising." Luryessa took a sip of her Shyrlan before continuing. "Sarron is the capital of Sarronnyn, and it is both an old city and a new one. It was founded by the last of the original angels to leave Westwind. That was nearly thirteen hundred years ago. Once it was a craft and trade center, through which flowed all the trade north of the Stone Hills and west of the mountains. In time, the rulers of Lornth decided that Sarron was too powerful and independent. They attacked. They were right. The women warriors of Sarron destroyed the forces of Lornth. From those battles came Sarronnyn . . ."

Kharl listened intently.

LXV

Threeday night, after refreshments with Luryessa that had lasted until past sunset, Kharl had returned to his envoy's residence—and to the library, where Erdyl was waiting.

"What did you find out from the weavers?" asked Kharl.

"The cloth didn't come from Brysta. It was made on steam looms in Hamor. That was what Derdan told me. He said that none of the weavers here in Nordla can make cloth that cheaply. The Hamorian cloth isn't as good—that's what he says—and it's all cotton that wears out sooner."

"It's probably more comfortable in summer," mused Kharl, "but they'll freeze in a hard winter. Egen wouldn't care about that."

"That's what the factor said, not about Captain Egen, but about the cotton. He said that he'd tried to suggest summer and winter uniforms, but the patrollers said those would have to wait."

"What about the other weavers?"

"That fellow Gharan—he's got some quality cloth there. It's a small place, just him and his consort and one other girl. She looks young, sort of sandy hair. First pretty young woman I've seen in Brysta. Good smile."

Kharl stiffened inside, but managed to reply, keeping his tone wry, "I'm sure there are others." Even as he spoke, he had to wonder at his reaction. Was it just that he didn't want young Erdyl thinking of Jeka as just another pretty young thing? She'd saved his life, and she deserved more than being a fleeting pleasure to a young lordling.

"I haven't seen any others, ser."

"I'm sure you will," Kharl replied. "What did Gharan say about the cloth?"

"He said it was decent cotton, but not much more, and that the patrollers would wish for warm wool come the turn of winter. He wanted to know if we were thinking of trying to ship cloth here. I told him that I didn't know of anything like that. I also said that we didn't grow cotton or much flax in Austra. Then he wanted to know if we'd like to buy anything."

"Did you see anything that caught your eye? Besides the girl?" Kharl wished he hadn't said the last words, but they'd burst out by themselves.

"He has some wools, lambs' wool, very soft, and some striking weaves, ser."

"We should visit, then, if we have some time." Kharl nodded. "What about Soret?"

Erdyl frowned. "There was something about him. I didn't like him. He didn't look at me, not straight. He kept asking why I wanted to know all this. I hope you didn't mind, ser, but I told him that envoys tell their secretaries what to do, and we don't ask too many questions, not if we want to keep being secretaries. I did tell him that you'd once been in trade and liked to know what was being traded where. That seemed to settle him some. He didn't say much, except that the cloth was Hamorian cotton and not up to the standard of good Nordlan linen."

"Is there anything else I should know?"

Erdyl's brows narrowed in concentration, and he cocked his head slightly, almost squinting, before he finally spoke. "There is one thing. Derdan . . . he said something about having trouble meeting prices when harbor tariffs had been lowered on cotton. It was almost under his breath, but when I asked him, he just shook his head."

"Did it look like any of them had added or lost weavers?"

"I never saw Derdan's back room, but I didn't see new looms or empty looms with either Gharan or Soret . . ."

After another quarter glass, Kharl stood and led the way to the dining room.

There, he didn't say much at supper, his thoughts partly on the cotton from Hamor. Given how many patrollers he'd seen already, there must have been hundreds, if not thousands of yards of the cloth, and all of a uniform dye. If none of the three weavers were complaining too much about lost business, then Kharl judged that not much cloth besides that had been shipped from Hamor . . . but that was a guess.

He was still concerned about Jeka, glad as he was that she was still with Gharan. He could still call up that gaminelike smile, infrequent as it had been in the cold days between the walls.

After supper, he retired to the library, where he tried to sort out all that he had learned since he'd arrived in Brysta. It didn't seem to help. Finally, he turned out the lamps and headed up to the overlarge bedchamber. He doubted that he would sleep all that well, but pacing around the library wasn't helping, either.

LXVI

Kharl had been right. On threeday night, he had not slept that well, worrying about what Luryessa had said, about what all the cotton for uniforms meant, about why he had reacted so strongly to Erdyl's almost casual observations about Jeka. He also found his thoughts swirling over the question of whether he was hopeless as an envoy.

All the matters that Luryessa had brought up did not surprise him.

Hagen had prepared him for the worst concerning Hamor's intentions. Nor had Luryessa's wealth of knowledge surprised him. She had asked nothing, but had learned more than Kharl would have liked to reveal. Yet he knew he could not be a hermit. He also knew that within another eightday or so, Lord West and the other envoys would learn more about him once they received word from the envoys and spies in Valmurl and elsewhere in Nordla. That was, if they had not already learned it. He doubted that he had more than another eightday at most before word would be everywhere in Brysta that he was a mage—or might be one.

When Kharl woke on fourday, he was still worrying, but he had some ideas. He washed and shaved, and dressed quickly, before making his way down to the smaller breakfast room, where a mass of egg toast and ham and breads awaited him, with both cider and ale—more of everything than either he or Erdyl or Demyst would ever be able to finish.

Erdyl was already eating, heartily, with all the zest of a growing young man. He looked up with a contented smile. "Good morning, Lord Kharl."

"Good morning." Kharl seated himself. After he had several bites, and some cider, he looked across the breakfast table at Erdyl. "We will need to offer entertainment to the other envoys."

"It is summer, Lord Kharl." The secretary looked puzzled. "One does not entertain before late harvest."

"Harvest will be here before that long, and it will take time to plan out such an event. I would like you to contact other secretaries once more and work with Fundal and Khelaya. We need to host a party or reception, or whatever they are called, as soon as it is acceptable to do so."

"Yes, ser."

"You will contact the other secretaries. Explain that you have never done this, and that is why you are talking to them so soon again. Pretend to be what they think you are, a younger son of a lord who knows little."

"You want me to find out everything I can?"

"Yes. But make sure that you keep talking about our reception."

Erdyl nodded brightly. "I can only be stupid for a while before I should have learned something."

"That is true. Also, if you seem not to know much . . ."

"They won't expect as much of me."

"Or of me." Kharl hoped that was so. "I'm going to watch Lord Justicer Reynol this morning, and then, this afternoon after we eat, the undercaptain and I are going to take a walk. That will leave the carriage for you to use this afternoon, if you need it."

"Yes, ser."

"A walk?" asked Demyst. "Not even a ride, ser?"

"We won't be learning much about Brysta if we don't look at it. We'll walk down Crafters' Lane. We can go into shops and talk to people. A ride may come later."

"Ser," began Erdyl, "envoys don't usually—"

Kharl just looked at Erdyl. Doing what other envoys did would only make matters worse. They had spies and retainers and knew how to use them. Kharl didn't.

"Yes, ser."

"You put it that way, ser, sounds like a good idea," added Demyst.

Kharl thought so, but that depended on what they learned.

"I was looking through the armory, and I found something that might be useful, ser."

"You know I'm useless with a blade, and carrying a staff would mark me." He snorted. "Envoys don't carry cudgels, either."

"Ah . . . ser . . . I found a long truncheon. Must be years old, but it's sound, and it's got a scabbard. Looks like a shortsword, but it's heavy. Lorken or black oak, I'd say."

That brought Kharl up short, but only for a moment. If it looked like a blade, at least from a distance, the truncheon might serve several purposes. It certainly couldn't hurt. "That's a good thought. I'll wear it this afternoon."

"Not this morning?"

"I'm going into the Hall of Justice itself. They won't allow weapons inside. They don't care if I am a lord and envoy. You can leave your blade behind, or you can wait outside for me."

"Outside, ser."

Kharl finished eating quickly, then went upstairs to finish getting dressed while Demyst and Mantar readied the horses and carriage.

In his large bedchamber, Kharl pulled on the black jacket, then fingered his chin as he looked into the floor-length mirror. He still had trouble recognizing himself without the beard. He hoped others in Brysta did as well. Then he descended to the library, where he picked up the leather case he had been using for his studies.

Mantar had the carriage drawn up beside the residence by the time

Kharl stepped outside, into what promised to be another hazy, sultry day. He'd forgotten how steamy Brysta could be before the late-summer rains finally arrived.

"Let's go." Kharl climbed up into the carriage.

Demyst followed.

The streets of Brysta looked no different on fourday than they had on any other day. There were still fewer people than Kharl remembered, and neither beggars nor unaccompanied young women. He could still recall Charee running through the streets before they had been consorted, and Tyrbel's daughters coming and going—until the time Egen had attacked Sanyle. Had things changed that much in little more than a year?

Just before Mantar brought the carriage to a stop outside the Hall of Justice, Kharl realized something else. Not only were there Watch patrollers on almost every block, but he had not seen a single regular armsman or lancer since he had returned to Brysta. There had never been many, but there had been some.

"Have you seen any armsmen or lancers?" Kharl turned to Demyst.

The undercaptain frowned, tilting his head slightly. "Just the Watch patrollers."

"I haven't either."

"You wouldn't see many in Valmurl."

"But you'd see some."

Once he left the carriage, Kharl walked swiftly to the outer double doors of the Hall of Justice, then through them and into the foyer. He could sense the eyes of the two guards turning toward them.

"I'll wait here, ser," said Demyst, halting just inside the foyer and stepping back against the stone wall, taking a position from which he could watch both the doors out of the building, the staircase, and the doors to the main hall.

"I'll likely be a while."

"Yes, ser."

Kharl made his way toward the double doors at the end of the foyer, doors he had only been through once before—as a prisoner accused of a murder he had not committed. He swallowed, then smiled as he neared the two patrollers.

"Please be quiet, ser . . . The hearing has already started," said the patroller on the left.

"What is the case?"

"Some fellow disturbing the peace now. Murder after that."

Kharl slipped inside the doors and took a seat on one of the benches in the fourth row back. He repressed a smile. Had he been dressed as a cooper, he doubted that entry would have been so easy.

The hall chamber was larger than the one in Valmurl, with a width of thirty cubits, a length of fifty, and a ceiling height of ten. At the end of the chamber away from Kharl were two daises, one behind the other, each holding a podium desk of age-darkened deep brownish gold oak. At the seat behind the lower dais sat a round-faced, blocky, and gray-haired man—Reynol. The square-bearded justicer wore a blue velvet gown, trimmed in black.

The single seat on the upper dais, its high carved back gilded and upholstered in blue velvet, was vacant. In the single seat before the benches on the right side of the chamber sat a dark-haired figure. Once more, on each side was a Watch patroller, and not the regular armsmen Kharl recalled from his own trial.

At the long narrow table on the left side between the benches and the dais sat Fasyn, along with a younger man. Both Lord Justicer Reynol and Fasyn glanced at Kharl, but their eyes returned quickly to the patroller who stood before the dais, speaking slowly.

". . . picked up a stool and tried to break it over Hunsal's head . . . had too much ale, I wager, 'cause it just banged his arm, not all that hard—"

"He attacked one of the Watch, then?" asked Reynol.

"I wouldn't say that, your lordship. He'd drunk so much that he didn't much know who was even around. He just went down without any of us touching him. Had to put him on a cart to get him to the gaol."

"If he had not attacked anyone, why did you put him in gaol?"

The patroller looked down.

"Answer the question, patroller."

". . . 'cause, your lordship, Serjeant Quant said we had to . . . said it was an order from Captain Egen, and we didn't want to go against that . . ."

"Enough."

Reynol gestured to the man sitting in the armless chair. "Senekyt, stand and step forward."

The man stood. Even from behind, Kharl could tell that he was young, probably not more than eighteen. The man trembled as he straightened and waited.

"You stand accused of disturbing the peace and of attacking the Watch.

You have heard the accounts and the charges against you. Do you have anything to say?"

"Ser . . . your lordship . . . sure as I'm standing here, I drunk too much ale. I know that, ser, but also sure as I'm standing here, I didn't attack no Watch. I'd never do that, ser. I know what comes of that. That's work in the quarries. I didn't attack no Watch, ser. I didn't."

Kharl could sense both truth and desperation in the words.

"Senekyt. You are a foolish young man, but there is some question about all that happened. You are hereby found guilty of disturbing the peace. Your sentence for attacking the Watch is suspended."

"Ser . . . your lordship? Suspended? What does that mean?"

"If you are brought into the Hall of Justice at any time in the next year, you will be found guilty of attacking the Watch, and you will be sentenced to a term in the quarries."

"If I do anything at all?"

"That is correct." Reynol cleared his throat. "You are sentenced to five lashes for disturbing the peace, and one silver for costs." He turned to the patrollers. "Have him lashed and released."

"All stand!" ordered the bailiff from behind Kharl.

Kharl stood with the others and watched. Young Senekyt lowered his head as he was led out of the Hall.

The bailiff's staff rapped on the stone floor three times. "Is there one who would take the Justicer's Challenge?" The bailiff did not even pause before continuing. "There being none, the felter Myondak is here, accused of murder, to be brought before justice!"

"Bailiff, bring forward Myondak the felter."

The same pair of burly patrollers marched a graying man past Kharl and up to the dais. The man limped, and Kharl could sense the chaos of injuries that had not healed.

"You, the felter Myondak, have been charged with the murder of your consort Salynia. What you say or believe is not a question. We are here to do justice, and that justice is to determine whether you killed your consort." The justicer seated himself.

From behind Kharl came a rap of the staff. "All may sit."

The hearing was brief, and unlike the first, there was no question of the felter's guilt, not even to Kharl, but he forced himself to watch the entire proceeding, until after the felter had been marched away and after Reynol had left the chamber.

Then he made his way out and rejoined Undercaptain Demyst in the foyer.

"Mantar has the coach outside, ser. Been waiting near-on a glass."

"It's still well before noon."

"He said he'd rather wait here than fret."

Kharl shook his head as he made his way to the carriage. The sky was brighter, but still hazy, and Kharl was dripping sweat from his forehead by the time he was seated in the coach. Even with the windows open, he was even hotter by the time they returned to the residence.

Erdyl was waiting inside. "I have a listing of the envoys and their secretaries and assistants, and the possible dates in harvest that we could host a function, ser."

"Have you talked to anyone yet?"

"No, ser. I had to go over the calendar. One cannot have a function on eightday or oneday, or on any of the Lord's holidays, and I checked with Khelaya to see what produce and fruits might be coming ripe when . . ."

"After we eat, and after I've had a lager." Kharl blotted his forehead with the back of his hand, before belatedly recalling that he had a handkerchief tucked inside his jacket. He almost hated to use the fine linen, but he pulled it out and blotted both hand and forehead.

"Dinner is ready, ser," announced Fundal, from the back of the foyer. "The lager and white wine are chilled."

Kharl led the two others into the dining chamber, where Khelaya had set out three bowls of cold gourd soup. On one platter were cold fowl breasts, with a pearapple glaze. Three different wedges of cheese sat on cutting boards, with baskets of both rye and dark bread. A bunch of red grapes was also on each man's platter, beside the cold soup. The pitcher holding the cool lager already had droplets of water on it, a good measure of the dampness of the air.

After seating himself, Kharl filled the crystal beaker with the lager, then handed the pitcher to Demyst. Erdyl was having white wine.

"What is the Hall of Justice like, ser?" asked Erdyl. "You've spent much time there."

"In some ways, I imagine they're all alike. Everyone wants something, and they all can't have it."

"Ser?"

"The accused doesn't want to be there, and he wants to be acquitted. The accuser wants the accused convicted. The clerks would rather be reading than watching and giving advice. If the lord justicer is fair, he wants to hand down something as close to justice as possible, and if he's not, he wants to do whatever benefits him." Kharl shrugged, then took a spoonful of the soup, slightly peppery and tart, but not too heavy.

"You don't sound like someone who wanted to study the law, ser." Erdyl's tone was almost accusatory.

"I needed to learn about the law, Erdyl. That's not the same as liking it."

"Aye," added Demyst. "A good lancer knows his blade well, but he'd rather not use it. If he uses it well, he lives, and the other fellow dies. If he uses it poorly, he dies. I'd wager that an advocate is like a blade."

Kharl found himself surprised by Demyst's observation. Then, Hagen hadn't actually said that the undercaptain had been stupid, just that he'd never make a good captain. There were many reasons for that besides lack of brains.

"Do you think magery—" Erdyl broke off his words with a wince.

"That's a question we don't discuss." As he spoke, Kharl repressed a smile. He'd heard Demyst's boot strike the secretary's shin. "Not now."

"Ah . . . yes, sir."

Little was said for the rest of the meal, with Erdyl's eyes jumping back and forth between Demyst and Kharl.

Finally, Kharl took a last swallow of ale and rose. "I'll be in the library. Demyst, if you would tell Mantar to ready the carriage?"

"Yes, ser." The undercaptain inclined his head slightly and departed.

Erdyl followed Kharl into the library, closing the door behind them.

He squared his shoulders and looked at Kharl. "Ser . . . I'm sorry."

Kharl looked squarely at the red-haired young man. "Erdyl. There are times when an apology means nothing. It might make you feel better, but the damage has already been done. This was not one of those, but it could have been, had anyone else been present. Even so, one never knows who might be listening."

"Are you going to dismiss me?"

"Demons, no. Everyone makes mistakes. Just don't do it again." He wanted to add something about not making the same mistake over and over, the way Arthal had, denying it every time. There was no point to that. Kharl had learned that people either learned from their mistakes or didn't, no matter what was said. Erdyl's actions would tell which kind he was.

"About the function, ser . . . We need to decide on a date . . ." ventured Erdyl.

Kharl laughed. "Pick the earliest date that you think is possible. Make it a date that will get others to wonder, but still attend."

Erdyl nodded. "Do you want just the envoys or the envoys and their principal secretaries?"

"See what you think after you talk to the other secretaries."

"What do I say if they ask about the magery in the rebellion?"

"Just tell the simple truth. That Lord Ghrant has two mages, and that you really don't know that much about either one, and that your envoy has suggested most strongly that you not discuss what you don't know."

A faint, if worried smile, appeared on Erdyl's face.

"That's the truth, isn't it?"

"Yes, ser."

"Good. I'll send Mantar back with the carriage after he drops us off. I suppose you could ride one of the mounts, but the carriage might be easier."

Erdyl nodded dubiously.

There was a rap on the library door.

"The carriage is ready," called Demyst.

"I'll see you later," Kharl told Erdyl, "and we'll talk over what you've discovered." He nodded and opened the door.

Undercaptain Demyst followed Kharl to the carriage.

Neither spoke until they had left the drive of the envoy's residence.

"I'm sorry, ser. The young lord wasn't thinking."

"You were right. He wasn't thinking. I had a word with him."

"I thought so, the way he looked when you left the library."

Had Kharl been that hard on Erdyl? Or was the young man too sensitive?

"Never make a lancer officer," Demyst went on. "Frets too much about what others think. That stuff about what other envoys do. Had Lord Ghrant wanted someone who did what other envoys did, it'd not be you, begging your pardon, ser."

Kharl burst into laughter. "You're so right." He was also beginning to see more clearly why Hagen thought Demyst would be helpful to Kharl and not necessarily that good a senior lancer officer. A properly deferential officer would never have put a boot on Erdyl's shins.

"He'll learn," the undercaptain went on. "Not like he's stupid or anything. Just hasn't seen enough."

Kharl wondered if he himself had.

Before that long, Mantar stopped the coach at the head of Crafters' Lane. "You sure you don't want me to meet you somewhere, ser?"

"No. I need the walk, even in this heat." He also needed a better feel for what was happening in Brysta. It almost didn't feel like the same city he had left. That could reflect the changes in him, but he didn't think so, not with what Erdyl and others had said.

Kharl stepped out, at the intersection of Fifth Cross and Crafters' Lane. He stood almost directly in front of the shop of Zabyl, the tinsmith, and he turned to take in the small leaded-glass windows, but, clean as the glass was, the display space was empty, as it had always been. Zabyl had never displayed any of his work.

"Tinsmith doesn't show anything," said Demyst. "Must be good, or real cautious."

"Probably both." Kharl could smell the odor of hot metal, despite the closed front door. He also had the feeling he was being watched. Slowly, he turned as if surveying the shops. A young Watch patroller in his crisp maroon-and-blue uniform on the opposite corner made no secret of his observations.

Kharl smiled politely before turning and walking past Zabyl's to the adjoining shop. There, Kharl stopped to study the bolts of woolen cloth shown in the square window. One was a muted plaid of blues and greens. Kharl frowned. The cloth looked more like something that Gharan might have woven. Was the weaver doing so well that he could sell in his own shop, and place cloth in Derdan's small factorage as well? Even with the cotton from Hamor? Beside it was a bolt of black wool, clearly from Recluce, along with another of white. Had the white come from Austra? From his neighbor, Arynal, who had boasted of his fabled white wool? Kharl shook his head. That, he doubted.

He studied the window again, then leaned forward and looked down, then up. Derdan had added brackets to hold bars behind the heavy shutters.

"Not bad wool," offered the undercaptain. "Black has to be from Recluce. Wouldn't be surprised if it cost a good silver a half yard."

"It costs a half gold a yard." At least it used to. Kharl regretted saying that much, but the words had popped out because he had once asked, when he had been thinking that it would have made a warm and stylish coat for Charee.

"That's right. You'd know. You were on a merchanter. Everything from Recluce costs a lot."

"It does." Even the knowledge, Kharl reflected. He turned away from the woolen factor's and looked across the lane, taking in the two shops, side by side there, that of Hamyl the potter on the left, and Gharan's weaving shop on the right. Gharan had never used a window to display his work, just a sample board at eye height beside the doorway.

Kharl wanted to see Gharan—and Jeka, he had to admit. But with the patroller watching so closely, and after Erdyl had visited just the day before, he wasn't sure that was wise. Still . . .

He stood there for a long moment, before finally deciding against it, then wondering if he were being too foolishly cautious.

Absently, as he used his handkerchief to blot his forehead, before turning to head toward the cooperage, he noted the barrel of sand to the left of Derdan's window. It was the same barrel of sand he'd used to put out the fire in Tyrbel's scriptorium on the day that his whole life had finally changed.

The cooperage was no longer boarded up, as it had been the last time he had seen it, and the paint on the sign that proclaimed MALLAMET, COOPER looked faded, although it could not have been much older than a year. A year? Just a year? So much had happened, since Charee . . . since Arthal had left . . . and Warrl had gone off with his aunt. For a long moment, Kharl just looked.

Then he straightened and studied the cooperage. The windows were dusty on the outside, and Kharl could see that sawdust clung to panes on the inside. Sawdust? A good cooper didn't create that much sawdust. Either Mallamet wasn't that good, or he hadn't cleaned in a long time. From what Kharl knew of Mallamet, both were doubtless true. The door was open, inviting a breeze that had not appeared.

Kharl kept walking, slowly, until he came to the scriptorium. Heavy iron shutters were drawn back from the inside of the small display window, shutters that had not been there before. The display area held several books on pale blue wool, but not, of course, Tyrbel's masterpiece, the red leather-bound *Book of Godly Prayer*—a work that Tyrbel had done as an offering to his faith. That had been destroyed in the oil fire Kharl had fought that fateful morning.

The sign on the scriptorium had changed as well. While it had once borne Tyrbel's name, now it now announced one Dasult as a scrivener. Kharl had never heard of Dasult. He wondered what had happened to Sanyle. Did he dare risk asking? If he had not heard of Dasult, scrivener, it was unlikely that the scrivener would recognize him.

"Just wait here at the door," Kharl told Demyst.

"Ser . . . that'd be dangerous."

"There's no one inside but the scrivener, and you'll be out here in case anyone else comes along. Keep your eye on that patroller. He's been following us."

"Thought so," murmured the undercaptain. "You sure about inside?"

Kharl nodded, then opened the door and stepped into the scriptorium, ready to use his sight shield to vanish, if need be.

A young man, more like Erdyl's age, stepped forward. Kharl thought he had seen him, recently, but he could not say where.

"Ser . . . could I be of service to you?"

"It is possible," Kharl replied. "It would not be quite . . ." He paused. "You're Dasult?"

"Yes, ser."

"I have not been in Brysta in some time, and I recalled that there was a scrivener here, but he was much older. Your father, perhaps?"

Dasult shook his head. "No, ser. That was Tyrbel. He was a most noted scrivener, but he was murdered, I'm told, on the street outside. I purchased the building from his daughter. She wished to leave Brysta."

"Hmmm . . . sad when those sort of things happen. I suppose she went off elsewhere in Nordla or to somewhere in Candar."

"Vizyn in Austra, I believe. She said she was going to help an older scrivener, a friend of her father's."

Kharl nodded. If Sanyle had reached Taleas, then she was in good hands. For the moment, he could only hope that she had. "I saw her once. She seemed a most sweet child."

"My consort said she was, and that she had suffered much."

"How do you find business?"

"It is improving. I have been accepted as a recorder at the Hall of Justice, and that has helped."

That was where Kharl had seen him, that very morning, but he had not connected the man to the scriptorium. "How do you find working there?"

"It is most exacting, but it pays well. Are you certain I could not interest you in one of these? Here is an illustrated rendition of *Tales of Cyad*. And here, I have the verses of Lenchret, a near-perfect copy of the one in Lord West's private library."

"You must have been privileged indeed to copy that."

"No, kind ser. Lord West wanted a copy, and allowed me to make a second in return for my charging but half what I told him."

"He got a bargain."

Dasult laughed. "In silvers, he did, but I always wanted that book, and I made a second copy for myself, as well as this fair copy. I hope not to lose too much."

"He must have quite a library."

"He does indeed, but I fear many of the volumes have not been read in years."

"That is often the case. How did you find him?"

"He was charming, but . . . preoccupied. I could not help but notice that he and his eldest had many visitors, even at the beginning of summer, when I was finishing the copying."

"Lords must deal with envoys and trade, and lancers, and all manner of people, I would wager. Even in summer. I'd wager, though, that you saw none from Recluce."

"No, I did not. They were never announced, but many were clad as are Hamorians, and more than a few were in uniforms I had not seen before."

"There are several Hamorian merchanters in the harbor, and there was a Nordlan trader an eightday or so ago."

"The Hamorians laughed at my work." Dasult stiffened. "They claimed to have built a machine that can make hundreds of copies of a book. Of what use is that? There are not that many people who would buy so many." He forced a smile. "Did you see *The Art of Healing*?"

Kharl ignored the sales effort. "Perhaps the Hamorians did not understand the craft that goes into creating a book the way you do?"

"They do not. Books, especially those such as the verses of Lenchret, they should be read and treasured. What about *The History of the Ancients*? It is rare, but I can let you have it for a mere gold."

Kharl smiled. "It is not a bad book, but what would I do with two?"

Dasult's eyes widened, then he laughed. "I cannot sell you what you already have."

"I am not buying today," Kharl said, "but I may be back."

As he left, Kharl wondered if he could have discovered more. Possibly, but he was not a spy, and he didn't think he could have learned more without making Dasult wary. He also doubted that what else he could have learned would have added much.

"Did you see any interesting books?" asked Demyst, as Kharl rejoined him.

"He had one that I've been reading. He wanted to sell it to me for a mere gold."

"A gold?"

"Some books are costly."

Kharl did not glance at the Tankard, the tavern whose doors had not yet opened, as he passed. He did study quietly the shops and narrow dwellings as he headed downhill, passing a white-haired laundress with her wash in a tall basket on her head, then a teamster with an empty wagon headed uphill. Behind them, the Watch patroller followed.

The two continued down Crafters' Lane. Less than a block farther west, Kharl saw Dhulat's cabinetry shop. He'd bought a modest chest from the crafter years before, but, like most folk, Dhulat had turned away from Kharl once Egen had put out the word that he was after the cooper.

Another two blocks toward the harbor, and they reached the upper market square. With the heat, few of the peddlers and vendors remained, and the low stone wall that surrounded the near-empty square was vacant. Topped with redstone with rounded edges, the wall was a good place for sitting and resting, and there had always been a beggar or two there. Today, there were none.

Past the square another hundred cubits or so was Hyesal's apothecary shop, clearly marked with the crossed pestles above the door. But the door was boarded shut.

Kharl wondered if the apothecary had died, or had fallen victim to Egen and the Watch.

He kept walking, turning southward at the next corner, so as to head back in the direction of the envoy's residence. For the moment, he had seen enough.

LXVII

Halfway through the early-evening meal, Kharl cleared his throat, then waited.

"We're going to the White Pony tonight," he finally announced. "Right after we eat."

"Sounds like a tavern or an inn, ser," offered Demyst.

"A tavern, mostly, and it's not all that good. Cevor and Alynar will come with us."

Demyst nodded. Puzzlement warred with curiosity on Erdyl's face.

"I'd like to hear what people are saying." Kharl paused. "We'll walk, and I'll need to find or borrow an old tunic. I will wear the truncheon."

"You forgot this afternoon," Demyst pointed out.

"You had your blade," Kharl countered.

"Best one of us did, ser."

"That's true." Kharl smiled and went back to finishing his cutlet.

Less than a glass later, the five walked toward the open door of the White Pony. Kharl mopped his brow with his sleeve. The sun had been down for over a glass, but the evening was still too warm for his liking, and harvest was a good three eightdays away, although some fruits were appearing in the market, according to Khelaya.

"Five of you . . ." said the red-faced man who greeted them. "You'll not be making trouble, now?"

"We're looking for a cool ale," Kharl said. "It's hot out."

"That it is. Best you take the round table off the wall there."

Kharl led the way. A third of the tables were empty. Most of those in the White Pony were men, and most of those were men older than Kharl, men with leather faces, rough-cut beards. There were a few women, but all three of those were graying or white-haired, and they were with older men. So were the handful or so of younger men.

Kharl and those with him had barely taken the wall table when the murmurs began, mumblings that Kharl could hear through his order-senses, despite the louder conversation and bustle. Still, he had to concentrate.

". . . who they are?"

". . . who cares . . . long as they got coins . . ."

". . . big fellow . . . follow him . . ."

". . . others . . . look like a clerk and three guards . . ."

". . . more like mercs . . ."

". . . all those Hamorians pissprick Egen's got wouldn't like that . . ."

"Careful . . . don't know who's listening . . ."

"Sides . . . what could four mercs do . . ."

"Fellows!" called an angular server, who had appeared at Demyst's shoulder, "what you all want?" She brushed back a lock of short black hair, her eyes darting around the table before centering on Kharl.

"Pale ale," Kharl said, recalling that lager in most taverns was merely watered ale.

"Lager's a lot better. Doesn't cost any more. Everything's three coppers a mug. Wine's five."

". . . silver for bad wine?" murmured Erdyl.

"Look, fellows . . . times been hard . . . especially in the south."

"Lager, then." Kharl offered a smile.

"Make that two," added Demyst.

"Four," added Alynar.

Erdyl shrugged helplessly. "Five."

"Any eats?" asked the server.

"Got any dark bread?" replied Kharl.

"Cost you. Rye's one for a loaf, two for a basket. Dark's two and four."

"Basket of dark," Kharl said, showing a pair of silvers.

"You got it. Five lagers and a basket of dark."

The lower murmurs continued.

". . . got coins . . ."

". . . all of 'em got blades, and the two big 'uns'd break you in half . . ."

". . . always that way . . ."

". . . right it is . . . why they got coins and you don't . . ."

The server returned with five brown crockery mugs, setting them quickly on the battered wooden tabletop, so deftly that despite her speed, not a drop slopped onto the wood. "Lagers." Then she set down the basket of bread. "Be three silvers and four."

Kharl handed over four silvers, as well as two more coppers.

"Thanks." The broad smile was both warm and professional.

Before she could step away, Kharl spoke. "There used to be armsmen in here all the time, didn't there?"

"Haven't been any since spring. Say they all went south to get the brigands out of the hills. Said that was the reason we didn't get no produce and stuff from there." The server shrugged, tossing her head to flip the errant lock of black hair back. "Miss the coins. Don't miss the rest of it."

"Looks slow, even for mideightday."

"Slow all the time now, except when the patrollers get off." She glanced toward the door.

"They're as bad as the armsmen?" suggested Kharl.

The server just shook her head. "Check on you fellows later." She moved to another table, where three white-haired men and a woman sat. "Need a refill, gramps?"

"Hain't finished what I got, Selda."

"Way you're drinkin', gramps, you never will . . ."

Kharl smiled.

"She didn't want to talk about the patrollers," observed Erdyl.

"Seemed that way," added Demyst.

Kharl said nothing, but studied the lager with his order-senses. There was no obvious chaos in it. He took a sip. He'd had better. He'd seldom had worse. After a second sip, he broke off a chunk of the bread and chewed off some. Warm, crusty, and flavorful, it was far better than the lager. He hated to think what the ale tasted like. He held the mug as though he would continue to sip, but concentrated on hearing what was being said at the other tables.

". . . sent Gorot home last fiveday . . . said wasn't enough work for two . . ."

". . . Melanya . . . thinks her Fradol's got eyes for Jaela . . ."

". . . knocks her up and looks elsewhere . . . Ought to knock him up . . ."

"She'd come home then, and your coppers'd be flowing then . . ."

". . . have children . . . always keep paying . . . they never notice . . . good times and bad . . ."

". . . seen better times . . ."

"Haven't we all?"

Kharl had been slowly studying the servers as they passed, but he hadn't seen Enelya, from whom Kharl and Jeka had wheedled, begged, and bought food. The long-faced blond server handing the tables in the far corner was familiar—but he couldn't recall her name. He gestured to her, holding up a silver.

"Yes, ser?" She glanced toward the kitchen nervously. "Selda's your server . . ."

"Not about servers," Kharl replied. "A silver for you, if you can answer a question or two. Nothing more.'

"A silver?" Clearly, she didn't believe him.

He beckoned for her to lean down. "When I was here, a year ago, there was a dark-haired girl, very friendly. Enelya, I think her name was. She had a sister, too, except something terrible happened to her."

"Right awful it was. She drowned in the harbor. The sister, I mean. Poor thing."

"Does Enelya . . . ?"

"Left here, not more 'n eightday ago. Couldn't say where."

Kharl could tell she was lying. He added a second silver to the first. "You might know where she went."

"Couldn't say, ser." Her voice wavered.

"Is she in trouble?"

The server glanced to the door. "Please, ser."

"Egen?" Kharl added another silver.

Her mouth opened. "She told him no." Her eyes darted away. "Said she had to go. Knew a place to hole up, wasn't bein' used. Didn't say where."

"The urchin's place?"

The girl's eyes widened. "Don't tell."

Kharl pressed the silvers into her hand. "I won't. Tell the others that you're meeting me later." He smiled. "Then sneak away and get some sleep."

"Ser . . ."

"Go . . ."

She darted away, but Kharl noted that she had kept the silvers—out of sight.

"Ser?" asked Erdyl.

"Later." Kharl took another small swallow of the lager. He kept listening, but he heard nothing new.

After another half glass, he nodded to Demyst. "Time to go." He stood and could feel eyes turning to watch him and the others as they walked from the White Pony.

Outside, Kharl walked to the first cross street, Second Cross, and turned westward.

"Ah, ser," murmured Erdyl, "the residence is back that way."

"I know," Kharl said cheerfully. "We need to investigate something."

"You know where the missing server is, don't you?" Erdyl's tone was almost accusatory. "What does she know?"

"I don't know, but I'd like to find out. I'd also like to repay a favor, if I can." Kharl lengthened his stride. The air had cooled some while they had been in the White Pony, and a slight breeze blew out of the north, mixing the scent of harbor and dead fish with smoke, cooking oil, and other odors. A year before, he would not even have noticed the smell.

As they neared where Second Cross met Copper Road, Kharl could not only see but sense the Watch patrollers coming up the darkened Copper Road, even before he heard their boots on the yellow brick pavement of the street, not that he could tell the color in the darkness, but he recalled it all too well. "Patrollers are coming."

Demyst, Cevor, and Alynar all checked their sabres. Belatedly, so did Erdyl.

Kharl stopped at the intersection, waiting.

"Where are you headed?" The lead patroller barked at Kharl. Then as his eyes took in Demyst, Erdyl, and the two guards, he added, "Ser."

"I was taking an evening walk, patroller," Kharl said politely. "I was told it was unwise to walk alone. So I brought some friends."

The patroller looked at Kharl, then at Erdyl and the others. "Can be, ser. Take care. Best to avoid the area just above the harbor."

"Thank you." Kharl watched as the patrollers turned and headed back along Second Cross.

". . . hate that . . . have to tell the serjeant . . . five of 'em . . . three guards . . . think I'm going to take on that . . ."

". . . serjeant understands . . ."

"Captain doesn't . . ."

"Serjeant won't tell him . . . never does . . ."

Only when the patrollers were a good five rods away did Kharl turn onto Copper Road, heading toward the tannery and the rendering yard.

Kharl could smell the rendering yard long before they reached it, except the pungency was not what he had recalled. "That's the renderer's."

"Looks like the gate's boarded up," Erdyl said, stopping momentarily.

Kharl tensed momentarily, then took a deep breath. Werwal *had* been known for speaking his mind. "Is there a proclamation or anything posted there?"

"No, ser."

Werwal would have to wait. There was little Kharl could do now. There might be little enough he could do for Enelya, but if the other server at the White Pony knew where she was, she would not be safe from Egen long. Kharl kept walking.

Uphill from the renderer's was the serviceway off the alley, and Kharl recalled both all too well. He stopped and studied the short serviceway beyond the alley.

"You going in there, ser?" asked Demyst.

"There aren't any brigands or beggars here," Kharl replied softly. He eased forward along the alley, then turned into the serviceway, stopping short of the brick wall. Behind it were hidden two walls less than four cubits apart, one the brick wall of the renderer and the other stone wall of Drenzel the tanner. Even in the dim light the ancient and worn yellow bricks of the wall directly before him stood out from the newer red bricks paving the serviceway. He cast his order-senses beyond the wall that was but a head or so above his own height. One person crouched in the hidey-hole that had been Jeka's. Enelya? Who else could it be?

"She's alone," Kharl whispered to Demyst. "I'm climbing over."

"Ser!" hissed the undercaptain.

"I'll be careful."

Kharl scrambled up to the top of the wall, then used his order-senses to harden the air just outside where Enelya crouched in the hidey-hole Jeka had made—or found. He stumbled slightly coming down off the wall, but caught his balance. There was no sound from behind the worn burlap that concealed the hidey-hole.

"Enelya, I'm someone Jeka sent."

Still no sound.

"You stay here, and Egen'll find you, sure as I'm standing here."

She lurched from the hole, half-staggering, half-lunging at him, using a sabre broken off a span short of the tip—but with a sharp and jagged edge that almost came to a point.

Clang! Fragments of metal sprayed off the hardened air shield onto the summer-hardened clay between the two walls. Enelya went down in a heap.

Kharl could sense the knife.

"The knife won't help. You can either trust me, or wait for Egen to find you."

"Won't go . . . no one . . ."

Kharl stood there. What could he do? He didn't know the gentler uses of order. After a moment, he tried again, speaking softly and trying to use his order-senses to project a sense of truth and calm. "I'm trying to help you."

"No one can."

"I can." He dropped the air shield, but remained ready to call it up again if he needed to.

"Sure . . . and I'm Lady of Brysta." Enelya sat up, her eyes taking in Kharl. Abruptly, she swallowed, looking at the fragments of metal on the clay, then at Kharl. "You some kind of mage?"

"I know a little."

"Why didn't you . . ." She shook her head.

"It doesn't work that way. It's better for defense." Kharl didn't like mentioning magery, but he didn't know what else to say.

"You . . . you coulda killed me."

"I'm trying to keep you from being killed."

"Why me? You're some sort of mage . . . or a lord. Easier to buy a girl from the Bardo . . ." Enelya slowly stood, her eyes glancing past Kharl to the wall behind him.

"I'm not looking for that. I'm trying to pay a debt."

"Think I'd pay a clipped copper for that?" The woman snorted.

"For a friend. Jeka helped him, and he said you helped her. He said that you'd been through hard times. You lost your sister. Everyone thought she drowned in the harbor. Jeka told my friend that she almost drowned as a child. She was afraid of water, and wouldn't go near it."

"What do you want?"

"I want to give you a position in my house, as a helper to the cook and as a server for dinners. I'll pay you well, maybe not so much as you get at the White Pony, but you'll keep every copper, and you'll have a room of your own in a place where Egen won't find you. Even if he did, he'd have to cross his father and his brother to hurt you."

"He would? How's that?"

"I'm the Austran envoy here in Brysta. I've been here less than two eightdays."

"Sure . . ."

Kharl sighed. "Do you think that I'd go to the White Pony, and climb over renderer's walls just to find someone for bed? Besides, you need a bath."

Abruptly, Enelya laughed, if softly. After a moment, she said, "How are you going to get me to your place safe-like?"

Kharl gestured to the wall. "I have three guards and my secretary waiting to see if you'll accept the offer."

There was a long sigh. "Guess I've got little choice."

"Ah . . . the knife . . ." Kharl said. "If you want to keep it, then you go over the wall first."

"I'll keep it."

Kharl stepped back until he was almost against the stone wall. "Then you may go first."

Enelya nodded, then nimbly climbed the wall.

Kharl followed, half-amazed that the woman was waiting in the serviceway when he descended. Then, the four men had stepped back.

"This is Enelya. I've offered her a position as a retainer at the residence. You're not to mention her name to anyone except to people in the house."

"Yes, ser."

Kharl, his order-senses half on Enelya, led the way back to the residence. He did make one detour, to avoid another set of patrollers, but in half a glass, they stood in the back hall of the residence as Kharl rang the bell for Fundal.

The steward appeared, dressed in his trousers and boots, and in a hastily donned tunic.

Fundal looked from Kharl to the bedraggled Enelya. "Ser?"

"This is Enelya. She's going to help Khelaya . . . and you, when she's not working in the kitchen. She has some experience serving, but it's mostly in taverns."

"Ah . . . ser," stammered the steward.

"It's not like that," Kharl snapped. "She once helped someone I knew. Someone I owe a lot to. There's a man after her who'd kill her if he could. I'm paying a debt, and I don't want a word about her going out of the residence. It does, and you go with it." Kharl's last words were cold.

Fundal took a step backward and swallowed.

"She'll need some better clothes, but I imagine Khelaya can help with that, and she's to have something to eat and a chance to clean up."

"Ah . . ." Fundal kept glancing from the woman to Kharl, then back to Enelya.

"Fundal . . ." Kharl sighed.

"You seen what's happening to women here?" asked Demyst, glaring at the steward.

Surprised by the undercaptain's statement, Kharl glanced at Demyst.

"I have," came another voice—Khelaya's. The cook stepped into the foyer. She nodded to Kharl. "Begging your pardon, Lord Kharl, but I was checking the marinade." Her eyes went to Enelya. Her voice softened. "You need a bath, woman, and some clean clothes. We'll take care of you." She looked back toward the men. "There won't be any words out of the kitchen, and it's about time we got more help around here, ser, especially if you want functions."

Kharl suppressed a grin.

Khelaya looked at Kharl. "Lord Kharl . . . best you lay out that set of garments for cleaning. Look like you've been crawling through alleys."

"We have," Kharl replied. "And I will."

He was smiling as he headed upstairs. He only hoped that Enelya would realize that she was safer in the residence than anywhere else.

LXVIII

Kharl woke on fiveday to a gray drizzle outside his open windows. The air was so warm that he was covered in sweat, even though he had thrown off the light sheet sometime in the night. He struggled to his feet and to the bath chamber. There, after shaving, he splashed his face with cool water, knowing that the relief would be momentary and the afternoon would be even steamier.

Had Enelya stayed or sneaked off? He'd already decided that he would not pursue her if she had. One chance was enough. Still . . . he wondered what she really felt.

After dressing, but not with either waistcoat or jacket, he slipped down the back stairs to the kitchen, using his sight shield to conceal himself. There, in the rear washroom, off the kitchen, Enelya was scrubbing something, actually humming to herself. She wore a faded maroon shirt and gray trousers. Her dark hair was tied back.

Khelaya moved to the door, less than a rod from where Kharl observed through his order-senses. For a moment, she stood watching the younger woman, unaware of the concealed mage. Then she cleared her throat. "How's that coming?"

"Need more pumice, but it'll be clean. Hasn't been in a while, looks like."

"Way it ought to be, but never have enough people here to do things right." Khelaya snorted. "You stay here, and you'll be a big help. Don't really have enough retainers here for a proper envoy's residence. Lucky we are that Lord Kharl's a practical sort."

"Lord Kharl . . . that was Lord Kharl that found me?"

"Large as life."

"He's really the envoy from Austra?"

"Don't know of none other. Good enough sort, but don't mess with him. Set Fundal right about who had the best goods. I'd been telling Fundal that for years. Never listened to me. Lord Kharl had him straightened out in less 'n day."

"What kind of lord is he?"

"Can't rightly say. He's Lord Kharl of Cantyl, and he did a lot for Lord Ghrant when some of the lords rebelled. He's some sort of advocate or something, too. Say he was an officer on a trading ship when he was younger."

"I wonder . . ."

"What's that?"

"He knew about me. He said that he was paying back a favor because I'd been good to someone else. But . . . he knew where I was."

"He just showed up where you were hiding?" asked Khelaya.

"Like he knew all about it."

"Someone musta told him. Do you know who?"

"I'm not sure . . . there was an old man, a beggar . . . he was with a girl I grew up with in Sagana . . . I was hiding where she'd been. She got a better place here in Brysta. Never said how . . . Told me not to say where. Haven't. Won't."

"I'm not askin'," Khelaya said with a laugh.

Behind his sight shield, Kharl winced. Old man? Maybe he'd just looked that way when he'd been hiding from Egen while he had been waiting for the *Seastag* to return to Brysta.

"Tellin' you like it is."

"Just count yourself fortunate." Khelaya sniffed. "Sun doesn't always shine down the alleys." After a moment, she added, "There's more pumice in the storeroom. You can get it."

Enelya rose from beside the scrubbing tub. "I'll be right back."

Kharl slipped away and up the rear stairs before releasing the sight shield. Then he made his way down the main staircase and to the breakfast room. Old man?

He had barely seated himself before both Fundal and Khelaya entered the breakfast nook, almost behind Kharl.

"Lord Kharl, ser?" began the steward.

"Yes?"

"About Enelya, ser?" asked Fundal. "You never said . . ."

Kharl studied the two. Fundal shifted his weight from boot to boot. Khelaya wore a faint smile above the batter-stained apron.

"How much to pay her?" Kharl frowned. "Isn't there a standard wage for servers? Or wasn't there?"

"Last one we had was Chovara," Khelaya said. "She got a silver an eightday. That was two seasons back, though."

Kharl reflected. Khelaya received three silvers an eightday, as well as a large room in the rear quarters. "She's getting a room and food."

"Better than she had," said Fundal.

"She needs better clothes," added Khelaya, "if you want her to serve at functions."

"What do you two think?" Kharl nodded at Fundal.

"Silver an eightday."

"Silver and three," suggested Khelaya.

"How about a silver and two?" Kharl said. "But she gets three silvers for better clothes. Just this one time."

The two exchanged glances. Then both nodded.

"Why don't you both tell her?" Kharl paused, then added, "I checked the ledgers. You've both been paid the same amount for over two years. Isn't that right?"

"Yes, ser."

"Starting this eightday, you each get more. A silver an eightday more. Each. For now." Both smiled.

"And you can promise Enelya that she can look forward to more if you are both satisfied with her work."

"Yes, ser."

After Fundal had left, Kharl reminded himself that he also needed to raise Mantar's wages, but less than those of Khelaya and Fundal. From what he could see, Fundal and Khelaya were doing most of the work, although the steward did the dirty cleaning when he thought Kharl would not be needing him, something Kharl had become first aware of when he and Demyst had inspected the empty barracks spaces. He didn't know about the gardener. He'd have to talk that over with Fundal and perhaps Mantar.

Khelaya returned with a platter of fresh egg toast and ham slices, and a small pitcher of redberry syrup. "Here you are, ser."

"Thank you." He paused. "Do you think she'll work out?"

"I'd say so, ser, but the proof's in the pie."

Kharl laughed softly. Wasn't that always so?

After breakfast, he ushered Erdyl into the study, closing the door behind him.

The secretary waited, a faintly quizzical look on his unlined face.

"Erdyl . . . I have another task for you."

"Ser?"

"The renderer's place we passed last night . . . there's a tannery just above it."

Erdyl's quizzical smile faded.

"My neighbor raises cattle and sheep. I'd like to know what the rates are for hides here. See if you can get an idea from the tanner."

"Ser?"

"You have cattle at Norbruel, don't you?"

"Well . . . yes, ser."

"Then use that, too. Complain that I don't know anything, if you have to, but see what you can find out, about how their prices are, about what they see in the city, but get them to talk about anything, the more the better. And see if he'll tell you anything about why the renderer's place is boarded up. I've never heard of anyone shutting down a renderer. Brysta doesn't feel right, but . . ." Kharl did not want to explain. "Keep your eyes open, for just about anything. Oh . . . take Alynar or Cevor, but leave them outside and out of sight when you talk to the tanner. The tanner's name—I had it here somewhere . . ." Kharl walked to the desk where he shuffled through the small stack of papers, before looking up. He hadn't looked, but didn't want Erdyl to know that. "Drenzel, that's it."

"You want me to do that now?"

"The sooner the better. I'm going over to the Hall of Justice for a while. I'd have you come with me, but it would be better if you and Alynar or Cevor rode."

"Yes, ser."

Kharl could sense that Erdyl was puzzled, but Kharl didn't want to tell him much, not until he'd talked to Drenzel and reported back to Kharl.

Kharl had to wait half a glass before Mantar had the carriage ready, because he'd forgotten to tell anyone.

After a glass or so that morning in the Hall of Justice library, Kharl slipped back downstairs into the Hall, to hear several trials held by Lurtedd, the other lord justicer, who, as he recalled, was supposed to be more closely tied to Overcaptain Osten. After two very long glasses in the hot Hall, when the second trial was completed, and one Astolan had been convicted of disturbing the peace—and sentenced to a season in the quarries—Kharl had come to two conclusions.

There was little difference between the two lord justicers, and he was not about to find out any more than he already knew from studying what went on in the Hall of Justice.

He left the Hall, and he and Demyst made their way outside, finding a shady spot to wait for Mantar.

"They do it much different here, ser?" asked the undercaptain.

"The procedures are almost the same. I think the sentences are harder." Kharl really didn't wish to say more, not where anyone could hear.

Despite the shade, the day was hot, and Kharl was perspiring profusely by the time Mantar returned with the carriage less than a half glass later.

"We'll take another ride through Brysta, starting at the harbor and working up through all the cross streets," Kharl told the driver.

"Be a long trip to go a short ways, ser."

"That it will be, but we need to see some things." Kharl opened the door and stepped into the carriage, making sure the windows were open.

As they rode, Kharl counted Watch patrollers. In addition to the harbor inspectors, there were four patrollers at the foot of the piers, although there was only one non-Hamorian ship, and that had to be from Recluce, flying as it was an ensign of the black ryall on a white background. There were four patrollers at the lower market square, and two were mounted, the first time Kharl had seen that—ever. The two around the upper square were also mounted, and there seemed to be a pair on foot at practically every other corner of a cross street and road. By the time they returned to the residence, Kharl had counted over a hundred patrollers in an area that amounted to less than a quarter of Brysta proper.

Erdyl was waiting when Kharl returned and entered the library, followed by Demyst. The young secretary stood immediately. "Ser."

"What did you find out?" Kharl blotted his forehead once more.

"The tanner wouldn't say much, except that it all depends. Good bull leather, that will take splits, a good hide might fetch almost a gold. Sheep fleeces are cheap, three coppers, maybe a silver."

"Did he say anything about the Hamorians or Lord South?"

"Said that with the trouble in the south, lots of herders were selling off part of their flocks, those they couldn't keep under roof at night, and that was driving down prices. Might be why wool prices were going up, too. He claimed he didn't know anything about the Hamorians, and Lord South, except that Lord South was a doddering old fool."

"What about the renderer?"

"His place has been closed for an eightday, or thereabouts. The tanner said he was in gaol. Something about tariff farmers. He didn't let one in, and in the night the patrollers came and smashed up things." Erdyl shrugged. "That's what he said. I couldn't believe that he said the patrollers did that."

"The tanners and the renderers usually will say more than other crafters," Kharl said.

"No one else wants to do what they do," suggested Demyst.

Kharl turned and walked to the desk. Should he? If he didn't . . . He looked at Erdyl. "I'm sorry to have you riding all over Brysta, but I have another errand for you, after we eat. You'll need to go to the Hall of Justice, and see if you can find out what will come before each justicer in the next eightday, or the next two. If Fasyn or the clerks ask, tell them that I'm interested in listening to certain cases, but that, as an envoy, my time is limited. So I wanted to pick those of most interest to me."

"Ser . . . will they tell me?"

"They might." Kharl forced a grin. "They're supposed to post the dockets, but I've never found out where. You could say that, if you need to. Take some paper and a markstick. You'll probably have to copy them, or take them down."

"Ser . . . ?"

"A listing of those cases could prove very useful." *One way or another*, Kharl thought. "It's too bad they haven't kept the case files up to date. It doesn't help that the newest records are more than four years old."

"Do you think that's because the lord justicers don't want anyone seeing the records of the way they decided things?" asked Erdyl.

"The records only matter if the law means something," Kharl replied, "and if there's a way to make sure that the justicers follow the law. If the justicers are twisting the law to do what Lord West wants, they won't want recent records. Not accurate ones, anyway."

"You think they're doing that?"

Kharl nodded, a wry smile on his lips. "We can't do much about that. Now . . . let's get something to eat."

LXIX

After the midday meal on a hazy sixday, Kharl retreated to the library, waiting for Enelya. He would have liked to have waited longer to talk to her, but he needed to know more about what was happening in Brysta, and he would have felt odd trying to contact other envoys and immediately questioning them. He'd taken off his jacket and was debating whether to shed the waistcoat when there was a timid rap on the doorframe. The door was open.

"Come in, Enelya." Kharl gestured to the chair across from the desk, then settled into his own chair.

The serving girl sat down on the edge of the straight-backed chair. Her hair was drawn back from her face. She did not look at Kharl, and for the moment, that was fine with the mage. He waited to see what she might say.

"Ser . . . I'd been meaning to thank you . . ."

"I'm just returning a favor you did for someone else," Kharl replied, "and I'm glad that I could. Is your room all right?"

"Oh, yes, ser. Khelaya's been teaching me cooking, too." She still did not look at the envoy.

"Enelya . . . I'd like you to tell me what's been happening in Brysta."

"Ser?"

"The last time I was here, I saw girls and women on the streets. There were a few armsmen here and there, and a handful of Watch. Now, there are no girls on the streets. There are no armsmen, and there are scores of patrollers." Kharl waited.

"I . . . never thought 'bout such, ser."

"You were a server at the White Pony. You must have heard something. Something happened to your sister. Was that part of the reason why few women walk alone?"

"How'd you know that?"

"I heard it from a friend of mine." That was absolutely true, if not in the way Kharl intended the woman to take it.

"Not many folk knew about Josarye."

Kharl waited again.

"Ser . . . I served 'em. Sometimes, I listened. Most times I didn't want to stay close . . ."

"Especially to Captain Egen?"

Enelya shuddered. "Girls at the Bardo'd hide if they heard his voice. Liked the little ones, and the young ones. Always was hurtin' 'em. Got him excited."

"Was he the one who had the armsmen sent south?"

". . . what Lecy said . . . told her the south would change everything . . . told her she wouldn't want to cross him 'fore long. 'Just wait. You'll see.' That was what he said."

That was suggestive, but it could have meant anything, or could have been Egen's boastfulness. "Did he ever say anything, that you heard, about his brothers?"

"Never heard about the middle one. Folks said that Kolanat's place burned 'cause he was closer to Osten."

"The factor who had the big place off Cargo Road?"

"That was him. Packed up and took a ship to Lydiar, heard tell. Late spring, I think it was."

"Did you ever hear anything about the patrollers . . . why there are so many?"

Enelya's laugh was bitter. "Even me, I know that. Tariffs. Lord West's been pumping up the tariffs. Patrollers come see folks who don't pay. They pay, or they go to gaol. Sometimes . . . heard tell, they busted into places at night."

Kharl suppressed a frown. While Enelya was doubtless right about what the patrollers were doing, Egen didn't need so many patrollers to collect tariffs. A year before the patrollers had worn blue and gray, almost shapeless, tunics and trousers.

Abruptly, Kharl stiffened. Now they wore *uniforms*. Egen was building a personally loyal army that could hold—or take—Brysta. Were he a wagering man, Kharl would have bet that all the armsmen, especially those who might have other allegiances, were in the south, being readied for the invasion of the South Quadrant. There had never been mounted patrollers before. Were they the beginning of another corps of lancers? One personally loyal to Egen? Why hadn't he seen it sooner?

He concentrated on Enelya. "Do the patrollers ever talk or complain about drills or practices?"

She looked up, then down. "More than a few times . . . always talking about drills and formations, and even practicing with rifles. Folks'd think that was all they did."

"Why don't the girls feel safe on the streets?" Kharl pressed.

"Ser . . . saw where I was . . ."

"Captain Egen . . . does he . . . ?" Kharl let the words hang.

"Not just him . . . some of the patrollers . . . and heard tell that white wizards made off with some girls, too . . . say they take their lives to keep them young . . ."

"Wizards? Like the demons of Fairven?"

"Don't know about that, ser. Just know what the girls were sayin'. Just safer not goin' places alone, 'specially after dark."

Kharl could sense that Enelya had told him what she could, at least what she could unless he revealed far more than he felt he should. "Do you think you'll like it here? That you'll want to stay, at least for a time?"

"Oh, yes, ser . . . please . . ."

The abrupt pleading note in her voice tore at Kharl. "You can certainly stay, so long as Khelaya and Fundal are satisfied with your work."

"Thank you, ser. Thank you."

After Enelya left, Kharl stood, then stretched. Slowly, he paced back and forth across the library. He had the feeling that, except for the meeting with Lord Whetorak, he had learned all he was likely to in Brysta for the next few days. He also felt that he was running out of time. On the enddays, he and his small entourage would take a ride southward, to Peachill. With luck, he could find out more about the new south road, and also reclaim Warrl. He'd waited long enough, and there was little enough he could do in Brysta in the next few days.

He walked to the desk, looking down at the listing of cases that Erdyl had copied. For the coming two eightdays, there were over one hundred cases on the dockets for the two lord justicers. From what he recalled, Lord Justicer Priost seldom heard more than fifteen cases an eightday, if that, and never more than twenty. His eyes dropped to the sheets again.

Werwal's case was set for fourday of the next eightday—before Lord Justicer Reynol. That was just two days after Kharl was to present his credentials to Lord West. The docket only showed that the renderer was charged with both a minority and a majority against the Lord of the West Quadrant. Kharl would attend the trial. What more he did would depend on what he saw. He *might* be able to do something for Werwal.

What was certain was that Egen was positioning himself to follow his sire. Then, Kharl reflected, Osten probably was as well, and the Hamorians were doubtless planning to take advantage of the coming conflict, perhaps even encouraging both sides in one way or another. He took a deep breath, then blotted his forehead.

At a quarter before the fourth glass of the afternoon, after having washed up once again, Kharl stepped out of the residence, down the ancient brick walk, and into the carriage. Demyst followed.

"Can't say I like you going into the Hamorian residence," the undercaptain said, settling himself onto the bench seat facing Kharl, but more to Kharl's left, to allow each some legroom.

"It shouldn't be as bad as a battle. At least, I hope it won't be." That would most likely come later.

The Hamorian residence sat on the upper slopes of the hill less than a quarter kay below the ancient walls of the Quadrancy Keep, just off the Lord's Road that angled downhill to join Cargo Road in the middle of west Brysta. The grilled iron gates to the grounds were swung back, but two Hamorian armsmen stood under an open-walled but roofed guardhouse. They wore the same tan uniforms as the lancers Kharl had fought in Austra.

Mantar slowed the carriage but did not fully stop. "Lord Kharl, the Austran envoy."

"Up to the lower portico." The shorter armsmen gestured.

The drive rose on a gentle incline, but leveled out some hundred cubits farther eastward, at the edge of an expanse of grass. The residence was fully three times the size of the Austran envoy's, and the walls were of creamy marble, with a roof of split gray slate. The entire lower level was surrounded by a covered porch, easily twenty cubits deep. The drive extended to a courtyard on the north side of the dwelling, where the porch joined a covered portico with long mounting-block steps. Beyond was a large courtyard, clearly designed to hold a score or more of waiting carriages. Beyond that were outbuildings, one of which looked like a barracks large enough to hold more than a company of armsmen. Yet it felt empty to Kharl's order-senses.

Mantar eased the carriage to a halt.

"Good fortune, ser," murmured Demyst, before opening the door and exiting, to hold the door for Kharl. "We'll be waiting here."

"Thank you."

Rather than a footman or a steward, there was another Hamorian armsman, but this one wore a uniform of black and crimson. *Possibly a dress uniform*, thought Kharl, who felt very plain in his black and silver, trimmed with the dark green of Austra.

"Lord Kharl, Lord Whetorak awaits you in the fountain court," said the armsman. "If you would follow me, ser?"

Kharl nodded. As he followed the man, he extended his order-senses once more, but he could discern no strong impression of chaos, although there were faint traces of whiteness that suggested that chaos had been present at some time in the past.

The fountain court was exactly that, a walled courtyard set behind and below the covered porch at the rear of the residence. The walls were also marble, but barely visible behind the greenery. The residence shielded the courtyard from the late-afternoon sun, and a good half score of fountains played, spraying water skyward and cooling the shaded space.

"There, Lord Kharl." The armsman stepped aside at the top of the steps off the porch.

"Thank you." Even before he was halfway down the steps to the marble tiles of the courtyard floor, Kharl was appreciating the coolness.

Lord Whetorak had been standing before the central fountain, a sculpture depicting a man on horseback. Although he was not quite so tall as Kharl, the envoy conveyed both height and angularity as he turned. His hair was a golden brown, his eyes black. He did not wear a sabre or a belt knife, but a covered holster that had to have held some sort of small pistol. Kharl could sense that the weapon held several iron-jacketed cartridges.

Whetorak stepped forward, inclining his head slightly and smiling with his mouth alone. "Lord Kharl."

"Lord Whetorak." Kharl smiled. "I can see why you prefer this courtyard. Especially on days like today."

"It is most pleasant. But you have had a warm journey, I am most certain. Let me offer you something to drink. What would you like? We have a wide selection of various wines, and lager, ale, or even icenyl."

"I must confess that I know little of icenyl."

"Few do, save those in a small town in the north of Suthya, north even of Cape Devalonia, but it is an icewine of a particular freshness and pungency, and most refreshing in times of heat such as these." Whetorak smiled politely. "You would prefer?"

"I'll stick with lager, even in this heat."

"The choice of a wise and cautious man."

"Cautious," Kharl conceded. "I'm not yet old enough to be wise."

"The good lager and icenyl." Whetorak glanced at a serving girl who had appeared from somewhere.

Kharl had to admit that the girl was beautiful, and the filmy shirt and skirt she wore left very little to the imagination. He forced his eyes back to the other envoy. Whetorak moved gracefully toward the sole table in the courtyard, one set with just two chairs. Each chair had a thick black cushion.

"You must tell me of your trip from Valmurl," said the Hamorian as he seated himself. "You did come from Valmurl, and not your own lands, did you not?"

"My lands are not that far away, but I came from Valmurl. Are you from Cigoerne?"

Whetorak laughed. "All envoys are from Cigoerne. We are trained there, and we first serve as aides to other envoys, then return for more training. We are lords only so long as we serve. If we serve well and faithfully for more than twenty years, we remain lords."

"It is almost a lordly craft for you, then?"

"A lordly craft . . . I like that." Whetorak waited as the serving girl set a pale crimson crystal beaker before Kharl and a goblet of the same crystal before him.

Kharl studied the lager with his order-senses, but it appeared to be lager and nothing more.

Whetorak lifted his goblet. "In thanks for your safe arrival in Brysta."

"To your hospitality," replied Kharl.

"Your posting to Brysta was rather sudden," observed the Hamorian.

"We had no idea when a replacement for Lord Hensolas might arrive. A most impressive envoy. I was personally sorry that he found it necessary to oppose his lord. Doubtless I will receive full information from Cigoerne within an eightday or so. Until then . . ."

"It was sudden to me as well," Kharl admitted. "I had hoped to get on with several projects on my lands . . ." He shrugged. "It is hard to refuse a request from the lord-chancellor."

"Ah, yes. Lord-chancellor Hagen, an interesting figure. I understand that he was once arms-master to Lord Estloch, but that there was a falling-out. Most interesting it is that the son has turned to him."

"Lord Hagen is quite able," Kharl said politely.

"Ah, yes." Whetorak laughed. "In times of trouble, rulers turn either to friends or to those of ability. Those who turn to friends usually lose all their power immediately. Those who turn to ability lose it more gradually."

"That's if a ruler lacks judgment."

"Most times, if a ruler faces great troubles, he has poor judgment."

Kharl couldn't argue with that. He took another sip of the lager.

"There were also tales of a mage who appeared from nowhere," Whetorak went on, after a sip of his icenyl. "And who could tell who was lying and who was not."

"Most order-mages, even the least skilled, can do that, I understand," Kharl replied.

"No one seemed to know much about him. Some say that the lord-chancellor discovered him and that he was made a lord."

"Lord Ghrant has rewarded those who served him," Kharl agreed. "He would have been remiss not to reward a mage who served him well."

"I must confess that I have not heard of Cantyl," Whetorak went on.

"Most have not. It is a small estate, as they go, on the coast and to the southeast of Valmurl. We produce mostly wine and timber. There are enough fields and orchards and berry patches to feed all those on the land. I've recently improved the sawmill and added a cooperage."

"Those are improvements most would not make."

"I inherited what my grandsire and sire had improved," Kharl said, "and I would hope that I could improve what I hold for my son." He had inherited the cooperage in Brysta, and he did want to hand on more than he had obtained, and he certainly hoped that the truthful, but misleading, statements would also mislead Whetorak.

"You did not bring your consort and son here, then?"

"No. I thought it better that my son remain with relatives until I was more established here. My consort died a year ago."

"I am sorry to hear that."

"It is still a painful subject."

"I imagine so."

"Your consort?" prompted Kharl.

"She is spending some time with friends near Eolya, in the green hills there. It is much cooler there at this time of year."

"You did not go with her?"

"No. These days, an envoy's work is never done. That you must also know, for Lord Ghrant would not have sent you in the summer were it not so."

"He felt that Austra needed an envoy here. That is true." Kharl forced a smile. "I had heard that Hamor was providing assistance to Lord West in building roads." That was a guess, but Kharl felt comfortable with it.

"We do have much experience in building such roads. Already the Great Highway from Cigoerne nears the eastern port of Atla. It is the longest paved road in the world."

"It must have taken years to build and mountains of stone."

"Anything great takes time." Whetorak shrugged.

"And your engineers and experts are helping Lord West?"

"Hamor can spare an engineer or two. That, we can do."

"I have noticed Hamorian merchanters in the harbor. Have they brought tools for Lord West's road?"

"Who could say? No one tells an envoy of all the cargoes that pass through a port."

Kharl could sense that Whetorak was definitely lying. But why? What the other envoy said made sense, but it wasn't true. That meant Whetorak did in fact know what was being shipped into Brysta.

"How long have you been here . . . as envoy?"

"Just less than a year. A most pleasant place, and somewhat warmer than your Valmurl, I think. We of Hamor prefer warmth to cold."

"How have you found Lord West and his sons?"

"Ah . . . Lord West, a most charming man, and his sons are most devoted to seeing his heritage continue."

Kharl smiled. He was quite certain that the sons wanted to continue the heritage of ruling, personally and immediately, but he couldn't see any point in pressing that, or questioning Whetorak about it. It was more than clear that Whetorak wasn't about to reveal anything—except by forcing Kharl to reveal even more, because asking specific questions required revealing knowledge.

"I notice you do not wear a sabre, as do so many Austran lords."

Kharl laughed. "I bear weapons when necessary. Certainly not in company such as yours."

"Yet . . . what if you were attacked?"

"Brysta is most safe these days, I have been assured. My guards are also quite accomplished." Kharl shrugged. "If necessary, I will go armed." He glanced at Whetorak. "Don't you worry about chaos setting off the cartridges in your pistol?"

"It is most unlikely." Whetorak smiled. "It is no secret. The cartridges are formed of soft iron; the bullets are lead. There is more wear on the gun that way, but only the strongest of chaos-mages could set off the cartridges, and"—he shrugged again—"in such a case, those would be the least of my worries."

Not to mention that most of the chaos-mages were under tight Hamorian control.

Kharl just hoped that he could keep smiling—and not reveal too much to the Hamorian—until he could leave gracefully.

LXX

The first light of sevenday had barely touched the tallest oak on the hill above the Austran envoy's residence when Kharl swung up into the saddle of the chestnut gelding, awkwardly because he bore the long truncheon in its slightly oversized scabbard. He wasn't used to riding that much, especially not wearing a weapon. He wore his black jacket and a gray cotton shirt, good garments, but not necessarily lordly ones. Demyst, Erdyl, and the two guards were already mounted, and all bore sabres, but a sabre would have been worse than useless for Kharl.

"Are you sure you would not rather take the carriage, Lord Kharl?" asked Fundal, standing on the end of the brick walkway from the portico.

He looked across the five mounted riders, and the sixth saddled but riderless horse.

"The carriage wouldn't work. Not all the roads outside of Brysta are that good. We may have to ride where the carriage would not go."

"Yes, ser." Fundal looked at the envoy glumly. "You don't know when you'll be back, I suppose?"

"Sometime before twoday, when I present my credentials to Lord West. It could be late today, or tomorrow, or oneday."

"Yes, ser."

Kharl turned his mount and headed down the brick-paved drive toward the open iron-grilled gate. Demyst pulled his mount alongside Kharl's. Alynar and Erdyl were directly behind Kharl and the undercaptain, while Cevor brought up the rear, guiding the riderless mount, which also held provisions. The loudest sound as the party rode eastward and down the hill toward South Road was that of hoofs on brick pavement.

There were few souls out and about, although Kharl could see the haze from chimneys and smell cooking oil and smoke.

"How far are we going, ser?" asked Erdyl, from where he rose behind Kharl.

"As far as we need to. No one wants to talk about roads or about what's happening in the south."

Erdyl was silent, as were the others. Kharl concentrated on riding and not bouncing in the saddle, although his riding was far better than it had been when he had first been required to ride at Dykaru two seasons earlier. He also kept checking the streets, and roads, and the area through which they rode for signs of chaos. He found none; but he was well aware that, even so early in the day, several uniformed patrollers had been watching them.

As they passed the last dwellings of Brysta on the southeast side of the city and began to ride through the small plots that were neither true holdings nor just gardens, the ground grew somewhat more hilly to the east of the road, low hills that were more like rocky meadows, dotted with woodlots and irregular fields. Then the road swung due south—or mostly so in its winding path—to avoid a long ridge that rose a good fifty cubits above the road and angled to the southeast.

A half kay farther south, the packed-clay track turned back southeast, following the curve of a hill below the rocky ridge. At the end of the low hill the ground to the east of the hill flattened, and Kharl saw more clearly the barracks he had seen from the carriage earlier and heard about—four new plank-sided buildings—and two long stables. On the flat between the base of the ridge and the stables, Kharl could see at least two companies of mounted patrollers drilling.

"Those are lancer drills," said Demyst quietly.

"I thought they might be. I saw some mounted patrollers the other day—first time I've seen them in Brysta." Kharl had half expected it, but it was still a surprise.

Just past the barracks, the south road was joined by another, narrower road from the east that cut through a low spot in the ridge farther east of the barracks and stables and ran due west on the south side of the patroller buildings, ending where it met the south road.

As they continued south on the main road that would eventually lead to Surien—if hundreds of kays farther to the southeast—the holdings and cots became far less frequent, and the road itself was often bordered by hedgerows and holder fields. Yet they encountered almost no one, except an occasional cart.

Then, less than two kays south of the barracks, the road abruptly changed from packed clay into a gray stone highway. The paving stones were large, two cubits by one, and the road was a good rod wide, with gravel and pebble shoulders.

"This looks new," Kharl said. It was new, at least since the time a year before when he had walked southward to Peachill to see Warrl.

"It's cut off sharp as with a knife. Right here. Doesn't run all the way into Brysta. That doesn't make sense," replied Erdyl.

"They're probably still building it," Kharl offered.

"There's no sign of 'em doing any more, but maybe they don't want folks to know about it yet," suggested Demyst.

Kharl stood in the stirrups of the chestnut gelding, looking ahead, but the pavement stretched out at least three kays ahead before disappearing over a low rise, cutting through the wide curves of the old road like a crossbow quarrel, in places running through meadows and fields. "We'll see how far it goes." He eased his mount forward.

On the west side of the road was a stone wall that ended abruptly near the shoulder of the new road, which cut through an irregular corner of what had been a pasture. The stone wall had not been rebuilt along the shoulder, something Kharl certainly would have done to keep in grazing livestock.

He glanced at the cot immediately ahead and to his right. Despite the cool of the early morning, the shutters were closed when they should have been open. So was the door to the small barn to the south of the cot. He could sense no one in the buildings or nearby. Had they protested the loss of their land to the road?

Kharl shook his head, imagining what Egen would have done to anyone who protested. He was just glad that Dowsyl's orchards were well back from the old main road, and he hoped that they were also well back from the new road.

For the next two kays, they were the sole travelers on the gray stone high road. Perhaps half a glass passed before Kharl saw riders coming from the south, wearing the traditional blue-and-burgundy uniforms and moving in formation.

"Looks like lancers, ser," said Demyst. "What do you want us to do?"

"Let's stop here and wait for them. I'd like to see what they have in mind." Kharl didn't have any illusions. The only question in his mind was exactly what sort of trouble the lancers posed. He reined up, then turned in the saddle. "Close up. As close as you can get."

"Ser?" asked Erdyl.

"You heard him," hissed Demyst.

The others moved in.

Kharl watched carefully as the lancers rode toward them, double file, in good order. The half squad of lancers reined up less than two rods away. All the riders carried not only sabres, but rifles in saddle cases—Hamorian rifles from their order-feel, Kharl sensed. Their undercaptain reined up to one side.

Kharl eased the chestnut forward.

"Hold it right there, fellow!" snapped the undercaptain.

"I didn't want you to have to yell." Kharl reined up slowly, so that he was almost a rod closer to the officer.

"You're not supposed to be here," announced the undercaptain. "The south road is closed."

"There were no signs or barriers," Kharl replied politely. "Might I ask why?"

"That's ser, to you, fellow, and no, you can't ask why."

"No one in Brysta said that the road south was closed," Kharl said, his eyes and senses on the ten lancers, all of whom had their hands on their rifles, clearly waiting for a command. He'd wondered about riding south, but, since no one had been able to tell him anything, he'd felt that waiting would not be wise. Now he was seeing why. He almost smiled at the thought. He'd never liked waiting.

"Well, it is, and the question is whether you fellows will hand over your golds and head back peaceably, or whether you end up in the quarries."

"I thought the justicers or Lord West decided that," Kharl said, even as he extended an order-probe to the rifle the undercaptain was pulling from its case. He began to untwist the order-locks in the iron.

"The lancers decide here, and I've decided—"

Kharl *untwisted* the last of the order-ties, then flung up a shield around his group.

Crrummmpttt! The blinding white glare and heat of chaos flared over the undercaptain and the ten suddenly hapless lancers.

Despite the shield, Kharl felt as though he had been thrust inside a furnace, then shaken. He just grabbed the rim of the saddle with his free hand and braced himself, trying to stay in the saddle as the chestnut jerked sideways. He managed to hold both his mount and the order shield until the tumult and chaos had dispersed.

Even so, a good tenth of a glass passed before Kharl's eyes stopped watering, and he could see clearly. Except for an irregular patch of darkened gray stone in the center of the new road, and a number of fine cracks in the paving stones, there was no sign of the eleven lancers, except ashes as fine as mist drifting in the light breeze.

"Light-demons . . . burned 'em to less 'n ash . . ."

"Mean bastards . . . woulda shot us dead on the spot . . ."

Kharl had no doubts of that, or that the undercaptain had been ordered to act just that way.

"Now what?" asked Demyst.

"We keep riding. We still don't know why they don't want anyone here." And Kharl wanted to get to Warrl before things got worse—if they hadn't already.

". . . no sign of 'em . . . nothing but a blackened patch on the road . . ." murmured Erdyl.

Neither guard answered his comments.

Kharl eased the chestnut forward at an easy walk. He had to keep blotting his forehead. They covered another two kays before he began to cool off. When he began to feel light-headed, he took out some cheese and bread from the provisions in his saddlebag, an awkward task for him because he still wasn't that good a rider. He ate slowly and drank almost half the water in his bottle.

The light-headedness departed, and as they continued southward, Kharl used his order-senses to study the road and the holdings. Occasionally, there were traces of chaos-wizardry, seemingly in places where stony outcrops or rises had been removed or lowered, but most of the road had been built without wizardry. Along the way, there was only a scattering of empty dwellings, and those were where the road had been built across the land belonging to that cottage or hut—at least from what Kharl could tell.

Still, no one anywhere close to the highway ventured out as they passed. Twice, a more distant peasant holder scurried into his hut when he saw the five riders.

The second time, Demyst cleared his throat. "Doesn't look like they like riders, ser."

"After the way those lancers tried to kill us, I'm sure that they don't."

"Don't see why they were acting like brigands . . ."

"So that anyone who escaped would add to the stories about brigands dressed as lancers." Kharl wondered exactly what Egen was hiding.

Another glass passed. They saw no one else on the new highway, and the gray stone pavement still stretched before them, arrowing southward. They continued riding, and Kharl kept looking, trying to sense the lancers he knew had to be somewhere ahead. Yet he sensed nothing but the remnants of older chaos.

Just before midmorning, on the east side of the road, Kharl saw the burned remnants of a cot that looked familiar. He thought it might have been the one where he had persuaded the elderly woman who lived there to feed him.

"The well here should be good," he said to the others, riding though the open side gate.

Demyst glanced at Kharl.

"There's no one here." The mage reined up short of the well.

"Eerie," murmured Erdyl. "There's no one in these cots real close to the road, none of them. This is the first one that's burned, though. What happened, do you think?"

"They didn't want to give up their land, or part of it, to Lord West's road." Kharl dismounted and tied the gelding to the dead limb of a tree that had been charred by the fire and stood leafless between the burned cot and the well. He walked to the well. A bucket and rope still remained.

After drawing the water, he let his order-senses check it, but he could detect no chaos—natural or wizardly—in the water. "It's good."

"Mounts could use water. So could I," said Demyst.

After watering their horses and letting them rest for a half glass or so, Kharl and the others remounted. As he rode on, Kharl's stomach grew tighter and tighter. While there were no more burned cots, and only a handful of empty cots and pastures, with untended fields that lay fallow, they saw no more holders outside. At times, Kharl could see others in the distance, and carts and wagons on back lanes, but none on the gray stone highway.

A good glass before noon, Kharl could see, off to the west of the new gray stone road, a curving section of the old road—and the kaystone that announced Peachill.

"We'll cross to the older track now." He turned the chestnut and let his mount pick his way over the uneven ground until they reached the original road. Even the ruts were old and worn down by rain and weather. Merayni and Dowsyl's orchards were off a lane on the west side of the road, short of the hamlet itself. The small hutlike cottage where he had asked directions was also a heap of charcoal, burned at least a season before.

As he guided the chestnut westward along the narrower lane, his eyes looked for the other cots and dwellings. He could see none, only another heap of burned ruins. His stomach clenched even more tightly.

"Ser . . . ?"

"I need to see someone—if they're here. If they're not . . ." He forced a shrug.

"Doesn't look like they left anyone here," ventured Demyst. "Must have done something."

Kharl could only hope that the destruction remained near the old road, as he rode westward on the lane. Dowsyl's orchard and house were a good two kays from the road, with the dwelling and storage barns set amid the orchard, between the pearapples and the peach trees.

Less than a quarter kay farther westward, he came to another burned-out cot and barn. He swallowed, moistening his lips.

". . . worried, I think . . ."

". . . be worried, too . . . no one on the roads, empty cots, burned cots . . ."

Kharl glanced down the lane, toward the rolling hills to the west, hills covered with the full summer green of broadleaf trees, mixed with the darker green of the pines and firs. Ahead, to his right was the old stone wall that marked the beginning of Dowsyl's lands and orchards. The pearapples and the peaches were in full leaf, and he could see the gold of the peaches amid the green. His guts twisted as he rode closer. He could not see the thatched roof of the house above the stone wall, nor the roof of the barn in the space between pearapples and peaches. Dreading what he knew was beyond the wall, he eased the chestnut through the gateless opening in the stone wall.

At the other scenes of destruction, where the houses had been burned or just left deserted, there had been no indication of what had happened to the holders. At Dowsyl's, that was not so. In the garden to the south of the charred ruins, six clear graves had been dug—and filled—heaped high with extra loam so as to leave no doubt that they were graves.

For a long time, Kharl just sat in the saddle and looked. He could sense that they were indeed graves, with the faintness of old death. The graves were not new. They could have been dug within eightdays of when he had last visited Warrl. Within eightdays. Eightdays . . . and Kharl had not even known. Had not sensed it, even.

Egen had traced Warrl somehow, and because he could not touch Kharl, he had killed them all—Merayni and Dowsyl and their three children . . . and Warrl. Warrl. Kharl's youngest.

He did not know how much time had passed before he finally turned the chestnut and headed back out eastward on the lane, back through the ruins of Peachill.

"Ser?" asked Demyst, gently. "You knew them?"

"My consort's sister and her consort, their children." He did not want to mention Warrl. "He was a good man. An honest man." He knew he could not say a word about Warrl, not and hold himself together.

"Lord West's men, you think?"

Kharl just nodded, although he had no doubt that it was Egen's doing. His throat was dry. He wanted to swallow, but he couldn't. Beneath the grief, rage seethed, and his jaw kept tightening.

How could anyone be so viciously cruel? For Kharl, it was beyond explanation. Four children, helpless, and one of them had been Warrl, who had only gone to Merayni's to be safe.

The mage shook his head. Merayni hadn't been Kharl's favorite, but she'd done what she had thought best—and it had led to her death. Kharl had tried to rescue Sanyle and keep Jenevra from Egen, and for that Egen had killed Charee, and tried to have Kharl flogged heavily enough that he would not survive. That had driven Arthal to sea on the *Fleuryl*—and to his death. Then Egen had used overtariffing and Tyrbel's murder to drive away Warrl and send Kharl into hiding and eventually into flight from Brysta. Beyond that, Egen had burned every cot in Peachill.

And that hadn't been enough—all that because Kharl had stopped Egen from abusing one girl and rescued one of his victims?

Thoughts kept swirling through Kharl's head. Egen . . . always Egen. *Bastard* was too generous a term for Ostcrag's son. So was *pissprick* . . . or anything else Kharl could think of.

The other thing that bothered him was that, at least for a time, Jeka had not been harmed. Kharl frowned, then nodded. Egen had never known that Kharl had hidden with Jeka. That had to be the only reason. When Kharl had walked to Peachill to see Warrl, he had not gone as a beggar, but as himself. Had that pride doomed Warrl?

And why hadn't Egen done the same to Sanyle? Or had she fled to someone who could protect her? Kharl wondered if he'd ever know, but he just hoped that she had gotten safely to Vizyn. She had certainly known that it was not safe for her to stay in Brysta. Kharl shifted his weight in the saddle.

No one said a word on the ride back toward the gray stone highway.

As they neared the burned-out hut beside the old road, Demyst cleared his throat. "Ah . . . we headed back, ser?" asked Demyst.

"Not yet. We'll keep heading south. We know what they're doing. We don't know why." Especially now, Kharl had to know. What was Egen doing that required such cruelty, not just to Kharl, but to the holders he'd driven from their homes?

Not until they were a good kay south of Peachill did Kharl call another rest halt, once more at an abandoned—but not burned—cot—and one where they were shielded by a short hedgerow and not visible from the new highway. They ate and watered and fed the mounts, then rested for almost a glass.

No one said much to Kharl, respecting his silence and grief.

Finally, he cleared his throat. "We need to get riding."

"Ser," ventured Erdyl, "what are we seeking?"

Kharl laughed harshly. "If I knew that, we wouldn't have to be here. Lord West—or his sons—don't want travelers here. They've built a new stone road, but no one is using it, and they don't seem to want anyone using it. There aren't any armsmen in Brysta. They've been replaced by patrollers in new uniforms. There are no ships in the harbor except those from Hamor, and no one seems to know what's on them. The Hamorian envoy avoided telling me that. The Sarronnese envoy doesn't know. We can't even find most of the other envoys or their secretaries. Those secretaries that Erdyl's talked to don't know any more than we do. Or they aren't saying." He shrugged. "So we'll keep riding for a while."

"Yes, ser. I didn't mean . . ."

"I know," Kharl replied. "It seems stupid, but there has to be some reason for all this, and we weren't finding out in Brysta." He climbed into the saddle and turned the chestnut back toward the gray stone road. He did not turn in the saddle to look back. He could not have done that and maintained any composure.

They rode more than another glass, another five to seven kays, from what Kharl judged before he sensed another set of lancers riding northward toward them from beyond the low hill crest ahead. He glanced around before speaking. "Off the road, over by those trees. There are more lancers coming."

The five others followed, gathering around Kharl beneath an ancient black oak. "Before they get here, I'm going to put a sight shield around us. You won't be able to see, but they won't see us, either."

"No more fire?" murmured Cevor.

"No. Not this time." Kharl didn't want too many lancers disappearing. Also, doing too much of the order-release magery took a heavy toll on him. "Just be quiet. They won't be able to see us, but they can hear us."

Once he had raised the sight shield, Kharl could hear more than a few swallows and someone's fast and nervous breathing. He just hoped none of his group would do something stupid.

The second patrol was close to forty lancers—two full mounted squads. The riders were moving at a trot, and were out of sight before long. Kharl waited until he was certain before releasing the sight shield.

"Whew!" Alynar shook his head. "Felt like I was in a cave, ser."

"Strange," added Demyst. "I could hear the hoofs, but they just kept riding."

Kharl turned the chestnut toward the new road, heading southward once more.

Over the next glass or so, east of the gray stone road, a road that had gradually changed its course so that it now pointed south-southeast rather than due south, the hills became more rugged, with occasional gray escarpments. Kharl had the feeling that the same kind of stone had been cut and used for the highway.

By then, it was well into late afternoon, and the holdings were getting more scattered. Kharl frowned as he looked at a hillside to the west at the blackened ruins of what had to have been a mansion or a lord's dwelling. The cots below it were unharmed, and he could see some figures working the fields. Then he nodded. An unfriendly lord—or one independent of Egen—might well have been a threat. Now, the golds from rents doubtless went to Egen.

For the next kay or so, Kharl began to sense something ahead, but he couldn't tell exactly what, beyond the general feeling of people and chaos and order—almost like a sizable town. That would not have been surprising, although there were few large towns to the southwest of Brysta, from what Kharl remembered. Most were either on the coast, to the east or north.

Still, the feeling grew.

Then they had to take cover once more, as another patrol appeared from the south and rode northward.

Once the third patrol had passed, Kharl concentrated on what he had been sensing ahead. There were lancers, buildings, and the chaos left from wizardry, and not all that far away. From what he could tell, it was beyond the hillcrest on the east side of the road.

"This way." Without looking back, he turned the chestnut into the meadow to the left of the gray stone road and headed toward the woods or woodlot that looked to be a kay or so farther to the east, straddling the top of the low ridge. He hoped the woods would provide some cover.

A single holder at the bottom of the hill yelled something, but Kharl ignored him, and the man went back to digging out his irrigation ditch.

It took nearly a half glass for Kharl to reach the woods and guide his mount through the edges until he reached a place where he could look southward over the long and shallow valley that stretched to the southeast from the ridge. The gray stone road split the valley almost evenly. Another two kays to the southeast, between the road and a stream, Kharl could see what looked to be a town, except that the buildings were all long and low structures.

"Looks like barracks," ventured Demyst. "Rows and rows of 'em."

To the north of the area with the barracks were fenced enclosures filled with horses. Smoke rose from more than a score of chimneys. Farther to the east, beyond the streams, were rows of huts, and beyond them was a raw slash in the stony escarpment and a long and wide pit. Lines of tiny figures snaked in and around the pit.

"That's the quarry, one of them," Kharl said.

"Like a town . . ." murmured Erdyl.

"More like a fort, with the quarries there." Demyst frowned. "They don't need a fort to guard the quarries."

"The fort's not for that. It's to train armsmen."

"For a war against the Lord South?"

Kharl didn't want to answer that. Lord South was certainly what Egen wanted people to think, but the fort was far closer to Brysta than to Surien. As he studied the valley, Kharl could sense at least two white wizards, perhaps three. Two of them were strong, perhaps not so strong as the strongest he had faced in Austra, but not to be taken lightly.

After a moment, he turned in the saddle and looked at the undercaptain. "We've seen what we need to see. We can head back."

"Just . . . head back, ser?" asked Erdyl.

"You want us to charge an entire fort and all those armsmen?" asked Kharl. "Some of them are Hamorian, and the others are Nordlan. We're not at war." *Not yet, anyway,* he thought.

He eased the chestnut back though the woodlot. At the north side, he checked the road and the meadows, but both were clear. The holder still labored on the irrigation ditch. The man did not even look up as Kharl and the others rode back to the gray stone road and turned back north.

As Kharl rode back northward, his eyes and senses concentrating on discovering Egen's lancers before they spotted his small group, questions twisted through his thoughts. The gray stone road extended at least twenty kays south of Brysta, but how far did it go? One of the histories said that the forces of Fenardre the Great had been able to complete a kay of stone road a day. If Egen's forces had been working on the road for even half a year, and could do half as much, he might have already completed over a hundred kays. That still left close to a hundred more before the road reached the border of the south quadrant—unless the road-building had been going on in secret much longer. How long had it been going on? Was the refused consorting just an excuse? Were the Hamorians helping Egen with the road so that they could use it once they took over the South and West Quadrants of Nordla? Couldn't Egen see what they had in mind? Or did he think he could outwit them? More important, could Kharl do anything? What? How? When?

Kharl rubbed his forehead. For the moment, they needed to get off the road and find somewhere to spend the night. He doubted he would sleep well. He hoped he could sleep some.

LXXI

Kharl and his small group did not manage to get back to the envoy's residence in Brysta until close to dark on eightday. Kharl had avoided Peachill on the way back, not wanting to face it as a reminder that he had failed Warrl as well.

While they had been able to find shelter in one of the abandoned cots on sevenday night, time after time, all through eightday, they had been forced to leave the road and hide, to avoid being seen by armed road patrols, far more than they had seen on their way southward. Kharl hoped that was because of the disappearance of the one road patrol, and not because some armed action was about to begin.

After the evening meal, most welcome after two days of bread and cheese and dried meat, Kharl, Demyst, and Erdyl sat in the library.

"What do you think of the road?" Kharl looked at his secretary.

"I have never seen one so fine," Erdyl admitted. "We traveled more than twenty kays, perhaps thirty, and it must continue for at least another ten." He paused. "But, ser . . . I do not see the need. There were no large towns. According to the maps, Surien is more than five hundred kays to the south."

Closer to six hundred, Kharl thought. "So why are the Nordlans building such a high road? Is that your question?"

"The Nordlans and the Hamorians," suggested Demyst. "Hamor likes good roads."

"They make it easier to control a land," added Erdyl. "They make transport easier. If we had a good road from Norbruel to Bruel . . . Ghardyl was always saying that we could see another hundred golds a year."

"So Hamor is fanning the conflict between Lord West and Lord South to get Lord West to build the road?" Demyst set his goblet on the table, tilting his head slightly.

"They might even be paying for part of it." Kharl thought that the Hamorians were going farther than that. He would not have been surprised if they were even supporting Egen in a bid to unseat his father—and his brothers. That way, Egen would at the very least owe Hamor, and if his bid failed, Nordla would be weakened and racked with conflict. Either way, it would be far easier for the emperor to begin the conquest of all of Nordla than it would have been otherwise.

"What can you do, ser?" asked Erdyl.

That was indeed the question. What could he do?

"I'll have to think about that," he finally replied. "It's been a long eightday."

Later, he sat in the study, with but the single desk lamp lit, his eyes fixed on nothing, his thoughts spinning through his skull.

What should he do? Envoys were just supposed to report, weren't they? To let Hagen and Ghrant know what was happening? But he had no way to send a report, and by the time he could, the West Quadrant would be a battlefield—or a fiefdom of Hamor.

He didn't *know* for certain that Egen was going to replace his father, or when that might happen. Nor did he know what the Hamorians would do . . . or when. He didn't think that it would be that long. At the least, he needed to be ready, to plan what he could do.

Deliberately, he took out a sheet of paper and a markstick, slowly sketching out a rough map of Brysta, and the surrounding area. If Egen held the harbor and the south, then the only way to leave the city was by the east road—really the southeast road—to Eolya. The north road to Sagana turned into little more than a dirt trail after a half score of kays, and there were no roads worthy of the name to the northeast or due east. That suggested that any movement of lancers or white wizards along the ring road from the south might indicate the beginning of whatever might happen.

He leaned back, trying to recall the road.

After a time, he folded his crude map, uncertain that he had accomplished anything.

Then there was Jeka. According to Erdyl, she was still with Gharan. What should he do there? He hadn't been able to do anything for Jenevra and Charee, and they were dead. He'd tried to talk Arthal out of leaving, but his older son had been far too stubborn—like his father. He'd been too late to save Warrl, and Warrl had asked the very least of him.

He put his head in his hands. Why Warrl? He'd been only a child. He couldn't have hurt Egen. He was too gentle to have hurt anyone.

After a time, Kharl lifted his head. He had to look ahead. He couldn't undo what was done. What could he do for Jeka? Or Gharan? Did he have to do anything immediately?

LXXII

As he rose from the breakfast table on oneday, Kharl turned to Erdyl. "I'll be going out. I want to take another tour along Crafters' Lane."

"Do you want me to come?" The secretary scrambled to his feet. "I'll only be a moment."

"No. Not this time. Demyst will come with me. You'd said that the assistant to the Sarronnese envoy . . ."

"Jemelya."

"She said that she'd be happy to meet with you after I met with Envoy Luryessa. I think you should meet with her. Don't tell her about how far we went or about the fort and the quarries, but mention the gray stone road—and the new patroller barracks on the south side of Brysta—and the lancer drills. See what her reaction is."

"She's very sharp, ser."

"So is the envoy," Kharl replied dryly. He had the feeling that everyone was smarter than he was, and it wasn't the most cheering of thoughts.

"Do you want me to have Mantar ready the carriage, ser?" asked Demyst, rising from the table.

"Please. I'll be washing up, then in the library." Kharl forced a smile he did not feel before turning and heading up to his quarters. He had not slept all that long and certainly not that well. He'd dreamed of Warrl, a nightmare about what had befallen his son, and he'd been trying to reach him, and had never gotten close enough.

He felt as though everywhere he went, unrest and chaos followed. Or was he bound to follow trouble? Was it him, or just circumstances?

He laughed softly, wryly. Did it matter?

He washed quickly, then donned a lighter black jacket, also trimmed in Austran green, to go with the silver shirt. He made his way down to the library. Enelya was in the front hall, dusting the pair of portraits on the inside wall.

"Good morning, Enelya."

"Good mornin', Lord Kharl." Her eyes did not meet his.

"How are you feeling?"

"I've been sleeping. Wasn't doing much of that for more 'n few eight-days. Khelaya's teaching me to cook the better stuff, too."

"Good." He paused. "That's if you like it."

"Can't be a tavern server forever, specially not here."

Kharl smiled and stepped into the library. It was clear she didn't associate him with the ragged beggar who had bribed food from her almost a year earlier. Would Jeka or Gharan recognize him? There was only one way to find out.

Less than a quarter glass later, he and Demyst were seated in the carriage, riding through another warm and cloudless morning that promised to become a sweltering day.

"Are we looking for something special like, ser?" asked the undercaptain.

"In a way . . . I want to talk to the weaver—Gharan. He might have some cloth I'd like to buy and ship to Cantyl. I'll have to see. He's had some before that I liked." Kharl had liked some of what Gharan had woven, but he'd never been able to afford much, and some of it Charee had not liked at all. So, for one reason or another, he'd bought little from his former neighbor, and that had nagged at him as well.

As Mantar brought the carriage to a halt outside Gharan's shop, Kharl swallowed. Was he doing the right thing? How would he know? He'd waited far too long with Warrl. He shook his head. It wouldn't have mattered. Yet, no matter how much he told himself that, he still felt that he had caused Warrl's death. He wasn't certain, and probably wouldn't be, ever, what else he could have done—except confess to a murder he hadn't committed. If he had just let himself be hanged . . . then his consort and children might still be alive.

. . . and Ghrant and his consort and children would be dead, and Hamor would hold all of Austra . . .

"Ser . . . we're here." Demyst's voice was apologetic as he opened the carriage door and stepped out, holding the door for Kharl.

"I'm sorry. I was just thinking . . ." Forcing a smile, Kharl eased his frame through the narrow doorway. The faintest breath of wind swirled around him, then died away. "I'd like you to remain here and guard the carriage and the doorway, if you would."

"Are you sure that's wise?"

"I'm not certain that anything is wise anymore." Kharl studied the entrance to the weaver's shop. The door was half-open to catch what vagrant morning breezes there might be.

He squared his shoulders and stepped into the shop, past the racks just inside that showed four separate wool patterns. One was a variation on what was considered the "Brystan" design, a plaid of burgundy and blue, with faint lines of black. Beyond the display racks was the open main room that held the looms. There were three, one more than when he had left Brysta.

Gharan hurried away from his loom. "Ser? How might we help you?"

"It's me, Gharan. Kharl. The cooper."

The weaver's mouth opened. Then he closed it, and shook his head.

"My secretary was here last threeday. He asked you about the cotton cloth used for the patrollers' uniforms."

"He said . . . he said that he worked for the Austran envoy . . ."

Kharl grinned. "He does. He works for me. A lot's happened in the last year." He tried to look beyond Gharan without being too obvious, but neither Amyla nor Jeka had looked up from their looms.

"It'd be true then . . . that . . . that you're a lord? An Austran lord? Ser?"

"It is." Kharl's lips curled. "I took a position as a subofficer—after a while—on an Austran ship—the *Seastag*. Her captain was a lord, and he ended up as the lord-chancellor of Austra."

"A real lord . . ." Gharan shook his head. "Hard to believe."

"It's true. But I'm the same Kharl who gave you the silvers to try Jeka as a weaver, and you're the same man who warned me to flee before Egen got his patrollers after me."

"Egen . . . he'll never forget," Gharan said.

"He won't expect to see me as the Austran envoy, or without a beard. You're the only one who knows."

The weaver looked down for a moment. "And you're telling me?"

"I owe you—and Jeka—too much to deceive you. Besides, I always wanted to buy some of your wool, but I never could afford it before." Kharl smiled. "You had a pattern of dark and light green. I always wanted a set of blankets out of that."

"The green grid pattern." Gharan laughed. "Charee . . ." His face stiffened. "I'm sorry . . . I didn't mean."

"I know you didn't. She never liked it. I'd also like you to design a pattern for me, for my lands."

"Lands, too?"

"Some. Will you do it?"

"Why did you come back? If Egen finds out . . ."

"He's not likely to." Kharl wasn't so sure about that, but there was no point in telling Gharan that. "If he does, he does. I came back to get Warrl . . . and to see about some other things."

"How are your boys?"

Kharl shook his head. "Arthal was killed when a Hamorian warship sank the *Fleuryl*. Egen, some way or another, killed Warrl . . . and Charee's sister and her family. That's another reason why I'm here."

"Kharl . . . Lord Kharl . . . I'm sorry."

"Kharl . . . just Kharl."

"You're an envoy? Really?"

Kharl nodded. "How is Jeka?"

"Do you want her to know?"

"She saved my life. She can keep a secret."

Gharan grinned. "You'd best tell her yourself." He turned. "Jeka . . . please to come here."

From behind the second loom appeared a gaminelike face, but the face was framed by longer hair, and set above blue trousers and shirt. She walked toward the two men briskly. Her steps slowed as her eyes took in Kharl.

He watched her closely, amazed at the transformation from an urchin boy to a woman.

"Cooper . . . Master Kharl . . ."

"He's Lord Kharl of Austra, now," Gharan said. With the slightest of winks, he stepped away, moving toward the back room. "I'll be getting that pattern book. Might take me a while. Amyla . . . I'll need you."

The weaver and his consort left Kharl and Jeka standing in the loom room, alone.

"Master Kharl . . . you'd be looking far better dressed . . ." Jeka looked down abruptly.

"You look . . ." He wanted to say "beautiful," but only could come up with "good." He hadn't realized how green her eyes were, or how lustrous her sandy hair. He'd also forgotten how tiny she was, her head not even to his shoulder.

"So do you." Her eyes flashed. "Why'd you come here?"

"I owe you. Without you, I'd never have lasted until the *Seastag* ported." He found himself moistening his lips.

"You're a real lord?"

"Yes. With lands. I'm also the envoy from Lord Ghrant of Austra to Lord West."

"What you do want from me?"

Kharl almost laughed. Jeka was still Jeka, fierce and independent as ever.

"You're not saying. You think golds and lands make a difference?"

He did understand what she meant. "Not that way. I'm not here . . ." He wasn't quite certain how to say what he meant without being condescending on the one hand or crude on the other. "I'd never be like Egen or his type."

Her expression softened, but only slightly. "Why?"

"Because . . ." he swallowed. "Everyone I left . . . even if I had to . . . they're all dead—except Sanyle, I think, but she got away, the scrivener said."

"Your boys?"

Kharl nodded.

"Egen?"

"Warrl and his aunt. Arthal was on a ship the Hamorians sank."

Jeka shook her head slowly. "Shoulda stayed with you."

"I had to make sure you were all right."

"I'm fine. Better 'n a long time."

"I'm glad." He wanted to reach out and touch her, but he'd never touched her, except to break the bonds of the white wizard.

Their eyes met, hers fierce like those of an untamed hawk.

"You see me. Now what?"

Another good question, and one he didn't have an answer for, not that he wanted to state. "I worried about you so much," he finally said. "I didn't think much beyond that."

She laughed, not loudly, but almost melodically, and he realized that he'd never heard her laugh. He liked the sound.

"I'm not your daughter. Won't be a plaything, either."

"I know."

"Need to think about it. You're a lord. Me, I'm a weaver girl." She smiled wryly. "Amyla helped me finish learning my letters. I wanted to write a letter to Enelya. Don't dare go near the White Pony, but wanted her to know I was still safe. Probably Selda'd have to read it to her."

"Enelya was hiding from Egen behind Werwal's place. We found her. She's working in the kitchen at the envoy's residence. She's got a good room . . ."

"You collecting playthings?"

"No." For some reason, her question hurt.

Jeka looked down. "Sorry. Wasn't fair. You saved a lot of us."

"I didn't want Egen to get her. I've got guards and a staff there. She's learning to cook from Khelaya." Kharl paused. "She doesn't know who I am. She thinks I heard about her from a nameless old beggar who was with you. An *old* beggar." His last words were dry.

Jeka laughed once more. "You're older 'n us."

He was. That was true, but he didn't feel that old.

"You did leave in an awful hurry, too."

He almost missed the teasing sound in her voice. "You would have, too, in my boots."

"Never had boots. What you going to do 'bout pissprick Egen?"

"Whatever I have to," Kharl said. "He's not in Brysta right now, from what I've been able to find out." After a moment, he added, "Things are going to get bad here in Brysta, before too long."

"Gharan and Amyla and me, we wondered 'bout that. Lots of Hamorians around, and those patrollers are mean bastards, just like Egen." Her chin set, and her green eyes hardened. "You still got that staff?"

"No. I've learned how to do some of that without it."

Her eyes took in the black jacket and trousers, as well as the black boots. "Thought you might be a mage."

"Not a full mage, but enough to do some things."

"More 'n a few, I'd wager."

"Enough."

They stood there, looking at each other, and Kharl had no idea what else to say. He didn't want to leave her, and yet . . . in some ways, he knew her better than any woman, and in others not at all.

"Ah . . ."

At the sound of Gharan's voice, Kharl turned.

"You did mention the blankets and a pattern . . ."

Kharl smiled. "I did, and I meant it." He glanced at Jeka. "You stay here."

"Me?"

"You'll tell me exactly what you think, and since I don't have a consort or a sister . . ."

"No playthings . . ." Jeka's words were half-playful, half-warning.

"No playthings," Kharl agreed.

Gharan glanced uneasily from the lord to the weaver girl, then back to Kharl. "Here's the pattern book, and this one here is one I never wove for no one."

Jeka shook her head.

"It has to be black and green," Kharl added, "and the green should be close to the Austran green . . ."

"Not thin-fancy, either," suggested Jeka. "Lord Kharl's a solid type. Pattern needs to be solid, too."

Kharl wasn't certain he liked Jeka calling him Lord Kharl. Then, he wasn't certain about much of anything where she was concerned. But he did owe Gharan, and he did need new fabric for some of the chairs and some new linens.

As for Jeka, he needed to think, and he couldn't do that with her so close to him.

LXXIII

Once he returned to the residence, Kharl went to the library to await Erdyl's return from the Sarronnese envoy's. He and Gharan—and Jeka—had worked out a pattern for Cantyl—one that could be woven in linen or wool. Kharl had ordered forty yards, in various weights and fabrics—

enough to reupholster the not-quite-threadbare chairs in the dining room. Doubtless it was an extravagance of sorts, but Gharan had stood by him when few had.

As for Jeka . . .

Kharl walked to the window overlooking the garden. He shook his head. He'd forgotten her eyes . . . and her directness. It didn't matter to her that he was now a lord, and she'd suggested from the beginning that he was more than a cooper. Her insight and directness—those he had missed. And for all her blunt talk, she saw more than the educated and lordly young Erdyl. All that was fine. What had bothered him had been his physical reaction. He'd wanted to sweep her into his arms, to never let her go. It wasn't just that he hadn't been with a woman in a while, either. Herana—the second mate on the *Southshield*—had been attractive and had made a play for him. So had ser Arynal's daughters, especially Meyena. But Jeka . . . she was a good ten years younger than he was, maybe fifteen. She was older than she let on, probably close to five or six years older than Arthal . . . than Arthal had been.

Abruptly, Kharl turned and began to rummage through the stack of papers on one side of the desk, until he came up with the listing of cases before the lord justicers. His eyes ran down the sheet. Werwal's trial was set for fourday. Kharl would be there. What he could do for the renderer who had once befriended him was another matter.

At the rap on the door, Kharl turned. "Yes?"

"Ser . . ." Erdyl took a step into the chamber.

"I'd like to hear what you found out. She was there? The assistant?"

Erdyl nodded.

"Ah . . . you'd better have the undercaptain join us, too."

"Yes, ser."

When Erdyl returned momentarily with Demyst, the three settled into chairs around the desk.

"What did you find out from her?" asked Kharl.

"Jemelya?" Erdyl's voice was casual.

"You like her?"

Demyst smothered a grin at Kharl's question.

"She's years older than I am, ser." Erdyl smiled sheepishly. "She is beautiful, though."

"Beautiful women are dangerous," suggested the undercaptain. "Then, maybe all women are." He laughed nervously.

"What did she say?" asked Kharl.

"She didn't say all that much. Well . . . she talked a lot, but . . . She knew about the patrollers' barracks. She said that the one in the harbor has an armory, and that there are three companies billeted there, and none of the patroller rankers can have consorts."

"She said it that way?" asked Demyst.

"Yes, ser."

"They think of them as armsmen, then," Kharl said.

"She never said that . . . oh, I see . . . companies . . . billeted . . . rankers . . . armory . . ." Erdyl nodded.

"What about the other barracks in the south?"

"She said that held five mounted companies and another four arms companies. She also said that there was another new barracks to the east, just off Angle Road. I'm sure she said Angle Road. That only holds six foot companies, but there's an armory there that also has cannon."

"Loaded with grapeshot," Kharl suggested.

"She didn't mention that."

"No, but it makes sense. That's the road that Osten and Vielam would have to use to bring their armsmen back to Brysta," Kharl pointed out.

"It's not a Hamorian barracks," Erdyl said.

Kharl shook his head. He'd never said anything to them about his suspicions. Should he? He fingered his bare chin. There was no point in hiding his thoughts now.

"Ser?"

"I've been thinking about all this. All those patrollers are nothing more than a small army. They all report to Captain Egen. He's Lord West's youngest son. He's moved the regular lancers and armsmen—the ones that might be more loyal to Lord West or Overcaptain Osten—to the quarry fort in the south. That means they're farther from Brysta, and his patrollers control who travels south, or who can do so quickly, anyway."

"That means they can't know what's happening in Brysta, not soon," suggested the undercaptain, "unless this Egen wants them to know."

"Egen's also the one dealing with the Hamorians."

"You think he's trying to get rid of his brother and succeed his father?" asked Demyst.

"I don't know. He's an evil little bastard, and he wouldn't hesitate to do something like that if he thought he could get away with it. He's also tightened up the laws and is having the lord justicers sentence more men to work in the quarries and, I'd guess, on that road as well."

"The Hamorians are backing him?" Erdyl moistened his lips.

"The cloth for the patroller uniforms comes from Hamor. There are only Hamorian ships in the harbor. The Hamorians are supplying engineers, and they're often in the south." Kharl paused. "And more than half the envoys from other lands have left Brysta, for one reason or another."

"When is something going to happen?" asked Demyst.

"Soon, but how soon, I don't know. I'm hoping I can find out more from Lord West tomorrow."

"I'd better see about looking into hiring a night guard or two," suggested the undercaptain. "We can afford that, can't we?"

"You think they'll come after an envoy?" asked Erdyl.

"Egen will come after anyone he thinks he can best." Kharl snorted.

"You know a lot about him?" Demyst frowned.

"Enough." *More than enough,* Kharl added to himself. "The guards are a good idea. I should talk to them before you hire them, though."

"I'd planned on that, ser. Mantar has some cousins, used to be armsmen. Thought I could talk to them first."

"You might have Enelya get a look at them, too."

Erdyl and Demyst exchanged glances.

"She knows about some of the worst ones." Kharl looked to Erdyl. "Did Jemelya tell you anything else we should know?"

"She said that the roads to the east weren't usually passable during the late-summer rains. Not with any speed, leastwise."

"I think she's suggesting that when the rains finally come, so will trouble," ventured the undercaptain.

That made an unfortunate kind of sense to Kharl. "Anything else?"

"I can't think of anything. I mean, she talked a lot, about everything from the good taverns to Overcaptain Osten's consort only giving him three daughters and Egen not having a consort, and Vielam's consort and children dying last summer when their coach went off the road and into the river . . ."

Kharl winced.

"Ser?"

"I'd wager that the coach accident was planned. That leaves no heirs."

"Planned by who?" asked Demyst. "Egen or the Hamorians?"

"I'd say Hamor. That's just a guess." Kharl's eyes rested on Erdyl once again.

"That's all, ser. I think. If I recall anything else, I'll tell you."

Kharl stood. "After we eat, Erdyl, I'd like you to make the rounds of the envoys' residences. Ask for the secretaries or assistants. If they're there, ask about the date you've chosen for our function. What I really want to know is how many of them are still in Brysta and how many have left or are planning on leaving soon."

"Yes, ser."

"When you get back, you and I will go over what I'll need to expect when I present my credentials tomorrow. And some good meaningless phrases."

Erdyl bobbed his head.

"I'll start on trying to find some guards, ser, this afternoon. Unless you need me," said Demyst.

"Not this afternoon."

After Erdyl and Demyst left, Kharl paced back and forth across the residence library. Everything seemed calm in Brysta, but beneath that apparent calm everything was unsettled, and likely to get more so in the days ahead. He paused and looked out the window. The sky was still clear. So far.

Before long, Khelaya and Enelya would be serving the midday meal. Kharl wasn't that hungry, but he supposed that he needed to eat. The way matters were going, he might have to do magery at any time.

He tried not to think about Jeka, but the image of her eyes, and the sound of her laugh, remained with him.

LXXIV

Kharl stood in the library on twoday morning, waiting for Mantar to ready the carriage to take him to present his credentials to Lord West. He hoped he could remember all that Erdyl and he had gone over the evening before, especially all of the phrases and courtesies.

On Erdyl's advice, he wore his second-best finery, a silver-gray shirt, black jacket trimmed in green, and black trousers and boots. His eyes dropped to the silver box on the desk, shimmering from its recent polishing. The box had had been Hagen's suggestion for a token to Lord West. A handspan in length and half that in height and width, it was ornately chased silver, with three narrow courses of stone inset as a border on the hinged top. The outer course and the inner courses were black onyx, and the middle course was lapis lazuli. In the center was a silver replica of the seal of the West Quadrant.

"Something tasteful, but not something he can convert easily into golds," Hagen had said. "One never gives such to another lord. It's in poor taste and imprudent, besides."

Kharl had understood that well enough. He smiled at his recollection of Hagen's dry words. He eased the gift into a plain pouch of new soft calf leather, then slipped the pouch into the elaborately carved leather case that held his credentials as envoy. He set the case on the corner of the library desk and turned toward the window, looking out at the dark clouds to the west. Were the late-summer rains finally arriving, or would the clouds blow over and leave Brysta hot and close for another eightday?

What did he expect to find out from meeting Ostcrag, the present Lord West? Did Ostcrag know what Egen was planning? Did Osten? Did they have plans of their own? If the reception and presentation allowed any questions at all, Kharl might get a better idea about Hamor and Nordla.

All that wouldn't help with Jeka, though. There, he was at a loss. He'd worried about her, but he'd been stunned to feel his own reactions to her. That was something he'd never expected. He just hadn't, and he was thinking about her when he should have been worrying about Lord West and Egen.

Warrl—what had happened to his youngest also lay close to the surface of his thoughts, with the sadness sweeping over him when he least expected it.

"The carriage is ready, ser," Demyst announced, from outside the library.

Kharl picked up the elaborately tooled leather case with his credentials. As he stepped out of the library, he saw three men awaiting him—Erdyl, Demyst, and Alynar. He raised his eyebrows.

"You need to take a guard, ser, someone in addition to Undercaptain Demyst," Erdyl said quickly. "So we asked Alynar to accompany you."

"Thank you." Kharl glanced at the two armed men. "We'd best be going." He turned and walked down the corridor to the front portico, then outside.

While Kharl and Demyst entered the carriage, Alynar settled himself next to Mantar on the right side of the driver's bench seat.

The Quadrancy Keep was at the top of the hill to the northeast of the harbor, an ancient and sprawling pile of gray stone at the topmost end of the Lord's Road. At perhaps a quarter before the hour, the carriage rolled up to the iron gates—closed and with three guards stationed outside—all regular armsmen, and not patrollers. Kharl could see a raised stone tower on the right, just behind the wall and gates, and he sensed several more armsmen there.

"Lord Kharl, the Austran envoy," Mantar announced.

Kharl's name was relayed to another armsmen on the inside of the gate, and several moments passed before the gate began to swing open. As the carriage passed the iron gates, Kharl noted the heavy oak gates behind them, held flush against the outer stone wall. An inner and higher stone wall stood another rod or so inside the outer wall. The inner gates were open, and Mantar drove the carriage into a courtyard beyond the second set of gates. There he pulled up opposite an arched entryway.

Two more armsmen flanked the archway.

As Kharl descended from the coach, a man stepped from the archway.

"I'm Mihalen, Lord Kharl, secretary to Ostcrag, Lord West." The slender dark-haired man bore a sabre and looked as though he could use it. His eyes measured Kharl. "You look like you were once a marshal."

"I've seen a few battles," Kharl replied, with a slight laugh, "but not as a marshal."

Mihalen's smile was faint. "This way to the small receiving chamber, ser." He turned and walked through the archway leading into the keep building. Beyond the entry was a small foyer, then a wide but dimly lit corridor. Mihalen kept walking.

Kharl followed.

Close to a hundred cubits down the stone-walled hallway, the secretary turned and stopped at a doorway. There he tugged at a bellpull. After a moment, he spoke. "Lord Kharl, the Austran Envoy, to present his credentials."

"Show him in, Mihalen."

The secretary opened the door and gestured for Kharl to enter.

The envoy and mage extended his order-senses . . . and paused for the briefest of moments. Somewhere beyond the door was a white wizard. Ready to raise shields or harden air, Kharl stepped through the open door into a chamber no more than twenty cubits by ten. The walls were of dark wood, and without painting or ornamentation, and the ceiling above was of plaster once white, but yellowed through age. The two high windows were open, but no breeze issued from either.

Four men were on the low dais at the far side of the chamber. Lord West, wearing a dress tunic of Brystan blue and gray trousers, but looking grayer and more frail than the one time Kharl had seen him before, was seated in a carved ebony chair. At his shoulder stood a younger man, close to Kharl's age, with deep-set black eyes and blond hair cut carelessly short. His dress tunic was burgundy. Stationed at each end of the dais was an armsman, both in burgundy and blue.

Kharl took several steps forward before bowing. "Kharl of Cantyl, here to present my credentials as envoy of Lord Ghrant of Austra to the West Quadrancy, and its Lord."

"And to his son, Lord-to-be, Osten," replied Ostcrag. His voice was hoarse.

"Step forward, Lord Kharl," suggested the younger man, "so that we can see you face-to-face."

Kharl did so, stopping less than two cubits from the dais. "My credentials." He took out the proclamation and sealed letter and extended them.

Osten stepped forward. He broke the seal and read the letter, then the proclamation, quickly and seemingly almost casually, before handing them to his sire. "They seem to be in order."

Ostcrag took more time in reading through the documents. He kept the letter and handed the proclamation back to Kharl. "Welcome to Brysta, Lord Kharl. We honor you as envoy of Lord Ghrant."

"Thank you." Kharl inclined his head, then straightened. "In addition to my credentials, I bring a small token of Lord Ghrant's esteem and respect." Ignoring the probes by the white wizard for the moment, he extracted the pouch from his case and extended it.

Osten took the pouch as well, easing out the silver box, which he lowered for his sire to see.

"The Lords of Austra have always bestowed such small and exquisitely tasteful gifts," Ostcrag replied.

"That is because the taste of the Lords of the West Quadrant are well known," Kharl said, hoping he didn't have to deal with too many more implied slights, but grateful for the time Erdyl had spent going over some of the possibilities.

Kharl could sense that the white wizard remained behind the hanging at the back of the dais. The wizard was not one as strong as those he had faced in Austra, but one with enough strength to throw firebolts and possibly detect untruths. Yet Kharl could say little about it, without revealing his own abilities. Then, he considered, he could not conceal them.

He looked directly at Osten. "You could invite your wizard to join us. I'm sure he would be more comfortable here than behind the arras."

"There were rumors," suggested Ostcrag. "You seem to be affirming them."

"I have some order-ability," Kharl admitted. "Enough to sense a white wizard, anyway. That takes little enough."

"I am certain that Borlent feels more comfortable where he is," suggested Osten.

Kharl merely nodded. "We all have our places and preferences." Another phrase from Erdyl.

"Lord Ghrant has survived some difficult challenges in recent times. He must feel most confident—or most adventuresome—to send a mage of any sort to Brysta as an envoy." Ostcrag's smile did not extend beyond his lips.

"Times have indeed been difficult in Austra, but Lord Ghrant is most fortunate in having Lord Hagen as his lord-chancellor. Matters have improved greatly. Lord Ghrant is most interested in strengthening Austra within itself. He has little interest in adventures."

"Not even in Nordla?" Ostcrag raised his eyebrows as if in disbelief.

"Lord Ghrant would hope that matters remain as they have with the four quadrants of Nordla. He would certainly not wish to support any change here." Kharl managed to keep his expression pleasant, even as he could sense a swirling of chaos from the hidden white wizard. He stood ready with his shields, but the momentary spike of chaos behind the hanging subsided.

"Things always change," observed Osten, his voice languid, at odds with his almost rigid posture.

"That is true," Kharl admitted. "Lord West succeeds Lord West, and so long as the succession is proper, that is change as it should be."

"Yet . . . small as you claim your talent for order-magery may be, Lord Kharl," Osten said, "does not your presence suggest . . . a certain . . . proclivity . . . an indication that Austra might favor the policies of Recluce."

"I don't think so." Kharl paused for just a moment. "Hamor uses white wizards, but I would not claim that such use has ever meant that the emperor is inclined to follow the views of Fairven."

Ostcrag laughed harshly. "One would hope not. In either case."

"How are you finding Brysta?" asked Osten quickly. "Or have you been here before?"

Behind him, Lord Ostcrag nodded.

"I've seen Brysta from the deck of a merchanter before," Kharl replied. That was certainly true, if definitely not the whole truth. "And I've traveled the streets." He paused. "I could be mistaken, but I've seen no beggars at all on the streets since I've been here this time."

"I'm glad that you have not." Osten's voice was hearty. "My brother has taken it upon himself to ensure that no such riffraff bother honest people."

"I've also seen more Watch patrollers. They are most alert."

"The Watch was reorganized last winter. That was after several malefactors escaped . . ." Osten shrugged. "My younger brother was not pleased and took it upon himself to overhaul the entire Watch. We have had far fewer thefts and disorder since."

Kharl turned to face Ostcrag directly. "Your sons are most diligent."

"That they are, and a boon to the West Quadrant."

"Still . . ." mused Kharl, drawing out the expression, "all cities, save Brysta, seem to have beggars. How have you managed this miraculous feat?"

"By putting them to work," replied Osten, before his sire could say a word. "They earn an honest wage in the quarries and upon the new south road."

"The new south road? Where does it go? To Surien?"

"Not yet," answered Ostcrag. "Were Lord South to finish his portion, within a few years we would have a metaled road between Brysta and Surien. Not the poor clay track that is now a mere excuse for a road. Then we would have greater trade and prosperity."

"Just like the Great Highway the Hamorians are building between Cigoerne and Atla," added Osten.

"That would certainly improve trade, I would think," said Kharl.

"Exactly," replied Osten. "Have you such highways in Austra?"

"None of that length. Only a few shorter ones near Valmurl," Kharl admitted, before getting to his own questions. "The Hamorian envoy told me that you were using Hamorian engineers for road-building, but I had no idea that you were planning to build such a large highway. Is that why there are so many Hamorian merchanters in the harbor?"

"There are no more than usual," replied Ostcrag.

The older lord was telling what he believed was the truth, and that stopped Kharl for a moment.

"I understand that you are also a scholar of the law, Lord Kharl," offered Osten. "Is that why you've been spending so much time in the Hall of Justice? Or is it familiar to you for other reasons?"

Kharl offered a laugh. "I have studied the law, as the chief clerks will tell you, but an envoy's task is also to better understand the land. What happens in the Hall of Justice reveals much."

"What has it revealed to you in the very short time that you've been here?" asked Osten, his words pointed.

"You like Brysta to be a very orderly city. You do not permit beggars and thieves. You would rather sentence a careless man to hard labor than risk letting a thief go free."

"Carelessness can be as dangerous as theft," Osten countered.

Kharl smiled politely. "You asked what I saw, Lord Osten."

"Overcaptain. My sire is the only Lord."

Kharl nodded to Ostcrag. "I beg your pardon."

"Granted, Lord Kharl." Ostcrag looked hard at the envoy. "You are a large man. Few are so large, and you speak as though you have some familiarity with Brysta. Yet you have lands in Austra. How did this happen?"

"I was fortunate in being in the right place during the revolt against Lord Ghrant. I was an officer on a merchanter of Lord Hagen's and was part of a force that was called to support Lord Ghrant. I managed to be of some assistance when it was most useful."

"A merchanter officer who is now a lord, who has demonstrated prowess in battle, and who has studied the law. Most unusual."

"Perhaps, Lord West. Yet envoys must know about trade and battles, and knowing the law cannot hurt."

"Such abilities are useful, Lord Kharl," Ostcrag returned, "but they can be most dangerous when an envoy does not have a large force nearby."

"I would not go against your judgment, ser. I would think that the danger would only exist if the West Quadrant were ruled by a Lord without scruples and honor, and all say that you have exhibited both." Those words Kharl had managed to adapt, if in a scrambled form, from a phrase that he and Erdyl had worked out the night before.

Osten frowned.

Ostcrag laughed. "You would entrap me by my own honor, Lord Kharl. Indeed, you are a dangerous man." He stood. "It has been a most . . . intriguing . . . presentation. You may find you need more than words to represent Lord Ghrant in these times. Between Hamor and Recluce, the rest of us must tread with great care, even wizards and order-mages."

"I will remember your words," Kharl replied.

"Best you do. Good day, Lord Kharl." Ostcrag nodded.

Kharl bowed, then stepped back, his senses alert; but neither the hidden wizard nor the armsmen moved or acted as he left the chamber.

Outside, in the corridor, Mihalen waited.

"You must have intrigued them. Such presentations are usually shorter."

"I'm new to being an envoy," Kharl replied. "I'm sure that it showed."

"All envoys must have a first posting."

Kharl smiled politely. He just wanted to leave the Quadrancy Keep. The walls seemed to press in on him, although his order-senses detected nothing except a feeling of age and faint chaos throughout everything.

Mantar, Demyst, and Alynar were waiting in the courtyard with the carriage, and Demyst offered a smile of relief as Kharl stepped through the archway. Kharl did not bother with a parting greeting to Mihalen, whom he trusted even less than Lord West and his son.

Not until the carriage rolled out of the gates and onto Lord's Road downhill toward the residence did Demyst ask, "How did things go, ser?"

"Mostly as expected. They wanted to know more about me, and I wanted to find out things about them. I didn't find out much. They didn't either." He just hoped that he had not revealed too much, although he had expected more probing questions.

As he rode back to his own residence, Kharl pondered over the presentation. He still could not tell, not for certain, if Ostcrag and his son had received word about his magely exploits in Austra. From what he had sensed, he was also fairly certain that neither Ostcrag nor Osten fully understood what Egen was doing. But how could they not see what was so obvious? Was it because they did not wish to see it? Or because they liked the orderly streets of Brysta and did not wish to look at how that order had been created? Then, there was Ostcrag's parting comment about the conflict between Recluce and Hamor. Kharl was unaware of such a conflict, and he was confident he would have felt *something* when he had been in Nylan. Yet Ostcrag believed what he had said, and the implications of that belief were anything but good for Kharl and Austra.

LXXV

Midmorning on threeday found Kharl and Alynar in the carriage, heading through a warm drizzle toward the residence of the Sarronnese envoy. That was assuming that Luryessa would speak to him—if she was even still in Brysta. Kharl wasn't above begging for information, not after his meeting with Lord West, and not after Erdyl had reported late on twoday afternoon that none of the envoys who had been absent from Brysta had returned and that two others—from Lydiar and Delapra—had also left Brysta.

The outer gates to the Sarronnese residence were open, and Mantar brought the carriage up the drive and to a halt under the receiving portico. Kharl opened the door and stepped out of the carriage. "Just wait here with Mantar," he told Alynar.

"Yes, ser."

The duty guard stiffened as Kharl approached.

"I'm Lord Kharl of Austra. I'd like to see Envoy Luryessa, if she's here."

"Ser . . . I can't say. I'll summon her assistant."

"That's fine." What else could he say? So he stood under the portico, out of the drizzle. The rain wasn't strong enough to be a true late-summer rain, but sometimes several days of light rain preceded the downpours that announced the end of summer.

The door opened, and a dark-haired woman stood there. She wore a short-sleeved, plain, dark blue shirt and matching trousers. A lock of unruly hair crossed her forehead, and, as if she had noted his observation, she brushed it back. "Lord Kharl?" A sense of blackness—order—rather than the white of chaos—flowed around the woman. Somehow, after meeting Luryessa, he hadn't expected a Sarronnese order-mage.

"You must be Jemelya." Kharl offered a pleasant smile.

"I am. You must be here to see Luryessa. She thought you might come by unannounced at some time. You are fortunate. She is here, in her study. If you would like to come in?"

"Thank you."

Kharl followed her to the library, then to the open door to the private study.

Luryessa did not rise from the desk, but smiled. "Do come in. You might close the door for me."

Kharl did and settled into a straight-backed chair across from her. "Jemelya said you were expecting me."

"I thought you might come. You are inexperienced as an envoy, but most perceptive. If you came anywhere, it would likely be here."

Kharl found he was neither surprised nor angered by her calm presumption. "I'm sorry to stop unannounced—"

"Don't apologize. It's better that you didn't. Already, the word is out that you're a minor mage." A smile danced on Luryessa's lips and in her hazel eyes.

"You had something to do with that?"

"Only the 'minor' part." The smile faded. "We will be returning to Sarron for consultations with the Tyrant. So we will be closing the residence, tomorrow or the next day, whenever our ships arrive."

"Ships? Warships?" Then Kharl shook his head. "That's to make sure that they arrive."

Luryessa nodded.

"What else should I know? That you can tell me?"

The mischievous smile returned. "You have just met with Lord West and his eldest. You must know far more than a mere woman."

Kharl snorted. "I am most certain that you have noticed that there are no regular armsmen in Brysta and that the patrollers loyal to Captain Egen effectively control the city. Doubtless you already know that their uniforms came from Hamor, and that the road leading to Surien has been designed by Hamorian engineers. It is a very good road, by the way."

"Yes. You have a point?"

Kharl decided not to make it—not yet. "I am also quite sure that you know that Captain Egen controls—or influences strongly—the lord justicers and that they have been instructed to find any way possible to sentence those who commit minor offenses to the quarries or the road-building crew. And that at least some wealthy factors who support Osten have left Brysta."

"I suspected that, but I did not know that. Your point, Lord Kharl?"

"I don't think that either Lord West or Osten understands what all that means. You do, if I understood the message about the late-summer rains."

"You discovered this by some sort of magery?"

Kharl shook his head. "Just by talking and listening to Ostcrag and Osten. They also knew something about me, but I don't think they understood what that meant, either."

"You had best hope that they do not."

"No . . . I'd best hope that Egen doesn't. Or the Hamorians."

"I am most certain that they do know. All of them. The Hamorians only have two or three wizards here. At the moment." Luryessa smiled sadly. "A fleet was being provisioned in Swartheld two eightdays ago. It was being readied to head northwest. With at least several more white wizards."

Kharl couldn't say that he was surprised. He would have been astonished if Luryessa had suggested that all was well. "Lord West suggested that he—and Austra—were being caught between Hamor and Recluce and needed to tread carefully. He believes that. So does Osten."

"That is because Egen and the Hamorians have prepared the ground well."

"How soon?" asked Kharl.

Luryessa shrugged. "Soon, but I cannot name a date. It is not likely this eightday, but not impossible. You have changed everything."

"Me?"

"Oh . . . they do not know that. None of them do except Whetorak and his assistants, and Whetorak will say nothing until additional white wizards arrive. He has heard of your exploits in Austra, and he is most cautious. Otherwise, Egen would now be poised to take Brysta at the first true rains."

Kharl had surmised as much, but it was still a double shock to hear Luryessa's words—first, her casual revelation that she understood just who he was and, second, her confirmation that Egen and the Hamorians were indeed planning to topple Lord West.

"Egen feels his father is weak and that his brothers are little better . . ." Luryessa noted.

"Whetorak is encouraging that, I would wager."

"I won't take that wager." The Sarronnese smiled. "So what do you plan to do?"

Kharl really hadn't thought that through.

"Will you just watch? Or throw your abilities behind Osten and Lord West, incompetent as they are?"

"What would you do?" he countered. "You're a sorceress."

"I'm not in your class, Lord Kharl. Few are. That's why we're leaving. We could assassinate Egen, but the Hamorians would know we had. They'd make certain that all the world knew. That's why our departure will be soon and very public. I just hope that it's soon enough."

Kharl sat there for a time, silent. Once again, it seemed that he had created a bigger problem just by showing up and trying to find out what was happening. "A good envoy would have discovered all this without . . ." He broke off. He wasn't certain what he really meant.

"You're acting like too many men," Luryessa said dryly. "I expect better of you."

"You might explain that," Kharl replied, tartly.

"Oh . . . that's simple enough. You're here something like two eight-days, and you discover what it's taken the best envoys seasons to figure out, and because you don't have a ready solution, you're acting like it's all your fault. Men . . . you can't stand it if you don't have an answer."

Kharl winced.

"Of course, you don't have an answer. You can't. No one could. You still don't know everything. I don't either." She smiled sardonically. "I don't have to have an answer. I just have to get my people out of here safely."

"And I don't?"

"Were you sent here to leave at the first sign of trouble?"

Kharl smiled wryly. "I wasn't given any instructions at all in that way."

"Exactly. Lord Hagen is counting on your sense of responsibility."

"How large a fleet?"

"Not large. More like a flotilla. Six or seven vessels. Only one troop transport."

"Is Lord Justicer Lurtedd still close to Osten?"

Luryessa frowned. "He will not cross Egen or Reynol."

"Would he warn Osten?"

"I would doubt that. He understands that Egen holds more power."

Kharl nodded slowly.

"I do not envy you, Lord Kharl. Anything you do will have adverse consequences."

"Some acts less than others, I would hope."

"That is always true. Do you have other questions that I can answer?"

Kharl knew he should have had scores, but he could think of few, although he knew he would come up with the most important ones only after Luryessa departed. "Where does Egen store his golds—the ones he uses to pay the patrollers?"

"I do not know that for certain, but a storehouse with barred windows and stone walls was erected in the post that serves the south road and the quarries. There is also an underground chamber in the main new barracks on the south side of the city."

"Is Whetorak truly in command of the Hamorian forces here? Will he remain so?"

"No. Submarshal Teorak—he is the assistant envoy in name—controls all armsmen and lancers and probably will command any additional forces landed in Nordla."

"Will this Hamorian flotilla try to conquer Surien as well?"

"They will not attempt anything unless there is no one with a claim to rule."

Kharl wasn't sure he liked that. The implication was that Osten or Vielam—or even Lord West—needed to survive, for any plan to block Hamorian control to be successful.

"I said that none of the choices would be good," Luryessa said.

"And you think I should do something?"

"I think nothing. I suggest nothing. I will say that a powerful black mage who is not from Recluce is the only hope for the West Quadrant not to fall under the iron fist of Hamor. And that is but a hope."

"Most of kind of you."

"You wanted my judgment, not my flattery."

Kharl sat there silently for a moment.

Luryessa stood. "If you have no more questions . . ."

Kharl rose. "I should, but I can't think of any more."

"Do what you feel is right. Trust Egen to be himself, and the Hamorians to weigh and be patient, and you may have a chance to change what others think is inevitable." Luryessa smiled, faintly. "Good day, Lord Kharl. Our best wishes are with you."

Kharl turned and walked down the corridor to the portico, followed by

Jemelya. At the archway, he nodded to her, then walked toward the waiting carriage.

Once he was settled into the carriage, Kharl looked blankly at the faded green fabric above the seat across from him. What could he do? He had no ships. He had no lancers or armsmen. He didn't even know what Egen would do first—or when.

He paused. There was one thing he could do—and should have thought of earlier. He eased the carriage door open and leaned forward, calling to the driver. "Mantar!"

"Ser?"

"Take me to the Factors' Exchange!"

"The Factors' Exchange it is, ser."

Alynar looked at Kharl, but didn't speak.

"We might need a few more golds on hand," Kharl said. He wasn't certain the guard fully appreciated what he was saying, but Kharl didn't feel like explaining in more detail.

At the Factors' Exchange, Kharl managed to draw two hundred golds, claiming that the terms of his arrangement allowed two eightdays' draw at any one time. He doubted he'd get away with that again, but he hoped he wouldn't have to.

After the carriage left the Factors' Exchange, he tried to think about what was most likely to happen. While Egen would not need the Hamorian warships immediately, Kharl couldn't see the captain starting his revolt without them. At the very least, their long guns could reduce the Quadrancy Keep, if necessary. Luryessa was right about the timing. If the rains came, then Osten and Lord West could not move their loyal troops against Brysta and Hagen's patrollers that easily.

A quick campaign would also end before harvest, and that would leave Egen with the full amount of the year's tariffs in his coffers. Then, mused Kharl, while Egen planned for a quick campaign, that did not mean it would be so—or that Whetorak and the Hamorians would want a quick resolution.

When Mantar brought the carriage to a halt at the residence, Kharl headed for the strong room inside. He'd no more than locked the door, after putting most of the golds in the chest, and gotten halfway up the rear steps to the back hall when he saw Khelaya standing there.

"Lord Kharl . . ."

"What is it?"

"Best you talk to Enelya, ser. Some other tavern girl just left. The poor thing's sobbing her heart out, talking about leaving . . ."

"Where is she?"

"In the back pantry. You need to see to her afore she goes off wild-like."

Kharl took a deep breath. "I'll do that." Even if dealing with a sobbing Enelya was the last thing he felt like doing.

Enelya looked up as he stepped into the pantry. Tears coursed down her cheeks. She swallowed.

"What is it?" asked Kharl.

Enelya just shuddered. She said nothing.

Kharl forced himself to be calm. Then he reached out with his order-senses, trying to create a sense of reassurance. "You can tell me now."

"Selda . . ." Enelya's eyes widened, but she said nothing more.

"What about Selda?"

"Nalona . . . Marya . . . they found her with her throat cut . . . all her fingers broken . . ."

Kharl had a feeling he knew who the woman was, but decided he should ask. "Selda? Who is Selda?"

"She was another server . . . White Pony . . ."

"Long-faced, with blond hair?"

Enelya nodded, trying to stop sobbing. ". . . only friend . . . really . . . except . . ." She closed her mouth abruptly.

"Except Jeka, you mean?"

Enelya gaped at Kharl.

"Did Selda know about Jeka?"

"Don't know what you're sayin', ser."

"I know about Jeka, and I know where she is—and where she was. If Selda knew . . . how safe will Jeka be? Did Selda know?" Kharl's voice was hard, demanding. "What did she know?"

"Only knew she—Jeka—was in trade . . . somewhere on Crafters' Lane."

"Why was Egen after you? It wasn't just because you told him no, was it?"

". . . told him no . . . two things . . . he was askin' about a girl dressin' as a boy . . . told me I was lyin' when I said I didn't know."

"Why would he care about that?"

"The old fellow . . . the beggar . . . once was a cooper, they say . . .

killed one of Egen's killers and got clean away . . . Folks talk about it . . . guess it curdled him . . . folks saw 'em together . . ."

Kharl swallowed. Then he straightened. "You'll still be safer here. Don't go anywhere. We'll talk later." Kharl turned. "Demyst! Alynar! Cevor! Erdyl!"

"Lord Kharl?" asked Khelaya.

"We've got—I've got—another problem. You and Fundal and Mantar—make sure Enelya stays here. Tie her up of you have to, but she leaves here . . . they'll get her, too."

"Who'll get her?"

Kharl decided to ignore the question. He wasn't certain he knew, except that they worked for Egen. Or maybe Egen himself had killed Selda. He'd always liked to hurt people. "I don't have time to explain now."

Leaving Khelaya standing in the back hall, Kharl hurried up the stairs to reclaim the sabrelike truncheon and sword belt. He was still belting it in place as he hurried back down the front staircase.

Demyst was standing in the corridor. "Ser?"

"We'll need the mounts. As soon as possible, and one extra." Kharl winced at those words. The last time he'd brought an extra mount had been for Warrl. He'd only been three seasons too late.

"Yes, ser."

Kharl followed the undercaptain out to the stable. He chafed at every moment it took to saddle the mounts, and at his own slowness in saddling the gentle gelding he'd ridden south. The drizzle had turned to mist, then lifted into low clouds that still suggested rain, but none was falling as he led the gelding from the stable and mounted.

Once they were away from the residence, and headed westward toward Crafters' Lane, higher on the harbor side of the hill, Kharl turned in the saddle to the undercaptain. "We're headed to the weaver's—Gharan's. Egen's after . . ." He paused. He'd never mentioned Jeka. ". . . someone there who helped me a lot. I need to get her out of there and warn Gharan."

"Yes, ser."

Kharl studied both sides of the street as they rode down from Sixth Cross. He didn't see any sign of patrollers nearby. For that he was glad as he reined up outside Gharan's shop. "Wait here," he told Demyst as he dismounted, and handed the gelding's reins to the undercaptain. "Let me know if any patrollers are headed this way."

Demyst nodded. "Erdyl can come get you."

Kharl hurried into the shop.

Gharan looked up from his loom. "Kharl? I mean, Lord Kharl. What is it?"

"Where's Jeka?"

"She's upstairs with Amyla and the children. Why?"

"She's got to leave. Right now."

"You wanted me to take her, and now that—"

"Egen's after her. She stays here, and he'll find her." Kharl fumbled through his wallet, and finally extracted five golds. "Here. I don't think Egen is after anyone else. If he asks about your weaver girl, you tell him that she left and didn't say where she was going. If it looks like trouble, just come to the envoy's residence. If you can't find me there, or I've had to leave Nordla, the golds should be enough for passage to Valmurl. If it comes to that, I'll take care of all of you at Cantyl."

Gharan's mouth opened. Then he closed it. "We . . . Brysta is our home."

"If you don't have trouble, then you can keep the golds. Call them payment for my upsetting your life." Kharl saw a flash of sandy blonde hair. "Jeka!"

"What are you doing here?"

"Coming to get you."

"Just like that? Like a fancy lord?"

Kharl forced himself to take a deep breath. "It's not like that. I told you that Enelya was working for me? Well . . . you know Selda, at the White Pony?"

Jeka's face froze for a moment.

"Egen or his men cut her throat. That was after they broke her fingers. They wanted to know something. Egen was after Enelya, and Selda knew about you and that you'd been the one who'd told Enelya where she could hide from Egen. She knew some other things, too."

"Doesn't mean he's after me."

For a moment, Kharl didn't know what to say.

"Well?" asked Jeka, green eyes flashing.

"He is after you. He only knows you're somewhere on Crafters' Lane. Didn't I know when that wizard—"

Jeka's jaw tightened. "Doesn't change anything if I go with you."

"Not that way," Kharl agreed. "Just grab everything you can. I've got a horse outside for you."

"Can't ride."

"You'll learn, and if you can't, you can hang on to me."

"I'll learn. Right now."

"Just get your things. Don't leave anything. Otherwise, they might think that Gharan is hiding you somewhere."

"Already figured that out." Jeka turned and hurried toward the narrow rear steps to the upper level.

Kharl turned back to the weaver. "Egen might not ever come here. But he or his men might be here this afternoon. I can't risk losing Jeka. Not . . . after everything." He swallowed. "I didn't mean to cause you trouble. If you want to leave right now . . . you can. You can stay at the envoy's residence . . ."

Gharan shook his head. "Weaver girls come and go. Everyone knows that. I'll just let it be known that she said she had a chance to go home."

"You're sure?"

"I'm sure . . . Lord Kharl." Gharan flashed a smile. "If we see trouble, we'll be at your door. I'm not a fool. Don't think it will come to that, though."

Jeka reappeared, carrying a burlap bag and wearing a shapeless jacket over her blue shirt, as well as a cap, under which she'd swept up her hair. She looked boyish once more. "I'm ready." Abruptly, she turned to Gharan and hugged him. "Be thankin' you, always."

After a moment, Gharan bent down and murmured in Jeka's ear, low enough that Kharl wasn't supposed to hear it. "You did good work, better 'n almost all. But I wouldn't a' given you the chance, weren't for Kharl. Don't forget it." He straightened.

Kharl didn't say anything, appreciating Gharan's words.

"You two goin' to keep jawing? We stay here, just cause trouble for the weaver," Jeka said.

"Thank you," Kharl said to Gharan, inclining his head before turning.

"It was my gain," Gharan said. "I'll send to the residence when the cloth is ready."

"If I have to leave Brysta," Kharl said, "I'll have one of the merchanters pay for it and pick it up."

"Your word's always been good." Gharan grinned. " 'Sides, you left a good deposit."

Kharl hurried out of the shop.

"No sign of patrollers, not even a street Watch," Demyst told Kharl.

That was a troublesome thought as well. Where were the patrollers?

Kharl turned to Jeka. "This horse."

She looked at the saddle dubiously. Her face was pale.

Kharl reached out and lifted her, mostly by her arms and shoulders, and set her in the saddle. "Hang on to the reins with one hand, the saddle rim with the other. I'll take your bag until we get there."

He remounted the gelding and turned his mount back toward Sixth Cross. He glanced back at Jeka, riding beside Alynar. She grimaced at him. He gave an exaggerated shrug, then lurched in the saddle. He still wasn't that good a rider. He could sense her smothered laughter.

"Street's real quiet, ser," observed Demyst. "Could be trouble."

"Likely in the next few days. How are you doing on finding guards?"

"One's coming round this afternoon. Maybe two."

"Let's hope they're good."

"One might be. The others . . . who knows?"

Kharl keep watching the roads, both with eyes and senses, but he saw no patrollers, nor did he sense any unusual amount of chaos. Even so, he was relieved when they finally reined up in the open space before the residence stable. He dismounted and turned the gelding to Mantar, before walking over to Jeka's mount.

Kharl held out a hand. Jeka took it, but only long enough to scramble down. He took the mount's reins with one hand and gave her the burlap bag with the other before she could request it.

"Now what?" asked Jeka.

"You can take one of the empty rooms on the third level."

"Where's Enelya?"

"In the retainer quarters there." Kharl gestured.

"Why not put me out where she is?"

"Because you're not a retainer here. You're a guest."

"A guest in a lord's house? What kind of guest?" Jeka glared.

Kharl could feel Demyst and Erdyl edging away, leading their mounts into the stable with relief. Mantar stood by the open stable door, holding the reins to Kharl's gelding, waiting.

"You can have one of the large bedrooms on the second level, then."

"That where your room is?"

Kharl nodded.

"Third level's better. Door better have a bar."

"It has a latchplate. It's very solid."

"Good."

Kharl led the mount over to Mantar. "Thank you."

"Not at all, ser." The driver, who was also the groom, did not look directly at Kharl, but Kharl could sense his amusement.

The mage and envoy turned back to Jeka. "This way."

Fundal and Khelaya were waiting inside the rear hallway. Kharl could sense Enelya in the rear pantry. "Enelya, you might as well come greet Jeka." Kharl waited, ignoring the impatience of the steward and cook, until the serving girl appeared. "Fundal, Khelaya, this is Jeka. She'll be staying with us for a while. Up on the third level. Enelya already knows Jeka."

Fundal glanced at Jeka.

The small woman looked hard back at the steward.

Fundal edged back.

"Captain Egen is after her as well. Not a word," Kharl ordered.

"Yes, ser."

Kharl could sense Fundal's puzzlement, but he wasn't about to explain. He wasn't sure that he could. He turned to Enelya. "If you would take Jeka up to the third level? She can have any chamber she wishes—except the ones being used by the guards and Undercaptain Demyst."

"Yes, ser."

"I'm going to my chamber for a bit. Then I'll be in the library." Kharl left the four in the rear hall and made his way to the front staircase.

Once he was halfway up and out of sight, he called up a sight shield and hurried up and then along the corridor past his chamber and to the door to the rear staircase. There he waited until the two women passed the landing before opening the door just enough to slip inside.

". . . look!"

"Look where?" asked Jeka.

"Thought someone comin' from there. Maybe Lord Kharl just shut the door," replied Enelya.

"He's really a lord?"

"He is. Erdyl—he's sorta nice—he was telling me that Lord Kharl has lands with a vineyard and forests and a sawmill. And you know what he did? He built a cooperage with his own hands. A lord who wants to be a cooper. Doesn't that beat all."

Kharl listened, wondering what Jeka would say.

"Takes all kinds," the weaver replied. "He found you back of Werwal's? That right?"

"Didn't know where else to go."

The two reached the top of the stairs and turned toward the front of the residence.

"Best room left is in the front, west side. Sun doesn't wake you."

"Good enough." Jeka cleared her throat. "Lord Kharl . . . he . . . interested in you?"

Enelya laughed. "He's interested in you. He found out that Selda knew where you were . . . look on his face . . . think he woulda shaken me like a rat . . . he was runnin' for the stable." There was a moment of silence. "Good-looking fellow. Older, but not that old. Wouldn't mind someone like that . . ."

"No! Not even for a lord."

"Pretty choosy, you are. Especially for someone who was hiding as a boy. You ever—"

Kharl moved slightly closer as Enelya opened the door.

"Oh . . ." The involuntary exclamation from Jeka tore at Kharl. "Never . . ."

"He likes you," said Enelya.

"Leave me 'lone."

"All right." Another silence followed. "He's good to people. You don't bed him, fine. Leastwise be nice to him. Don't spoil it for the rest of us." Enelya slipped out of the front chamber, closing the door softly.

Kharl flattened himself against the wall, remaining silent while the serving girl passed him. Then he eased forward. Was Jeka humming? Singing?

He stopped. She was sobbing.

He swallowed, then turned and made his way back to his own chamber. Not until he was certain that he was alone did he release the sight shield. He stood at the window, looking down at the side garden. Jeka . . . sobbing?

He stood at the window for a long time.

At around the second glass of the afternoon, he finally went downstairs to the library.

For all his worry about Jeka, he still had to consider what he might do when Brysta erupted into fighting. The clouds had lifted more, and hazy sunlight bathed Brysta. Still, it would not be that long before the summer-end rains arrived.

He settled behind the desk and took out a markstick. He couldn't think of what to write. Or what he could do. Killing Egen made the most sense, and if there had been an Egen in Austra . . .

Kharl laughed, ironically. Ilteron had been much like Egen, except he'd been Ghrant's older brother, and Kharl had killed him with magery. But that had been in a battle. No, Kharl had killed when necessary, but was it something that he should do as an envoy?

Being an envoy made matters harder, not easier. As just a mage and cooper, and not an envoy, for what Egen had done to Kharl and those he loved, Kharl could have killed the captain without a qualm. But . . . would that be the best thing to do? For that matter, where was Egen? Kharl didn't dare try to travel south again. He frowned. Egen might well be at Werwal's trial the next day. Kharl could get a sense then. If Egen was not, he might be able to ask the others where the captain was. That would be far quicker than searching blindly.

He nodded, then began to sketch out a rough map of Brysta, using an older map in one of the histories as a rough guide, but updating it from what he knew. He needed to know how long it might take to get from the two barracks to the Quadrancy Keep—or to the harbor piers and other places.

Before Kharl knew it, Khelaya was standing in the doorway.

"Supper is served, Lord Kharl . . . the others . . ."

"Oh . . . I'm sorry." Kharl rose quickly and hurried to the dining chamber.

His place at the end of the table was empty, of course. The others stood behind their chairs, Erdyl was to his right, and Demyst to his left. Jeka stood to the left of the undercaptain. She still wore the weaver's blue, but it became her, especially in the soft lamplight of the evening.

"Please . . ." Kharl gestured for them to sit. "I was working on some maps."

"You missed the midday meal, too," Erdyl said.

Kharl hadn't even thought about eating then. That might have been why his stomach decided to growl. After he seated himself, he filled his beaker with lager and handed the pitcher to Demyst, knowing that Erdyl would have wine, as the secretary always did.

Khelaya set three platters in the middle of the table, the main dish, something like flankaar, closest to Kharl. He served himself and handed the platter to Erdyl.

"Ah . . . ser," Erdyl began.

"Yes?"

"Just a while ago, there were two warships standing off the breakwater."

"Sarronnese, I'd wager," Kharl said, taking a helping of some cooked and wilted greenery he did not recognize. "Did you find out?"

"Cevor said they looked Sarronnese. Oh, and the Gallosian envoy has decided to go hunting somewhere north of Sagana."

"Not much to hunt there," observed Jeka.

"He's not really hunting," Kharl said, "unless it's for a place to hide from what's coming."

The faintest look of puzzlement crossed Jeka's face, then vanished.

"We think that Captain Egen may decide he should be the next Lord West," Kharl said blandly.

"Won't stay lord long."

"Because he's too mean?"

"Likes to hurt people," Jeka said. "More people find that out, fewer folks'll support him, or fight for him."

Kharl laughed, softly. "You're right about that, but a lot of people could get hurt before people find out. Lord West—the present one—isn't too kind, either." He took a sip of the lager. It tasted flat, but that wasn't the lager, he suspected.

They ate in silence for a time. Kharl studied Jeka, trying not to be too obvious. One thing was clear. She watched the others, and copied their manners and how they used cutlery and how they drank. Finally, as he finished the last of the mutton flankaar, Kharl turned to her.

"Is your room all right?"

"It's fine."

Fundal appeared in the archway. "Undercaptain . . . I hate to intrude, but . . ."

"Sestalt is here?"

"Yes, ser."

Demyst looked to Kharl. "If you would excuse me, ser?"

"Go ahead."

Erdyl glanced at Kharl. "Ser?"

Kharl nodded.

After the two men had left, Jeka looked at Kharl. "You managed that nice."

"I didn't manage it. Undercaptain Demyst is trying to hire more guards. He told me that they would be coming this afternoon or evening."

"Don't want your assistant around me, either."

Kharl wanted to sigh. Instead, he laughed. "You're right. He said you were pretty. You are. But it bothered me."

"Never said that to me before."

"I shouldn't now," he said. "You told me nothing had changed."

"Hasn't. Woulda been nice to hear, though."

Kharl thought he understood. "I'm sorry. I didn't understand. I've thought about . . . everything."

"Friends . . . right now." Jeka looked directly at Kharl. "Please?"

"For now," Kharl agreed. Not that he had any choice, he realized.

To the side, there was a cough. Demyst stood in the doorway. "Ser . . . I thought you should meet Sestalt."

Kharl didn't know whether to be relieved or displeased as he rose from the table. But then, that seemed to be the way everything was headed.

LXXVI

On fourday, Kharl dressed to appear in the Hall of Justice. He wasn't sure what else he could do. He hadn't slept that well, with dreams about Hamorian warships bombarding Brysta from the harbor while he staggered through the streets looking for a black staff. He'd awakened from that dream with a start, gotten up, and walked around his chamber before climbing back into his bed. The second nightmare had been worse—Egen had burst into the residence with a squad of his patrollers, looking for Jeka. Kharl had not returned from his presentation to Lord West in time, and found everyone slaughtered. Jeka had been used—horribly.

He lay awake in the warm night for a good glass after that, and slept only fitfully, especially after a steady rain began to patter on the roof of the residence.

As he finished dressing, except for his jacket, he considered the day ahead. The rain continued, steady, but not quite a downpour. Should he still go to the Hall of Justice? He shrugged. What else could he do? Demyst was better at finding guards than Kharl would ever be. Besides, Egen might well be at the Hall for Werwal's trial, and, if he was, that would mean a few days—*one day at least*, he corrected himself—before any attacks began. Since Werwal's case was second on the docket before Reynol, Kharl had time to eat breakfast before heading to the Hall of Justice—if he hurried.

Kharl could sense Jeka and Demyst at the table, and he could hear that they were talking. He paused, then eased the sight shield around himself as he moved toward the archway into the breakfast room.

"Lands and all . . . why'd he come here?" asked Jeka.

"Lord Ghrant asked him to."

"Did he have to?"

"I doubt any man could make Lord Kharl do what he felt was wrong."

Kharl appreciated Demyst's words, but doubted their accuracy.

"We in trouble here?"

"That we are. There is no help for that, I fear."

"He's staying here and going to let it happen?"

Kharl winced at Jeka's question.

"In Austra, I questioned his actions. I was wrong. When he acts, there is none braver . . ."

Kharl heard steps above. Where he was standing in the narrow archway, one way or another, he was likely to be discovered. He released the sight shield, then coughed before he made his way into the breakfast room.

"Don't believe that business about bravery," Kharl said, with a smile. "He was far braver to accompany someone who rides badly and knew little about fighting."

"He is also modest," Demyst said to Jeka, standing as he did. "I fear I talked too long. I need to spend some time with Sestalt, and I am awaiting another man who may do as a guard." He nodded to Kharl. "Ser?"

"Do what you have to. At the moment, you're getting more done than I am. How are you doing with finding guards?"

"Not so well as I'd like. Sestalt will do, and so will Sharlak."

"Take them on, if they'll start today. Can you talk to Mantar, or Fundal, and see if we can get some more mounts and riding gear?"

A sheepish expression appeared on the undercaptain's face. "I was going to talk to you about that, ser. Already been scouting. We can pick up four pretty good mounts, but they'd be three to four golds each."

"Do it. I'll get you the golds after I eat." Kharl was glad that he'd thought about the need for golds and gone to the Factors' Exchange earlier, especially since it appeared that the summer-end rains had arrived. "What about sabres, or crossbows?"

"We have enough in the armory here. Fundal had them stowed out of sight." Demyst laughed. "He's most cautious."

"About everything."

With a smile, Demyst inclined his head, then slipped out of the breakfast room.

Kharl settled himself at the circular breakfast table. As he did, Khelaya appeared with a platter on which were cheesed eggs, thick ham slices, and a basket of bread. "Erdyl said you'd be leaving soon."

"I'll be at the Hall of Justice."

"No good comes from there," replied the cook.

"Not often," Kharl agreed. "Has to be a first time, though."

"When the hot springs of Kayol freeze, maybe."

Kharl laughed.

Khelaya shook her head, then glanced at Jeka. "You want more?"

"No." After a moment, Jeka added. "Thank you."

Because he wasn't sure what he could say to Jeka, Kharl took several mouthfuls of the eggs, then a swallow of the cider, tart, as early summer cider always seemed to be.

"Why are you going to the Hall of Justice? Thought you'd seen enough of that."

"Werwal . . . he's before Reynol today."

"You going to bust in there with horses, too?"

"No. I'll do what I can—if I can do anything. While I'm gone, you can use the library. Practice reading." Kharl kept eating. He didn't want to be late to the Hall.

"That's harder than weaving."

"Or you can talk to Enelya. I'd wager that she's still upset about Selda. I won't be back for a while."

"Like last time . . ." muttered Jeka.

Kharl winced. "I didn't have much choice, did I?"

"Suppose not."

"I did come back."

"For your boy."

"And for you."

Jeka looked down. "Your boy? Undercaptain said you went south . . . graves there."

"Egen and his men. They killed Merayni and Dowsyl, all the children and Warrl." He looked at Jeka, waiting until she met his eyes. "I couldn't let that happen to you."

Jeka looked back across the table at Kharl. "Wouldn't. You didn't have—"

"I was supposed to leave you?" asked Kharl. "Let Egen find you?"

"I could have hid."

"For how long?"

"I was a good weaver."

"You are a good weaver. You stayed with Gharan, and you might have been a dead one."

"What about Gharan and Amyla?" demanded Jeka.

"I told him that if he ran into any trouble to get out of there and come here. If he can't find me, to get a ship to Austra and go to Cantyl. I gave him some golds."

"You only gave me silvers." Her face was deadpan.

It took Kharl a moment to catch the hidden humor. "That was all I had then. I gave you half of all I had." He forced a grin. "Do you think you were worth it?"

Surprisingly, to Kharl, Jeka looked down at the table for a moment. Kharl didn't know what to say. Finally, he stammered. "I'm sorry."

"No need for that. You're a lord."

He felt like pounding the table. The last thing he wanted was to hurt Jeka. "Being a lord—it doesn't mean you hurt people. I don't want to be like Egen."

"Never be like that pissprick." Jeka looked up. "You're going to the Hall. What if Egen sees you?"

"He won't know I'm the same person. I don't think he'll believe a cooper could come back as a lord."

"Mean bastard. Doesn't forget much."

"Even if he does, he's not going to do anything in the Hall of Justice."

"Better be real careful when you leave."

"He might not be there."

"Why you're going, isn't it? See if he's there?"

"That, and Werwal."

"You really got lands in Austra?"

Kharl nodded. "I didn't expect it, but that was how it turned out. You'll like them." He tried to keep his expression pleasant as he realized just what he'd said.

"You think I'm going? Didn't ask me."

"You're coming to Austra. You'll be safe there. You can't stay here."

"Says who?"

Kharl took a deep breath. "I do."

"You been right about stuff." Jeka didn't quite meet his eyes. "Still doesn't change things."

"It might be a while," Kharl added. "Things could be dangerous here."

"No worse than hidin' from Egen between walls."

"No," Kharl agreed, although he wasn't so sure about that. He finished the last bit of ham and took a swallow of the cider. Then he stood. "I need to get to the Hall."

"Guess I'll talk to Enelya first."

"She can come with us to Cantyl, if she wants."

"You givin' her a choice, but not me?"

Kharl did catch the attempt at humor this time. "That's right." He grinned.

After a moment, Jeka returned the grin, although hers was shaky. "You be careful."

"I will." He turned and hurried up to his chamber, where he washed quickly, donned his black jacket, then hastened down to the strong room to get more golds for Demyst. Then he locked up the chests and the strong room, and made his way up to the front portico and the waiting carriage beyond. Demyst stepped out into the rain and opened the door. He slipped inside after Kharl.

On the way to the Hall, Kharl gave Demyst the golds for the mounts. Then he studied the streets, and, when he could see it through the rain, the harbor. There were two iron-hulled warships moored at the outermost piers, and several wagons on the piers themselves. Kharl could barely make out the ensign on one—mostly blue. Although he did not recognize the design, he had no doubts that the vessels were Sarronnese, and that Luryessa, Jemelya, and the rest of the Sarronnese at the envoy's residence would be boarding those ships—if they had not already.

"Sarronnese ships," suggested Demyst, looking past Kharl.

"They've closed their residence. If Erdyl's right, the Hamorian envoy is the only one left here in Brysta, except for us."

"How soon before the fighting starts, you think, ser?"

"I don't know. Another eightday. Could be sooner. Could be later."

"Even with guards, we can't really protect the residence."

"I know. We ought to have some supplies laid by so we could ride out in a hurry."

"Yes, ser. Already been working on that. Khelaya's been helping. Says she won't go with us, but she'll make sure we're ready to go. Any chance of catching a ship back to Austra?"

"No. Not that I know of." Besides, although Kharl wasn't about to say so, leaving now didn't feel right. Was that because he'd fled once before, and Warrl and Arthal had died? Was he being stubborn and foolish? What could he do?

Offer his services to Lord West? When the lord had sentenced and executed Charee, knowing she was innocent?

"Ser?"

"Just thinking."

It was just half past the second glass of the morning when Mantar brought the carriage to a halt outside the Hall of Justice. After getting out, Kharl turned and looked at the driver. "This time, I'd like you to come back in a glass, Mantar, if you don't mind. I'm sorry about the rain, but I'll need you. If anything changes, Undercaptain Demyst will let you know."

"Yes, ser. Thought that might be the way it was."

Kharl readied himself, extending his order-senses, but he could detect nothing more than the usual minute trace of chaos that existed anywhere frequented by people. Once the two men stepped into the front foyer of the Hall of Justice, Undercaptain Demyst halted, stationing himself just inside the doors. Kharl walked on toward the two patroller guards.

"Just finishing the first one, ser."

"That didn't take long."

"No, ser. Never does."

Kharl slipped into the chamber, past the bailiff, who gave him a quick glance. Outside of those involved in the trial, the chamber was almost empty, except for a handful of men and a single woman in the front row on the left.

A sturdy man was being marched to face the justicer seated behind the lower podium desk in his blue velvet gown—Lord Justicer Reynol, round-faced, gray-haired, and blocky. Behind him, on the upper dais, the single carved high-backed seat was vacant.

". . . you have been accused of disturbing the peace and assaulting a patroller of the Watch. The first offense is a minority. The second is a majority against the Lord West. For the first, you are sentenced to five lashes. For the second you are sentenced to two years' hard labor in the quarries."

"No . . ."

"Any further outbursts will add another five lashes. Justice be done."

"All stand!" ordered the bailiff.

As the patrollers led the prisoner out, followed by two other patrollers who might have been witnesses, Kharl eased up the side of the chamber. He stood waiting at the end of the first row on the right side.

Fasyn, sitting at the side table, glanced toward Kharl. Beside him was Dasult.

The young scrivener murmured to Fasyn. "That the advocate for the next one?"

". . . advocate . . . also lord and envoy from Austra . . . sometimes watches cases . . ."

The bailiff's staff thudded three times. "Is there one who would take the Justicer's Challenge? There being none, the renderer Werwal is here, accused of disturbing the peace, and a majority against the Lord, to be brought before justice!"

"Bailiff, bring forward Werwal, the renderer."

The doors at the back opened, and two patrollers stepped into the chamber, with Werwal between them.

As they marched Werwal in, Kharl noted that the eyes of the woman on the other end of the first row followed the renderer. Behind Werwal and the patrollers came Fyngel, the tariff farmer, and behind him, the slender figure of a captain that Kharl recognized too well—Egen. Ostcrag's son was surrounded by a mist of chaos, some of the chaos of having been exposed to magery and some the sullen reddish white chaos of evil. Kharl could also sense the chaos of a beating permeating Werwal.

Egen and Fyngel stood before the benches next to the aisle on the left side, less than ten cubits from Kharl.

"Does anyone represent the accused . . . Seeing no one—"

Kharl rose. "I would ask leave to represent the accused, your lordship."

The lord justicer stopped and looked to Fasyn, seated at the black table to the side. "Fasyn? Is he a registered advocate?"

Kharl could sense Egen's eyes upon him, but he did not turn.

"Ah . . . Lord Kharl is the envoy from Austra, your lordship," Fasyn said nervously. "You have seen his credentials. There is no bar in the law to his representing the accused. That is, if the accused chooses to accept him as an advocate."

Reynol looked directly at the renderer. "Werwal, the Austran envoy and advocate has asked leave to represent you. You may accept his offer or decline it."

"It can't be worse than it is," mumbled the battered renderer.

"Yes or no? And be civil."

"Yes, your mightiness. I will take aid from any quarter."

"Be it noted that the advocate from Austra represents the renderer."

Kharl stepped forward. He did not wish to get too close to Werwal. The renderer had been very perceptive. He might not be that observant in his current condition, but Kharl did not wish to offer him that choice.

"You, the renderer Werwal," Reynol announced, "have been charged with obstructing the tariff farmer in the performance of his duties and in using violence against the Watch. Both are majority offenses against the Lord West. What you say or believe is not a question. We are here to do justice, and that justice is to determine whether you did so act." Reynol seated himself.

From behind Kharl and Werwal came the rap of the bailiff's staff. "All may sit."

The patrollers sat Werwal in the armless chair of the accused. Kharl reseated himself on the bench.

The first witness called was Fyngel, the tariff farmer who had once tripled Kharl's tariffs on Egen's orders. Fyngel avoided looking at Kharl as he described his efforts to inspect Werwal's property.

". . . told him he had to let me see everything. He said that I'd already inspected his place, and I needed a warrant from the lord justicer for a second inspection. He barred the door. Wouldn't let me in. Told him I didn't need no warrant thing."

Kharl watched Reynol with his order-senses. From the lord justicer's reactions, Kharl got the impression that such a warrant was needed—or that Reynol thought it was.

"What did you do then?" asked the lord justicer.

"I went and told Captain Egen. Stopping a tariff farmer in his duties, that's for the Watch."

"What did you do after that?"

"I didn't do anything, your lordship. Heard that the Watch had taken Werwal, and I figured that was something for your lordship."

Reynol nodded, then turned to Kharl. "Do you have any questions?"

Kharl stood. "Just a few, your lordship." He faced the tariff farmer. "Has anyone ever asked you for a warrant before?"

"No, ser. Never needed one."

"Have you ever asked the justicers about the need for a warrant?"

"No." Fyngel looked puzzled.

"I would like to note, your lordship, that the renderer was acting within the precedents and the Code when he requested a warrant."

"So noted, advocate." Reynol looked to the patroller seated beside Egen. "Serjeant Feryt, please step forward."

The narrow-faced patroller with the two stripes on his shoulder stepped forward.

"Please explain what happened when you and your men went to the renderer's?"

"Not all that much to say, your lordship. We went there, like the captain said, and we knocked on the gate. There weren't no answer. We knocked again, and there weren't no answer then, either. So we broke out the hinges and went into the front courtyard. The renderer there, he had a staff, and he laid out Hionot and Jospak cold. Busted Calsot's arm so bad he'll be mustered out. Took the rest of us to lay him out." The serjeant shrugged.

"The renderer did not ask who you were?" asked Reynol.

"Not that I heard, your lordship . . ."

Reynol asked a number of questions, but all pertained to the injuries suffered by the patrollers, and Werwal's use of only a staff to attack the patrollers.

Abruptly, he stopped and looked, not to the serjeant, but to Egen. "Is that all?"

Egen stood and bowed his head briefly before speaking. "There is little more to be said about that, Lord Justicer. The renderer attacked the Watch in performance of its duties." He cleared his throat. "There is one other matter, Lord Justicer. Just yesterday morning, we discovered that vagrants had been using a hidden space behind the renderer's rear courtyard wall to hide from the Watch. One of those hiding there may have been a murderer as well. The murderer who was there has been reported to have left Brysta, but the renderer allowed him shelter."

"That will be considered, Captain Egen."

Egen smiled and seated himself.

The captain and the serjeant had both been lying throughout—or slanting things so much that what had been reported might as well have been lies. Kharl could sense that. But how could he make that clear without revealing that he knew it through magery?

Reynol looked to Kharl. "Are you ready to address the charges, advocate?"

"If it please your lordship."

"You may begin."

Kharl turned. "Serjeant Feryt?"

"Yes, ser?" The patroller stood.

"You said that you knocked on the gate twice?"

"Yes, ser?"

"Did you say anything?" Kharl projected a feeling that the patroller should tell the truth. He hoped it was strong enough. He also looked hard at the serjeant.

"Wasn't nothing to say, ser. We were there to do our duty."

Kharl had recalled what Erdyl had told him. "When was this? What part of the day?"

The serjeant glanced toward Egen.

"You must recall what time of day it was," Kharl suggested.

"We were late, ser, by the time we got orders."

"Was it dark out?"

"Yes . . . ser." The words sounded dragged out.

"It was dark. Did you have lanterns or torches?"

"No, ser."

"In the darkness, the renderer could not see your uniforms, then?" Kharl projected another compulsion at the patroller.

The man turned, opened his mouth, then swallowed. Finally, he answered. "No, ser."

"Was there any other reason why the renderer might not have seen you clearly? Any reason at all?"

Feryt did not answer.

"Serjeant?" Kharl intensified the projection of order.

"Captain Egen made us blacken our faces."

"Did you announce that you were Watch patrollers?"

The patroller serjeant swallowed again. He did not speak.

"You must answer the question," Reynol admonished the serjeant, "and you must answer with the truth."

"No, ser. The captain said he'd know well enough who we were."

Kharl looked hard at the serjeant. "You have said that the renderer was supposed to know that you and your men were patrollers. Yet it was dark. You carried no lanterns, and you have said that you had all blackened your faces. You never announced that you were Watch patrollers. How was the renderer to know that you were patrollers?"

"He shoulda known."

"Can you tell me how?"

"He shoulda known," the serjeant repeated, helplessly.

Kharl turned to the lord justicer. "I have no more questions for the serjeant. I do have questions for Captain Egen."

"Captain, would you step forward, please?"

Egen rose.

Kharl could sense the anger and the chaos within Egen. He ignored it. "Captain, your serjeant has said that the renderer was supposed to know that they were patrollers. Yet it was dark. They carried no lanterns, and they did not identify themselves. Their faces and uniforms were hidden. Was what the serjeant said correct?"

"I did not tell them to act that way," Egen lied. "They were supposed to tell him who they were."

"So you gave them proper orders?"

"Yes."

"You were not there?"

"No. That was their task."

"Then you were not there to enforce your orders?

"I just said that I was not."

Kharl nodded, then cleared his throat gently. "There is also the question of the space behind the rear wall. Captain Egen, you said that the hidden space was behind the rear wall. Most rear walls are solid. Was there any evidence of an entrance to the renderer's courtyard?"

Egen paused, as if he thought about lying. "No. But the renderer should have known about it."

"You said that the space was used to hide a murderer. Was this murderer ever charged?"

"He escaped Brysta. There was no point in charging him."

Kharl fingered his chin, turning back to Reynol. "Perhaps I have missed something, your lordship. While there may indeed have been a murder, I do not believe that the renderer can be charged with aiding a murder that has never been brought to the Hall of Justice."

"Your point is taken, advocate. That charge is dismissed." Reynol looked blandly at Egen.

Kharl could sense the growing anger and frustration in Egen.

Kharl addressed Reynol. "A Lord of a land has right to know what property a man has in order to set the tariff properly. The Lord also has the right to use force when his officers are opposed. That is the law. The renderer would not contest that. But he must know who the proper officials are. He must be able to identify them. Otherwise, he could lose everything to brigands posing as officials. Both the Code and the precedents allow a man to protect what is his against unlawful acts. The Watch has the duty to identify themselves. They did not do so. The accused did not know that he was opposing patrollers. He thought he was defending his property against brigands. That is not an offense in any land. Also, the renderer had the right to ask for a warrant from the tariff farmer. He may have been unwise, because such a warrant would be granted. But turning away the tariff farmer because he had no warrant was not an offense against the Lord."

"There seems to be a reasonable doubt in the eyes of all involved in this." Reynol glanced at Egen.

Kharl could sense the growing anger in the young captain.

"He still turned away the tariff farmer and attacked the Watch, Lord Justicer," Egen replied.

"What do you say to that, advocate?"

"The renderer did not use force against the tariff farmer, your lordship. He asked for a warrant. The tariff farmer did not show one. He did not show his medallion. The renderer was not wise, because the right to tariff is well established, but foolishness should be punished far less severely than defiance or a crime against the Lord."

"Your points are taken, advocate."

"Your lordship," Egen said. "At the very least, the renderer used force against others and disturbed the peace."

"Your point is also taken, Captain Egen." Reynol coughed, then spoke. "Werwal the renderer. Step forth."

Werwal was yanked into a standing position, not gently, but Kharl was not about to make a point about that.

"You are hereby sentenced to five lashes for disturbing the peace. You are ordered to make your premises open to Fyngel the tariff farmer, and to pay all tariffs imposed. You are also sentenced to pay one gold for the time and costs of this trial." Reynol paused. "Consider yourself most fortunate, renderer."

"Yes, your lordship."

"Take him away. The sentence is to be carried out immediately, and he is then to be released."

"All stand!" The bailiff's voice boomed through the chamber.

The patrollers led Werwal out of the Hall.

Almost as the renderer went through the doors, Egen stepped up to Kharl. "Lord envoy, you are a most effective advocate." The captain's voice dropped slightly. "Might it be that you have had other . . . means? Magery, perhaps?"

Kharl offered a smile. "It is doubtless no secret that I do have a very slight ability with order. It is just enough to see who tells the truth and who does not, Captain Egen. That can be helpful, I will admit, but I cannot make anyone tell a lie or what is not so. Not even the greatest of order-mages can do that." His eyes met those of the smaller man.

"Even envoys must recognize what is, Lord Kharl, and I do not forget."

Kharl smiled again, politely. "I am certain you do not, Captain. I hope that you are not suggesting that I should suffer for pursuing justice within the law."

Egen's smile was cold. "I would never say that. Good day, envoy." He turned and strode stiffly from the chamber.

The woman who had been in the front benches eased toward Kharl. "Ser?"

"Yes."

"Thank you. I would pay you all I have for my consort's life, but we . . ."

"You have paid enough." Kharl lowered his voice. "As soon as he is released, come to the Austran residence on the east hill. You can stay there."

"Ser?"

"Captain Egen will find someone, I would judge . . ." Kharl let the words hang.

"Ser?"

"Tell Werwal what I said, then. Let him decide."

"Yes, ser." The woman backed away.

At that moment, Fasyn hurried up. "Lord Justicer Reynol would appreciate it if you would do him the honor of seeing him in his chamber, Lord Kharl."

"I would be happy to see the lord justicer."

Kharl followed the chief clerk through the side entrance behind the dais, and to a chamber not all that much larger than that of the chief clerk's. Unlike Fasyn's chamber, Reynol's did have a window that looked out on the courtyard.

"Lord Kharl, ser." Fasyn bowed, then stepped back and closed the door, leaving the two men alone together.

"Lord Justicer." Kharl bowed his head briefly, then looked directly at Reynol.

"I have the sense that we may have met before, Lord Kharl, although I cannot recall where." Reynol's smile was brittle.

Kharl could sense that the justicer was being truthful. He did feel that he had seen Kharl before, but he did not recognize the former cooper. For now, that was just as well. "It could be, Lord Justicer, that I have watched in the Hall so often in recent eightdays that you feel that you should know me."

"That might be." Reynol took a long pause before continuing. "Might I ask why you chose to defend the renderer?"

"I cannot say, your lordship." That was true. Kharl could not say, not yet at least. "He looked honest. I might have been mistaken, though. That would not have been the first time I have been deceived."

"I do not think you are often deceived, Lord Kharl. Still . . . you are fortunate you are an envoy. The captain is not pleased."

"I would hope justice would always be served."

"We all hope that, even the heirs of Lord West, but justice is a tool, and it can be turned many ways."

"Heirs of Lord West? Is the captain . . . ?"

"His youngest."

Kharl forced an ironic laugh. "I *am* glad I am an envoy. I will have to tender my apologies. I had not thought . . ."

"Having arrived so recently, it is not something that would have come to your attention."

Kharl understood the reproof. "It should have come to my attention, and I will discuss this at some length with my secretary." Again, he was being truthful, but the discussion would not go the way Kharl implied.

"It is not all that great a problem," Reynol lied. "Captain Egen will understand that there are often . . . unforeseen circumstances in life."

"I would rather not have contributed to that . . . understanding."

This time Reynol laughed. "I understand that." He paused. "I have read your letter of recommendation from Lord Justicer Priost of Austra. Seldom does one get that fine a recommendation, and particularly for a lord who does not practice often as an advocate. Might I ask your scholarly interest?"

"I would have to say that my interest is more practical," Kharl said, drawing on what Hagen had stated. "I am the envoy to the West Quadrant. I need to understand Brysta to be a good envoy. Studying the way laws have been made and how they are carried out and judged helps in understanding."

Reynol tilted his head slightly, as if pondering what Kharl had said. He waited several moments before replying. "I do not recall any envoy before being so assiduous. I also note that your choice of garb is almost . . . magely."

"I have been told I have some small abilities in that area, Lord Justicer. I do have some ability to know when people are not telling the truth. I do not believe that this should be any bar to representing an accused. I doubt that anything I can do is of the scope of the great mages of Recluce or of the past."

Reynol nodded, then laughed softly. "You are a dangerous man, Lord Kharl."

"I am?" Kharl replied, almost without thinking.

"A scholar of the law, a talented, if unpracticed advocate, a man who is physically imposing, and who can tell when others are not telling the truth—those are traits that make a good envoy, but a dangerous opponent. It is a good thing that you represent a ruler who has no designs on Nordla."

"I can assure you that Lord Ghrant does not," Kharl said. "He wishes nothing more than for the Quadrants of Nordla to remain as they have always been. He was most clear about that."

"Were that all rulers were so impartial." Reynol offered another smile. "Do you intend to make a practice of appearing in the Hall?"

"No, your lordship. I fear that I may already have appeared more than is wise. If you encounter the captain, you might convey that to him as well."

"I will indeed."

"Thank you."

"Good day, Lord Kharl. It may be that your appearance was indeed for the best." Reynol nodded.

"Good day," Kharl replied, before turning and letting himself out of the chamber. He had not liked the thought that his appearance was for the best, because Reynol had been truthful, and anything that the lord justicer thought was for the best was not likely to be good for Kharl—or for Brysta.

Kharl followed Fasyn, who had been waiting in the corridor outside, back to the front foyer, where the undercaptain waited. Neither said a word until they were in the carriage. The rain continued, steadily falling, neither heavier nor lighter than earlier in the day.

"What happened, ser?" Demyst's voice carried concern.

"I represented the renderer. Captain Egen was not exactly happy. Did you see where he went?"

"He looked less than pleased, but he rode off up the hill."

"The renderer may show up at the residence. We might as well use him, if he does. He has some ability with a staff. Enough to take out three of Egen's patrollers."

Kharl glanced out the carriage window, toward the harbor. One of the Sarronnese warships was swinging clear of the pier, and the other looked to be ready to follow the first.

If matters in Brysta simmered on, and no conflict appeared in the next few days, Kharl would have to have Erdyl write a letter begging Egen's indulgence, but he could do that. He'd also have to tell Fundal to expect Werwal.

Kharl smiled. At the least, if Werwal could fight off Egen's patrollers, he wouldn't make a bad guard until Kharl could make arrangements to have the renderer and his consort leave Brysta.

LXXVII

Belatedly, Kharl had ordered Mantar to drive up Lord's Road from the Hall of Justice. Even from just outside the Quadrancy Keep, Kharl had not been able to sense the kind of chaos that surrounded a white wizard. Nor had there been any chaos near the Hamorian residence. In fact, the Hamorian envoy's residence had felt deserted. Kharl had not liked that at all.

After checking the Hamorian residence with his order-senses, Kharl had Mantar swing back by the harbor. Both Sarronnese warships were well beyond the breakwaters, and a single iron-hulled warship was making its way past the harbor forts—a Hamorian ship. Despite the muting effects of the water and the iron, Kharl could sense that there were several white wizards on board.

"Ser?"

"More white wizards on that ship."

"With them and the rain, won't be long before things get tight," suggested the undercaptain. "You thinking we should move out?"

"That would be a good idea, if we had anyplace to go." Also, even using the wagon and the carriage, Kharl doubted that they had mounts and space enough to take everyone housed at the residence. Given Egen's vindictiveness, Kharl had no doubts that anyone remaining would be in great danger, and the captain could always claim that none of them were protected by being part of the envoy's staff because they were all from Brysta.

"Sure would like some more armsmen."

"That would help," Kharl agreed, not voicing his thoughts that even a full company of armsmen and lancers would not make that much difference.

The streets were not quite so busy as usual on a fourday, but they were far from deserted. Kharl found the situation almost like a dream—or a nightmare. Egen had a private army ready to take over the city. The rain would keep falling, and make it hard for anyone else to contest Egen's control, and the Hamorians now had at least four white wizards supporting them. Kharl also suspected that the white wizard who had been in the Quadrancy Keep might well have left to join Egen—or the Hamorians.

Yet, with all that, nothing in Brysta looked amiss.

"We'll have to mount some sort of guard," Kharl said.

"Yes, ser." After a moment, the undercaptain added, "Sure would like a good squad of lancers."

"That would help," Kharl said. *So would being in a position to strike at Egen.* One of Kharl's problems was that neither Ostcrag nor Osten seemed to understand, or want to acknowledge the depth of Egen's treachery. Every other envoy seemed to see it. Then, reflected Kharl, perhaps Ostcrag and Osten did as well, but had their own plans. Or found themselves unable to act because they had discovered too late that they had been outmaneuvered.

What made it worse for Kharl was that he didn't care for any of them. It was just that the idea of Hamorian control of Nordla was even less appealing.

He took a deep slow breath.

"Piss poor situation, ser," offered Demyst.

"It is." It was even worse than that. If he could find Egen at the moment, killing him might well help Kharl and those with him. It would not help Ghrant and Hagen, because they would be seen as wanting to meddle in other land's affairs. That would not help Kharl over the long term. And that was if Kharl could even find Egen and kill him against the opposition of the Hamorian white wizards. Then, he might not have to find Egen. Egen might well soon be after him—and everyone close to Kharl.

Kharl looked out the coach window. Once more, everything that he tried to do to help those he cared for seemed to turn back against him. Yet, if he had not stood up for Werwal . . . who would have?

Kharl just hoped Werwal listened to his consort and hurried to the residence.

LXXVIII

In the late-evening air, misty and damp, Kharl stood in the darkness on the front portico of the envoy's residence. He could barely see Sestalt, stationed by Demyst on the corner of the portico overlooking the brick drive and the now-closed gate, but the newly retained guard's presence was more than clear to Kharl's order-sense.

In the end, after talking matters over with Demyst, Erdyl, and Jeka, Kharl had decided to remain at the residence for a time. While staying was far from good, in the rain and without the support of armsmen or lancers, until he had a better idea of what was going to happen, trying to leave could well place them in a worse position, at least. He was definitely missing such necessities for the road as scouts and supplies. For the moment, at least, he was also in city that he knew.

The rain had subsided into a foggy mist a glass or so past sunset, but the clouds above remained, and the next few days would likely bring more rain.

There were two concentrations of chaos. One was centered near the harbor, probably at the newer barracks at the old slateyard or at the Hamorian warship. The other was somewhere to the south, near the new south patroller barracks. There was another fainter hint of chaos even farther south, but that might have been seemed fainter because it was at the quarries and more distant, although Kharl was guessing about that. The nearer chaos to the south was moving slowly toward Kharl.

The rain would not help the white wizards, but Egen also faced a tradeoff. He needed the rain to slow any reinforcements to his sire and brothers, although, from what Kharl had heard, it was likely that Vielam was also backing Egen. For the moment, Kharl could not tell exactly how far away the chaos might be, except that it had to be several kays away.

"What you doing?"

Kharl jumped slightly. He'd been so intent on tracking the chaos that he'd not paid any attention to his immediate surroundings, and Jeka had seemed to appear from nowhere. "There's a white wizard heading in our direction, maybe more than one. I was trying to find out how far away he was."

"Why'd you come back? Really?"

"I had to."

"Don't tell me it was for me."

"I can't lie about that." Kharl paused. "I was worried about you and Warrl. For different reasons." His laugh was soft and bitter. "I really thought Warrl would be mostly safe. I wasn't sure about you."

"I was safe."

"I didn't know that. I was wrong about both of you. You were safe, and he wasn't." Kharl looked out into the darkness, all too aware of Jeka's warmth and presence.

"Don't know what to make of it, do you?"

Kharl understood. He also understood that he didn't have a good answer.

After a silence, Jeka said, "Can't sleep. Mind if I stay here?"

"I'd like that," Kharl admitted.

Neither spoke for a time.

Kharl continued to track the white wizards. The one from the harbor area was clearly headed up in the direction of the Quadrancy Keep, while the one from the south was nearing the residence, and was less than a kay away. With him were at least two squads of lancers.

"Jeka, would you go find the undercaptain, and tell him that there are lancers headed our way?"

"I'll find him." She turned, then stopped. "You can tell that?"

"Yes."

Kharl kept tracking the wizards, but, in the few moments that passed before Demyst hurried across the front portico to where Kharl stood, the lancers and the accompanying wizard had not moved that much closer. "Ser? How long before they get here?"

"Somewhere between a quarter glass and half a glass." Kharl looked through the darkness at Jeka. "Would you wake the retainers, Fundal and all the others, and have them go down to the cellar in the main residence?"

"Not staying there."

"You don't have to. I'll need you for messages."

Jeka was off.

"Mind of her own, that one," Demyst said quietly. "Beauty, too, if you look close. She hides it."

Kharl was all too aware of both.

"How do you want to handle this, ser?"

"They've got two squads or so. I don't think they know who I am. You know what I mean?"

In the darkness, Demyst nodded, then replied belatedly. "They think you're Lyras, maybe?"

"Something like that. We've got a couple of crossbows, don't we?"

"Three."

"Why don't we just wait, and let them get close. I'll just keep behind the stone pillars there at the corner. If our men can use the third-floor front windows, that might give them an angle."

"You don't want to be inside?"

"I can't do what I need to do if I am." That was always the problem for Kharl. While he had means of releasing great force or redirecting the chaos of a white wizard, he had to be fairly close to do so.

"I worry . . . someday, ser . . ."

"So do I," replied Kharl.

"I'd best be getting them positioned." Demyst slipped away into the darkness.

The force approaching the residence through the darkness was less than half a kay downhill, when Jeka reappeared. "Got everyone down in the cellar. Wanted to know why. Told 'em that Egen sent a white wizard. Better stay down there 'less they want to get burned. That right?"

"That's right."

"Undercaptain's got Cevor, Alynar, and Erdyl up top with crossbows. Erdyl said he was a good shot."

"Probably is." Kharl felt a slight twinge of something. Jealousy? He was too old to be jealous, and in too much trouble to worry about it. "He doesn't boast."

"You don't, either."

"I try not to."

The street and the other dwellings seemed suddenly silent, hushed as if the very structures knew that danger neared.

Kharl thought he heard hoofs on brick, but that might have been his imagination.

He kept waiting until he was certain that the muffled *clop-clop-clop* was indeed nearing and not something he just thought he heard.

"They're almost here. Keep down!" he hissed at Jeka.

"I'm down." She was crouched beneath the low stone half wall that formed the outside edge of the portico around the residence.

As the lancers drew up in the street below the residence, Kharl wondered why they were waiting—and for what. He could sense but a single white wizard, and an effort to collect free chaos.

Four lancers rode toward the gate. Between them they carried some sort of ram-sling that swung into the gate. *Thud!*

The four backed off, then rode forward again.

With a second *thud*, the gate, more decorative iron than barrier, broke open, and the four lancers turned their mounts.

As the remainder of the lancers shifted formation in some fashion, Kharl forced himself to remain behind the shelter of the stone. Then something flew past him, and the window behind him and to his left shattered, spraying glass into the residence. Flame flared up. The crossbow bolt had carried chaos.

What could Kharl do? For a moment, he just stared. Then he reached out with his order-senses, and hardened the very air around the chaos-flame, clamping a small order shield around it. The flame died. After a moment, he released both barriers, but the flame did not rekindle.

He could sense another flare of chaos headed toward the residence, and he threw up an order shield. Chaos flared against the shield, lighting the night like a lightning flash that vanished. In that moment, Kharl peered out.

Crack!

He jerked his head back. The lancers had rifles, and they were using them.

Crack! Crack! . . .

Another chaos-filled bolt smashed through a window to Kharl's left. This time, he managed to smother it immediately with order and hardened air.

The reports of the rifles came more quickly, and Kharl could feel the bullets flying toward the residence and past him.

What could he do about so many rifles? He hadn't faced those before, not in such numbers. He tried to think. Rifles meant powder, even if kept within soft iron.

He extended his order-senses, but all but two or three lancers were beyond his reach for what he needed to do, and sweat was already streaming down his face.

Those he could reach would have to do.

All he needed was just to unlink a small bit of the order in the iron . . . just a small bit. His entire body felt hot, as if he were about to catch fire. Then, the unseen, but strong links began to unravel, and Kharl flattened himself against the stone.

Whhhstt . . . CRUMPT!!!

The entire residence shook. Flames shot up from the front rank of the lancers, and parts of the trees overhanging the street began to smolder.

A wave of death surged over Kharl.

The lancers were dead, and so were their mounts, so quickly that there were no screams—just ashes and several charred figures of men and horses, those farther away from the point where Kharl had unbound order and released pure deadly chaos.

For all that, Kharl could sense the shields of the white wizard, just beyond his reach. Raising his own shields, he eased sideways across the portico.

"No . . ." whispered Jeka.

Kharl kept moving, taking the steps down to the drive.

Whhhstt! A firebolt arced toward him, splashed across his shield.

So much sweat was streaming down his face that his eyes stung, and he could barely see. He had to get to this white wizard before the man tried to flee. Kharl didn't want the other white wizards to know any more than they might gather from a distance about him, and he certainly didn't want to deal with three or four at once. That could happen if this one escaped. Kharl had barely managed two at a time before, and that had been chancy, even with lancers supporting him.

Two firebolts flashed at Kharl, one right after the other. Both sheeted around him. Kharl felt as though he were standing in the middle of one of his coopering fire pots, but he kept walking toward the attacking wizard.

The white wizard was still mounted. Even from fifty cubits away, Kharl could see that he was young. He didn't look that much older than Erdyl. A look of surprise had appeared on his face as he saw Kharl walking through the gate that the lancers had battered open.

Whhstt! Another firebolt flared toward Kharl, spraying around him as he walked forward, readying his own attack.

With the next firebolt, Kharl created the shield that deflected the chaos back at the young wizard, then struck by hardening the air around the man.

The wizard froze in the saddle, then slowly toppled sideways. A flicker of chaos whispered toward Kharl, then died as the younger man struck the bricks of the street. Kharl still had to hold the hardened air shield for a time before the other man died.

He took a deep breath. He still knew of no way to capture chaos-wizards—not that would keep them from escaping. From what he knew, he wasn't sure that there was a way. Or maybe he just didn't know enough.

When he released the shield, the figure of the wizard, young as he had looked, shimmered, and disintegrated into dust.

Kharl turned and trudged back to the residence.

Demyst and Jeka were waiting on the portico—both shielded by stone pillars.

"Ser?" asked Demyst.

"They're dead. All of them." Kharl sank onto the half wall, half-sitting, half-leaning. White points of light flickered in and out of his vision. "Need to eat, drink. In case someone else comes." He straightened slowly, then walked into the residence.

He hadn't done that much heavy magery recently, and it showed. He also hadn't eaten that much the night before, and that hadn't helped, either. So many things to think about.

Demyst headed up to the third level. Kharl knew someone up there had died, and he hoped that it hadn't been Erdyl. Then, he hadn't wanted anyone to die.

He settled into a chair in the breakfast nook.

Jeka reappeared with a wedge of cheese and some bread. "You want lager?"

"Please."

"The others can come up from below?"

Kharl nodded, then, realizing she might not see the movement in the darkened room, added, "Yes. Won't be anything happening for a while."

Kharl sat in the darkness, slowly chewing some bread. His mouth was so dry he was having trouble swallowing, and he was grateful when Jeka reappeared with a pitcher of lager. She found a beaker and filled it. He took a careful swallow, then sliced a piece of cheese off the wedge with his belt knife. He had trouble holding the knife, but managed.

As Kharl slipped the cheese into his mouth, Demyst entered the breakfast room, followed by Erdyl.

"They shot Cevor," the undercaptain said.

"I'm sorry. I felt it. I didn't know who, though."

"One man . . . against forty-odd of theirs and a white wizard—there was only one, wasn't there?"

"Just one." Kharl took another sip of lager. The worst of his weakness and light-headedness was beginning to subside. "Hate to lose even one of our own. The thing with the chaos-bolts and the windows. Hadn't seen that before."

"What?"

"The windows they broke . . ." Kharl went on to explain how the bolts had been infused with chaos to set the residence on fire. ". . . probably wanted the place ablaze so that they could pick off people trying to escape."

"Sounds like the Hamorians," said Demyst.

"More like Egen." Jeka's voice was hard.

"He wasn't with them, I don't think," Kharl said.

"'A course not. Let someone else do the dirt," Jeka replied.

That would only work for a while—at least Kharl hoped so. Eventually, he needed to face Egen, if only for his own sake.

After a time, Jeka, seated across from him, asked, "You . . . you coulda done this before?"

"No. I didn't know I could. The staff started it, but I never knew." Kharl smiled sadly. "A lot of lancers and armsmen died because it took me a while to learn what I know."

"More of 'em lived than would have otherwise," suggested the undercaptain.

In fact, he and Demyst were both correct, but it didn't make Kharl feel that much better about it.

LXXIX

By just after dawn, and only a few glasses of sleep, not only could Kharl still smell smoke, and the ashes of burned men and mounts—and foliage, but despite the clouds, he could also see a pall of thick gray smoke still rising from somewhere near the top of the hill. The only place it could have come from was from the Quadrancy Keep. Whether Osten or Ostcrag had survived was another question, but that speculation could wait. Regardless of that, Kharl needed to deal with Egen and the Hamorians, especially the Hamorians.

Alynar was standing watch out front, and one of Demyst's guards in the rear, as Erdyl, Demyst, Kharl, and Jeka ate hurriedly in the breakfast room.

"How many men do we have?" Kharl asked Demyst.

"We lost Cevor, and Sestalt's pretty bruised. Why?"

"We're going after Egen."

"Better 'n sitting here any longer."

"We couldn't start a war. Egen started it," Kharl said. "We can try to make it very short."

"Why didn't—" Erdyl broke off his words.

Kharl understood the unspoken remainder of the question, and he didn't have the best answers. He hadn't wanted to overreact to Egen's evil viciousness. He hadn't really understood what being an envoy was all about. He'd worried about setting up a situation where all the rulers of the Quadrancy and Candar would back Hamor in invading Austra—because Austra, in the person of Kharl, had tried to upset the established order in Nordla. Worst of all, while he had understood how evil Egen truly was,

Kharl hadn't realized the true depth of Egen's ambition until the last few days.

"Because," was all he said.

"Lord Kharl's been here less than three eightdays," Demyst pointed out. "Not very long to learn what's happening and do something about it. Especially when we got no lancers or armsmen, and Egen's got wizards and his own private army."

"Envoys aren't supposed to bring private armies," Kharl said dryly. "We're just supposed to watch and report." Had it been less than three eightdays? He felt as though he'd been back in Nordla forever. He forced himself to eat another helping of egg toast, followed by a healthy swallow of the too-tart early cider.

"Where are we headed, ser, if I might ask?"

"To the south barracks, the ones out by the new road, just south of the city." Kharl had already used his order-senses to determine that there were no chaos-wizards remaining at the new harbor barracks, or anywhere around the harbor, and the chaos that surrounded them appeared to have come from the south. He was guessing, but he didn't think the white wizards who had been at the quarry fort had joined Egen's patrollers. He didn't know about the wizard who'd been in the Quadrancy Keep before, either, except that he wasn't there any longer.

Demyst frowned.

"He'll be there. Or his patrollers will be. That's where his golds are. If he's not there, he'll be at the fort off the east road."

"Why there?" asked Erdyl.

"That's where they can block any lancers from the north and east who might support Ostcrag and Osten."

"Do we know if they're still alive?"

"I'd guess that at least one of them is. If they were both dead, Egen and the white wizards would already be holding the Quadrancy Keep."

"What about the other son—Vielam?"

"I don't know. He favors Egen, I've heard. Doesn't matter, though. Either Ostcrag survived the attack on the Quadrancy Keep, or one of the older sons did. Otherwise, Brysta would be crawling with patrollers and white wizards."

Jeka grimaced, but said nothing.

Kharl rose. "We'd better get ready." He turned to Khelaya, standing in the archway to the kitchen. "We'll need some provisions, and I'll need a hefty bag, and my water bottles filled with cider."

A quizzical look momentarily crossed the older cook's face.

Demyst raised his eyebrows in a different inquiry.

"It's not much of a secret now," Kharl said. "I'm an order-mage. I can't keep using magery without eating a lot."

"After last night, it had to be something like sorcery," Khelaya said. "Never seen anything like that."

Behind Khelaya stood Enelya, and the serving girl's mouth opened. She shut it quickly, and her eyes went to Jeka, who gave the slightest of headshakes.

"We'll make sure you have enough," added the cook.

"Thank you." Kharl hurried up to his chamber, where he donned a black riding jacket and quickly washed, before heading down and out to the stables. As he crossed the stretch of gardens, he glanced up. The clouds had lifted some, but had also darkened slightly, suggesting more rain later.

Mantar had the chestnut gelding saddled and waiting for Kharl. Demyst and Alynar were packing provisions into their saddlebags. Erdyl had already mounted, as had Sestalt, bruised as he was. Enelya stood to the side, holding several more bags.

Kharl looked to the serving girl.

"Jeka already packed yours, ser," Enelya said quickly, not meeting Kharl's eyes.

Kharl followed her glance to the side of the stable yard. Jeka was already mounted. She wore a gray jacket, and she'd cut her hair boy-short once more. Before Kharl could say a word, she spoke. "I'm going. I can run messages. Do stuff."

Kharl didn't say anything. He just stood there for a long moment. He didn't want Jeka anywhere near the fighting.

"Don't leave people," she added. "Told you that once."

She had. More than once. And Kharl had let Merayni take Warrl away for his son's safety. Warrl and Merayni were dead. Who could protect Jeka at the residence if Egen sent men after her? He didn't like the idea of her coming with them . . . but . . . with all the chaos and Egen's viciousness, she well might be safer with him.

Finally, he took a deep breath and nodded slowly. "Stay out of the direct fighting. Thank you for taking care of the provisions."

"Yes, ser. You got two bottles, both filled with the cider. I got three bottles, case anyone needs some."

"Good." Before mounting, Kharl used his order-senses to make sure that the saddlebags were indeed filled, but did not touch them, not wishing to suggest that he doubted Enelya or Jeka.

As was all too often the case, he was the last mounted. He looked to Khelaya and Mantar. "Take care."

"That we will, ser."

Kharl eased the gelding forward and past the side of the residence. As he rode past the sagging gates, he studied the street. The on-and-off rain of the night and early morning had dampened the ashes into a black-and-gray paste that mottled the ancient yellow bricks, but the few charred lumps that had been the men and mounts not totally turned to ash by Kharl's magery had disappeared. Marks in the sodden ash indicated that a wagon had been used. Kharl suspected that Mantar and the gardener had taken care of that. He could worry about that later. He looked back at the residence. He still worried about those remaining in the residence, but Mantar insisted that they'd be safe, and that they could retreat to the cellar if need be.

"Don't wait," Kharl had said.

"No, ser, but there's just ash out there now," Mantar had explained with a smile. "A bit more rain, and no one'll see anything except some blackened trees, and that happens when lightning strikes."

Thinking about it, Kharl wasn't so sure that the groom-driver wasn't better prepared than Kharl was. Once well into the street, the envoy-mage turned the gelding downhill, then, at the next street, southward.

Demyst moved up alongside Kharl. "City's quiet this morning. Can't say I'd expect otherwise."

"Everyone's hiding and waiting."

"What'll we be facing?"

"Several companies of lancers, and two or three white wizards. Maybe more of either."

"We have to do this?"

"We don't, and our children will be fighting Hamor in Austra." After he'd spoken, Kharl realized that he didn't have children, not any longer, and Demyst had never had any. "Or all those who do have children will."

"Sad choice, ser."

"Most are," replied Kharl dryly.

As he rode, his eyes and senses alert, Kharl felt—more than once—the brush of chaos that meant a white wizard was trying to keep track of him. From what he could tell, all the white wizards around Brysta were in the same place to the south—unless one was using chaos-skills to hide himself.

He wanted to look back and see how Jeka was doing, but decided against it although he wasn't certain he liked that she was riding with Erdyl. Then, he had his doubts about her coming, except that her staying behind might be even worse.

Ahead, near where the side street joined the south road, a young man looked at the riders, then sprinted across the bricks and into a single-story dwelling, whose shutters were closed. For just a moment, the echo of the slammed door drowned out the *clopping* of hoofs.

As they neared the southeast side of Brysta, the bricks of the south street gave way to the packed clay. Each step of the gelding threw up some mud. Because few had traveled the road since the rains had begun the day before, only parts of the road were muddy, and there were but a handful of deep wagon ruts.

On the less-traveled and unpaved section of the south road beyond the city, a company of lancers would churn up the road enough to stop any wagon, and after the first two or three companies traveled it, the later riders would have great difficulty traveling with any speed, and the lower-lying sections would become, if not impassable, places where men and mounts bunched into groups making their way through slowly.

"Road's going to be slow from here on," observed Demyst.

"It's only a kay or so." Kharl studied the small plots that were neither true holdings nor just gardens that now bordered the road.

To the east of the winding road, the low hills were covered with rocky meadows, and dotted with woodlots and odd-shaped fields. Farther ahead, the road turned due south to skirt the long ridge that overlooked the new patroller barracks and camp.

Kharl held up his hand and reined up. Somewhere ahead, coming up the back side of the hill just ahead, were lancers, more than a few, but not an entire company. "Close in! Right behind me!"

Before he finished his orders, the half squad of Hamorian lancers reined up on the low rise of a field to the east of the road and less than a quarter kay south of where Kharl had halted. As he watched, they drew weapons, blades he thought, until they raised them to their shoulders. More rifles.

Kharl hardened a space of air just in front of him.

Crack! Crack! . . .

The reports of the rifles sounded muffled. Abruptly, Kharl could feel the force of bullets on the air shield, leaching away some of his strength, if only a slight bit.

As quickly as they had come, the lancers wheeled, then rode back over the rise.

Kharl released the shield. He reached for his water bottle and took it out, taking a long swallow of the still-cool cider before corking it and replacing it in its holder.

"Why'd they do that?" asked Demyst.

"To tire me out," Kharl replied.

He sat in the saddle, thinking. The rifles changed everything, at least in the open field. Facing sabres or even crossbows, he could get close enough to use his order-magery—or his disorder-magery. With the white wizards tracking him with their sorcery, he couldn't use a sight shield to get closer without the lancers seeing him—and they could keep firing at him until he was exhausted before he could ever get close enough—on the road or open ground.

He glanced toward the ridge ahead and took in the woodlots. From what he recalled, there was a narrow road through the ridge from the east. The ridge was steep enough that the lancers and patrollers couldn't fire directly at him and his small party without getting close—very close.

"Ser?" asked the undercaptain.

"We'll have to leave the road. We're headed up toward that ridge, using the hills and woodlots for cover." Kharl turned the gelding off the road and through a gap in the low stone wall that bordered the meadow.

He kept his order-senses looking for lancers, or patrollers, but could not sense any as they rode up the sloping meadow almost directly east. A slight gust of wind swept across them, bringing a few scattered drops of rain, then died away, as did the rain droplets.

As they reached the first woodlot, Kharl could sense no one near the trees, but to the south, another squad of lancers—or the same squad—was using the lower ground between the hill and the ridge as an approach to the road—to try another attack. Kharl smiled, because by the time the lancers reached a point overlooking the road, their quarry would be to the east and south of them, and the lancers would have to ride uphill to catch Kharl.

Still, he didn't like the fact there were lancers between him and the ridge.

The woodlot ended just short of the flat hillcrest, and Kharl reined up while still in the trees, looking southward.

"We could follow these hills. There's that other road," Demyst said, pointing to the brown track a good kay to the south. "Cross the road and follow those hills on the south till we get to the gap in the ridge."

Kharl nodded. At least until they reached the road, they would either be in the trees or close enough to cover, and mostly on higher ground than any attacker. He had to remember that his goal was not necessarily to kill lancers, or patrollers, but to get close enough to kill Egen and the white wizards.

They covered another half kay to the south before a company of mounted patrollers rode eastward on the narrow road through the ridge gap. Behind them were what looked to be several oblong, canvas-covered carts.

Kharl looked farther south. The next hill had an escarpment of gray stone that faced south and slightly west, and looked to afford some protection, at least for men on foot, and they could tie the mounts farther back in the woodlot.

"Can we make it to that next hill there, you think?" Kharl asked the undercaptain.

"Easy, ser. Won't even take more than a fast walk. That grass down there is long, and the ground's soft. Harder here near the crest. You thinking about that rock there." Demyst grinned.

"I was. Is there something wrong with it?"

"Not so long as we don't let 'em circle to the southeast and come up through the woodlot. Could trap us then."

"We could have Jeka watch back there."

"Might be a good idea."

Kharl urged the gelding forward.

Demyst was right. Kharl and the five other riders reined up just above the jagged upthrust gray rocks before the patrollers had stopped riding the road. There were far more than Kharl had realized—a good three companies. The mage turned in the saddle. "Jeka?"

The former urchin and weaver rode slowly toward Kharl, then reined up. Kharl thought that she was far more graceful on horseback than he was, even though she'd only ridden twice in her life.

"You want something, ser?"

"You said you wanted to be helpful. We need some help." Kharl pointed to the southeast. "We're going to see if they attack us here. We don't want someone sneaking up the back side of the hill on us. Can you ride over to the edge of the woodlot there, on the higher ground, and keep watch. If they start something like that, ride back, but don't come out of the woods. Just call out and let us know."

"I can do that."

"Thank you."

"You want me to go now?"

"Be best if she does, ser," suggested Demyst.

"If you would," Kharl said to Jeka.

She turned the horse and rode steadily up the gentle slope until she was riding beside the trees.

After watching her for a long moment, Kharl turned his mount uphill toward the nearest part of the woodlot. By the time he had had tethered his mount well back in the woodlot, remembering to pull out his provisions bag, all three companies of mounted patrollers were drawn up on the flat to the north of the narrow road. Kharl hurried back downhill and into a position behind the rocks. Behind the patrollers, surrounded by two squads of lancers in the tan uniforms of Hamor, were the white wizards—three from what Kharl could tell.

"Like as they were waiting for us," muttered Alynar from the rear.

Kharl had no doubts that they had been, not after having felt one of the wizards tracking them. He still didn't understand why the patrollers and wizards were going to attack him. "If they waited," he murmured, "we'd have to come to them."

"Ser," said Demyst, with a crooked smile, "they don't know that. Best we don't tell them."

Still, Kharl wondered as he peered out through a gap in the gray rock. He would have liked to have gotten closer to the barracks as well. Something was happening behind the patrollers, with the carts, but Kharl couldn't see exactly what it was. The mounted patrollers, their lines dressed, moved forward slowly across the flat, but less than a third of a kay before halting once more. That left them at the base of the slope, a quarter kay downhill from Kharl and his small party. Kharl could see that these patrollers also had rifles—every last patroller.

Thwump! Soil and rock and mangled vegetation exploded from the ground less than a hundred cubits below and to the right of Kharl.

"Cannon," murmured Demyst. "Friggin' cannon."

What could Kharl do about cannon? If they tried to reach their mounts . . . at least some of them, if not all of them, might get shot . . . or run down. And Kharl couldn't do magery on the run, either.

Thwump!

The second blast was to the left, but more like seventy cubits away.

Kharl forced himself to concentrate on the cannon. While they were too far away for him to affect with his order-senses, he had felt the mixture of chaos and order that had accompanied the shell and the explosion. Was there any way to channel that? To turn it back?

He could sense the expansion of chaos and the near-instant flight of the next shell—and it landed less than fifty cubits directly in front of the rock outcropping. Soil and rock fragments sprayed above his head.

"Ser?"

"I'm working on it!" Kharl snapped. There had been a channel of order and chaos, the path that the shell had taken.

Kharl watched and waited, sensing the next shell.

The moment before it exploded, he focused all the energy, order and chaos, back along the flight path.

What seemed like a brownish red streak flashed back at the cannon, half-burying the weapon in rock and soil, and hurling the cannoneers aside. Kharl sensed at least one death, but focused his efforts on the second weapon.

This time, he not only returned the explosive force, but boosted it with a touch of released chaos—enough so that the second cannon, and the shells beside it, exploded in a gout of flame.

Cannoneers fled from the third and remaining cannon.

Kharl sat down, slightly light-headed. He took a swallow of the cider and tore at the bread. After several mouthfuls, he looked over at Demyst. "Tell me if, or when, they start to ride uphill."

"Yes, ser."

Kharl kept eating, biting a chunk out of the hard cheese, glad that there had only been three cannon, and that the cannoneers of the third had fled. The effort of handling just two shells had almost exhausted him.

"Those Hamorian lancers, the ones in tan," Demyst said, "they're riding across the flat up behind the patrollers."

Kharl could sense the growing mass of chaos on the flat below the slope. He took a last swallow of the cider and stood. Most of the light-headedness had subsided.

As he looked down through the rocks, he could see the patrollers beginning to spread out into a wider line, with more space beside each rider. None of them moved forward.

Kharl could sense three white wizards, but the three had linked somehow.

A single trumpet triplet sounded, and the patrollers started riding uphill. Their tactics were simple enough. Each patroller rode, then slowed and fired, then rode more quickly. The erratic nature of the advance would have made it difficult for anyone with a rifle or a crossbow to fire back effectively. But since Kharl and his small group had neither, the only effect was to make them to keep their heads down. And with fire coming from such a wide front, Kharl couldn't erect a hardened air shield that would be strong enough and broad enough to protect them—not without exhausting himself within a fraction of a glass.

Whhssttt! A chaos-bolt arced uphill, aimed directly at Kharl. Caught half–off guard, he could only deflect it, but he was ready for the second one, and using the linkage back to the white wizard, he turned it back.

Instead of slipping inside the white wizard's shields, it splashed across the linked shields of the three.

Kharl swallowed. He hadn't thought about that effect. The back-linkage didn't exist for the other two, and by linking their shields, they effectively blocked his technique.

Whhstt! Another firebolt flared uphill.

Knowing that the whites' shields would hold, Kharl just redirected the chaos across the first rank of the patrollers, who were within three hundred cubits of Kharl.

Death voids washed across Kharl, and he staggered. He'd never gotten used to dealing death, not really.

Whhhsttt!

Whhhstt!

The firebolts kept coming, one after the other. Kharl kept throwing them aside and across the ranks of the patrollers.

"That's the last of 'em, ser!" announced Demyst. "The patrollers, I mean."

Kharl was well aware of that. He was also aware that he was light-headed, and having trouble seeing.

The three white wizards and their Hamorian lancer guards had remained beyond his own effective range for unbinding order and releasing chaos—or for hardening air. If they kept flinging firebolts, sooner or later, they'd break through his defenses. Kharl couldn't think of what else he could do. He couldn't make his way downhill undetected.

He stopped. He didn't have to make his way downhill undetected. With the patrollers and the cannon gone, all he needed was to get closer to the white wizards.

After diverting another chaos-bolt, Kharl turned to his left and scuttled from point to point behind the rocks until he was at a gap that he could take straight downhill.

He almost stepped through the gap when he saw the squad of lancers flanking the white wizards, all three mounted. Wearily, Kharl called up a sight shield, and moved through the rocks and down onto the grass, trying to move in a zigzag fashion, and not trip because he could not see, except through his order-senses.

He could only hope that by the time the wizards explained to the lancers where he was and the lancers got out their rifles, he'd be close enough—

He stumbled and pitched forward, releasing the sight shield for a moment to right himself, and catch a glimpse of a flatter slope to his left.

Crack! Crack!

He thought he felt something fly by, and he staggered back to his right, heading downhill, covering yet another fifty or sixty cubits.

Whhsst!

He parried/deflected the firebolt, and kept moving.

Sweat was running into his eyes, and he was seeing flashes across the darkness through which he stumbled and shambled downhill. He could tell he was getting almost close enough.

"See that dust! Fire there, or charge him! Do something!"

Kharl half jumped, half flung himself sideways in his own private darkness, then charged downhill, reaching out toward one of the lancers closest to the wizard on the left.

The vibration in the ground told him he didn't have much time.

Desperately, he reached for a chunk of soft iron in the lancer's cartridge belt, using his senses to unlink it.

Eeeeeeee . . .

A terrible whining screeched at him, through him, as he fumbled at unlinking the iron in more cartridges . . . as many as he could.

Then chaos flared, and with his last strength, frantically, he tried to throw up his own shields.

Redness, whiteness . . .

. . . and hot blackness flashed over him, and swallowed everything.

LXXX

When Kharl woke, he was flat on the ground looking up. It was late afternoon. That he could tell from the light, despite the drizzle that sifted through the trees.

"Did yourself in, almost," Jeka said, sitting on the gnarled root of a tree, looking down at him.

"I . . . didn't have . . . much choice." His head was splitting, and flashes flared across his eyes. Slowly he sat up, looking around the clearing in the woods. His face was dry. He looked at Jeka, who had her jacket across her arm. Her blue shirt was damp across the shoulders.

She looked away for a moment, before she spoke. "Brought you up here out of sight. Not that there was anyone down there left to see anything."

"The whole flat is burned grass and ashes," said Erdyl. "I've . . . never seen anything like that."

"Hope you don't see it often," added Demyst.

Jeka extended an uncorked bottle to Kharl. "Better drink."

"Thank you." He took it and drank the cider, slowly.

"I don't think Egen was down there, ser," offered Erdyl.

"I don't think so either." Kharl lowered the bottle. "In a while, we'll move closer to the barracks, but I'd wager they're empty."

"They'd just leave?" asked Erdyl.

"Without any white wizards to back them up? I think so."

Demyst nodded.

"Then what?"

"We *sneak* north to the other fort. That's the one with the cannon that guards the main east road. If there are any cannon or powder left there, we destroy it."

"Just like that?" asked Jeka.

"Like this." Kharl gestured downhill, in what he hoped was the right direction. "Then we see what's left." He didn't like where matters were pointing him, but another effort like the last would get them all killed.

"What about the fort at the quarry? The one in the south?"

"That's where most of the regular armsmen who will probably support Egen are. That's where most of the white wizards are. I'd like to see if we can drag up some lancers to help before we take them on." Kharl didn't want to consider—not yet—dealing with the southern forces without some sort of support.

"You gonna throw in with Lord West?" asked Jeka.

"Osten, I hope," Kharl admitted. "He may not be any better than his sire, but he can't be any worse than Egen."

"Some choice," muttered Jeka.

"You have a better idea?" Kharl took another swallow of the cider. Jeka handed him some bread, and he began to eat. He mixed the bread with some of the hard cheese as well.

After a time, he looked up again. "We might have some influence on Osten—or even Ostcrag, especially if we get rid of Egen and the Hamorians. Egen doesn't listen to anyone. I don't think he ever has."

" 'Sides, pissprick doesn't deserve to live," Jeka pointed out, more practically.

Kharl had to agree with that.

LXXXI

Kharl's guess had been right. There was no one in the southern barracks. All the buildings were deserted—except for one elderly groom who could only say that everyone had left "soon after the big battle" and that they'd all headed south on orders from Overcaptain Vielam. While some gear had been left, there were no provisions, and no rifles or cartridges. There were bags of powder in an iron-lined, stone-walled magazine building well away from the others, but nothing besides cannon shells and powder.

The quick departure confirmed Kharl's secondhand impression of Vielam, both of his abilities and his courage, since Vielam couldn't have been in the force that faced Kharl. It might also reflect Vielam's intelligence in assessing the situation, Kharl reflected.

Kharl and the others settled back into their saddles and rode northward. Less than a kay from the deserted barracks area, they turned from the south road onto the ring road that led northward to the east road. Like the south road leading out of Brysta, it was packed clay, turned sloppy by the rain, but there were few tracks, and nothing to indicate that any large body of lancers had traveled in either direction, or that armsmen had marched the road recently. Hadn't Vielam sent any messengers northward? Was the eastern road camp or barracks even held by Egen's forces?

Kharl shrugged. In a sense, that didn't matter. If all of Egen's forces were already regrouping in the south, then finding Ostcrag or Osten might well be easier. If they weren't, Kharl needed to do something to neutralize the camp ahead.

As he rode along the ring road that he had once walked with Jeka, fleeing a white wizard before he'd even known he was a mage, that journey seemed ages ago, for all that it had been slightly less than a year before. So much had changed, and was still changing.

After a glass or so, he turned in the saddle and called to her. "It's faster riding."

"Sorer, too," she responded, with a faint smile.

Erdyl looked puzzled, and, after turning to watch the road ahead, Kharl extended his order-senses to hear what his secretary might ask.

". . . why did he say that?"

"Been this way before, time back. He can tell you," Jeka said pleasantly.

"How did you come to know him?"

"Better if he told you." Her voice remained pleasant.

Kharl couldn't help but smile at Jeka's responses.

Less than two glasses later, Kharl turned his mount off the ring road, a good kay before it intersected Angle Road, and followed a lane that looked to head east. After less than a kay on the lane, half a kay away to the north, across the hills, he could see the south side of Vetrad's sawmill and lumber barn.

Ahead, the green hills steepened into irregular and rocky shapes, and the lane turned sharply south. Kharl reined up, extending his order-senses once more, feeling for the camp and lancers that he knew could not be that far to the northeast of where he was. There was no concentration of chaos that would have marked a white wizard, but Kharl did gain a sense of the muted chaos that often marked large groups of people—almost due north. He studied the ground, mostly small meadows marked by stone walls and hedgerows, and infrequent cots and huts.

About two hundred cubits ahead on the left side of the lane, just before it turned, was a gap in the low, piled-stone wall, and a narrow track *seemed* to head north. They could try that, Kharl decided, and he urged the gelding forward.

The track was more like an animal trail, or a lane that had once seen more traffic and since been largely overgrown. There were no tracks in the damp clay, except for those of coneys and other small animal traces that Kharl did not recognize. He had to duck continually, or brush away branches that poked out from the two hedgerows that framed the track.

They had traveled less than half a kay when the track turned leftward, but more to the northwest, rather than straight west. Kharl could sense that they were still slightly to the east of the camp. He kept checking with his order-senses, since he could not actually see beyond the trees and bushes that had once been a better-kept hedgerow.

Another three hundred cubits or so later, they neared a gap in the vegetation on the right side. Kharl reined up and looked through, out onto what had once been a meadow, but now sported a forest of saplings that ranged from knee high to as high as his mount's ears. From what he could tell, the camp lay beyond the former meadow, even beyond the woods on the far side.

"This way."

As he rode slowly through the saplings, he wondered why the area had been deserted. Land was life to a holder, and Kharl couldn't imagine it being neglected without some reason. Had the holder let the lands lapse back to the local lord? Why? Or had the holders been removed by Ostcrag? Or Osten?

The light was beginning to fade by the time Kharl reined up on the far side of the narrow woods, at the edge of a short bluff that began within a half score of cubits from the end of the trees. Below the bluff was a gully cut by another stream flowing out of the hills. In the middle of the rise on the far side of the gully stood what he had sought.

The eastern camp was more like a fort than the barracks to the south of Brysta. Gray stone walls a good six cubits high surrounded the buildings and stables. There were gates to the south and west, but not to the east.

There the low hill had been cut away, and cannon mounted on the top of the wider walls faced the main road. The road was on the north side of the stream that had cut a narrow canyon through the higher hills to the east, giving the fort control of the road. Given the rocky and rugged nature of the hills—and the crumbliness of the rock—the fort clearly controlled the east road. The area around the fort had been cleared of brush, although the grasses looked to be almost knee high.

Even in the dimming light, the rising fog, and the growing mist, Kharl could tell that the walls were manned not by Nordlan armsmen from the West Quadrant, but by Egen's patrollers, and the gates were closed.

He eased his mount back into the trees, toward a small clearing they had passed less than fifty cubits back. There he dismounted, tied the gelding, and stretched. The others followed his example.

"What are you going to do?" asked Jeka.

"Eat and rest, and when it gets full dark, I'll slip under the walls on the east side and blow up the cannon," Kharl said. "Then come back here."

"Like before?"

"Mostly. Except I won't be facing white wizards. There aren't any near."

"Do you have to, ser?" asked Erdyl.

"No. I can wait until they leave and swell Egen's forces. Or I can wait until Egen shows up here with white wizards, then face them all alone. Or we can ride northeast to Hemmen and catch a ship back to Valmurl, where I'll tell Lord Ghrant that I failed and the West Quadrant will soon be a possession of Hamor."

Erdyl took half a step backward. "I'm sorry. It's just . . . you've done so much, and we haven't been that much help."

"And I look like second death, probably," Kharl added. After a moment, he laughed. "You know, when I found out I was a true lord, I asked Speltar, the steward at Cantyl, what that meant. You know what he told me?"

No one answered.

"He said it meant that, if I did something wrong, I had the privilege of being beheaded instead of being hanged."

Jeka and Demyst were the only ones who smiled. Erdyl just looked bewildered.

Kharl rummaged through his provisions sack. There was still some bread and cheese left, and he knew one bottle held cider. He could use all the sustenance he could get before he took on the fort on the other side of the gully.

After eating, Kharl propped himself against a tree and closed his eyes. He thought he might have dozed, but started into full awareness at the sound of a bell tolling.

"Watch bell," Demyst said. "First glass of the night watch."

Kharl rose, stiffly, and stretched. He couldn't help yawning. He stretched again, then looked through the darkness to the undercaptain. "Time to get moving."

He could feel Jeka's eyes on him, but she said nothing.

"I'll be back as soon as I can. If this works, you'll hear things long before I get back."

He moved slowly along the rough track the horses had made earlier, stopping at the edge of the woods—or former woodlot, he suspected—where he surveyed the open space beyond and the dark gray mass of stone. There was still no sign or sense of a white wizard.

Kharl couldn't say that he understood, but he wasn't going to question the absence of a chaos-wizard, not when he'd faced more of them than he'd expected all too many times.

He took a deep breath and moved toward the gully.

The low bluff was steeper than he'd recalled, and he ended up grabbing roots to slow his descent to the stream—less than two cubits wide, although full to its banks after the rain. He jumped across and promptly found his boots sinking into the spongy ground on the other side. The slope on the north side was more gradual, but longer, and he was breathing heavily when he reached the top. He stayed low, not wanting to be silhouetted against the lighter-colored soil on the south side of the bluff, as he began to cross the meadow toward the south wall of the fort.

He kept his order-senses extended but did not use a sight shield, although he was ready to raise it at any moment. He was tired enough that he wanted to avoid any unnecessary order-magery.

He tried to move quietly, but the swishing of the wet grass against his boots and trousers sounded to him like it carried for kays. He'd only covered a hundred cubits or so before his trousers were soaked below the knee, and water was seeping down into his boots. Step after careful step finally brought him to the south wall, about a third of the way toward the southeast corner.

He extended an order-probe toward the magazines beside the cannon, but they were too far—or rather, the combination of distance and cold iron defeated Kharl's efforts.

He flattened himself against the gray stone blocks and began to edge his way westward toward the southeast corner of the fort.

Above him, he heard a rustle; and he raised a sight shield and froze in place.

"Serjeant . . . serjeant . . ."

Under the sight shield, Kharl kept moving, if more slowly and deliberately. Behind and above him he heard boots on stone, then voices.

". . . thought I saw something down there . . . grasses moving . . ."

". . . ought to be able to see a man, Navoyt . . . might be a fox . . . Keep watching . . . don't want Osten's men slipping up on us . . ."

"Yes, ser."

The voices got fainter as Kharl reached the corner and began to ease his way down the section of the hill that had been cut away, a drop of another three cubits. Even for all that, he was getting closer to one of the magazines holding powder—or cammabark—and the locked chaos of the powder was definitely stronger to his order-senses.

At the base of the hill-wall, he edged northward, until he stood directly below one of the magazines. Slowly, Kharl extended the finest line of order, upward toward the magazine almost directly above him. Even so, it was an effort. Carefully, he began to unlink the order of a small section of iron on the inside of the magazine, directly beside bagged powder loads for the cannon.

At the moment the linkage began to spray apart of its own momentum, Kharl concentrated and surrounded himself with a shell of hardened air.

CURROMPTTT!!!

Despite the shield, Kharl's ears rang so badly that he could hear nothing. He felt, rather than heard, the successive explosions of the other magazines. For all his caution, he was thrown against the inside of his own air shield, then hurled back the other way, bouncing back and forth.

Stones and stone fragments crashed down against the shield.

Another wave of explosions followed the first, and yet another after that.

Reddish white waves of death cascaded across Kharl, and his guts tried to turn themselves inside out. He swallowed, convulsively.

Another round of explosions shivered the ground beneath his feet, and more stone hammered at the air shield.

More waves of death buried Kharl, each a knife of reddish white, yet a gaping emptiness as well.

The ground shifted, jerking Kharl against the air shield once more. He struggled to stand erect.

Kharl waited until he was sure that not only the explosions had stopped, but that no more rocks and fragments of the fort were falling. Then, he forced himself to expand the air shield slightly, just to make sure nothing was resting on top of it that would fall on him once he released the shield. Several more chunks of stone rumbled and rattled away.

When he finally released the shield, he was standing in a pit surrounded by stone piled somewhat above his head.

Almost a quarter glass passed before he had climbed out of the pit—most carefully—and started back toward Jeka and the others. He stumbled more than a few times, and half fell into the spongy ground on the north side of the stream, coming down on his knees. He struggled upright and jumped across the stream, then searched for a place where he could use roots to help him climb the bluff that had seemed so much shorter coming down.

Jeka and Demyst were waiting at the top of the bluff. They reached out and pulled him up.

"Thank you," he panted.

"Not much left," Demyst pointed.

Kharl looked back. Before, the fort had looked solid and gray. Now, sections glowed red, and even in the darkness, the trails of smoke that wound up toward the overhead clouds were easily visible. It looked like a vision from the time of the white demons.

Kharl turned away, almost stumbling again.

Jeka steadied him. "Now what?"

"We find a place to wait where we don't get too wet. There should be some cots or something near here," Kharl said tiredly. "When Lord West—or Osten—or whoever—discovers that the fort is gone, they'll ride down toward Brysta, or they'll send scouts."

"If they don't?" inquired Demyst.

"Then Egen will move his troops back up here to guard the gap to the east. That won't happen. Even Osten isn't stupid enough to stay blocked away to the east, not if he wants a chance at succeeding his father. He might not confront Egen, but if his lancers and armsmen are where they could attack, he'll be in a stronger position."

"Why haven't they fought over Brysta?" asked Jeka.

"Because Brysta is what brings golds into their coffers. They fight over the city itself, and everyone loses, no matter who wins." Kharl took a deep breath. Demons, he was tired. "If the fighting goes on, they might. I don't think so, because even the Hamorians wouldn't want Brysta that badly damaged."

He made his way toward the gelding, hoping he could mount. He really didn't want to remain too close to the burning ruins of the fort. He thought, tired as he was, that he could lead them back the way they had come, using his order-senses and night sight. He stifled a yawn. He hadn't been sleeping that well, and he needed sleep. He wasn't certain that he'd get that much, but anything would help—after they put some distance between them and the destruction he had created.

LXXXII

Kharl did not find a cot or a hut, but they did find a shed with a thatched roof that had once been used to store hay and shelter a flock. After pulling off his damp boots, Kharl had collapsed on a scattering of very dry hay. His dreamless sleep lasted but a short while before the nightmares began.

The first one was almost like the battle against the three white mages, except this time, he could not find a way to break their shields or to get close enough to them to unbind order and release chaos—because there were scores of cannon pounding at him.

Abruptly, he was running through the streets of Brysta, looking for Jeka, because she had slipped away while he was considering what sort of magery to use against the harbor forts that were still held by Egen's patrollers. After that, he fought against shadowy demons—both black and white. Sometime in the night, however, he dropped into a deeper and dreamless sleep. Or, at least, he didn't recall any other dreams.

Both Jeka and Demyst were looking at him when he finally struggled awake and sat up.

"Cloudy, but it's not raining now. Might not, either." Demyst paused, then added, "There's lancer scouts coming down that east road."

"You've been out scouting?"

"Took Sestalt with me, ser, but I thought it might be a good thing."

"It was. I'm sorry. I wasn't thinking all that well—" Kharl wrestled his all-too-stiff boots back on his feet, then stood.

"You've been doing enough for three men. Time for some of the rest of us to earn our keep." The undercaptain grinned.

"You'd mentioned that we needed to do something with Osten or Ostcrag . . ." ventured Erdyl.

"We do. We'll need lancers and some support to face Egen and the Hamorians. Whether it's Lord West or Osten, they need us, or they'll get burned into ashes. I'd like to meet Ostcrag or Osten, or both of them, on the flat before the ruins of the fort. If it will make them comfortable, they can bring some guards, but not many."

"Do you think they will?"

"After they look at the fort?" Kharl raised his eyebrows. "If they don't, then we'll have to wait until they get beaten, and hope that there are enough left for a second battle."

"If that happens—"

"We'll worry about that if they won't meet me."

"I don't know . . ." muttered the undercaptain. "Don't know as I like you just riding up there to them."

Kharl had thought about that, and he didn't like it, either, but he was the envoy.

"I'll do it," Erdyl said. "Besides Lord Kharl, I'm the only one any of Lord West's people might recognize. It'd be better if I went."

"Thank you," Kharl said, hoping that he wasn't sending his secretary out to his death, but knowing that Osten and Ostcrag were such traditional lords that for Kharl to ride up and announce himself would lessen his stature and increase their contempt for the envoy-mage—despite what he had already done. To overcome that would require more magery and force. He held in a sigh. Magery would probably still be required. "You'd best take both Sestalt and Alynar."

"I'll get ready." Erdyl started for the shed door, then paused and called back, "You ought to eat whatever you can, ser."

Kharl was already looking for what remained of his provisions. There was some bread, and a chunk of cheese. That was all.

The undercaptain had followed Erdyl, leaving Jeka and Kharl in the shed.

"Don't like sending him, do you?" asked Jeka.

"No," Kharl admitted, after chewing a mouthful of bread. "But he's right."

"You can't do everything."

While Kharl knew that, it had never been easy for him to let others do things for him, especially when he had been a cooper, perhaps because so seldom had they done them well, and he'd usually had to do them over again—or live with the consequences. But then, he reflected, as he felt the uneasiness within himself that suggested he was not being accurate, there were all too many times, especially in the last year, when he had not done so well, and it might have been better in some cases to listen to others.

"Can you?" pressed Jeka.

"No."

"Leastwise, you know that." She offered a smile.

Kharl just took it in.

Abruptly, Jeka rose. "Be back in a while."

Kharl finished his meager provisions, and waited. While Jeka drifted in and out, she never stayed long, and that worried Kharl.

Erdyl returned almost two glasses later.

Demyst and Jeka joined Kharl as Erdyl dismounted in front of the ramshackle shed.

"Lord Osten has agreed to meet with you in front of the fort in half a glass," were Erdyl's first words.

"He doesn't want you to try any trickery," suggested Demyst.

"How much trouble did you have?" asked Kharl.

"It took a while, and a lot of words," Erdyl admitted. "I just kept pointing to the fort and asking if they wanted the mage who did that on their side or against them. It helped that they finally brought Mihalen to see me. After that, it only took about half a glass."

Kharl shook his head. He wasn't certain he would have had Erdyl's patience. "It was a good thing you went. Thank you."

"Ah . . . yes, ser. He said that he'll have guards, and a crossbowman ready to cut you down if there's any trickery."

Kharl snorted. "If I wanted to do him in, I wouldn't be stupid enough to try it there." Osten's reaction didn't do much for Kharl's opinion of the rightful heir. "Did he mention Lord West, or Ostcrag, or say anything about what happened?"

"No, ser. I thought it was best I didn't press."

Erdyl was probably right about that as well. Kharl looked toward the gelding that Demyst or Sestalt had already saddled for him. "I'd better be going."

"Ah . . . and you're to ride ahead of your guards, ser."

"So that his bowman has a good shot, I'm sure."

"Can you—" began the undercaptain.

"I'll try, but I can't hold shields the whole time." Kharl climbed into the saddle. He still couldn't vault up the way Demyst and Erdyl, and even Alynar, could.

Demyst and Erdyl rode back along the lane, north on the ring road, then out Angle Road. While two companies of lancers were drawn up on the road to the northeast of the ruined and still-smoldering fort, the space before the fort where Kharl was to meet Osten was empty.

Kharl halted in the middle of the open space.

"He has to make you wait," Erdyl said quietly from where he had reined up behind Kharl. "To prove he's more important."

The more Kharl dealt with lords and rulers, the more he just wanted to return to Cantyl.

Almost a quarter of a glass passed before Osten, at the head of a squad of lancers, rode across the deep and damp grass toward Kharl.

He reined up.

Kharl eased the gelding forward, then also reined up a good ten cubits from Osten. "Lord Osten." He inclined his head.

"You asked to meet me, Lord Kharl." In the dark blue riding jacket, with silver piping, Osten looked more imperious than he had in the receiving hall of the Quadrancy Keep.

"I did. The night before last, your youngest brother's patrollers and a Hamorian white wizard attacked my residence in Brysta. We prevailed, but I discovered the next morning that he had also attacked the Keep. We were less than pleased that he appeared to be attempting to remove you and your sire. I attempted to track him through the white wizards."

"How fared that?"

Kharl shrugged. "We fought three white wizards and several companies of patrollers to the east of the barracks just south of Brysta. All were destroyed, but Overcaptain Vielam had not taken the field. After the battle he fled southward before we could reach him. I would wager that he has rejoined Captain Egen somewhere to the south, perhaps at the fort Captain Egen built along the south road."

Osten said nothing.

"Because we knew of *this* fort, I decided to attack it last night. I thought that would make it easier for you to bring your lancers to Brysta and south against your rebellious brothers—if that is your intent."

For the slightest moment, Osten's eye strayed to the smoldering pile of stone that had been a fort. "Could you not have spared the fort?"

"Magery does not work that way," Kharl replied.

"Why did you come to me?" Osten's tone was dismissive.

"When I presented my credentials," Kharl said, "I suggested that everything was not as it should be. You chose not to listen."

"You *knew* of my brother's treachery . . . and you let—" Osten's face darkened. "That is insufferable—"

"Osten . . . you chose not to listen." Kharl's patience was wearing thin. "Do you want my help or not? If I walk away, your brother and his Hamorian wizards will do even worse to you than I did to this fort."

"Why do you care?"

"I don't care about you very much. The alternatives are just worse. Your brother would be the most evil ruler the West Quadrant has ever had, and before a handful of years had passed, Hamor would rule both the West Quadrant and the South Quadrant. Austra does not want Hamor gaining a foothold so close."

"So you will help me, whether you like me or not?"

Kharl could see Osten beginning to scheme.

"No. If you don't promise to make the justicers more fair, and tariffs lower, and a few other things . . . I'll walk away and let all of you fight over it. Then, when you're dead, and your brother thinks he can take his pleasures, I'll have to destroy him and the Hamorians, and then I'll probably have to make someone like your justicers next Lord West." Kharl wasn't certain of any of that, but he was determined to try, and probably Reynol and Lurtedd wouldn't be much better, possibly even worse.

"You seek to bargain."

"No," said Kharl coldly.

Osten's sabre appeared from nowhere, and whistled toward Kharl.

Kharl raised the hardened air shield, and the sabre shattered against it.

Wincing, Osten dropped the useless hilt. "You . . . you mages . . ."

Kharl released the shield, but was ready to raise it instantly. "I am not bargaining. I am giving you terms. You don't keep them, and I can return to Brysta anytime and kill you. And I will. Do you understand?"

The lord-heir swallowed.

"I am not interested in being a ruler, but I want *you* to be a good ruler. The kind people respect and praise, not the kind that people fear and flee."

"You're weak, mage."

Kharl laughed. "Am I? Tell me that when you must have scores of guards. Tell me that when you need to have someone taste everything before you eat."

Osten's face darkened once more.

Alert to any movement, anyone nearing them, Kharl waited, saying nothing.

Finally, the young lord nodded. "I must accept your terms. Better you, insufferable as you are, than to lose all to Hamor."

Kharl waited once more.

"What do you want from me?"

"To accompany you when you ride south to confront your brother. Two squads of lancers who will keep stray patrollers from getting too close to me while I attack their mages."

Osten's brows wrinkled. "You could do that—"

"It's easier that way. Otherwise, I'd have to chase him. Also, he might avoid me and attack your lancers with his forces and the Hamorian wizards. They'd destroy you."

"They still might destroy you," Osten pointed out.

"They might. But you're no worse off that way." Kharl laughed ironically. Talking to Osten was more than a mere chore; it was painful. "He has at least three white wizards. You have none." Kharl paused, then asked, "What happened to the one you had in the Quadrancy Keep?"

Osten's face narrow face froze. For a moment, his black eyes hardened. "He was the one who betrayed us and killed my sire."

Kharl had suspected something like that, from the wizard's reactions when he had presented his credentials to Ostcrag, but there was little point in letting Osten know that. "You are the rightful successor to your sire."

"What is that to you, ser mage?"

"As a mage," Kharl shrugged, "not enough to risk my life. But as Lord Ghrant's envoy, and one who has seen what the white wizards will do to a land, it means a great deal to me. I would not see any land fall to Hamor—or to anyone who might be their tool."

"You think my brother is their tool?"

Kharl was ready for that question. "Don't actions speak louder than any flowery words? What do you think?"

"I think that I need you, whether I like you or not." Osten's laugh was hard.

"As I need you, Lord West," Kharl replied, "so that Hamor will be kept from both our shores. How long before all your forces are gathered?"

"Tomorrow, at the earliest."

"Where will you assemble them?"

Osten frowned, but replied, "At the Quadrancy Keep. There is no other place suitable. It once was just that, and it will suffice for now."

"Then I will send my secretary to yours early tomorrow, to learn when we should join you."

"Are you leaving Brysta?"

"No. We've destroyed two of Egen's forces, and one fort. I'm going to get a good meal and some rest." Kharl smiled politely.

"Till the morrow, ser mage."

As Kharl rode off the flat and eastward along Angle Road to rejoin the others, followed by Demyst and Erdyl, he kept his senses alert. He trusted Osten not at all. His problem was that Egen and the Hamorians were far worse.

LXXXIII

Brysta was quiet as Kharl and the others rode back to the residence. While there were some souls about the city, they were few, and they scurried away at the sound of riders and hoofs. For the moment, that was fine with Kharl.

The moment Kharl reined up before the stable, Mantar and Fundal appeared. They assured Kharl that no one had even neared the residence.

He had not stepped into the rear hallway when Khelaya confronted him and protested, almost as if she needed to complain, that she could have fixed a better meal than they would receive if Kharl had only sent word ahead.

"I couldn't, but it will be a good meal, and far better than anything we have eaten," he had replied. Then, of course, before the evening meal was even being prepared, he had to explain, briefly, but in more detail than he wished, all that had happened.

From that, Kharl escaped to his chambers, where he indulged himself with a bath, followed by a nap—one without nightmares.

Around the table that evening, everyone looked far cleaner and more rested than the night before, and there was little conversation for the first moments.

"You think we'll ride out tomorrow, ser?" Erdyl finally asked.

"No. Egen won't rush north. We may even have to ride to him. Osten will find that he lacks something. It will be the next day, perhaps even the day after."

"Is that wise?"

Kharl shrugged and looked to the undercaptain.

"There's a time for haste, and a time to wait, and times when it matters not," the undercaptain volunteered. "When Lord Kharl destroyed the fort, that was time for haste, because there were no white wizards to protect it. I can't see that haste matters that much now."

"Unless the Hamorian fleet shows up in the harbor," Kharl said dryly, "with more white wizards."

"I've been thinking; ser. Those patrollers had rifles—the ones in the south. They were shooting well, more like trained lancers. Have we ever seen patrollers with rifles anywhere?"

Kharl felt that he should have seen that. "You think that they off-loaded their troops somewhere, then left, and that the lancers were wearing patroller uniforms so that folks wouldn't think that Hamor was playing too big a part?"

Demyst, his mouth full of lace potatoes, nodded.

"You're right. He had more patrollers there than we ever saw on the streets, and they could use those rifles. They were trained, better than I've seen except with the Hamorian lancers," mused Kharl.

"That's because they were Hamorian lancers, I'd wager," said Demyst.

"It was all planned from the beginning, then," Erdyl said. "The cloth came from Hamor . . ."

All the pieces fit. Kharl just wished he'd seen them earlier. But it was another case where his lack of experience showed—all too clearly.

"If that's so," said the undercaptain slowly, "they can't land any more lancers soon."

"We don't know how many more white wizards there are," Kharl said. "There were three in the south before, and that doesn't count the one that killed Ostcrag. He's probably with Egen. I count four of them with the rebel forces." *At least.*

"Handled three of 'em yesterday," Jeka pointed out. "Didn't have any lancers with you, either."

"I've never faced four at once," Kharl said. "Two or three, and I almost didn't make it. We can't trust Osten much, either, especially if we win."

Erdyl frowned, momentarily, then nodded.

"Can't trust none of them," observed Jeka. "Never could."

"No. That's the problem."

"Not if you do away with them all."

"That's a bigger problem. There are no heirs, and there's no one else who's sufficiently well known to take over without blood in the streets. Who will take over the West Quadrant? Lord East? Lord North? The Emperor of Hamor?"

"You're a mage," Jeka pointed out.

"That's a problem, too. People don't like mages as rulers, not since Fairven. I've seen how folks here in Brysta feel about blackstaffers and order-mages—and they're considered the good mages."

"A good mage is a trusted advisor and a feared ruler," Erdyl said.

"Hated," Kharl suggested, recalling Charee's repugnance at Jenevra—and Jenevra had been little more than a girl.

"You mean . . . you'd put Osten up as Lord West?" asked Jeka. "Really would?"

"Does anyone have a better idea? We don't want Egen or Vielam, and we don't want the Emperor of Hamor or one of his tools."

Jeka looked away.

Kharl couldn't blame her. Once he would have felt the same way. But he'd seen the other side. When Egen had turned against him, most of the people he had known and trusted had refused to stand up for what was right. Only Tyrbel and Gharan had. And Jeka, especially Jeka. Wassyt the miller and Werwal had done what they could without making it public. Everyone else had gone along.

He frowned. That wouldn't have happened in places like Recluce or Southwind. He'd seen that. Even in Austra, there were men of power—like Hagen—who had risked everything to do what they thought was right. Why was Nordla—or the West Quadrant—different?

He wasn't sure he had an answer.

He also worried about Werwal, since he hadn't seen or heard from the renderer; but he couldn't be in all places, and he didn't have enough retainers to send them through a city where anything could happen at any time.

Lost in those thoughts, he said little for the remainder of the meal. No sooner had he stood than Jeka slipped away the moment his eyes left her.

After dinner, Kharl walked into the kitchen to talk to Fundal and Khelaya, because he had worried about provisions for the residence. "Do we have enough for the next eightday or so?"

"That'd be tight for full meals, ser," Khelaya had answered, "but there's plenty to fill stomachs."

"You can pay more if you can find what we need." After what he'd told Fundal earlier, Kharl thought he needed to say something about prices.

"Good to know," Fundal replied.

When Kharl returned to the dining area, he saw no one. Erdyl and Demyst were sitting on the front portico, but Jeka wasn't there.

He'd known he'd upset her, but he'd wanted to explain in private why he didn't have any good choices in the matter of whom he supported. Yet he didn't want to chase her all over the residence.

He shouldn't have to do that, should he?

Besides, unfortunately, he needed to figure out how to deal with the white wizards. If he could work out a better shielding for his innate order, so that they could not sense where he was, he might be able to surprise at least one of them. Musing about that, he walked toward the library.

LXXXIV

Although Kharl had stayed up until late in the evening, working on and refining a shield to hide the concentration of order around him, he was up early, still worrying about Jeka. When he came down for breakfast, she was not anywhere on the first floor of the residence. Enelya was in the kitchen, helping Khelaya with the egg toast.

"Have you seen Jeka this morning?"

"No, ser. Didn't see her none last night after supper, either."

"Thank you." Kharl turned and walked up the back stairs to the third floor. He could sense that she was in her room.

He knocked.

"Go away."

"I wanted to talk to you last night."

"Don't want to talk."

Kharl stood there. What exactly was he going to do? He didn't want to hammer down the door. That wouldn't help. "I'm not going away until you let me in."

"Can't bust in here with horses."

"I don't want to break in. I want to talk to you."

Jeka said nothing.

"Do you think I'd want to do anything to hurt you? Do you think I like what's happened?"

There was still no answer.

"Do you want patrollers and lancers and mages tearing up all of Brysta—and then Sagana, and wherever else they'll go?"

Jeka opened the door and stepped back. "Just talk."

Kharl stepped inside, slowly. The room was neat—spotless. He almost said so, but realized that wouldn't be good at all.

Jeka seated herself cross-legged on the bed. She was wearing faded gray trousers and an equally faded blue shirt. She was barefoot.

Kharl pulled the side stool out and straddled it, facing her.

"You didn't say you were going to . . ." Jeka shook her head.

"It's not good," Kharl admitted. "Everything else is worse."

"That's what you say." Her green eyes flashed.

"I've made mistakes," Kharl admitted. "You know that. Do you think I like making Osten the next Lord West?"

"Another mistake."

"It might be. But . . . bad as he might be, the choices are worse. You see how folks feel. Did anyone stand up for you in Sagana when the tariff farmer turned out your mother and tried to get you sold to a pleasure house? Did anyone want to buy my barrels after Egen put out the word on me? I was the only one who even stopped to see if Jenevra was hurt—"

"Jenevra?"

"That was the blackstaffer girl that Egen raped, then had killed while I was fighting the fire."

"Oh." Jeka's brows knit together for a moment.

This time Kharl was the one to be silent, much as he wanted to say more.

"Shouldn't be that way." Jeka sighed.

Kharl kept waiting.

"You being a mage. Guess I thought . . . don't know what I thought."

"I can do some things . . . I'll do everything I can to make sure Egen doesn't hurt another girl, doesn't murder another person. I can't change the whole land. People have to want to change."

"Osten. He doesn't want to change."

"He will," Kharl said. "I told him that if he wasn't a better lord than his sire, I'd come back and kill him. I told him that was something I could do." He grinned ruefully. "That was why he tried to hit me with his sabre. It broke."

"Told him that?"

Kharl nodded. "Wasn't all that smart, I guess. If we win, he'll try to kill me if he thinks he can. But I wanted him to know that he couldn't be like his sire or his brother."

"You'd come back and do that?"

"I came back for you," Kharl pointed out.

"Not just me."

"No. But I did."

Jeka uncrossed her legs and reached for the scuffed shoes. "Need to eat. So do you."

"Once this is over, we need to get you some boots."

"See about that, then." But there was a faint hint of a smile.

As he headed down to breakfast, following Jeka, Kharl realized something else. He still hadn't seen Werwal or his consort. There was no one he felt comfortable sending to the rendering yard. If he went, he'd need to take at least Alynar or Sestalt, and that would leave the residence poorly protected with Osten's lancers coming into the city. Jeka was good at sneaking around, but Kharl didn't want her where he didn't at least have a chance to protect her. He didn't want to send anyone, in fact, until he knew that Brysta would remain relatively orderly.

Everything he did, he felt, was some sort of compromise between what ought to be and what could be. Belatedly, as always, he realized, that was why Lyras wanted to stay away from the Great House and the Lord of Austra. There was always conflict, a need for compromise in ruling, and in law, as the clerk Jusof had pointed out to him in Valmurl. Law was not justice, and given people's differing feelings about what they deserved, and what they wanted, it couldn't be.

That was another reason why he shouldn't ever try to be more than he was, a mage and a lord. He'd just make matters worse—or tear himself up inside—or both. He'd precipitated the second revolt in Austra by trying to second-guess what Ghrant had needed. Now, in less than a season, he'd created swaths of death and destruction just trying to do his job as envoy to the West Quadrant.

Still, he fretted about both Werwal and Jeka, for very different reasons.

LXXXV

As Kharl had suspected, Osten's forces were not ready on sevenday, although Kharl had been able to sense the approach of Egen's white wizards by late in the day. By sunset, he felt as though they were still well south of Brysta proper, south even of the barracks on the south side of the city.

Early on eightday Kharl and his group rode out to join Osten's forces. The day had dawned with a hazy sky, but Kharl had the feeling that it would clear. That meant that Egen was more likely to attack, since the white mages preferred not to fight in the rain. By midmorning, all of Osten's forces were moving southward on the ring road, less than a kay from where it joined the south road. The lancers led the column, and the armed foot brought up the rear, with the supply wagons trailing, and having a hard time of it in the muddy clay left by the combination of summerend rain and the mounts and men traveling before them.

Kharl and his small party rode just behind the vanguard, in the second body of troops, following Osten and his personal guard—lancers clad in a blue so dark it was almost black, with a thin piping of silver-gray. Osten had detailed—not quite grudgingly—two squads of lancers as support for Kharl. Kharl's trousers were mud-spattered, and there were even a few splotches on his sleeves, although those had dried quickly even under the hazy morning sunlight.

The ground on both sides of the road held low hills, but the those on the eastern side were higher and presaged the more rugged hills to the south. Kharl could just make out, over the tops of the woodlot trees ahead to his left, the beginning of the long ridge to the north of the southern patroller barracks.

"How far away do you think Egen is?" asked Demyst.

"About four kays south of here, close to the barracks where we were before." Kharl's order-senses gave him a rough idea. Over the past day, he had pondered whether he should have destroyed the structures, but at that time, he'd been more worried about the eastern fort and whether more white wizards might appear. If he had, he certainly wouldn't have had the strength for at least another day to deal with the eastern fort, and who knew what those patrollers might have been able to do?

"They moving?"

"They don't seem to be."

"Waiting for us to come to them."

Kharl nodded as he sensed two scouts who rode back toward Osten. He just hoped that Osten would tell him what they had discovered, although he had more than a few doubts about Osten's judgment. Not for the first time, and certainly not for the last, he wished he had been faced with better choices as to whom he needed to back on behalf of Lord Ghrant.

After perhaps a quarter glass, a lancer pulled his mount from the column ahead and began to ride back toward Kharl.

"Lord Osten wants something, I'd wager," offered Demyst, riding beside Kharl.

"All lords do," Kharl said dryly, realizing as he spoke the words that he'd condemned himself as well. His wry smile was brief.

The lancer turned his mount to ride on the shoulder, alongside and matching pace with Kharl and his escort. "Lord Kharl, Lord Osten would like you to join him."

Kharl eased his mount forward and onto the shoulder, where he rode past the rear of Osten's guard until he neared Osten himself.

"Lord Osten . . ."

The blond lord turned his head. "Join me."

Kharl eased his mount beside Osten, momentarily conscious of just how much bigger he was than Osten.

"Lord Kharl," Osten began, "what can you tell me about the would-be usurper's position?"

"I do not have scouts, as you do, but the main body of his forces, and three or four white wizards, are somewhere ahead. I would judge about three kays."

For a moment, the narrow-faced Osten was silent. Then, he nodded. "Almost exactly two and a half kays ahead. His wizards or his patrollers killed one party of scouts. The two who just returned tell me that we face three companies of mounted patrollers and two companies of patroller foot, with almost ten companies of regular Nordlan lancers. The entire rebel force has retaken the southern barracks area."

"There was nothing to stop them. The barracks were empty, and they took everything with them when they retreated earlier."

"All the supplies?" Osten's voice was disbelieving.

"All of them except some cannon powder, but the cannon were damaged in the battle." *Except one.* And Kharl wasn't about to mention that.

"The scouts did not report cannon."

Kharl nodded, waiting to see what Osten would say next.

"They have blocked the road, and hold the flat to the east and the high ground to the west. They have fixed crude pikes across the road to block our lancers there or to force us into the marshy part of the flat or uphill against the patrollers with rifles."

"Most of the patrollers are probably Hamorian lancers in patroller uniforms," Kharl suggested.

"That *is* like him. Ungrateful wretch!" Osten spat to the side away from Kharl. "I found it hard to believe that *he* could have trained so many in a year, even with . . ." The lord-heir let the words trail away.

Kharl noted that Osten had yet to refer to his brother by name. "He didn't. That way, the emperor—"

"The white demon can claim that he only supplied a few wizards and some training to the men of the would-be usurper. That is so like Hamor. Be that as it may, what great aid do you offer us?"

"The hills to the west are not at all that high, and the slopes are gentle. That is where the white wizards are. If they were not there, you could take the hills and flank . . . the usurper. Then he and his men would be trapped against the ridge and the marshy ground."

"You want me to send men against the wizards?" Osten's voice turned scornful.

"No. I intend to deal with the wizards—with the two squads of lancers you loaned me, of course. We'll circle behind them and attack them from the west. From what you've said, and from their positions, they expect you to attack. They plan to use the wizards to kill as many lancers as possible before you can reach them." Kharl smiled politely. "What I suggest is that you ready your men for such an attack, and take a great deal of time doing it. When I have dealt with the white wizards, you take the hills to the west and begin to encircle them."

"What about the rifles?"

"They'll go when the white wizards do." *If I am successful.*

"Pardon me, ser mage. What happens if you are not successful?" Osten's voice was cold.

"You have lost nothing but two squads of lancers, and your enemy is that much weaker," Kharl pointed out. "You hazard little. From where his forces are set, he cannot attack quickly."

"When will you begin your attack?"

"When we get there," Kharl said flatly. "You will see chaos-fire and much else."

Osten offered an excessive half bow from the saddle. "We await your efforts, Lord Kharl."

"Thank you, Lord Osten." With a smile he did not feel, Kharl turned his mount, his shields ready for any treachery, although he did not believe such an attempt would come until later.

As he rode back northward to his own small detachment, when he passed the last rank of lancers, he infused a small mass of order into the saddlebags of one of the lancers. When he later cloaked his own order, he hoped that the white wizards would perceive the order in the saddlebags as him—or as his failure to shield himself adequately.

Even so, Kharl couldn't help but wonder what new tactics the white mages with Egen might try. He had no real idea, but he did know that almost every time he had faced one of the Hamorian mages, they had done something he had not anticipated. That might also reflect his own lack of training and experience. From what Whetorak had revealed, Hamor trained its envoys extensively, and Kharl would have been surprised if its mages had not also had some type of instruction. He could have used some of that himself, rather than having to discover everything by trial and error.

He snorted quietly. That blade had two edges. On the one edge, he'd had to learn late things others had known early. On the other, he'd discovered techniques no one else seemed to know.

Kharl rode directly to the subofficer in charge of the two lancer squads accompanying him. "Serjeant."

"Yes, ser?"

"We're going to be heading west from here. We're breaking off, and we'll be circling around."

"Ser?"

"The white wizards are on high ground ahead to the west of the road. We'll be attacking them . . ." He paused. "I'll be attacking them, and you'll be there to make sure that someone doesn't send a squad or something at me. Also, with two squads, we'll look more like a scouting party, and they won't think so much about it. You ride with me, and we'll lead the way."

"Ah . . . yes, ser."

Kharl looked past the serjeant to his own undercaptain.

Demyst nodded, although his face carried a worried expression that was not quite a frown.

After raising the shield to cloak his own order, Kharl eased the chestnut gelding back onto the shoulder of the road, then over a soggy depression into a field that looked to hold some sort of beans. At the western end of the field, there was a lane that wound to the southwest. That was the general direction they needed to go.

As he and the serjeant rode down the rows of the bean field, Kharl was conscious of the words of the lancers who followed Demyst, Erdyl, Jeka, and Alynar.

"One mage . . . and he's gonna take on the white devils?"

"You see what he did already? Nothing but rocks . . ."

"Rocks aren't wizards . . ."

Kharl was well aware of that. He turned in the saddle and managed to get out some of the bread and cheese that he had taken from the residence, knowing he would need it. He managed several bites before they reached the lane—barely wide enough for two mounts abreast.

"How far, ser, before we reach the wizards?"

"They're about two kays over there"—Kharl pointed south-southeast—"but the way we're going is more like three or three and a half. Lord Osten will be slowing his advance and preparing. He won't attack until we're done."

"We're not going to charge the wizards, now, are we?"

"Not all the way. Just to get me close enough to deal with them." And that was far closer than Kharl wanted to be.

Although there were cottages and sheds amid the meadows and fields, Kharl saw not a single soul. That was scarcely surprising, not with a long column of lancers and armsmen visible on the south road stretching back toward Brysta.

After less than a kay, the lane turned westward and downhill, arrowing straight west toward the seacoast cliffs and ridges. Once more Kharl turned off the lane, this time across a meadow toward another set of hedgerows.

A good glass later, he reined up on a low rise, one roughly half a kay to the south of the rise where the white wizards and the mounted "patrollers" waited, although from where he was, Kharl could only see the southernmost of them. He looked more to the northeast, out onto the lower ground. Egen's regular lancers held the flat to the north of the barracks area. Two hastily constructed lines of angled and sharpened posts blocked the road and ran a good ten rods to either side, while mixed companies of foot patrollers and armsmen were drawn up in formation behind the posts.

Kharl looked back to the north. He thought there were four wizards, but he wasn't about to probe to find out. That would only reveal where he was. He turned. "Follow me."

He started the gelding down the slope, mostly grassy, but with some scattered bushes, and a handful of isolated blue oaks.

They had ridden no more than a few hundred cubits down toward the swale between the two hills that were little more than large rises, when the serjeant cleared his throat loudly. "Ser . . . looks like some of those patrollers might be breaking off, heading toward us."

"We'll ride through the swale toward that pair of low oaks on the lower part of the slope there, above that woodlot."

"Ser . . . ?"

"The woodlot is right below. They'd have to break formation to follow us through the trees, wouldn't they?"

"Yes, ser . . . but . . ."

"We aren't going to do that, but I want them to think that. I need to get closer to the wizards." Kharl eased the gelding into a trot, trying not to bounce too much in the saddle.

The others followed.

Kharl kept checking the hillside to the north as he rode across the grassy swale between the two rises.

Once he started up the other side, where the slope of the grassy rise blocked sight of the main patroller force and the other white wizards, Kharl turned the gelding more to the northeast and began to angle up the side of the larger rise that the patrollers were riding down. The patrollers were riding far faster.

With the patrollers—what looked to be half a company—rode a white wizard. Although Kharl was still shielding himself, he got the impression from the other's projected chaos that the man was the wizard who'd betrayed Lord West.

Whhstt . . . A firebolt arced from behind the leading riders.

Rather than extend any great effort until their pursuers were closer, Kharl used his shields just to nudge the chaos into the ground uphill of them.

"Ser?" asked the serjeant.

"Don't worry about this one," Kharl snapped. The patrollers were almost close enough.

Another firebolt flared at them, and Kharl slid it behind the short column. "Halt. Right here." He reined up, and concentrated on the oncoming riders, now less than fifty cubits away.

Whhsttt!

This time, Kharl *twisted* the chaos-energies through the back linkage into the white wizard, beyond him across the sixty-odd riders. Death voids flashed across him, but many of the trailing riders escaped. Within moments, the score of survivors had turned and galloped eastward, not uphill but along the side of the hill.

"Now! Straight uphill!" Kharl called.

This time, while he pulled his shielding cloak back together, he knew that the other wizards would know that he was somewhere behind them. He needed to get as close as he could before they could turn their forces and force him to fight his way to them—if he could.

Kharl reached a point several hundred cubits below the hillcrest on the west side when he saw that perhaps half the patrollers on the rise had finished a wheeling maneuver into a formation to face his small force. He dropped the cloaking shield that had kept him from the full perceptions of the white wizards.

Between the two sets of mounted patrollers were the white wizards, and to their right was another group of riders—wearing dark blue and burgundy. At their head was a slender figure he recognized even at a distance—Egen. The would-be lord's chaos—that of evil and not of chaos-force—was clear enough to Kharl.

Kharl permitted himself a smile that vanished as chaos mounted from within and around the white wizards.

Whhsttt! Whssst! Whsstt! The three firebolts that arced from behind the line of charging patrollers were linked together, feeding off each other, seemingly expanding into a wall of chaos flame.

Kharl had already sensed the linked shields of the three. He couldn't use the wizards' tie to the firebolts to funnel that chaos back at them, but instead, he created his momentary hardened air shield curved to fling the chaos back across the first wave of patrollers—much as he would have preferred to throw that massive force at Egen and his personal guard.

More than two companies of patrollers vanished as the wall of fire flared across them.

A swath of knee-high grass was no more—just a bare stretch of blackened earth, with occasional low rocks protruding from the baked soil.

While the wizards retained their shield, the early-afternoon sky was empty of firebolts.

Slowly, the remaining patrollers began to wheel toward Kharl.

Kharl grabbed for his water bottle and took a long swallow of cider, watching the hillcrest to the east. Then he urged the gelding forward, not at a walk, but at what he thought might be a canter. He could see what was likely to come, even before the patrollers began to raise their rifles. After a moment, Demyst, Erdyl, Alynar, and Jeka followed him, as did some of the two squads of lancers, although Kharl thought that some of the lancers had dropped back. So had the serjeant, but there was no help for that.

Kharl glanced over his shoulder, then shouted, "Demyst! Jeka! Erdyl! Get right behind me! Now!"

"You heard him!" ordered Demyst.

Kharl snapped his head back forward. He kept riding, watching the patrollers as they brought their rifles up. At what he thought was the last moment, he threw up a shield of hardened air—a good fifty cubits in front of him—and wide enough, he hoped, to shield him and his small party. He couldn't spare the energy to shield the lancers behind him, spread as they were.

Crack! Crack! Crack! . . . The rifle reports sounded like continuing whip cracks.

Behind him, Kharl felt one death, then another, as he narrowed the gap between him and the patrollers and the white wizards behind them. In those moments when he thought that there was a lull in the firing, he dropped the air shield and rebuilt it farther ahead. Each time he wondered if he would be shot in that brief instant when he was unprotected.

Yet, for all the rifle fire, there were no firebolts, no use of chaos by the white wizards, except to maintain their linked shields. Had they realized that Kharl was using their own chaos against them? How could they not?

Kharl kept riding, trying to reach a point where he could extend an order-probe to where the white wizards stood, impervious, waiting, and to the right, Egen and his personal patrollers.

All the time, the patrollers kept firing, and lancers behind and flanking Kharl dropped, wounded or killed. Before him, chaos drawn from somewhere began to mount behind the shields of the three white wizards. His entire body was hot, burning like a fire pot, it seemed, and he was drenched in sweat, squinting as the salty stuff ran by and into his eyes.

He was less than two hundred cubits from the first line of patrollers, and the ground shivered. With that shivering, the chaos behind the white shields intensified. Kharl could sense chaos building everywhere—in the ground under him, in the air above him—and yet he was still not close enough to unbind chaos against the wizards.

But . . . if he unbound it against the patrollers . . .

He reached out and unlinked the order within the iron of the rifle of the patroller closest to him.

Currumpttt!!!

White-and-red chaos-flame flared back across the mounted patrollers, pressed by the shields Kharl threw up hastily. Those patrollers and mounts who were not turned into instant pillars of ashes flared like trees blackened in a firestorm—then toppled. Abruptly, the chaos-flare vanished, sucked into the swirling vortex of brilliance that rose around the three Hamorian wizards, a whirlwind of energy burning brighter than the sun, so bright that not a single figure remaining on the hillcrest cast a shadow, a pitiless searing light, with which nothing Kharl had ever seen or felt could have possibly compared.

Yet behind that vortex, protected as the other patrollers had not been, remained the enemy wizards—and Egen and his personal guard.

Egen—coward, betrayer of his own family, and destroyer of Kharl's. Egen . . . protected by the chaos energy of the white wizards.

From somewhere deep within Kharl a cold rage began to build. They would not protect Egen!

A high whining sound began to build.

Kharl raised both an air shield and order shield directly in front of him.

The air itself vibrated, and the shrilling penetrated Kharl's ears like sharpened needles. As it did, a line of white light flared from the shielded chaos toward Kharl. As that light lance struck the air shield, coruscating, strobing light exploded like cannon shells going off in all directions.

The well of white chaos that surrounded the three Hamorian wizards throbbed. The white vortex dimmed—but only for a moment. Then the ground shivered once more, and the shrilling began to build again.

Kharl kept riding, although he could sense that few remained riding with or behind him. He had to get close enough to reach Egen—and the chaos-wizards. He had to.

Now, he was on the flat of the hillcrest, and only a hundred cubits from the wizards and their linked shield . . . and the blindlingly brilliant chaos vortex that rose like an inverted triangle into the sky—and Egen!

As he neared the vortex, he struggled, through sweat and heat, and exhaustion, to rebuild his air shield and order shield. Exhausted as he was, he had to . . . just to get close enough to do what he could, what he had to do.

What could he do? The blinding lightsword he had never seen before, never even read about or thought about. Could he turn it against their shield?

The shrilling rose until he could hear it no longer, until his eyes were watering with agony from the unseen needles stabbing through his ears and into the depth of his skull . . . and still it rose. Kharl forced more order into the air shield, waiting, watching, trying to pick out Egen as well.

The lightsword flared toward him.

He tried to grasp it with order, and it was like trying to grasp smoke or fog. Yet it struck his shields so hard that he rattled back and forth in his saddle. Explosions of brilliance and light made the noon sun in summer seem as dark as night in the deepest cave that had never seen light.

Once more he was without shields, his defenses shredded.

The chaos-vortex dimmed more than the last time, but the ground shivered, and the vortex began to regain its brightness once again.

The gelding was barely walking forward, and Kharl was panting, breathing heavily. His face felt burned as if he had spent days in the sun without shade, and he knew much of his exposed skin was blistering. It was hard to keep his eyes open from the swelling around them.

What could he do?

The ground quivered once more.

Kharl tried to swallow, but his throat was so dry he nearly choked.

What . . . how?

He looked at the glowing chaos shields and the brilliant vortex rising once more like a hammer that was about to strike and smash him flat.

The ground trembled more strongly.

The ground?

With what felt like his last strength, Kharl reached toward the white wizards, not directly, but toward the chaos tap that extended deep within the very earth. There was the slightest chink, one of necessity, he felt, just beneath the earth, where one kind of chaos met another and was transformed.

Kharl did not try to change or force anything created by the chaos-wizards. Instead, he began to work on a simple red stone, one mostly of iron, to release the order bounds within that chunk of rock lying just between the two kinds of chaos—and directly beneath the wizards and Egen.

As those bounds dissolved in the iron-stone rock, Kharl drew back his order-probe and flung shields around himself and those just behind him, hoping that his party was all there.

The ground rumbled.

A firebolt flared toward Kharl, a fraction of an instant too late, exploding against his belatedly drawn shields.

Somewhere to the east, he could sense a handful of riders galloping southward from the Hamorian forces, trying to put part of the hill between themselves and the battle; but he would have to worry about them later, after dealing with the wizards.

Then . . .

A sound like iron being ripped apart, like the agony of a mother losing a child, knifed through Kharl.

The light of the great vortex was nothing compared to the flaring chaos-inferno that exploded skyward. As each chaos-wizard's shield failed, the explosion lanced higher. Kharl shuddered in his saddle, hanging on with both hands as the gelding reared, screaming.

As the whitened redness of death flared around him, he knew, could sense, that none of those opposing him on the hill had survived.

A grim smile crossed Kharl's face, if but for a moment.

Slowly, so slowly, it seemed, everything faded, and the afternoon sun returned, so dim by comparison that the sunlit afternoon looked like late twilight.

Kharl, Demyst, Jeka, Erdyl, and Alynar remained alone on a fire-scoured rise. The air was like a furnace, and fine ash drifted everywhere.

Kharl forced himself to turn the gelding, although he could see nothing, except through his order-senses. His face was aflame, and he felt as though every bit of skin had been blistered away.

"We need to get away." His voice came from a great distance, it seemed to him, and patches of blackness appeared before his eyes, then vanished.

Deliberately, he rode southwest, picking a path down the hill away from the area where the scattered grass and brush still smoldered, down to where he could turn westward, then back toward Osten and his forces.

Before long, riders appeared, moving from the east. Kharl squinted. There had to be close to half a company, and all were wearing patroller uniforms—except for one figure in blue.

"Ser!" called Demyst.

The patrollers spurred their mounts toward Kharl and his small group. Several had their rifles out.

"Behind me!" Kharl ordered, hoping that Jeka, above all, was close enough for his shields, shields he only hoped he could hold long enough for Egen to approach more closely.

"Fire! Aim for the mage!" Egen's voice carried across the ten-odd rods that separated the two groups.

Crack! Crack! . . .

Kharl rocked in the saddle at the force of the patroller's volley, and he could feel his grasp on his shields slipping.

"Keep firing! He can't hold on!" snapped Egen.

Kharl forced himself to reach out, to stretch for a bit of iron, sensing a small amount in Egen's belt, and untwisting and releasing the order-bonds.

Crumpt!

More light flared across the hillside. When Kharl could see again, his eyes took in another patch of blackened ground.

Somehow . . . after all that had happened, Kharl just wished Egen had known, really known, who Kharl was. But life didn't always work out the way one hoped. There hadn't been a real confrontation, just a footnote to a battle, and Egen was dead. It didn't seem that Egen had paid enough for all his villainy, not near enough.

"Ser?" Demyst's voice broke through Kharl's reverie. "It's not that safe here, still."

"You're right." Kharl urged the gelding downhill and more to the west.

They had ridden less than half a kay when yet another group of riders appeared, these in Brystan blue.

Kharl blinked when he saw the serjeant who commanded the squads of lancers that had accompanied him—and the half score of lancers who remained, though the lancers hung back from the serjeant.

"You stayed here?" Kharl asked.

"As would any smart man, ser mage."

Kharl could feel his own party closing up behind him.

"Lord Osten is now Lord West," Kharl announced, using almost his last strength. "He has the field. You can tell him that he will know where to find me."

Kharl swayed in the saddle.

The serjeant smiled, driving his mount toward Kharl and lifting his sabre. Kharl tried to turn, but he was sluggish, so sluggish.

The blunt edge and the hilt of Erdyl's sabre—thrown end over end—slammed into the serjeant's shoulder and neck.

Then Demyst and Alynar struck, and the serjeant sagged in his saddle.

Another lancer slashed at Erdyl, who had no sabre.

Somehow . . . Kharl managed to unlink the tiniest bit of order from something—whatever was easiest—in the lancer who had slashed Erdyl. As the chaos flared, Kharl flung up a half shield, one that directed the force across the rest of Osten's lancers.

Not only blackness, but strobing light-flashes flared across and before Kharl, clouding his order-senses. He could barely feel Jeka, riding closer to him.

"Get me out of here," he hissed to her. "Can't hang on much longer. If Osten gets to me . . ."

At that moment, the deeper blackness swept over him.

LXXXVI

Kharl woke up in a bed. He thought it might be the large bed in the residence, but, since he still could not see, and since his head throbbed so much that he could not use his order-senses, he was far from sure.

His throat was dry, and he tried to sit up.

"Easy there." The voice was Jeka's.

"Thirsty . . ." The single word was an effort.

"Got some ale here."

"Can't see," he tried to explain.

Jeka guided a mug into his hands.

He drank slowly. After several small swallows, he could feel the ale easing the dryness in his throat. Some of the throbbing in his skull subsided, enough that he could tell that he was in his own chamber and that Jeka was the only one with him.

"What happened?"

"Undercaptain got me onto your horse. Held you, and we rode back. Alynar helped Erdyl."

"How is he?"

"Khelaya thinks he'll be all right. Arm's pretty smashed up. Hope it doesn't get wound chaos."

"That takes a few days," Kharl said. "When I'm feeling better, I think I could help there." He took a longer swallow of the ale.

"Told you not to trust Osten. Bastard, always," said Jeka. "Stupid, too."

Kharl could agree with both Jeka's judgments.

"Still think he ought to be Lord West?"

"Who else? If Vielam's still alive, he's worse. He'd betray anyone. The two lord justicers don't have any guts . . ." Kharl stopped and coughed. His head throbbed more. When the spasm passed he took another swallow of the ale.

"Anyone shown up," he asked, "looking for me?"

"Not so far . . ."

"What time?"

"Close to midnight. Could be Osten's still out there . . . grabbing coins and booty."

"He doesn't know what happened," Kharl said. "The only ones close enough to see . . . We don't know what happened, either."

"That was Egen at the end, on the hillside, wasn't it?"

"Yes. He abandoned the wizards, I think, just before . . ."

"Too quick for that pissprick."

Kharl had to agree. Egen didn't deserve a quick death, or just to die once, not after all he had done. "Best I could do."

"Hope it hurt—a whole lot."

"With Egen gone . . . and the white wizards . . ." Kharl paused for another sip of the ale to forestall a second bout of coughing.

"You think Osten managed to come out on top?"

"He might not have had to fight that much," Kharl suggested. "The regulars might have accepted him as Lord West. You think they want to die for someone who's dead?"

"What about the other one?"

"Vielam? He might have tried to rally them around him, but that's hard to do in the middle of a battle." Kharl stifled a yawn.

"You need sleep," Jeka insisted.

"So do you."

"Won't get it unless you do."

He could hear a hint of humor in her words. "Thank you . . ."

"Nothing . . . did what . . ." Her hand touched the back of his briefly, then squeezed gently before taking the mug from his hands. "Go to sleep."

Kharl leaned back into deeper darkness.

LXXXVII

By twoday evening Kharl had regained his eyesight, at least most of the time, although he had moments when everything turned black. Brysta remained quiet, from what he could see and hear and from what Mantar and the other retainers had observed. The lower market square was almost as filled as usual, according to Enelya, who was more willing to venture out, although there were no patrollers around. The upper market square was less frequented, with but half the vendors and buyers. That could have been because it was closer to the Quadrancy Keep, where many of Osten's forces had returned.

While he recovered, Kharl spent some time considering exactly how to deal with Osten, and how he might handle matters—if he had to meet with Osten, as well as if Osten decided to avoid or ignore Kharl. He still had not heard anything from or about Werwal, but he still didn't have retainers to spare to go inquiring, not at the moment. Nonetheless, it nagged at him.

As with everything else involving Osten, matters took longer to sort out, and Kharl heard nothing from the new Lord West until midmorning on threeday, when a pair of Osten's personal guards escorted an undercaptain to the residence.

Kharl, Erdyl, and Demyst met with the undercaptain in the library. Kharl stood in front of the desk and did not seat himself, nor did he offer a seat to the lancer officer.

"Undercaptain Huard." The young officer gave a perfunctory nod.

"Greetings, undercaptain." Kharl did not smile. "You have a message from Lord Osten."

"Lord *West* had noted that you did not remain long on the field." The undercaptain's words were delivered in a matter-of-fact tone. "And that none of the lancers who accompanied you have been since seen."

Kharl had thought that a few might have escaped either the white wizards or his own wrath, but he couldn't have said he was surprised that they had not.

"I thought it unnecessary to remain," Kharl replied coldly, "since Lord West had conveyed the message that he had no further need of my services after I had defeated the white wizards and destroyed the Hamorian lancers."

"Ser?"

"The message was both direct and personal, undercaptain, and Lord Osten is well aware of it. What do you want?"

Huard looked from Kharl to Demyst, then to Erdyl, his arm bound and in a sling. All three looked coldly at the junior officer. Huard swallowed. "Ah . . . I was not aware of any such message . . ."

"It was sent, nonetheless," snapped Erdyl. "Your lord should have been more respectful of a mage who salvaged his rule for him."

Kharl repressed the faintest of smiles.

"Nor is it exactly respectful," Erdyl continued, "to send a boy of an undercaptain after displaying such disrespect."

"But . . . he is Lord West . . ."

"Lord Kharl represents Lord Ghrant, the ruler of all Austra, and a domain many times the size of the West Quadrant." At the chill in Erdyl's words, Huard looked almost helplessly at Demyst.

The older undercaptain remained stone-faced.

"What has happened has happened," Kharl said evenly. "Why did Osten send you?"

"Ah . . . he wishes to meet with you, ser."

"Why?"

Huard glanced around the library, then finally looked back at Kharl. "I do not know."

Kharl could sense that was not quite the truth. "Then I would suggest that you guess," he said dryly. "I am not interested in meeting with Osten unless I know why."

"It . . . might be about the harbor forts. The remaining rebels hold them. There are no cannon remaining, and the two gunships cannot be found."

Kharl suspected that the two small warships of the West Quadrant would never be found, not unless someone found a way to search the bottom of the Eastern Ocean. "I will meet Lord Osten—at the foot of the oceangoing piers. He is not to bring more than a squad of personal guards."

"He had thought . . . the Quadrancy Keep."

"At the foot of the piers, at the third glass past noon. I will be there."

"Ah . . ."

"You heard Lord Kharl." Erdyl's voice was cutting. "Lord Osten requested a meeting. He has it."

"Ah . . . yes, ser."

"Oh . . . undercaptain," Kharl said politely. "I would also request your presence at that meeting. If you are not there, I will not meet with Lord Osten, either."

"Me, ser?"

"I am only thinking about your health, undercaptain," Kharl said.

At those words, Huard paled. "Yes, ser. Thank you, ser." He bowed.

When the captain had left, Demyst laughed softly. "Scared the piss out of him, you did. Little snot deserved it."

Jeka opened the door and slipped into the room. She looked at Kharl. "Bastard Osten wants something from you. What?"

"He wants me to bring down the harbor forts, I'd wager. We're meeting at the third glass after noon on the ocean piers."

"Bastard tried to kill you."

"He'll deny it," Kharl said.

"Still did."

"There's no proof. Osten and the five of us are the only ones alive who know what happened. That may be for the best."

Jeka snorted. "You're still going to meet him?"

"Yes. So long as the rebels hold the harbor forts, there won't be any merchanters in here. We can't leave, and neither can anyone else." Kharl fingered his chin. "The rebels probably wouldn't be holding out if Vielam didn't happen to be with them, and Osten's afraid that so long as he's alive, the Hamorians will keep meddling. That's not good for anyone."

"Don't like it," said Jeka.

"You think I do?" asked Kharl.

"What will you do?"

"Take some precautions." Kharl turned to Demyst. "Can you find a pair of good pistols that you can use?"

"Yes, ser."

"Good. Now . . ." As he spoke, Kharl just hoped that, among the four of them, they could cover most of the possibilities that would allow him to deal with both the harbor forts and with Osten's treachery and duplicity.

LXXXVIII

Erdyl had suggested that Kharl keep Osten waiting. Kharl had demurred. "It's better if I'm there first." For one thing, Kharl could sense any changes that might reveal any treachery Osten planned. Also, Kharl saw no point in mere pettiness.

With Alynar seated beside him on the driver's bench, Mantar drove Kharl, Demyst, and Jeka to the piers. Jeka was still attired as a young man, wearing openly the knives she had learned to use so well in her days as a street urchin. The carriage came to a halt at the first ocean vessels' pier at half before the third glass.

Before getting out, Kharl turned to Jeka. "I'd prefer that you stay here with Mantar and Alynar, but if you see anything that looks like trouble, let me know."

"I can do that." She nodded solemnly.

Kharl caught the gleam in her eye. He hoped she didn't see trouble, because she'd be in it if she did. He got out and looked up to Mantar. "I'd like you to wait, but more toward the slateyard—that new barracks there—a little away from where Osten will show up."

"Yes, ser."

As the carriage moved away, Kharl walked onto the pier a good thirty cubits, stopping next to one of the heavy bollards nearly as tall as he was.

Demyst took out one of the pistols. "Good weapon. Wasn't quite sure we could get these, but Sestalt has his ways."

"We ought to make him the head of guards at the residence. Start a regular guard corps. It'll have to be small."

"I've mentioned the idea to him. Besides Sharlak, he has another man who might do well."

"That's all we can afford," Kharl said. "For now, anyway."

The moments drew out.

"You think he'll come?" Demyst finally asked.

"Osten? He wants something that no one else can provide. He'll come."

"He won't be happy."

"He never will be." After the words left his mouth, Kharl looked down at the worn and graying timbers of the pier. Was he like Osten? Not exactly, because he'd been satisfied with being a mage, even being a cooper—the undeniable satisfaction of a task well-done. But what about happiness? Joy even?

He glanced along the seawall toward the slateyard, where the carriage waited. "What do you think of Jeka?" he asked Demyst.

"Why, ser, if I might ask?" Demyst's voice was quiet, deferential.

Kharl wasn't certain what to say. "I came back here for her. Not just for her, but more for her than I knew."

"That says something, I'd wager." Demyst half smiled. "She didn't leave your chamber that night after the battle. Don't ever tell her I told you."

"She doesn't like to let people know she cares," Kharl said.

"Begging your pardon, Lord Kharl, ser . . . but neither do you, not in words. You'd walk through chaos to save a friend, but you'd find it hard to tell him he was your friend."

Kharl started to protest, then stopped. Had he ever told anyone he'd cared, or loved them? Warrl—but only when he'd had to leave his son with Merayni. After a long silence, he said quietly, "Thank you."

"Ser . . ." Demyst broke off. "Riders coming down Cargo Road, ser. Looks to be Lord Osten, or . . . Guess he's probably Lord West now."

Kharl extended his order-senses toward the short column of riders. So far as he could tell, there was no chaos, and none bore rifles. That would doubtless change in the seasons and years ahead, now that the Hamorians had discovered how to keep the powder from being set off except by more powerful mages. Still, he stood ready to throw up shields.

"I count just two squads. Think he's got a company holding farther up the hill."

Kharl reached out farther to the north, then smiled. "He does."

"He's the type. Like your little Jeka's words for him."

"She's not mine," Kharl said with an embarrassed laugh.

"She'll never be anyone else's, ser."

"She won't belong to anyone. She has to be herself."

"So do you, ser," the undercaptain said.

"When you want to point out something, Demyst, you get very formal."

"You are a lord, ser." The undercaptain's words were delivered in a humorously sardonic tone.

Kharl would have said more, but Osten had reined up at the foot of the pier and dismounted. Kharl focused his senses on the new Lord West, and upon the squad of armsmen that followed him. Leading the squad was Undercaptain Huard. His face was set . . . and pale.

Kharl could sense Demyst easing back, to give the two lords space to themselves.

"Well, Lord Kharl, mage of mages, I have received your messages," said Osten, his voice cold, "and I am here to attend you."

"You requested the meeting, and I obliged," Kharl replied. "I also must apologize," he went on smoothly and politely. "I fear that Undercaptain Huard did not appreciate all that occurred. You will understand if I did not enlighten him. I would hope that he has a long and rewarding service under you."

Osten frowned. His eyes fixed on Kharl. "Your face is blistered, ser mage."

"Chaos can get very hot, when facing four Hamorian mages." Kharl paused. "Undercaptain Huard did not convey the reasons for your wanting this meeting. Your youngest brother had garrisoned the harbor forts with his patrollers. He was killed in the battle south of Brysta. It appears as though the forts have not surrendered, and I would also surmise that Overcaptain Vielam is now commanding the remaining rebels and has taken refuge there."

"You surmise much, Lord Kharl."

"That is what envoys for rulers are supposed to do."

Osten did not quite meet Kharl's eyes. "It is true. The last of the rebels still hold the harbor forts. The . . . other rebel . . . is in one of them."

"They will not surrender?"

"No. They say they'll be killed anyway." Osten laughed, harshly, bitterly. "Killing is too good for them. For him."

"They—and the Hamorians—have caused much trouble," Kharl observed politely.

"Could you not have captured the two traitors?" asked Osten. "Especially the one?"

"Egen?" asked Kharl. "He was hiding behind the white wizards. When their chaos turned on them, everything around them was blasted into ash." That wasn't quite the truth, but Kharl didn't feel like explaining.

"That was too quick a death for him."

"What would you like of me?" Kharl asked.

"I would like the harbor forts captured and the remaining traitor taken alive. He betrayed my sire, and he betrayed me."

"Do you want personal revenge more than you want to hold Brysta?" asked Kharl.

"What do you mean?"

"I can destroy the harbor forts. I can bring them down around Vielam. He will not escape. I cannot do that and save him for you to kill later."

"Would that I could let them sit there and starve . . . slowly," said Osten.

Kharl thought briefly of how he would just as soon wring Osten's throat or turn the new Lord West into ashes.

"But . . . that will not do," Osten admitted. "They have some cannon, and the harbor chains, and they can stop traders from porting. There will be no trade. Before long we will be paupers."

"The people in Brysta would suffer and blame you, and some might even turn to Hamor once more," Kharl pointed out.

"You think I do not see that?" Osten glared at Kharl. "What will you do for me in this?"

"I will do nothing for you." Kharl held up a hand to stop the lord from reacting. "I will destroy the forts for your people. They will not defend the harbor against the warships of Hamor in these days, anyway. The Hamorian guns would pound the forts to crushed stone and gravel."

"I like that not."

Kharl ignored the lord's words. "Find me a good boat and a pair who can row it well. Position your armsmen at the ends of the breakwaters, as far from the forts as they can be and still capture anyone who might try to leave."

"That . . . I have already done."

"Good. I will return here a half glass after sunset. If the boat is ready, we will take care of the forts tonight."

"Why not now?"

"Because it will be easier and quicker tonight." *Because I'll have less worry about their sighting cannon at me.*

"So long as it is done."

"It will be."

A silence fell between the two men on the pier.

Osten was the one to break the silence. "For all that you have helped me, ser mage, after this matter is over, I think both our lands would be best served by another envoy."

Kharl wasn't surprised. "That is not my choice." He paused. "I will return to Valmurl and convey your request to Lord Ghrant. I will leave my assistant, because Lord Ghrant does not wish to be ignorant of what may happen here in Brysta. Lord Ghrant will do as he sees fit. He may insist I return. He may appoint another envoy. He may decide to make Lord-heir Erdyl the envoy."

"Mihalen had thought your assistant might be of lordly birth."

"His sire is lord of Norbruel."

Osten looked as though he might say something about that, but then merely said, "The boat and rowers will be here before sunset. I trust you will not request my presence."

"No. It would be best if those in the forts saw nothing."

Osten nodded. "Good day, Lord Kharl."

His shields still ready, Kharl watched as the latest Lord West turned and walked off the pier.

Demyst moved closer to Kharl. "He is not to be trusted, not so far as one could heave his mount."

"I don't intend to trust him." Kharl also had his own plans for making the best of a bad situation. "We need to get back to the residence. I'm going to need a very solid meal before this evening." He began to walk toward the carriage.

Neither Mantar nor Alynar said anything as Kharl and Demyst approached, but both men looked relieved.

"We're heading back." Kharl stepped into the carriage.

"Yes, ser."

Once Demyst closed the carriage door, Mantar turned the coach up Cargo Road.

"What did he want?" asked Jeka.

"The last rebels hold the harbor forts. Vielam's in one of them," Kharl said. "Vielam's probably worse than Osten, at least as a ruler, because he's not only cruel, but weak." He didn't know that, not for certain, but based on what he'd seen it seemed more likely than not. Vielam had played all sides and betrayed both his father and his eldest brother. Like everything Kharl had had to deal with in Nordla, he had no good choices. "So long as he's alive, he'll betray whoever he can, and the Hamorians will try to make trouble."

Kharl turned to Demyst. "Are you willing to come with me . . . with your pistols?"

"Pistols against forts?"

"No. They're for you to shoot the two rowers if they try anything."

Jeka laughed.

"We also won't row back to where we leave. Mantar can bring the coach down to the old wharf off the lower market."

"Good," declared Jeka. "Alynar and I will be with Mantar. Sharlak, too. He's got a hunting rifle. Good shot. Even in the dark. He potted one of those patrollers that night they came against the house."

Kharl looked at Jeka, trying not to be too obvious, taking in the brilliant green eyes, the short-cut sandy hair. She was good-looking, but it was not that which appealed to him, he realized, but that she was *alive*. Even when she had been scrounging out a living by her wits, she had not just gone through the motions.

"You all right?" she asked.

"Thinking," he replied.

She just nodded, as if she knew those thoughts were not for saying aloud in a coach.

Within a glass of returning to the residence, Kharl sat down to a solid early-evening meal, one that Khelaya declared—again—was not up to her standards because no one was selling good produce and meat, not at any reasonable prices, not in the upper market square, and she wasn't about to frequent the lower one.

At sunset, Kharl and his party climbed into and onto the carriage, with Alynar inside with Kharl, Jeka, and Demyst. Sharlak, a long-barreled rifle in his hands, sat beside Mantar.

When Mantar brought the carriage to a halt at the end of the pier, Kharl could see a half squad of lancers there—again commanded by Undercaptain Huard. "Poor Huard."

"Poor . . . and stupid to serve Osten," Jeka said.

Demyst nodded, but added, "Could be he had little choice. Younger lordly sons have few."

Jeka frowned.

"They cannot inherit. Trade is considered beneath them, and some are trained to be lords in case their elder brothers die. If the brothers survive, the younger ones are ruined for anything else. Especially honest work." Demyst laughed.

Jeka even smiled.

Carrying a small bag of provisions, Kharl followed Demyst from the carriage, glancing to the west, where the two forts were outlined against orange-tinged clouds. He moved toward the half squad of lancers, nodding to Huard. "Undercaptain."

"Lord Kharl. The boat and boatmen are ready for you."

"Thank you." Kharl kept his shields ready, but there was no sense of treachery or chaos, although Kharl couldn't help but feel sorry for Huard.

Halfway down the pier, two older men—fishermen, Kharl suspected—were waiting with a high-sided dorylike boat, moored on the shoreward side, well out of direct sight from either fort. The craft was smaller than most dories Kharl had seen.

"You're the mage, ser?" asked the taller of the two, a muscular man with graying hair perhaps ten years older than Kharl.

"He's Lord Kharl. He's a mage and the Austran envoy," Demyst replied.

"Do you understand what we're going to do?" asked Kharl.

"No, ser," replied the older man, "except we're to do what you want."

"How did Lord West find you?"

"He sent an overcaptain to the Fishers' Guild. Offered a gold each for the two best rowers to row a mage where he wanted to go this evening. Overcaptain said if someone didn't volunteer, wouldn't be a Fishers' Guild tomorrow. Gerrik and me, we figured a gold each was better 'n pissin' off a hothead lord. Beggin' your pardon, ser."

"Gerrik," Kharl asked, "is he telling the truth?"

"Yes, ser, Holyt's right fair, excepting that we didn't need to be threatened. Can't take our boats out now, nohow. Cannon blew poor Jotrok right out a the water this morning."

"I'm not threatening. We get through this, and I'll add a gold to each of you from my own purse—once we get to the old wharf there." Kharl gestured to the south.

"Beggin' your pardon, ser," said Holyt, "but it seems a mite strange for an Austran to be doing something for Lord Osten . . . Lord West."

"I'm doing it for the people in Brysta, and because Lord Ghrant of Austra doesn't want the Hamorians any closer than Hamor."

The younger man laughed. "We don't either."

Kharl studied the pair. "You'll be rowing blindly. The way we're going you won't be able to see a thing. I'll give you directions. Do you understand?"

The older, slightly graying Holyt nodded. "Don't much care, ser mage, so long's as we get back."

"That's why." He looked toward the breakwaters. From the end of the pier the northern fort would be closer. He eased down and sat on the forward thwart, not exactly comfortable, but a position from which he could direct the two rowers.

Demyst settled aft of the pair. He did not reveal the pistols.

Twilight was settling across the harbor, but they would still be visible against the shimmer of the water for a time.

"You can cast off," Kharl said.

"Yes, ser."

"You'll be able to see until we reach the end of the pier. Then, everything will go black. You won't be able to see, but the lookouts on the fort won't see us, either. Once we get close to the breakwater, we'll need to be quiet. They won't be able to see us, but they can hear us."

"So long as you know where you're going, ser."

"How close can we get to the breakwater on the harbor side . . . without going aground?" asked Kharl.

"In this craft, ser?" Holyt smiled. "Maybe a cubit from the rocks. Oars'd hit the rocks before we'd ground."

"Good."

As the small dory's prow reached the end of the pier, Kharl raised the sight shield, extending it a good five cubits behind the stern. In the dim light, he hoped that would be enough so that the ripples from the oars would not be that obvious to the forts' lookouts.

"Bring her starboard," Kharl said.

"Coming starboard."

Kharl used his order-senses, trying to get a course line from the end of the pier to the northern breakwater.

"Just a touch more starboard," he said.

After a moment, he added, "Steady as she goes."

"You been at sea, ser?" asked Holyt.

"Merchanter subofficer," Kharl admitted.

In a murmur Kharl was not meant to hear, Gerrik murmured to Holyt, "Maybe we got a chance."

Kharl certainly hoped so as the dory moved across the twilight-calm waters of the harbor toward the northern breakwater.

Nearly a glass later, he could sense the stones of the breakwater and the port. "Port a quarter."

"Coming port."

"Hold on this line," Kharl said quietly. Just thirty cubits ahead was the northeast corner of the harbor fort. The stone walls ran straight down into the harbor.

Less than a quarter of a glass later, the dory was little more than an oar's length from the wall, and less than twenty cubits north of the southeast corner.

"Back down and stop here," Kharl said.

He just sat in the prow of the dory, extending his order-senses toward and around and through the stones of the ancient fort, searching out the magazines and the linkages he might be able to make between them. As he did, a sense of profound sadness settled over him.

He could not but help recall what Jusof had first said to him about the law, that it was a tool and a necessary evil—and that, bad as it was, without it, matters were inevitably worse. That was the position in which he found himself. Bad as what he was about to do was, not doing it would lead to worse evil, and because he was but one mage, his choices—those that seemed to be effective—were limited to the use of great power applied seldom and violently.

He swallowed, and began to undo the linkages in the iron-lined walls of the largest magazine that he could reach, at the same time creating order-tubes to the other magazines nearest.

As chaos flared, the first magazine exploded.

Kharl released the sight shield and clamped a shield of hardened air around the small dory.

The early-night sky flared into red and whitish orange flashes that streaked out from the northern harbor fort. Beneath the colors of powder and cammabark exploding was the red-tinged white of released chaos.

"Friggin' demons!" hissed one of the fishermen.

". . . poor bastards . . ."

Kharl just sat in the prow, holding his shields. The chaos voids of death washed over and around him. Stone fragments, chunks, pebbles, and other things he didn't want to think about pelted the hardened air. The dory rocked back and forth, wildly for at time, then bobbed up and down within the shield. As he had half expected, his eyes saw nothing.

Finally, he released the air shield. Hot air washed across them, air laden with the smell of ashes, hot metal, and all manner of burned things.

"It's time to start rowing again," Kharl said. "Across toward the south fort."

He forced himself to ignore the odors. Instead, he opened the provisions bag and slowly began to eat, interspersing food with ale from the water bottle.

Not until Holyt and Gerrik had rowed the dory halfway across the channel between the burning and sundered north fort and the southern fort did Kharl raise the sight shield once more.

As they neared the southern harbor fort, Kharl could make out voices from the battlements above. He set aside the provisions bag and tried to hear exactly what was being said on the walls above them.

"No ships out there, ser!"

"Nothing in the harbor."

"There must be something. Forts don't explode by themselves."

"Chaos or fire in the powder magazines could do it."

Kharl listened, using his senses to discern the dory's progress. "A touch to starboard," he whispered.

The dory eased to starboard.

"Steady."

As the dory neared the harborside wall of the southern fort, Kharl began the process of seeking out the magazines and setting up another set of links. He pushed aside the sadness and concentrated on the task at hand.

Once more, as the order links parted, and chaos flared into the first magazine, Kharl dropped the sight shield and set the hardened air shield in place.

Currumptt!

Light and chaos once more flared across the harbor, though Kharl could only sense that brilliance, rather than see it, followed by the voids of death.

When the stone fragments and blocks finished falling onto the shield and into the dark waters of the harbor, Kharl released the air shield. His hands and arms were shaking. Point-lights flared across the blackness that was all he saw with his eyes.

"Ser?" asked Holyt.

"Back to the old wharf . . . just row where the undercaptain tells you . . ." He could barely get the words out. He hoped he had some strength left by the time they made the old wharf because, even though he hadn't told Osten what he planned, he didn't trust the new Lord West any more than his sire, or than Egen.

As the dory turned eastward, toward the old wharf, Kharl looked back over his shoulder, extending his shaky order-senses. At the end of each breakwater, a pile of stone burned and smoldered, glowing red in places. From the diffuse chaos, Kharl could tell that trails of smoke spiraled upward in the still night air.

After a long moment, Kharl turned his unseeing eyes toward the shore, clasping his hands together to keep them from shaking.

Jeka was waiting at the old wharf. So was Sharlak, his long rifle held at the ready. Kharl climbed out of the dory, then fumbled with his wallet, extracting two golds. He handed them to Holyt. "I promised. Here are your golds."

Holyt bowed his head. "Thank you, ser." He looked up with a crooked smile. "We just might not want to try to collect from Lord West."

Kharl walked slowly to the carriage, without turning back. He could still sense the death and the ruins across the harbor behind him.

LXXXIX

On threeday night, Kharl had managed to remain alert on the return to the residence, but he had barely managed to undress and climb into bed before succumbing to exhaustion and order-weariness. He slept late the next morning, but still could not see when he finally rose, bathed, shaved, and dressed.

After breakfast, taken alone because the others had already eaten, Kharl sat in the chair behind the library desk, a beaker of lager on the wood before him. He picked it up and took another sip before setting it down carefully.

He had not unlinked nearly so much order, or released as much chaos as he had in the battle south of Brysta. Was his present blindness because he had not fully recovered when he had dealt with the forts?

Thrap.

"You can come in, Jeka," he called.

"Scary," she said, settling into the chair across the desk from him. "You not being able to see and still knowing."

"It's scary not being able to see."

"You'll get better."

Kharl shrugged. "Hope so. Lyras told me that Creslin couldn't see most of his later life."

"Lyras? Creslin? Who are they?"

"Creslin was the weather mage who founded Recluce. Lyras is a mage in Austra. You'll probably meet him."

"Me? Not likely."

"You'd agreed that you would come to Cantyl," Kharl said. "Even with Egen and Vielam dead, it's not all that safe for you here."

"Safe enough."

There was something in Jeka's voice, and Kharl wished that he could see the expression on her face. Demons! He wanted to see her face again. He swallowed.

He would. It would just take time, he told himself.

After a moment, he spoke. "It's not safe enough. You . . . I wouldn't want anything to happen to you."

"Be fine."

Kharl took a long, slow breath. Demyst's words from the night before came back to him. ". . . You'd walk though chaos to save a friend, but you'd find it hard to tell him he was your friend."

"Jeka . . ."

"I'm here."

As she spoke, he realized one other thing. He would always be who he was, at heart, and Jeka knew who that man was. The young ladies like Meyena never would know, never would understand. He swallowed once more, before speaking. "I . . . want you to come to Cantyl. I don't want to leave you here."

"Told you. Can't come like that. Won't be a plaything. Rather take my chances here."

"I'm not asking you to come as a plaything. I'm asking you to come to see if you like Cantyl well enough to be my consort."

For a long moment, there was silence.

"Don't need to come to Cantyl for that."

Kharl shook his head. "I . . . we can't stay here. I'd have to spend every moment worrying about what Osten was trying to do next."

Jeka laughed, the melodic laugh that he had heard so seldom and loved so much. "Wasn't what I was saying. Be your consort anywhere. I don't need to see Cantyl. Doesn't matter whether you've got more lands or less. Matters that you want me."

Kharl swallowed again, not unhappily. "You mean that?"

Another warm and rich laugh answered his words. "You saved me. Two, three times. You did everything you could for me. You came back, partly for me, ran to find me when you thought Egen might be after me. You're handsome. You're good. Used to watch you, you know? Would have been a cooper's consort." There was a pause. "You sure?"

"Very sure." Kharl didn't even hesitate.

Before he could take another breath, she was beside him, her arms around him.

For the moment, and those that followed, Kharl did not worry about blindness, or anything else.

XC

Kharl, Jeka, Erdyl, and Demyst sat in the library. Jeka perched on a stool beside Kharl's desk chair. He couldn't help but keep looking at her. He had persuaded her to have some new outfits made—still trousers and shirts. She wore dark green trousers and a matching shirt, with a lighter green leather vest, not quite so shapeless as those she had worn before, but not form-clinging either. She also still bore the pair of belt knives, not to mention the hidden blade.

". . . someone had to have been waiting at the rendering yard, Sharlak said," Demyst finished.

"One of Egen's people." Kharl shook his head. With everything that had happened, it had taken days before he'd been able to send someone out to check on Werwal—and as in the case of Warrl, even if he'd sent someone the next day, it would have been too late. He'd warned Werwal's consort, but he should have waited and taken Werwal straight to the residence. Another case where he hadn't quite finished the task at hand, and another one of those who had supported him had died.

"You can't do everything, ser," offered Erdyl.

Somehow, those words didn't reassure Kharl very much.

"You two going to have an official ceremony?" asked Demyst quickly.

"As soon as we get to Valmurl," Kharl said.

"Consorted now," replied Jeka. "He never breaks his word." She looked sideways at Kharl with a grin.

"That shouldn't be that long, then. When will the *Seastag* be ready to leave?" asked Erdyl, shifting his weight in the chair to avoid banging the edge of the side table with his injured arm, still in a sling.

Kharl had tried to use order to speed the healing. He'd definitely kept any wound chaos from forming, and probably his efforts would result in Erdyl's earlier recovery, but it was clear that he was no healer.

"She just ported two glasses or so ago," said Kharl. "Why do you think we're leaving? Why are you in such a hurry?"

"I'm not so sure I did very well, ser." Erdyl glanced down at his injured arm.

"I wouldn't be in that much of a hurry." Kharl smiled.

So did Jeka, from beside him, knowing what was coming.

"We aren't going back to Austra, ser?" Erdyl's face fell. "I saw you and Jeka packing."

"Oh, *we* are." Kharl drew out the words. "You aren't."

"Ser? What did I do wrong?"

"Nothing." The mage grinned at the younger man. "That's why you're staying. Lord West—the new Lord West—has requested that I return to Austra. I insisted that Lord Ghrant needed to keep someone here, at least an assistant envoy. You get to be that assistant envoy. Either Lord Ghrant confirms you as envoy or he doesn't, but either way, it's a better position, and you'll get to be in charge here—at least as much as Undercaptain Demyst and Khelaya let you."

"I worry about Lord West," Erdyl said.

"Don't worry too much," Kharl said. "He knows that, if anything happens to you, I'll be back. He'd much rather have you as an envoy."

"Me . . . I don't know . . ."

"You will do much better with the functions, and being polite. You understand that. Every time I had to meet with them, I spent glasses learning just a handful of the proper phrases," Kharl pointed out.

"When will you leave?"

"Tonight. There's not that much cargo to onload, and Furwyl really just returned this way to check on us before heading back to Valmurl. Lord Hagen had ordered him to."

"Thoughtful of him," said Demyst dryly.

"He does worry. Occasionally." Kharl turned back to Erdyl. "Besides, you can send a letter to your sire. You can sign and seal it as the envoy in charge in Brysta."

Erdyl laughed. "You think—"

"Lord Ghrant can't send another envoy for a season. Besides, he can trust you, and there aren't many that he can. You can write well and report on what Osten does. That's what envoys are supposed to do." Kharl stood. "We need to get ready. I'll tell you what I think that you might not know while we do . . ."

It took Kharl less time than he'd thought to do both, perhaps because he didn't know as much as he'd thought, and because Erdyl had been more observant than Kharl had realized, and because Jeka had little to pack.

The sun was low in the west, almost ready to set, when Kharl watched the last bag being loaded into the baggage cart, along with the first bolts of fabric from Gharan. The others would have to be shipped on one of Hagen's ships when Gharan finished them. Demyst had the two mounts saddled and ready.

Jeka stood beside the carriage. She looked at Kharl. "Still think you've done enough."

"No. This is . . . I have to do it."

"You think that it'll work? That he'll be there?"

Kharl shrugged. "I don't know. Not for sure. He was there earlier today, and Sestalt's people say that he didn't ride out. I have to try. I can't leave this job unfinished."

"Don't let anyone get close enough to hurt you." Jeka's green eyes flashed as she looked up at him. "Rather be with you."

"I have to do this alone." He opened the carriage door for her, then stood aside as Alynar stepped into the carriage. Sharlak sat beside Mantar. "Straight to the *Seastag*."

"Yes, ser." Mantar smiled, then gave the reins the slightest flick.

As the carriage headed down the drive, followed by the cart, Kharl turned and looked at the envoy's residence. With all that had happened, it was hard to believe that he'd been back in Brysta less than a season. Less than a season, but as the druids had predicted, a necessary season.

He walked to the gelding, took the reins from Demyst, and mounted. Neither man spoke until they were well away from the residence.

"You're all right with staying?" Kharl asked the undercaptain.

"Yes, ser. Erdyl, he'll need me." Demyst smiled. "Done the hard work, and I'd like to enjoy what comes next. Besides, I sort of fancy Enelya."

Kharl hadn't even noticed that, but that wasn't something he would have noticed. "She seems a good sort."

"Not like your lady, ser, but good. None like yours."

Kharl laughed softly. He'd never met anyone like Jeka, not even close.

As they turned their mounts uphill, shadow fell across the hillside.

"You sure this is necessary, ser?" asked Demyst.

"Not for me. For Brysta."

"Doesn't deserve it. Deserve what they put up with."

"If I don't, they won't know anything better, and they'll come to put up with worse. Then we'll have to," Kharl countered.

"That's one way of looking at it, ser."

It was the only way Kharl could look at it. The Lord's Road was almost deserted at twilight, and no one even seemed to look at the two riders as they passed the entrance to the Hamorian residence—the gates locked and the guards absent. How long before Whetorak or another envoy returned? Kharl shook his head sadly. Hamor wouldn't change. He didn't see it happening in his lifetime, maybe not ever.

Kharl turned at the next side road, the one that turned east and bordered the lower gardens of the Quadrancy Keep. After about fifty cubits, he reined up under an ancient oak, one that shielded him from direct view from the southeast tower, and dismounted.

"I'll be hereabouts somewhere, ser," said Demyst.

"I'd guess it won't be much longer than a glass," Kharl said.

"Be careful."

Kharl nodded. He intended to be most careful. He waited for a brief time until Demyst was another fifty cubits farther east, then turned to the tree.

While the oak had been trimmed and pruned to eliminate any lower branches, Kharl visualized a set of steps made of hardened air, then created the stairs as a form of air shield. He released the air shield as soon as he was in the branches of the oak.

He climbed up several more branches until he was above the wall. Then, creating a sight shield, he eased himself down onto one of the stone merlons and slipped down onto the guardway.

Walking swiftly but carefully, he followed the guardway back west, then northward toward the main section of the keep. Kharl had to step into embrasures twice as guards passed, but his sight shield was enough, and none even paused.

From what he had discovered earlier in the eightday, Osten had taken apartments on the third level while the Lord's quarters were being repaired and rebuilt, and his study was directly above where the battlement ran beneath and adjoined the west wall. There was a balcony outside the study.

Kharl stopped a good ten cubits short of the balcony. He let his order-perceptions reach upward. As he had anticipated, Osten was in his study alone, as he usually was in the glass before the evening meal. Because it was still summer, the door to the balcony was also open, providing air to the study.

Kharl smiled, briefly. For most, a six-cubit sheer wall would have been a problem. Kharl created another set of steps out of hardened air and made his way up to the balcony. Holding the sight shield, Kharl made his way unseen up his invisible steps. He was sweating profusely by the time he stepped over the parapet and released the steps of hardened air.

Still, he was inside Osten's defenses. While there were guards throughout the keep, the closest pair was stationed outside the door to the bedchamber, beyond the study. Kharl eased through the open balcony door.

Osten sat at a table desk, a large ledger before him, his back to Kharl.

Kharl stepped slowly to the door between the empty bedchamber and the study. Once there, he quietly closed the door, which had been only slightly ajar, and slid the lock plate closed. Osten did not look up or turn his head.

Kharl hardened the very air around Osten, leaving only space for his nostrils and ears, before stepping forward and releasing the sight shield so that Osten could see him.

"Osten, Lord West," he said quietly. "I don't think you believed me when I said that I could always get to you."

Osten tried to struggle, but could move not a muscle.

"This is to show you that I can. If I *ever* hear of cruelty or unfairness—the way your brother and father acted—I *will* return, and you will no longer be Lord West. You will no longer be anything."

Osten's breath rasped in and out of his nostrils.

"If you ever try to send assassins after me, or after whoever is envoy for Austra, the same thing will happen. It is very simple. All you have to do is your best to be a fair and just ruler. You do that, and you have nothing to worry about." Kharl laughed softly. "You didn't see me coming, and you didn't hear me, and all your walls and guards meant nothing." Kharl took the pen from the stand and dipped it in the inkwell, then wrote across the open page of the ledger: "Be fair. Be just, and fear nothing."

He set the pen back in the stand, then looked at the red-faced Osten. He smiled and said, "Good night, Lord West."

After stepping back, Kharl raised the sight shield around himself. Then he walked to the balcony. He took a deep breath and wiped the sweat from his forehead, then re-created the air-steps, releasing them as soon as his boots touched stone once more. Not until he was on guardway below and halfway to the garden oak did he release Osten's bonds.

This time, short of the oak, he used the stairway of hardened air to the ground beside the lower garden wall.

Behind him, he heard no alarms, no outcries, and he sensed no guards moving. Was that because Osten had decided against telling anyone what had happened? Because it showed he was vulnerable? Kharl didn't know, and didn't much care, so long as he reached the *Seastag* safely.

He did not see Demyst immediately and began to walk eastward. He'd been walking almost a quarter of a glass before he sensed the undercaptain and the two mounts. Releasing the the sight shield, he stepped out from behind one of the hedges.

"I'm back," he said quietly.

"Getting worried, ser."

"So was I." Kharl grinned, then mounted, and wiped his forehead.

They rode quickly downhill through the darkness toward the waiting *Seastag*—and to Jeka.

Epilogue

There won't be any great mages in the future," Kharl said, standing on the front porch and looking out at the small harbor of Cantyl—his harbor, or his and Jeka's. "I had trouble stopping rifle bullets when a whole company was firing. Before long, they'll start building bigger cannon with soft iron shells, maybe even black iron shells. Then they'll build something bigger, because the next Emperor of Hamor, or the one after that, or the one after that, can't stand the thought that someone stopped Hamor from grabbing another land."

"Doesn't matter," Jeka said, squeezing his hand. "Always someone making trouble. You fixed things now. When the time comes, folks then, they'll have to fix things for themselves."

"I suppose so."

"You've done enough. 'Sides no one's going to bother Lord Ghrant so long as you're his mage. Folks are stupid, but not many stupid enough to get you after them."

"I didn't really create all that chaos," Kharl pointed out. "The chaos-wizards did."

Jeka laughed, the musical laugh that he loved so much. "Who knows that, except you and me?"

Kharl squeezed her hand back and looked at the smooth silver of the harbor water, calm in the late fall evening.

GRE
WES
OCEA
RE